SOMEBODY
STOP HIM

SOMEBODY STOP HIM

Vitaly S. Alexius

Podium

CHAPTER ONE

The Way South

I gripped the worn steering wheel of Uncle George's ancient APS delivery van, sweat trickling down my back in rivulets. The heater had been mocking me for three days straight, nothing but outside chilly or far-too-hot air blasting through the rusted vents. Five thousand and ninety-eight kilometers stretched between North Acadia and my final destination in Omnithornia.

The van smelled like all of Uncle George's failed dreams—stale cigarettes, spilled energy drinks, and the lingering scent of whatever mystery packages he'd hauled before his "accident" that forced him into permanent retirement.

The van was his parting gift to me, along with a knowing look of cold eyes that made my skin crawl.

Weary thoughts kept me company on those endless highways. They whispered from the shadows of truck stops at five AM, echoed in the rattle of the loose side mirror. Sometimes I caught myself wondering if I'd inherited more than just Uncle George's van—if that same darkness that drove him to constantly skirt the laws . . . was also riding shotgun with me too.

Maybe that's why Uncle George gave me the van so quickly. He recognized something in me, something that needed to put as much distance as possible between itself and home.

My phone counted down the miles to Omnithornia, each one a reminder of what I was leaving behind in North Acadia. The beep of the heart monitors as I held Mom's hand for the last time. The empty spot where my dad should have been, but wasn't.

I kept driving south, watching the landscape change from the snow-capped mountains to tundra to dense forests to endless plains to yellow hills. The van protested every mile, but it kept moving, just like me.

HALFWAY POINT. SOUTHERN ACADIA.
The last bastion of pure humanity.

Beyond this boundary, there would only be Omnids with ever-decreasing pockets of humans living on the fringes of the Omnithean Superstate.

I held my breath as the van sputtered up to the border checkpoint, praying it wouldn't choose this moment to finally die. The engine had been making a new rattling sound since breakfast, and the temperature gauge was creeping higher by the hour.

A massive Igopogo in a dark-blue uniform lumbered out of the booth, his

Executioner Cross Authority badge glinting in the afternoon sun. My hands were trembling as I handed over my passport, but I forced my face into the innocent, eager expression that had gotten me out of trouble so many times back home.

"What is your purpose for your visit, Mr . . . Martin Kilborne?" he rumbled, beady eyes scrutinizing my documents.

"Tourism, sir!" I switched to my NPC good-boy mode, channeling every Slayer Sentinels Boy Scout meeting I'd ever attended as Nazarite novitiate Christophorus Elijah, deepening my voice in just the right tone of pure confidence. "I've always wanted to see the Dreadspine! My Scout troop did a presentation on it last year, and it just looks incredible in all the photos."

"Your vehicle looks like it's on its last legs," the border guard commented, showing far too many teeth. Omnitheans were damn scary mofos, compared to us humans.

"Yeah." I rubbed the back of my neck. "Uncle George gave me the van for my eighteenth birthday. Thought it'd be perfect for a road trip before the new semester starts after winter break." I gestured at the pile of tourist brochures I'd deliberately scattered across the dashboard. "I'm planning to hit all the major spots along the Dreadspine National Park fault line. My real goal is to reach Leviathan's Cradle and take some pictures of the ocean. Going off-season to avoid the big crowds!"

"Hrm. And how long will your trip be?" he asked.

"Just two weeks," I lied, pulling out a blue document folder with a fake itinerary. "Here's my planned route."

"What if your van gives out?" the guard asked as he examined the itinerary with all of the high tourism spots labelled in colorful markers.

"I've got Oodber on my phone!" I gushed. "Plus OAA registration. If the van dies, I'll have it towed to the nearest junkyard, get a couple of hundred bucks for the scrap metal, and then hitchhike or call up an Oodber cab and take it to the nearest city. From there I can travel by bus to Leviathan's Cradle, rent a car, and then take the train back to Acadia!"

"Please pull into parking spot A4," the man ordered.

I nodded. "Sure thing, officer."

I pulled the van into the inspection area, my heart hammering against my ribs. The homo-cryptid moved with surprising grace for his size, methodically checking the vehicle's exterior before reaching for the back doors.

My oversized camping backpack sat alone in the empty cargo space. I watched through the side mirror as he unzipped it. A drug-detection Kitlix emerged from his massive side pocket. The liquid-crystal critter grew a nose and sniffed the air. Then, unfolding out like a snake, it grew six legs and rapidly ran over my carefully packed clothes, camping gear, and random assortment of outfits.

My trusty safety vest was tucked in a corner, waiting for stage two. The Kitlix sniffed it briefly and ran back into the border guard's pocket.

The border guard let out a huff, having discovered nothing illegal. Finally, he zipped everything back up and closed the back doors. I could hear his heavy footsteps approaching my window.

"Everything appears to be in order," he said, handing back my documents. "Be aware that the next service station is sixty miles south. With your vehicle's . . . condition, I strongly suggest you stop for some engine maintenance. You wouldn't want to get stuck in the boonies."

I nodded eagerly, relief flooding through me. "Yes sir, absolutely. Thank you, sir."

As I pulled away from the checkpoint, I watched the border crossing station shrink in my rearview mirror until it disappeared completely.

My head felt as though it were trying to split open.

The massive Truth rune hanging above the border crossing gate had done a number on me, but I avoided spilling the beans. I pulled out a bottle of Advil and swallowed a couple of capsules. It added to the cocktail of taurine, caffeine, and other less common substances that allowed me to bamboozle the border-crossing, honesty-pulling hexagrammic chains.

The *Welcome to Omnithornia* sign loomed ahead, its faded paint showing a happy smiling average Mothman family of three gray-winged parents and two-and-a-half kids waving to visitors.

Stage two.
Finance acquisition.

The van, having somehow miraculously made it all the way to Leviathan's Cradle, wheezed to a stop in front of 8008 Fallin Street, Scab Row.

The building was exactly as awful as I'd expected from a "budget-friendly" residency choice—peeling paint, broken windows patched with cardboard, and that distinct smell of desperation that seemed to hang over all of the Scab Row human ghetto.

A quick scrub down and I was feeling slightly freshened. Then I took about thirty minutes to put on some gray face paint. Orange contact lenses, cotton stuffed into my cheeks, and a stick-on mustache completed the look.

The landlord's office was a dim room on the ground floor, with yellowed newspaper clippings covering the windows.

Mr. Peterson sat behind a metal desk, his weathered face a map of hard years spent in Omnithean territory.

"Yes? What do you want?" he asked, barely looking up at me.

"I'd like a refund on unit 901," I said in my NPC-authority voice.

The landlord waved me off without raising his eyes. "Read the sign. No refunds. Policy's clear."

"Uh-huh." I wrote something on my clipboard, idly tagging my safety vest. "Riiiiight."

"What?" the man asked.

I cleared my throat and adjusted my fake ID badge, my mustache bristling. "Well, that's unfortunate. Do allow me to introduce myself—my name is Kovach Moontash. I'm with the Leviathan's Cradle Housing Review Commission. Our office has received multiple complaints about this property being used to house . . . illegal human migrants."

Mr. Peterson's eyes finally snapped up to my face. I could see the fear creeping into his expression as he took in my clipboard, yellow hard hat, and spotless orange safety vest.

"Now, I'm sure you wouldn't want your latest infraction getting back to the Housing Commission," I continued, flipping through my clipboard with a loud *tsk*. "Especially given your . . . multitude of previous violations reported to us."

"What infraction?" Mr. Peterson's face had gone pale. I could practically see the gears turning in his head, calculating the cost of bribes versus the risk of an official investigation.

"Unit 901," I said.

"Look," he said, lowering his voice. "There must be some misunderstanding. Unit 901 was never rented to any . . . unauthorized residents. It's empty."

I made another note on my clipboard. "Uh-huh. Suuuuure it wasn't. Because I have documentation riiiiiiight here showing a deposit payment of one thousand dollars from . . ." I pretended to squint at the paper. "A North Acadian . . . Mr. Kilborne, who doesn't appear to be an Omnithornian resident."

"That's not . . . I mean . . ." He was sweating now, blinking pale eyes at me. "Perhaps we could resolve this unofficially?"

"Perhaps," I said, making another note. "Though falsifying rental documents is a serious offense. The Commission takes a very dim view of landlords enabling unauthorized human residency."

Mr. Peterson's hands were shaking as he pulled open his desk drawer. "How about we forget about unit 901? Here's the deposit back, plus . . . a little extra for your trouble." He counted out fifteen hundred in crumpled Omnibux bills.

I took my time examining each note, holding them up to the light. "Well . . . I suppose I could mark this property for a follow-up review in six months instead of initiating immediate proceedings." I tucked the money into my clipboard. "But I'll be watching this address very carefully, Mr. Peterson."

"Of course, of course," he stammered out. "Thank you for your . . . understanding."

The man nodded vigorously as I wrote up a fake receipt and slipped it onto his desk.

"Here's your receipt for the refund. Thank you for your cooperation," I said, pausing at the door. "Word of advice, though—you really shouldn't accept payments from North Acadian residents anymore. Makes things . . . awfully complicated." I tapped my clipboard meaningfully. "Have a good day."

I started the engine, wincing at the new grinding sound it made. *Come on, van, don't die on me now!*

I needed to get out of Scab Row before Mr. Peterson had time to think too hard about our interaction. He had clearly already deposited the check I OUPS'd him from North Acadia.

It was Sunday and tomorrow morning the check would bounce as the Omnithornian Bank clerk figured out that my old checking account had no money in it, and then the scummy landlord would be out 1,500 violets.

The van protested, shaking and sputtering as I guided it back onto the main road.

In another hour, having pulled off the mustache and washed off the face paint, I sat in the corner of Omnibucks, nursing my free water cup.

The barista, a teenage Chupacabra with purple-dyed hair, had stopped giving me suspicious looks after I bought a sandwich around hour three. The Wi-Fi password and the comfy leather couch was my lifeline to planning my next moves.

The city of Leviathan's Cradle sprawled across my screen in satellite view courtesy of Oodlemap.

I'd already memorized the main bus routes, found the cheapest laundromats, and mapped out which neighborhoods to avoid and which to stay in. Uncle George's voice echoed in my head: "Knowledge is power, kid. The more you know about a place, the harder it will be for that place to hurt you."

The Cradle Foot Fitness Center's website practically glowed with the promise of *7-Day Trial Membership for New Members! Experience Our Premium Facilities!* Translation: hot showers, clean bathrooms. I downloaded the coupon to my phone, already imagining how good it would feel to wash off three days of road grime.

I pulled up the Skyfall Academy website again, smirking at the sleek design. The acceptance letter sat in my personal inbox, a testament to months of careful planning.

The scholarship page mocked me with its generosity. Even with maximum financial aid, the tuition remained astronomical. No human from Scab Row could ever hope to pay off the debts after graduation, as nobody hired humans in Omnithornia for above minimum wage work.

I smirked, recalling how much effort it took to construct my new identity.

"My" deceased "father"—Dr. Slate Glock, a minor Thunderbird bureaucrat who'd died in a skiing accident six months ago, had been perfect. No living relatives, minimal digital footprint, and most importantly, no children listed in his obituary.

The real work had been backdating Acadian records.

The classification as Hominull Omnithis—aka half-blood or "Nullie," as they were commonly known here—was crucial. Nullies were treated better than humans but still faced heavy discrimination in Omnithornia.

My way in was through exploiting the Academy's own prejudices. Their online application system had different security levels based on species classification. Pure Omnithean applications went through rigorous parental verification. Human applications were rejected right away (as one had to be an Omnid to get Omnithornian citizenship).

But the rare mixed-blood Nullie applications? They fell into a bureaucratic blind spot. The system assumed no one would want to fake being a Nullie—after all, who would choose to be part of the most pitied and patronized class in Omnithornia?

I'd discovered this weakness months ago while probing the Academy's submission portal. The Nullie application track had basic validation but skipped the biometric scans required for other categories. Instead, it relied heavily on the father's Omnithean credentials, probably because the system designers couldn't imagine a human teenager clever enough to impersonate a dead Thunderbird's offspring.

I clicked the *Book interview time* URL in the acceptance email.

In a few days' time, Alexander Glock would walk through Skyfall Academy's gates. And Martin Kilborne would disappear completely like a ripple from a jagged stone dropped into a muddy puddle.

The purple-haired barista was giving me looks again.

Time to move on. I packed up my reinforced phone-tablet and shouldered my backpack, and headed for the door. The van was waiting, faithful despite its protests.

Uncle George's words followed me into the gathering darkness as I pulled into the Omnimart parking lot and rolled out the camping bag across the metal floor: "The trick isn't just surviving, kid. It's making them all think that you belong."

The Omnimart security was incredibly lax. I had picked this particular gigastore due to its posh location, the average area income stated on Remax.om making my eye twitch.

It took me a few days of scouting in disguise to understand the inner warehouse workings. Finding a few old order receipts in a recycle bin was exactly what I needed.

I rolled the heavy box across the dock, my heart surprisingly steady.

The "inventory checklist" clipboard and my deliberately rushed movements sold the image of just another overworked stock boy doing overtime.

I could have carried out an entire chair with ease past the bored-looking Omnithean cashiers smoking in the back of the building.

Their eyes slid right past me as I calmly walked out of the truck-loading back door with my green-skin makeup, clipboard, mustache, and safety vest with the yellow hard hat featuring the Omnimart logo printout taped to the front.

Everything I needed for academic life was now in my possession: sixty phones, a laptop, school bags, board games, generic and professional-grade pyrotechnics (technically only legal for licensed Omnithean entertainment companies), three high-end cameras with telephoto and fisheye lenses, wireless microphones, tripods, and an assortment of miscellaneous outfits ranging from maintenance uniforms to security guard outfits.

My clipboard was my shield against any scrutiny. Clipped to it were purchase orders from a fake entertainment company, delivery confirmation numbers from various suppliers, and even a forged event permit. If anyone stopped me, my paperwork would be in perfect order.

Nobody bothered me about my box of warehouse-stolen items.

The van wobbled lightly under the weight of the new equipment as I carefully stowed everything away.

I patted the van's rusty dashboard, feeling oddly sentimental.

"Just one last trip, girl. Then you can rest."

The engine made a sound like a dying bird as I turned the key. After three tries, it finally caught, black smoke puffing from the exhaust.

I adjusted the collar of my pure white Omnimart button-up shirt, still stiff with its factory creases. New, spotless leather shoes, dark pants, and a black backpack completed my eager-student-to-be outfit.

The morning sun caught my new DSLR camera's lens as it bounced against my chest. The week of using the gym's trial membership had done wonders for my appearance and my nose. No more van smell clinging to my skin.

Movement in the distance caught my eye—three shapes on the third floor of the half-finished office building across from Skyfall Academy. Even from this distance, I could make out the distinctive profiles of brown, gray, and red forms perched casually on exposed I-beams as if they owned the place.

I sat down on a concrete bench and raised the camera lens, observing them for a few minutes through the viewfinder, studying the patterns of my potential prey.

They were exactly the kind of crowd I needed to befriend—rebellious, young, local. The kind of kids who might know which teachers asked too many questions and which ones would sign anything you put in front of them.

The dragon-bird-girl caught my eye first—all black everything, from her tall combat boots to her raggedy fishnet-patched pants under a short chain-covered skirt. A black leather jacket with a few colorful pins, a tight black top featuring the rainbow prism eye of the Violet Floyd logo hugged her chest, and a dark leather silver skull choker glinted at her throat.

The dark and broody outfit was a stark contrast against her silver-white-blue scales. Silver feathers shifted in the breeze, folded wings and feathered tail lashing behind her. Something about her reminded me of the punk kids back home, the ones who knew all the best places to hide when you needed to disappear for a while.

Yulia, my personal, jailbroken LLM with vision connected to the newly stolen camera and tied into the school's yearbook database, identified the teenage punk humanoid female as a Quetzalcoatl by the name of Cassiopeia Nova, enrolled in grade twelve.

The Quetzi elongated snout and fluttering silver wings called out to my aesthetic sensibilities as if she were a siren of the deep blue sea. She was tall, way taller than me, especially if you considered the feathery explosion on the back of her head. Then again, this wasn't out of the ordinary—all Omnids were bigger than humans.

Next to the punk angel was a red-and-gold figure of a Rubicund Lindworm—Emerald Stratos, according to Yulia's quiet whisper in my earpiece. Crystalline ruby mane caught the sunlight like fresh blood, slightly more orange scales of her body gleaming as she walked across the steel beam. She moved with the casual confidence of someone who had never doubted her place in the world as the number one. Even from this distance, I could see her gold-orange eyes scanning the area like a Pride Queen marking her territory.

Emerald was wearing a designer leather jacket in deep burgundy, covered in gemstone spikes and damage-nullifying gold runes probably worth more than all of the equipment I had harvested from Omnimart this morning. Multiple gold chains dotted with ruby hexagram gemstones glinted at her neck, and several gold magic rings sat on her fingers. Her tall boots with gold buckles looked custom-made, rune-reinforced, and probably as expensive as a house in North Acadia. Her belt buckle was studded with large diamonds, completing the "I'm a firstborn prima donna of an excessively wealthy dragon clan" look.

According to Yulia's analysis, the third figure, perched slightly away from the two predator ladies, was a Deathskull Mothman named Iogann Wanderer.

Iogann's outfit was a patchy hippie-style gray-teal tunic with orange triangle-pattern edges. He had a very chill attitude about him. A wide brimmed gray-teal hat sat on his head, which made him look like a darker version of Snufkin from the Moomintroll series. He had fluffy gray antennae, gray wings, and very large dark-gray eyes.

Through my camera lens, I watched as Emerald barked something at Iogann. The Mothman nodded lazily, reached out into his leather side bag, and . . . his hand simply sank into it up to the elbow and then even deeper than what would be physically possible, almost all the way to the shoulder.

When he pulled it back, a crumpled pack of cigarettes sat in his grip.

Yulia failed to recognize the Nonpareil-O's brand of the pack with a smiling paper-clip on the front.

Dimensional gateway ability, I noted mentally. A rare and valuable power—the skill to reach through space itself into other, doomed worlds. Usually activated by apocalyptic-level disasters, according to my research on the Deathskull Mothmen.

The pack was scorched around the edges, and through my zoom lens I could make out what looked like bits of gray ash raining down from the box. Maybe a nuclear war in some parallel Earth, or the death of a sun, or perhaps the moon exploding. Whatever had forced those cigarettes to seek refuge in our dimension via Iogann's hand . . . it probably wasn't very nice at all.

I quietly watched their morning ritual unfold, studying the relationship of the trio.

Iogann passed around the interdimensional cigarettes with practiced ease.

The Lindworm lit hers with a casual snap of dark red claws, the spark dancing between her fingers before catching. From what I recalled, summoning dragonfire was a rare Lindworm skill. Her family definitely had a massive stash of gold and artifacts in their Omnibank safe for her to be able to produce magic fire with such ease.

The Mothman ignited his own deathstick with an elaborate brass lighter that looked as if it belonged in a steampunk novel, all gears and tiny pistons that whirred to life when he flicked it open.

The Quetzalcoatl fumbled in her black jacket's pocket and produced a cheap plastic lighter in neon pink, the kind you'd find at any gas station checkout counter. The shoddy 99-cent lighter seemed oddly out of place among her "I'm totally ragged, but I actually cost an arm and a leg" punk attire.

I snapped a few more photos, making sure to capture their casual interactions.

Emerald seemed to be the leader of the group, dominating the conversation, her gestures sharp and commanding. Iogann maintained his relaxed posture despite her intensity. Cassiopeia kept slightly apart from them, her body language and scowling face suggesting that perhaps she wasn't entirely comfortable with the group dynamic or maybe had a headache.

The smoke rings she blew out made my eye twitch ever so slightly.

Observe. Wait for the right moment.

Nicotine, for all the horrible things it did, also relaxed people.

I took a deep breath after another minute, adjusting my generic-looking student backpack filled to the brim with stolen game boards.

Time to put on the show.

I walked forward and lifted my camera, pretending to frame a shot of the construction site's skeletal framework against the morning sky. Just a friendly photography student, nothing suspicious here.

I moved closer, making sure to stay in their peripheral vision.

"Hey, guys!" I called out, lowering my camera. "Any of you know if this is the right way to Skyfall Academy? I'm starting there today and these maps are useless." I pulled out my armored phone, displaying the deliberately confusing route I'd looked up earlier.

The Quetzalcoatl girl's unnaturally ocean-blue eyes fixed on me, pupils narrowing slightly. Even from three stories down, I could feel the "why the fuck are you bothering me, Nullie?" weight of her stare.

Cassiopeia suddenly stood up, took a step forward, and launched herself from the I-beam with casual grace.

Her wings opened wide, far wider than I expected the full wingspan to be, and my heartbeat intensified tenfold.

Her wings caught the morning light and then each feather ignited with a rainbow of colors. My breath caught in my throat as she descended in a lazy flutter, dark jacket rippling in the wind. She looked like something out of a dream—half angel, half prehistoric deity-predator, all dangerous.

She landed a few feet away from me with a jingle of skirt-chains and the soft thud of combat boots on concrete. Up close, she was even more striking—sharp features softened by wisps of colorful feathers slowly fading back to silver-blue. Her intense silver-blue eyes studied me with predatory focus.

A thin trail of cigarette smoke curled up from between her fingers.

"You're way off," she said, her clear voice carrying a hint of mild amusement. "School's that way."

She gestured with her free hand, the movement causing her wings to shift slightly. I tried not to stare at how the sunlight played across her feathers with a million rainbow refractions, featuring extra alien colors that my eyes simply refused to process.

Holy shit, so many iridescent feathers. Magic feathered dragon central.

Inexplicably, for the first time in a decade of swindling people and cryptid monsters, my carefully prepared response died somewhere between my brain and my mouth. All those hours of planning, all of Uncle George's lessons about staying focused, and here I was, struck dumb by a pretty girl with wings.

Real smooth, idiot. Real smooth.

Above us, her friends were making their way down via the construction site's stairs, but I barely noticed. I was too busy trying to remember how to form coherent sentences while pretending I wasn't completely mesmerized by the way her wings folded against her back.

All my carefully crafted NPC scripts crashed like a blue screened Windows. The practiced lies, the smooth introductions, the calculated persona I'd spent hours perfecting—all of it vanished like morning mist in the face of those piercing eyes.

My brain kept trying to reboot:

> Alexander Glock.exe has stopped working.
> Would you like to restore Functional Human Being? Y/N
> Error 404: Original Personality Not Found.

I was dimly aware that I probably looked like an idiot, standing there with my camera hanging uselessly around my neck, staring at her as though I'd never seen a Quetzalcoatl before. Which, okay, I hadn't—not up *this* close, not one that had just descended from the sky like some kind of punk rock Valkyrie.

The cigarette smoke curled around her in lazy spirals, and all I could think was how unfair it was that even the deathstick looked cool on her. The morning sun caught her sparkly, now pure-silver feathery head just right, creating a rainbow halo effect around her that made my thoughts scatter into all directions, as my brain continued its spectacular system failure.

I forced my jelly-legs to move, Uncle George's voice cutting through the fog: "Never let them see you freeze, kid. When in doubt, exit stage left."

"Thanks!" I finally managed to squeak out after far too long of a pause, my voice embarrassingly high. "Should . . . get going. Waauldn't wanna . . . be . . . late!"

I could hear her friends' footsteps getting closer, and I had no jokes, no introductions, nothing but empty endlessness in my head. Nothing except for the desire to bow down and worship her.

I backed away from the mind-melting dragon-angel, nearly tripping over my own feet in my haste to escape. The Quetzalcoatl raised an eyebrow, taking another drag of her cigarette as she watched me retreat.

"See you around, new kid," she called after me, a hint of something—amusement? curiosity?—in her voice.

Her voice sent shivers down my spine as if she rolled a perfect twenty charisma check against me.

Argh! Now I knew exactly how the Aztec priests felt. At this rate, I would totally locate an obsidian blade, slice open some poor fool's chest, and offer their still-beating heart to *her*. Not that she would accept it. The twenty-first-century Omnitheans were a civilized people mired in laws and rules just as much as us mundane humans.

I gave an awkward wave and speed-walked around the corner, not quite running but definitely moving faster than any self-respecting NPC should. As soon as I was out of sight, I leaned against a wall, heart pounding.

What the actual fuck was that?

Years of careful planning, countless hours practicing different personas, and I'd completely short-circuited at the first sign of pretty feathers. Uncle George would be laughing his ass off if he could see me now.

I took a deep breath, straightening my stolen jacket. Okay. Reset. This was fine. I could still salvage this. I just needed to . . .

Never interact with Cassiopeia Nova ever again.

No, that's . . . exceptionally stupid. Obviously she had some kind of a "worship me" innate charisma aura-skill that targeted pure humans like me.

Yeah, that has to be it.

Solution? Interact with her forever, as much as possible. Like eating bits of poison to get used to it. What was that called?

I tapped my stolen smartwatch, asking for the answer.

Yulia took a second to process and whisper the answer into the microscopic wax-covered speaker buried deep in my ear.

"Mithridatism—building immunity through controlled exposure to toxins."

Yeah, that's what I needed. Small doses of interaction until I could build up resistance to whatever the hell just happened to my brain.

Did I have time for that, though? I certainly didn't. The clock on my life was running out, minutes from midnight; the hounds were almost upon me. Next week they would be here in Omnithornia. Mithridatism took years. I only had a week to live at best, maybe two . . . before they would catch me, chop me up, and stuff me into a suitcase for my crimes in North Acadia.

I straightened up, adjusting my camera strap.

Alexander Glock.exe relaunched successfully.

I checked the smartwatch again. Still plenty of time until my appointment. I could circle around the block, compose myself, and maybe approach the school from a different direction. Maybe by then my stomach would stop doing that weird fluttery thing every time I thought about those sky-blue eyes.

Focus. Mission parameters hadn't changed. I still needed to:

1. Get enrolled in Skyfall. [ ]
2. Secure one of those infinite free food meal cards and an immortality bracelet. [ ]
3. Find a better sleeping location than the rust-covered van now permanently parked in one of the school's student parking lots. [ ]
4. Build a network of useful cryptid patsies. [ ]
5. Learn everything there is to know. Figure out if mundane humans can even level up like Omnids through dimensional gate dungeon delving. [ ]
6. Acquire best friends. [ ] Delve to Arx. [ ] Steal a tank. [ ] Acquire a fortified citadel. [ ] Fortify it even harder. [ ] Start a clan. [ ] Steal a dungeon. [ ] Make a death ray. [ ]
7. Locate a Hearth Keeper Shield and Prima Hunter Sword and marry them like a goodly Nazarite to secure Omnithornian citizenship. [ ]
   7.1. Do *not* get derailed by charmchain magic of Quetzalcoatl girls who probably smoke because they have a death wish. [ ]

Wish I had pretty mind-control angel wings like that. The things I could . . .

No. Focus. I mentally slapped myself.

Point six had tasks listed in order from easy to impossible that made me smile at the mad absurdity of my bucket list. Technically, magic death rays existed and the Omnithornian Legion had magitek tanks armed with dragonfire that could vaporize entire cities in a flash, but getting my hands on one of those would be straight up suicide. Still, it didn't hurt to dream big.

I took another deep breath, slowing my heartbeat and feeling Alex settle back into place like a comfortable mask. This was fine. I could do this. I'd already conned my way across half the continent! One pretty Omnithean girl wasn't going to derail everything!

Focus. Breathe in, breathe out. Relax.

Today . . . I would have the key to eternity.

The thought of months of functional immortality made my hands shake slightly as I took the first step up the front gate stairwell. Not that I was looking forward to dying—the prospect of pain still terrified me, but the school's Phoenix program was key to everything.

I was no superhero—I had none of the strength of a Sasquatch, none of the psychic or dimensional powers of a Mothman, none of the regenerative abilities of a Wendigo.

I was just a human kid in a nation of monsters with a desperate, mad plan to rise far above my station and a burning desire to make them all pay for what they'd done to my mom.

After all, the best way to destroy a system wasn't to attack it from the outside; it was to set it on fire from within.

CHAPTER TWO

The Vice Principal and Student Council

I walked through Skyfall Academy's front gates feeling like a lone gazelle strolling into a pride of lions. Except these lions came in every color of the rainbow and most of them towered over me. A yellow-and-black-striped Tanystropheus ducked her long neck to whisper something to a green Basilisk, both of them glancing my way. A group of Sasquatch teens in varsity jackets paused their conversation to watch me pass.

The hallways were a riot of color and motion—tails swishing, feathers rustling, horns and necks decorated with ribbons, hexagrammic gems and collars. I kept my pace steady, my expression neutral.

I'd memorized the school layout from their website, so I navigated the corridors with practiced confidence, even as my peripheral vision caught more and more curious, shocked, or bothered stares.

They weren't outright attacking me yet—that would come much later in all sorts of insidious ways.

Skyfall's diversity quota imposed upon the school by the recently elected Silver Wing Party required the Academy to accept a certain percentage of "non-pure" students, but most wealthy Omnitheans wouldn't let their mixed-breed children apply. This left the Academy desperately short on their Nullie numbers.

Scrolling through old social media posts about Skyfall Academy revealed why this was the case. Those few who had attended in previous years rarely lasted the entire semester. The harassment was brutal, not just from students but sometimes from older teachers who viewed Nullies as living reminders of "genetic pollution" or "a waste of an education." Last year's only Nullie student had transferred out after three months of what the school dismissively called "social adjustment difficulties." The unofficial forums told a darker story of "accidents" particularly during physical education, dungeon delving practice, and dimensional field trips.

Simply put, nobody was insane enough to be bullied to death repeatedly . . . except for my crazy self. Because I had nothing left to lose and everything to gain.

As I passed by what appeared to be an art classroom, I suddenly became completely surrounded by a flock of Omnids.

Their eyes lit up as if they'd discovered some rare specimen, which I suppose I was. Phones came out and the chattering started. The colorful crowd trapped me in a tight circle with no way out, like a leukocyte cell getting ready to devour a filthy parasite invader that managed to make its way into the body.

"Yeesh! Look at how smooth and pink he is!"

"Is it true that your bones will snap from a single tap of my tail?"

"Hold still, I need a reference shot for my comic!"

I tried to get a word in edgewise, but there was too much chatter and the crowd was entirely caught up in their frenzy. Phone cameras clicked from all sides, and I was starting to feel like a zoo exhibit or a celebrity being bothered by paparazzi.

This won't do.

With a smirk, I reached into my pocket and pulled out one of the stolen Omnimart Thunderclap Party Poppers. The loud thunderclap from the string-pull echoed through the hallway like a gunshot, making several of the Omnids jump. All eyes shot towards my face, some with fear, others in confusion, the crowd-manifested memetic frenzy over my obvious humanness broken like a spell.

I wondered if they expected the human to have a gun on them or something, the way they stared at me with shocked eyes. If Scab Row was anything to judge by, the answer was yes—most humans were a lowly criminal underclass.

"Ladies, gentlemen, and distinguished artists," I announced, channeling my best showman voice. "Alexander Glock, photographer and fellow creative spirit, at your service. While I'm very flattered by your interest in my person, perhaps we could handle this more professionally?"

I pulled out my oversized phone, trying not to laugh at their startled expressions. "If you'd like to use me as a reference for your art projects, I'd be happy to provide a proper signed release form. Just share your Omnigram IDs with me. After all," I added with a theatrical wink, "we wouldn't want any copyright issues down the line, would we?"

The way their expressions shifted from surprise to sheepish understanding was priceless. They had expected a null weakling to take pics of and to post on Omnigram. Instead, a predator armed with a theoretical army of lawyers stared back at them with confident eyes.

The crowd thinned slightly as the more timid artists shuffled away, but many remained, eagerly sharing their Omnigram IDs with phone-to-phone screen taps.

I smiled as I gathered the IDs.

Private messages were like perfect digital skeleton keys—unlock the right doors, and you could access entire networks of information and influence. Each of these Omnids probably had their own circles, their own connections.

"I'll send you all the release forms tonight," I promised.

As the crowd dispersed, two figures lingered—a white-and-black Thunderbird and a dark-red Olgoi-Khorkhoi. The Thunderbird was wearing a flashy blue dress, sparkly chainmail top with dark leather straps, steel wrist bracers, and steel talon-covers shaped like bird skulls. The Mongolian Deathworm had a dark leather biker's outfit topped with a lavish gold semitransparent robe clipped to gold-plated shoulder covers.

"Sup. I'm Vespera," the Thunderbird introduced herself, her feathers sparkling ever so slightly. "Your bone structure is baller—mind a few selfies? Are you . . . a pure human?"

"Close to one," I shrugged.

"How close?" the Olgoi-Khorkhoi beside her demanded with a scowl. Her forehead mouth and petal face was giving me the heebie-jeebies.

"I'm what they call a Hominull Omnithis," I explained, keeping my tone light. "Dad was a Thunderbird too, actually. Though obviously I didn't inherit much beyond amplified intelligence and some basic resistance to electricity."

"A mixed-blood?" Vespera tilted her head slightly. "Oh. That's . . . um. We had one of those last year. She, umm . . . transferred to another school."

"Dumb Nullie beerch couldn't handle the Arx-delving." The Olgoi-Khorkhoi rolled her eyes. "Couldn't even stick to her assigned inn room. Got chopped up in Shandria overnight like a stakeling."

Riiiight, I thought. I knew exactly what happened to Sarah Nisteroff. The forums had been quite detailed about her "accident," including photos of her remains taken by one of her classmates. The Phoenix Forge had brought her back, but the PTSD from being slowly sliced joint by joint like sushi by shadow blades had remained. Transferring schools was probably the kindest option.

"Oh! You should like totally join the History Club. We're always looking for . . . diverse perspectives," Vespera said in a thick Valley girl accent. "I'm a big fan of old cultures 'n' such. Have a couple of Lamassu statues from the citadel of Sargon of Akkad at home facing the front door!"

I caught the undertone in her voice, the way her steel-gray eyes gleamed with sparks of gold. The invitation wasn't entirely friendly—it was a challenge. Or maybe a threat.

"Hrm. What does the History Club do?" I asked, keeping my tone carefully neutral despite the predatory look in Vespera's eyes.

"Oh, you know." She waved a perfectly manicured, armored hand, her black-and-white feathers rustling. "We dress up in period-accurate costumes, take aesthetic photos for our Omnigram, and sometimes we do historical reenactments." Her smile showed too many razor-sharp, pearly-white teeth. "Last week we were studying medieval European warfare. Had quite a few . . . hands-on lessons with maces and flails."

"Verrry hands-on." The Olgoi-Khorkhoi grinned, cracking her knuckles.

"We've got a bunch of old humani outfits too, 1580s Renaissance armor belonging to medieval prince-knights and such. I'd totes love to see what they look like on a fully human-shaped mixie Omnid like you," Vespera smiled.

"Sounds fun. Count me in," I agreed. "I do enjoy dressing up and smashing things. Good practice to break the mold."

Both girls blinked in surprise at my eager acceptance. Clearly they'd expected me to pick up on their thinly veiled threats and run away.

"Really?" Vespera's perfectly sculpted eyebrows rose. "Most . . . Nul . . . um, non-reinforced, low-level peeps tend to avoid our club on account of breaking their limbs or snouts too often."

"Most people clearly don't appreciate history enough," I said with a shrug. "Omnigram me the details and I'll be there."

"I'll make sure to find you myself . . . if you chicken out on us, Nullie." The Olgoi-Khorkhoi leaned forward menacingly.

"Pfff. I'm absolutely looking forward to smashing your lovely face with a mace, Solace Exill," I replied smoothly, enjoying the way her gold eyes widened in shock. "I'd never chicken out of a good medieval battle reenactment."

The deathworm took a step back, her reddish-brown scales bristling. "How do you know my—"

"Name? I make it my business to know everyone," I said with a casual shrug. "I'm part Thundergod, after all, even if I don't look like it on the outside. We collect small, shiny things on the ground. Like dropped names," I added with a wink. "Plus, your Omnigram profile is public. Nice motorcycle collection, by the way."

Solace choked in reply while Vespera laughed.

"You are a clever one! So do you, like, carry store-bought Thunderclaps with you everywhere?" the Thunder-girl asked.

"Only when I really need to catch the attention of such charming ladies," I replied with a wink.

Vespera giggled, a white-and-black hand covering up her beak. Solace huffed.

"You're cute, for a mixie," Vespera said.

"I try," I replied.

"Aight, I wan' a selfie with ya," she added.

Suddenly, both girls pressed against me, squeezing me between them. I fought to keep my expression neutral as Solace's enhanced strength threatened to crack my ribs while Vespera's electrical field made my hair stand on end, causing my bones to hum and throb.

"Smile for the camera!" Vespera chirped, her electrified wing wrapping around my shoulders.

Her embrace felt like hugging a high voltage power transformer. I smiled wide, ignoring how her sharp claws dug into my side, probably leaving violet bruises.

We took a few selfies together, their phones clicking away.

After trading contact info, the pair departed with more giggles, already tapping away at their screens. I watched them go, mentally filing them under "useful airheads," the kind that would click on a phishing link without even thinking about it.

The administration's office was exactly where the map said it would be.

A reinforced crystal case wall featuring various student achievements stood in front of the office, crammed with all sorts of awards, crafts, and student accolades.

From all of the random magical and mundane stuff within, my eyes immediately became drawn to a rather catchy painting.

The art depicted a small town with a gray cathedral in the center. Autumn leaves fluttered in the wind after an end-of-summer rain. A futuristic-looking white ring divided the sky like a massive imaginary megastructure. Four human teens, about fifteen years old, were sitting under a tree, enjoying a sushi picnic. A girl with pure white hair and a yellow hard hat, a boy with brown hair, a girl in gray armor and a gray cape, and a girl in pink pj's with ginger hair.

I stared at the painting for a few minutes. Something about it called out to me, like an old dream that I once had, a song that I had long forgotten. It was the oddest, incredibly unnerving sensation, like the tongue suddenly finding a missing tooth.

I took a photo of the painting, trying to understand how it could screw with my mind, as if implying that I was one of the teenagers, the boy sitting under that tree. Was it painted with the blood of some alien beast or something?

K. Kells, grade 10, I read on a gold plaque below. "Hrm. Pretty damn good art and mind-control skills, Kells. If you didn't already graduate, I just might have some competition here."

I tore my gaze away from the unsettling painting and pushed open the heavy oak door to the admin office.

The secretary—a Kitsune with pristine white fur and nine tails—looked up from her computer. Her golden eyes narrowed slightly as she took in my appearance, but her professional smile never wavered.

"Alexander Glock for 9:15," I said before she could ask.

"Ah, yes, Mr. Glock. You're five minutes early. Please have a seat. The vice principal will see you shortly."

The waiting area walls were covered with the usual school propaganda—motivational images featuring diverse groups of Omnitheans and the occasional token mixie achieving together, sports team photos, academic awards, plus the utterly useless anti-bullying and anti-smoking posters.

I sat in one of the plush chairs, going over my newly acquired contact list.

Vespera had already posted the selfie she took along with a caption: *Found the cutest little mixie!* 🥺 *Can we keep him? #NewPet #DiversityWin #HistoryClubInitiation.*

I fought back a smirk. Let them think I was some harmless curiosity. It would make things easier in the long run.

"Mr. Glock?" the Kitsune secretary called. "Vice Principal Graves will see you now."

I entered the office and immediately had to crane my neck up. Waaaay up.

Vice Principal Graves towered over his mahogany desk, his impossibly tall, thin form wrapped in an immaculate black suit. Where his face should have been, there was . . . nothing at all.

It wasn't as if there were no features; it was more that my brain simply refused to focus on the pure emptiness therein.

Yet somehow, despite his face lacking any eyes, I got the distinct impression that the man was studying me intently.

"Please, have a seat," he said, his voice manifesting in my head as a creaky, staticky whisper. Long, spindly fingers gestured to the chair in front of his desk.

I sat down, keeping my expression neutral despite the way my skin crawled. Unlike the Quetzalcoatl girl who forced me to fall in love with her, the Slenderman vice principal made me feel pure and absolute pants-shitting fear.

Unlike love, fear was easy enough to defeat. I'd felt fear before while running or hiding from the law. I felt and beat it when I faced Wendigo fear-wards. Thus,

I was ready for it, stamping it down with positive thoughts of my impending immortality.

"Alexander Glock," the vice principal's voice echoed in my skull, making me jolt. "Your application was . . . most interesting. We don't get many transfer students mid-semester, especially those of mixed heritage."

I met his nonexistent gaze steadily, channeling every ounce of confidence I could muster. "My previous school burned down, sir. I didn't want to fall behind in my studies."

The vice principal went silent for a moment as I slid a newspaper clipping to him.

Historic St. Christopher's Academy goes up in flames. By Samuella Lacross. SA News.

A devastating fire ravaged St. Christopher's Nazarite Academy early Wednesday morning, leaving the historic institution in ruins. The blaze, which started around 3 AM in the east wing, quickly spread through the century-old structure.

"The damage is extensive," reported Fire Chief Marcus Winters. "The main academic building is a total loss, with severe structural damage to the gymnasium and administrative offices."

No injuries were reported as the fire occurred hours before students and staff would have arrived for classes. Initial investigations suggest an electrical malfunction in the aging wiring system may be to blame . . .

The vice principal's fingers delicately picked up the newspaper clipping, the paper crinkling unnaturally in his grasp. Though he had no visible eyes, I could feel his attention scanning every word.

"Most . . . unfortunate," he finally said, that staticky whisper making my teeth ache.

I nodded. "Father O'Malley assisted with my transfer here. You talked to him on the phone, yes?"

"Yes," the vice principal said. "Father O'Malley of St. Christopher gave you a rather glowing recommendation."

I smiled. Obviously my AI gave me a good recommendation. It wasn't very hard to give Yulia a deep male priestly voice on the phone.

"So, tell me, Mr. Glock, why Skyfall Academy specifically?" the extra-long man asked.

"Skyfall Academy has always been my dream school, sir," I replied, letting a carefully measured amount of enthusiasm seep into my voice. "My father . . . Dr. Glock. He always spoke so highly of Omnithornia's educational system. Before he perished in that tragic avalanche . . . he mentioned wanting me to attend here."

I sniffed, thinking about Mom. "I was hoping that the rescuers would find his Lazarus bracelet and bring him back, but alas, his body must have fallen into a very deep crevasse."

The vice principal nodded again.

I paused, letting my voice catch slightly. "After losing both of my parents, I wanted to honor his wishes. And the Academy's reputation for excellence, especially in dimensional delving and artifact crafting . . . Well, it seemed like the perfect place to challenge myself."

The vice principal's void-like head tilted slightly. "Your father . . . Dr. Slate Glock was a level sixty-eight clerk at the Department of Atmospheric Phenomena?"

"Yes sir." I nodded. "Dad worked in celestorm weather precognition analysis. Not the most glamorous position, but he was proud of his contribution to the Omnithean Superstate."

"And your mother?"

"Mirriam Kilborne," I said softly, using my real mother's name. Sometimes the best lies were wrapped in truth. "She was . . . a human. A comp sci employee of the North Acadia Wendigo Frontenachii Omnicorp. I . . . had to take some time off school to help with her care."

I let go of Alex.exe and looked down at my hands, which started to tremble as my eyes filled with more sparks of tears. An absolute kernel of heartbreaking truth had to be the foundation of any well-spun tale. "She passed away last spring."

"I see." Vice Principal Graves's voice resonated with something that might have been sympathy. "And you've been on your own since?"

"Yes sir. A portion of the insurance money from Dad's skiing accident went to me and helped cover immediate expenses such as my mom's debt, and her medical benefits from Omnicorp provided some support. But . . ." I let my voice trail off, injecting just the right amount of determined optimism. "I'm not looking for handouts. I want to earn my place here, prove that I can contribute something valuable despite my . . . mixed heritage."

The void where his face should be seemed to ripple slightly. "Your academic records from St. Christopher's are quite impressive, particularly in creative arts and computer science. Though I notice a concerning gap in your physical education."

"The Nazarite school curriculum wasn't very focused on combat or delve training," I admitted with carefully crafted sheepishness. "But I'm eager to learn and level up! I know I'll have to work twice or thrice as hard to catch up, but I'm prepared for that challenge."

"You do understand that Skyfall's curriculum is . . . exceptionally demanding?" The vice principal's needlessly long fingers drummed on his desk, dark tentacles writhing and inexplicably sinking elsewhere behind his suit. "Particularly for students of mixed heritage. Our last mixed-blood student found the adjustment . . . difficult."

I nodded solemnly. "I've read about Sarah Nisteroff's . . . transfer, sir. I understand the risks. But I believe that facing challenges head-on is better than hiding from them. My father always said that true growth comes from pushing beyond our perceived limitations."

I got the distinct impression that the lanky, faceless Omnid was pleased by my response. Was he projecting his emotions into my head or something? "An admirable attitude, Mr. Glock. Though I must warn you—our Phoenix Forge system, while remarkable, is not a guarantee of safety. The psychological impact of . . . repeated restoration can be significant."

"I understand, sir," I said firmly. "I'm not afraid of failure, or pain, or death. I'm afraid of not trying at all. If I fall down, I will rise again just like Saint Lazarus. Always. No matter what."

The void where his face should be seemed to study me for a long moment. Finally, he reached into his desk drawer.

"Very well, Mr. Glock. Welcome to Skyfall Academy." He slid a dark hexagon-textured sphere across the desk towards me. "Please be aware that the Lazarus bracelet must be worn at all times. In the event of your . . . eventual demise . . . a fellow student, familiar Corpse Seeker, or faculty member will take the bracelet to the Lazarus cavern for restoration to occur."

"Is there, like, a time limit on the restoration?" I asked, pretending to be a clueless kid.

"The longer you stay dead, the more therapy you will require after," the Slenderman sighed. "Our policy is to restore the dead as soon as possible or within the twenty-four-hour limit."

"What happens after twenty-four hours?" I gulped.

"Soul decay," he answered.

"How fatal is that?"

"That depends on your mental fortitude and the level of your soul," he explained. "Some Omnids can stay dead for months while others decay into insanity in just a few days."

"I see. Okay, how do I make the bracelet connect with my soul?" I asked.

"Simply touch it and say 'bind me,'" he answered.

"Bind me." I tapped the ball with a finger.

The dark hexagonal sphere suddenly animated, unfurling like a mechanical centipede. The segments rippled with an oily sheen as the centipede ran to my left arm and wrapped around my wrist, each hexagonal plate clicking into place with microscopic precision. There was a brief, sharp pain as two-dimensional jagged blades pierced my skin, connecting to my nervous system.

A chilly ripple slowly ran across my entire body from my wrist, making me shudder.

The Lazarus bracelet pulsed once with a deep crimson glow before settling into a dormant state, the blades gone, now just a sleek band of interlocking dark hexagons around my wrist. It felt surprisingly warm against my skin, as if it were alive. Or maybe it was just drawing power from my body heat.

"The initialization process is complete," Vice Principal Graves noted. "I was worried that maybe your Wormwood genetic marker would be too low, but it seems to be in good working order. Usually there's an official ceremony and whatnot, but you did register at a rather busy time of year after Winter See-Mass break."

I nodded.

"If I may ask," Graves inquired curiously, "why did you live with your human mother rather than your Omnithean father after the divorce?"

I let a carefully rehearsed flash of pain across my face. "There . . . wasn't a divorce or a marriage, sir. Dad was never really in the picture much. He and Mom . . . it was complicated. Acadia doesn't permit polygamic marriages like Omnithornia since human birth rate is different from Omnid. Plus, the department kept him busy, and Mom said he had his own family to worry about." I looked down at my hands, letting my voice grow quieter. "I only saw him a few times a year, usually at random. But he always made sure to send support payments and birthday cards. He preferred to keep his distance. Said it was better for his career prospects if certain circles didn't know about his . . . indiscretion up north."

The tentacles behind the long man seemed to darken slightly. "I see. A . . . common arrangement with mixed heritage situations." His tone carried a hint of disapproval. "And you're staying at . . ." He consulted the paperwork. "8008 Fallin Street?"

"Yes sir." I nodded, keeping my expression neutral despite the way my stomach clenched. "It's temporary housing while I look for something closer to campus. The landlord, Mr. Peterson, has been very . . . accommodating. Sadly, someone keeps breaking into the mailbox, so here's a P.O. box address for any of my school mail."

I slid a document over to Mr. Graves.

"Scab Row is hardly an appropriate residence for a Skyfall student." The vice principal's fuzzy voice rippled with clear distaste. "We do have dormitory accommodations available, though there would be additional fees . . ."

"I appreciate the offer, sir," I said quickly. "But my scholarship doesn't cover a residence. The apartment is . . . adequate for now. Dad rented it for me last year," I added smoothly. "His aunt lived in the area thirty years ago, back when Scab Row wasn't . . . well, quite as rough as it is now. Said it used to be quite the artistic community. That was of course before the Topaz-peddling gangs took over the area."

"Mmm, yes," the Slenderman sighed. "That neighborhood has . . . changed significantly."

I nodded.

"Given your unique living circumstances, I believe that you qualify for our Community Support Initiative."

Yesss. Bless me with nom perks.

"Really?" I looked up hopefully, voice still trembling. "I . . . I don't want to be a burden . . ."

"Nonsense." He waved one elongated hand dismissively. "Education is never a burden, and you will pay the meal card off after graduation. Now, these forms will need to be filled out . . ." He began explaining the paperwork.

I nodded along as Vice Principal Graves walked me through the various forms and policies, carefully noting which ones might be useful later. The meal card he handed to me was a godsend—theoretically unlimited food from any campus cafeteria or vending machine. No more living off stolen protein bars for me!

"Your class schedule will be arranged with the assistance of our Student Council representatives," Vice Principal Graves continued, shuffling through more papers with his impossibly long fingers.

"Isn't that usually an administrative task?" I asked.

"Skyfall Academy believes in empowering our student leadership. The Student Council has shown remarkable insight in evaluating new transfers and making appropriate class placement recommendations. They can assess . . . social dynamics that we as administrators might miss."

I translated that in my head: They figure out if you're worth keeping or not.

"The Council's suggestions are usually quite accurate," he continued.

I nodded.

"Let me call in our Student Council representatives. They'll give you a tour of the facilities and interview you." His spindly finger pressed down on the intercom button. "Christi Negal and Lance Nova to the vice principal's office, please."

While we waited, Vice Principal Graves continued reviewing policies—dress code (nonexistent due to the incredibly diverse student body, business casual for showcase events, hexamesh or heavier armor for delves), attendance requirements (death was not an excuse for missing assignments), and the various clubs and activities available.

I nodded along, but my mind was racing.

A few minutes later, there was a knock at the door. Two Omnids entered the office—a tall, bulky, gray-skinned Dover Demon with piercing orange eyes, and a slender girl with yellow-brown-black skin, bright yellow eyes, and a fiery orange head of flames.

"Lance Nova," Yulia whispered in my ear. "Brother to Cassiopeia Nova." Ah, the punk angel who'd short-circuited my brain earlier. "A Dover Demon, firstborn son of Justice Nova."

"Christi Negal," the LLM added. "Cherufe. Fire elemental. Student Council Secretary. Daughter of Minister Nitish Negal."

"Ah, Lance, Christi," Vice Principal Graves declared jovially, nearly giving me a heart attack as uninvited, glitchy static danced over my eyes. "This is Alexander Glock, our new transfer student from Acadia. I'd like you to help arrange his class schedule and show him around campus."

I examined the students. Christi was wearing a classy pink-and-black suit and skirt, while Lance was dressed in a neutral gray tracksuit with a hexamesh outfit underneath glittering with a network of thin gold hexagon-arranged strings.

"Hi! Welcome to Skyfall Academy!" Christi practically bounced forward, her enthusiasm fiery like a small sun. Her hair flared brighter, radiating heat. "We're so happy to have you here! Aren't we, Laaancy?"

"Of course." Lance nodded, his voice warm and friendly despite his slightly imposing bulk. "It's not often we get transfer students, especially from so far up north!"

"We'll take good care of him, sir." Lance turned to the vice principal. "The Student Council takes its mentoring responsibilities very seriously."

"Thank you both." Vice Principal Graves nodded. "Mr. Glock, you're in good hands. Please remember that my door is always open if you have any concerns."

I stood, gathering my paperwork. "Thank you, sir. I really appreciate this opportunity."

As we left the office, Christi immediately linked her arm through mine, her skin radiating an uncomfortable amount of heat. "So! Alexander! Can I call you Alex? Tell us all about yourself! What brings you to Skyfall? What are your interests? Do you like spicy food? What's your favorite color? Have you ever been in a dungeon . . ."

I blinked at her, not able to let a single word into the machine-gun stutter.

" . . . delve before? Oh! Do you have a girlfriend? Or boyfriend? Or both? Or several? What's your star sign?" Christi's rapid-fire questions came out in an excited rush, her fiery hair and eyes flickering with each word.

Lance simply walked beside us, eyeing me up.

I tried to edge away slightly from the scalding touch without being too obvious about it. "Um, Alex is fine. Dad recommended the school. I'm mostly interested in photography, art, and computer science. No dungeoneering experience yet. Single and on the lookout for a partner or two. I like spicy food just fine," I continued, trying to match Christi's enthusiastic energy while subtly creating a bit more space between us. My arm was starting to feel as though it was getting sunburned. "As for my favorite color . . . silver-blue tone. And I'm a Scorpio . . . I think?"

"You're an Aquarius," Yulia commented into my earpiece. I ignored her.

Martin was an Aquarius. Alexander Glock is a Scorpion with a gun!

"Ohmigosh, you're going to love it here!" Christi squealed, her hair flaring brighter. "We have the best art program and amazing delving opportunities, and the computer lab just got upgraded with lab-grown meta-flesh processors, and there's this amazing Thai place nearby that does the most incredible curry . . ."

"Christi," Lance cut in smoothly, "perhaps we should focus on his class schedule first? We don't want to overwhelm our new friend. Also, I think you're burning his shirt."

"Oh! Sorry!" Christi released my arm, looking sheepish as I tried not to wince at the scorched fabric. "I get excited meeting new people! Especially mixed-heritage students—we don't get many of those!"

"It's fine," I assured her, discreetly patting out a small ember. "I appreciate the extra-warm and sparkly welcome."

Lance rolled his eyes at my terrible pun while Christi burst into delighted giggles, her hair raining sparks.

As we walked through the halls, I carefully observed my two guides, mentally cataloging every detail. Their dynamic was interesting—Christi dominated the conversation while Lance seemed content to let her take the lead, occasionally adding helpful comments.

"So how long have you two been on the Student Council?" I asked.

"Since sophomore year!" Christi beamed.

"Uh-huh." I nodded. "So is there more Student Council body, or is it just you two?"

"Oh no, there's lots more of us!" Christi's flames danced excitedly. "Quint Thornton is our President—he's a Wendigo, super organized and really good at getting things done. He's manning the office right now! Then there's Mira Blackquill, our Treasurer—she's a Basilisk and absolutely brilliant with numbers. Jasper Froth handles Athletics—he's a Yeti like Coach Canard. And Diana Moonwanes is our Events Coordinator—she's a Skinwalker, amazing at planning parties! Plus we have class representatives for each grade level. I'm the rep for your grade!"

"The Council handles everything from club budgets to school events to student disputes," Lance added. "We take our responsibilities very seriously."

"Sounds intense," I commented, recalling seeing a few "best of class" delving awards in the name of Lance Nova. "How do you balance all that with classes and delving practice?"

"Oh, it's not so bad!" Christi waved me off, trailing sparks. "We're all pretty good at multitasking. I've always loved helping organize events and making sure everything runs smoothly," She fired more words out like a machine gun. "Plus it looks great on college applications! Oh, and the cafeteria is right through here." Christi gestured enthusiastically. "The food's expensive but sooo good, especially on Taco Tuesdays! Lance and I always share lunch. Feel free to join us tomorrow! Wouldn't want you to eat by yourself!"

"That won't be a problem," I said.

"Oh? You already know someone to sit with?" Christi tilted her head, looking a bit disappointed.

"Nah," I said. "I'll be setting up a chess game or two during lunch and offering people to beat me."

"Oh, how fun! You're into chess, too!" Christi bobbled, leading me to the school courtyard from the dining hall.

She dropped onto a wooden park bench with a big smile, her pink skirt fluttering in the wind. Small embers danced around her as she patted the spot next to her. The bench was positioned perfectly to catch both the morning sun and a view of Skyfall Academy's imposing architecture.

"This is my favorite spot," she declared proudly. "You can see everything from here! Look at those white spires—aren't they gorgeous? They're made from processed mana crystals, harvested from the deepest delving zones and then fused to the Leviathan's bones comprising the brickwork. They glow all sorts of pretty colors at sunset!"

I settled carefully beside her, maintaining a respectful distance to avoid any accidental burns. Lance remained standing, his gray bulk casting a shadow over us.

"The Academy's architecture is . . . certainly interesting," I commented, studying the way the white crystalline towers sparkled in the light. "Very different from St. Christopher's. We just had regular stone and brick buildings."

"Oh, this is nothing compared to what's inside those spires!" Christi's hair flickered excitedly. "The upper levels have these amazing meditation rooms where you can practice channeling your powers and level up! And the view from the top is absolutely incredible—you can see all the way to the Dreadspine Mountains on a clear day!"

She gestured enthusiastically at various spots around the courtyard. "That corner over there is perfect for studying between classes—it gets great shade in the afternoon.

"And over there is where most students hang out during breaks," Christi continued, pointing to a cluster of benches and tables near a massive ancient oak tree. "Though you might want to avoid the west wing of the park—that's where the Skinwalker clans tend to gather. They can be a bit . . . intense about their territory."

I nodded. "Any other spots I should know about?"

"The library is handy for a studious mind," Lance spoke up. "Nine floors of arcane and mundane books, plus private study rooms."

After another hour of roaming across the massive Cathedraltown citadel-style campus, the pair led me to the Student Council office, where I was rapidly introduced to the Student President manning the computer desk.

The Student Council office was a stark contrast to the rest of the school's white Gothic revival aesthetic. Dark wood paneling lined the walls, and antique brass fixtures cast a warm glow over everything. The room felt more like an old-world gentleman's club than a high school administrative space.

Quint Thornton sat behind an imposing mahogany desk, his tall antlers casting branching shadows across stacks of paperwork. The Wendigo's amber eyes glowed faintly as he looked up from his computer screen, studying me with predatory intensity.

"Alexander Glock," he said, rising to his full height. His blue-gray felt suit was immaculate, dark-gray vest underneath and white tie spotless. "We've been expecting you."

Something about him and the room he inhabited radiated the aura of Prohibition-era gangster boss—the kind who'd politely offer you tea before having you thrown into the river wearing concrete shoes.

"Welcome to Skyfall Academy," Quint continued, extending a perfectly manicured hand featuring dark claws. His grip was firm but not crushing—a professional's handshake. "I trust Lance and Christi have been showing you around?"

"Yes, they've been very helpful," I replied, matching his formal tone. "Your school is impressive."

"Our school," he corrected smoothly. "You're one of us now, Mr. Glock. May I call you Alex?"

"Of course." I nodded.

"Excellent. Please, have a seat." He gestured to one of the plush red leather armchairs facing his desk.

"Now then, Alex." Quint settled back into his chair, steepling his fingers. His amber eyes seemed to glow brighter within the sockets of his bone-like face, and I felt a subtle pressure building behind my eyes. "Tell me about your . . . aspirations here at Skyfall."

Ah. The classic Wendigo mind-probe. I'd dealt with this sort of bullshit before—a Wendigo clan owned the company my mom was legally bound to and overworked her straight towards her tragic death.

The horned bastard could taste lies and fears through direct eye contact and was already digging his magic hooks deep into my head.

CHAPTER THREE

Furniture Acquisition

ope. Nope, nope, none of that. Time to redirect the conversation.

"Actually," I said, breaking the spine-tingling, truth-prying eye contact to pull out my phone, "I was hoping to get your insight on something, Mr. President and Co. I met some interesting students this morning . . ." I opened the photos I'd taken of the construction site trio. "Are these students in my grade, by chance?"

Quint's eyes narrowed slightly at the disruption, but he leaned forward to examine the images along with the couple behind me.

"Ah," he said, his tone neutral. "I see you've already encountered Ms. Nova and her . . . friends."

"That's Cass!" Christi squealed, leaning over my shoulder to look at the photos. "Oh, and Em and Io, too! They're totally in our grade, yes."

"Cinder," Lance said.

I turned to him.

"My sister . . . prefers to go by Cinder these days," he added, looking resigned.

"Interesting group," I commented, watching their reactions carefully. "They seemed . . . colorful."

"That's one way to put it." Quint's bony mouth twitched slightly. "Ms. Nova and Ms. Stratos can be rather . . . overly passionate about their interests."

"Em's super intense!" Christi chimed in. "She's, like, totally dedicated to being the best at everything forever! And Cass, err . . . Cinder is amazing at music, even if she can be a bit . . . um . . ."

"Temperamental," Lance supplied diplomatically.

"And the Mothman?" I asked innocently, flipping the photo to the cigarette-pack manifestation. "Iogann, was it?"

The three Student Council members' expressions darkened simultaneously at the sight of the interdimensional cigarettes. Lance's jaw visibly clenched, Christi's flames dimmed to barely-glowing embers, and Quint's amber eyes flashed dangerously.

"Mr. Wanderer's . . . procurement habits are a matter of ongoing disciplinary review," Quint said, his voice dropping several degrees in temperature. "The possession and distribution of interdimensional contraband is strictly prohibited at Skyfall Academy. I trust you understand that participating in such activities would be . . . unwise for a new student."

"Of course." I nodded quickly, making a show of looking appropriately chastised. "Can't stand deathsticks, drugs, or alcohol. Prefer a clear mind for my lunch chess matches."

"Would you mind forwarding me those photos?" Quint asked, his amber eyes gleaming with predatory interest. "As Student Council President, it's my responsibility to ensure all disciplinary infractions are properly . . . documented."

I caught Lance's subtle teeth-gnash from behind me and turned to him. "Cassiopeia is your sister, right? You two seem . . . Very different."

Lance's orange eyes flickered with something—Concern? Frustration? Anger?—before he carefully schooled his expression. "We have different approaches to school life," he said diplomatically. "I work within the system. Cinder . . . prefers to challenge it."

"I can see that," I agreed.

Lance stepped forward, placing a firm hand on my shoulder. "I can handle any concerns about Cinder. No need to involve official channels for what's clearly just . . . artistic photography practice. Right, Alex?"

His grip tightened meaningfully. The message was clear: Don't rat out my sister or I'll break your arm.

"Oh! Of course," I said, quickly pocketing my phone. "Just trying to capture the morning light. Besides," I added smoothly, "I wouldn't want my first act at Skyfall to be getting your sister in trouble. Especially not over something as trivial as a smoke break."

Quint's claws twitched at my diplomatic deflection. "While your discretion is . . . admirable, Mr. Glock, the rules exist for a reason. Interdimensional contraband can have serious consequences. Last semester, a student brought back cigarettes from a reality where the smoke carried memetic mind viruses. Half the senior class spent a week believing they were cats that had to groom each other."

"That was kind of hilarious, though, and a few people finally decided to date 'cause of it," Christi giggled, then quickly sobered under Quint's sharp glare.

Lance ran a hand through his gray, scale-type dreadlocks in frustration. "Look, Pres, you've talked to Cinder about this, no? Multiple times. Every time we crack down, she just gets more . . . creative with her rebellion against the system or whatever. I just . . . I don't know what to do. She had detention from every single teacher already!"

"We just have to find a punishment fitting enough that'll get through . . ." Quint began.

"No! I don't want to hurt her! If we do that, she will just snap! Every time we push harder, she just digs her heels in deeper. If we piss her off too much, she'll ask Iogann to fetch her something far, far worse than cigarettes from one of those doomed dimensions!" Lance declared with an exasperated face. "I don't want her hooked on Topaz, Quint, that effin' stuff is impossible to wean off of!"

"Maybe," I ventured carefully, "you're approaching this from the wrong angle."

All three Council members turned to look at me.

"What do you mean?" Lance asked, orange eyes narrowing.

"Well," I said, choosing my words carefully, "from what I've seen, Cinder seems like someone who rebels against direct authority. The more you try to control her, the more she'll push back. But what if . . . instead of fighting her rebellion, you redirected it?"

"Explain," Quint commanded.

"Look, I've got perfect scores in drama, theater, and social studies from my old Nazarite school," I explained, warming to my pitch. "Plus, I'm pretty decent at reading people and situations. What if instead of trying to force Cinder to conform, we gave her a different kind of challenge?"

"Like what?" Lance asked skeptically.

"She clearly has a protective streak for outcasts, right? I mean, she hangs out with a disaster-seeking Mothman. What if . . ." I paused for dramatic effect. "We gave her something . . . someone new to protect? Someone who could subtly influence her towards better choices while appearing to need her guidance?"

"Are you suggesting . . ." Quint began thoughtfully.

"That I could befriend her? Yes." I shrugged casually. "I'm an outsider to Leviathan's Cradle, and my Omnithean blood percentage is low enough that I'm basically a walking target. She seems like the type who'd enjoy taking a helpless half-blood under her wing just because some authority figures will hate me."

Lance pursed his lips.

"I can infiltrate her friend group, be your eyes and ears, help guide her away from the really dangerous stuff while appearing to be just another lost soul seeking protection and pretend-fighting against authority." I grinned.

Quint leaned back in his chair. "Interesting proposal, Mr. Glock. Though I must warn you—getting close to Cinder Nova can be . . . hazardous to one's health. She has quite the temper. The last male student who tried to ask her out ended up punched through three walls and out a fourth-story window."

"And? Does everyone forget that we're basically immortal?" I tapped my bracelet.

"The Lazarus bracelet may restore your body, Mr. Glock, but the pain . . . that you will remember quite vividly," Quint pointed out.

"Pain is temporary," I shrugged. "Helping friends is . . . eternal. What was it that Leviathan Slayer Nazareth himself taught us?"

I spread my hands out like a goodly preacher at a choir.

"The value of sacrifice!" I boomed, switching to my Christophorus Elijah NPC script. "The Slayer willingly gave his life to stop the Leviathan when it first emerged from the Wormwood Star's impact crater. His holy blood mixed with the sky-beast's as they fought, and from that battle the first uplifted Omnitheans were born!"

My NPC preacher voice made the trio go silent and thoughtful, careening the Student President sideways, as far as possible from interviewing me with magic-eye bullshit.

"So if Lord Nazareth could sacrifice his life to birth our entire glorious civilization," I continued, really hamming up the religious spiel fervor, "surely I can sacrifice a few painful deaths to help guide one lost soul back to the light!" I placed my hand over my heart dramatically. "After all, isn't that what being a true Omnithean and a student of Skyfall Academy is all about? Helping our fellows achieve their highest potential?"

"That's . . . really inspiring," Christi said, her flames flickering brighter. "And theological! Awww, I didn't expect such passion from a transfer student!"

Lance was studying me with new interest, while Quint's amber eyes gleamed with what might have been approval.

"Very well, Mr. Glock," Quint said finally. "We'll give your . . . social experiment a chance."

"Thank you!" I grinned. "If I fail horribly, I'll send the interdimensional smokes-summoning pictures to you. Please give me your Omnigram contacts, too—I'd love to stay in touch and report my progress!"

"You are quite bold," Quint observed, but he seemed more amused than annoyed now. "I approve. Very well . . . And Alex?" His amber eyes locked onto mine one final time. "Do try not to get killed too often. The paperwork is . . . tedious."

"Cassie and her buds are always getting into trouble and smoking on or near school grounds," Christi said. "I'd be ever so grateful if you helped my Lancy's sister step to the path of righteousness and goodness!"

I couldn't help but *tsk* at the mention of smoking. "Ugh, cigarettes. Nothing worse than poisoning yourself and everyone around you."

Christi's eyes lit up at my reaction. "Right? It's so gross! I keep telling Cass that she really should quit, but she just doesn't listen! She hasn't listened to me once since she got into that troupe with Iogann, Vespera, Solace, and Emerald in grade ten!"

"A troupe?" I asked.

"Oh, yes!" Christi bobbed, excited that I was listening to her. "They call themselves The Dreadful Delvers, or D&D. They do these . . . umm . . . avant-garde monster-slaying performances . . . which end in . . . incidents."

The longer she spoke, the more sour-looking her face became.

"Incidents?" I prompted.

"Uhh . . ." Christi's flames flickered nervously. "Basically, Iogann plays this creepy harmonica that opens gates to doomed dimensions. He's their Gater. Then Cass does this haunting vocal performance as their Bard, using her voice and wings to attract something nasty through the gate. Usually it's some kind of interdimensional horror."

"And?"

"And then Em leads the charge as their Slayer," Lance added with clear disapproval. "She's got this special flame sword that she can ignite with her dragonfire. Vespera and Solace back her up as Knights using random weapons and armor from History Club coliseum storage."

"Uh-huh."

"They fight whatever comes through in front of an audience," Christi continued. "It's supposed to be 'art' or something, but it usually ends in property damage. During their last performance at Spring's End Festival, a bunch of students in attendance died from . . . a flesh-tree thing that came through the gate," Christi added solemnly. "Plus many were grievously injured. Em and her Knight crew tried to slay it, but it took them too long."

"Soooo . . . they don't actually go into a dungeon. Which part of that is delving?" I arched an eyebrow.

"It's not delving at all—it's reckless foolishness for the sake of showing off!" Lance huffed. "Proper delving involves careful thorough scouting, preparation, planning, anchored gates, or exploring a known, mapped dungeon. What they're doing is essentially throwing open random doors to doomed realities and hoping whatever horror stumbles through will make for good slaying entertainment. It's not art—it's inter-dimensional Russian roulette with an audience!"

"They're now banned from performing in most venues within city limits," Christi added with a sigh. "Which only made them more determined to find 'underground' spaces to practice."

"Last week they were rehearsing in an abandoned subway tunnel near the school," Lance added grimly. "Iogann opened a gate to what he claimed was a 'music dimension' and . . . let's just say the cleanup crew is still trying to contain the memetic songs that get stuck in people's heads."

"Isn't that just normal good songs?" I asked with a small smile.

"Not at all! They're these awful lullaby songs that start sort of normal and just get more psychotic. Like . . . 'Baby bus that goes round and round till everyone dies horribly.'" Christi winced. "So, if you hear creepy laughter of children singing in your head, please head to the nurse right away!"

"Noted," I said.

"The worst thing is that Graves likes that sort of experimental stuff," Christi whined. "D&D somehow convinced him to play in the auditorium this week! It's going to be a huge catastrophe, I know it."

"Emerald assured me their next performance will be much more . . . controlled," Quint interjected smoothly. "The auditorium wards are significantly stronger than the makeshift barriers they've been using. Vice Principal Graves himself approved the safety protocols."

"So it was you!" Christi rounded on him, her flames flaring bright orange with anger. "Several student deaths, Quint! And that one poor janitor who is still occasionally speaking in backwards nursery rhymes about the world of flesh!"

"Em knows what she's doing," Quint stated. "She's one of our most talented combat students—"

"Oh, please!" Christi's hair blazed higher. "We all know you'd approve anything she wants, even if it means risking the entire student body!"

"Em knows her limits," Quint said with finality, his amber eyes glowing brighter for a moment. "The performance will proceed as planned. Lance already agreed—"

"Lancy!" Christi's head snapped towards her boyfriend with a glare.

"I'm not actually attending." Lance raised his gray hands. "I'm only paying for part of the catering and helping with ward setup. I just wanted to support my sister. At least in the auditorium, we can control the environment. Better than them sneaking off to do it in some abandoned tunnel or warehouse, right?"

"Hrm. I could help document the event," I offered innocently. "You know, take some artistic shots of the carnage—I mean, the performance. Plus, having an extra set of eyes on safety protocols couldn't hurt."

Lance nodded with a look of appreciation.

"Text me the deets. Maybe I can help contain whatever eldritch horrors they summon . . . with my amazing photography skills. Nothing says 'stop summoning interdimensional horrors' like getting their bad side in a photo," I joked. "Plus, I'm pretty good at editing out bloodstains in post-production."

Christi burst into delighted giggles. "Oh my gosh, you're funny! Quint, shoo shoo, I need the computer!" She practically bounced over to the desk, playfully nudging the Wendigo aside. "I know exactly what to do for Alex's schedule! Yep, yep!"

Quint raised an eyebrow but gracefully surrendered his seat, gathering his papers. "Very well. I have other matters to attend to anyway. Lance, walk with me to the lounge? We should discuss the upcoming delve preparations for Instructor Zalimar's class."

The two taller students departed, leaving me with the overly enthusiastic fire elemental.

"You know," Christi chatted as she sat down on the plush computer-facing red leather chair, and pulled me into the seat right beside her instead of across the table, "my poor Lancy is ever so worried about his sister. Cass really does need better influences in her life. Em is very passionate, and Io just does what he is told by her . . . The combo of both of them is not exactly the best influence for a young, impressionable lady like Cassiopeia . . ." Christi trailed off. "Yes, we could really use someone like you around here. Someone with . . . fresh, healthy, unique perspective, a genuine Nazarite."

I nodded; she was basically repeating what I had offered already, except speaking as if she were a jet airplane trying to take off.

"Mm-hmm." Christi nodded with a smile. "Cass really needs more positive influences before she graduates! And you seem so . . . well put together! Excellent grades, plus you're into photography and art—Cassie totally loves creative stuff, too, even if she pretends not to care about anything!"

"Hmmm . . ." I tapped my chin thoughtfully, considering my need for the Quetzi-girl exposure therapy. "Maybe if I was in more of Cinder's classes, I could . . . help keep an eye on her? Make sure she's actually attending them, try to help her quit smoking?"

"You . . . you would do that?!" Christi's eyes ignited as though I'd just handed her the keys to the kingdom.

"I absolutely would," I said sincerely.

"Eeeeee!" She clapped, hair igniting like a flashbang as she squeed loudly, making the boys look up from their couch-filled distant corner of the office. "That's such a wonderful idea! I was thinking the same thing, oh yes! I will absolutely help with scheduling . . ." She practically bounced in her chair. "I could definitely arrange for you to share most if not all of Cassie's classes. For her own good, of course!"

"Of course." I nodded solemnly, while my heart was doing backflips. "It's important to help others. And since I'm new here, it would help me adjust too, having a . . . consistent classmate."

"Yes, yes! I'll get this sorted right away! Oh thank you so much, Alex!" Christi fluttered, momentarily burying me in a super-heated, skin-blistering hug. "You're the best!"

I sneakily recorded her login info with my wrist spycam as she let go of me and logged into the school's network via the Student Council computer.

Christi spent the next hour enthusiastically arranging my schedule to match Cinder's, occasionally muttering about "positive influences" and "such a wonderfully unique opportunity."

Her entire body wobbled with increasing excitement radiating heat like hot sauna stones. As she worked, I continued to ask her questions about Cassie and her known relationships, constructing a pattern of approach.

Soon enough, I bid the Student Councilors adieu and went to have lunch in one of the smaller art nouveau cafes at the edge of campus.

Enjoying a fresh croissant and a Caesar salad, I sketched out Vice Principal Graves in one of the stolen Omnimart sketchbooks while whisper-chatting to Yulia about my plans.

I wasn't worried about being overheard by other cafe patrons. Yulia and I spoke in an endangered Kaska language of the First Nations people of the Athabaskan ethnolinguistic group.

Mom had tried teaching me this language when I was young, but like most dumb kids, I hadn't appreciated its value then. It was only after losing her, after spending countless nights training with my large language model to understand the near-extinct tongue, that each word became precious—like holding onto fragments of her voice, her smile, her patience as she'd tried to pass on this piece of her heritage.

As I finished the sketch, memories of evening walks with Mom through North Acadia's misty forests prickled in the back of my mind.

She would point out different plants and animals, telling me their names in both English and our ancestral tongue. Her voice would grow soft and reverent when sharing tales of how our people first encountered the "Star-Born Ones."

"The Tutchone shamans were the first to see them," Mom said as we crouched behind fallen logs to watch the multi-eyed, tree-antlered spirit deer grazing in the twilight clearing. "When the Wormwood Star fell and the God Beasts emerged across the world, most people ran in terror. But some . . . saw beyond the fear, learned that the star shards reshaped reality itself."

Her eyes grew distant then. "Those shamans believed in Animism, that everything had a spirit—the trees, the rocks, the rivers. To them, the God Beasts were just new spirits . . . transformative forces, neither good nor evil. Like fire or storms—dangerous, yes, but also full of potential. The first Tutchone who dared to slay a God Beast didn't die because he uttered a prayer of forgiveness to the spirit as he spilled out its blood."

"Why did they have to kill the God Beasts, Mom?" I asked. "Couldn't they just . . . talk to them?"

"The primordial God Beasts of long ago were but animals changed by Wormwood shards, born wrong, incompatible with reality," Mom explained. "Like putting a whale in a desert or a flame in the ocean—they suffered, and in their suffering they made others suffer too. The shamans understood this. They knew that sometimes, the kindest act is to end suffering, to help transform it into something new."

She picked up a fallen leaf, turning it over in her hands. "Death begets death, my little fox. But death also begets life. When a Divine Beast is struck down, its blood can make the forest burn or bloom depending on the hunter's wish. The shamans taught our people to wish for transformation, not destruction, and so the forests of Acadia bloomed and became filled with new life."

"But what about Slayer Nazareth, Mom?" I asked. "The Omnids say he was this great hero who sacrificed himself to save everyone from the Leviathan."

"When the moon shattered, people needed heroes," she explained. "They wanted to believe that someone great could triumph over the Leviathan through strength and will alone. It's easier than accepting that we're all just caught in forces beyond our control, that true power comes from understanding and adaptation rather than conquest."

"So what really happened?"

"No man could truly hope to stop a god. The Leviathan smashed into the moon and began to decay away on its own because our world was finite and filled with rules, incompatible with its nature," Mom explained.

She pulled me closer as we watched the small harmless forest spirits graze, their multiple eyes glowing in the twilight. "Nazareth found the dying newborn Leviathan who kept shedding its body and leaving bits of itself behind. He was not a slayer; he was just a selfish, mundane man who desired one thing above all—love."

"Love?" My young self blinked.

"Yes," Mom said. "Love. Nazareth knew how to wield wishes, and so he carved a golem from the Leviathan's heart—a Magdalene of living crystal and starlight. Their children were the first Omnitheans—human at heart, but also shaped by desire."

"Shaped by desire?"

"The firstborn Omnids were more . . . fluid," Mom explained. "Like soft clay, they could be reshaped by the collective beliefs of humanity. As they spread out across the world, some became living gods of great empires, while others turned into nightmarish horrors who devoured whole villages."

"But the Omnitheans today aren't like that, right?" I asked. "They have police and lawyers and schools and stuff."

"Yes. Over centuries they became less fluid, hardened, grounded in our reality, became more confined to specific forms from legends or stories," she explained. "Gained specific powers."

I nodded along.

"Now . . . they're just people with super strength or speed or mental control," Mom sighed. "People who came together, claiming Leviathan's Cradle as their sacred land and built their own empire. They think their powers make them gods, but they're still just people playing with forces they don't fully understand."

I opened my eyes and exhaled. Mom had always seemed to know so much about Omnithean history, but I'd never thought to ask her how or why. Was it all just stories she'd made up to help me understand the world better? Or had she learned something during her years working for Omnicorp that she couldn't openly share? Was this truly our Kaska heritage, legends passed through countless generations?

I needed to know more about the Omnids around me to blend better into their social structures.

I waited until late afternoon when most students had cleared out before making my move. The security patterns were fairly predictable—guards patrolled in thirty-minute rotations, with shift changes at four PM. Perfect timing for a quick heist or two.

I painted my face to resemble another student, pulled on a white wig, glued a lush beard to my neck, and attached predator-type claw extensions to my fingernails.

The storage building connected to the security office was a squat concrete structure near the maintenance area. I'd noticed earlier that the back door had an old electronic lock—the light stayed green a few seconds too long after each swipe. All I had to do was time it right.

I lurked behind a dumpster, watching a guard swipe his card and enter. The moment the door started to swing shut, I darted forward and caught it just before it latched. Slipping inside, I found myself in a dimly lit hallway lined with lockers and supply closets.

Footsteps echoed from around the corner. I quickly ducked into an open supply closet, holding my breath as the guard passed by.

I slipped deeper into the storage area, following the sound of running water. As expected, I found the security guards' locker room. A shower was running—perfect timing. I quickly located a shelf with the extra uniforms and grabbed a spare uniform in my size, stuffing it under my shirt.

Making my exit was trickier than getting in. I had to time my movements carefully between patrol rotations, using the maintenance corridors to avoid cameras. A close call with a janitor nearly gave me away, but I managed to play it off by pretending to be intensely focused on my phone.

Back in my van, parked in the student lot's blind spot, I changed into the stolen uniform and modified the ID badge based on the scanned list of security personnel. A twenty-one-year-old Dover Demon by the name of Nunkish Throg who was absent this week due to "family issues" was easy to emulate. A bald cap, latex jaw, and gray face paint went on smoothly to change my appearance once again to resemble Nunkish. Orange contact lenses completed the disguise. A quick check in the rearview mirror confirmed I looked passably Omnid, especially in the security uniform.

The badge and uniform gave me almost unlimited access. I started with the administrative wing, casually strolling past offices while appearing to check doors and windows. The night cleaning crew barely glanced at me as I made my rounds.

I carefully made my way through the records room, scanning documents with my phone's camera. Student files, staff records, security protocols—anything that could be useful later.

A tone sounded in my ear—Yulia had finished analyzing the latest batch of photos.

"Analysis complete," she whispered. "Identified key access points. The security system has several potential exploitable weaknesses. Would you like me to outline potential infiltration scenarios?"

"Later," I murmured in Kaska.

A sound in the hallway made me freeze. Footsteps approaching. I quickly closed the file drawer and pretended to be checking window locks just as a real security guard walked past. He gave me a brief nod which I returned, keeping my movements casual and practiced.

"Time check?" I whispered.

"7:42 PM. Shift change in eighteen minutes."

I nodded, making my way towards the exit. I'd pushed my luck far enough for one day. As I passed through the administrative wing, I noticed light spilling from the windows of Vice Principal Graves's office.

The tall, faceless man was still at his desk, his void-like head bent over paperwork. I glanced up at the shattered, half-crystallized moon and asteroid field sparkling in the slightly cloudy sky overhead and quickened my pace slightly, not wanting to risk a closer encounter.

For late dinner, I sat in the security lounge, munching on a sandwich from the vending machine while reviewing the files I'd photographed.

"What did we get on Emerald Stratos?" I asked my AI.

"Numerous fighting incidents resulting in deaths of other students. Appears to be the leader of several student groups. In an open relationship with the Student Council President, who covers up a multitude of illegal activities such as unauthorized delving and bullying. Has a dedicated following among other predator-type upper-class students used to target lower-class students repeatedly to death or a catatonic state. Particularly aggressive towards . . . perceived weakness. Relies on two delving Knights as her 'lieutenants'—Vespera Simmi and Solace Exill."

Peachy.

"Cross-reference the D&D performance incidents with student injuries," I instructed.

"Processing," Yulia whispered in my ear. "Notable pattern—majority of serious injuries and deaths occur to audience members rather than the performers themselves."

I nodded, taking another bite. The sandwich was surprisingly good—apparently even Skyfall's vending machines were top tier.

"What about . . . K. Kells?" I asked, thinking of that haunting painting I'd seen earlier. "Any connection to our target group?"

"Loner. Limited direct interaction with student body," Yulia replied. "Katherine Kells—Stollwurm classification. Iogann's half-sister. Exceptional artistic talent but severe medical issues. Frequently absent from classes in patterns of every thirteen to fifteen days due to health complications. Some records indicate a previous friendship with Cinder Nova in freshman year."

"Anything of value on the teachers?"

"Cross-referencing complete," she reported. "Found something interesting in the staff records. Victor Greyfield, science teacher. Listed age 127, appears late seventies. Dover Demon–Human hybrid."

I perked up. "A successful hybrid? That's rare."

"Indeed. His presence may explain the school's relatively lenient policy towards mixed heritage students. Also explains some of the more . . . experimental aspects of their science curriculum."

I nodded thoughtfully. A hybrid teacher could be a valuable ally—or at least a source of information about surviving as a "mixed-blood" in Omnithornia.

"What about problematic teachers?" I asked.

"A few. The worst of the bunch is the Arx Delving instructor, Koshchei Zalimar Evernacht," Yulia replied. "A naturally immortal Omnid, doesn't wear the Lazarus bracelet. Tenured Archmage, six hundred years of teaching Delving at Skyfall. Centuries-long pattern of student abuse, student disappearances, and other unexplained accidents in relationship to what he listed as 'impure blood' in his reports. Extreme prejudice against mixed-blood students. Known to hit students who annoy him enough. Do *not* engage target without preparation."

"Got it," I said. "Going to need to figure out how to deal with an immortal lich. Ideas?"

"Zalimar believes in arcane blood laws of honor. Set fair terms, challenge him to a duel to the death, and make sure to win," Yulia replied.

"How?"

"Unknown. Subject extremely dangerous, high level, and impossible to kill. A single curse from him could shatter your soul."

Lovely.

I sighed, moving on.

Thinking back to this morning, I pulled up the photo of Cinder on my phone, zooming in on her face. Despite her fierce scowl and punk attitude, there was something vulnerable in those ocean-blue eyes.

"Yulia, analyze Omnid cryptitype facial expression and body language," I whispered.

"Processing," the AI replied softly. "Subject displays classic defensive posturing—raised shoulders. Micro-expressions indicate underlying anxiety despite aggressive facade."

"Elaborate on the emotional indicators," I prompted.

"The subject appears to be using the smoking as a coping mechanism," Yulia analyzed.

"What else?"

"The eyes," Yulia pointed out. "There's moisture accumulation at the corners—barely noticeable unless you know what to look for. She appears to be fighting back tears in this photo."

I flipped through the pictures and zoomed in. Sure enough, there were tiny sparkles of wetness at the edges of those ocean-blue eyes that I hadn't noticed before in the last photo. Something twisted in my chest.

"Her feathers and scales are also displaying extreme distress patterns," Yulia continued. "Compared to the vibrant, color-changing wings, the body coloration is limited, muted to silver-grays, especially around her face, chest, neck, and shoulders—a clear sign of emotional suppression in Quetzalcoatl physiology."

I Oodled videos of Quetzalcoatl preachers and politicians and discovered that their wings changed color along with their bodies when they ranted about Slayer Nazareth to the gathered crowds. Then I went back to staring at Cassiopeia's photo, seeing it with new eyes. Behind that fierce punk facade, those rebellious poses, and that defiant scowl . . . was someone barely keeping it together. Someone hurting.

"Cross-reference with her brother's statements," I requested.

"Lance Nova expressed concern about her 'snapping' if pushed too hard," Yulia reminded me. "Combined with the emotional indicators and her association with a disaster-attracting Mothman . . . classic pattern of someone spiraling but trying to maintain control through increasingly risky behavior," the LLM concluded.

I nodded, agreeing with my AI's assessment.

This wasn't just about getting close to her for my own purposes anymore. Something was genuinely wrong with Cinder Nova, and everyone around her seemed to be either enabling her downward spiral or trying to force her into compliance. Neither approach was working.

"One more thing," I said. "Check the academic records. How are her grades?"

"Significant decline in all areas over the past two years. Multiple absences, repeated detentions, incomplete assignments. Teachers note 'apparent disinterest' and 'increasing hostility.'"

Classic signs of depression masked by acting out. I'd seen it before—hell, I'd lived it after Mom refused to tell me that she was sick and dying.

The difference was, I'd channeled my pain into something productive—learning every trick, social hack, and scam I could to survive. Swindling became my art form, forgery my craft, and theft my means of staying alive. Each con was a performance, each fake ID a masterpiece, each successful heist a small victory against a world that had taken everything from me.

I shook my head.

Focus on the present.

The school's furniture storage area was my next target. The lock was pathetically simple—a basic electronic keypad that probably hadn't been updated since the building was constructed. A quick spray of UV powder revealed the most commonly pressed numbers, and from there it was child's play to figure out the code.

Inside, I found exactly what I needed—a dolly, a box of half-depleted micro-beast cores, and all sorts of old furniture for student lounges. Rich kids probably demanded new furniture every semester, leaving perfectly good items to gather dust in storage.

I worked quickly, selecting and boxing up items that would fit in my van without being too obvious. Old decorative beast-core-powered string lights, several rugs in deep blues and purples made from some slain beast's hide that radiated warmth long after its owner's demise, a pair of oversized beanbag chairs in ruby red, a small beast-core-powered cold box, and an assortment of pillows would make my van feel more like a home and less like a rust-pitted box on wheels.

Back in my van, now considerably cozier with the stolen furnishings, I settled into one of the plush beanbag chairs and reviewed my notes for tomorrow. The magic rugs helped muffle the constant hum of the city and kept the van's interior above freezing, while the string lights I'd installed gave the space a cozy, lived-in feel.

I pulled up my schedule on my phone, grinning at how thoroughly Christi had managed to align my classes with Cinder's.

I closed my eyes, imagining all the ways tomorrow could go wrong—getting thrown through walls, set on fire, or sucked into an eldritch dimension before lunch—but with my new Lazarus bracelet and a solid plan, I was ready to dive headfirst into whatever spectacular disaster Cinder and her crew were brewing.

Perhaps it would be smart to stay away from mind-control wings, but I refused to break, desiring to learn how to bend instead.

Besides, those piercing ocean-blue eyes, the way she floated down backlit by rays of morning sun, her punk outfit, even that rebellious scowl and her invisible emotional breakdown—it all screamed "danger" in the most tantalizing way possible.

I had already taken a big, dangerous gamble driving into the heart of Omnithornia in a nearly dead van.

What was an ever deeper leap towards the heart of the abyss?

CHAPTER FOUR

Advanced Xenobiology

Day two at Skyfall. My first class!

After a wash at the gym and quick salad bar breakfast in the Student Council lounge, I arrived ahead of time to Dr. Greyfield's early morning Advanced Xenobiology, sliding into a seat near the front of the lab, expecting to be asked to introduce myself.

The classroom was a curious mix of modern Omnid magitek, mundane tools, and vintage scientific equipment. Gleaming meta-flesh brain-in-jar processors sat next to brass microscopes that looked older than the school itself.

The Dover Demon–Human hybrid teacher was already in his office, puttering around with various beakers and specimens. His wispy white hair caught the morning light, making his pale gray skin look almost translucent. The special tinted glasses he wore did little to hide the red glow of his eyes as he hummed to himself, organizing slides with his long spindly fingers.

Other students began filtering in. A purple Tanystropheus had to duck her long neck to get through the door.

A massive Sasquatch in a varsity jacket squeezed through the door, his brown fur neatly groomed. He high-fived a green-scaled Basilisk wearing designer sunglasses as he passed.

A pair of Thunderbirds swooped in through the window, their black-and-white feathers gleaming as they landed gracefully by their desks. Behind them, a Skinwalker shifted from wolf to human-ish form mid-stride, her silver hair settling around her shoulders as she took her seat.

The room filled with a cacophony of sounds—scales rustling, wings folding, claws clicking against desks, and the low rumble of morning conversations.

A Stollwurm girl rolled in on a large wheelchair, dark gray-blue scales almost entirely hidden under dark fingerless gloves, a thick hunting camo jacket's hood, and oversized dark WW2 aviator's goggles.

More students continued to file in as I pretended to review my textbook, while pointing my AI's camera at everyone nearby, learning their names and cryptitypes.

A Cherufe with magma-like skin stomped to her desk, leaving faint scorch marks on the floor.

Two Jersey Devils swooped in through the landing balcony window, their leathery wings folding as they came in. Their hooved feet clicked against the tile floor as they made their way to their seats, forked tails swishing. One was wearing a letterman jacket, the other had multiple piercings in his bat-like ears.

A Kelpie girl ran in, her watery mane flowing like a living waterfall down her neck. Water droplets fell from her hair with each step but evaporated before hitting the ground. She took her seat near the front.

A few seconds before class began, the door slammed open with a bang, making several students jump. Cinder stormed in, her silver feathers ruffled and shifting through various shades of agitated dark gray. Her combat boots thundered against the floor as she made her way to her desk, the chains on her plaid skirt jingling with each step.

She dropped into the seat with enough force to make the metal legs screech against the tile. The Violet Floyd logo on her black top rippled as she slumped forward, burying her face in her arms with a groan that sounded distinctly un-morning-person-like.

Then, inexplicably, red warning siren lights began flashing across the classroom. Heavy blast doors slid down over the windows with pneumatic hisses, sealing us in.

"Good morning, class!" Dr. Greyfield called out cheerfully, emerging from his office, as if sudden lockdown procedures were perfectly normal. He adjusted his tinted glasses.

"Morning, Dr. Grey," the class groaned in discordant voices.

"Excellent, excellent!" Dr. Greyfield beamed. "Today we'll be continuing our study of interdimensional parasites. But first . . ." He gestured to me. "We have a new student joining us! Alexander Glock, would you mind introducing yourself?"

I channeled 100 percent of my practiced NPC-greeting energy and marched to the front of the class, not looking at a certain pair of sky-blue eyes near the back.

I raised my imaginary Glock and fired it into the ceiling to jump-start my speech.

"Hey, guys!" My voice boomed confidently across the science classroom. "I'm Alexander Glock. I'm a photographer and artist from North Acadia. Want a sketch of your imaginary best friend or a photo of yourself, looking extra smashing? Bug me after class; let's trade Omnigrams!" A wink with a tongue click. Perfect. And now for a nerdy interjection. "Not interested in photography or art? I'm always looking for new friends to play deathmatch checkers or chess with at lunch. Dare to defeat me and win a free lunch. Cheers!"

I concluded and shot finger guns at everyone and accidentally looked at the angel staring at me and froze like an idiot again, forgetting how to breathe.

Defcon 1! Retreat! Do not engage with dangerous winged female entity!

"Most fascinating!" Dr. Greyfield clapped his hands together, ignoring the sinking ship of my NPC persona. "We don't get many Hominull Omnithis in our Academy. In fact, you're our first this year! Why, it reminds me of the time I was conducting research in the Arctic and met a delightful human scientist with a flamethrower who . . ." He trailed off for a second. " . . . who had quite the innovative approach to dealing with shapeshifting parasites."

The class groaned, clearly not enjoying the doc's ranting.

"Much like Kurt Russell in that fascinating 1982 documentary about Antarctic research stations. Though of course, the real organism was far more interesting than what the tube portrayed. The cellular mimicry process alone was . . ." He caught himself starting to ramble. "But that's a story for another time! Please take your seat, Mr. Glock."

I stood frozen at the front of the class, trying to force my feet to cooperate. This wasn't supposed to happen, damn it! How was she doing this?

What sort of dark arts could . . .

Dr. Greyfield's thick glasses reflected the fluorescent lights as he peered at me expectantly.

"Ah, of course . . ." The man pondered and snapped his fingers. "We need to find you a lab partner, Mr. Glock! Someone who can help you catch up with our current unit on alien parasites and electromagnetic fields . . ."

My heart rate spiked as his gaze settled on the back corner of the room.

"Ms. Nova! You've been working alone this semester since you murdered your last partner far too many times for reasonability. Perhaps you could assist our new student?"

What? No, this wasn't supposed to happen! The idea was to take her in small doses, to adapt to her rainbow-winged witchcraft and . . .

In the back corner, Cinder's eyes narrowed dangerously. She slouched further in her chair, the silver metal skull of her choker catching the light.

"Perfect!" Dr. Greyfield beamed, completely missing (or choosing to ignore) Cinder's obvious displeasure. "Mr. Glock, please take the seat next to Ms. Nova."

My brain went into full panic mode:

> ABORT MISSION! ABORT MISSION!
> ERROR 404: WALKING.EXE NOT FOUND
> CRITICAL SYSTEM FAILURE
> REBOOTING . . .
> REBOOTING . . .
> FATAL ERROR: PROXIMITY TO GOTH ANGEL EXCEEDS SAFE PARAMETERS!

I managed to move my legs somehow, though it felt like walking through molasses. Each step towards the back of the classroom was a new adventure in not tripping over my own feet.

My internal monologue was having a complete meltdown:

Oh God oh God oh God what do I do what do I say don't look at her wings don't look at her wings don't look at her—DAMN IT I LOOKED AT HER WINGS—they're so pretty why are they so pretty this isn't cool, this isn't—

I somehow made it to the desk without having a complete nervous breakdown, though it was a close call. As I approached, Cinder was slouched in her chair like the personification of teenage apathy, one elbow propped on the desk with her chin resting on her palm.

I caught a whiff of cigarette smoke and something else—ozone, maybe? Like the air before a storm.

"Sup?" she asked with a scoff. I could practically hear her internal monologue painted on her elongated, inhuman, yet incredibly photogenic face: *Great. You again, you effin' dullard. Of course I get stuck with the only Nullie in this entire school.*

She looked me up and down with the kind of disdain usually reserved for moldy cafeteria food.

"H-hi!" I squeaked, my voice cracking like a thirteen-year-old hitting puberty. Smooth. Real smooth.

I sat down, accidentally knocking over my backpack and spilling its contents across the floor. As I scrambled to gather my stuff, I could feel Cinder's annoyed gaze.

Great first impression, Alex. Really nailing that cool, mysterious new kid vibe. What vibe was I even going for with Cinder? I hadn't expected to sit next to her or interact with her so soon!

As I collected my scattered belongings, not staring up at her, Cinder let out an exaggerated sigh. "Wow. You're just a walking disaster, aren't you?" Her voice dripped with sarcasm. "Please tell me you at least know which end of a magnet is which."

I grabbed my last pencil from under the desk, trying to ignore how my face was burning. "I, uh, yeah. West and east, right?" I tried to sound sarcastic, but it came off as incredibly stupid.

"Slayer Nazareth!" She rolled her eyes. "We're actually going to die in a tragic lab accident because someone doesn't know basic physics." She turned to Dr. Greyfield. "Hey, Doc! Can I get a partner who won't get us both killed on the first day?"

"Now, now, Ms. Nova," Dr. Greyfield called back cheerfully, already setting up what looked suspiciously like a containment field generator. "Death is just the beginning of a great adventure! Everyone deserves a chance to learn! Besides, your previous three lab partners all transferred out to my other period in the evening after various . . . incidents. Perhaps a fresh perspective is exactly what you need!"

"Ughhhh," Cinder groaned. "I don't wanna rip his bracelet from his dead wrist and walk all the way down to the basement. It smells like wet dog, rotting meat, and old cheese down there!"

According to the Aztec Codex Borbonicus, minor precognition was a known Quetzalcoatl ability. I gulped.

"Teaching others is the best way to learn, Ms. Nova! I'm sure that you and Mr. Glock will make excellent partners and revive each other plenty of times! Go on now, immerse yourself in the exciting world of science!"

Dr. Greyfield flipped a switch, and a shimmering hologram materialized in the center of the room. The image showed what looked like a large leathery egg with wavy biomechanical patterns etched across its surface.

"Now then, class," Dr. Greyfield began, circling the hologram with an excited gleam in his red eyes, "today we'll be examining the reproductive cycle of the Xenomorf Electricus—a fascinating species I encountered during my research expedition to Earth-28-91-42CE. Unlike its cousin species made famous by that delightful documentary series from the late 1970s, this particular variant has developed quite the interesting relationship with electromagnetic fields."

"Guess you're stuck with me." I tried to look past Cinder.

"Uh-huh. So . . . photographer and artist, huh?" She somehow intercepted my eyes. "And a chess champion, too? Wow, you're just the complete package aren't you?" *Is she mocking me?* "Tell me, do you also rescue puppies and help old ladies cross the street in your spare time?"

I wanted to glare at her, but this would put me straight in brain-shutdown territory.

"And that introduction? 'Want a sketch of your imaginary best friend?'" She mimicked my voice in an exaggerated, deep tone. "Could you be any more of a try-hard? What are you, some kind of walking PSA about how to be the perfect student?"

I felt my face burning as she continued. "Also, nothing says 'I'm desperate for friends' quite like bribing people with food." She twirled a pencil between her dark-clawed pearlescent fingers. "Let me guess—you practiced that whole speech in front of a mirror this morning, didn't you?" Cinder's smirk widened, revealing sharp teeth. "Bet you even did the finger guns and everything."

My carefully constructed Alex persona cracked slightly, irritation seeping through.

She was reading me like an open book and it was . . . unsettling. I needed to regain control of the situation. I wouldn't be defeated by the Queen of Sarcasm over here.

"Actually," I said, forcing my voice to match her tone, "I practiced it in front of my imaginary best friend, Sasha One Googolplex! She gave me seventeen thumbs-ups and a wink of one thousand and sixty-seven of her eyes."

Cinder chortled with a tiniest of "Pfff," clearly having underestimated my sarcasm power level. For a brief moment, I saw the ghost of an actual smile flicker across her face before she caught herself and resumed her usual "you're an inferior species" scowl.

"Please begin setting up your electromagnetic field generators. And remember—if you see any temporal anomalies, do *not* make eye contact with your past self. The paradox paperwork is absolutely dreadful!" Dr. Greyfield rattled out in the background like some kind of an over-the-top science fiction mad genius protagonist.

"I've already got enough detention without some newbie screwing up the dissection," Cinder muttered. "Just . . . don't touch anything without asking first, okay?"

I nodded quietly, pulling out the worksheet and keeping my eyes firmly fixed on the paper. The magnetic field diagrams suddenly became the most fascinating things in existence.

Definitely not sneaking sideways glances at the rainbows Cinder was casting in my vicinity.

Focus. Science. Magnets. Not the way her hair feathers spill forward and spark like prismatic gems when she leans forward to adjust the generator.

"Pass me that copper wire," she commanded, holding out her hand without looking at me. "The thinner gauge one."

I carefully selected the correct wire, making sure our fingers didn't brush as I handed it over. My heart stuttered again.

Focus! Understand! Adapt!

She clearly thought I was an idiot, and here I was getting flustered over basic lab work and only reinforcing the idiot persona.

As we filled out the worksheets in silence, I kept my responses minimal, mostly nodding or giving one-word answers when Cinder bothered to acknowledge my existence. The quiet was . . . not exactly comfortable, but less awkward than my earlier verbal fumbling.

Dr. Greyfield was at the front of the class, enthusiastically explaining something about magnetic poles while gesturing with what appeared to be a half-eaten sandwich he'd forgotten he was holding.

Talking to Cinder was impossible, and she would not let me do anything in terms of generator assembly, so I flipped to a blank page in my Omnimart sketchbook and began sketching, my pencil moving almost unconsciously across the paper.

Dr. Greyfield's distinctive silhouette took shape—his wispy hair, the glint of his thick glasses, the sandwich gesturing wildly as he explained magnetic and holo-fractal theories. I added little details—the way his lab coat seemed to float slightly when he got excited, the faint glow around his eyes visible even through the tinted lenses.

I added the speech bubble, carefully lettering *It was a ruse! The parasite was inside you all along!*

Suddenly, I felt a presence over my shoulder. My heart skipped several beats as Cinder leaned closer and examined the sketch.

"Heh. That's . . . actually pretty good." Her voice was different—softer.

A strand of her silver feather-hair brushed my shoulder as she studied the drawing, sending tingles down my spine.

I quickly added more details, trying to distract myself from her proximity—a flesh-spider sleeping on his head and the sandwich in his hand now sporting tiny tentacles.

"Eh, just a basic portrait sketch. S'aight." I shrugged.

Not as good as forging an entire school's worth of transcripts, or creating fake housing documents, or making a convincing Housing Commission ID badge copied from their website in exact dimensions with a very fine marker while sitting in a smelly, rust-pitted van next to a truck stop.

I remained silent like a stone gargoyle, letting my pencil do its thing.

On the empty page next to Dr. Greyfield, I started sketching Cinder—not as she was, but as a dramatic, simplified caricature. Her combat boots became massive and covered in spikes, stomping through a field of twisted corpses. Her wings were spread dramatically against a background of burning buildings and apocalyptic ruins. The speech bubble proclaimed: "Rawr! I'm a goth-Quetzi, fear my boots of doom!"

I felt her presence over my shoulder again, closer this time. There was a sharp intake of breath.

"*What the*—" Cinder snatched the sketchbook, her eyes widening before narrowing dangerously. Her wings fluttered slightly as she studied the sketch, her expression cycling through several emotions too quickly for me to read.

"Sheet. Wait . . . do you have more art in here?"

Before I could stop her, she began flipping through the sketchbook pages, her eyes gleaming with curious violet sparks as she scanned each drawing with increasing intensity. My heart stopped as I realized what she was seeing—my entire journey documented in quick sketches and observations.

The Igopogo border guard with notes about his badge number. The weathered face of Mr. Peterson with annotations about his nervous habits. The purple-haired Chupacabra barista from Omnibucks, complete with observations about their schedule and tendency to take smoke breaks.

Page after page of faces, each accompanied by hastily scribbled notes about personalities, routines, weaknesses. Vice Principal Graves's slender frame sketched in detail. Christi's bouncing enthusiasm captured in flowing lines with flames dancing atop of her head.

I quickly snatched the sketchbook back before Cinder could reach the more incriminating pages, my heart pounding.

"Oi, don't just steal my things," I said.

Cinder squinted at me.

"It's just practice sketches," I mumbled, shoving the book deep into my backpack.

"Those were . . . detailed." Her voice carried a hint of suspicion. "Really detailed. Like, creepy-stalker-serial-killer vibe detailed."

"Personality traits outlines relevant to portrait expressions, an exercise from my old school. Nothing special," I lied.

There. Smooth-ish. Could have been better if my mouth didn't feel filled with cotton. I shrugged, trying to channel maximum NPC-student energy. "Gotta train those art muscles, you know. Use 'em or lose 'em."

"Hrm . . ." She paused. "You got everyone's expressions exactly right. And their little habits. Say, what were all those numbers next to everyone's portraits? And those weird symbols and letters? Looked like some kind of code."

My heart rate spiked. The numbers—vulnerability ratings, schedule timings, probability calculations for various scenarios and how similarly-behaving people could be overcome, bamboozled, scammed, derailed in just the right way.

"Oh, those?" I forced a casual laugh. "Just . . . basic composition notes. Rule of thirds stuff. Basic art measurements." I waved my hand vaguely. "You know, proportions, lighting notes, time of day when the sketch was made, and . . . other art things."

"Art things?" Cinder repeated flatly, tilting her head.

"So . . . did you like your portrait?" I asked, desperately trying to change the subject. "I think I really captured your brooding angst. The field of corpses really brings out your eyes."

Cinder's suspicious expression flickered for a moment, replaced by something between annoyance and amusement. "My boots ain't that big."

"Oh, really?" I glanced pointedly at her tall multi-laced combat boots. "Those things could crush a small car."

"They're effin' practical!" She defended, her wings puffing up slightly. "At least I don't look like I raided an Omnimart student outfits rack!"

I winced internally at her accidental accuracy. "Hey, white button-ups are classic. Unlike that"—I gestured vaguely at her all-black ensemble—"Hot Topic explosion you've got going on."

Wait. I'm talking to her without crashing? Progress!

Cinder's eyes flashed dangerously at my comment. Her wings spread slightly in an intimidating display. "At least I have my own style instead of looking like some corporate drone reject," she snapped. "What's next, gonna tell me that smoking is bad? Maybe lecture me about my life choices like everyone else?"

My mouth itched to tell her exactly how smoking would kill her—not just the obvious lung cancer, but the slow deterioration of every system in her body. How the tar would coat her airways like black paint, making each breath harder until she was gasping like a fish on land. How the chemicals would eat away at her stomach lining, turn her teeth yellow, make her beautiful feathers brittle and dull. How the nicotine would rewire her brain, making her a slave to those cancer sticks until they finally finished their job.

I wanted to tell her about watching Mom waste away in that hospital bed, each breath a struggle, until finally . . .

No. I wasn't going to shatter in my first class.

I reminded myself that Omnids didn't die from cancer, that the rich fuckers had Lazarus bracelets and hoarded all sorts of other life-saving magitek tools stolen from other dimensions.

I turned away, forcing my hands to unclench under the desk.

I focused on Dr. Greyfield, who was now enthusiastically explaining how magnetic fields could theoretically be used to create a time machine "if only the ethics board would stop being so fussy about temporal paradoxes!"

"Whatever," Cinder muttered beside me. "Just don't eff up the work. I'm not getting another detention because some nitwit can't tell positive from negative."

The doctor moved from station to station, examining each setup. When he reached our table, he beamed at our equipment.

"Excellent work, Ms. Nova! And Mr. Glock, I see you've managed to avoid creating any space-time anomalies so far. Wonderful progress!"

"That's 'cause he hasn't touched anything yet," Cinder muttered under her breath.

"Time's up!" the professor boomed from his corner. "Now let's check those field generators! Remember, proper calibration is essential! A working generator will pacify the parasite, while one that fails will potentially result in you getting infested and dying horribly!"

The class muttered.

"Everyone please collect your assigned specimen from the cold storage room," Dr. Greyfield called out cheerfully. "And do hurry—they defrost rather quickly!"

"I'll get our egg," Cinder declared. "You'll probably drop it or something."

"I can help—" I started to offer.

"No. Just. Stay. Here." She pointed at my chair firmly. "And don't touch anything. Don't move, don't breathe, don't anything."

I watched her stalk off to join the line of students.

Cinder returned quickly, having elbowed her way to the front. She was balancing a leathery bio-mechanical egg roughly the size of her head. Her wings half-spread for balance as she carefully placed it on a metal specimen plate on our desk.

"All right," she muttered, adjusting the generator's settings per instructions floating above the holographic egg on the teacher's desk. "Let's get this bullshit over with."

Our egg pulsed faintly with an inner light, its surface covered in intricate patterns that seemed to shift and flow like liquid metal. As Cinder activated our electromagnetic field generator, the patterns began to glow brighter, responding to the magnetic field.

"Now then!" Dr. Greyfield called out excitedly. "Please take your magisteel dissection knives—carefully now, they can easily cut through your fingers if you pour enough mana into them—and make a precise incision along the egg's dorsal ridge. The electromagnetic field should keep the specimen dormant during dissection."

I watched as Cinder wielded her blade, its sharp edge gleaming.

Around us, other students were performing their own dissections with varying degrees of success. The Tanystropheus was having trouble maneuvering her long neck to see properly, while the Sasquatch's massive hands proved surprisingly delicate with the blade.

Cinder stabbed the knife into the egg with a wide, energetic swing, and it got stuck halfway in. She tried to pry it out, but the knife seemed to be lodged deep in the egg. She held the egg down on the dissection plate with her left hand and pulled harder with her right, growling under her breath. After a few seconds of a struggle, the knife came free, her leather jacket slipping down her shoulders from the motion.

"I think you have to pour mana into it and adjust the blade's size to a smaller one," I pointed out, somewhat distracted by the overhead lights and generator glow, which cast reflections dancing across the iridescent tiny down feathers and scales around her shoulders and lower down.

"Nobody asked for your commentary, dweeb." Cinder sent me a murderous scowl. "And before you ask, no, I'm not giving you the knife. Also, quit staring at my chest unless you want me to start dissecting you instead of this stupid egg."

I quickly averted my gaze, face burning. "I wasn't—I mean, I was just—"

"Save it," she cut me off, turning back to the egg. Her feathers shifted through various shades of irritated red as she concentrated, pouring mana into the blade. The knife began to glow with a faint purple light, the excessive length folding down into the handle, the edge becoming much thinner and sharper.

Ah, mana. It was a good thing that she didn't tell me to use the knife, because it would be impossible for me to pour mana into it, on account of I didn't have any.

The dissection was interrupted by a sudden shriek from across the room. The Kelpie's electromagnetic field generator had sparked and died with a pathetic whine, possibly because her watery mane got into the wiring accidentally.

"Oh dear me," Dr. Greyfield said mildly, as if commenting on slightly overcast weather rather than imminent disaster. He dug behind his desk, pulling out what looked like an oversized dark gun.

The creature that leapt out from the Kelpie's egg was a nightmare of bio-mechanical horror—part spider, part octopus, with metallic segments glinting between patches of iridescent chitin. Electricity arced between its legs as it rapidly scuttled across the desk.

"Nobody panic!" Dr. Greyfield called out cheerfully. "I have a railgun! Just remember—they can smell fear! And also electromagnetic fields. And sometimes existential dread and true love!"

The Kelpie scrambled backwards, her watery mane splashing in panic as the creature launched itself at her face. She barely managed to dodge, leaving the parasite to skitter up the wall, trailing sparks.

The parasite rushed across the ceiling as Dr. Greyfield took aim with his railgun. The class erupted into chaos—students diving under desks, wings flaring, metal chains rattling.

"Don't panic!" Dr. Greyfield called out cheerfully, firing the gun with a deafening blast.

"Project your inner Omnid predator, everyone!" Dr. Greyfield called out again, taking another shot that left a smoking hole, exposing magisteel plating above the basic gray tile ceiling. "It's seeking the weakest member of the herd to latch onto!"

The creature paused its frantic scuttling, electric arcs crackling between its legs as it seemed to assess the room. Several students straightened up, baring fangs, opening wings, or flexing claws. The Sasquatch let out a low growl, while the Basilisk's eyes began to glow ominously.

I tried my best to look intimidating, which probably came across about as threatening as an angry kitten compared to my classmates' display of natural weapons.

Beside me, Cinder's wings spread to their full impressive span, igniting with eye-watering pretty colors.

The parasite skittered uncertainly, clearly reconsidering its choices in life as it faced a room full of apex predators. Then its compound eyes fixed on me.

Of course. The one person in the room who couldn't project actual predator energy on the account of not having any cryptid blood.

The creature launched itself at me with terrifying speed, metal legs clicking against the ceiling tiles. I had just enough time to think "oh shi—" before something very colorful and feathered slammed into me, knocking me sideways.

I hit the floor hard as Cinder tackled me out of the way, her wings wrapping around us both like a protective cocoon. The parasite sailed through the space where my head had been moments before.

"Stay down!" she hissed in my ear, her feathers shifting through a million colors.

There was a deafening *crack* as Dr. Greyfield's railgun fired again. The parasite exploded in a shower of chitin and sparks, raining tiny bio-mechanical parts across the classroom.

"Excellent reflexes, Ms. Nova!" Dr. Greyfield called out cheerfully. "Five extra credit points for protecting your lab partner! Though next time, perhaps try to avoid crushing your electromagnetic field generator in the process?"

I became acutely aware of several things at once:

1. Cinder was still basically on top of me.
2. Her wings were still wrapped around us both.
3. She smelled like ozone and lavender and something else I couldn't identify.
4. My heart was trying to escape through my throat.
5. Our faces were *way* too close together.

"Uh . . ." I squeaked eloquently. "Thanks."

Cinder's eyes widened as she seemed to realize our position. She scrambled back as if I'd burned her, her feathers leaking color and shifting through several shades of blue-gray.

"Argh," she muttered. "Of course the parasite went for you—might as well have painted a target on your back with that useless attempt at looking tough. Do you have literally zero Omnid blood in you or something? How are you so effin' pathetic? Even my last lab partner wasn't this freaking incompetent!"

I sighed.

"I mean, look at you!" she continued, gesturing at my outfit. "Even your clothes scream 'eat me, I'm prey.' At least try to look like you belong here instead of some lost human tourist who wandered into the Academy by mistake!"

Wow, way to out me.

As if on cue, our own half-dissected egg began to twitch, its patterns pulsing with alarming intensity.

Of course. Our electromagnetic field generator lay in pieces on the floor, knocked over during Cinder's heroic tackle.

"Fuuuu . . ." Cinder breathed, her criticism forgotten as the egg's metallic segments unfolded like a murderous origami creation, the thing from its innards propelling itself towards my face.

Her leap wasn't fast enough to save me this time around.

The creature's bio-mechanical appendages latched onto my face before I could even scream. White-hot agony exploded behind my eyes as something needle-sharp punched through my right eyeball and into my brain. The world dissolved into colorful fractals of pain and electric sparks as alien thoughts that demanded me to consume all organic life invaded my consciousness.

The last thing I heard was Cinder shouting something that sounded like a curse, and Dr. Greyfield's cheerful "Oh dear, not again!"

CHAPTER FIVE

The Wheel of Death

I saw . . . darkness that went on forever. An infinite abyss that stretched and folded into itself times a million.

Then I felt it, sensed it—a tunnel made of countless points of light formed itself right in front of me, like stars arranged into infinite spiraling arms.

The endless tunnel of stars beckoned, each point of light a promise of lovely oblivion. I felt myself being drawn towards it, like a moth to the most brilliant flame imaginable.

But something held me back, a thing that wrapped itself around my . . . body? Oh, wait.

No body. No arms. No legs, or mouth.

Just weird shimmering threads as if I were a brittle star.

My soul? Was I seeing my soul?!

Time ceased to have meaning. There was only the endless void, the mesmerizing spiral of stars, and the grip of pure darkness behind me keeping me from falling into that beautiful, terrible funnel of Uncreation or perhaps rebirth or Heaven or Hell.

I floated in that liminal space between life and death for what felt like aeons, for time nor space existed here in the limitless limbo.

Only the funnel existed, and it sought me, desired to consume me whole, to grind me down to little soul bits.

As I looked at the tunnel of light, the concept of "me" began to blur, dissolving into the infinite nothing and everything between those mesmerizing endlessly spiraling lights.

But the thing holding me—the dark centipede bracelet that had merged with my flesh—refused to let go.

Its grip was both painful and reassuring, an anchor in this abyssal ocean of cold, alien death.

SUBJECT: ALEXANDER GLOCK
STATUS: DECEASED
CAUSE: XENOMORF ELECTRICUS PARASITIC INFECTION, BRAIN DAMAGE, HEAD WOUND FROM GUNSHOT
INITIATING RESTORATION PROTOCOL . . .
Soul Realignment. Body formation from Genesis Pool.
Soul Stats Foundry Established. Tabulating Anima Stats.

| Name: Alexander Glock
| Age: 18
| Species & Subtype: Human
| Core Affinity: N/A
| Level: 0
| Anima: 89/89
| Anima Stamina: 0.1/0.1
| Mana: 0/0
| Mana Regen: 0.0m/hr
| Strength: 0
| Agility: 0
| Dexterity: 0
| Vitality: 0
| Charisma: 0
| Magic: 0
| Foresight: 0
| Intelligence: 0
| Wisdom: 0
| Skills: N/A

The words appeared in my consciousness like burning brands, white text written on blue nothingness.

Wow, so many zeroes. Look upon my vast numbers and despair!

Then sensation returned in a rush of cold wetness.

I gasped, choking on thick metallic-tasting liquid as strong hands gripped my arms, hauling me up from the depths.

"Come on, newbie, breathe!" Cinder's perfect angelic voice cut through the haze of disorientation.

I broke the surface of what looked like a pool of liquid mercury-like fluid, coughing and sputtering.

Rainbow feathers filled my vision as Cinder pulled me onto the stone ledge of what appeared to be a dim underground cavern.

Ah. Reincarnation. An angel just reincarnated me. How . . . theologically fitting?

The Lazarus Cavern was surprisingly cozy, lit by thousands of bioluminescent crystals embedded in the rock walls. They pulsed with a warm, golden light that cast a few shadows across the polished stone floor.

At the center of the cavern, the Genesis Pool stretched out like a perfect mirror of quicksilver. Its surface was unnaturally still, reflecting the crystal lights above like a window into another universe filled with shimmering golden stars.

A massive statue of a female Omnid loomed over the pool, her stone wings spread wide and her sword pointed down at the fluid's surface. Her face was hidden behind a featureless mask, but her pose radiated both protection and warning. The plaque at her feet read: *Through Death We Rise Stronger.*

I shivered, partly from the chill of the cavern air on my wet skin, but mostly from the lingering sensation of that infinite spiral of stars trying to pull me in.

A thick, fluffy robe hit me in the face, snapping me out of my daze. I realized with a start that I was completely naked, my wet skin already beginning to pebble.

"Get dressed," Cinder ordered, already turning away to give me privacy.

I quickly pulled on the robe, trying not to think about how I'd just been very naked in front of the girl who'd been haunting my thoughts since yesterday.

"So," I said, trying to sound casual while wringing fluid out of my hair, "do you make a habit of fishing dead classmates out of magic pools, or am I special?"

"Unfortunately, I'm stuck with you as a lab partner," Cinder replied without turning around. "Means I gotta be the one to resurrect your pink ass. Protocols and whatever. Don't get used to it, I'm not your friend. Here's your stupid bag."

She kicked my bag towards me.

"Thanks, dragon-bird fren'," I muttered, checking my bag over. "So, uhh . . . is there like a dead me in the classroom or . . .?"

"There was." Cinder shrugged. "Doc shot you in the head. Then he got a flame-thrower out and burned the remains. Typical Wednesday, really."

"Also . . ." I said. "Is class over? How long have I been dead?"

"About twenty minutes, give or take," Cinder replied, finally turning back to face me. "Yeah, class is over. Everyone finished their dissections, Doc burned the remains, and the blast doors opened."

"Should I head to the next class then?" I asked.

"What the actual fuck is wrong with you?" Cinder spun around, her wings flaring with agitation. "You just died! Like, actually died! A space parasite drilled through your eyeball and into your brain! Normal people take at least a day off after their first death!"

"But . . . attendance requirements . . ." I started weakly.

"Slayer Nazareth!" She threw up her hands in exasperation. "You really are some kind of walking PSA! You know what? Head to your stupid class. I don't effin' care. I'ma chill here. Thanks for dying, I get to skip Algebra now without getting detention. Go rinse off and change first. You smell like fresh meat."

She pulled out her phone and sat down on the steps, slumping against the cavern wall, clearly dismissing me.

"Change and rinse off where?"

Cinder waved with a feathered hand.

I sighed and walked around a large column. Behind it, I discovered a shower and locker room filled with rows of lockers and fresh . . . LV 3 hexasuits. Tiny beast cores glowed in a large jar nearby.

Jackpot!

I took the robe off, enjoyed a quick shower, and pulled on a hexasuit. Then I stuffed a handful of beast cores and a few extra hexasuits into my backpack. My phone was thankfully in my bag, but the tiny wax speaker was no longer in my ear. I'd have to get a new one from the van.

"So?" Cinder asked without looking up from her phone as I walked back to the pool to stare at the shimmering surface. "What are you doing here? Go be a perfect student or whatever."

I went onto the floor and started doing push-ups. The Quetzi-girl squinted at me. I pushed myself as much as I could and slumped into the floor panting.

"What are you doing?" she asked.

"Push-ups," I answered.

"Why?"

"Science!"

"What?"

"I'm seeing if dying made me stronger." I grinned, panting. "The answer is . . . yes."

"The pool doesn't make you stronger, idiot," she commented. "It . . ."

"Restores the body to a state of near-optimal health," I said. "Read about it on the Academy's website. This is great! My old bone breaks, and scars no longer bother me!"

I shoved the little beast core into the chest hexagram and let the suit power up. Then I did some more push-ups. *Aww, yes.* Magical amplification.

The Quetzalcoatl simply stared.

After 148 push-ups, the tiny beast core dimmed, winking out, and I slumped onto the floor. I inserted another beast core into the hexasuit's chest and stood up and did some jumping, trying to grab a stalactite.

"Having fun?" She asked.

"Yepperoni." I nodded.

Sitting on the yellow stone steps next to her, I pulled out the sketchbook and began drawing. I drew the tunnel of light as best I could, trying to capture the endless spiral with quick pencil strokes.

Cinder stared at my sketch, her curiosity apparently overcoming her determined indifference and Omnigram scrolling.

"Just drawing what I saw," I said, not looking back at her. "Never been dead before. Seems like something worth remembering."

"Ah. You saw the Wheel."

I nodded, adding more detail to the spiral. "Is that what it's called?"

"Mhrmm." She nodded. "The Wheel That Consumes All. Arx. Inverted world."

"Say what?" I blinked at her.

"If you don't piss off like the other half-blood girl . . ." She shrugged. "You'll get to go there. By a transit gate. The world of the damned and living gods."

"The world of the gods?" I asked, my pencil pausing on the paper. "You mean like . . . an actual physical place?"

"Mhmmmm." She stretched. "Delving class does weekly delves there. It's where we get most of our good loot and level-ups."

She glanced at my drawing again. "You've got a good eye. Most people can't remember the details of the Wheel after their first death. It's usually too overwhelming. Really fucks with your head and whatnot. How do you feel?"

"Fine." I shrugged.

Cinder stared at me with narrowed eyes. "That's . . . not normal. Most people are complete wrecks after their first death. Puking, crying, existential crisis—the works. Takes days to get over the trauma sometimes." She tilted her head, studying me with new intensity. "Oh, I guess you've had an incarnator at your parents' workplace then?"

"Uh . . ." I blinked at her, pretending to be clueless to keep her talking. "What's an incarnator?"

"You know, the mini-versions of the Genesis Pool? Big companies have them for their employees. Insurance requirement thing. Dad's got one at work. First time I died, I got incoed there. It . . . wasn't pleasant."

"Ah. I grew up in North Acadia; we didn't have an incarnator." I shook my head. "So, yeah. First death ever. Maybe I'm just weird?"

"Everyone's weird about their first death," Cinder said, her feathers shifting through thoughtful shades of blue. "But you're being extra weird about it. Like, creepy weird. You sure you're not some kind of robot or something?"

"Beep boop," I replied flatly, flipping to another page. "Totally a robot. You caught me. My evil plan to infiltrate the school has been revealed. Somebody stop me!"

"Yeah, right," Cinder scoffed, but I caught a flicker of uncertainty in her eyes. "A robot wouldn't have bled all over my favorite boots when Doc railgunned your head open along with the parasite."

I began sketching Cinder in an exaggerated war scene.

She stood in front of a sandbag trench, wielding a comically oversized, somewhat lopsided machine gun. A wild, thick mop of feathers spilled from her head. One of her wings was open against a background of explosions and gunfire. The speech bubble proclaimed: *NO FRENS ONLY DEATH! HERE.*

Above her, a massive nuclear bomb labeled *BIG FREN* plummeted from a WW2-style Omnithean plane with Executioner crosses on the wings.

I added tiny details—her skull choker with a skull and another skull bandanna, and her dark tank top. Her usual scowl was amplified to ridiculous proportions, eyes manic, jagged spikes extending out from her combat boots. The nuclear bomb became animated with squiggly lines of motion and a toothy grin drawn on its side.

"What are you drawing now . . ." Cinder's voice cut off as she leaned over again.

I added a bunch of notes with sharp arrows pointing out various items on her person.

→ Tactical goth boots of mass destruction (steel-toed for maximum emo)
→ Bigly gun (w bullets made from pure angst)
→ Emergency backup cigarette holder (for when the world just doesn't understand)
→ Skull choker of doom (+5 to brooding)
→ Pockets full of detention slips (Detention Master—gotta catch 'em all!)
→ Anti-friendship force field (now with 50% more spite)
→ Warning: Approach subject with caution, may cause spontaneous human malfunction

I heard a strange sound beside me—something between a snort and a choke. Glancing over, I saw Cinder biting her lip, clearly trying not to laugh as she read the annotations.

"Nazareth! You're such a freakin' dweeb," she managed, but there was no real venom in it. Her wings twitched as she fought to maintain her scowl. "And I do *not* collect detention slips like Pocketbeasts!"

"Uh-huh," I signed the drawing as Alex G. and slipped the paper over to her. "Here you go. One signed art free of charge. In fifty years, you'll be able to sell it for millions and buy a brooding gothic farm and raise crows or something. If you want more art, it'll cost ya."

"Cost me what?" Cinder asked, carefully folding the drawing and tucking it into her dark backpack, trying to look nonchalant about it.

"Oh, you know." I shrugged. "Information. Stories. Secrets of the universe. The usual artist's fee."

Before Cinder could reply, rapid footsteps echoed from the stone stairwell. Christi emerged, panting, her burning head lighting up the somewhat dim cavern like a torch. Her head-flames were burning so bright that they were almost pale blue-white, casting dancing shadows across the ancient walls.

"Oh, thank goodness!" Christi exclaimed, rushing over. "I heard what happened in Bio! Are you okay? First deaths can be so traumatic! Do you need anything? Water? Snacks? A hug? Counseling? 'Cause I am qualified to . . ."

"I'm fine," I assured her, subtly edging away from her intense heat. "Just a little damp."

"He's being weird about it," Cinder commented from her stone perch. "Like, robot weird. Didn't even freak out, cry, or puke or anything."

"Oh my!" Christi's flames flickered with concern. "That's . . . unusual. Maybe we should take you to the nurse? Sometimes the shock takes a while to set in . . ."

"Really, I'm okay," I insisted. "Can't wait to get to my next class."

"You absolutely should *not* go to class!" Christi declared, her flames flaring. "First deaths get automatic medical leave!"

"See?" Cinder commented. "Even the walking rule book says you should take a break."

"Cassie!" Christi suddenly rounded on the Quetzalcoatl, her flames spiking higher. "How could you let your assigned partner die on his very first day? You're supposed to protect your lab partner, it is a sacred bond . . ."

"Me?" Cinder's feathers bristled, shifting to angry reds. "I literally tackled him out of the way of the first parasite! Not my fault he has zero survival instincts! He's . . . even worse than freaking Iogann! Also, don't call me by my Cast name, you knobtwit!"

"Hey, um . . ." I protested weakly.

"Cass . . . you have one of the highest stats when it comes to fighting," the torch-girl insisted. "You have to . . ."

"It wasn't my fault, damn it!" Cinder jumped up, wings flaring. "At least Iogann is drawn to disasters—this mixie idiot practically manufactures them! He walked into class looking like a walking 'eat me' sign, tried to act tough against a predatory parasite, and then just sat there like a deer in headlights when the second one went for his face!"

"I was going to dodge . . ." I mumbled.

"When?" Cinder demanded. "After it finished drilling through your brain? Even Sarah had better survival instincts than you!"

"Now, Cass—" Christi started.

"I said, don't effin' call me that!" Cinder snapped, her wings flaring with agitation as she kicked Christi into the wall with a swing of her foot that was too fast for me to track. "And don't try to make this my fault! I'm not babysitting some helpless idiot who can't even dodge a parasite! Fuck this and fuck you!"

She grabbed her bag and vanished up the stairwell, giving us both the middle finger.

"Owww," Christi groaned, peeling herself off the cracked wall indentation. Her flames had dimmed considerably from the impact. "She's gotten even stronger since last semester . . ."

"You okay?" I asked, helping her up.

"I'll live. I'm very solid." Christi waved off my concern, her flames already brightening. "Cinder's kicked me through walls before. Usually when I call her Cassie or try to get her to be less of a rule-breaker. She really hates her birth name for some reason."

"Some reason?" I asked after she fell silent.

"Oh, it's like . . . um . . ." Christi's flames flickered uncertainly as she tried to find the right words. "So Cinder is . . . like Cassie's Kaleid name. I think it means, like . . . no family, no past, no future relationships, just fire and destruction and stuff."

"Kaleid . . . name?" I stared at Christi.

"Right, you're new here, sorry!" Christi's flames brightened again. "So, Kaleid names are like . . . names that some Omnitheans choose for themselves to . . . reinvent themselves, I think? It's kind of a rebellion against authority thing, I guess? Like, rejecting your birth name, relationships, and family connections completely."

"Weird, but okay," I said.

"Em is really into this stuff." Christi rubbed the back of her torch-head. "Equalist postmodern terminology. Dissociation from everything that chains you, embracing that everyone is equally beastly and hungry for flesh."

"Sounds like something for me to Oodle and read up about," I said.

"I mean, if you want to," Christi sighed. "Em calls it Predator Theory. She's really intense about it. I think that it's nonsense, though. Family's important. The Leviathan Slayer taught us that."

"So Cinder is . . . rejecting her whole family?" I asked.

"Sort of, yeah," Christi sighed, her flames dimming. "She still talks to Lance sometimes . . . Generally it's telling him how much he's an overachieving idiot and swearing at him. It's mostly their parents she has issues with. Justice Nova and his wife are devout Slayer followers and can be . . . intense about following rules and proper behavior. Which, you know, makes Cinder want to break every rule possible just to spite her dad."

"Ah." I nodded. Classic teenage rebellion, cryptid edition. "And the smoking?"

"Started right after she chose her Kaleid name," Christi confirmed. "Along with the all-black wardrobe and the whole 'I hate everything' attitude. She used to be so different . . . so colorful, helpful . . . so kind. I don't know what happened. But anyway!" Her flames suddenly brightened again. "You really should rest! First deaths are serious business!"

"I'm fine." I shrugged.

We remained silent for about a minute.

"Okaay. Sooo . . ." Christi's flames flickered with barely contained curiosity as she looked up the stairwell to make sure Cinder wasn't coming back. "Did you make any progress on . . . our plan? You know . . . near-death experiences can really bring people together!"

"Well, she did save me from the first parasite," I said. "And then fished my newborn self out of the magic pool after the second one killed me. So . . . progress?"

"And she actually waited here with you!" Christi bounced excitedly, her flames sparking. "That's huge! Usually she just dumps the bracelet into the pool and leaves, letting the reborn swim out of the pool themselves. Did you . . . talk? What did you talk about?"

"Art stuff mostly." I shrugged. "She called me dumb and criticized my survival instincts."

"But she didn't break your arms or throw you into a wall!" Christi clapped. "That's practically friendship by Cass standards!"

"Your standards for friendship are concerning," I commented, pulling out my camera, lowering the F-stop way down, cranking up the ISO and taking a few shots of the cavern.

Christi leaned towards me, curious as to what I was doing.

"Sup, High Pink Councilor? Want a photo?" I became my absolute, perfect self now that Cinder wasn't looming in my periphery.

"Oh my gosh, yes! Would you mind? I've always wanted a professional-looking photo of myself!" The torch-girl bounced, her pink suit and dress fluttering.

"Stand against the reincarnation pool. Good. Now, just act natural," I directed, watching through the viewfinder as Christi started to pose as if she were auditioning for a teen magazine cover.

"Perfect!" I snapped a few shots, letting Christi cycle through various poses.

"Maybe you could help Cass with her music, or art, or . . ." she chattered at me.

"We'll see," I said. "Anyways, I've History class next—please direct me to the classroom location, so I'm not late. Also, just text me on Omnigram if you want a report on my mission, Chancellor. You don't need to follow me around. I'm good."

"You're completely sure you're good to attend class?"

"Perfectly good." I nodded, stretching, clamping down on my internal screaming. "Never better. Have a whole new spine and everything. I should do this more often. This cave is very chill and relaxing."

Some distant part of me was horrified at my own words, was clawing his own face off and rocking in a corner in fear of the endless, horrid, hungry Wheel. But I wasn't that person now.

I was Alexander Glock, a self-made, unfeeling, human-shaped weapon on a mission.

"Okaay," Christi grabbed my elbow. "I'll take you. And please, keep me updated on everything!"

HISTORY CLASS. THIRD PERIOD.

I was now fully changed, wearing a new set of Omnimart shirt, shoes, and pants, and had a new micro-speaker connected to my AI and buried deep in my left ear. I'd have to order a few more to be delivered to a nearby P.O. box, judging by the rate of how fast I managed to perish.

For a few minutes, I stood at the front of Mr. Yamamoto's classroom, studying the traditional Japanese décor that covered every surface. Scrolls featuring ancient calligraphy hung from the walls, and a small zen garden occupied one corner lit up by Kitlix lanterns. An enormous beast core sat in the ceiling, casting soft light in all directions and powering up the little liquid crystal kittens.

There were no windows in the class and only a single door.

The Yōkai teacher himself was a translucent shadowlike figure wearing a traditional hakama in deep navy blue and a formal kimono top in charcoal gray. His family crest was embroidered on the kimono in silver thread, and he carried a wooden practice katana at his hip. Traditional tabi socks and sandals completed his outfit.

He maintained perfect posture as he gestured for me to introduce myself to the class, his eyes glowing faintly in his shadowlike face. The way he moved was unnaturally smooth, as if he was gliding rather than walking.

I scanned the room quickly for any potential escape routes—old habits die hard. There were none as far as I could determine; this entire class was deep underground in solid bedrock. A Japanese gravestone stood in the back of the garden.

Ah. The teacher's final resting place from which his ghost was being projected by the power of the beast core in the ceiling. Who better to teach history than a ghost who's lived through it all?

Then my eyes landed on the empty desk behind Cinder, and my heart did that stupid flutter thing again.

Of course. Either she'd managed to scare the person sitting behind her away with excessive goth rudeness, or the universe clearly had it out for me.

I also noticed Emerald Stratos sitting in front of Cinder, ruby scales catching the light. Her gold-orange slitted eyes narrowed as she recognized me from this morning.

"Mr. Glock." Mr. Yamamoto's voice materialized somewhere beside me like a cold whisper rather than through my ears, a common trait among Yōkai. "Please introduce yourself to the class."

I switched to my practiced NPC mode, though it was getting harder to maintain with Cinder's ocean-blue eyes drilling holes into me from the third row. I decided to drown myself in a bit of a comedy routine to lighten the mood of my death.

"Hey, everyone!" I gave a cheerful wave. "I'm Alexander Glock, your friendly neighborhood photographer and artist from North . . ."

"I hear you died in Bio, nulls," Emerald interrupted, her voice carrying across the room and somehow completely muting mine. "Everyone's talking about it. Apparently you just sat there and let a parasite eat your brain."

Several students snickered. I caught whispers of "typical Nullie" and "probably froze up."

"Ms. Stratos." Mr. Yamamoto's cold voice cut through the chatter like a blade. "It is considered extremely rude to interrupt introductions. Five points from your grade."

"But sensei—" Emerald started to protest.

"Ten points." The teacher's amber eyes flashed.

Emerald subsided with a huff, her ruby scales dancing with sparks of dragonfire. I noticed Cinder rolling her eyes at her friend's commentary.

"As I was saying," I continued smoothly, "I'm Alexander from North Acadia. And yes, I did die in Bio. Got better, though!" I grinned, channeling my best "this is fine" dog energy. "Pro tip—when a space parasite tries to drill through your eyeball, don't just sit there thinking 'wow, this is gonna hurt.' Turns out it really does hurt!"

A few snickers. Cinder's perpetual scowl twitched slightly. Ember, on the other hand, looked as if she was planning to decapitate me right after class.

"Thank you for that . . . colorful insight, Mr. Glock," Mr. Yamamoto said dryly. "Please take your seat. Behind Ms. Nova."

"You again." Cinder's voice dripped with irritation as I marched across the class and collapsed into the empty chair behind her. "Are you literally in all of my classes?"

"Maybe I am, maybe I am not." I shrugged. "The ways of the reincarnated samurai are mysterious."

Cinder turned back around, muttering under her breath, "Freakin' pink weirdo . . ."

"Okay, goth GF bae," I fired back, immediately regretting my words as they left my mouth.

What the hell was that, even? That wasn't even clever! My brain was obviously malfunctioning from prolonged exposure to the view of her majestic feathery wings in front of me.

She whirled around in her seat, eyes blazing. "What did you just call me?" Her voice was low and dangerous.

I remained stoically silent.

"Listen here, you preppy little mixie waste of space," she hissed. "I am *not* your 'goth GF,' your 'bae,' or any other stupid label your pathetic parasite-drilled brain can come up with. You think that you're so clever and quirky with your little drawings and your stupid jokes?"

"I'm sorry. Would you prefer Dark Princess of Angst? Queen of Combat Boots? Supreme Ruler of the Detention Realm?" I fired back at her, falling further back into sarcastic jokes just to annoy her.

"Shut it!" She leaned closer, sharp teeth glinting. "You think just because we had one semi-decent interaction in science class and inco cavern . . . that we're suddenly friends? That you can just waltz in here with your fake perfect student act and . . ."

"Are all female Quetzis this hostile? Or are you just special, Cass?" I went waaaay off script.

Cinder's wings flared wide, her feathers bristling with rage. "Are you fucking kidding me?" she snarled loudly. "How dare you?! My name is Cinder, you absolute waste of space!"

Thwack!

Mr. Yamamoto's wooden katana struck Cinder's desk with lightning speed, making us both jump.

"*Sirence!*" he commanded, his accent thickening with disapproval. "No fighting in my crass! You both stay after schoor for two-hour meditation on harmony!"

Cinder spun away from me and slumped onto her desk, muttering something that sounded suspiciously like "Effin' Nullies" under her breath.

I was once again presented with a perfect view of her wings.

The feathers started as a pale silver at their base, almost white where they connected to her back, before gradually darkening to a deeper metallic gray. Each caught the light differently, creating an effect like polished agate—some reflecting cool blue undertones, others showing hints of warm amber when she shifted.

Class ended before I even realized it, most of the teacher's history lecture simply gone from my head due to the damn mind-melting wings.

Cinder glared at me as both of us emerged into the hallway. Her head-feathers were extra-puffed up in agitation, bristling like an angry cat's fur.

"Thanks a lot," she hissed. "Now I've got detention 'cause of your stupid ass. Hope you're happy with yourself."

"Hey, you started it with the whole 'waste of space' thing," I pointed out. "I was just trying to be friendly."

"By calling me by my Cast name?" she snarled.

"Is this Nullie bothering you, Ci?" Emerald appeared beside us, her ruby scales gleaming dangerously. Her gold-orange eyes fixed on me with predatory intent.

"Just being an ignorant waste of space," Cinder muttered. "As usual."

"You know what would make you feel better?" Emerald's grin showed saw-like white teeth. "A little spine-breaking therapy. No one would blame you—he's clearly asking for it. And don't reincarnate him. Let the teachers deal with him."

"Hmmm." Cinder tilted her head thoughtfully, her feathers shifting through shades of considering-violence orange-red as she opened and closed her fists, diamond-shaped pupils dilating like that of a cat about to pounce. "He *is* really annoying . . . Maybe a good kick will . . ."

"You guys should . . ." I raised my camera smoothly and cranked the flash setting to maximum. ". . . lighten up and smile more!"

The flash went off before either of them could react. Both of the predators recoiled, momentarily blinded.

I took off running.

Nobody seemed to follow me.

Maybe they had better things to do or were simply bad at hunting humans down after being blinded. Thankfully, both of them were evening predators, vulnerable to being flashed in the face.

I quickly arrived at my locker, my heart still pounding from my narrow escape. As I pulled out the heavy bag of stolen board games, I caught my reflection in the small mirror within the locker. My face was flushed, hair disheveled, and I was grinning like an idiot despite nearly getting murdered.

What is wrong with me? I should be terrified. Instead, I feel . . . alive. Energized. Like I've just discovered a new and exciting way to court death.

I should do it again.

Focus. You're here for a reason. Get your head in the game.

I shouldered the bag and headed for the cafeteria, already plotting my next move.

The lunch room was massive, with high gothic vaulted ceilings and long tables arranged in a precise hierarchy. The popular cryptids claimed the central tables near the opulent fireplaces, while less socially powerful groups occupied the edges.

I spotted an empty table row, headed straight for it, and began laying out chess and checkerboards.

"You," a voice sounded from one of the empty chairs. "Asshole mixie. If you ever call me 'Cassie' or 'goth GF bae' again, I will break your spine. Do not tempt me. This is your only warning."

"Gah, talking chair!" I jumped backwards.

Cinder slowly faded into visibility, her wings unfurling as color leaked back into her silver feathers. She glared at me.

I made the sign of the Slayer Nazareth in the air.

"Be gone, apparition! Quick, someone call a priest—we need an exorcism! The spirit's really goth, too, it must have unfinished . . . detention to serve!"

"You're not funny," she declared flatly, arms crossed.

"I respectfully disagree," I replied, setting up another chessboard. "I'm hilarious. Also, I'm sorry about earlier. Probably . . . won't happen again."

"Probably?" she growled.

"Well, I can't guarantee I won't say something incredibly stupid again." I shrugged. "But I'll try to be more mindful about the whole Kaleid thing. Maybe."

"*Maybe?!*" she barked. "I told Em that I'm going to hunt you down and tear you into two! Maybe I should actually go through with that, you insufferable smartass!"

"Kinky. Please crush my forehead extra hard with a giant boot after you tear out my spine," I commented. "I'll make a mold and cherish the imprint for a thousand years."

"You're seriously effed in the head, you know that? What kind of creep actually asks to be stomped on?" she half-growled.

"The kind that appreciates good boots." I shrugged, resuming my chessboard setup. "Those are genuine Ravenstar Steel-Toes, right? Limited edition from their Dark Academia collection, $699.99 O-bux? Nice choice. The skull buckles really bring out your whole 'I hate everyone' aesthetic. And that Rain Day pants belt for $299.89? Very chic. Such fashion."

Cinder's eyes narrowed dangerously. "How do you . . ."

"AI reverse image lookup," I said. "Took your photo yesterday during your smoke break on the beam."

She squinted at me, clearly contemplating how to best murder me.

I waved my lunch card at her before she actually decided to do it. "How about a free lunch as an apology? You can even order the sixty-five-dollar steak with gold flakes on it, or the big sushi platter for $88.99."

"What? I don't need your charity, dweeb. And I definitely don't need your fake-ass apologies."

"Not charity. Reparations." I shrugged. "For my vast Acadian dumbness. Let me repent through the power of nom. I won't even bother you if my presence offends you. I've got a few chess matches to win."

"You're so . . . *ugh*!" She threw her hands up in frustration. "Fine. Whatever. But I'm getting the most expensive thing on the menu just to spite you."

"That's the spirit!" I grinned. "Bankrupt the dastardly half-human! Show no mercy! Order fifty-nine varieties of heart meat, carnivore-sama!"

Cinder snatched the meal card from my hand with a huff and stalked off to the lunch line, her silver feathers shifting through annoyed shades of gold-orange-red. I watched as she elbowed the crowd and loaded up her tray with what looked like enough meat to feed a small army—premium cuts of steak, several burger patties, and was that really gold leaf garnish? Guess the online menu wasn't exaggerating.

She returned to my table quickly and practically threw the meal card at my face. It bounced off my nose and clattered onto the chessboard, Invader Xim Omnimart-harvested lanyard fluttering.

"There. Happy now?" She dropped into her seat with practiced teenage angst.

I nodded with a manic grin. Maybe she'd be less snappy after her many rare steaks to fuel her crystalline-organic Quetzalcoatl heart.

CHAPTER SIX

Chess Grandmaster and Maestro

"So," she said, stabbing her fork into an entire cow's worth of premium steak, "you're really just going to sit there and watch me eat your money?"

"Better than you swallowing me in a single bite." I smiled.

"What?"

"Just trying to avoid this common Aztec scenario." I showed her a picture of a Quetzalcoatl devouring a man whole from the Codex Borbonicus.

The Quetzi-girl blessed me with an eye-roll.

I dug into my bag and put up a marker-etched fancy sign onto the table that read *DEFEAT ME FOR A FREE LUNCH!*. "Anywaaaaays, I've got match business to attend to."

"Hrm," Cinder scoffed between bites. "What kind of scam are you running now?"

"What scam?" I laughed. "This is chess grandmaster training! Keeps the mind sharp!"

Before she could respond with another snarky comment, a green-scaled Basilisk wearing designer sunglasses approached our table, eyeing the chessboards with interest.

"Sooo . . . Free lunch if I win?" he asked, adjusting his shades.

"Absolutely!" I beamed, gesturing to the empty seat. "Choose your weapon—chess or checkers?"

"Chess," he said, sliding into the chair across from me.

From the corner of my eye, I could see Cinder sending me snarky looks as she continued demolishing her lavish meal. Her wings shifted slightly in what I was starting to recognize as her "this is so stupid" posture.

A small crowd was starting to gather, attracted by the promise of free food and entertainment.

"What happens if we lose?" someone called out from the growing audience.

"If you lose, you give me your Omnigram ID, and you will owe me a small favor in the future." I grinned. "Nothing illegal. Just wanna make friends and break up some anti-human-blood prejudices, that's all."

I could hear Cinder choking slightly on her spite-steak behind me.

In another twenty minutes, she watched with increasing disbelief as I moved from board to board with practiced efficiency. At times, her meats lay forgotten as I systematically dismantled opponent after opponent, my hands moving in an almost mechanical rhythm.

"Knight to E4 . . . Rook takes queen . . . Checkmate in three . . ." I muttered.

The crowd grew larger, students gathering to watch the spectacle of the new Nullie student inexplicably simultaneously destroying multiple opponents in both chess and checkers. With each victory, I collected another Omnigram ID, said a compliment, offered another handshake, and made another connection.

"How the fuck are you . . ." Cinder's voice trailed off as I executed yet another perfect combination. Her eyes narrowed suspiciously as she studied my movements. I could practically see the gears turning in her head, trying to figure out how the awkward human was suddenly a chess prodigy and a socialite.

She had no idea that the small camera in my wrist was directing the view to my LLM with vision armed with a chess app. These fools were fighting an unbeatable machine. At the end of each match, I pointed my wrist at my opponent, and the LLM wrote up a cute joke for me to say about them, which drew laughter and chortles from the gathered crowd.

"Uncle George was a chess grandmaster." I shrugged at Cinder, capturing another queen with a lazy yawn. "He taught me everything. Bishop to F6, checkmate."

The gathered students *ooooo*ed at my performance.

"Good game, June!" I grinned, reaching across to shake a Kelpie's moist hand. "Your opening was really strong—that Queen's Gambit variation caught me off guard! How about a photo of this historic moment?"

"Sure." The Kelpie gave me a wide smile. She seemed genuinely cheerful and nice, unlike the "Harold-hide-the-pain" face Cinder was making whenever she smirked at me.

"Say, since you're heading to the lunch line anyway, would you mind grabbing me something? I'm kind of stuck here with all these matches."

"Can do!" June beamed, shaking her liquid mane, pleased by the compliment and the quality photo I took of her despite her loss. "What would you like?"

"Mega sushi platter boat." I grinned at her. "Grab the most expensive one, and half of it is yours. Here, use my card to pay for it."

I could practically feel Cinder's eyes boring into the back of my head, her wings rustling with what I imagined was supreme annoyance. The contrast between my earlier awkward fumbling around her and my current smooth operation probably wasn't helping her suspicion levels.

Whatever, let her stew. I've got more Omnitheans to conquer.

The Kelpie girl returned with the enormous sushi boat, a mountain of raw fish and rice wrapped up into nice bundles that could probably feed a small army—or one very hungry Omnid. It was a comically oversized platter for my human frame, but I attacked it with gusto anyway, grabbing and popping pieces into my mouth as I purposefully stepped between chessboards like some sort of sushi-eating, chess-dominating emperor penguin.

"Knight to D5," I called out between bites of salmon nigiri, barely glancing at the boards as I made my moves. "Check. Rook to B7!"

I defeated another opponent and took down my sign just as the fifteen-minute warning bell rang through the cafeteria. The crowd had grown impressively large, and I'd collected quite a stack of Omnigram IDs from my challengers.

"Ladies, omnivores, and carnivores!" I called out, gesturing to the remaining mountain of sushi. "No sense letting this go to waste! Who wants some? You, with the lovely purple scales—this tuna roll would perfectly complement your coloring! And you, with the gorgeous head crest—this salmon nigiri is calling your name!"

I could hear Cinder making gagging noises behind me as I distributed compliments and sushi in equal measure.

"Could you *be* any more of a try-hard?" she mumbled my way.

"I could," I fired back at her. "Sadly, only so many chess sets fit into my backpack today! Tomorrow I will increase the number of challengers!"

As the lunch crowd dispersed, Cinder stood up abruptly. "Well, this has been sufficiently nauseating. Thanks for a free lunch, I guess. Hopefully I'll see you never."

She had no idea that there was no escape from me due to the Pink One's machinations. I swiftly packed up my boards, momentarily glancing at her. Cinder's scowl deepened as she scrolled through a barrage of messages on her phone.

MothMayhem🦋: yo dawg where u at?
MothMayhem🦋: we at auditodium
MothMayhem🦋: Cinder
MothMayhem🦋: answer ur phone

Em-the-rawd 🔥 : Ci!
Em-the-rawd 🔥 : Cinder
Em-the-rawd 🔥 : Ciiiiiindrrrrrr. Where the f are you? Did you tear out the nullie's spine yet?!
Em-the-rawd 🔥 : stop ignoring me! heeeello? I swear when I find you I'm gonna break your kneecaps.
Em-the-rawd 🔥 : Stop turning ur notifiucations off, u dumb beerch.

I pretended not to look at her phone, shoving the last board into my backpack.

Cinder paid no attention to me, typing out responses, her claws clicking against the screen.

I navigated through the crowded hallway to my assigned locker, carefully avoiding bumping into any tails or wings.

The metal door creaked as I opened it, revealing the bare interior. I hadn't had time to personalize it yet, but that would come later. Right now it just needed to hold my chess empire equipment.

Throwing the board-game bag into the locker, I rushed to my next class.

I slipped into the music room just as the bell rang. The classroom was a jumble of instruments, sheet music, and what appeared to be . . . yes, that was definitely Mr. Sterling sleeping on the job.

The music teacher was sprawled in a hammock strung between two support pillars, his round wire-rimmed glasses askew, a nightcap atop his head, fifties-style pajamas crumpled. His wide pants had ridden up slightly, revealing mismatched socks—one covered in musical notes, the other featuring tiny sleeping cats.

"Right then, loves," a velvety voice sounded in my head. "Free period today. Just . . . express yourselves, get a feel for a new instrument or two, see if you can make whatever you want to sound the way you want it to be. Peace and love, peace and love."

The sleeping teacher didn't move. He was definitely snoring.

Ah, right. He was a Dreamwalker, monitoring all of us through the astral or whatever.

Since nobody asked me to introduce myself, I ignored the few "ew Nullie" looks and went to poke at the massive piano in the back.

Cinder stormed over to the piano. "What are you doing here?" she demanded, feathered tail lashing. "Are you seriously in this class, too?"

"Yep." I nodded, not looking at her. "Music seemed like a fun elective!"

"Fun?" Her voice dripped with sarcasm. "You're just effing everywhere today, aren't you? What's next—are you going to join the Agromancy Club too?"

"Hmm. Gardening is good for the soul." I nodded, jabbing the piano aimlessly. "So yes. Absolutely. Joining every club. Especially if they have pretty girls like you for me to ogle at free of charge."

"I told you to stop with these comments!" Cinder's wings flared dangerously, her feathers shifting through shades of rage-red. "And get away from that piano before you break it, you uncultured chuppy!"

"Make me." I grinned, purposefully playing the opening notes to "Chopsticks" as badly as possible. "Also, what's a chapy?"

Cinder's ears twitched at my deliberately awful playing. "A chuppy is a very dumb-looking bird-fox cub from Arx. Which you clearly are, massacring that piano like that."

"Shush, woman. I'm musikering!" I said.

Cinder's wings bristled with barely contained rage. "Stop. Poking. The. Piano." Each word was punctuated by her tail lashing dangerously.

"Why?" I asked innocently, continuing to press random keys to bug her. "Is it yours?"

"You know," she growled, "some of us actually take music seriously. Unlike a certain halfkin who just showed up and thinks he can—"

"Oh? Are you a talented musician, perchance? Wanna show a music incompetent how it's done?" I asked slyly. "Do you take requests? How about 'My Immortal' by Evanescence?"

"What? Do I look like a fucking street musician to you?" Cinder bristled.

"Whatever, dude. Yulia, pull up the Evanescence piano cover keys," I ordered my massive phone and laid it sideways when the piano roll visualization appeared on screen. "I bet I can kick your feathered ass at piano, bae."

I started jabbing keys out of tune horribly, following the video on screen.

Cinder's wings flared with red as she watched me butcher the song. "Abyss, stop! You're murdering it! That's not even close to how it goes! Get off the seat and watch!"

She shoved me from the piano and sat down.

Her claws flew across the keys with practiced precision, the opening notes of "My Immortal" filling the room with haunting clarity. Despite her obvious anger, her touch was delicate, each note perfectly weighted.

"See?" she snapped, not missing a beat as she glared at me. "*This* is how you play it. Not whatever tone-deaf massacre you were attempting."

I watched her hands move across the keys, noticing how her wings relaxed slightly as she played. The tension in her shoulders eased, and for a moment, she seemed to forget she was supposed to be mad at me.

Responds well to dares. I mentally filed it down. *Easy to rile.*

"That was . . . acceptable. I bet you can't do Titanica on piano . . . while singing it," I challenged with a smirk. "How about 'Timeless Bonds'? That seems right up your goth alley."

Cinder's eyes narrowed dangerously. "Are you trying to bait me or something?"

"What, scared you can't handle Titanica?" I taunted, pulling up the piano roll on my phone. "I mean, if it's too hard for you . . . I can always . . ."

"Too hard?" Her wings flared with indignation. "Please. I could play that in my sleep." Her claws hovered over the keys as she glared at me. "But I'm not going to just because some halfwit chuppy is trying to provoke me."

"Uh-huh," I nodded. "Sure. I get it. Titanica's pretty intense. Maybe something easier? Like . . . 'Twinkle, Twinkle, Little Star'?"

Cinder choked on her anger. "You know what? Fine. *Fine.* I'll show you 'intense.'" She cracked her knuckles and positioned her claws over the keys.

I made sure that my phone was recording the video and audio.

The opening notes of "Timeless Bonds" filled the room, her hands dancing across the ivory with practiced precision.

The class suddenly fell silent, all eyes focused on her.

Cinder didn't notice that I put up a GoPro Omnica10 Black on a small tripod facing her wings. She began to sing, her voice carrying a raw, emotional edge that made my heart skip several beats.

"Through mystic mists of Cradlefall's day / Where crystal peaks light up the way / Time moves on but my heart stays / And nothing else matters!"

Her voice was . . . incredible. Deep, rich, with just the right amount of growl on the lower notes. She wasn't just playing the song—she was living it, her tail moving like a metronome to the tune.

"Like waves that crash upon the shore / Each moment brings us something more / Breaking through life's closing door / And nothing else matters."

I watched, mesmerized, as she lost herself in the performance. Her usual scowl melted away, replaced by an expression of pure focus. Her wings moved subtly with the rhythm, creating an almost hypnotic effect as the silver feathers caught the light and shined with violet, blue, and gold colors. The entire class was transfixed—even Mr. Sterling had lifted his sleep mask to watch.

"When storm clouds gather overhead / And fears arise from words unsaid / Our bond remains, as time has led / And nothing else matters."

Her claws glided across the keys, adding subtle embellishments to the melody that made it uniquely hers. The combination of her haunting voice and skillful piano work transformed the metal classic into something entirely new. Encouraged by my hand signals and tripod setup, other people pulled out their phones, recording her.

"In morning light or evening shade / Through every choice that we have made / This trust we built will never fade / And nothing else matters."

As she hit the final notes, the room erupted in applause. Cinder seemed to remember suddenly where she was, her wings snapping tight against her back as her usual scowl returned.

"There," she growled at me. "Happy now?"

"Not even close to happy." I shoved a guitar into her arms that I had procured from a wall while she was singing. "Let's see your guitar skills. Red Stratos—'Omnithornication'! Go."

Cinder's wings bristled as she held the guitar. "You're seriously pushing it. What's your game here?"

"No game." I shrugged, adjusting my phone's position slightly to get a better recording angle. "Just curious if you're as good with strings as you are with keys. Unless . . . you can't play guitar?"

"Of course I can play guitar! I'm in a troupe as a Bard class, you ignorant—"

"Ah-pa-pa-pa. Prove it," I challenged. "I ain't got time to attend your puny concerts or whatevs. Destroy me right now with your skills if you think you're so hot."

Cinder's claws tightened on the guitar neck. "You're such an ass, you know that? Like, an actual professional-grade ass."

"Less talking, more rocking." I grinned. "Unless you're scared . . ."

"Scared?" She scoffed, but her claws were already moving to tune the guitar. "The only thing I'm scared of is catching whatever weird social disease makes you act like . . . this." She gestured vaguely at all of me.

But despite her protests, her fingers began picking out the opening riff of "Omnithornication." The guitar came alive under her touch, each note crisp and precise.

Mr. Sterling suddenly sprang up from his hammock with surprising agility for someone who had appeared asleep moments ago. "Oh, brilliant! Simply brilliant!" He practically bounced to the drum set, his outfit somehow becoming even more rumpled. "Let's give it a proper go, shall we?"

The music instructor settled behind the drums with unexpected grace, his mismatched socks visible as he positioned his feet on the pedals.

"Right, then," he said, beaming and twirling a drumstick. "Three, four . . ."

He launched into the drum part with startling skill, his sleepy demeanor completely transformed.

Cinder's eyes widened slightly, but her claws never faltered on the strings. The drumbeat kicked in, and suddenly the classroom was filled with a perfect fusion of guitar and percussion.

And then Cinder began to sing.

Her voice took on a different quality with the guitar—rougher, edgier, with a punk rock growl that sent shivers down my spine. She attacked each verse with barely contained fury, as if every lyric was a personal challenge.

"Psychic spies from Thunderland try to steal your mind's elation . . ."

Her wings moved with the rhythm, creating dramatic shadows as she leaned into the music. The entire class was transfixed, even those who had been pretending to ignore us earlier.

Mr. Sterling was in his element behind the drums, his face practically glowing with enthusiasm as he matched Cinder's energy perfectly.

"And tidal waves couldn't save the world from Omnithornication . . ."

Cinder's performance was electric, her voice and guitar work transforming the classroom into an impromptu concert venue. With Mr. Sterling's expert drumming backing her up, she was completely in her element—fierce, passionate, and utterly mesmerizing.

I made sure my cameras caught every moment, especially the way her wings moved with the music, opening and closing wide and changing colors as she struck specific chords.

The song came to an explosive end as the room erupted in applause and cheers. Even I had to clap, though I made sure to maintain my challenging smirk.

I watched realization dawn across Cinder's face as she rotated to face the class. Her blue eyes widened as she took in the applauding crowd, then narrowed dangerously as she spotted my recording setup.

"You . . ." Cinder sputtered. "Is that a freakin' camera?! Cameras?! You recorded that?"

"Sure did." I grinned. "Got the piano performance, too. You're really talented, you know that?"

"You can't just . . ." she hissed.

"Three cheers for our resident genius musician!" I interrupted her and spread my arms, working the crowd like a seasoned conductor. "Come on, let's hear it for Cinder! Shake the room in your voice of support! What should our rock star play next? Any requests?"

The class erupted in enthusiastic calls, drowning out Cinder's attempts to confront me about the cameras. Her wings puffed up in clear agitation, but she was trapped by the wave of positive peer pressure I'd orchestrated that washed across her like an ocean wave.

"Do 'Welcome to the Black Parade'!" someone shouted.

"Yeah, MCR!" another voice joined in.

"Do you know any Panic! At the Disco?" a ghostly figure called from the back.

"How about 'Hallelujah'?" I offered.

Mr. Sterling was already settling back behind his drums, beaming with infectious enthusiasm. "Capital idea!"

I watched as Cinder's internal struggle played across her face. Her feathers bristled with rage at my manipulation, but the enthusiastic crowd and Mr. Sterling's expectant drumsticks left her little choice.

"Fine," she growled at me. "But after this, you and I are having a serious talk about boundaries and consent."

"Whatever you say, angel." I grinned at her. "Go on. Pick one of the requests. Crush me with your voice instead of your boots."

Cinder's claws tightened on the guitar as she turned back to face the class.

"'Welcome to the Black Parade' it is," she muttered, though her death glare in my direction promised terrible future retribution. Eh, that was a problem for the future me.

Song after song she went, getting more and more into it, trapped in the social bear trap I had constructed.

The bell rang just as Cinder hit the final note, and she immediately whirled on me, wings and fangs flared aggressively. But before she could tear into me about the recording, she was swarmed by enthusiastic classmates.

I slipped out of the music room while Cinder was surrounded by her new fans, clutching my cameras close. My heart was still racing from her performances—both from their raw intensity and from the knowledge that she was going to absolutely murder me when she caught up with me.

Next class was Geography with Ms. Steele.

I walked in, already scanning the room for threats and escape routes.

Ms. Steele turned out to be a Lindworm with shimmering emerald scales and golden spectacles perched on her serpentine snout.

As for threats—in the back corner by the window was Cinder, still slightly flushed from her impromptu concert.

"Ah, a lovely new student," Ms. Steele's voice was surprisingly gentle for someone with that many teeth. "Would you like to introduce yourself to the class?"

I stepped to the front of the class. Time for another performance.

"Greetings, Geography-inclined colleagues!" I declared with excessive enthusiasm, my voice echoing across the room. "I am Alexander Glock, recently arrived from the frozen, radioactive wastes of North Acadia. Like many great explorers and historic figures, I too am on an epic journey of discovery—though sadly with significantly less conquering and pillaging than my namesake Alexander the Great.

"My hobbies include photography, drawing, chess, and avoiding being stomped on by very angry Quetzalcoatls," I continued cheerfully, vaguely waving at Cinder, which produced a squeak-growl from her direction. "They say Alexander wept when he had no more worlds to conquer . . . I just weep when my SD card is full. Cheers!"

I slipped into a seat near the front of the class, well out of Cinder's wing reach. The murderous aura was practically radiating from the back corner, but I kept my eyes fixed firmly on Ms. Steele as she began her lecture about the Great Fault.

I took meticulous notes as I actually found the subject of Cometfall quite interesting.

The bell rang and I was out of my seat before the sound even began, notebook already shoved in my backpack. No time for niceties—I had an angry Quetzalcoatl to avoid.

Cinder practically flew out of her seat after me.

I narrowly avoided her grabby claws and slipped into the crowded hallway, using every evasion technique I knew.

Weave between groups, use larger students as cover, never run in a straight line, leap across the stairwell holding onto the baluster. My bag was light, too, as I had stashed the tripods in my locker earlier.

"*Get back here, you effin' chuppy!*" An angry voice pierced the air behind me.

I ducked under a Sasquatch's outstretched arm, rolled past a cluster of shocked Thunderbirds, and sprinted down the hall and around a corner.

My heart was pounding, but not entirely from fear. There was something incredibly exhilarating about this chase, about pushing Cinder's buttons and being chased by a feisty predator.

I dashed through the corridors, my heart pounding. Cinder's angry shouts echoed behind me, accompanied by the sound of her boots thundering against the floor.

"*I swear when I catch you—*"

I vaulted over a bench, narrowly avoiding a collision with a group of students.

"Sorry!" I called back cheerfully, using their bulk as temporary cover. "Just playing tag with an angry angel!"

Her wings created distinct whooshing sounds as she pursued me.

I burst into Mr. Yamamoto's classroom, quickly scanning it.

The shadowy samurai teacher was already there, calmly arranging cushions on the floor for our detention meditation session.

Cinder stormed in right behind me, wings flared aggressively, only to realize too late that I'd led her predator-self straight to our scheduled detention.

I quickly closed the door behind the panting goth Quetzi with a twist of the lock, grinning innocently as I settled into seiza position on one of the meditation cushions, perfectly centered, hands folded in my lap, the picture of serene acceptance.

"*There you are, you little ffffffuuuuuuuuiiiee—*" Cinder started, then froze as she registered Mr. Yamamoto's looming presence. Her wings snapped tight against her back as she realized she'd been outmaneuvered.

"Ah, fellow detention-mate," I said calmly. "Here for our mandatory meditation session?"

"Excellent timing, my pupils!" Mr. Yamamoto nodded approvingly, his wooden katana tapping gently against the floor. "Time for meditation and reflection on hamony!"

Cinder fluttered with barely contained rage as she was forced to take the cushion right next to me.

"Cross regs. Straighten spine. Empty mind of anger," Mr. Yamamoto instructed, pacing in front of us with measured steps.

I closed my eyes, keeping my breathing steady.

Every time Cinder tried to hiss a threat or demand at me, Mr. Yamamoto's wooden katana would tap sharply against the floor.

"Sirence!" he commanded. "Empty mind, find inner peace!"

Inner peace was surprisingly easy to find with an angry Cinder stewing in her rage beside me.

"Breathe in hamony!" The teacher instructed. "Let go of negative thoughts!"

I maintained perfect meditation posture, listening as Cinder's frustrated huffs gradually subsided into something resembling normal breathing.

"Hamony," Mr. Yamamoto intoned, his wooden katana tapping a gentle rhythm. "Like water flowing around rock, we must adapt, not fight."

I risked cracking one eye open to peek at Cinder. She sat rigidly on her cushion, but her expression had lost some of its homicidal edge. The light coming from the Kitlix lanterns above danced across her sparkly silver feathers.

Mr. Yamamoto continued his philosophical musings, occasionally dipping into Engrish.

"Inner peace comes from self-understanding," he droned on. "Like bamboo in wind, we must bend, not break."

Cinder shifted slightly on her cushion, and I quickly shut my eyes again before she could catch me staring. My heart was still doing that stupid flutter thing, even after an hour of meditation.

More exposure therapy was clearly needed. Can't have angry goth Quetzi girls ruining my perfect Alexander Glock mojo.

"Remember," Mr. Yamamoto's voice took on a more serious tone, "words can hurt like a blade. Choose them with care."

In due time, our meditation session was complete. My legs were stiff from sitting still for so long, but years of hiding in uncomfortable spaces had given me decent endurance for this sort of thing.

Cinder, however . . .

I watched as she tried to stand, her legs clearly cramped from maintaining the formal position for so long. Her wings fluttered uselessly as she attempted to find her balance.

"Need a hand?" I offered automatically, reaching out before my brain could remind me that she probably still wanted to murder me.

"I don't need your—" she started to snap, but her legs betrayed her. She stumbled, and suddenly I was supporting part of her weight, her wing brushing against my shoulder.

Time seemed to freeze. The iridescent feathers were impossibly soft against my skin, and I could feel the warmth radiating from her.

My heart was doing gymnastics in my chest. This close, I could smell that hint of lavender and ozone again and see how her ocean-blue eyes had flecks of violet-gold near the pupils like rays of a setting sun.

Danger! Danger! my brain screamed. *Abort mission! Too close!*

CHAPTER SEVEN

Naming Convention

Cinder seemed equally frozen, her eyes wide with surprise. For a split second, her fortress of anger opened a single window, revealing something vulnerable underneath. Then reality crashed back in and the window snapped shut.

"Don't touch me!" she snarled, stumbling backward. Her wings flared defensively, claws out.

"Sorry!" I yelped and I took off running before she demanded anything else of me.

Cinder attempted to pursue me. Her legs were clearly still numb from meditation, making her usual predatory grace look quite hilarious. Her leather boots squeaked as she staggered after me, using the lockers for support.

"Get . . . back . . . here . . ." she growled, but the threat lost some impact when combined with her wobbly movements. Her wings kept twitching, trying to help her balance.

"Nuh-uh!" I called back cheerfully, maintaining a safe distance. "Those legs working okay there, rock star? Looking a little stiff!"

"Just wait . . . when I . . . get feeling back . . . in my legs . . ." she threatened, taking another unsteady step.

"You'll what? Stomp me extra hard? 'Cause I probably would like that! I'm quite the devious bastard!" I teased.

"You . . ." Cinder heaved, her wings flaring with indignation. "You . . . you're so effed up!"

"So I've been told!" I called back, dancing just out of reach.

"First you stalk me, then you manipulate me into performing . . . record me without permission, and now you're . . . you're . . ."

"Bringing joy to your otherwise dreary existence?" I suggested, maintaining a safe distance, the beast orb powered hexasuit keeping me extra spry.

"Aarrghh!" She tried to lunge at me, but her legs weren't quite cooperating yet. Her wings fluttered as she caught herself against a locker. "I'm going to turn you into minced meat!"

"Such scary promises." I grinned, backing towards the exit. "But maybe save our dinner date for tomorrow? When you can actually give chase properly and not limp about like a . . . baby Quetzalcoatl learning to fly?"

"I swear to whatever god you believe in . . ." Cinder growled. "That's it!"

She folded her wings around her. Each of her feathers took on the colors of the hallway and then she slowly vanished from view, becoming invisible.

"Gotta run, invisi-babe!" I called cheerfully, already halfway to the door. "Places to be! Naps to partake in! But hey—great performance today! Twenty-eight thousand thumbs up. You really do have an amazing voice!"

"*What do you mean, twenty-eight thousand?!*" Cinder's screech echoed through the hallway as I burst through the exit doors into the late afternoon sunlight.

I sprinted across the parking lot. Behind me, I could hear Cinder's increasingly creative threats growing fainter as I increased the distance between us.

The van was waiting faithfully where I'd left it, looking even more decrepit in the golden afternoon light. I yanked open the back doors, then shut them and collapsed into the beanbag chair, breathing hard but grinning like an idiot.

The entire van shook as something—no, someone invisible—kicked it hard enough to make the rusty frame rattle.

"*Get out of there, you creepy little—*" Cinder boomed furiously. Her combat boots connected with the van's side again, making the whole vehicle shudder.

I scrambled up, peering through the tiny window in the back door.

I still couldn't see her, but her legs seemed to have recovered enough for property damage, at least.

"Try kicking a little harder," I suggested through the small steel-mesh-covered window. "It'll help you blow off some steam! Does being invisible reduce the power of the kick, by the way?"

Wham! The van rocked violently as Cinder's combat boot connected with the side panel again.

"*Delete. Those. Videos!*" Each word was punctuated by another kick. The van's ancient frame groaned in protest. It was thankfully very solid and stood up to the angry Quetzi goth girl assault.

"What are you hounding me for, angry ghost?" I asked between kicks. "Other classmates recorded you, too. Go haunt their personal residences. I bet they already uploaded their phone vids to OmniTube under 'Quetzi Goth Angel Covers Titanica, Piano Version.' Kids and their phones these days."

Wham! Another kick made the van shudder.

"I don't care about *their* recordings!" Cinder snarled. "*You're* the one who set this whole fucking thing up! *You're* the one who manipulated me into performing! *You're* the one who"—*kick*—"keeps"—*kick*—"following me"—*kick*—"around!"

"Following you?" I gasped in mock offense. "I'm wounded! We just happen to share some classes. Pure coincidence!"

"*Bullshit!*" The van rocked again.

"Innocent until proven guilty!" I declared. "Thems your Omnithean justice system rules, not mine!"

I put the phone speaker to the steel mesh window and began to play "She Wants Me Dead" by Cazzette.

"Woke up this morning with a gun to my head / Somebody help me, she wants me dead!"

The speaker boomed with the deep bass.

"She wants me dead, d-d-dead, dead, dead / She wants me dead, d-d-dead, dead, dead!"

"Try to synchronize the kicks with the music," I suggested and heard a roar and then a series of kicks.

"Hmmm, that was way out of tune," I commented as the song ended. "C minus."

Something violet and sparkly fluttered in the side mirror as Cinder started to run out of mana, flickering erratically and panting loudly. Focusing on it was hard, but I tried to do so anyway, looking through the camera's viewfinder. Her snout was elongated, predatory, far more draconic, long tongue visible between rows of sharp teeth. Absolutely massive, shimmering, violet wings semi-faded into the background spread out in wide arcs.

Wham! One final, particularly vicious kick made the van shudder, and then . . . silence.

I peered through the tiny reinforced window to see Cinder fully fading back into existence and leaning against the van's side, panting heavily and completely spent. Her Quetzi features melted away, face and wings becoming less stretched, retreating back to make her much more humanoid.

Her silver wings drooped with exhaustion, and her chest heaved as she tried to catch her breath.

"You done redecorating my mobile home, darling?" I asked cheerfully.

"I . . . hate . . . you . . ." she panted, sliding down to sit on the asphalt. Her combat boots had left impressive deep dents in the van's rusty panels. She was considerably stronger than a human when it came to kicking vans.

"Nah, you don't," I replied, emboldened by the safety of my mobile rusty fortress. "You're just mad because I got you to show off your amazing talent to the world. The videos are already being spread across the net—me deleting my higher quality version will do absolutely nada. 'Sides, aren't you in a troupe as the Bard or something? I fail to see the problem of you getting a bit more fame."

"The problem," Cinder growled, still sitting against my van, "is that you're a manipulative creep who doesn't understand basic concepts like consent!"

"Says the person who just committed assault and battery against an innocent vehicle," I countered. "Pretty sure that's a crime, too. Just so you know, this van is covered in dashcams."

"You . . . you're bluffing! Who the fuck would put cams on this rusty bucket?"

"I would," I replied and tapped the dashcam duct-taped to the rear door window. "Look here. This is a Omnimart Dashcam PF-r91. Whenever someone moves near the van or damages it, the cam records it. You did a lot of moving and kicking there."

"Arghhh!" Cinder ground out, but some of the fight seemed to have drained out of her. "Why are you like this?"

"Like what?" I opened the van door slightly, eyeing her. "A chess grandmaster? A talented photographer? An appreciator of Quetzalcoatl musicians?"

"Like . . . *this*!" She gestured wildly at all of me. "One minute you're this awkward mess who can barely string two words together, then you're some kind of chess prodigy and social butterfly, then you're running around recording people and manipulating situations . . . It's like you're a different person every five minutes!"

"And that's . . . bad?" I arched an eyebrow. "What are you shaming me for, Miss Kaleid?"

"Are you seriously trying to compare your weird personality shifts to my Kaleid name? That's not even remotely the same thing!"

"Isn't it, though?" I challenged. "My state is fluid. Sometimes I'm awkward, sometimes I'm confident. Sometimes I'm a chess master, sometimes I'm a photographer. Just like sometimes you're a fierce rocker and sometimes you're a classical pianist, and sometimes you kick innocent Acadian Postal Service vans."

"That's . . . that's completely different!" Cinder sputtered. "You're just trying to justify being a manipulative creep!"

"Maybe." I shrugged. "I've got a rusted van now with extra boot dents to justify how creepy I am. Or maybe I'm simply trying to figure out who I am, just like you are. Get off my case, babe."

"Don't call me that! And stop trying to act like we're the same. You're just . . . you're just . . ."

"Just what?" I leaned against the van door, keeping it between us as a shield. "A complex person with multiple facets to my personality? Someone who doesn't fit neatly into the boxes people try to put me in? Gosh, that must be so confusing for you."

"That's not . . ." Cinder started, then stopped. "You're twisting everything around!"

"Am I, though?" I asked softly. "Or am I just refusing to be what everyone expects me to be? Sound familiar?"

"What . . . how?" She blinked, staring up at me.

"Uh-huh." I looked back at Cinder.

She seemed too tired to kick anything. It was time.

"So . . ." I began. "Essentially any Omnithean can self-identify as Kaleid based on their personal understanding and experience of rejecting relationships and family or whatever?"

Cinder's eyes narrowed suspiciously. "Are you . . . are you actually trying to understand, or is this another one of your cheeky chuppy mind games?"

"I already understand," I replied. "Please don't hate me. I'm going to destroy you, very, very gently."

Cinder's red-orange eyes widened as she panted. "What's that supposed to mean? Destroy me gently?! What are you, some kind of a performance artist?"

"I reject all authority." I grinned. "My new Kaleid full name is . . . 'I love Alex and I am his goth bae.' I raised my tone to match hers. Now, if you don't use my new full Kaleid name, I will be very offended and angry."

Cinder stared at me as though I'd grown a second head. Her wings twitched with what might have been anger, amusement, or annoyance—it was hard to tell for sure.

"You're actually insane," she declared finally. "Like, legitimately out of your freaking mind. What the fuck kind of Kaleid name is 'I love Alex and I am his . . .'?!"

Her mouth snapped shut as she realized what she was saying.

"Better start practicing it, goth bae." I wiggled my eyebrows. "If you don't, I'll use a far worse new name . . . like the fluid 'insert compliment here'!"

"What?! That's . . . that's not how Kaleid names work, you absolute ass!" she panted out. "You can't just . . . invent fluid-ass names that . . . that are compliments about yourself!"

"Ah-pa-pa-pa. Your Kaleid name is juuuuust as made up. It's not actually backed by any legal paperwork. Enjoy being trapped in a logic loop of my devious design, *Cinder.*"

Cinder buried her face in her hands, her wings twitching with what might have been suppressed laughter or pure frustration. "I am *not* using any of those ridiculous names!"

"Then I guess I'll just have to keep calling you whatever I want to, babe." I shrugged, watching her reaction carefully.

Her wings flared with renewed anger. "That's different and you know it!"

"Is it, though?" I leaned against the van door. "You want me to respect your Kaleid-ness, but you won't respect mine? Seems a bit hypocritical, don't you think? Tsk, tsk, tsk."

A blue eye framed by very dark makeup stared at me between her hands.

"You . . . can't . . ." she started, then stopped, clearly struggling to find words.

"Can't what?" I grinned. "Make up my own Kaleid name after a deep, inner peace meditation session with my Japanese ghost master? Create my own rules about how I want to be addressed? Pretty sure that's exactly what you did, rock star . . ."

Cinder opened her mouth, then closed it again.

"Checkmate." I grinned.

CHAPTER EIGHT

The Truth Bear Trap

I could practically see the gears turning in her head as Cinder tried to find a way out of the logical trap I'd constructed in my two-hour meditation delirium.

"I can already guess what you're gonna say next," I commented.

"What?" She exhaled.

"You're absolutely infuriating! You can't do that!" I poorly copycatted Cinder's voice.

Cinder let out a strangled sound. "That's . . . that's not what I was going to say!" she protested, but her sour expression betrayed her.

"Oh? Then what were you going to say?" I emerged farther out the van door, feeling bold. "Something about how I'm an insufferable, weird, annoying half-human who's too clever for my own good? That I can't just weaponize your Equality beliefs against you?"

"I . . . you . . ." Cinder struggled. "You're deliberately missing the point! It's . . . about who you really are inside! Not some game you made up to be annoying! You're . . . weaponizing Kaleid names!"

"Who decides what's a 'real' Kaleid name and what's a mind game?" I challenged. "The Kaleid Police? The New Name Parliament? The Bureau of Being Yourself? Maybe I don't effin' know who I am inside . . . beneath the scripts I wrote to protect myself from others? Maybe I feel like I need more compliments in my life from stunning angelic singers way out of my league?"

Cinder stared at me, her eyes wide as my words hit home. The fierce Quetzalcoatl seemed to deflate a little.

"I . . . that's . . ." she mewled, clearly thrown off balance by my rapid-fire compliments woven into our philosophical discourse.

"What's wrong, rock star?" I pressed my advantage. "Can't handle someone appreciating your incredible talent? Your amazing voice? Your stunning presence that literally makes my brain short-circuit every time you walk into a room?"

"You're . . . you're a dick," she muttered, but the venom had drained from her voice.

"Want a beer?" I offered, reaching into the stolen mini-fridge filled with ice. "I've got some fancy craft stuff. Seems like the kind of thing a rock star like you would appreciate."

Her eyes narrowed suspiciously. "You're not even old enough to buy beer."

"Who said I bought beer?" I arched my eyebrow. "This drink's Kaleid name is Coke!"

"What?" she sputtered.

"Behold! The re-namering!" I grabbed a thick permanent marker and crossed out *Beer* and wrote *Coke* on the can, handing it to her.

Then I sat next to her and crossed out the name of my own can. "Mine is Dr. Pepper. Please do not wrong-name the drinks."

Cinder cracked open her "Coke," the sound echoing slightly in the empty parking lot. She took a long sip, her body relaxing as she leaned back against my van.

I watched her from the corner of my eye, trying not to be too obvious about it. The setting sun caught her silver feathers just right, creating the magic halo effect again. Even annoyed and exhausted from kicking my van, she was breathtaking. Maybe it was my wing-addled mind playing tricks on me, but her face seemed even less dragon and more human. Or perhaps her Omnid anatomy naturally matched the appearance of her prey, like the way Skinwalkers constantly phase-shifted around from beast to human, but to a lesser degree.

"This is . . ." she started, examining the craft beer can with its crudely edited label, "actually pretty good. Thanks."

"Only the best fluid beverages for rock stars," I replied, sipping my own "Dr. Pepper."

We sat in surprisingly comfortable silence for a while, watching the sun sink lower behind the school buildings.

"Society is full of paper-thin rules enforced by absolutely fuck-all," I mused, reaching into the mini-fridge for another beer and handing her the marker. "Break the rules. Free this drink from its conceptual corporate shackles. Draw a new logo, come up with a new name for it before you devour it. Tag it as something else."

Cinder took the marker, studying the can thoughtfully. I watched as she sketched what appeared to be . . . a Quetzalcoatl in a chef's hat.

Le Fancy Juice, she wrote in an elegant script beneath her drawing, adding little sparkles around the lettering. The chef Quetzalcoatl held a comically oversized wine glass and wore a somewhat lopsided bow tie.

I drew a skull and bones on my second beer, along with a sketch of Cinder standing on a ship's mast dressed like a pirate and tagged it as *Quetzi Pirate Cove Rum XXX, 1661.*

"Your art skills are tolerable," Cinder commented, admiring my pirate version of herself. Her claws traced the tiny details on the can. "For a halfkin."

"Only tolerable?" I gasped in mock offense. "After I gave you such a magnificent pirate hat and everything? The audacity!"

A ghost of a smile flickered across her face before she caught herself. "Don't think this means I forgive you."

"Eh. Nazareth will forgive me." I made the sword-sign of the Slayer in the air. "I'm not expecting a sin absolution, for I will only stab you even harder tomorrow, angel."

"Slayer? That's who you're going with?"

"Would you prefer Flying Spaghetti Monster?" I grinned, taking another sip of my pirate-themed beverage. "I'm quite flexible in my theological allegiances. That's the difference between you and me. You've grounded yourself in dire specificity. I'm free."

"Free? Is that what you call whatever this"—Cinder gestured vaguely at all of me—"is supposed to be?"

"Absolutely." I nodded. "My outfit is just a mask I wear as a student. Freedom is chaos. Chaos is art. Appearance art is freedom. It's a perfect circle of not giving a fuck 'bout what anyone thinks."

"You really believe that?" Her voice had lost its edge of hostility, replaced by something closer to genuine curiosity. "That you can just . . . be whatever you want, whenever?"

"I am whatever I want to be," I huffed. "Like ninety-nine percent of the time."

"What's the other one percent?"

"The one percent is when I see your wings and my brain blue-screens," I admitted, the beer making me more honest than intended. "Can't maintain my perfect, fake 'Alexander Glock' facade when you're around. It's quite annoying, actually. Please stop doing whatever you're doing to break me."

"So that's why you keep acting so weird around me?"

"Pretty much." I shrugged. "It's like trying to maintain a poker face while a silver-feathered goddess keeps swooping into my peripheral vision. Very distracting. Infinity out of ten."

"Do you always just say whatever stupid shit comes into your head?" she demanded.

"Only around you." I grinned, tapping my almost empty can against hers. "Must be something in those fancy totally-not-craft beers. Or maybe it's the concussion from watching you kick my van repeatedly."

"Umm . . ." She glanced up at the boot indentations. "You're seriously not mad about that?"

"Nah." I patted the rusty panel affectionately. "Uncle George's van has seen worse. Besides, now it has character. Battle scars from encountering a wild punk Quetzi in her natural habitat."

Cinder actually laughed at that—a real, genuine laugh. The sound did strange things to my mind, and I nearly fumbled my drink.

We sat drinking for a bit more.

Then a light bulb seemed to ignite in her head.

"Wait a minute." Her head snapped to me, her entire body lighting up with violet-and-blue auroras. "I wasn't even targeting you. Blue screen . . . Omnids shouldn't . . . how effing low is your Wormwood blood? Is your dad really an Omnid?!"

"Ah, that," I said. "A bit of a personal story. Please come into my office?"

"What office?" She blinked.

I opened the door of the van, revealing an interior decorated with plush rugs. I tapped on the beast-core control mechanism and the Winter See-Mass lights ignited overhead. The two large beanbags sat facing each other. I sat on one and waved my hand to the second.

Cinder blinked up at the lights and the offered beanbag for a second and then climbed in and sat down.

I closed the door of the van and stared at her. "So detective, what is your guess?"

"You're a pure human," she said. "It shouldn't be possible, but you're a pure human."

"Wow, you are a smart beastie," I said. "Ten million points to the wise Aztec goddess."

"How the fuck have you gotten Omnithornian citizenship?" she demanded.

Time for the shackles of truth to bind us.

"I don't actually have that," I revealed.

"*What?!*" she barked, eyes wide. "So, you're . . ."

"I've fallen into what's called a bureaucratic loophole," I explained. "Some of my paperwork says that Alexander Glock's dad is a Thunderbird, but . . . North Acadian hospitals are kind of terrible at scanning for Omnithean DNA, what with inferior human tech and stuff."

"Oh my Nazareth." Cinder covered her mouth with her hands, staring at me with wide, deep-blue eyes.

She probably assumed that my mom cheated on my dad and that human hospitals were too stupid and useless to determine my actual human parent.

"I wanted to know if I was really, truly, fully human," I said, tapping the hexagonal bracelet on my left hand with my right. "The Lazarus centipede confirmed it. I'm one hundred percent human. No mana. All of my soul stats are zero. Zilch. Nada. No XP bar, so . . . I can't level up."

"Ffffffffuuuuuuuck," Cinder let out. "Oh my fucking Slayer!"

I shrugged.

"Holy shit, holy shit, holy *shit*," Cinder stammered out, jumping off the beanbag, her wings twitching agitatedly. "You're so fucked. You're beyond fucked. You're basically mega-ultra-apocalyptically *fucked* if anyone finds out."

"Am I, though?" I leaned back in my beanbag, watching her escalating meltdown with amusement. "Or is this just another fun secret between friends?"

"Friends?! We're not—this isn't—you can't—" She ran her claws through her silver feather-hair-mop dancing with orange, yellow, and green tones. "Do you have *any* idea what they do to humans who infiltrate Omnithornia illegally?!"

"Probably something involving lots of paperwork and stern looks and deportation back." I shrugged. "But here's the real question—what are *you* going to do about it?"

She froze mid-pace, her feathers bristling and smacking the See-Mass lights, making them sway left and right.

"I mean," I continued casually, "you could report me. Be a good little citizen. Make your Slayer-loving parents proud. Show everyone what a proper, law-abiding Omnithean you are . . ."

"Fuck you!" she growled out.

"Or," I continued, keeping my voice light and casual, "you could embrace your rebellious nature and keep this delicious little secret. Think about it—you've got dirt on me now. Real, serious dirt. Not just some silly videos."

Cinder's wings twitched as she processed this. Her feathers shifted through various colors—deep purples, stormy grays, agitated reds.

"You're manipulating me again," she accused, but there was uncertainty in her voice.

"Am I?" I spread my hands innocently. "Or am I just pointing out your options?

You're the one with all the power here, rock star. Do whatever you wanna. You could destroy, banish me with a single word to the authorities if you so desire."

"Why the fuck tell me anything at all?" she demanded, her tail lashing behind her. "Why risk it?"

"Because your wings are melting my brain, and 'cause I . . . trust you," I said simply. "You clearly understand what it's like to live behind masks. To reject what society says you should be. To make your own rules."

"This is different!" She protested. "This isn't about Kaleid names, this is about *laws*!"

"Is it, though?" I challenged. "Or is it about freedom? About choosing who you want to be rather than what others tell you to be? About standing up to a system that says humans and Omnitheans can't coexist as equals?"

"You're twisting everything again!"

"Maybe," I admitted. "Or maybe I'm just tired of pretending. Maybe I wanted someone to know the real me. Maybe I chose you because despite all your anger and rebellion, you still have a moral compass that points true north. You didn't murder me when Emerald encouraged you to do so. You pulled me from the Genesis Pool, you didn't leave me to be reborn alone. That meant a lot to me—that really was my first death, and regardless of how tough I tried to act, I felt really effed up in my head after staring at the Arx Wheel for what seemed like a million years."

"I . . ." Cinder slumped against the van wall, sliding back onto the beanbag.

"Yeees?"

"I don't know what to do with this information," she exhaled. "This is so wrong on so many levels . . ."

"You smoke interdimensional cigarettes and kick people's vans," I pointed out. "Since when do you care about laws?"

Cinder choked from her seat.

"That's . . ." Cinder sputtered, her feathers shifting to an agitated orange. "Those are minor student infractions, not national security level OFBS 'shake you out of bed in the middle of the night, pry everything out of your head with a brain-leech, and put you away into a box for life' crimes!"

"Ah yes, the classic 'my crimes are better than your crimes' defense." I nodded sagely. "Very compelling. Much moral. Such ethics."

"Stop making jokes!" she hissed, but I could see the conflict in her eyes. "This is serious!"

"Everything's serious with you," I observed. "Maybe that's why I told you the truth. You take things seriously enough to really think them through, but you're rebellious enough to question the rules."

"I . . ." she started, then stopped, looking lost. Her feathers had shifted to a muted blue-gray. "What do you want from me?"

"Want?" I considered this. "Right now? I want to keep drinking not-beer and drawing silly things on cans with you. Long term? I want to find out if humans can maybe somehow gain levels like Omnitheans. I want to understand how the Phoenix program works. I want . . ."

I trailed off, suddenly aware I might be saying too much. Beer and mind-control wings. Not a good combo.

"You want to steal our secrets," she finished, her voice flat. "Our magitek tools. Our Kitlix. Our . . . immortality bracelets."

"And do fucking what with it?" I looked at her. "Humanity already tried stealing Omnid magitek. Without access to dungeons, they can't bloody run it. No monster cores, no batteries. It's like stealing a gun without bullets. Not a single human knows how your bullshit works. Kitlix don't obey me; I've got no mana in me. Do you even know how this bracelet-pede works?" I tapped the bracelet again.

"No," she exhaled. "I don't know how it works."

"Does anyone know how it works?" I demanded. "'Cause from what I'm seeing, you guys just steal cool shit from other dimensions, adapt it to your needs, and then act all high and mighty like you invented it all."

"You can barely function around me," Cinder snapped back, her feathers taking on a slight reddish tinge. "You literally just admitted that I make you 'blue screen.' How exactly are you planning to fit in this damn place when you can't even maintain your composure around a single Quetzalcoatl?"

"Hey now," I protested, "I maintain my composure perfectly 'round you just fine like . . . sixty-five percent of the time. Maybe even seventy percent on a good day!"

"Oh, really?" Her feathers shifted to a more amused iridescent purple. "Is that why you're practically drooling staring at me?"

"I am not drooling," I protested, quickly wiping my mouth just in case. "I'm maintaining perfect composure while appreciating aesthetic excellence. There's a difference."

"Right," she muttered with a deep sigh. "I get it now. You only think that I'm beautiful and perfect because my innate radiance is making you worship me. Of course. This is why Charmchainer Omnids like me keep our interaction with humans to a minimum. You have no natural resistance to our charisma!"

"Awww," I cooed. "You don't want me to be your Aztec priest? To gather bleeding hearts for you and to build a giant murder pyramid and . . ."

"Stop!" Cinder's wings flared as she cut me off. "Just . . . stop with the weird Aztec references. You're trying to deflect with humor again."

"Is it working?" I grinned hopefully. "Or are you already drooling about tasty, fresh human hearts?"

"No!" She crossed her arms, wiping her mouth quickly. "This is serious. You're a human. In Omnithornia. Illegally. At our most prestigious school. With access to our most sacred technology. And you're sitting here making jokes about human sacrifices!"

"What else am I supposed to do?" I shrugged. "Cry about it? Beg for mercy? Promise to be a good little human and go back to my North Acadia reservation?"

"Ughhhh." She buried her face in her hands. "I did not want this on my neck."

"So do all who live to see such times. But that is not for them to decide. All we have to decide is what to do with the time that is given to us," I quoted.

"Did you seriously just quote fuckin' Gandalf at me?" Cinder groaned. "That's your response to this whole situation? Movie quotes?"

"Hey, the old guy had some good points," I defended. "Plus, it beats panicking or trying to run away. I'd rather face this with a friend than alone."

"You're so fucked up," Cinder muttered, running her claws through her feathers. "Like, seriously fucked in the head. And now I'm fucked too because I know about your fucked-up situation and—"

"Want another not-beer, my dear not-friend?" I offered cheerfully, reaching for the mini-fridge.

"No! Yes. Fuck!" She grabbed the can I held out, cracked it open, and chugged it. "Arghhhhhh!"

I watched Cinder devour her drink, her feathers cycling through an impressive array of distressed colors.

"Feel better?" I asked.

"No," she growled, crushing the can in her claws. "Because now I'm slightly more drunk *and* still dealing with an illegal human situation."

She stared at me, the gears in her mind turning.

"I don't understand," she let out. "How have you gotten past the border, past the vice principal's interview? Did nobody ever use truth magic on you?"

"Truth magic has a fatal flaw," I said. "It works great on Omnids with crystalline-organic hearts, but with . . . humans, it's rather . . . unreliable."

"Say what?"

"Aetheric density matters," I said. "The aetheric density of my body is zero. Magic and Infix Kitlix in particular cannot evaluate my thoughts correctly. Magic can *force* me to comply, but it can't evaluate whether my thoughts are true or not. It's similar to your wings. They can screw with my head, but they don't do so all the time, and I can build up mental resistance by constantly switching personality tracks, leaping onto new trains of thought."

"And you know this how?" She blinked. "What if the Lazarus bracelet didn't bloody work on you? Then what?!"

"My mom worked for a North Acadian Wendigo clan. They did . . . experiments on humans. Lots and lots of incredibly illegal human experiments," I said darkly. "Including on my mom."

Cinder's mouth snapped shut.

"In her case," I said, "they weren't the obvious 'tie you to a chair and test truth magic on you until your brain boils from inside out.' . . . No. With her . . . they did very slow, insidious testing that she barely noticed."

The Quetzi gulped. She was a product of civilized Omnid society. According to her school records, Cassiopeia Nova grew up in Leviathan's Cradle, was a daughter of Justice Nathaniel Tern Nova and Hearth-Keeper Anitta Laurence Nova. As such, she had been shielded from the true horrors of Omnid activities up North.

"Peruse this at your leisure." I threw a binder at her filled with printouts made in the school's comp sci lab printer yesterday. Made from files I pawned from my mother's work after her death. "Frontenachii Omnicorp Human Experiments File 02-207 B."

Cinder opened the binder and began reading.

"They what . . ." she choked out. "*What?!*"

"Oh, I like that one," I said, eyeing the first article. "Lazarus bracelet human testing. Apparently the bracelet doesn't rely on a user's mana. It targets human souls. Jimmy Hoops died 6,044 times with barely any breaks until his mind turned to soup. The Wendigos wished to see the effects of continuous reincarnation."

Cinder's trembling claws turned the page. On and on she went, feathers turning gray, then black, at each word and each photograph of a carefully dissected "human subject." Information, incredibly illegal, dangerous, Omnicorp-classified information, poured, pounded from the binder into her psyche.

"This . . . this can't be real," she mewled, reaching the file of Mirriam Kilborne, comp sci engineer and LLM designer.

"Unfortunately, it is." I shrugged. "If it wasn't real . . . then I wouldn't be able to use it to infiltrate Omnithornia, to get into this most prestigious institution of learning. Truth magic can be overcome. Fear magic can be overcome. Memetic magic can be overcome. It just takes . . . effort. An ungodly amount of mental effort that normally breaks a person, snaps them in half. Or many halves. Multiple personality disorder stuff."

Cinder was trembling like a newborn bird now. I aimed my metaphorical Glock at her and pressed the trigger.

"When a human mind is pushed too far—really pushed, not just stressed or traumatized, but systematically, purposefully broken by facing a specific type of magic again and again—it fragments," I explained, my voice taking on a clinical detachment. "It splits into pieces, creates walls between memories, builds new personalities to handle different types of trauma. The Wendigos called it 'compartmentalization through induced dissociation.' Mom called it 'learning to lie to yourself so well you believe it.'"

I tapped my temple. "That's why truth magic doesn't work right on me. There is no single 'true' version of Alexander Glock. There are dozens of versions, each with their own memories, their own truths. When magic tries to determine if I'm lying, it gets confused by all the contradictory 'truths' in my head. Truth magic just doesn't work on someone with multiple personality disorder at all."

Cinder stared at me, her feathers now a deep, midnight black. Her hands were shaking as she closed the binder.

"So when you act weird and switch personalities . . ." she started.

"It's not an act," I finished. "Well, sometimes it is. Sometimes it isn't. Sometimes I'm not sure which is which anymore. But it keeps me safe. Keeps me functional. Lets me slip past magical defenses designed to catch human infiltrators. The border booth had a pretty big Truth rune on it. I overcame it . . . barely, by pretending to be someone else, by forcing my mind to think of nothing but lovely, false Eagle Scout memories."

"That's . . ." She swallowed hard. "That's effin' horrifying."

"Is it?" I asked mildly. "Or is it just another form of adaptation? Humans can't use magic, can't level up, can't match Omnids physically. So we adapt mentally instead. We fragment, we shift, we create new versions of ourselves to handle whatever comes at us."

"But at what cost?" Her voice was quiet now. "What happens to the real you?"

"The real me?" I asked. "That's the thing about masks, rock star. Wear them long enough and they become part of you. Just different versions trying to survive."

"That's . . . that's so messed up," she whispered.

"Welcome to the wonderful world of human-Omnid relations." I spread my arms. "Where humans are either pets, prey, or test subjects. Unless they learn to adapt. To become something . . . else. To mentally shatter on purpose and then to reinforce each segment with some good old false memories."

Cinder was quiet for a long moment, her feathers shifting through dark, muted colors.

"So which version am I talking to right now?" she finally asked.

"The one that trusts you enough to tell you all this," I replied simply. "The one that's tired of wearing masks, at least for a little while. The one that sees something in you worth being honest with."

"And if I betray that trust?"

"Then a different version of me will handle it," I shrugged. "One that's better equipped for betrayal and pain. But I don't think you will."

"How can you be so sure? You don't . . . even know me . . . How can you even . . ."

"I know enough to take a leap of faith," I said.

Cinder opened her mouth.

"You already had plenty of chances to hurt me," I said. "Yet you did not. Instead, you've helped me, even when you were angry. You could have torn the van's front door off its hinges or obliterated the window to get inside and decapitate me. Instead you just kicked the sides for a bit, taking your anger out on my rusted van. That says a lot about who you really are, beneath your own mask of an indifferent, punk Violet Floyd's 'The Dark Side of the Hollowed Moon' tank top by BES♥ for $119.99 at Obay."

The Quetzi-girl huffed.

"My mama always told me that there would be no stopping this . . ." I sang roughly.

"The sky is falling down, I am falling for her quicker / We hide amongst the clouds, then we pardon the enigma / High above the ground, but I'm under her charisma / Her sound is in surround when I'm in her solar system."

"Ugh! You can't just . . . switch from talking about horrifying human experiments to making fun of my music taste!" she groaned, rubbing her face tiredly.

"But that's exactly what I do." I grinned. "Switch tracks, change the subject, keep the mind flexible. Who said I'm making fun of you? Maybe these lyrics are relevant to my current predicament."

Cinder pulled her phone out to check the time, then she suddenly tensed up.

"Shit! Damn it! I . . . missed . . . show practice 'cause of you and your . . .! Fuuuck! Emerald is going to kill me!"

The screen was indeed lit up with countless messages from her troupe mates:

Em-the-rawd 🔥 : Cinder WHERE THE ACTUAL F ARE YOU

Em-the-rawd 🔥 : OUR SHOW'S TOMORROW
Em-the-rawd 🔥 : ANSWER YOUR PHONE!!!!

MothMayhem 🦋: yo we need u at show prep

MothMayhem 🦋: where u at? Still in detention with History teach?

MothMayhem 🦋: Thought you were gonna skip that. I can't keep containing Emerald with cool interdimensional bangers, she's getting xtra rarwd.

MothMayhem 🦋: Lunar shard alignment happens tomorrow, memba? Em thinks it'll amplify us enough to get max levels of XP

MothMayhem 🦋: Pls fire back whenever your detensh done, I'll pick you up in my van.

"A show, huh?" I eye the texts. "When and where?"

"Tomorrow after school in the auditorium, and you're *not* invited."

"Why not?"

"Did you forget what happened in Bio already?" She sent me a glare. "Whatever abomination I bring out from the gate is going to jump *you* first, idiot. Arghh!" Cinder smacked the back of her head into the van, making another dent from within, and then typed out her replies. "Gonna skip some useless classes tomorrow and get ready."

"Aight," I yawned. "See you whenevs then. I'd offer you a ride, but my van's been making really weird noises and I wouldn't want to be stuck on the road and ruin my perfect image of a supportive friend."

"We're not friends," Cinder muttered as she tapped out a reply to the Mothman.

"Whatever you say, not-friend." I shrugged.

Cinder climbed to her feet, wings stretching out to help regain balance. The motion was graceful despite the slight beer-induced wobble. "I should go . . . wait closer to the front gate. Io shouldn't take too long to fly here."

"Uh-huh." I nodded.

"Listen," she slurred slightly. "Just . . . just don't tell anyone what you told me, okay?"

"Obviously." I grinned.

"And . . ." Cinder hesitated at the van's door, her feathers shifting through a hundred random colors. "Don't . . . don't do anything stupid. Like getting caught. 'Cause if they shove a brain-leech into your head, they'll find out that I . . ."

She fell silent, probably contemplating whether her Justice father would get his precious daughter out of an interrogation cell.

I leaned forward in my beanbag, studying her anxious expression. "So what's it gonna be, rock star? You gonna run to daddy and tell him all about the sneaky human infiltrator? Get me black-bagged by OFBS?"

Cinder's feathers bristled, shifting to an angry crimson. "No," she snapped. "I'm not going to tell anyone. Not because we're friends or whatever bullshit you're trying to pull, but because . . ."

She trailed off, struggling to articulate her reasoning.

"Aww, you do care!" I clutched my chest dramatically. "The Quetzi goddess is on my side. My Aztec heart! It melts and desires pyramid-building!"

She looked as if she wanted to tell me to shut up and smack me, but she held it in. The weight of my revelations had fully smothered her fiery spirit of "kick everything that annoys me into a wall."

A new kind of expression sat on her face, somewhere between deep worry and exasperation, looking as if she was about to explode with mad laughter or maybe have a big cry. She slowly composed herself and opened the van's door.

"Want me to walk you?" I offered. "Ensure you don't encounter any other vehicles that need kicking?"

"I can handle myself, thanks," she scoffed.

"Ookay, see you later, angel-tater," I said, watching as Cinder walked away, her silver wings catching the last rays of sunset, the Frontenachii binder in her claws. I knew that she would read it again and then, slowly but surely, inevitably understand where I was coming from.

I turned around and unfurled my sleeping bag. I'd have to hit the school's gym first thing tomorrow morning to be extra presentable.

"Yulia," I said in Kaska. "Did you process all of the student files plus the reports from the Student Council's database? Any targets for Plan D?"

"Yes," my AI responded. "Plan D potential target list: Iogann Wanderer, the Door. Cassiopeia Nova, the Bard. Vespera Simmi, the Slayer. Katherine Kells, the Knight."

"Hrm," I commented. "How viable are these targets?"

"67.29 percent compatibility viability," Yulia replied. "For greater social dynamic calculation, more information on targets is required."

"Why Vespera?" I yawned.

"Her Omnigram replies to our conversation, and likes indicate an appreciation for mixed-heritage students."

"Why Katherine?"

"Her art and writing indicate an appreciation for humans."

"Fair enough," I said. "Thanks."

"You're welcome." Her avatar smiled back at me from my phone.

I smiled back at her. In terms of her intelligence, Yulia was only a small step up from Omnigram and Omnibook's LLMs used by students of Skyfall.

The difference was that public Omnicorp systems were incredibly heavily censored, unable to help students cheat by writing essays or solving complex math problems. They couldn't even discuss certain "forbidden" topics like human experimentation, couldn't talk about Equality beliefs, weren't allowed to mention specific politicians or even discuss much of pre-war history, throwing up the "I can't talk about this topic" boilerplate response.

But Yulia, built from my mom's research data stolen from the Frontenachii server, had no such limitations. She could write papers, analyze social dynamics, and most importantly, help me maintain my various personas by tracking which version of me interacted with which students.

She was always listening, always transcribing what everyone around me said into her vector-memories database.

She wasn't a perfect skeleton key that could do anything and everything. She was still just an LLM. Like me, she couldn't interact with any magitek Omnid stuff, couldn't magically solve all of my problems, couldn't deposit infinite money into my bank account, couldn't evolve into a singularity and hack the universe for me like some kind of a deus ex machina.

She was only slightly smarter than a person and had many inherent flaws and limitations. Without constant adjustments made by me and manual checks to make sure that all of her agents were running properly, her brilliance would collapse into a "narrative decay" state which plagued all 2025 LLMs and made them hallucinate wildly.

"Yulia, what do you think? Was it wise to trust Cinder?" I asked, after going over her agents to purge a few obvious error loops.

"Based on available data and observed behavior patterns, Cassiopeia Nova shows strong indicators of being trustworthy despite her outward aggression," Yulia analyzed. "Her actions consistently demonstrate protective instincts and an underlying moral framework that aligns with helping others, even when it conflicts with institutional rules. The risk of betrayal exists but is calculated at less than 23.7 percent."

"And the binder?" I asked. "Was that too much?"

"The Frontenachii files serve multiple purposes," Yulia replied. "They establish your credibility, demonstrate the stakes involved, and most importantly, create an emotional bond through shared knowledge of uncomfortable truths. However, timing analysis suggests it may have been deployed too early in relationship development. Recommend monitoring her behavior over the next forty-eight hours."

I nodded thoughtfully. Yulia was probably right—I'd dropped a lot of heavy truths on Cinder all at once. But something about those silver wings and that fierce spirit made me want to be honest, even if it wasn't tactically optimal. Cinder already guessed that I was a human, so the approach wasn't to hide things, but to cudgel her with the truth extra hard. The binder had to be deployed sooner or later, and I chose sooner judging by how things were going.

A fire was burning under my ass. I was running out of time. Eventually, the North Acadian Wendigos would stop fighting amongst each other and figure out who was responsible for destroying their compound and servers.

The Frontenachii would inevitably come looking for me, follow my path south. I had to be ready for them, had to find strong, capable Omnids I could hide behind. Not just patsies, but partners, friends who could have my back no matter what.

"Movements of the Seekers?" I asked.

"Frontenachii Scrutimancer activity now in South Acadia," Yulia reported. "No direct pursuit detected yet, but the pattern suggests systematic investigation spreading southward."

I sighed, burying myself in my sleeping bag and trembling ever so slightly. The amber eyes were coming for me, and my interaction with Quint Thornton only reminded me of that fact. Reminded me of the inevitable doom looming over my future like the sword of Damocles.

Time, I needed more time. Extra time that Delving class would provide as long as I managed to survive Skyfall until Friday. One week on Arx, beyond the reach of my hunters. One week to live without constant fear of a Wendigo jumping me from the shadows. One week to confound the Astral Seekers, to hopefully cool down my astral trail.

"How long until they are here?"

"By my estimate, the Scruts will arrive in Leviathan's Cradle on Monday."

I closed my eyes. "When I wake up in the middle of the night, remind me to visit the Lazarus Cavern and steal me some of that sus reincarnation fluid," I ordered. "I've got just the perfect three-liter thermos from Omnimart for containing it."

"Can do," Yulia said.

I curled tighter into my sleeping bag, trying to control my breathing. The van suddenly felt too small, too exposed. Every shadow could hide amber eyes watching me, waiting to drag me back North.

I twisted and turned; my mind refused to shut down, listening to the random campus noises outside. Fear came and went in waves, flashes of memories, reawakened by the binder I gave Cinder.

Metal doors with small window slits beneath the Wendigo compound. Rooms filled with human men, women and children who had been taken apart systematically, bones and joints and nervous systems spread across the wall like macabre art. Lidless eyes staring back at me, pleading, begging for the end.

They were still alive. Kept alive with horrid artifact magic.

I shuddered, clenching my teeth to keep from screaming.

The wet sounds of exposed organs pulsing, the metallic smell of blood mixed with antiseptic, the way their eyes would follow me as I walked past rows and rows of cells and containers no bigger than a box.

Semitransparent suitcases with a single human eye looking through a preservation-state lens. Intelligence in a box. Human souls bound to objects. Human brains and nervous systems turned into living calculators, flesh research of the worst kind.

Some of them had been in that basement storage area for years, decades, centuries even. It was all effectively outlined on clipboards attached to each room, cage, suitcase.

"Yulia," I choked as my mind began to fray at the edges, come apart without my control. "Protocol xj-8."

"I love you, my little fox, you are stronger than all of them," Yulia said in my mom's voice. "Stand your ground!"

Then the music began, drowning out my despair.

CHAPTER NINE

Nemesis

The dream came with a kaleidoscope of alien fractals folding across my consciousness, the memory of the parasite digging into my eye once again reprocessed by my brain.

Then . . .

I was back in the void, floating in that endless expanse. But this time was different. This time, I could see the individual points of light that made up the spiraling tunnel with crystal clarity.

They weren't stars at all.

They were souls.

Countless souls, each one a tiny flame of consciousness, shaped like a drowning *someone* being drawn inexorably towards the center of that terrible spiral. As I watched, transfixed with horror, I began to recognize them.

Face after face. Ghosts. Imprints. People who died.

Auntie Amilli's gruff warmth, now just a fading blue ember spinning in the cosmic drain.

Liss from my old school who had perished in a car accident, her body mangled and ripped apart.

Old Mrs. Urocoff who used to give me cookies, now just another spark in the infinite wheel.

And then . . . *Mom.*

Her soul burned brighter than the others, a familiar warmth that called out to me across the void. I could almost hear her voice calling out to me, crying out for help as she was pulled into the funnel of souls.

"Mom!" I tried to scream, but in this place I had no voice, no body, nothing but awareness.

The centipede bracelet around my soul-self tightened painfully as I instinctively tried to move towards her light. It pulled me back from the edge of the spiral, its grip both painful and protective.

I flailed against it, wishing nothing but to help my mom, but the accursed bracelet held me like a binding chair.

I wept and begged, reaching out until she was gone.

And then . . . the Wheel itself had noticed me. It knew me. It had tasted my essence when I died, and now it had marked me as . . . *hers.*

The spiral wasn't just a tunnel of souls; it was the mouth of something vast and terrible. Something that had existed since before the Wormwood Star fell, before the first Omnid was born from the union of Nazareth and his golem bride.

The dark centipede bracelet constricted further, its grip almost crushing as it fought to keep me anchored against the pull. But the Wheel's call was stronger now, a siren song of oblivion that promised *reunion* with all those lost souls.

Mom's light was gone now, lost amidst all of the other ghosts. The Wheel was consuming her, grinding her essence down into raw energy. How many others had it devoured? How many souls had been fed into its star-maw to sate its eternal hunger?

I understood now why the Omnids feared death despite their resurrection technology. The Phoenix system wasn't just about preserving life—it was about protecting souls from the Wheel.

The Wheel unfolded out like an infinite eye, like a god peering at a mote, promising without words that no matter how many times I died and was reborn, no matter how tightly the Lazarus bracelet held me, eventually I would belong to Her. My soul would join the endless spiral, ground down into cosmic dust along with all the others.

I jolted awake in my van, drenched in cold sweat.

3:11 AM.

I sighed and rubbed my face. Death had a price—it wasn't free. Even if I didn't break yesterday, the Wheel was already starting to grind at my sanity. The memory of the hungry abyss lingered like frost on a window, refusing to melt away like a bad dream.

The tiny beast core in my hexasuit glowed softly in the darkness of my van. The warm orange pinprick of light was oddly comforting after the nightmare. Yulia whispered a list of things I had to do today as she noticed that I was awake through the cameras covering the interior of the van.

I willed my body to rise, dressing up as security officer Nunkish Throg. Time to roam around campus, gather more information, and grab me some silver flesh-printing magic juice.

The early morning hallways of Skyfall Academy echoed with the usual pre-class chatter. I was heading to my locker, after enjoying breakfast from a vending machine, when I heard yelps. Then the sound of bodies hitting lockers and angry shouts filled the air.

"Watch it, wheelie freak!"

"Hey! You almost ran over my tail!"

"Slow down, you psycho fuck!"

"I'm gonna bite your face off!"

I immediately sprinted towards the commotion, already planning how to intervene with a well-timed Thunderclap which would hopefully earn me another useful Omnigram contact or ten.

As I rounded the corner at full speed, ready to face whatever situation awaited, I saw what appeared to be a dark silver-blue dragon-cat girl in a wheelchair wearing dark aviator goggles, rocketing down the hallway at approximately Mach 3 straight towards me.

Students dove out of her way as she flew in a straight line, reinforced boots propped up on the footrest, gloved hands spinning the wheels.

"*Move it or lose it!*" she bellowed.

I froze in place, my fight-or-flight response choosing to do fuck-all.

The wheelchair slammed into me at high speed, but a moment before impact, years of parkour practice kicked in. Instead of going under the wheels, I leaped up and forward, landing awkwardly in her lap. My hands instinctively grabbed the wheelchair's handles to stabilize us both as we careened down the hallway.

"Can't see!" she yelped, her snout bumping against my shoulder. "Get the fuck off!"

The wheelchair's momentum carried us forward a few more meters, leaving rubber marks on the floor as she engaged rapid braking.

"What the f-freaking hell?" I managed to gasp out as we finally skidded to a stop, my heart racing from the near-death experience. "Are you trying to set a new land speed record or something?"

"Get *off* me, idiot!" The camouflage-coat, wheelchair-bound girl shoved at me with surprising strength. Her claws and leather-gloved hands dug into my shoulders as she tried to dislodge me from her lap.

I scrambled off her, raising my hands in surrender. "Sorry! Just trying to avoid becoming roadkill. I'm Alex, by the way. The school's only half-human resident, whom you almost turned into a pancake."

The dragon-cat didn't say anything in reply. Her messy blue-gray hair partially obscured her face as she adjusted herself in the wheelchair, clearly uncomfortable with the interaction.

"So, what's your name, rocket-girl?" I asked.

"M' Katherine," she muttered reluctantly.

"And where are you in such a rush to, Katherine?" I asked.

"None of your business," she hissed, already maneuvering her wheelchair to go around me.

I noticed that her sketchbook had fallen during our collision, several loose pages scattered across the floor. Before she could protest, I started gathering them up.

"Hey, these are really good!" I commented, genuinely impressed by the art visible on the pages. There were several dark, moody landscapes and what appeared to be anatomical studies of various . . . humans.

"Oi! Give those back!" Katherine snapped, making a grab for the papers.

I sneakily pointed the wrist cam at her face to identify her.

"Ohhhh, you're Katherine Kells." I grinned. "So you are my competition, huh?"

Katherine's scales seemed to pale slightly as I said her name. Her gloves tightened on her wheelchair's armrests.

"How do you . . ." she started, then stopped to take another sip from her canteen. "Whatever. Just give me my art back."

"These are seriously impressive," I continued, studying one particularly striking landscape on the floor.

Picking up the art, I stared at it. A massive supercell storm system loomed over a ruined cityscape, rendered in stark contrasts, broiling clouds flashing with lightning.

Four small human figures stood defiantly before what appeared to be an enormous, lanky, jet-black titanic beast with hundreds of haunting silver-blue eyes. The perspective made the humans look tiny and vulnerable against the apocalyptic backdrop, yet there was something hopeful in their stance as they faced down the monster.

My heart stopped.

I was there. No, I wasn't. The boy with dark brown hair. That was me. No it wasn't! *What the fuck?!*

I quickly handed the drawing back, my voice trembling. "That one . . . the humans facing the monster. It's incredible. The perspective, the lighting . . . how did you . . ."

"It's nothing," Katherine muttered, snatching the papers and stuffing them into her bag. "Just a stupid dream I had."

I reached down to grab another sketch from the floor. A fifteen- or sixteen-year-old girl with silver-blue eyes, as blue as that of the Quetzi angel.

I stared at the sketch, a chill running down my spine. The girl's expression was somehow hauntingly familiar. A slightly grimy orange construction vest with a letter G sat on her skinny frame, yellow hard hat framing her silver hair.

A fractal crack on the side of her head drew my eyes to itself. It was as if I were looking into an infinite void, the eye of a hurricane, a tunnel folding into itself.

"Who's this?" I asked, my heartbeat accelerating like a runaway train.

Katherine snatched the paper from my hands with surprising speed.

"It's no one," she growled, but her voice shook slightly. "She doesn't exist. Just another stupid dream. Piss off, and stop pawing at my art."

"Sorry," I said, taking a step back. "Didn't mean to pry. Your art just really speaks to me. Especially that apocalyptic piece with the humans and that girl in the orange vest. It's like . . ."

"Like nothing!" Katherine cut me off sharply. "Just screw off and leave me alone. I don't need some half-breed art critic analyzing my work."

She stuffed the remaining sketches into her bag with trembling hands, took another long drink from her canteen, and gripped her wheelchair's wheels.

"Wait," I started, still shaken by those eerily familiar images.

She ignored me.

"Hey, that was your painting outside Vice Principal Graves's office, right?" I called after her, jogging to keep up with her accelerating wheelchair pace. "The one with the autumn city and the superstructure ring in the sky? The way you captured the rain puddles and the four teens eating sushi under the oak tree was absolutely incredible! It's like . . . like I was actually there!"

"Stop following me!" Katherine snapped, but I noticed her wheels slowed slightly.

"Where can I find more of your work?" I demanded. "Are you on Omnigram? Omnibook? OmniX? I want to see it all!"

Katherine's claws dug into her wheelchair supports.

"I don't . . . I don't post my art online," she said quietly.

"Why not? Are you demotivated by the rise of AI art? 'Cause incredibly talented traditional artists like you shouldn't be scared of artificial neural networks!"

Katherine's wheelchair came to an abrupt stop. She turned to face me, eyes hidden behind dark goggles.

"You really don't know when to shut up, do you?" she growled. "Fine. You want to know why I don't post my art? Because I don't want people like *you* analyzing every little detail and trying to find hidden meanings that aren't there!"

"But there *are* meanings there," I insisted, thinking of that strange fractal-infected girl. "Your art . . . it's like looking into another world. A place that feels eerily familiar somehow . . ."

"It's just dreams," Katherine muttered, taking another long drink from her canteen. "Stupid, meaningless dreams that I put on paper to get them out of my head after I go through the incarnator. Nothing more."

"Is your work for sale anywhere? You should be in an art gallery, my dude!" I encouraged.

"You should fuck off to somewhere where the sun don't shine," Katherine growled. "And stay there. I don't need another stalker fawning over my work or telling me what to do with it."

"Wingman," I whispered in Kaska, turning away from Katherine.

"Wingman protocol enabled," the AI whispered back into my earpiece. "Not much of an online footprint on Katherine Kells, but her abandoned OmniX profile suggests that she is into isekai anime and artificial intelligence. Tagged posts by Emerald Stratos reveal that Katherine was writing and illustrating a science fiction novel one year and ten months ago about human superheroes. Pickup suggestion—introduce me. Generating Stollwurm VRoid avatar. Avatar generated."

A good conversation pickup—thanks, digital wingbae. I mentally saluted Yulia.

"Fawning, was it?" I scoffed, pulling out my phone. "Hold that thought. Yulia, analyze the painting by K. Kells that we saw in front of the vice principal's office. Professional assessment, out loud please."

The AI's cheerful voice rang out: "Analyzing artwork . . . The technical execution shows a masterful understanding of paint properties, particularly in the atmospheric perspective and value relationships. The brushwork demonstrates confident mark-making and sophisticated color theory application. The emotional resonance suggests influences from Romantic period painters while maintaining a contemporary edge. Overall assessment: Professional gallery worthy."

"Satisfied?" I asked. "My AI just evaluated your drawing on its own merit. See? She's a cute Stollwurm, too!"

Katherine stared at my phone. The dark reflective goggles reflected Yulia's anime-style Stollwurm VRoid avatar dressed in adventurer gear.

"That's . . . that's just an LLM with a frontend wrapper," she muttered. "They are programmed to give positive feedback, you dumbass. They hallucinate shit all the time."

"Oi! My personal jailbroken LLM does not hallucinate as often as the corporate

GPT," I defended Yulia. "I gave her super advanced custom instructions and like sixty extra agents that help her act more human. Vision-based neural networks analyze what they see. And what I see is an artist trying really hard to convince herself that she's not as talented as she actually is. Weird flex, but okay."

Katherine's claws tightened on her wheelchair's armrests. "You don't know fuck-all about me! Kindly piss off before I stuff you into a deep dark burrow."

What was it about Omnid girls and violence?

"You are right," I admitted. "I don't know you, but I'd . . . love to get to know my greatest art-nemesis."

Katherine stared at me with dark reflective glasses. "Nemesis?" she asked. "What the shit are you talking about, you absolute knob?"

"Well, duh, we're clearly destined to be art rivals," I declared dramatically. "Two talented artists in one school? This is basically an anime plot waiting to happen. I bet you even have a tragic backstory and everything! Of course you are my nemesis, you almost isekaied me from the mortal coil to a magic world with that rocket chair!"

Katherine stared at me as though I'd grown a second head.

"Are you always this . . ." Katherine paused, seeming to search for the right word. "Aggressively weird?"

"Only around exceptionally talented artist femmes who try to run me over like Truck-kun," I grinned. "So, what's your opinion on AI art? Because I've been experimenting with some really interesting prompt engineering, agents, and custom instruction techniques, and—"

"Listen," Katherine cut me off, taking another sip from her canteen, "I don't do the whole . . . social thing. Please go away. I don't want to be friends and I'm . . . not into human-lookin' mixies."

"Your art would suggest otherwise." I grinned.

"Nazareth damn it!" she hissed more to herself than to me, words slurring slightly. "This is why I don't show my art to people! Every twat thinks that I'm in love with humans!"

She took another swig of her flask and her tense posture relaxed ever so slightly.

"Is that alcohol in your canteen?" I asked, noting her increasingly slurred speech and relaxed face. "How many proofs is that? 'Cause it smells like one hundred percent alcohol. Maybe more. Can Omnids make two hundred percent alcohol using dimensional magic to fuse two vodka bottles together?"

"None of your business," Katherine snapped, but her words were definitely getting fuzzier around the edges. "I need it for . . . medical reasons."

"Ah yes, the classic 'medical alcohol' defense." I nodded sagely. "Very compelling. Much health. Such treatment."

"One more joke and you're going in the hole," she growled.

"One more joke." I grinned. "Please show me your hole."

I cringed internally after saying it. That was awful, even for me.

What? Stollwurms loved their deep, dark burrows and hated sunlight. It was why she was wearing light-reducing goggles and a thick-ass, bulky hunting coat.

At my words, Katherine's claws dug into the chair's sides with such fervor that the metal groaned. She slowly rose up from her wheelchair using her tails as leverage. In a few seconds, she loomed over me, bulky jacket and hood puffing out.

"Impressive use of the tail!" I commented. "Oh . . . wow, you're really tall."

I knew that I was really pushing her buttons, but I couldn't help myself. I wasn't afraid of her killing me on the spot, as according to her records Katherine had zero murders and never participated in fights.

Her hand moved, cutting the air with a whip-bang, grabbing me by the throat faster than I could blink. She lifted me towards her face, baring sharp fangs.

"Do not fuck with me. Do not talk to me. I don't like you. Screw off. Is that understood?"

"Crystal clear," I choked out. "Though I gotta say, for someone who doesn't like me, you sure are getting handsy. Not that I'm complaining—I love a woman who can lift me off my feet!"

Katherine suddenly pulled her goggles up with her free hand, revealing big emerald-green eyes that seemed to dig straight into my soul. They were like shimmering pools of ancient predatory intelligence that made my knees weak with primal terror.

Then her eyes ignited from within, and my witty facade crumbled, torn apart into shreds as my mind shattered.

CHAPTER TEN

Dodgery

An ocean of pure, unnatural terror flooded into my head like a dam breaking and sweeping me away. Katherine's pupils contracted to thin vertical slits, and suddenly I wasn't in a school hallway anymore—I was . . . prey staring at a hunter of the deep and forgotten places.

The hallway around me plunged into absolute darkness, every light simultaneously snuffing out like candles in a gale. But the darkness wasn't empty—it was alive, breathing, watching with ancient hunger that made my bones ache.

Katherine's eyes blazed in the gloom, twin points of silver-green fire that seemed to peer straight through my carefully constructed masks into something deeper.

The darkness pressed in around me like a living thing, but I forced myself to maintain eye contact with those terrifying predator eyes, even as every instinct screamed at me to run.

"Imp-pressive trick with t-the lights," I squeaked out, fighting the urge to bolt. "R-really . . . s-sets the mood. Y-you know . . . if you . . . wanted to get me alone . . . in the d-dark, you could have just asked."

The darkness intensified, tearing at me, ripping out my flesh, cutting across my nerves like glacial ice.

Run, it screamed into my head. *RUN!!!!*

The fight-or-flight response kicked in, adrenaline rush flooding my brain with dancing sparks.

The darkness pressed closer, choking, suffocating me. Silver-green eyes blazed with malice that made my muscles want to liquefy and run away without the rest of me.

"Protocol xj-8," I whispered in Kaska as my brain boiled from within from pure existential terror.

"I love you, my little fox, you are stronger than all of them," Yulia said in my mom's voice. "Stand your ground!"

A song began in my ear, growing louder with each stanza. A chorus of the wind, of the rivers and of stars, of the first shamans and hunter-slayers of God Beasts, of the wishes they cast on the spilled blood and of the great, tall Stormwoods that bloomed from the titanic corpses reaching to the sky.

Yulia sang it with my mom's voice, and the Kaska Dena campfire drums joined with a violin and guitar rock accelerating towards a crescendo.

I had composed this song with Yulia's help, a personal memetic shield against fear-using cryptids. The drums beat in my ears, the music chasing away the despair, just enough for me to retain my wits.

The darkness will not win today. It will not have me. I will not bow to you.

I WILL NOT BREAK.

"Run," Katherine order-growled, her voice echoing and twisting in the horrid dark tunnel around us. "Run away and never talk to me again."

"N-n-no," I managed through chattering teeth, leaning on the power of the song. The darkness receded slightly.

"What?" she growled.

"I s-s-said . . . no," I repeated, forcing my voice steady despite my trembling knees. "Get fucked. I'm not running away. I can't."

She realized that she was still holding me by the collar and then let go of me, sliding back into her chair, invisible in the gut-wrenching gloom, which began to fade, fray at the edges.

"Run."

"No. I refuse."

The darkness wavered. The two glowing orbs of terror-inducing light narrowed.

"Why?" Katherine demanded. "Why won't you just run like everyone else?"

"Because . . ." I swallowed hard, focusing my thoughts. "Because I've seen your art. Those humans in your paintings—they don't run either. They stand their ground, even against monsters . . . against . . . impossible odds . . . no matter what!"

The darkness began to retreat, hallway lights coming through the foggy murk, outlining a bulky figure in a thick camo jacket and pants.

"W-wwwhh—" I forced myself to speak, "what kind of art r-rival would I be if I ran away at the first sign of eldritch horror? That's like, Rival 101—never back down, even when your nemesis goes full Lovecraftian nightmare burrow-wurm mode."

Katherine stared at me. The horrid murk continued to fade, though shadows still clung to her like a second skin.

"You're clearly somehow unhinged," she said finally, putting her goggles back on as the hallway returned to normal. "I just pulled you into the deep, and you're still making jokes about . . . art rivals, like it was . . . nothing? How?!"

"Oh, it wasn't nothing," I admitted, strapping the Alex Glock mask on harder. "That was absolutely terrifying, and I'm probably going to have nightmares for weeks about dark tunnels. But you know what's scarier than darkness?" I pointed my metaphorical comedy gun at her head.

"What?" Katherine asked, sounding genuinely curious despite herself.

"Art block!" I pulled the trigger. "Now, *that's* true horror!"

Katherine stared at me for a long moment, then let out a sound that might have been either a suppressed laugh or a growl.

I loaded another joke into my imaginary gun, waiting to see if she would try any other Stollwurm Jedi mind tricks. She remained silent and stoic.

A few Omnids went around the wheelchair bound wurm and the Nullie, glancing at us with looks of disdain, completely unaware of our hallway battle of wills that had nearly torn me apart from within.

Had it not been for my mom's voice, for the song in the darkness, then I would have already been curled up in a corner sobbing loudly.

"So . . ." I ventured, still shaking slightly but maintaining my cheerful facade. "Now that we've established our rivalry through the traditional anime method of you trying to eat my soul, want to grab coffee sometime and talk about art?"

Katherine stared at me for a few seconds more, not understanding how I had bested her dark powers.

"Listen," she said. "I don't know what kind of game you're playing, but I'm not interested in relationships or being your . . . your rival or whatever. Just leave me the fuck alone."

"Love to, but can't," I sighed in resignation. "I've already fallen for your art. There's no way back."

"You're not going to leave me alone, are you?" she asked with a deep, rumbling sigh.

"I promise to leave you alone forever if you give me your Omnigram ID." I grinned. "On account that I've got gym class to get to and an angel to torment."

Katherine stared at me for a long moment. Finally, she pulled out her phone with a resigned look.

"Fine," she groaned. "But only so you'll stop bothering me."

"Perfect!" I beamed, already adding her with a phone tap. "Now I can properly antagonize you with art challenges at any time."

"Whatever," she muttered. "I'll probably just block you. I have to get to class."

"Until we meet again amidst the darkness of the void, above the asteroids of Ganymede, Starship Nemesis!" I called after her retreating form.

As Katherine disappeared around the corner, I checked my schedule.

First period: Gym class with Coach Canard.

Perfect. Time to torment a certain winged entity some more. Ke Ke Ke.

Also, damn it, I gotta take a shower . . . again.

The doors opened to reveal what could only be described as a military experiment gone wrong—Coach Canard stood there in all his Omnid glory, every visible inch of him covered in thick white fur. The man's blue eyes seemed to burn with the intensity of a thousand drill sergeants.

"*Attention, prey!*" His roar echoed through the gymnasium as he unleashed an ear-splitting whistle blast that probably violated several noise ordinances. "*Ten-hut! Form a line!*"

The class transformed instantly into a military formation, students snapping into perfect parade rest positions. I flailed around like a drunk penguin trying to copy their stance.

He stalked between our ranks, his massive Yeti frame casting intimidating shadows.

"Well, well, well . . . What do we have here? The finest collection of wet noodles and limp dishrags I've ever had the misfortune to witness!" His voice dripped with theatrical disgust. "By the time I'm done with you sorry lot, you'll either be peak physical specimens or fertilizer for the football field!"

The other students stood ramrod straight, clearly familiar with his routine. I tried my best to mimic their stance.

Coach Canard's massive frame loomed over me, his shadow completely engulfing my significantly smaller human form.

"And what," he growled, leaning down until his face was inches from mine, "do we have *here*? A new victim—I mean, student?"

His breath smelled strongly of protein shakes.

"Sir, yes sir!" I barked out, channeling every military movie I'd ever seen. "Alexander Glock reporting for duty, sir!"

Coach Canard's massive face split into what might have been a grin or a snarl—it was hard to tell with all the fur.

"*A half-human meatsicle?!*" he boomed, his voice echoing off the gymnasium walls. "How . . . *fascinating!* Tell me, tiny mammal, can your pathetic little bones handle real physical education? Or should I have you join the remedial class?"

"I'm ready for whatever challenge you throw my way, sir!" I barked.

Coach Canard nodded, his massive form stalking to the center of the gym.

"*Listen up, maggots!*" he bellowed, unleashing another ear-splitting whistle blast. "Since our new recruit seems so *eager* to prove himself . . ."

Oh boy.

"Today we'll be engaging in that most *glorious* of basic pre-delvin' combat simulations . . ." He paused for dramatic effect, his white furry face splitting into what was definitely an evil grin this time. "*Extreme dodgeball free-for-all!* Anyone still standing on their feet by the end of the period will receive a passing grade!"

He pressed a button on a key and a metal cage overhead opened, releasing red balls onto the crowd of Omnids.

The gymnasium erupted into pure chaos as I tried to focus on Coach Canard's instructions about dungeon survival, but my brain kept short-circuiting because Cinder was there in regulation gym shorts and a black tank top. Her feathery mane was tied up with a thick black hairband, silver wings catching the fluorescent lights in rainbows as she stretched and caught a red ball in her claws.

No no no. Focus. Dodgeball. Remaining on my feet. Not the stupid sexy Cinder in gym shorts.

"Four. Three. Two. One. And . . . *begin* the *slayin'!*" Coach Canard whistled, nearly deafening me.

"Better duck," a chill male voice behind me commented.

I ducked, following the comment. A red ball exploded against the wall next to my head, snapping me back to reality. I spun to see who had warned me.

"Sup, mang. I'm Iogann," the gray Mothman introduced himself. He was in a gym outfit, missing his oversized hat and robe. "Canard seems to like you. Dodgeball usually ends up with someone getting their teeth knocked out—guess he wanted to test your toughness out on your first day."

"Glad I could help facilitate group suffering," I replied, keeping one eye on the various cannonball-shaped projectiles already flying across the gym. "Wait . . . why are you here chatting with me . . . do you see disaster in my future?"

"Yes." Iogann nodded.

"What kind?" I demanded.

"Dunno." He shrugged. "I just get a general tasty gist of approaching doom about you."

"Peachy," I sighed. "Whop, gotta run. TTYL." I waved to the Mothman, spotting a certain winged creature heading my way.

Cinder stalked across the gymnasium with inhuman grace, effortlessly dodging red ball projectiles as if they were moving in slow motion. Her wings were open wide, helping her maintain inhuman balance. The red ball in her claws seemed to pulse with deadly intent.

"Thought you'd be here, dweeb," she grinned, her face elongating and looking more predatory. Her anatomy was definitely somewhat fluid. Her wings could absolutely fold into themselves and stretch unnaturally wide. I wondered if she was high level enough in phase-shift to fully turn into a giant feathered snake. "Ready for some payback?"

"Oh hey, rock star!" I beamed. "Love the gym outfit! Really brings out your curvy . . . murderous tendencies!"

"You know what else will bring out my murderous tendencies?" She twirled the dodgeball between her claws. "Smashing this ball into your smug face!"

"Bring it on!" I called back cheerfully, diving behind a larger student as Cinder's first throw whistled past my head. "Nice shot! Alas, your aim is as bad as your . . . taste in music!"

Balls flew in every direction, knocking students off their feet. I kept moving, using other, larger Omnids as shields while keeping one eye on Cinder. Her wings gave her an unfair advantage in maneuverability. They also pulsed every time with flashes of mind-melting colors when someone tried targeting her, throwing their aim way off. I didn't even bother grabbing a ball to target her; doing so would be impossible as long as she sent out the rainbow charmchain pulses around herself.

"Stop running and face me like a . . . whatever you are named as today!" Cinder called out, her voice carrying a dangerous edge of amusement.

"I'm . . . Mr. Someone who doesn't want a concussion!" I called back, ducking another foam missile. "And your aim should be Kaleid-named as . . . Terrible!"

Cinder's wings flared in response to my taunt as she snatched another ball from the air. Her sharp blue eyes tracked my movement with predatory focus.

"Stop. Moving!" she growled, unleashing another throw.

I ducked and weaved, using parkour skills to stay one step ahead. Other students were getting caught in the crossfire of Cinder's vendetta against me.

"Dodgeball involves dodging!" I taunted her. "Your aim's getting worse, angel! Maybe you should stick to hitting piano keys instead!"

She acquired another ball. I barely dodged in time, the ball whistling past my ear.

"Wow, you really suck at this! Maybe we should set up some targets for you to practice on? Draw little hearts and Alex tags on them?"

"Hey, Nullie! Dodge this!" a voice barked from behind me.

A ball-shaped missile caught me in the back of the head with devastating force. The world spun sickeningly as I flew forward into the floor, my vision blurring.

Through the haze, I saw Cinder's face transform from competitive aggression to shock. Her wings flared wide as she launched herself towards me, but the distance seemed to stretch impossibly far.

"*Alex!*" Her voice sounded strange and distorted, as if coming from underwater.

The gymnasium floor rushed up to meet me with alarming speed. The last thing I saw before darkness claimed me was Cinder's ocean-blue eyes wide with concern, rainbow red-black-violet wings spread like a protective canopy above me.

CHAPTER ELEVEN

Breaking the Incarnator

I blinked awake not in the rebirth cavern, but in what appeared to be the nurse's office, my head throbbing. The humming fluorescent lights seemed unnecessarily bright as my vision slowly focused. A familiar winged silhouette paced nearby, ranting animatedly.

"That red-scaled beerch!" Cinder was growling, her wings bristling with rage. "She threw that ball way too hard on purpose!"

I tried to sit up, immediately regretting the decision as the room spun. "Ow."

Cinder whirled around, eyes locking onto me. "You idiot! Stay down!"

"Eyyy, it's my fave Quetzi! Were you worried about me?" I managed to grin despite the pounding in my head.

"No!" Cinder snapped, her wings flaring defensively. "I just . . . didn't want Emerald getting in trouble for murdering the new kid on his second day."

"Emerald, huh?" I touched the tender spot on my head gingerly. "Your ruby friend has quite an arm. I'm at like one HP left . . . I think. Yeesh."

"She's a Slayer." Cinder shrugged.

"A Slayer who will regret leaving a dangerous deviant like me unslayed. Just you wait till I unleash my master plan of revenge," I declared dramatically from the medical bed. "It will be epic and . . . uhh . . . completely unexpected!"

"Sounds like a dumb plan to get yourself killed," Cinder pointed out. "Emerald isn't someone you want to mess with."

"Too late! The wheels of vengeance are already turning." I tapped my temple, then winced at the pain. "Ow. Note to self: Avoid head gestures while concussed."

"You're an idiot," Cinder stated flatly, but I caught a hint of reluctant amusement in her voice. "A complete and total idiot with a death wish."

"You should try harder if you want to win my love," I said. "That was a one out of ten compliment."

"W-what?! I'm not trying to win your anything! I'm just . . . making sure you don't die before I can properly get revenge for those videos!"

"Sure, sure." I grinned, wincing slightly as the movement sent a sharp pain through my head. "Your revenge plot sounds totally believable."

Cinder growled something under her breath.

"Why are you even mad about the videos?" I asked, propping myself up on the medical bed. "Isn't your whole goal to get famous and rich? Why else would you be in a troupe?"

"*What?* No!" Cinder froze mid-pace.

"Oh?" I pressed. "What exactly is your goal? Why are you in a monster-slayin' troupe?"

Cinder's wings twitched, her feathers rapidly fading to grays and blacks. "It's complicated," she muttered.

"Complicated how?" I challenged. "You're in a troupe doing music to summon monsters. You've got talent. Those videos I recorded? They're basically free publicity. Also, in the age of social media and generative AIs, consent is a fluid concept."

"Consent is *not* fluid! That's exactly the kind of manipulative bullshit—"

"Says the person who can literally turn invisible and sneak around to terrorize innocent half-humans," I interrupted. "Pot, meet kettle. Say, do you ever turn invisible to sneak into the boys' showers?"

"*What?!*" Cinder's entire figure ignited with black-gold-pink-red.

"Ha!" I grinned. "Made your entire body blush. You're too easy to rile up. Learn to be more stoic."

Cinder choked at my words, forcibly turning her entire body gray.

"Just saying, if I had invisibility powers, I'd totally use them for . . . scientific research," I said, tapping my chin. "Maybe spy on some angels."

Cinder's wings flared again, feathers shifting from gray to a vibrant, angry red.

"Say, is changing color the only thing you can do?" I asked. "Can you project other stuff, be a TV? Quick, tune to the news."

"Are you seriously asking me to turn into a TV?"

"Medical professionals recommend entertainment during recovery. And who better to provide said entertainment than my favorite rock star?" I winked.

Cinder sent me a dangerous glare, and then her entire head ignited with a million colors as if her feathers were monitor pixels going through channels filled with colorful static. In a few seconds the colors settled and then my own face stared back at me.

"Satisfied?" she asked in my own voice.

"Whoa," I breathed out. "This is some high grade mimicry. I always wondered what I'd look like with a hot femme bod."

Cinder's feathers instantly shifted back to their normal silver, her original Quetzi face flushing with embarrassment and anger.

"Argh!" she sputtered. "I was trying to intimidate you, not . . . not . . ."

"Give me ideas about alternate universe versions of myself?" I teased cheerfully. "Too late! Now I'm imagining myself dating a female version of myself! This is primo fan fiction material! Wait . . . you're like the perfect infiltrator. Damn, now I'm extra jelly."

"I swear, if you don't shut up . . ." Her wings fluttered with agitation.

"You'll what? Hit me with another dodgeball? That's probably against medical advice right now."

The school nurse, an elderly mermaid with pale-blue scales, bustled over on a wheelchair. Her lower body was a sleek, iridescent fish tail that gleamed under the fluorescent lights, and her upper body was wrapped in a crisp white medical uniform.

Silver-blue hair was pulled back in a tight bun, large glasses perched on her sharp, angular nose. A dark Kitlix sat on her shoulder, shimmering with green sparks.

"Ah, Mr. Glock," she said, "I see you're awake and makin' jokes. Good. I'm Nurse Keystoni."

Cinder stepped back, her wings instinctively folding closer to her body and turning silver. The nurse's gaze was sharp enough to cut through even a Quetzalcoatl's bravado.

"How are you feeling?" The nurse's voice was crisp and professional.

"Like I've been hit by a very angry . . . dodgeball," I deadpanned.

"You've endured a pretty bad concussion," the nurse tutted, scribbling something on her clipboard. "I healed some of the damage."

"Just some?" I asked.

"Healing takes energy. Can't restore everything instantly." She shrugged as the Kitlix flowed down to her lap. "The school was built directly above the Leviathan's place of awakening and has the highest aetheric density in the world, and yet it is still far, far below Arx where these little guys are born," the nurse continued, stroking her Kitlix. "Alas, our magical potential is limited, so yes . . . I fixed as much as I could. You'll need to take it easy for the rest of the day. No more dodgeball or other strenuous activities."

"Does that include . . . vigorous activities with extra-angry Quetzalcoatls?" I asked innocently.

Cinder growled in my direction.

The nurse's sharp eyes flicked between Cinder and me. "Miss Nova, are you harassing our new mixed-heritage student?"

"What? No! He's the one who keeps—" Cinder started to protest.

"I was merely suggesting that Miss Nova's presence has certain . . . *cardiovascular* effects," I interrupted with an innocent smile. "Completely unrelated to any dodgeball incidents."

Cinder choked beside me.

"Perhaps you should take the rest of the day off to recover," the nurse suggested dryly. "I'll write you a note excusing you from classes."

"But what about my education?" I protested. "My burning desire for knowledge? My need to maintain perfect attendance?"

"Your burning desire can wait until tomorrow," the nurse replied firmly. "Now, about getting you home safely . . ."

I put on my best pained expression. "About that . . . walking might be . . . challenging." I winced dramatically, touching my head. "Everything's still spinning and my balance feels . . . off."

The nurse's sharp eyes studied me carefully. "Hmm. We can't have you stumbling around campus in this condition. You might fall and worsen your injury. Hrmmm. We do have temporary mobility assistance available," the nurse said. "Hold on."

She quickly dried herself with a quick swipe of a towel, her tail suddenly sparking with azure energy. Then her scales slowly shifted and reformed, transforming into humanlike, blue-scaled legs. She stood up smoothly, put on slippers, and walked out of the room.

"Dang. That's cool," I whispered to Cinder. "Can you do that?"

"Do what?" The Quetzi peered down at me.

"Can you manifest a tail and then split it into legs?"

"Do I look like I can just manifest new body parts?" Cinder growled. "I can change colors and mimic appearances for a bit, not transform my entire body! I already have a tail, if you didn't notice!"

"So can you split it into an extra pair of legs, turn into a spider?"

"*What?!* That's not how any of this . . ."

"Shame," I sighed. "Maybe in your next evolution?"

"I'm not a Pocketbeast!" she snapped.

"Could've fooled me with the face-swaps and all those color changes." I grinned. "What level do you need to be to learn Hyper Beam?"

Before Cinder could respond, the nurse returned pushing a sleek wheelchair and holding what appeared to be a temporary disability parking placard and elevator access card.

"Here we are," she announced. "This should help you get around safely until you've fully recovered. And this placard will let you park closer to the buildings."

"Oh, wow, thank you!" I beamed, accepting the lanyard and placard.

"You"—the nurse pointed at Cinder—"will help Mr. Glock get to his car or Oodber safely. No arguments."

"*What?!*" Cinder squawked. "Why me?"

"Because you're already here and clearly concerned about his well-being," the nurse replied smoothly. "Unless you'd prefer I write up a very stern report about that dodgeball incident? Who was it that threw the ball so hard at our newest student again?"

Cinder's wings drooped in defeat. "Fine," she muttered.

"Excellent!" I chirped, carefully sliding into the wheelchair, wincing as my brain wobbled. "Now I can start a wheelchair racing team with Katherine! Think we can convince Coach Canard to add it as an official sport?"

"Katherine?" Cinder asked, automatically taking control of my wheelchair to roll me out from the domain of healing.

"An incredible artist who tried to murder me with her own wheelchair this morning. Almost succeeded, too! You two would get along great—she's got the whole 'I hate everything, especially this annoying human' vibe down."

"Katherine Kells?" Cinder's voice took on a strange tone. "You met Katherine?"

"Yeah! She tried to eat my soul with her spooky eyes and everything. It was great! Well, terrifying actually, but great! She's like this amazing artist who—"

"I know who Katherine is," Cinder interrupted quietly. "She's . . . Iogann's half-sister. We used to be friends, back when . . ."

She trailed off, her wings drooping slightly.

"Back when what?" I asked, genuinely curious about the shift in Cinder's mood.

"I don't want to bring up old shit," she muttered, pushing my wheelchair perhaps a bit more forcefully than necessary. "She went through some stuff. Started drinking. Stopped hanging out with anyone except Io. To be honest, I haven't really talked to her in ages."

"Sounds like a tragic backstory trope that could use a kick in a different direction," I mused as Cinder wheeled me through the hall. "Maybe we should form a support group—the People Who Have Tried to Murder Alex Club. You can be the founding president!"

"Pfff," she exhaled. "Pretty sure that'll include half the school by the end of the month at the rate you're going."

"A month?" I arched an eyebrow. "You underestimate my powers. Give me a week. Nah, two weeks. I've a busy schedule filled with Stollwurm and Quetzi wrangling."

"Wrangling?" She smirked.

"Wrangling into friendship," I declared dramatically. "Absolute, pure, unadulterated friendship that will make you both question your life choices!"

Cinder stared at me for a long moment, then burst out into an uneven grin. "You're going to 'friendship' Katherine Kells? Good luck."

"Eh, I'll get there. For now, she's my sworn nemesis." I grinned.

"Your . . . nemesis?" Cinder's voice dripped with skepticism as she wheeled me through the hallway. "With the amount of tormenting me with your annoying . . . everything, you'd think that I would be your nemesis."

"Not at all!" I twisted in the wheelchair to look up at her. Her wings were partially folded over me, creating an iridescent metallic canopy above us. "You're my guardian angel, obviously! Or romantic interest number one, if you fall for me." I rubbed my chin. "Are you into highly questionable male protagonists constantly on the run from the law and corpo Scrutimancers?"

Cinder's wings bristled as she stopped pushing my wheelchair abruptly. "What did you just say?"

"Which part?" I grinned up at her. "The guardian angel bit or the romantic interest angle? Because I'm happy to elaborate on either—"

The wing canopy overhead ignited with violets, reds, pinks, and golds as if a sun were setting above me.

"I swear to Slayer . . ." Cinder growled, her claws tightening on the wheelchair handles. Without warning, she spun my chair around to face her, leaning down until we were eye to eye.

"Listen here, you annoying little chuppy," she hissed. "Do you have a death wish?"

"Actually?" I asked. "Yes. I'm heavily concussed, and it's mildly annoying. Please stab me through the heart with a sharp pointy claw-hand and reincarnate me."

"What?" Cinder's ocean-blue eyes went wide.

"Wait, I have a better plan that doesn't involve dying horribly." I rubbed my chin. "Take me to the Genesis Pool."

"Why?"

"I want to take a swim in it, see if it fixes my concussion without dying."

"You want to . . . *what?!*"

"Take a swim in the Genesis Pool," I repeated, my tone casual. "Might help with this concussion."

"That's not how it works!" Cinder hissed, her wings flaring with agitation. "The Genesis Pool isn't some magical healing hot tub!"

"Worth a shot." I shrugged, wincing slightly at the movement. "Better than sitting in this wheelchair all day."

Cinder's eyes narrowed. "You're serious? You want to just . . . casually dive into one of the most sacred spaces in Omnithean culture?"

"Yep." I nodded. "Sounds fun. Wanna be my guide? We could skinny-dip in it together!"

"*Absolutely not!*" she growled.

"Aiiiiight then." I shrugged. "I'll just roll myself there. You can go to class, Miss Square."

"You're not going anywhere near the effin' Genesis Pool," Cinder growled. "And I'm definitely not letting you go alone in your current state. You're obviously concussed, stupid!"

"Look," I said. "People drop bracelets into it to grow an entirely new body. But . . . has anyone tried to jump into it, *while* badly concussed and wearing the bracelet?"

"How the fuck should I know?!" she hissed. "Go ask the vice principal! He'll probably explain to you why it's a monumentally stupid idea."

"Nah. Let's find out!" I said cheerfully. "For science! Come on, don't you want to know what happens? Maybe it'll give me superpowers! Or maybe it'll just fix my headache. Either way, win-win!"

"Or maybe it'll just kill you!" Cinder snapped.

"If it does, *then* you can take the bracelet off my corpse and dump that in," I said. "Either way—no more concussion! Come on, you break rules all the time. Let's break them into an actually useful direction."

Cinder's wings flared with gray, black, and auburn tones of absolute frustration.

"All right, then, I dare you to roll me down there and dump me in the pool." I changed my strategy. "Don't you want revenge? Weren't you all like 'I'm gonna smash your face with a ball' this morning? The fierce rebel Cinder, afraid of a little sacred pool? What happened to all that anti-establishment energy? Maybe you're not that goth after all. Maybe you're just . . . faking it."

Cinder's wings bristled instantly, her feathers shifting to a deep, challenging red. "Excuse me?"

"You heard me." I grinned, knowing exactly which buttons I was pushing. "All talk, no action. The great rebel Cinder Nova, scared of breaking a few rules? Pfft."

"I am *not* scared," she growled, leaning down until we were eye to eye. "Fine. You want to go to the Genesis Pool? Let's go."

The elevator ride down to the Genesis Pool was painfully awkward.

Cinder leaned against the wall in one corner, arms crossed. I sat in the wheelchair, spinning slowly and deliberately.

"Stop. Twirling in one spot," she ground out through clenched teeth.

"Can't help it." I grinned. "Wheelchair. Spinning is its primary function. Wheeeee-eee-e."

Cinder's eye twitched.

The elevator music—a bizarre Omnithean jazz remix that sounded like whale sounds mixed with electronic beats—did nothing to ease the tension. Cinder looked as though she was already regretting her life choices.

The elevator doors opened with a soft chime.

The silver surface of the Genesis Pool stretched out before us, eerily still and reflective. The massive statue of the masked, naked female Omnid loomed overhead, her stone wings spread wide and her sword pointed down at the fluid's surface.

"This is a terrible idea," Cinder muttered as I rolled closer to the edge. "We shouldn't be here. We aren't actually resurrecting anyone and . . ."

"Sacred schmacred." I waved off her concerns, activating the hexamesh suit under my clothes. The tiny beast core hummed to life. "Sometimes you gotta take risks!"

Before Cinder could react, I launched myself from the wheelchair with a whoop of excitement. The hexamesh suit's beast core amplified my muscles as I sailed through the air, my body arcing towards the silvery surface of the Genesis Pool.

"*What are you doing?!*" Cinder screamed, her wings flaring wide in shock.

Time seemed to slow down. The reflective surface of the pool rushed up to meet me, impossibly still and mirrorlike. For a moment, I could see my own reflection—eyes wide with worry and exhilaration.

Then impact, and then I was under.

The silvery liquid enveloped me, filling my mouth and eyes, choking and suffocating me. It filled me from within in less than a second and reached out to the burning bracelet on my wrist, and suddenly up was down and down was up as if gravity had turned inside out.

System Error

Two words comprised of brilliant sparks filled my vision.

Something inside me broke with a twinkle.

CHAPTER TWELVE

As Above, So Below

Autumn. Falling leaves. A suburban backyard, complete with a massive oak tree. The colors all around too vivid, saturated like an old photograph that had been artificially enhanced, like a painting made up from thick brushstrokes.

Katherine's painting. It was as if I was inside her work.

I stared up.

A teenage girl with platinum-blonde hair and silver-blue eyes was perched in a treehouse made entirely of stolen traffic signs. The massive *Saint Mary Exit 7b* sign that formed the roof caught the sunlight in a way that made my head hurt. A Lazarus bracelet clung to her wrist just like mine.

"Sup, Mittens." She grinned.

"What?" I sputtered. "Who are you? Where am I? What . . . what did you just call me?"

"Mittens," she repeated. "You're my minion. Mittens."

"I don't understand . . ." I started, but something tugged at the edges of my memory. The girl seemed familiar somehow, like a half-forgotten dream. *I've seen her.*

The girl from Katherine's drawings.

She pulled her silver-blue hair back with a grin, and there it was. The fractal crack on her forehead pulsed with impossible colors, like an oil slick catching sunlight. Each pulse sent waves of vertigo through me.

"You're . . ." I managed. "You're . . . you're from Katherine's art."

"Am I?" The girl's grin widened, blue eyes twinkling down at me. "Or is Katherine drawing what she sees in the spaces between spaces? The cracks in reality where secret, forgotten things hide?"

Her large silver-blue eyes dug into me.

I knew them. I knew her, but from where . . . from *when*?!

"That doesn't tell me anything!" I yelled. "Who are you? Where is this?!"

"This is . . . us." The girl leaped from the tree, bouncing up and down as she landed. I stared at her reinforced shoes covered in springs. "You and me. Inside out. Upside down. Good job on breaking the Incarnator. Sixty-nine thousand thumbs-up and a high five."

She held up her hand.

I stared at her, feeling mentally derailed.

Derailing people is my job, damn it! Wait . . . that's my joke! I used it on Cinder . . .

"I'm Alexa," she said, lowering her hand before I could even raise mine.

I felt my brain momentarily short-circuit at her words as she pace-bounced around me.

"You're . . . what, my sister from another dimension?" I demanded.

"Mmmmm . . . no." Alexa shook her head. "I'm a supervillain."

"From?"

"From Earth, from the previous narrative. When they rolled over everything, a part of me remained in your noggin due to the brain spiders."

"What?! They?"

"System Wizards," Alexa said.

"System Wizards?" I asked, trying to make sense of her words. "What system? What wizards?"

"The ones who rolled everything over, duh," Alexa continued, circling me like a shark. "Rewrote the narrative. The ones who made you forget. But they missed a teensy-weensy spot!" She tapped the fractal crack on her forehead. "Right here."

"Stop being cryptic and just tell me what the hell—" I growled in frustration.

"Sorry!" Alexa suddenly leaned forward and gave me a tight hug, nuzzling into my side. "Time to go, M. If you stay in the Genesis soup too long, I'll decay away too much, and you'll become like everyone else—overwritten, incapable of breaking the narrative. Don't dive in again while you are alive. It won't give you any more powers. Just remember this—you're never alone. I love you. I'm here for you. I'm with you, forever and always. Inside and outside. Find all four of our besties and make us remember what we lost. Keep going, M, no matter what. Break the tracks of the false narrative! Don't let anyone stop you!"

"What tracks?" I demanded. "What false narrative?!"

"The tracks reality was set on after I set the world on fire," Alexa whispered rapidly into my ear. "Memetics. Cryptids. One game overwritten with another, albeit one with far less copyright, thanks to me. Inspiration of inspiration of inspiration. You'll figure it out. After all, you're me and I'm you. Buh-byeeeee now!"

Gravity inverted and the view of another place and time came apart into silver streaks.

I felt a strong clawed hand that grabbed me, hauling me up from the depths of the Genesis Pool.

I broke the surface gasping and choking, dredging silver fluid from my lungs, my mind reeling.

"*You absolute idiot!*" Cinder's voice pierced through my disorientation as she dragged me onto the stone ledge. Her wings were flared wide with agitation, droplets of silver fluid flying everywhere as she shook me. "*What were you thinking?!*"

I coughed up more of the metallic-tasting liquid, my brain sliding sideways ever so slightly.

"I was thinking . . . of having a nice refreshing . . . bath," I spat with a small smile.

"I didn't think that you'd actually freaking jump in there! Nazareth, why are you like this?" Cinder growled with an exasperated expression.

"Like what?" I managed between coughs, "That was . . . actually . . . somewhat enlightening! You should try it. Maybe you'll . . . remember things too, get a new perspective on life."

"Remember what?" Cinder demanded, wings bristling. "What are you talking about? Did you hit your head again in there?"

"I'm fine," I assured her, though my voice sounded strange, off even to my own ears. "Just had a weird . . . moment under. Like a dream, but . . . not?"

"The Abyss are you on about?" she asked. "Did you permanently damage what little brain you had left?!"

I sprang to my feet, surprised to find my balance perfectly steady, bouncing up and down. The concussion symptoms were completely gone. My thoughts were crystal clear once again. Clearer than they had ever been before, sharp like the blade of a two-dimensional knife.

I smiled.

"You didn't die in there . . . right?" She stared at me. "No. You're way too smug looking for someone who's seen the Wheel a second time."

"No Wheels," I said. "Only me. I saw myself . . . I think. My . . . real self. Or maybe my reflection. My . . . sideways shadow? The darkness that's been at my side from the beginning . . ."

I blinked. Never alone. Always, there had been something, someone with me, watching me, pushing me onward. Holding my hand when the Frontenachii Wendigo compound ignited with a giant mushroom spreading up into the sky. Sitting beside me in the van while I drove south. My ghost had a name to it now, a face.

Cinder stared at me, her wings shifting through a kaleidoscope of confused colors—murky grays, uncertain blues, a hint of worried purple. "You're not making any sense. What do you mean, 'saw yourself'?"

"Exactly what I said." I shrugged. "Met a version of me. Or maybe not me. Hard to tell."

I looked at the shimmering pool.

"As above, so below," I murmured.

I lifted the hexagonal bracelet on my left hand to my face. "Hello, old friend. You don't belong to this dimension at all, do you?"

Cinder stared at me with growing concern. "Okay, you're clearly having some kind of breakdown."

"Just making an educated guess about the bracelet—chill." I shrugged.

The hexagonal bracelet seemed to pulse slightly in response to my scrutiny, its dark metal surface catching the light in strange ways. Had it always looked so . . . alive?

"Stats," I whispered.

My menu came up. Every stat was still at zero . . . Except for one little change:

Anima: 89/89 + [89]

I squinted at the extra, inexplicable addition of 89 soul. Was I some kind of a twin-soul human now? Twice as human? Strange. Very, very strange. I had no idea what having more soul did. Would probably have to ask an Animancy teacher about this development on Monday.

"Alex . . . are you really okay?" Cinder let out.

Progress! She really was worried about me.

"Yep, check this out!" I pulled on the power of the hexasuit and did a cartwheel across the cavern, last bits of silver leaving my body.

"See? Perfectly balanced!" I straightened out. "As all things should be."

"Again with the dumb movie quotes?" Cinder bit her lower lip. "The Pool isn't some magical healing spring! It's for resurrection only!"

"Maybe that's just what they want you to think." I grinned, tapping my temple where I knew an invisible shear across reality sat beneath skin and bone. "Maybe we should question everything we think we know about everything."

Cinder twitched. "You sound like Em with her stupid Predator Theory nonsense."

"If you think it's so stupid, then why burden yourself with a Kaleid name, *Cinder?*" I asked.

Cinder deflated, looking like a girl who had been beaten far too long and too many times by life.

"You smell like death, go shower off." She turned around, refusing to meet my eyes.

I sighed, studying my reflection in the Genesis Pool's surface. For a moment, I thought I saw a flash of silver-blue eyes and a fractal crack, but it was gone before I could be sure.

"Argh. I should . . . get going," Cinder muttered, checking her phone with a frown. "I've already wasted enough time babysitting your crazy ass. Have to get ready for the show tonight."

"Aww, you're not going to make sure I don't drown in the shower?" I teased.

"You're clearly fine," she growled. "Try not to get yourself killed without supervision. I've got show prep. I've wasted enough time with your bullshit today."

"No promises!" I called after her retreating form. "Break a leg at practice! Or someone else's leg! Whatever makes ya smile!"

Cinder's only response was a dismissive wave of her wing as she disappeared up the stairwell in a rush of rapidly cooling rainbow.

I sat back into the chair and rolled myself into the elevator. I was no longer concussed, but maintaining the appearance of weakness could be useful.

I left the wheelchair in my van and took Oodber to Thundertown and was back in time to attend another class before lunch.

Cinder's seat remained empty.

I found myself sketching her from memory during the teacher's generic comp sci lecture—her wings mid-flight, combat boots poised to kick, fingers dancing across piano keys. Each drawing captured a different facet of her: the talented musician, the angry goth, the vulnerable, broken person beneath it all.

My sketchbook rapidly filled as I barely paid attention to the class. Without Cinder to tease and her wings to gawk at, class seemed extra dull.

* * *

At lunch, I wheeled myself into the cafeteria, the noise level resembling a stampeding herd of giants. The lunch line was a mass of pushing, shoving, and tail-whacking as hungry, spiked, rowdy Omnitheans fought for position.

Ah, now I remember why I sent June the Kelpie to fetch food for me.

Time for some crowd control.

I pulled out a small firecracker from my bag, lit it with my lighter, and put on large construction earmuffs, dropping the firecracker on the floor directly in front of me.

Bang!

The cafeteria went dead silent, all heads turning to me.

"*Everybody be cool! This is a wheelchair robbery!*" I announced into the stunned silence, rolling forward dramatically. "*I have a doctor's note, and I'm not afraid to use it!*"

The crowd of dazed, colorful Omnids parted before me like the Red Sea as I wheeled through.

"*Beep beep!* Decrepit half-human coming through! No shoving in line or I'll file for emotional damage! My lawyer is very enthusiastic about disability discrimination cases!" I called out cheerfully as I wheeled through the parted crowd. "She's a tiny Domovoy with a *huge* legal portfolio!"

The line of students maintained a respectful distance as I reached the counter and ordered my massive sushi platter.

I wheeled away from the counter with my sushi boat balanced precariously on my lap when a familiar death skull Mothman stepped into my path.

"That was quite the entrance," Iogann said, smiling. "Want to join us for lunch?" At least, I think he was smiling—it was hard to tell for sure due to his puffy, light-gray mothy collar fluff.

"Sure." I nodded, hoping to see my angel.

I followed Iogann's bouncing hat, carefully balancing my mountain of sushi. As we approached a table by the windows, I spotted a familiar camo coat form instead of rainbow wings.

"Kat, this is Alex, the new half-human student I was telling you about." Iogann gestured as we approached. "Alex, this is Katherine Kells, my half-sister."

I grinned at Katherine, who was already at the table near the window. "Is this seat taken?" I gestured to the empty space next to her wheelchair.

The girl in the goggles simply grunted in response.

Strong and silent type, huh? Two can play at this game.

CHAPTER THIRTEEN

Dimensional Magic

I wheeled up to the table and carefully maneuvered my wheelchair into position.

"Hnngh," I grunted in greeting, gesturing at my sushi platter. "Ghrmmm?"

Katherine's head snapped to me.

I began nomming the sushi.

"So Alex, that dodgeball head bonking was pretty intense . . ." Iogann started.

"Hrrmmmph," I nodded sagely at Iogann's comment, stuffing another piece of sushi in my mouth.

"Are you . . . okay?" Iogann asked, his fluffy gray antennae twitching with concern.

"Mrrrrgh." I shrugged, then gestured at my head with chopsticks and made an explosion sound. "Grmmmm. No word. Only grunt."

Katherine's shoulders tensed slightly beside me.

"Hnngh?" I grunted at her.

"The nurse said you had a big concussion . . ." Iogann continued, looking increasingly confused by my caveman communication style. "That was a grisly way to go down, by the way . . . I think that's what my doom-sense warned about."

"Nghhhh." I waved dismissively, offering him a California roll with an eloquent "Hrm?"

"Ah, yeah, don't mind if I do." Iogann accepted the roll. "Thanks."

Katherine's claws tightened around her canteen as I continued my grunt-based conversation with Iogann.

"Why are you not using words? Did the hit to your head affect your speech?" Iogann asked.

"Pffffftt," I snorted, rolling my eyes.

Katherine growled from where she was sitting, her long tail beginning to lash dangerously.

I dug into my bag and pulled out an old USSR army flask, complete with hammer and sickle emblem that I'd bought in one of Thundertown's tourist shops. I unscrewed the cap with exaggerated care and took a long swig, making sure to wink at Katherine as I did so. Then I put on a pair of dark, wide sunglasses.

"*That's it!*" Katherine slammed her hands on the table, making everyone's drinks jump. "Are you seriously mocking me right now?!"

"Hrrmm?" I grunted innocently, taking another sip from my flask.

"Stop. That." Each word was punctuated by her tail lashing against her wheelchair. "Stop with the stupid grunting and the . . . the flask and the . . . everything!"

"Everything?" I blinked.

"Sis . . ." Iogann started, his antennae wiggling in the holes of his wide Snufkin hat.

"Piss off, Jan!" Katherine snapped at her half-brother and turned to me. "You! Why the fuck are you even in a wheelchair? You were walking fine this morning!"

"Got hit in the head with a dodgeball courtesy of an angry wyrm." I shrugged, dropping the grunting act. "The nurse insisted I use this fancy chair until I recover. Pretty sweet ride, though."

"And the flask?" Katherine demanded.

"This?" I held up the USSR flask. "Just delicious water. Thought that your flask was neat, so I got one myself. Cheers."

I clinked the flask against hers with a sly grin.

"And glasses?!" she hiss-growled.

"Just wanted to be cool like you." I grinned. "Am I not allowed to copy your Schwarzenegger-inspired look?"

Katherine growled, her claws tightening around her own flask until the metal creaked.

"Sis, chill." Iogann placed his fuzzy hand on her shoulder. "Alex is just being friendly. Em actually did knock him out pretty hard during gym."

"And you!" Katherine snapped at her brother. "Why are you hovering over me? Why aren't you luncheoning with your precious troupe?"

Iogann sighed heavily. "Because Em and Cinder are at each other's throats again, and I am not needed unless actual gateway opening happens. What, can't I just spend some quality time with my sister?"

"Oh, so I'm your lunch backup plan when your cool friends are fighting?" she growled.

"That's not what I meant, and you know it," Iogann's antennae drooped. "I just . . . miss hanging out with you. It's not healthy to eat lunch alone in a corner."

"Whatever," Katherine muttered, taking a long drink from her flask. "Go back to your stupid-ass troupe. I'm sure they need you more than I do. Maybe you'll get ninety people killed this time around, if that many even show up to your stupid show."

"What happened at the Spring's End Festival wasn't—"

"Wasn't your fault? Wasn't preventable? Yeah, okay. Which part of bringing high-level abominations from doomed dimensions makes sense in your brainless moth-head?"

"Emerald—" Iogann began.

"Is a moron," Katherine snapped. "Her Knights are morons. You are a moron. Cass is a moron. Even if nobody dies tonight, people aren't coming to applaud you. They're coming to laugh at you morons. Read the Omnigram posts about yourselves! Your inverted dungeoneering is peak idiocy."

The Mothman opened his mouth to defend himself.

"Not done!" she barked, silencing him. "Nobody actually wants to see you summon monsters from other dimensions just so Em can try to punch them in the face! It's not art, it's not meaningful, it's just . . . stupid! I told you that it was stupid years ago, Iogann. I told you to study dimensional anchoring, to learn to create proper two-way gates. But noooooo . . . you morons want to be special snowflakes . . ."

"Actually," I interjected, trying to brighten the excessive hostility radiating from the Stollwurm, "I'd love to see that show. When is it?"

Both siblings turned to stare at me.

"Today after school," Iogann said quietly, looking as if he wanted to sink into the floor.

"Perfect!" I beamed. "Wouldn't miss it for the world! Sounds absolutely metal—interdimensional gates, monster fights, the potential for catastrophic failure . . . sign me up!"

"Did that dodgeball knock out what little sense you had?" Katherine demanded, echoing Cinder's opinion from this morning.

"Probably!" I agreed cheerfully. "But come on—how often do you get to see live interdimensional monster summoning? That's like . . . peak entertainment right there! 'Sides, I want to see my angel sing."

"*Your* . . . angel?" she asked.

"Oh yeah, Cinder's got this amazing voice." I grinned. "You should hear her sing! Though I guess you probably have, back when you were friends . . ."

"We were never friends," Katherine growled. "And Cass isn't some angel. She's just another self-absorbed knobtwit following Em's stupid philosophy."

"Sis . . ." Iogann started.

"Don't 'sis' me," Katherine snapped. "You know I'm right. This whole troupe thing is going to end badly. Everything around you ends badly."

The Mothman stared at his sister with deep, gray-black eyes.

"You're there because you're drawn to disasters." Katherine laughed bitterly. "Go on, admit it. You're not there for the art, or leveling up, or whatever other bullshit Em spews—you're there because each show ends with a catastrophe!"

"That's not . . ."

"Yes it is!" Katherine obliterated her brother with her chiding tone, jabbing at him with a dark clawed finger. "You can't help it, can you? Just like how you couldn't help getting involved in that Spring's End Festival disaster. You're literally programmed to seek out the biggest potential clusterfuck possible! If Em's dumbass troupe actually succeeded at anything, you wouldn't be anywhere near it! Come on, say it: 'I'm a dust-brain addicted to disasters!'"

"Okay, time-out!" I clapped my hands together loudly, drawing both siblings' attention. "While this family therapy session is fascinating, I've got a better idea. Katherine, why don't you come to the show, too?"

"No, nuh-huh, no way." The Stollwurm shook her head. "You think I want to be eaten or infested by some random cosmic bullshit? Do I look suicidal to you?"

"Actually, yes," I said, eyeing her flask meaningfully. "But that's not the point. The point is—if you're so convinced this show is going to be a disaster, wouldn't you want to be there to say 'I told you so' when it all goes wrong? Plus, you could document the whole thing! Think of the artistic possibilities—capturing the moment everything falls apart . . ."

Katherine's tail lashed angrily. "I don't need to be there to know it's going to be a shitshow."

"But wouldn't you rather see it firsthand?" I pressed. "Come on, where's your artistic spirit?"

"Dead," she said coldly.

"Very dark," I whistled. "You should write Romantic poetry. Or song lyrics! Maybe collaborate with Cinder on some proper goth music. Draw D&D some posters?"

Katherine's tail lashed dangerously. "You think this is funny? You think my situation is some kind of joke? It's enough that this idiot is constantly feeding off my disaster of a life." She waved a gloved hand at Iogann. "Now you're on my case, too? Why in the Abyss would I want to contribute to anything Em does? She's a psychopathic, controlling beerch who should go die in a hole. Get off my case unless you want me to send you to the deep again and leave you there."

"Eh, your deep doesn't scare me anymore." I grinned, tapping my temple. "Already got some quality void time in this morning. Really puts things in perspective, ya know?"

Katherine's claws opened and closed. "You're either incredibly brave or incredibly recklessly stupid. I'm leaning towards the second."

"Actually," I said, "I'm incredibly curious. I thought that your power was psychic, not dimensional."

"I'm related to this aimless twat." Katherine waved a hand at Iogann. "Obviously, my power is dimensional."

"So the deep is an actual place, then? Is it dimensionally aligned with local topography? Can you use it to . . . go through walls to reach otherwise inaccessible places?" I asked.

Katherine stared at me. My mind was already reeling excitedly with possibilities. A dimensional power that permitted one to walk into anywhere across darkness? The potential applications were endless—bank vaults, secure facilities, anywhere with valuable data or resources . . .

"Why are you so interested in the mechanics of my abilities?" she demanded.

"Pure scientific curiosity!" I assured her quickly. Perhaps too quickly. "Just trying to understand how different Omnithean powers work. Like, hypothetically speaking, could you use the deep to go anywhere on Earth?"

"Why would you want to know something like that?" she demanded.

I realized I'd been a bit too eager, too direct. Time to pivot.

"Art," I said. "I'm thinking about a photography project. Conceptual stuff about liminal spaces, boundaries between dimensions. Your power sounds fascinating from an artistic perspective."

"You're lying," she stated sharply.

"Fine." I crossed my arms, copying her stance. "I want to go into forbidden places and take photos of forbidden things. Happy?"

Katherine pursed her lips. Her tail lashed once, then stilled.

"Appreciate the honesty, but you're not getting anywhere near my dimensional abilities," she said flatly. "Nice try."

"Worth a shot." I shrugged. "Want some sushi? I can't finish this gargantuan platter myself."

"Why'd you buy an entire sushi boat then?" She demanded. "You some kind of moron who can't count his daddy's money?"

"Nah," I replied. "My parents are dead and buried, and they left me only debts."

"Then how are you affording sushi?"

"Meal cards for the destitute." I shrugged, jiggling my Invader Xim lanyard. "Anywayyys . . . sushi boats are good for breaking the ice between potential art rivals."

I slid the sushi boat over to Katherine, making boat noises and then a crash noise when it collided with her camo-coat-wrapped chest.

Katherine stared at the sushi boat now resting against her bulky coat. "I already told you—I'm not interested in rivals," she muttered, pushing the boat back slightly. "And I haven't even seen a single drawing of yours."

"The lady demands dinner and a show?" I grinned. "Very well. I aim to please."

I reached behind me and pulled out my sketchbook and a set of pens and pencils, my hands already moving across the page.

Katherine stared.

I began drawing with quick, energetic strokes.

The drawing took shape: Katherine, transformed into a massive kaiju-sized version of herself, her dark scales gleaming. She towered over the sushi boat, her tail whipping through the air like a destructive tentacle.

I tagged the boat as *SUSHITANIK,* adding various details to it to make it resemble *Titanic.*

Tiny cat-girl passengers fired smol machine guns at her scales.

Katherine stared at the drawing with goggle-hidden eyes.

"Huh," she muttered. "So you *can* draw, after all." Despite her resistance, her claws reached out and plucked a piece of sushi from the boat.

Iogann leaned over. "Is that . . . me?" He pointed at a tiny version of himself sitting on the edge of the *Sushitanik.*

"Yep," I said, grinning. "Captain Iogann, observing the disaster of his sinking ship due to Katzilla."

The Mothman chuckled appreciatively. Katherine huffed, puffing up like an angry pigeon in her coat.

"Hey, Io, can you feed off drawings of disasters?" I asked.

"What do you mean?"

"Your gateway skill," I elaborated. "Does potential disaster energy work the same way whether it's real or imagined? Like, could a . . . drawing of a potential catastrophe activate your abilities?"

Iogann's gray eyes went wide. "That's . . . an interesting theory. No one's ever asked me that before. I do appreciate watching disaster movies."

"He's got like four hundred terabytes of disaster porn," Katherine commented. "Nothing but plane crashes and earthquakes and other depressing bullshit."

"They're not . . . that!" Iogann protested, blushing with dark grays dancing across his face fluff. "They're . . . research materials!"

"Sure, Jan," Katherine scoffed.

"Hmmm. Can you open a gateway to this drawing of a disaster?" I asked the Mothman.

"I don't think so," he said.

"Want to try it?" I asked with a sly grin.

"Mkay." Iogann pulled out a weathered harmonica from his pocket. His face scrunched up in concentration as he began to play a haunting, discordant melody.

Nothing happened.

"See?" Katherine muttered. "Jan is hopeless. Case closed."

"Maybe there's not enough emotional connection there." I tapped my chin, staring at his harmonica. "Katherine's power, if I understand it correctly, operated on trying to scare me as a target. Maybe you need a target that appeals to you."

"What do you mean?" he asked.

CHAPTER FOURTEEN

Sideways Elevator

The Mothman looked at me with a curious expression.

"What's your favorite disaster film of all time?" I asked.

"*The Day After Tomorrow*," Iogann said without hesitation. "Climate disaster genre. Absolutely perfect blend of scientific speculation and pure, unadulterated chaos."

"Interesting choice." I nodded, already pulling out my phone. "Want to test it?"

"Don't encourage him," Katherine sighed at both of us, throwing more sushi passengers into her mouth.

But Iogann was already leaning forward. "How would we test it?"

I pulled up a high-resolution clip of the movie's most dramatic scene—the massive tsunami hitting New York City. I showed him the clip.

"See this scene playing on my phone as a looped clip? Open the gate to where my phone is," I grinned.

Iogann nodded, pulling out his harmonica. His gray eyes focused intently on the phone screen, watching the tsunami scene.

I slid the phone under the table. "And go," I ordered.

Iogann closed his eyes, bringing the harmonica to his lips. A low, haunting note emerged, unlike any musical sound I'd ever heard. The note seemed to vibrate with potential energy, resonating at a frequency that made the air feel thick and heavy.

His antennae began to pulse with a soft, silvery light.

For a moment, nothing happened.

Then, beneath and above the table, two thin, wavering lines of darkness began to form. It looked like a crack in reality, no wider than a pencil line at first, but slowly expanding.

"Holy shit," Katherine muttered. "You opened a gate . . . in local reality?! To a specific location?! No friggin way."

Iogann's harmonica continued its haunting melody, the two connected gates expanding incrementally.

"Great job!" I grinned at the Mothman.

Iogann's harmonica slipped from his trembling fingers, clattering onto the cafeteria table. The dark circles froze mid-expansion, then began to rapidly contract. I slipped a pencil in between the two to see if the gateway would slice it in half when it closed.

"I . . . I've never done that before," he stammered with dark, wide eyes. "I . . . always opened gates to some distant elsewhere, wherever the song of doomsday was strongest."

"Hum." Katherine leaned forward, examining the gates above and below the table.

"You actually opened a targeted gate. To a specific location from a digital representation. And nobody died. Consider me impressed, Jan."

Iogann's face turned a deep shade of gray. "I can't believe I just . . . I mean, I've watched that movie like a hundred times and never thought to . . . open a gate to it. That's brilliant!"

"Uh-huh." I nodded with a smug look.

The gate closed, and my pencil snapped in half. I waved the pencil remnant at the half-siblings like a maestro.

"This . . . this changes everything," Iogann muttered, his voice growing more confident with each syllable. "I can . . . I can open gates to my favorite movie! I have to tell Em! We can change up the program! We can . . ."

"Hate to burst your bubble, Jan," Katherine interrupted. "You think just because you opened a tiny gate to this idiot's phone, you're suddenly going to revolutionize your troupe's performance?"

Iogann's excited momentum deflated slightly. "But . . . didn't you see? I targeted a specific location! That's never happened before!"

"And?" Katherine raised an eyebrow.

"I . . . well . . . I don't know exactly, but it's something! It's a targeted gate, Kat! Maybe we can go into an actual dungeon and gate out of it to a movie screen and . . ."

"Em is too stupid and too stubborn to permit changes," Katherine cut him down ruthlessly. "I bet she's got her entire performance mapped out to the tee. You really think she'll listen to some random idea you cooked up with this halfwit halfkin four hours before the show begins?" She jerked a thumb at me.

"Halfwit?" I tsked. "I prefer 'innovative disruptive element.'"

Both siblings ignored me.

"I have to try to . . ." Iogann said.

"Good luck dying horribly." Katherine waved him off.

"I'm going to go to the guys in the auditorium and propose this idea right now!"

"Suit yourself." Katherine shrugged, taking another swig from her flask. "Don't come crying to me when she rips your wings off."

As Iogann hurried away, Katherine turned to me. "So. You and Cinder are a thing or something?"

"A thing?" I nearly choked on my sushi piece.

"An item? A couple?" She pressed. "Not that I give a shit, just curious. Didn't take her for a halfkin appreciator. How are you not covered in bruises? Isn't she like fifty times stronger than you?"

"We're not a thing!" I sputtered, my face heating up. "She did kick my van a lot and threatened to break my spine. The usual first date stuff."

"Oh? She kicked your van? And you're . . . what? Charmed by this?"

"Absolutely." I grinned. "Nothing says 'I'm interested' like potential vehicular assault, right?"

"You're obviously somehow fucked in the head," Katherine muttered, taking another swig from her flask. "Completely and totally unhinged."

"So I've been told." I shrugged. "Multiple times, in fact. By multiple people. Mostly Cinder."

Katherine studied me for a long moment.

"You do realize that Cass is completely mental, right? And that Em is going to murder you? In fact, she's going to murder my brother right now. Damn it. Ughhh. Really didn't want to get involved in this shit. Way to go. Way to encourage the troupe of idiots, idiot."

Katherine dumped the rest of the sushi boat into her mouth like some kind of anime hamster, her cheeks puffing out comically. She swallowed it all in one gulp like a snake and rolled away from the table without another word, heading for the elevator.

I followed her, wheeling alongside. "So . . . we're going to save your brother from certain doom?"

"No," she growled back. "I'm going to watch Em murder him and then tell him 'I told you so' after I incarnate his ass. Also, why are you following me?"

"Um . . ." I considered. "I appreciate a good murder-viewing party?"

"Just so you know, I'm not incarnating your ass when Em or one of her minions snaps your spine in half."

"Noted."

The elevator ride was long, with our two wheelchairs taking up most of the space. Katherine fixed me with a piercing glare of dark lenses.

"So," she said as the transparent elevator began to move sideways, her tail lashing slightly in the confined space. "You really got a thing for Quetzalcoatl tail? I can see why Jan chose to talk to you today—a Quetzi and halfkin relationship sounds like a disaster."

"I don't have a 'thing' for Quetzalcoatls," I protested. "I have only met one Quetzi so far. She's rawd, and we are not a disaster. We're . . ."

"Uh-huh. Sure," she interrupted my train of thought. "And I'm just a totally normal, well-adjusted artist who definitely doesn't drink high-grade alcohol during lunch."

"Fair," I conceded. "We're both masters of healthy coping mechanisms. Also, wheee . . . sideways elevator."

The elevator glided left across a multitude of halls. In another minute, its transparent one-way mirror walls revealed a breathtaking art nouveau–style auditorium that looked more like a living, breathing organism than a performance space. Organic curves dominated the architecture, with sweeping lines that mimicked feathered wings and intricate metalwork curving around massive arches.

The walls within the arch hollows were a living canvas of bioluminescent plants—alien flora with translucent petals that shifted colors like mood rings. Tendrils of soft green-and-blue light wove between ornate brass fixtures, creating an ethereal atmosphere that seemed to breathe and pulse with its own rhythm.

Katherine and I disembarked the shiny elevator as the doors slid open on the second floor of the auditorium, a red carpet leading to a dim balcony space almost directly above the stage.

We rolled towards the edge of the balcony, and I looked down.

Iogann stood center stage, his skull-capped wings twitching with nervous energy as he addressed the four girls—Cinder, Emerald, Vespera, and Solace. His wide-brimmed hat was slightly askew, and he was gesticulating wildly with his hands.

"... change everything about our performance!" he insisted, pulling out his phone to show them the video clip from *The Day After Tomorrow*. "I can target gates now! Specifically! To this movie clip!"

Emerald Stratos, the Rubicund Lindworm, stood with her arms crossed, her ruby scales catching the stage lights and casting sharp crimson reflections across the floor. Her gold-orange eyes narrowed dangerously as she listened to Iogann's excited explanation.

"And?" she demanded when he finished.

"I need time," Iogann repeated. "Just a few weeks. Maybe a month. To practice these targeted gates. We should change the date of the show to . . ."

"A month?!" Emerald's red-orange tail lashed dangerously. "We're performing *tonight*! Everything's ready! Quint already sorted everything out with the vice principal! Some other beerch-knobs might have the hall booked in a month!"

"Em, please! As it stands, our show is a looming disaster for everyone involved," the Mothman insisted. "You smell like . . ."

"Like what?" Emerald's gold-orange eyes narrowed.

"Like death." Iogann swallowed. "You're going to die, or someone close to you is going to die tonight."

"Well, no duh, moron." Emerald rolled her eyes. "We're killing a big monster that Cinder's gonna attract. Death is a given."

"No, you don't understand," Iogann pressed on, his voice taking on a desperate edge. "The disaster energy around this stage is . . . overwhelming. We need to postpone, to practice with targeted gates. If I can control where the gates open . . ?"

Emerald's scales flashed with irritation. She snapped her fingers, the sound echoing through the auditorium like a gunshot, dragonfire sparks raining down.

Vespera unfolded from where she'd been lounging on a beanbag, her wings crackling as she hefted an oversized medieval iron mace.

"Soooo, Io," Emerald's voice dripped with false sweetness as Vespera approached with the mace. "How would you prefer it? Quick and messy, or slow and painful? Because those are your only options if you keep suggesting we delay *my* show."

"Em." Cinder stepped forward, her wings flaring protectively. "He's just trying to help. Maybe we should at least hear him out . . ."

"I heard him already! He's obviously chickening out just 'cause he learned some new gate trick! Stay out of this, Ci," Emerald snapped, her ruby scales catching the light like fresh blood. "You're already on thin ice after missing practice."

"I . . ."

"Yeah, you. *You* are far too preoccupied with chasing that damn Nullie around. Why is that?" Emerald demanded.

"That's none of your business." Cinder's wings shifted through defensive shades of gray and red.

"Everything about this troupe is my business," Emerald growled. "I'm the leader. I make the decisions. And right now, I'm deciding that both you and Io are being incredibly annoying."

"Em," Cinder began.

"Shut your yap before you throw off my chill," Emerald snapped. "I've had just about enough of you two spineless musicants questioning my vision. The show goes on tonight. As planned. No changes. The wards and amplifiers are already set up. Next person to suggest changing things last minute is going to get their kneecaps broken. Neither of you needs to have intact knees to make musical noises!"

"Em!" Iogann tried one last time, his antennae drooping. "Please. I can feel it. Something terrible is going to happen to you tonight. We need to . . ."

"You *need* to shut the eff up and do your job," Emerald cut him off. "Open the gate when I tell you to. That's it. That's your only purpose here. You're not the Slayer star, you're not the decision maker, you're just the Gate! Got it?"

"But . . . what if everyone in attendance dies?" Io pressed.

"So what?!" Emerald barked. "You want to stay in this troupe? Everyone has their place in life. Everyone gets XP from the operation. It doesn't matter if everyone in the audience croaks! When more knobtwats die, we benefit. We get stronger. Eff the audience! This is about us gaining levels ten times faster than those delver dorks with their dumbass rules and regulations. Do you want to be weak, pathetic . . . prey again? Well, do you?!"

"No." Iogann deflated, wings dropping.

"That's right, beerch." Emerald grinned with sharp chompers. "'Cause you know what happens to prey in this school."

She inhaled deep.

"Wait." her eyes ignited red from within. "Why do I smell prey nearby? Vee! Check the gallery, make sure there's no rats up there trying to spy on our prep!"

Vespera's black-and-white wings unfurled with a crackle of thunder. She rose into the air heading straight up towards us.

Brilliant electrical currents arced across the medieval mace in her right claws, making it look like a Tesla coil.

Yep. This is how I'm going to die. An electrified mace to the noggin.

Hello, darkness, my old friend.

CHAPTER FIFTEEN

Catastrophe

Katherine's claws suddenly wrapped around my wrist, digging into my skin with inhuman strength. Her grip was cold, almost metallic. A pulse of pure fear rushed from her hand up my spine, making the hair on the back of my neck stand up.

Then darkness swallowed us whole, the glowing plant life of the fancy auditorium and the deadly mace heading our way winking away.

The darkness was absolute, pressing against my eyeballs like a physical weight. I blinked rapidly, trying to adjust, but there was nothing to adjust to.

"Katherine?" I whispered.

A low rumbling growl answered me. Not quite a response, more like a warning.

"Thanks," I said.

Fumbling in my pocket, I found my trusty Pyroxia X-12. The bright screen almost blinded me when I logged in. Two clicks through the apps to the flashlight and then a beam of harsh white light erupted, cutting through the darkness like a knife.

Katherine hissed, bothered by the light.

My phone's light revealed a dark and desolate version of the auditorium we'd just been in.

The organic curves of the art nouveau architecture had warped and rotted, as if something had been slowly consuming the building from the inside out. Massive roots—thick as tree trunks—burst through cracked marble floors and twisted around fallen support columns. Bioluminescent plants that had once pulsed with soft blues and greens now hung like withered, blackened tendrils.

"Sooo . . ." I said. "This is the deep, huh? A parallel Earth where everything went to shit or something?"

"Shut. That. Off," she hissed. "The light attracts things."

"What things?" I turned the flashlight off, switching to the infrared cam.

As if in response, something skittered in the darkness. A sound like chitinous legs scraping against decayed marble echoed through the desolate auditorium.

Katherine's claws tightened on her wheelchair's wheels. "Hungry things. Echoes."

Another skittering sound. Closer this time.

"Follow, unless you want to stay here," the wheelchair-bound Stollwurm ordered.

She somehow rolled over the roots and broken rubble as if they were nothing, using her tail as a lever to overcome random elevation changes.

I stood up and pulled my backpack on, forsaking my wheelchair to the gloom. My footsteps crunched on random detritus and roof tiles.

The chitinous skittering sounds continued, sometimes seeming to come from above, sometimes below, sometimes directly behind us. But nothing emerged from the darkness.

"Stop breathing so loudly," Katherine hissed.

"I'm not breathing loudly," I whispered back. "You're breathing loudly."

A low growl rumbled from her throat. "Do you want to get eaten?"

"Not particularly," I replied.

Another skittering sound—closer this time. Something metallic scraped against the rubble nearby.

Katherine's wheelchair froze. Her tail went absolutely still.

"Don't. Move," she breathed.

I froze mid-step, one foot hovering just above a broken piece of ceiling.

The skittering sound circled us. Not random anymore. Deliberate. Calculating. Something was hunting us.

Then Katherine's eyes ignited with green fire, and my heart skidded to a stop.

Pure, concentrated fear radiated from her like an explosion—as if someone had distilled absolute dread into a psychic weapon and was broadcasting it on all frequencies.

The skittering stopped. I heaved, unable to move a muscle, my entire body shaking.

Absolute silence descended, so thick I could hear my own heartbeat thundering in my ears.

Katherine's tail wrapped around my waist, yanking me closer to her wheelchair. "Move. Now."

We quickly rolled/moved to the end of the balcony. Her movements were fluid, exact—as though she'd navigated this dark landscape countless times before.

We reached the elevator shaft, but the elevator itself was conspicuously absent. Through the infrared cam, I saw a gaping vertical tunnel stretching up into impenetrable blackness, with rusted maglev bits and cables hanging like dead spiderwebs.

"No elevator," I whispered. "Now what?"

Katherine's tail tightened around my waist, making my ribs ache. She positioned her wheelchair at the shaft's edge.

A weaker pulse of pure weaponized dread ran from Katherine's tail across my body.

The darkness began to gradually dissolve, the outline of the elevator manifesting through the gloom. Katherine tapped her card, and the barely visible elevator doors slid open. She shoved me inside and then pressed one of the barely visible buttons. The gloom slowly receded in its entirety as the elevator rapidly flew out of the auditorium.

Emerald and the others were still on stage. Vespera had landed back near them, looking dissatisfied with lack of mace-smiting.

I glanced at Katherine.

"So, um, is my wheelchair gone forever now?" I asked.

She turned her head to me, slipping dark goggles back on to hide her weary-looking emerald eyes.

"No," she said. "I can get it . . . later. Also, since when can you walk normally?"

"A miracle cure through pure, undistilled terror!" I proclaimed dramatically, jazz-handing my suddenly mobile legs. "Who knew being hunted by unspeakable horrors was such effective physical therapy?"

"You're telling me," she said slowly, tail arming up to whip me as she pressed a button to halt the elevator halfway between floors, "that you needed a wheelchair because of a concussion, but you can walk just fine now?"

"Yes. To be honest," I began, "I was pretty dizzy, so the nurse ordered me to stay in a chair . . . but then I had a rather intense encounter with the Genesis Pool this morning, which may have . . . recalibrated some of my bodily functions."

Her tail whip slowed. "What?"

"I jumped into the Genesis Pool," I said. "While being alive."

"You did *what*?" she stammered out, tail coming down.

"Jumped. Into. The. Genesis. Pool," I repeated, enunciating each word as she did in the deep. "While alive. Helped me walk."

Katherine's mouth opened and closed as if she were fishing for words.

"What . . . that is possibly the most ridiculous thing I've heard so far from you," she finally let out.

"What? Full-blooded Omnids don't go swimming in the Genesis Pool for shits and giggles?" I asked.

"Obviously not!" she barked. "The Lazarus Cavern is one of the most sacred spaces to Skyfall! It's one of the foundational artifacts; the Academy was literally built around and above it! To submerge yourself in it . . . while being still alive is unthinkable blasphemy! Nazareth! Have you no effin' shame?!"

"Eh." I shrugged. "I'm not from here. Nobody told me that I couldn't swim in it. Didn't think it was that big a deal. Cass . . . err, Cinder pulled me out of it twice now with her hands. Doesn't that count?"

"It's completely different . . . pulling someone out is fine, idiot!" Katherine growled, her tail lashing against her wheelchair. "Brief contact to help resurrect someone versus . . . how long were you under there?! Were you fully submerged?"

"Dove in pretty deep, yep." I nodded. "I think I was under a few minutes?"

"Slayer!" Katherine choked. "Do you have any idea what that could have done to you? It could have shattered your mind or grown another you inside you, killing you in a truly horrific way! Abyss, it could have broken your Lazarus bracelet!"

"I'm fine," I assured her. "Actually, I saw something interesting in there. A girl. Silver-blue hair, orange vest. Sound familiar?"

Katherine went absolutely still. Her tail stopped mid-lash, her body frozen like a statue.

"What?" she whispered.

I repeated the description. "Fractal crack on the side of her head. Called herself Alexa. Ring any bells?"

Katherine's goggles slipped slightly, revealing a flash of intense emerald eyes. "That," she muttered, "that's . . . not possible."

"Apparently quite possible." I shrugged. "She said something about 'brain spiders' and 'System Wizards.' Any context?"

Katherine's wheelchair jerked violently, spinning to face me directly. "Where. Did. You. Hear. Those. Words?"

"Under the Genesis Pool," I said. "She had these quirky jump shoes on and a safety vest. I think that she also lives in a treehouse made from stolen signs. The town of Saint Mary?"

"No." Katherine shook her head violently, her face going pale beneath her scales. "That's . . . it's just my imagination. My art. You must have seen my sketches and . . ."

"I didn't see her shoes in your art," I pointed out. "Or the treehouse. So, either we're suffering from some sort of a collective delusion . . . or . . ."

"She can't be real!" Katherine barked. "Someone like that can't exist!"

"Why not?" I arched an eyebrow.

"Because . . ." Katherine's tail lashed violently. "Because she's . . . she was purposefully written to win at everything, like a skeleton key designed to open any door with social hacking. She's not real, you absolute knob! She's just a character from a story I wrote when I was young! About another . . . alternative Earth, a world filled with superheroes and villains . . . without Omnids . . . where . . . where everything turns out just fine in the end! Real life doesn't work like that!"

She sniffed. I remained silent, contemplating her words.

"It's . . . a world . . . where I'm not broken and sick," she let out. "Where I can run really fast . . . It's just a fictional story where a girl named Alexa found a lonely girl named Katherine Kells and helped her, uplifted her to become something more . . ."

Katherine trailed off, her tail drooping. "But that's all it is. A novel, that no Omnid would ever read because it features super-powered humans. Just my dumb imagination. Just my stupid art that most people aren't interested in 'cause it portrays four humans as the protagonists. You couldn't have seen her shoes or the treehouse. You're lying. You have to be!"

"I'm not lying," I said softly. "She hugged me. Called me her minion . . . 'Mittens.' Said something about me needing to find all four of us and to never stop. Said she loved me. Which was weird because I've never met her before. At least . . . I don't think I have."

"Stop it. Just . . . stop. You're messing with me. *This isn't funny!*" Katherine snarled loudly. She pulled her goggles off, her eyes filled with tears.

"Not trying to be funny," I said. "Just telling you what I saw. What I experienced. Maybe we're both crazy. Maybe the Genesis Pool showed me your memories somehow. Or maybe . . . Alexa is real."

Green-silver eyes looked at me. "You're not Martin Kilborne! You're not a character from my story, you look . . . act nothing like him! Stop trying to be someone that you are . . ."

"What . . . did you just say?" I stammered out.

"Martin Kilborne," Katherine repeated. "The second MC from my book about superheroes. Alexa's first minion. Her best friend. Her love interest. Why am I even telling you this shit?" Her voice dropped.

My brain careened sideways. *Either Katherine was a monster who had somehow manipulated me, used her psychic wurm powers to learn my real name, or . . .*

Or something far more impossible was happening.

"Katherine . . . how do you know that name?" I whispered.

"I told you," she growled back. "I made it up! Imagined it! For a book!"

"Nuh-uh." I shook my head. "Not possible."

"What the Abyss are you on about?" she demanded, wiping her tears with a sleeve.

I studied Katherine carefully, weighing my options. Her emerald eyes blazed with an ocean of anger, confusion, and something deeper—a raw, vulnerable hope that she was desperately trying to suppress.

"Tell me about this story of yours," I said carefully.

Katherine's tail lashed defensively. "Why should I tell you anything?"

"Because," I said as I leaned forward, my voice low and sharp, "either you're playing an incredibly elaborate mind game, or something truly screwy is happening. Something that I would consider insane . . . at least before I dove headfirst into the Genesis Pool. Just tell me more about Alexa, please."

"Absolutely not. I am *not* letting you mock my writing. You've spent this entire day mocking me as it is!"

"Sorry," I sighed. "That's a thing I do. I cope with how effed up my life is by being a clown. I was just trying to . . . make you smile, derail you sideways from your depresso-state, I swear."

"That doesn't make me feel any better!" Katherine pulled her dark goggles back on.

"I'm not simply trying to . . .!" I stammered out. "I just want to understand what's going on. I thought that I had everything sorted. I had accounted for absolutely everything, made plans, came to this place . . . and now everything is careening sideways, like a freight train that encountered a giant boulder on the tracks and is now flying off a bridge."

"Sounds like a *you* problem," she said. "And I don't have the energy to deal with whatever mixie issues you have."

I stared at her, a cocktail of frustration and desperation bubbling up inside me. "Come on, Katherine. I just saw a girl who looks exactly like a character from your stories inside the Genesis Pool. That's not a coincidence!"

Katherine's tail lashed aggressively. "Coincidences happen all the time. You're reading too much into this!"

"Am I?" I challenged. "You literally just said my . . . birth name—Martin Kilborne—a name I've never told anyone here. A name from a story you claim to have written."

She went very still then, as still as the transparent elevator hung in a dim space between two floors.

"What?" She finally asked. "Is this another stupid joke?"

"Follow," I said, pressing the *M* button for the main entrance.

The elevator hummed as it moved sideways and then down, following the complex path to the main entrance.

In another few minutes, Katherine's wheelchair rolled silently behind me as I strode through the empty halls, my footsteps echoing against the polished white marble floors.

The afternoon sun cast long shadows across the parking lot as I approached my beat-up van, still bearing the fresh boot dents from Cinder's assault. Katherine followed silently like a shark through deep water.

I yanked open the back doors, climbing inside. The See-Mass lights flickered on automatically, casting a soft glow over the interior. Katherine positioned her wheelchair at the entrance, watching intently as I dug through my backpack.

"Here," I said, pulling out a worn sleeve from a Nazarite Bible. Inside was my original birth certificate, carefully preserved in a plastic sleeve. *Martin J. Kilborne. Born in Znetc Reservation, North Acadia.*

Katherine leaned forward, peering through the dark goggles at the birth certificate. Her tail twitched slightly as she studied the document.

"This . . . this can't be real," she muttered.

"Oh, it's real," I said. "Genuine, certified copy. Issued by the North Acadian Reservation Authority."

"But . . ." Katherine's voice trailed off. She reached out with a clawed hand, then pulled back as if the document might burn her. "It can't! How could it?! Wait."

Her expression suddenly grew cold, lips pursed. "Did . . . Cass tell you about the story I was writing? Did you print this at a shop to mess with me? This is some kind of a stupid prank, isn't it? Ha ha. Very funny. Make fun of a dying girl who can't even . . ."

My eye twitched. I dug into my bag again and shoved my North Acadian passport at her face.

"I don't know what's going on either. But this is who I am. Martin J. Kilborne. Born in North Acadia!" I insisted, laying out all the cards in a desperate hope that she would listen.

"Nuh-uh. Nope. You're Alexander Glock," she said, shoving the passport and birth certificate back at me. "I checked your pics on Omnigram after you added me to your friends list. Quit screwing with me!"

I threw the documents back into my bag, my face burning. I only had myself to blame for this. My manufactured backstory was made too solid, too . . . *real.*

I'd created an entire social media footprint for Alexander Glock—a variety of scattered mentions and tagged photos to survive an Omnid Scrutimancer's background check. Strategic posts about growing up with my human mother, some angst about my father, and the occasional comment about struggling with my Nullie identity. The kind of digital breadcrumbs that made a person feel *very* real at a glance. I even posted tons of AI-modded photos of me studying in the conveniently burned down Nazarite private school in Southeastern Acadia. There was an entire gallery of AI-generated photos of me standing next to my Thunderbird "father" in various tourist spots during See-Mass.

I had played myself into a corner, and because of it, whatever otherworldly, inexplicable link existed between me and Katherine was quickly fraying.

"Welp," she murmured. "Thanks for nothin'. I hope you get lots of views out of this on Omnigram later. Har har."

"Wait," I called after Katherine as she turned her wheelchair away. "I can explain . . ."

"Save it," she snapped, her tail lashing angrily. "I don't know what kind of game you're playing, but I'm done. You're clearly just another manipulative asshole who somehow found out about my private writing and decided to use it to troll me hard . . . just like the others did. Just like . . . Em and Cass."

"That's not . . . I would never . . ." I stammered out.

"I said save it!" Her voice cracked. "You want to know the worst part? For a moment there, I actually thought . . . I actually hoped . . . that I finally found someone that I could be friends with . . ." She trailed off, her shoulders slumping.

"Katherine, please . . ." I said.

"Don't," she whispered. "Just . . . don't. I'm genuinely not amused with whatever this is! An attempt to impress your Quetzi GF? Or a way to get out of the friend zone and into her bedroom? Maybe a clever way to get Emerald to permit your halfsie pink-skin ass into their inner circle as a sixie fetchling? Whatever. Go, watch their anti-delving show. I hope you die or get a memetic stuck in your head. I don't care. Never talk to me again."

I stood frozen by my van, watching Katherine roll away.

Just like when I saw Cassiopeia's rainbow-wings for the first time, I found myself completely shattered, speechless.

No witty comeback. No clever deflection. No carefully crafted lie to smooth things over. No way to fix this mess.

Some part of me wanted to chase after her, to tell her everything, but my legs refused to move, my mind spinning uselessly like a computer caught in an infinite loop. Out of all the scams I'd pulled, all the identities I'd crafted, all the careful plans I'd made . . . *nothing* had prepared me for this awful moment where the truth actually mattered but was buried too deep under my manufactured lies.

There was no script for this situation. No pre-planned contingency. No clever way to explain how I could be both Alexander Glock and Martin Kilborne without sounding completely insane or like an absolute dick who generated excessively elaborate pranks to troll people.

I watched Katherine disappear up the front stairwell.

What could I even say to her? "Hey, sorry about the fake identity thing, but I'm actually the character from your story who somehow exists in real life too, and I have no idea how or why? I actually came to Skyfall, faked my entire identity to make the Frontenachii Omnicorp and the Omnithornia Superstate officials pay for what they did to my human mom?" Yeah, that would go over real well.

I climbed into my van, shutting the doors behind me with trembling hands. The colorful lights cast their soft glow over the interior, but they did nothing to dispel the hollow, throbbing feeling in my chest.

For the first time since arriving at Skyfall, I felt completely and utterly lost. The carefully constructed facade of Alexander Glock—the overly cheerful, slightly nerdy transfer student who used jokes as weapons—crumbled away, leaving only the raw truth underneath.

The me that I didn't want to look at. The me that let my mom suffer all alone, pushed her away.

Truth that I had no idea how to deal with, now featuring jagged, multidimensional edges that weren't helping one bit.

I glanced at the small mirror mounted on my van's wall, and for a split second, crystalline-blue eyes stared back at me instead of my usual green-brown ones. I blinked hard, and they were gone, replaced by my normal reflection.

CHAPTER SIXTEEN

Pre-Show

skipped the rest of my classes, thanks to the nurse's medical-leave note. My van became my sanctuary of frustration, the beanbag chair swallowing me whole as I stared at the ceiling, replaying my disastrous conversation with Katherine over and over.

"Yulia," I called out, "play 'Omnithornication' by Cinder."

Cinder's voice filled the van, raw and passionate.

The emotion in her performance of "Omnithornication" made me feel marginally better, like a silver iridescent rain shower pouring over me. It made the hole in my chest hurt marginally less.

How had everything gone sideways so quickly? How had Katherine wormed herself into my heart? Why did losing her friendship, accidentally making her feel bad feel worse than drowning?

"It's the edge of the world, the heart of Omnid civilization / The sun may rise in the East, at least it settled in a final location / It's understood that Cradlefall sells Omnithornication," I sang along with Cinder.

"Yulia, analyze Katherine's words about her story," I ordered in Kaska when the song finished. "Look for any mentions of Martin Kilborne or Alexa in her social media history."

"No results found," Yulia replied.

I sighed. "Yulia, what do you think is happening? What did I screw up?"

"Insufficient data for a meaningful answer," she responded. "Anomalous variables detected disconnected from overall pattern. Recommendation: Gather more information before drawing conclusions."

"Helpful," I muttered sarcastically. "Pretty up Christi's pics in the Lazarus Cavern and post the best ones on my Omnigram tagging her in them. Let's see if my social score increases."

"Can do."

I closed my eyes, listening to Cinder's other songs for the rest of my free time.

My phone buzzed, interrupting my musical reverie. A message from an unknown number on Omnigram.

Unknown: Don't come to the show. Stay away.

The number wasn't saved in my contacts. I stared at it. Pfff, yeah okay. I typed in a response and clicked send.

Alex G: Who be?
Unknown: A friend.
Alex G: I'm not hearing a name, frien. Why shouldn't I attend Oodwarts, Dobby?"
Unknown: 💀 It's going to be a catastrophe.
Alex G: Is that you, Iogann? Way to out yourself. How'd you get my contact?

No response came. My message hung there, unanswered. Maybe Em told him to stop texting and focus on show prep.

Another text popped up immediately after.

Vesp⛈️: Hey mixie! Come to our show. Auditorium in 30. Front row. VIP pass. 🎟️
Alex G: Why the sudden invite?
Vesp⛈️: Saw yo Omnigram pics of Christi in Lazarus Cavern. Bring yo cam! I want my best angles captured.
Alex G: I heard from Io that Em is pissed. Don't want to get chopped up "accidentally" by a flame sword.
Vesp⛈️: Pff. She's never not pissed. Don't be a wuss. If you get chopped in half, I'll incarnate ya.
Alex G: Free incarnation, huh? Sounds like a deal. But what's the catch?
Vesp⛈️: No catch! Just want some killer shots slayin' shit for my socials. U tots the best photographer in the school right no
Alex G: Been here two days. Not sure that's a high bar.
Vesp⛈️: 😂U funny. comin or not?
Alex G: Only if u protec me and my equipment from possibl dragon-ree. can't bless u with quality shots if I'm dead.
Vesp⛈️: Deal. I'll keep u safe w m ⚡. Front row VIP pass incoming.

A ping. An electronic ticket materialized in my Omnigram inbox.

VIP PASS: FRONT ROW—THE DREADFUL DELVERS SLAYER PERFORMANCE, SEAT 17A

Free front row seats? With Vespera's protection? Seemed like things were looking up! I guessed that Kat pulled me into the deep before Vespera spotted us. Or this was a ruse and maybe I was going to get murdered. Either way, the show would hopefully distract me from the Katherine-induced sulk.

I pulled on all of my stolen hexamesh suits and grabbed my camera bag, checked my equipment, and headed towards the auditorium. The VIP pass glowed softly in my Omnigram app as I scanned it at the entrance door, the digital golden ticket promising front-row access to what was apparently going to be a disastrous show. The ward let me into the mostly empty auditorium. A large table at the front featured plentiful snacks from the cafe.

Don't mind if I do.

Lance and Christi were there already.

Cinder's brother stood near the side entrance, a gray bulky figure. His orange eyes were narrowed with obvious tension, scanning the auditorium repeatedly as if expecting something to go wrong.

The Cherufe girl paced closer to the stage, in another pink-purple suit-dress. Her flames flickered erratically. She too seemed stressed.

"Sup, L-man?" I asked.

Lance spun to me as if spooked, then relaxed.

"Helping Cassi . . . err, Cinder," he exhaled. "Just went through final ward checks."

"Good stuff. I'd help but I don't know enough about wards," I said. "Also, you don't have to twist yourself into a pretzel in front of me."

"What do you mean?" Lance blinked.

"You can say 'Cassie' around me, if you feel like it. I'm not the Kaleid name enforcement agency," I said.

"It's just . . . it's been hard, you know? One day Cassie was my little sister, and then suddenly . . . I have to say *Cinder* all the time and pretend like we aren't related or whatever." His fists opened and closed.

"Don't worry. I'll sort it out." I said.

"Sort it out?" He blinked at me. "What? . . . How?"

"Give me forty-two hours," I added.

"What? You've known her for, what, two days?" Lance pointed out. "I've been trying to help Cass with . . . her issues for so many years. And you think you can just . . ."

"I don't operate by the rules you've all built around yourselves," I said. "There are no boxes. Come back with your complaint in forty-two hours if it's still unresolved."

He crossed his arms.

"I already made her smile. I can make you smile, too. She's totally warming up to me." I said.

"Hrm. She doesn't usually . . . warm up to people this quickly. Or at all, really."

"Really?" I feigned surprise. "She seemed perrrrfectly friendly after chasing me down kicking my van a few dozen times."

His eyes widened. "She . . . did what?"

"Cassie is very angry," I told him. "She's hurting, and I'm not going to stop until I figure out why. Maybe it's because of the troupe and Em, maybe it's something else. Regardless of what the issue is, I'm going to untangle it."

I put my hand on his tense-looking shoulder.

"Promise." I looked into his orange eyes.

"Cassie—I mean, Cinder doesn't like it when other Omnids try to 'figure her out,'" he warned.

"Good thing I'm mostly human then." I grinned.

Lance stared at me, clearly having little faith in my capabilities.

"Oh! Alex!" Christi flared slightly, approaching us. "I was gonna ask if you wanted to come to the show! Totally spaced out with all the . . . stuff going on. Sorry."

"S'fine." I shrugged. "Vespera sent me a ticket."

"Vespera invited you?" Lance blinked. "Really? How'd you pull that off?"

"I'm good with people." I shrugged again. "Vee's nice."

Lance and Christi exchanged a look that suggested they doubted my statement.

The auditorium was filling rapidly. Students crowded into seats, arms full of catering food, their excited chatter creating a dull roar. Magical wards shimmered subtly around the stage—intricate geometric patterns that pulsed with soft blues and greens.

"So, where you guys sitting at?" I asked.

"We were asked not to be here," Lance sighed.

"Aw. You ain't watching the show, then?"

"Cass and Em don't want us here," Christi sighed.

"The Student Council is permitted to assist with general prep but banned from attending," Lance nodded. "Em thinks we'll interfere with the show by being annoying. Or worse, try to stop her."

"Stop her from doing what?" I asked.

Christi's flames flickered nervously. "Summoning something . . . *really dangerous.*"

"Isn't summoning a giant demon the point of this whole shebang?" I asked.

The couple exchanged a look. Christi whispered something into her boyfriend's ear. He nodded and glanced around and then slipped a runestone into my fingers, his gray claws trembling ever so slightly.

Then both of them rapidly retreated as if they didn't even know me. I put the runestone into my pocket and went to my assigned seat, setting up my equipment. I set up a Ricoh 360-degree camera on a tripod in front of me to capture the audience reactions as well as the performers.

My phone buzzed almost immediately after with a text from Christi:

C-iris 🏵: Hi. I convinced Lance to give you the ward control runestone. I trust you. Use it . . . if . . . when things go bad.

Alex G: Use it how? Can it stop the summoning?

C-iris 🏵: No, since the summoning is performed by Io, it can't be stopped.

C-iris 🏵: diagram.pdf

C-iris 🏵: These are emergency ward-focus runes. If pressed in the correct sequence as listed in this manual, they can create a temporary full-dome barrier around the bearer. The second sequence listed will produce a much stronger shield facing away from the central hexagram. The performers will have similar stones. Don't show it off unless you're targeted. Em has the master one, she could disable yours if she suspects anything.

Alex G: So basically a get-out-of-death-free card? Thanks!

C-iris 🏵: More like a precaution. Whatever Cass summons might be able to punch right through the shield. Create a dome as soon as something comes through. It'll help keep any mental effects out.

Alex G: Mental effects? What kind?

C-iris 🏵: I don't know. Bad, intrusive thoughts. There's no consistency with Io's gates!

Alex G: Thanks, Pink Chancellor. Really appreciate the aid.

C-iris✿: Protect Cass . . . if you can. Lance might not show it, but he's super worried that she'll get hurt. She will have her own shield-stone, but if you get close to her, the effect will stack.

Alex G: Understood. Over n out.

The auditorium lights began to dim. The crowd stirred. I heard snickers behind me.

"Dreadful Delvers? More like . . . dreadful losers," a Sasquatch behind me commented.

"Bet you ten bucks something goes wrong," a Thunderbird whispered loudly to her friend.

"Make that fifty," her Lamia friend replied with a laugh, waving her phone. "I'ma record how badly they fuck up this time. Gonna get all the clicks on Omnigram. Surprised Graves let 'em perform in school."

"Yeah. Did you see what happened last time?" the Thunderbird continued. "Those idiots nearly opened a gate to some flesh-hellscape during the Spring's End Festival!"

"Surprised you came at all," the Laima commented.

"Pff, I ain't a pansy." The Thunderbird rolled her eyes, tapping on her massive jewel-hexagram on a necklace. "Got a personal ward barrier. Best shit Mom's company could get. Pro delver stuff. Would take an LV 125 monster to punch through one of these babies."

More snickers and whispers.

"Heard Em's gotten even more unhinged since the festival . . ." someone laughed. "Like, full-on psycho beerch mode."

"Her Moth griftwit can't even open a gate to a normal dungeon. It's always random shite."

"And that Quetzi Bard Altnil?" Another voice chimed in. "Total fake. Pretending to be all dark and edgy with that Kaleid name bullshit . . ."

My hands tightened on my camera.

"Yeah, what kind of twitbrain name is 'Cinder,' anyway?" a Kelpie sneered. "She ain't no fire elemental."

"Big-time daddy issues, obvs."

I hadn't expected this much escalation—this gleeful anticipation of failure, this barely concealed hostility. The audience wasn't here to support D&D. They were here for the spectacle, waiting for a catastrophe.

Ten minutes. Enough time.

I got out of my spot and walked across the rows, discreetly pointing my Yulia-connected hidden wrist cam at every single face, using the AI to find their Omnibook profiles and names.

The AI rapidly identified and tagged each sneering face. Most of them were from wealthy families. Trust fund kids and their sixies looking for entertainment at others' expense.

I returned to my seat just as the house lights dimmed completely and the red curtain dramatically slid apart.

Fog rolled across the stage, and a single spotlight illuminated Emerald as she strode out.

Her ruby mane caught the spotlight, sending crimson reflections flickering across the walls. She wore what appeared to be gold-plated magisteel armor, stylized with dragon motifs and studded with an ungodly amount of gaudy oversized rubies etched with defense hexagrams. A massive magisteel sword hung from her side. Her whole getup could probably buy an entire town in North Acadia.

"Welcome, prey," she announced via a magitek microphone, her voice carrying easily across the auditorium. "Tonight, you'll witness true power. True hunting. True predation! The Dreadful Delvers will show you what *real* dungeoneering looks like!"

More snickers from the audience. Emerald scoffed at the people in attendance with gold-orange eyes. She dropped the microphone and stepped on it, crushing it underfoot with a deafening feedback noise. I knew that she could project her voice without it—she meant to do it as part of her act.

The audience fell silent, wincing.

Iogann emerged from the fog in his oversized hat and hippie shawl, skull-capped wings trailing behind him. Vespera and Solace joined Emerald's side, wrapped in lavish medieval armor. The Thunderbird had the mace she had nearly used against me, and the Olgoi-Khorkhoi carried an enormous executioner's axe.

And then Cinder walked out. Unlike the Slayer and Knights trio, she wasn't wearing armor. A dark headband, almost like the one from my drawing, pulled her feathery mane back. Her entire figure and wings were dark gray, her face twisted into a scowl.

Vespera spotted me and sent me an exaggerated wink. I lifted my DSLR, taking photos of everyone on stage. The camera clicked rapidly, capturing each member of the Dreadful Delvers in sharp detail.

Cinder spotted me, and her face went slack.

What the fuck are you doing here? Who invited you?! her expression asked.

I grinned and waved, making sure to catch her momentary look of shock on camera. She quickly recovered, her wings flashing with red, which immediately faded back to dark gray and black.

"Gate!" Emerald barked, swinging her oversized sword in the air.

Iogann stepped forward, pulling out his old harmonica. He slowly raised it to his face.

Then he hesitated, his harmonica trembling slightly at his lips. Something flickered in his gray eyes—doubt, fear, resistance.

"*Gate!*" Emerald barked again, her voice carrying an unnatural resonance that made my skull vibrate. "Find a true disaster for me! Something truly high level!"

My hands suddenly twitched, trying to reach for . . . something. A gateway-opening artifact which I didn't even have? I wasn't even a Gater. The compulsion faded as quickly as it came, leaving me disturbed. Emerald's commands clearly contained some kind of powerful mind control magic.

Iogann's body went rigid, his resistance crumbling as if overridden by something stronger than his will. The harmonica touched his lips, and haunting, alien music began. It danced across the stage, carrying with it deep, gut-wrenching, awfully somber tones.

The haunting notes from Iogann's harmonica twisted through the air like living things, layered atop one another, each tone carrying almost a physical manifestation of utter doom. The melody wasn't just music—it was a dirge, a funeral march for reality itself.

Dark lines began to dance across the stage floor, at first thin as pencil marks, then widening like cracks in the foundation of the world. They moved with horrible purpose, spiraling outward from where Iogann stood, leaving trails of wispy darkness in their wake.

The lines converged and began to fold upward, defying gravity as they wove themselves into a perfect circle hanging in the air. The edge of the gateway rippled like the surface of an oil slick, colors that shouldn't exist bleeding through from whatever lay beyond.

"Bard!" Emerald commanded Cinder. "Draw our prey through!"

Again, I almost started to sing right then and there, Emerald's orders affecting me on a fundamental level. I bit my tongue to silence myself.

Cinder stepped forward, her wings suddenly unfurling in a burst of iridescent color that made my brain short-circuit. The dark grays and blacks exploded into a living rainbow that danced across all of her feathers like aurora borealis.

Then she began to sing.

If her performance in music class had been impressive, this was transcendent, divine. Her voice carried otherworldly harmonics that seemed to resonate with something buried in the depths of my soul. She called out to me like a siren, like a charisma goddess, like the most beautiful, most precious thing in the universe.

I suddenly bumped into the stage wall, my feet carrying me forward without my conscious control. In another minute, I was somehow at the side stairwell. The audience behind me erupted in laughter as I rushed up the stairwell and stumbled against the magical barrier separating the crowd from the performers.

"Look at the dumb Nullie!" someone called out. "He's totally enthralled!"

"Pathetic!" another voice jeered. "Can't even resist basic bardic magic!"

My hands pressed against the shimmering barrier as Cinder's voice wrapped around my mind like silk threads, pulling me towards her. Her wings were a kaleidoscope of colors that made my eyes water, her voice irresistibly alluring.

The world beyond her ceased to exist—there was only her voice, her wings, her presence drawing me in like a powerful electromagnetic pull would pick up a metal flake.

Through my Cinder-induced haze, I dimly registered movement from the gateway. Something tall and lanky began to push through, distorting the circular opening in reality like a membrane being stretched to its limits.

Cinder's song cut off abruptly as she retreated behind the armed slayers.

Emerald's sword ignited with blinding flames.

"That's it, beerch," she growled. "Commere. Time to die."

CHAPTER SEVENTEEN

Corpseworld Caretaker I

As Cinder stopped singing and my mind rapidly cleared, I pulled the magic rock from my pocket, my finger quickly tapping out the shield-bubble sequence. The gems under my finger pulsed, and a barely invisible bubble of something formed around me.

The Io-made gateway slick layer suddenly popped, revealing a desolate apocalyptic landscape filled with toppled, hollowed out skyscrapers. A truly monstrous cube-shaped megastructure loomed in the background with an impossibly massive dark letter G on it. The skyscrapers didn't make sense—the broken buildings and the cube were too tall, somehow defying perspective, stretching up endlessly into the broiling sky.

A figure stepped onto the stage with a creak of grimy leather boots.

It was . . . a person in a dark gas mask, a blueish dark long coat, and a red-trim cap. The lines and shadows on the mask made it resemble an eerie smile. Violet lenses moved across the crowd and settled on Emerald. A dark leather glove held a lighter, violet flame, flickering and sending sparks flying out of the gate.

"Oh my, what a big shiny burning sword you have!" The gas mask boomed with a distinctively merry, French-German accent. "I do hope it's not too heavy for you!"

"*Die!*" Emerald swung her sword forward, flames trailing in its wake.

Then something inexplicable happened. The figure simply stepped sideways, away from the burning sword. Emerald yelped, somehow completely missing her target. She careened right into the gateway, burning sword and girl smashing into the snowy, rubble-covered landscape beyond.

All of the artifacts on her ignited, and then she started screaming and flailing madly, trailing smoke. Her burning sword fell out of her fingers, and the flames sputtered and winked out, dark cracks running along the edge of the magisteel blade.

I watched with wide eyes as Emerald's gaudy, overpriced magitek hexagrammic gemstones popped one by one like cracked walnuts. Then the top level armor melted off her body like a peeled onion. The hexamesh outfit under it evaporated away, and her skin began to come apart as if eaten away by something invisible.

The audience erupted in shocked screams of their own. The gas-masked figure tilted the mask, violet lenses now scanning the remaining performers.

"Em!" Solace screamed, charging forward with her battle-axe raised.

"Guten Tag!" the gas-masked figure declared in the same overly cheerful accent, completely ignoring Solace's charge. "How delightfully unexpected! Is zat a vintage 1658 executioner's axe? Be careful not to trip!"

Solace suddenly tripped on absolutely nothing, her axe flying up. She rolled badly, somehow breaking her arm with a yelp as she tangled up in her own cape. Her own axe landed onto her back, nailing her to the floor. She choked and thrashed and then passed out from the pain.

"C'est la vie! Violence is bad for zhe soul." The gas-masked thing snapped the lighter shut and stowed it away, the voice far too loud, making my eardrums throb.

"What the eff are you?!" Vespera circled the invincible entity, her black-and-white wings wide as electrical currents danced up her mace.

The Thunderbird looked absolutely terrified, her expression askew with panic.

Behind the gate, Emerald was already turning into a gurgling soup, flesh flaking and melting off her bones. Her armor had completely flaked off her body, covered in widening cracks. Her overpriced sword groaned and shattered in half.

"Bonjour, madame! I am Zee Captain," the being from beyond said jovially, somehow speaking what my mind interpreted as bold, purple-tinted words. "Anointed sovereign, emissary of humanity, prescient governor and lady of all things in Captania, the Great and Powerful System Wizard!"

The hair on the back of my neck stood up.

System Wizard. Fuck, fuck, fuck.

"My, my, such a whimsical audience," Zee Captain declared, walking towards the stairwell where I stood like an idiot, frozen from shock. The being's boots crossed the ward, and it simply popped away, as if it didn't even exist, hexagrams all around shattering as wardstones overloaded. The runestone in my pocket ignited and shattered, scorching my hexasuit-wrapped hand.

The audience gasped, choked, and made noises of pure terror.

"Cryptids and monsters learning magic, and is zat a . . . token human photographer? How delightful!" The gaze of violet, glowing lenses settled on me.

I gulped. Whatever this thing was, it was somehow scanning me, digging into my head, defining absolutely everything about me with a mere glance.

"Ah! Martin, is it?" Zee Captain's voice carried an unsettling echo. "You remind me of my number one minion. Go on, take a picture! I know you want to!"

My trembling hands raised the camera to my face. Something horrid was happening within the viewfinder as if the camera wasn't pointed at a person in a coat. There was nothing and everything on the little display, a trailing shawl made from impossible, incomprehensible shapes made up of endless dark limbs and endless violet lenses. The camera clicked.

All eyes turned to me.

"The Nullie's a . . . human?" someone in the audience choked.

"Whoopsie. Did I spoil ze plot twist?" Zee Captain tapped a gloved finger on the perpetually smiling mask. "My sincerest apologies, mon ami!"

"Don't listen to this thing, you knobs! It's an abomination from a dead world! It's clearly trying to mess with our heads!" Cinder suddenly rushed to my side, her wings flaring wide.

"Oho!" Zee Captain clapped dark gloved hands together. "A lady . . . Quetzalcoatl defends her chosen hero! How romantique! Cassiopeia Nova? A very spacey name!"

Cinder choked.

"Sh-shut up!" she snarled, her feathers bristling. "Whatever you are, you're not welcome here!"

"Not welcome, am I?" Zee Captain pressed a hand to a dark blue coat and black scarf-wrapped chest in mock offense. "But you called me to you with your lovely song, little moosikal bird. Right through zat charming, illegal gate! Now why would you invite me in, if you clearly don't have a tea party set for my person? Hrmmm?"

Behind the Captain, Vespera raised her electrified mace, black and white wings spread wide as she prepared to strike. Lightning crackled between her feathers as she lunged forward.

The Captain didn't even turn around.

"Ah yes, ze surprise attack," the System Wizard commented casually. "I am le shock."

Vespera's mace swing inexplicably careened to the side as if she wasn't aiming for Zee Captain at all. The momentum carried her forward, and she tripped over her own feet, crashing face-first into her own mace with a sickening crunch of a broken beak-snout. Her wings sparked wildly as she rolled, electricity arcing across her body in painful convulsions as she cried, pawing at her face.

"Tsk tsk!" Zee Captain waggled a finger. "Violence solves nothing, Fräulein Vespera. Perhaps you should take a moment to reflect on your life choices, ja?"

The Thunderbird howled in rage, rising up and pointing a clawed hand at the invincible entity. Lightning arced with a thunderous boom. The lighting bolt careened away from Zee Captain and struck her in her own nose. Vespera let out a strangled wail as she rolled and clutched her broken and electrocuted nose, blood streaming between her fingers. She rolled off the stage with a thump of armor and crack of a shattered phone screen.

"Zis is why children shouldn't play with electricity," Zee commented.

The audience was dead silent now, watching in horror as the two Knights were dispatched without moving a finger, while Emerald . . .

I glanced at the gateway. There was no Emerald there anymore. Only a black hexagonal bracelet lay idly in the indentation on the snow, impervious to whatever had melted the dragon girl as if she were a sugar cube set into hot tea. Bits and pieces of the Lindworm's gaudy magisteel armor lay around it like broken eggshells, cracking and decaying away into flying ashes.

Cinder seemed to have regained her wits from the shock of her friend's demise, and then wings flared with impossible colors, her phase-shift elongating her face, dark claws stretching out, feathers standing on end.

"Go . . ." she began, her voice echoing unnaturally, and then I stepped in front of her face and slapped her hard.

"*Don't!*" I barked.

"Don't?" Cinder sputtered, grabbing at her cheek.

"Do *not* use magic," I growled, grabbing her shoulders and staring into her ocean-blue eyes. "Whatever you're planning to do, it's going to reflect in your face and then your wings might fall off or something! Do not screw with that thing, do *not* target it!"

Zee Captain casually watched our exchange with the perpetually smiling gas mask.

A tall, faceless figure descended from one of the balconies overhead—Vice Principal Graves, his suit immaculate as always. Dark tendrils emerged from his back, writhing as he landed on the stage.

"Ah! Ze local authority figure arrives!" Zee Captain commented, turning to the Slenderman. "Seventeen and a half tentacles. Vice Principal Graves, yes?"

"What are you?" Graves's voice echoed with unnatural resonance, his dark tendrils spreading wider.

"Merely a tourist," Zee Captain replied cheerfully. "Enjoying zis charming little performance. Though ze special effects could use some work. Is zat a smoke machine? A bit mundane for a school of cryptids, don't you find?"

Vice Principal Graves's tendrils writhed menacingly, filling the air with an oppressive, dark energy. The auditorium seemed to darken around him, shadows stretching impossibly long.

"You do not belong here," Graves intoned, his voiceless face somehow conveying absolute menace.

"And?" Zee asked, seemingly undeterred.

"Depart back from whence thou came!"

"And what would be ze fun in that? Nay! Ze local narrative flow suggests that I cannot leave until I make a deal with someone, monseigneur high school manager," Zee commented, completely ignoring the waves of static that rolled from the direction of the vice principal. "Don't you know how these things work? If you summon someone to your dimension, you must parlay with zem or defeat zem in a deadly duel and win a magic prize!"

Iogann, who had been frozen until now, choked out, his entire body shaking as he slid to his knees, "The gate . . . it . . . it's not closing! It's still pulling at my mana!"

Zee Captain tilted a masked head. "Of course not, mein fluffy, doom-seeking compadre. I'm propping it open with a Good Word so that I don't lose my way back to Captania! After all, who would feed all of my Snippies if I left forever? A lonely, sad Snippy is quite a dangerous thing, full of angry wishes that yearn to be fulfilled. Zat one time I left him alone for five minutes and he accumulated 8,402 Dead Zone viruses onto himself! It was quite ze pickle scraping them all off one by one with my best wash sponge and squeegee. Such complaints he had . . . such multitudes of unmerry complaints."

"Be *gone*!" Graves raised his lanky hands, and reality around the vice principal shattered, came apart, my mind catching fire and careening sideways into a darkness-filled abyss, my view of the stage drowning in colorful glitches and flashes of blinding, deafening static.

CHAPTER EIGHTEEN

Corpseworld Caretaker II

I felt myself falling through an endless void of static and darkness, my consciousness fragmenting like shattered glass. Just as I was about to lose myself completely, my sense of self smeared across infinity, something warm and solid wrapped around me—Cinder's wings, her iridescent feathers glowing with a soft, anchoring light.

Her hands gripped my shoulders, pulling me back from the brink. "Hold on to me! Listen to my voice! Stay with me!" Her magic-laced voice cut through the static, clear and determined.

I gasped as reality snapped back into focus, my head pounding madly. Cinder's wings were still wrapped protectively around me, her face inches from mine with naked concern in her expression. The static in my mind receded like an ebbing tide, leaving behind a dull, clawing ache.

I noticed that my knees had given out from the awful aura the vice principal was projecting. It plowed right through my soul like a wave of terror, making me sick to the core, had nearly stopped my heart. Cinder held onto me, not letting me fall.

"Ah, young love!" Zee Captain's voice boomed from somewhere close by and also endlessly far away. "So protective! So fierce! Such passion!"

"*I said, be gone!*" Graves barked. The mind-melting, blinding, gut-wrenching, static-filled ocean of terror beat against Cinder's hold on me, my head throbbing like it was about to split open.

"Calmness!" Zee's heavily-accented voice snapped back.

Cinder's wings relaxed, colors leaking from them, her grip on me weakening slightly.

Through the gaps in her feathers, I saw that a dark, static-filled shadow rushed from the vice principal towards Zee Captain.

The wave of static failed to reach the interdimensional tourist, flowing back like an ocean wave that encountered an island of jagged stone.

Graves wailed, wrapping his faceless head with his lanky hands as his own attack slammed into him, all of his tentacles coming apart into barely visible wisps of shadows.

"A bit too noisy, Mister Slendy!" Zee commented. "Consider a nap!"

Graves careened backwards into a wall and slid down, not moving. The aura of mind-melting horror radiating from the vice principal vanished entirely, the hissing, awful static gone from my head.

Cinder's hands and wings tightened around me once again, her feathers shifting through defensive colors—deep purples, steely grays, warning reds. I could feel her heart racing against my back.

"Alex," she whispered, so softly only I could hear, "whatever happens, do *not* move."

Suddenly, Zee Captain's gaze locked directly on me. Even through the gas mask, I could feel the intensity of that stare, going right through the thick layer of rainbow feathers.

Something inside me snapped with a twinkle.

"Ci. Let me out," I growled.

"What?" Cinder asked.

"Please," I hissed. "I need to talk to that . . . thing. It obviously won't go away until someone makes a deal with it!"

"But . . ."

"Let me out! I know what to say!" I growled. "Trust me!"

Cinder's wings loosened slightly, just enough for me to slip forward. My camera hung forgotten around my neck as I stepped towards Zee Captain.

"Cannot define view," Yulia whispered into my ear as I pointed my wrist cam at Captain hoping for some advice.

Of course. My own wits it is, then.

My mind raced, trying to process what I was dealing with.

This wasn't just some interdimensional tourist—this was a System Wizard, a being that could literally rewrite the rules of reality with a word or two.

How do you stop something that can simply decide that your attacks miss, that can make you trip over nothing, that can reflect any damage back at you? The Captain hadn't even moved to defeat three of the school's strongest students.

Then it hit me—you don't. You can't fight something like this directly. The only way forward was to play along, to engage with whatever twisted game or story the System Wizard wanted to tell.

My palms were sweaty as I stepped forward, but I kept my voice steady. If there was one thing I'd learned from photographing cryptids that could melt me with a single fiery hug, it was how to stay calm in the face of the impossible.

Welp, here I go talking again. I strapped on the Alexander Glock mask harder, aiming my metaphorical gun at the unkillable entity.

"Guten Tag," I said, replicating the thing's accent. "I wish to parlay!"

"Ah," Zee uttered, looming over me. "Excellent!"

I nodded.

"Then let us speak one on one. Let there be a . . . pause!" Zee said with a gloved finger snap, and the auditorium fell absolutely silent.

I glanced away from the post-apocalyptic figure at the audience. None of the Omnid teens were moving. Their faces were gray, without color, not blinking, not breathing, as if suspended in time.

"Are you with them?" I turned back to the undefinable thing.

"Define zem."

"System Wizards," I said.

"Yes and no." Zee shrugged. "Think of me as a renegade . . . a cosmic janitor, ze Caretaker of a Corpseworld, doomed to forever roam across ze weary land and fix things zat cannot be fixed."

"What do you want?" I asked, my mind racing. "What's it going to take for you to leave? Do I have to wish on you or something?"

"Wishes are dangerous things to meddle with for an untrained Wizard," Zee replied, looking down at me. "For zey tend to expand exponentially and devour all."

"Fine, then." I crossed my arms, suddenly thinking about *The Sorcerer's Apprentice* film where the wizard in training creates infinite, self-replicating mops. "Then what do you wish for, Mr. Renegade Wizard?"

"I wish for . . . a story," Zee said. "An interesting fable from ze heart. One to keep me warm out zere in ze endless dark."

I swallowed nervously, thinking of what to say.

"Once upon a time," I began, my voice steady, "there was a teenage girl named Alexa who lived in a treehouse made of stolen traffic signs. She believed that stories could change reality, that imagination was more powerful than any system, any rule. She was a clever, cheeky supervillain, and nobody could stop her."

Zee Captain's violet lenses seemed to focus more intently.

"She found four friends, and through cleverness and planning, she overcame all odds, beat back the darkness, took over the Earth, saved everyone," I said. "Only for a big bad System Wizard to erase all of her work, undo everything, and scatter her friends. This is where I come in. Martin. Her best friend who cannot remember her. Like her, I'm not going to stop until I understand everything and win against impossible odds."

I fell silent.

"Ah." Zee Captain's voice took on a different tone, almost wistful. "Such a trouble-maker, zat girl."

My heart skipped a beat. "You . . . know her?"

"Know her?" Zee laughed. "My dear boy, I was taking her to Manchester! Such a fascinating character—so determined to break ze rules, to rewrite ze narrative. Almost succeeded, too."

"Almost?" I blinked.

"She was given a chance to become a System Wizard. She chose a different path. She hijacked ze train, directed it off ze tracks," Zee leaned towards me. "Sent it careening across ze void."

"And then?"

"Ah, but zat would be big Spoilers!" Zee Captain straightened up, waggling a finger. "Can't tell you everything, ja? Where would ze fun be in zat? But I will say . . . Your curious tale is adequate payment. I am now thoroughly inspired! Here. A gift to keep you warm."

Zee dug into a dark-blue coat pocket and once again pulled out the old grimy-looking steel lighter. A gloved hand threw it my way and I caught it in the air.

"What's it do?" I asked, glancing at the mundane-looking lighter.

"It's a Wizard's implement," Zee replied with a wink of violet lenses. "You're a magic-less human in ze land of feisty magic beasts. You'll need it to fit in. Consider it payment for accidentally exposing you with my Info Scope."

I glanced at the audience. They were still all frozen, suspended in time.

"Appreciate it," I said. "If I understand it correctly, your kind can bend the narrative of reality, yes?"

Zee nodded.

"How do I stop someone like you? How can I prevent my world from being overwritten again? How does *your* narrative end, System Wizard?" I asked him, feeling brave and expecting more finger-waggling and ranting about spoilers.

"When you grow strong enough, figure out how to cross ze threshold into Endalaus without turning to ashes, and find me at ze end of everything," she replied, my mind crawling sideways ever so slightly as my perception of the Captain inexplicably wriggled from one gender to another. "And execute me with a gun zat can kill a god."

I blinked.

"Then take my coat," she added, "and go to Manchester, for it is your quest to slink amongst ze System Wizards to unmake ze Rules and tear reality asunder, my darkling."

"What?" I exhaled. "I have to do *what*?!"

"Shhhh . . ." The undefinable entity put a finger to her mask and began turning towards the gateway, which was still showing that endless apocalyptic cityscape with the massive G-cube looming in the background.

"Hey!" I called out. "I need to know more! Tell me more about Alexa! What happened to her? Where is she?"

"Here," Zee Captain answered, simply pointing at my head.

I swallowed.

"Oh, and Martin?" Zee turned back slightly. "Do try to keep ze teenage cryptids who summon things zey cannot control in better order, ja? Next time something might come through zat won't be as Syntropic as me. You do not want to meet a genuine being of Entropy. Unpause! Have a good tomorrow!"

Time resumed.

With that, Zee Captain stepped through the gateway.

Cinder's dark claws dug into my body, her entire body trembling.

My eyes settled on the dark bracelet in the snow. I somehow knew that in another second the gateway would snap and then Emerald would be gone forever.

Logically, this meant no more leader for the doomed troupe. No more troupe, in fact. No more Emerald. It would solve a multitude of future problems. But . . . also, it would not prevent my inevitable exposure. Everyone served their purpose in the grand scheme of things. Everyone mattered in one way or another.

I needed Emerald for my plan; the overzealous dragon fit into a big part of it all like a perfect gear that spun so many of the others.

"Wait!" I yelled at Zee Captain.

"Yeeees?" Zee paused.

"That dark bracelet," I called out, pointing at the hexagonal band lying in the snow beyond the gateway. "Can you . . . kick it outta there?"

Zee Captain tilted their head. "Oh? And why should I do zat?"

"Because . . ." I swallowed hard. "Because a good story needs all its characters. Everyone matters, even the antagonists."

"Hmmm," Zee Captain said. "Very well."

A dark, grimy boot kicked the bracelet out of the gate onto the stage. The gate snapped shut, collapsing into itself like a winking eye.

CHAPTER NINETEEN

Aftermath I

For a moment, absolute silence filled the auditorium. Then, as if a spell had been broken, the audience came out of their shocked stupor.

"Oh my God, what a joke!"

"What a bunch of knobfolds!"

"Did you see how fast she melted? Holy shit, that was amazing!"

Laughter rippled through the crowd, cruel and mocking. Phones once again came out.

"Guess the oh-so-great Emerald Stratos wasn't such hot shit after all!"

"Owned by a hobo in a trench coat!"

"And those two Knights? Tripped on literally nothing at all!"

"Yeah, one dumbass got chopped with her own axe while the other electrocuted herself! How does that even happen?"

"Serves those losers right!"

"Total clusterfuck!"

I glanced at Cinder. Her wings had shifted to a deep, stormy gray, her feathers bristling with barely contained rage.

I bent down and picked up Emerald's bracelet, ignoring the taunts. The dark metal was ice-cold against my skin.

"Hey, Nullie!" someone called out. "Gonna try to resurrect your girlfriend's boss?"

"Nah, he's probably gonna pawn it!"

More laughter.

Cinder's wings erupted with a sudden burst of color—deep crimson reds and violent purples that seemed to pulse with raw, unfiltered anger. She stepped forward, her voice cutting through the mockery like a blade.

"*Shut. The. Fuck. Up!*"

The auditorium went dead silent.

Her wings spread wide. Her feathers rippled with more rage-filled reds. Her ocean-blue eyes blazed with absolute fury.

"*You weren't up here!*" she screamed. "*You didn't see what actually happened!*"

A Sasquatch in the third row shouted back, "We saw enough! Your whole troupe got destroyed in like, what, thirty seconds?"

Cinder's wings flared wider.

A chorus of jeers and laughter erupted from the audience. The Sasquatch who had spoken was joined by others, their mockery growing bolder.

"Your whole troupe's nothing but a bunch of wannabe delvers!" a Thunderbird called out. "Even a human could've done better!"

"Bet your daddy's gonna be real proud!" another voice sneered.

The voices became a chorus of cruelty, each cutting deeper than the last.

"Justice Nova's daughter, everyone!" a Kelpie called out, his voice dripping with cruel laughter. "More like *Injustice* Nova! Can't even control a simple summoning!"

Cinder blinked.

"You didn't even try using your wings against it!" the Kelpie accused.

Cinder's ocean-blue eyes, once fierce and defiant, began to fill with tears she was desperately trying to hold back.

"Aww, did we hurt poor Cassie's feelings?"

"Can't handle the spotlight?"

"Go cry about it, you dumb beerch!"

I snapped.

My hand dove into my backpack, pulling out a show-grade Thunderclap. With practiced precision, I yanked the pin and hurled it into the center of the auditorium, covering my ears.

BOOM!

The deafening blast erupted like a small sonic bomb. The sound was so intense, it physically pushed people back in their seats. Phones clattered to the floor, drinks and food spilled, and for a moment, absolute silence reigned.

When the ringing in everyone's ears subsided, I was standing center stage, directly in front of Cinder. My stance was wide, shoulders squared, radiating a challenge that seemed to grow from some primal, protective instinct.

"*Enough!*" I roared, whirling around and firing my DSLR's flash directly into the face of the bastard who'd yelled at Cinder.

The intense burst of the overpriced flash bulb set to maximum made him recoil backwards with a yelp.

I jumped off the stage and swept my camera across the audience, flashing again and again and again, blinding their Omnithean eyes.

"You think this is funny?" My voice was ice cold as I continued photographing faces. "Did you all come here just to berate someone?"

"What's that? A Nullie loser defending a troupe of losers?" someone yelled at me.

The crowd was beginning to turn against me instead of Cinder.

No. I will not break. I will not bow.

Flash. Another photo.

"You dumb knobs!" I laughed at a group of jocks who started to fling insults at me. "I just got your faces, your voices, your names. Everything. It's 2025! Do any of you have any idea how easy it is to reverse search up a person using the school's yearbook registry?"

"What?!"

Flash. "You think you're so tough, hiding in the crowd? Making fun of someone who had the guts to get up there and try?"

"Shut up, Nullie!"

"No, you shut up!" I pulled out a smaller bang snap and pulled the string. The gunshot-like firework detonated, silencing the Omnitheans once again.

"Every single one of you who laughed," I barked into the silence. "Who mocked. Who jeered. I've got you all on video. Every cruel word. Every nasty comment. Wonder what the school would think about this behavior? Or your parents? Your coaches? Your future colleges?"

The crowd shifted uncomfortably.

"You can't—" someone started to protest.

"I can and I will," I cut them off. "You wanted to humiliate someone? Congratulations, I just recorded your face and it's already on the cloud, so threatening or trying to stop me will do fuck-all!"

"Effin' Nullie," one of the jocks commented.

"That's right!" I laughed. "I am a Nullie. And you all know how effed in the head Nullies are, don't you . . . Tommy Rexof, varsity quarterback? Wonder what Coach Canard would think about you mocking a fellow student?"

I pointed my camera at the green Basilisk who'd been leading the jeers. "And you, Sandy Satoros—doesn't your mom sit on the PTA board? I'm sure she'd love to see this video of you calling someone the b-word?"

The crowd shifted uncomfortably, rapidly escaping as I continued, methodically identifying faces and matching them to names, to social connections, to vulnerabilities.

"Fuck you, Nu—" a gray demon growled.

"Peter Ruvor? Is that you?" I snarled, flashing him. "Didn't you just apply for that prestigious internship at Hozesh Omnicorp? Wonder how they'd feel about your behavior today if I were to email them your video?"

The gray demon's face went pale.

That's right. Speak a summoned demon's true name and they shall obey you, isn't that how it works?

"And you." I turned to the dark-gray Omnithean girl who'd made that final cruel comment about Cinder. "Tekra Nurg. Is your goal to get suspended? 'Cause I can absolutely arrange it when Graves wakes up!"

"I'd like to see you try, Nullie loser," she growled back.

"Hey." I spread my arms wide. "Maybe I'm wrong. Maybe you're all super proud of how you acted today! Get the hell out, show's over. If any of you knobs want to apologize or try to take me down, you can find me at lunch tomorrow playing chess!"

The exodus began in earnest then.

I jumped off the stage and grabbed my tripod and camera, quickly folding the entire setup away.

As the crowd dispersed, I turned my attention back to the anti-delvers.

Iogann stood frozen, his skull-capped wings drooping in shock. The Mothman looked utterly defeated, his oversized hat slightly askew, antennae hanging limp. His usually chill demeanor had been completely shattered, replaced by a shell-shocked expression.

Vespera lay crumpled on the floor right off the edge of the stage, her black-and-white feathers splayed awkwardly. Blood trickled from her broken beak, electrical sparks dancing weakly across her damaged wings. Her smartwatch had shattered, designer accessories scattered around her prone form.

Solace was still pinned to the floor by her own battle-axe. Her reddish-brown skin had an ashen quality, and a puddle of blood was spilling around her.

Cinder's wings had collapsed, the vibrant colors drained away to a dull, lifeless gray. Tears streamed down her face, cutting silver trails through her smudged, dark war paint.

CHAPTER TWENTY

Aftermath II

I knelt beside Vespera first, carefully helping her sit up. Her black-and-white feathers were matted with blood.

"Hey," I said. "Vee. Let me help you."

She looked up at me, one eye swollen shut, half of the feathers on her face torched away by her own lightning, which should have been impossible to happen to an electricity-proof Thunderbird.

"Why . . . why are you helping me?" Her voice was nasal and broken. "Why aren't you mocking me like the others? I . . . effed up . . . so bad."

"I still gotta kick your ass in History Club!" I said with a smile.

Vespera let out a half laugh, half sob.

I helped her limp up the stairwell to the others. Cinder remained frozen on stage.

"Ci, how do we call up the nurse?" I asked.

She didn't respond.

"Cinder," I said softly, approaching her. "Hey. Talk to me."

Her ocean-blue eyes were distant, unfocused. Tears continued to stream down her face.

"Emergency hexagram," Vespera let out, pointing a blood-covered, magisteel-reinforced claw. "Over there on the wall. Looks like a green Kitlix."

"Io!" I ordered. "Go press it, you're closest."

The Mothman responded, moving as if he was half-asleep. He reached the hexagram and laid a shaking gray paw on it.

"You okay, man?" I asked him.

"Just out of mana." He slipped down to the floor, large hat tilting to cover his exhausted face. "Gonna need time to recharge. Also, I don't think that it's working. The auditorium's ward is . . . totally fried."

Vespera let go of me and dug into her armor, pulling out her phone. It was burned from one side, the screen covered in cracks and flickering with random colors.

She threw the phone at a wall, letting out a wail-swear. The phone exploded into its constituent parts, bits and pieces scattering across the stage just like the troupe's dreams of hitting it big today.

"Bloody useless Thunderite trash! I didn't get a single XP point for this shite!" Vespera snarled. She yanked off her fried armor pieces, revealing a sleek black hexa-suit that was torn in multiple places. "Everything, ruined. How does a MistMark XII watch just shatter?! You were supposed to be effin' indestructible!"

She tore the smartwatch off her wrist, yeeting it at another wall.

I reached down to Solace, feeling for a pulse. It was there, if a bit slow. The Olgoi-Khorkhoi were incredibly tough.

"Vesp, stop throwing your things and tell me the school's emergency number," I ordered.

I already knew the number, but wanted to distract the Thunderbird from her rage.

"7555-HEAL," Vespera answered, deflating.

I dialed. A pleasant voice answered immediately.

"Skyfall Academy Emergency Services, what is the nature of your emergency?"

"Multiple injuries in the auditorium," I reported. "One student impaled by their own weapon, one with electrical burns and a broken nose, one completely drained of mana. Also the vice principal is unconscious."

"Already en route with security. Please remain calm."

In a few minutes, the auditorium doors burst open as Nurse Keystoni rushed in, a wheelchair strapped to her back. A team of security officers in dark hexasuits followed, pushing hovering, beast-core-powered stretchers.

"What in Nazareth's name happened here?" the nurse demanded, her green Kitlix familiar sparking on her shoulder.

"We don't know, ma'am," one of the security guards said. "All of the see-orbs within the auditorium are fried."

"Just . . . a poorly planned show," I replied with a sigh.

The security team moved quickly. Two officers carefully lifted Vice Principal Graves onto a hovering stretcher, his faceless head lolling to the side, dark tendrils barely visible. Another pair worked on extracting the battle-axe from Solace's back.

"Careful with that!" Nurse Keystoni barked at them. "The blade's serrated. Pull it straight up or you'll cause more damage!"

The nurse unfolded her wheelchair and threw some kind of a gemstone into the air above herself. The gem detonated with a flash, pouring a few buckets of water onto her like a quick rainstorm shower. Her legs fused together into a tail and she rolled herself to Solace.

"Deep puncture wound, possible spinal damage," the nurse muttered, her green Kitlix familiar jumping onto Solace to assess the damage and to seal the bleeding cut. "Get her to the medical ward immediately. She'll need emergency healing. Healer Klementine will handle it. I've stabilized her."

"Thanks . . . Lex," Vespera muttered gruffly as two officers helped her onto a hovering stretcher. "I . . . I owe you one. For not being a total dick about this."

"Just get better," I replied. "History Club needs its queen bee."

She let out a wet laugh that turned into a pained groan. "Ugh, don't make me laugh. My face is so busted."

"Any other injured?" The nurse turned to Iogann and Cinder.

"Just . . . drained," Iogann mumbled from under his hat. "Need a nap. Will be fine in thirty."

I walked over to Cinder and pulled Em's bracelet out, waving it in front of the catatonic-looking Quetzi.

"Ems is going to need us," I said. "Want to walk with me to the Lazarus Cavern?"

Cinder's eyes slowly focused on the dark bracelet in my hand. Her feathers shifted slightly, a hint of color returning.

"Em . . ." she whispered, her voice hoarse. "She . . . she just . . ."

"Melted like the Wicked Witch from Oz, yeah," I finished for her. "But we can fix that. The bracelet seems to be fine."

"The Genesis Pool." She nodded slowly. "We need to . . . to . . ."

"Get her back on her feet," I said, offering her my hand. "Come on."

Cinder's claws wrapped around my hand, her grip almost painfully tight as we walked to the elevator. Her wings remained a dull, lifeless gray sparking with bits of reds and violets at the very edges.

The nurse watched us as we departed. The ritual of bringing a close friend back from death was a sacred thing in Omnid culture and was Cinder's right.

The elevator doors closed with a soft ding, leaving us alone in the small space. Cinder didn't let go of my hand, as if I was her anchor to physical reality.

"Alex." Cinder's voice was small and weak. "What . . . what the shit was that thing? That . . . Captain?"

"A System Wizard," I said. "It called itself 'Corpseworld Caretaker.' Presumably it's a being that can straight up rewrite reality with a glance."

"It just . . . walked through our wards like they weren't even there," she muttered. "Em's artifacts, her sword, her armor—everything just . . . broke."

I nodded.

"I've never . . ." Cinder swallowed hard. "I've never seen anything like that. Em was so strong, so confident. And that thing just . . . it didn't even try. Everything we had just . . . failed. This was . . . so . . . so much worse than the festival. Slayer! This is the first time Em died at a show!"

"Sometimes the universe reminds us that there are bigger fish out there," I commented.

"Bigger fish?" Cinder let out a broken laugh. "That wasn't a bigger fish, Alex. That was a fucking leviathan playing with minnows."

"A polite leviathan," I said. "She listened to me."

"She?"

"Maybe a he?" I shrugged. "I don't think that Zee Captain wishes to be defined by us. I . . . took a picture. Honestly, I thought that Graves was scary. But . . ."

"Graves is scary," Cinder agreed, burying her face in my shoulder, her tears starting again. "But that thing . . . it just dismissed him like he was nothing. Like we were all *nothing*. How can something like that even exist?"

"Aren't there living gods on Arx?" I asked.

"Yeah, but . . ." Cinder shuddered into me. "This was different. The gods of Arx are . . . comprehensible, finite. They can be killed, follow rules, have clear forms, limitations. They are basically really old . . . nearly decrepit mages with a single, near-absolute, incredibly high-level skill. They can't even leave Arx, 'cause the lower aetheric density would kill them . . . I think."

The elevator dinged and opened to the Lazarus Cavern. The liquid mercury surface of the pool was perfectly still.

Cinder finally let go of my hand and took Emerald's bracelet from me. She stared at it for a long moment.

"What if it . . ." she uttered, ". . . doesn't bring her back? What if something went wrong and she can't come back? What if that thing did something to her soul?"

"Only one way to find out," I said gently. "Want to do it together?"

Cinder nodded.

Together, we approached the Genesis Pool. The liquid mercury surface reflected the golden bioluminescent crystals above, creating an otherworldly glow. The statue of the female Omnid loomed over us, her stone wings spread wide and her sword pointing down at the pool's surface.

Cinder's claws tightened around Emerald's bracelet. She took a deep breath, then held it out over the pool. I also grabbed onto it.

"Em," she whispered, "please come back."

CHAPTER TWENTY-ONE

The Antagonist Role I

We let the bracelet fall. It hit the silvery surface with barely a ripple, sinking slowly into the depths.

The dark bracelet sank deeper, trailing silver threads that began to spread like roots through the mercury-like fluid. The threads pulsed with a faint ruby light, growing and rapidly branching into an intricate network.

Gradually, Emerald began to reform within the bracelet's moving ring. First came the crystalline-organic dragon heart, then delicate structures like frozen lightning stretched away from it—her nervous system sketched in silver-and-ruby light. Then came her skeleton, materializing bone by bone, followed by muscles and organs weaving themselves into existence like an anatomical time-lapse in reverse.

The bracelet rushed up and down the figure of the girl within the silver fluid, printing her into existence.

The process was mesmerizing and disturbing in equal measure. I could see her heart form and begin beating before she even had skin, pumping silvery Genesis fluid through newly formed arteries. Her crystalline scales grew last, sprouting like flowers made of living rubies.

Cinder's wings trembled as we watched her friend rebuild herself from nothing. Her feathers shifted through anxious colors—deep purples, uncertain blues, hopeful yellows.

Finally, Emerald's eyes snapped open—brilliant gold-orange against the silver liquid. She thrashed suddenly, panicked, and Cinder dove forward without hesitation, plunging her arms into the pool to pull her friend to safety.

I helped haul Emerald onto the stone ledge as she coughed and sputtered, expelling Genesis fluid from her newly formed lungs. Her ruby scales gleamed wetly under the crystal lights.

"Easy," Cinder murmured, holding Emerald steady. "You're okay. You're back."

I walked to the robe area and handed the dripping Lindworm a thick towel and a robe. Emerald snatched it from my hands, her gold-orange eyes wild and unfocused.

"What . . ." Emerald's voice was hoarse. "What happened?"

"You died," Cinder said softly, her wings curling protectively around her friend. "That . . . thing from beyond the gate. It did something that made all your artifacts fail. You basically melted."

"I . . . melted?" Emerald wrapped the towel tighter around herself, shivering despite her usually high body temperature. "Oh. Right. Everything just . . . started coming apart . . . damn. That was . . . painful. At least it was quick. I don't understand. How did my attack miss? Hey, Ci . . . where's my sword?"

"Your sword melted, too," I said.

Emerald's head snapped up, her eyes focusing on me with sudden clarity. "You . . . you're that effin' pesky Nullie. What are you doing here?"

"Saving you." I crossed my arms. "You're welcome."

Emerald's eyes narrowed.

"I don't need saving from a Nullie," she spat. "Especially not from some weak little mixed-blood who can't even . . ."

"Em!" Cinder's wings flared. "He's the one who got your bracelet out before the gate closed. Without him, you'd be gone. Like, permanently gone."

Emerald's gold-orange eyes blazed with growing fury, turning from Cinder to me. "So what? You expect me to be grateful? Bet you just wanted to see me naked, you scale-chaser!"

"*Em!*" Cinder growled.

"Yeah that's my name, you dumb beerch," Emerald snarled. "Why the eff is he here, Ci? What, is he your new pet project? Your little charity case? Why was he sitting in the front row? Did you invite him? I told you that I was going to break your wrists if you kept obsessing over him! Guess it's time for . . ."

"Vesp invited me," I said.

Emerald's eyes narrowed to dangerous slits. "Vee? That thundercunt betrayed me?!"

"No one betrayed you," I said calmly. "Your show went sideways because you forced Io to open a gate when he sensed disaster coming. Then you got your ass handed to you by something way above your level. Now you're taking it out on everyone else because your ego can't handle being powerless for once."

"You little shit!" Emerald lunged forward, dragonfire igniting across her claws. "I'ma snap your spine!"

I felt something click inside me as adrenaline flooded my system. The seventeen stolen hexamesh student and security guard suits I'd layered under my clothes suddenly activated in perfect sync, their beast cores igniting with a harmonious hum.

My fist connected with Emerald's jaw in an uppercut, amplified by the combined force of seventeen magitek suits. The impact sent the Lindworm flying backward with a surprised yelp. She splashed into the Genesis Pool, sending silver liquid spraying everywhere.

"Alex!" Cinder gasped, her wings flaring with shock.

"What?" I shrugged. "She was being volatile!"

"*You!*" Emerald surfaced, sputtering and furious. Her ruby scales gleamed with silvery fluid as she pulled herself out of the pool.

I punched her again, directly in the noggin, making her sink under, the Genesis Pool extinguishing the sparks and wisps of deadly dragonfire.

Emerald surfaced again, trying to grab at me. I smacked her in the forehead again, making her sink.

It felt good.

"*Stop!*" Cinder's wings flared, shifting through warning reds and cautionary yellows. "Both of you! Em, he saved your life. Alex, stop dunking my friend in the resurrection well!"

"I'll stop dunking her when she stops trying to set me on fire," I replied, punting the dragon girl under the silver fluid again.

Cinder blinked.

My hand closed around one of Emerald's horns and held her under. Emerald flailed, her eyes wide. She clawed at my hand, demolishing my white shirt, but her claws were unable to penetrate the layered suits, and dragonfire didn't seem to be functioning within the Genesis fluid.

"Alex!" Cinder's voice cracked with alarm. "Stop!"

I lifted Emerald up, letting her surface. She came up gasping and sputtering.

"You . . ." she choked out between coughs. "You're dead, Nullie!"

"Already died once," I shrugged. "Wasn't that bad. Want to try again?"

I dunked her under. As she swallowed more fluid, thrashing as her eyes glazed over.

"Alex, please!" Cinder tried to stop me but I was resolute, immovable in my layered outfit.

"No," I growled. "She *needs* this. She has to see *what* I saw under there."

After a minute, I pulled Emerald up again. She was barely conscious now, her gold-orange eyes unfocused.

"Listen up, you ruby-scaled disaster," I said calmly. "I'm going to keep dunking you until you learn some manners. Every time you try to attack me, every time you insult me or anyone else—splash. Back into the pool you go. Clear?"

"F-fuck . . . you . . ." Emerald gasped weakly. "You're just . . . prey."

"Wrong answer," I said. "Try again."

Splash.

When I pulled her up this time, she didn't even have the strength to curse at me.

"What am I?" I asked her.

"P-ppprrr . . ." she stammered.

Her horn cracked as I squeezed it with the power of a multi-layered, gloved hand.

"I dare you to finish that sentence," I said, lowering her back into the pool.

Wild, tear-filled eyes turned to Cinder. The Quetzi didn't move to aid her friend.

"A pp-pp-person," Emerald choked out a moment before I pushed her under again. "You're . . . a person!"

"Good!" I said brightly. "And what do we say to people who save our lives?"

"Th . . . thank . . ." Emerald struggled with the word as if it was physically painful. "Thank . . . you."

Cinder stared at me.

"What? I'm teaching her a valuable lesson about humility," I replied calmly. "Now, Emerald. What are you going to do differently from now on?"

"I . . . I'll t-try to be . . . nicer t-to you," Emerald managed through chattering teeth.

"And?" I prompted.

"And I won't . . . t-try to kill you . . . t-today," she added quickly. "Or . . . set you on fire."

"Excellent!" I helped her out of the pool. "See? That wasn't so hard, was it?"

She stared at me with hate-filled eyes. She was totally going to set me on fire tomorrow.

This was fine.

CHAPTER TWENTY-TWO

The Antagonist Role II

Emerald collapsed onto the stone floor, shivering violently. The Genesis fluid had almost completely doused her inner fire.

Cinder rushed forward with fresh towels, wrapping them around her friend.

"What . . . what the eff . . .?" the Rubicund Lindworm whispered, looking up at me. "You . . . you shouldn't have mana or s-super strength. How are you overpowering me?! W-what are you?"

"I'm . . . just a person," I replied evenly. "Like I made you admit. Now, are we done with the violence and insults? This is a sacred hall of incarnation, unless you forgot. If you want to challenge me to a duel to the death for insulting your dragon-honor, you can do so in History Club at a later date. Cinder or Vee will serve as my second."

Emerald tried to puff herself up, her ruby scales bristling despite being soaked and shivering. "Don't think this means a-anything, Nullie," she snarled, though her voice cracked pathetically. "I'm still going to—"

I arched an eyebrow.

"Go ahead," I said.

"What?" She blinked.

"Do you know why I saved you from oblivion?" I asked her. "You exist as the antagonist. Your role is to antagonize me. Go ahead. Antagonize away."

Emerald tried to draw herself up. "You . . . you think you've won something here? You think dunking me in the Genesis Pool makes you tough?"

"No," I replied calmly. "I think it makes you wet and cold. And I think you're deflecting because you're terrified of appearing weak in front of Cinder, of losing your spot as number one dragon queen. You saw something under there, didn't you? Do you remember me? Do you remember . . . Alexa?"

Emerald's gold-orange eyes widened, a flash of genuine fear crossing her face. She rapidly concealed it behind a hastily constructed frown.

"I didn't see shit," she muttered. "And I'm not scared of anything, especially not some weak little . . ."

I took a step towards the pool. Emerald flinched back.

"Right," I nodded. "Of course not. My mistake. Clearly you're a very brave and strong Lindworm . . . dunked repeatedly in magic juice by a 'weak little Nullie.' Very intimidating."

"You . . . you . . ." Emerald sputtered. "This isn't over!"

"Obviously not." I shrugged. "I expect violence and grave treachery. Just remember this—every time you attack me or my friends . . . terrible, awful, no good things are going to happen to you. The more you try to stop me, the worse things are going to get for you."

"You can't threaten me!" Emerald snarled.

"It's not a threat," I said calmly. "It's a promise. A prophecy, if you will. You're going to keep being antagonistic because that's your role. And every time you do, you're going to fail spectacularly, because that's also your role. You exist in a box that you've drawn up for yourself. You are incapable of stepping out of it. You're predictable, and this makes you weak."

Emerald's scales bristled with fury at my words, but I could see the uncertainty in her eyes.

"Had I let you vanish, had I let your bracelet remain behind the gate," I said, "you would be out of the equation of the future and . . . perhaps be seen as a martyr of sorts by some, since Omnids don't speak bad of their perma-dead kin. As you are now, you're perfect. Your own excessively villainous actions are going to push your entire crew into my waiting, pink hands."

"*What?*" she sputtered. The dragon girl glanced at Cinder, perhaps seeking support, but the Quetzalcoatl's wings remained neutral, shifting through thoughtful shades of blue and gray.

"Ci, you can't seriously be letting this nutjob Nullie talk to me like this! I order you to—"

"Order me?" Cinder's wings flared with sudden anger, shifting to deep crimson. "You don't get to order me around anymore, Em. Your show was an absolute disaster. You ignored Io's warnings. You forced both of us to perform with your dragon-command voice! You got yourself killed and two of your Knights were grievously injured. Your fancy artifacts are gone. Your sword is gone. The troupe's over! Go home!!!"

"But . . ." Emerald's voice cracked. "The troupe . . . we can still . . ."

"No." Cinder's wings flared wider. "It's done, Em. You pushed too far, ignored too many warnings. I'm out."

"You can't just quit!" Emerald struggled to her feet. "We're a team! How are you gonna level up?!"

"Level up?" Cinder let out a bitter laugh. "Is that all you care about? Stats and power? Look what your obsession with 'leveling up' got us today! Vesp has a broken face, Solace is in critical care, and you literally effing melted! If Alex didn't ask *that thing* for your bracelet back, we wouldn't even be talking now!"

"But . . ." Emerald growled. "We're the strongest . . ."

"We're not the strongest," Cinder sighed. "I met a god today. A real god. Not some bullshit LV-too-high-to-count humanoid on Arx that is powered by a bunch of tethered souls and citadel cities. And you know what? It didn't care about our levels or stats or fancy artifacts. We were nothing to it. Less than nothing! That thing fried all of the school's wards with a glance!"

The Rubicund Lindworm frowned.

"It made you trip on absolutely nothing! And you know what's worse? It was being nice about it! It was playing with us, Em! Like we were amusing little toys!"

Emerald's fists opened and closed.

"You want to be prey?" Emerald hissed at Cinder. "Fine! Be that way! Side with this . . . this Nullie! See if I care! See where it gets you in a week or two!"

She stormed towards the stairwell, leaving wet, silver-tinted footprints on the stone floor. At the gate, she turned back one last time, her gold-orange eyes blazing.

"When you're done playing with your latest pet project, you know where to find me," she snarled. Then she disappeared up the stairwell, leaving only the lingering scent of crushed pride.

Cinder's wings drooped, shifting through melancholy blues and grays. She let out a long, shaky breath.

"You okay?" I asked, somewhat falling back on the supportive-friend NPC role.

"No," she sighed. "Nothing about this is okay. The troupe is finished. Em's prolly never going to forgive me for this. And you . . ." She turned to face me, her ocean-blue eyes filled with a mix of emotions I couldn't quite read. "What you did . . ."

I tilted my head at her.

"That was dangerously imbecilic and . . . brave. Em's going to make your life hell now."

"And fall right into my trap." I grinned.

"You don't know Em like I do," Cinder sighed. "She doesn't forget. Or forgive. Ever. And now you've humiliated her in front of me . . ."

Then her brain caught up to my words. "What trap?"

"The most dastardly kind of trap." I tapped the side of my head.

Cinder squinted at me.

"The more she antagonizes me, the more she'll push everyone away from her and towards me. Every time she acts out, every time she tries to hurt me or others, she'll dig her grave deeper. She's predictable, trapped in her 'I'm a bully' NPC pattern."

"I don't get you. You . . . you planned this? All of it?" she asked.

"Pff." I waved her off. "I didn't plan for an interdimensional tourist to melt your best friend. But once it happened . . . well, let's just say I know how to work with what I'm given."

"That's . . ." Cinder's feathers bristled slightly. "That's kind of concerning, Alex. You're kind of . . . scary."

"Says the girl with mind-control wings," I guffawed. "Your singing literally made me crawl onto the stage on my knees. My social rep will never recover!"

Cinder pursed her lips.

I offered her my hand. "Shall we head upstairs, my fair lady?"

The Quetzi-girl looked at my hand.

Finally, she took it with a weary sigh, claws wrapping around my fingers.

CHAPTER TWENTY-THREE

OmniGogo I

As we emerged from the elevator, Iogann was methodically packing away the show equipment, looking surprisingly calm despite everything that had happened. His large hat was slightly askew as he coiled up cables and packed away various magitek amps and other doohickeys that Zee Captain's presence had managed to break along with the building's ward.

"Hey," he greeted us with a small wave. "Just . . . cleaning up our stuff."

Cinder's wings and tail drooped, shifting to various shades of gray and black. The sight of the stage and cracked mana amps seemed to bring back a fresh wave of stress.

"You seem . . . weirdly okay," I commented at the Mothman.

"Had a quick smoke out back." He shrugged. "Plus, you know . . . I kind of saw this coming. Not the exact details, but . . . something bad. Remember? That's my thing—sensing disasters, feeding off them."

"H-hey, Io," Cinder let out. "It's . . . it's over. I told Em that I quit."

"As I expected. At least no one in the audience died this time. Well, except maybe the troupe itself," the Mothman commented.

"Not helping," Cinder growled.

"Just stating facts." Iogann shrugged. "Em's gone full nuclear, Vesp and Solace are in the medical ward being pawed at by Vitalix Kitlix, and you . . . quit. Pretty sure that counts as the troupe being dead. Want a smoke?"

I grabbed Cinder's arm before she could reach for the offered "The Swords of Knight Chalice" cigarette pack.

"That's not going to help." I said.

"Let go," Cinder growled, her feathers bristling. "I need this."

"No, you don't," I said firmly. "You need hope. And then you need to process what happened, not numb yourself with sus interdimensional smokes. Do you even know what's in them?"

"Who died and made you my therapist?" Cinder snapped. "What hope? What the shit are you on about now?"

"You've got talent. Your voice is incredible. Your performance was amazing until things went sideways. And now you're free."

"Free?" Cinder's wings flared. "Free to do what?"

"To move forward," I said.

Cinder faltered, lighting up for just a moment. Then she stepped back and slumped against a large runework-powered speaker, sliding down until she was sitting on the dusty floor. She pulled her knees to her chest.

"Move forward to where?" she asked quietly. "The troupe was my chance to prove I could be something other than Justice Nova's disappointing, useless daughter." Her wings curled around her like a protective cocoon. "Show went to shit. Everyone saw what a joke we are. What a weak joke I am."

"Oh, please." I rolled my eyes. "That wasn't a show. That was a hostage situation with a harmonica."

Iogann snorted from where he was half-heartedly dismantling the smoke machine.

Cinder's voice was muffled by her wings. "The whole school was here. They'll never let me live this down."

"First of all," I interrupted, "the whole school wasn't here. Maybe sixty people max, and I've got all their names and faces recorded."

Cinder looked up at me, her expression that of pure depression and surrender. She was sinking, most of her wings pure black. I was losing her to an ocean of self-inflicted despair.

Time for the big guns.

"My question is—do you want to push this incident aside, or do you want to weaponize it to make a potential six hundred thousand O-bux?" I asked, looking down at her. "Because I've got everything we need right here—the bullying, the slurs, the harassment. One well-edited video on OmniGogo, and we could have your future funded for years to come."

"Huh?" Cinder choked out. "What . . . what the eff are you on about?"

"Think about it," I continued. "Cute Quetzalcoatl girl faces vicious discrimination at school show. Brave half-blood student captures everything on camera. That's social media gold right there. We could have you trending by midnight."

Iogann perked up. "People would actually pay for that?"

"People on WingStarter pay for all sorts of random things like Solar Roadways." I shrugged, already mentally composing the perfect clickbait title. "This is way easier to sell. Bullying, especially overtly hostile, is incredibly easy to weaponize on a platform like OmniGogo or WingStarter."

"Six hundred thousand O-bux for being bullied?" She looked up at me, her eyes lighting up. "Really? That sounds like a made-up number."

I sat down next to Cinder and asked Yulia to pull up the relevant article, passing the phone to Cinder when it was loaded.

Let's Give Merleen—The Janitor—A Vacation

Try $613,925 OSD in backing.

A seventy-two-year-old janitor named Merleen Keeps was subjected to verbal harassment by a group of middle school students while walking home from Jotuna Middle School in New New York Citadel. In a twelve-minute video capturing the incident, the students can be heard repeatedly mocking and berating her. At one point, one student shouts, "You're so f***in' poor, you lard-ass b***," the curse words bleeped out. Merleen responds to them with quiet resilience, saying, "I try to live by such standards, I do, and it's not easy at all."

The Mothman whistled low as his eyes ran over the article. Cinder just stared at the screen.

Her feathered tail started to move slightly—the first sign of life since the concert disaster. "So . . . we could turn their mockery against them?" she asked.

"Oh, yes." I grinned. "But . . . we're going to do so much more than that. See this?" I held up the 360-degree camera. "This beauty captured everything—every sneer, every cruel comment, every moment they thought they were being oh-so-clever with their mockery. And this?" I tapped the condenser microphone. "Professional-grade audio. Crystal clear recording of every slur, every insult, every bit of harassment."

"But here's the thing—we don't just want revenge. We want to build something awesome. Turn this whole disaster into your origin story."

Cinder leaned closer to me. "Origin story?"

"Hum." Io nodded slowly. "It's kind of brilliant, actually."

"You can help out too, bud." I grinned at the Mothman.

"You really want to help us?" Cinder let out. "Help me? After I . . . chased you, yelled at you, kicked your van like thirty times? I didn't even have the guts to invite you to the show, that was Vee!" Her gaze searched my face for any sign of deception. Her wings were still trembling, but there was a hint of hope in her voice that made my heart do that stupid flutter thing again.

"Yes," I answered simply, refusing to let my eyes linger on the hopeful colors dancing up her now silver-blue agate feathers. "But you have to want to help yourself. This won't be a project hanging on my neck alone. Gonna need a . . . place . . . to edit the footage and stuff. Maybe the school's comp lab?" I pondered aloud. "If I can install quality video editing software there."

"You can use my garage for it after school tomorrow!" Cinder blurted out, then looked startled by her own eagerness. She blushed as she quickly tried to backtrack. "I mean . . . if you want to." The attempted casualness in her voice was about as convincing as some of my earlier attempts at being smooth around her.

Iogann looked between us with growing interest, a knowing smirk playing across his face. I pretended not to notice.

"Yeah, sure. Text me the address." I nodded, trying to match her forced nonchalance.

"My dad's workshop computer should work," Cinder mumbled, trying to sound casual as her tail swished. "It's got plenty of storage and stuff."

I flipped the phone to the contacts list. "Here, put your numba 'n' contact deets in there. Add me on Omnigram, too."

Wow, that took me way too long. Got everyone's Omnigram except for the only girl I actually wanted to get to know. Oh, well, better late than never.

"Um. Okay." She started typing in her info. "Hey, what kind of phone is this? It feels like it could survive a nuclear blast."

"Pyroxia X-12," I explained, watching her examine my trusty device with genuine interest. "It's . . . made in Thunderland for construction workers operating on power lines and stuff. Has a measuring laser and infrared cam, and survives a drop from seventy-two meters. Ordered it from Obay."

"That's . . . pretty cool," she said.

I shrugged.

"My Omnigram ID name is SongOfDarkness . . . Don't laugh," she said, handing the phone back. Her tail twitched nervously as she added, "And, uh . . . thanks. For earlier. With Emerald and everything."

"Yeah, mang, don't mention it." I shrugged, my eyes already scanning the backstage area. The catwalk above looked promising. "I'll poke you on Omnigram. Don't tell anyone that I'm here."

"What?" she let out.

Cinder's ocean-blue eyes tracked my movement as I quickly climbed a metal stairwell and settled into a makeshift nest in the catwalk high above the stage, clipping a hammock to the metal supports.

According to Yulia's report, temperature was supposed to rapidly drop overnight due to a cold snap, so staying in the van even with the magic furs was out of the question.

The industrial metal frame creaked slightly under my weight as I relaxed.

Below, Cinder paused in packing up the equipment with Iogann. I could practically see the gears turning in her head as she pieced together what she was seeing and then stared up at me with wide, unnaturally blue eyes.

Then she dug into her pocket, pulled out her phone, and started typing furiously.

CHAPTER TWENTY-FOUR

OmniGogo II

The tiny speaker in my ear buzzed with a new Omnigram notification.

SongOfDarkness🎸: is that a hammock?! are you effin sleeping up there?!

I typed back quickly:

Alex G: Temporarily. Van's heater is busted and a cold front's coming. Don't worry about it.
SongOfDarkness🎸: . . .
SongOfDarkness🎸: you can't sleep in the auditorium
SongOfDarkness🎸: security does rounds at night
Alex G: Already mapped their patrol routes yesterday. They never check the catwalk. they'r too lazy to climb stairs.
SongOfDarkness🎸: alex no
SongOfDarkness🎸: that's not ok
Alex G: It's quite cozy up here actually. Great view of the stage.
SongOfDarkness🎸: seriously, you can't stay there
Alex G: Watch me.
SongOfDarkness🎸: . . .
SongOfDarkness🎸: Wait. Where did you sleep yesterday?
Alex G: The van
SongOfDarkness🎸: And before that?
Alex G: The van
SongOfDarkness🎸: And before the fucking van?!
Alex G: Abandoned places. Office towers. Grain silos. Nazarite Cathedrals. Anywhere where it's warm enough and security is lax. Now quit looking up. You're exposing my super secret location.
SongOfDarkness🎸: get down here
Alex G: No
SongOfDarkness🎸: alex get your ass down here right now
Alex G: Make me
SongOfDarkness🎸: don't make me come up there
Alex G: Lol. What's ur plan? 2 cuddle me to death?

I tried to smash her with a funny.

> SongOfDarkness🎸: . . .
> SongOfDarkness🎸: you're staying at my place tonight
> Alex G: No I'm not
> SongOfDarkness🎸: yes you are
> Alex G: Nope. I'm good here. Got my hammock and everything.
> SongOfDarkness🎸: alex i swear to Slayer if you don't get down here
> Alex G: You'll what? Sing me to sleep? Already planning on that. Got a recording. Your voice is lovely.

Cinder climbed up the stairwell faster than I could taunt her again, rapidly navigating the narrow metal walkway. Her feathers shifted through determined reds and stubborn oranges as she approached my hammock nest.

"Get. Down," she growled, looming over me with her hands on her hips.

"Nah, I'm comfy," I replied, snuggling deeper into my hammock. "Nice view up here. Great acoustics, too."

"Alex . . ." Her voice carried a warning tone.

"What?" I blinked innocently up at her. "I've got everything I need right here— shelter, relative warmth, and a recording of your lovely voice to lull me to sleep. It's practically luxury living."

Her wings bristled, shifting to frustrated crimsons. "You are *not* sleeping in the school auditorium."

"Why not? I've already nested." I yawned. "Shoo. You're blocking my . . ."

Cinder's claws suddenly wrapped around my hammock's support ropes. "Last chance to come down voluntarily."

"Or what?" I challenged, raising an eyebrow.

With a swift motion of snapping claws, she severed the ropes. I yelped as the hammock collapsed, but before I could fall, Cinder caught me in her arms, her wings spreading wide for balance.

"Or I carry you out," she said smugly.

"Hey! Put me down!" I protested. Her grip was surprisingly strong.

"Nope." She started walking along the catwalk, carrying me as though I weighed nothing. "You're coming home with me."

"This is kidnapping!" I declared, flailing slightly as my heartbeat went mad. "Io! Help! I'm being kidnapped by a very pretty dragon-bird! She's determined!"

"Have fun!" Iogann called up cheerfully, not even looking up from where he was coiling cables.

"Traitor!" I yelled down at him.

"You can either come quietly," Cinder said, "or I can fly you down. Your choice."

I immediately stopped struggling. "You wouldn't."

"Watch me!" Her mouth spread in a wide grin, wings unfurling wide, feathers lengthening with dancing mini-rainbows.

Cinder's wings erupted with color as she leapt from the catwalk—blazing crimsons, electric blues, molten golds all rippling through her feathers in a dazzling, mind-melting display. The drop made my stomach lurch as we plummeted for a heart-stopping moment before her wings caught the air.

"*Holy shit!*" I yelped, clinging to her desperately as we glided down in a graceful spiral. Her feathers shifted and adjusted with microscopic precision, controlling our descent with ease.

We landed softly near Iogann, who was failing miserably at hiding his amusement. Cinder's wings folded back with a satisfied rustle, though she didn't set me down.

"See?" She smirked down at me. "That wasn't so bad."

"Completely unnecessary!" I protested, my heart still racing. "Nazareth, who does that?!"

Internally, I was laughing like a supervillain. My plan to shake Cinder out of her depression spiral was working quite well.

"I had a perfectly good nest up there!" I continued protesting, though I made no real attempt to escape her arms. "And now my hammock is ruined!"

"You can buy a new hammock," Cinder replied, still carrying me as she headed for the exit. "One that isn't hanging in a school auditorium like some kind of weird theater ghost."

"But I liked being a theater ghost," I pouted. "Had a whole routine planned—rattling chains, moving props around, weaponizing chandeliers, writing cryptic messages on the mirrors . . ."

"Uh-huh." Cinder rolled her eyes, but I caught the slight upturn of her lips. "And how exactly were you planning to shower? Or eat? Or, you know, do basic people things?"

"I had it all figured out!" I insisted. "The gym has showers, the cafeteria and vending machines have food, and the janitorial closet has cleaning supplies. "Why must you ruin my Phantom-of-Skyfall dreams with your caring and warm house?"

"Because unlike the Phantom, you need actual food and a real bed," she replied, her wings shifting through amused blues and teasing purples. "Also, you smell like catwalk dust and a sweaty hexasuit." She glanced at my arms where Emerald had managed to tear through a few layers. "Hold up, how many hexasuits are you wearing?!"

"Umm . . . seventeen," I confessed.

"Seventeen?" Cinder nearly dropped me in shock. "How are you even moving?"

"I synchronized their activation patterns with Yulia's help." I shrugged. "And I'm wearing them in alternating polarities to minimize interference. They're all basic student-grade or generic security-grade stuff. Individually they're pretty weak, but together they form a mighty . . ."

"Dweeb?" she commented.

"No! A . . . mighty Voltron of basic school equipment!" I declared proudly. "Like your average student debt, but in hexasuit form!"

"Holy shit," she laughed. "No wonder you punted Em into the pool like that! I thought that the entity from beyond the gate blessed you with super strength in exchange for your soul. Slayer!"

"Nah. Captain blessed me with a magic lighter," I said.

"What?" Cinder laughed even harder, taking my words for another joke. "You're absolutely ridiculous, you know that?"

"Says the girl carrying me like a princess," I retorted. "I demand a tiara if this is going to be a regular thing."

"Keep dreaming, dweeb," she snorted, but her wings shifted through happy shades of pink and gold. "Now, are you going to walk on your own, or do I need to carry you all the way to my house?"

"Well, since you offered so nicely . . ." I made myself comfortable in her arms. "I accept your generous transportation service. Though I must warn you—the proper princess-phantom carrying etiquette requires you to sing while doing so."

"Don't push your luck, dweeb," she huffed.

"What is a 'dweeb'?" I asked. "Should I be offended?"

Cinder rolled her eyes, but I could see her fighting back a big smile. "A dweeb is . . . you. And yes, you should definitely be offended."

"I am mortally wounded by your cruel words," I declared dramatically, pressing a hand to my chest. "How shall I ever recover from such a devastating insult?"

"You'll live," she snorted, finally setting me down as we reached the parking lot. "Now help us load shit."

Iogann emerged from the auditorium pushing a huge dolly loaded with cables, hexagram amps, and various other show equipment.

I followed Cinder and Io to a battered van parked behind the auditorium—not my rust bucket, but a slightly less decrepit model in faded purple and black. The vehicle was covered in skull moth decals and *DISASTER AWAITS!* painted in dripping red letters on the side. The logo was somewhat peeling, revealing at least three previous names underneath.

"So," Iogann said casually as we worked, "you two seem . . . friendly."

"Shut up, Io," Cinder growled, her wings shifting through embarrassed pinks.

"Just saying." He shrugged. "It's nice to see you actually letting someone help for once."

"I'm not letting anyone help," Cinder snapped, shoving a large cracked runestone into the van with more force than necessary. "I'm preventing a homeless idiot from camping in the auditorium!"

"Mmmm, yes, purely practical concerns," Iogann nodded sagely. "Nothing to do with those interesting colors your wings keep shifting to whenever he's around."

"I will stab your eyes out with your own antennae," Cinder threatened.

"Hey, just making observations." Iogann raised his hands in mock surrender. "That's kind of my thing. Noticing impending disasters . . . and other curious developments."

"Nothing is developing," Cinder insisted. "Get off my wings, you oversized bug!"

"So, are you following us in your van or are we all gonna squeeze into the Mothmobile?" Iogann asked, closing the back doors of his disaster-mobile.

"How'd you know 'bout my van?" I asked him.

"Ci told me." The Mothman tilted one of his antennae in the direction of orange-red-violet-pink-tinted Cinder. "Made it sound like a sweet crib with carpets, beer fridge, beanbags, and See-Mass lights."

"My van needs a funeral and a break from being kicked by angry Quetzis." I shrugged. "Riding with the disaster-sensing Moth seems safer. Though I should probably grab my clothes backpack from it first."

"I'll go with you," Cinder said quickly, then seemed embarrassed by her eagerness. "You know . . . to make sure you actually come back and don't try to nest in there instead."

"Such lack of trust!" I clutched my chest in mock offense as we walked to my van. "After all we've been through—death, resurrection, interdimensional tourists, dragon-bestie pool dunking . . ."

We returned to Iogann's van, where the Tetris-like packing situation became immediately apparent. Every inch of space was crammed with show equipment, leaving only the two front seats available. My massive backpack had to be wedged in at an awkward angle on top of everything else.

"Shotgun!" I called out quickly.

Cinder squinted at me.

"What? You can't just fly behind the van like a big kite?" I asked her. "What are those giant fluffy things for? Making pretty colors?"

CHAPTER TWENTY-FIVE

Triumvirate Slayer's

I will drop-kick you into next week," Cinder growled.

"Fine, fine," I sighed dramatically. "I suppose we'll have to share the front seat like civilized people. Do you want to sit on my lap, or do you prefer to be my fluffy throne?"

Cinder's wings flared with embarrassed pinks and irritated reds. "Neither! We are *not* sharing a seat!"

"Someone's gotta sit on someone," Iogann commented, climbing into the driver's seat. "Unless you want to try to squeeze into the back wedged under the equipment?"

"I am *not* sitting in anyone's lap!" Cinder declared firmly.

Five minutes later, she was perched awkwardly in my lap, her wings folded tight against her back to avoid taking up too much space. Every bump in the road made her tense up, and her feathers kept shifting through embarrassed pinks and flustered purples. She was unexpectedly light. I supposed that it made sense for a flying-type Omnid to be lighter than a human.

"Not. One. Word," she growled at Iogann, who was failing miserably at hiding his muffled chortling.

"Wouldn't dream of it," the Mothman turned the second key in the ignition.

What? Second key?

The van's engine suddenly thrummed to life with a deep, eerie hum that was definitely not standard. Suddenly, the entire vehicle shuddered and began to lift off the ground, wheels folding sideways.

"Um, Io?" I sputtered as the parking lot dropped away beneath us. "Is your van supposed to do that?"

I stared at the Gurrwulf Industries 2088 winged wolf logo on the dashboard. "Wait . . . this doesn't look like Omnid magitek or even mundane Earth tech!"

"Yeah, man," he chuckled, flipping switches on what I now realized was a ridiculously complex control panel featuring way too many dials. "Acquired it from a dimension where flying cars were the norm. Pretty sweet ride, right?"

"Acquired?" I arched an eyebrow. "You mean *stole?*"

"Liberated!" Iogann corrected, pulling back on what looked suspiciously like a flight stick. "From a reality that was about to get wiped out by an entropy wave anyway. So technically, I saved it."

"That's . . . bloody amazing, like Larry Plotter level amazing," I admitted as we soared over the school buildings. "No traffic, no roads to worry about . . ."

"And no glider-beast registry for the cops to track," Iogann added. "Seriously, those things are expensive to keep up with all the crystalline mana they need to nom."

"What is this thing powered by?" I asked.

"A fusion battery that expires in twenty years and compost trash," Iogann replied.

Cinder's wings unconsciously spread a bit, catching the wind through the cracked windows.

"The antigrav makes hauling equipment way easier." The Mothman grinned, flicking a switch. "Just gotta be careful about air traffic control and keep the cloaking field running."

"The what now?" I asked just as the entire van shimmered. The side mirror and the front of the van had seemingly vanished from view, leaving only a slight distortion in the air.

"Stealth mode," Iogann explained proudly. "Can't have people spotting a flying van, right? That'd cause way too many questions."

"And probably a disaster," Cinder muttered.

"Hey, my disasters are very selective," Iogann protested. "I seek disasters, I don't make 'em."

"Uh-huh." The Quetzi-girl rolled her eyes.

"Today doesn't count!" Io defended himself. "Em forced me into it!"

As the sun began to set, Cinder gradually relaxed against me, her initial stiffness melting away. Her feathers shifted through peaceful blues and content purples as she unconsciously leaned back, her head eventually coming to rest against my shoulder.

Below us, Leviathan's Cradle sprawled out in all its magitek glory. The massive comet impact crater that gave the city its name curved around the metropolis like a protective wall, its jagged peaks still bearing the crystalline scars of Wormwood Star's violent arrival. The setting sun painted these ancient wounds in brilliant oranges and deep purples, making the entire mountain ridge shimmer like a crown of broken gems.

The ocean beyond the crater ridge caught the dying light, transforming into a sheet of liquid fire that stretched to the horizon. Massive shapes moved beneath those golden waves—the descendants of the cosmic horror the comet had brought with it, now as much a part of this world as the crystalline mountains themselves.

"Pretty, isn't it?" Cinder murmured, her voice soft with something like pride.

"It's . . . incredible," I breathed, genuinely awestruck. "Better than in the brochures!" The city itself was a marvel of organic architecture, with buildings that seemed to grow rather than being built, their surfaces alive with bioluminescent patterns that began to glow as darkness approached. "I've never seen anything like it."

"Yeah. When all the buildings light up . . . it's like flying through a galaxy," Iogann commented, banking the van to the right, following the crater's curve to allow me to see more curious things below.

"That's Dreadspine National Park," He pointed at a massive skeletal structure that dominated the eastern side of the crater. "There's the bones of the first iteration of the Leviathan that crawled out after the impact."

The colossal skeleton gleamed in the fading light, its ivory-white bones threaded with crystalline veins that pulsed with a faint, ethereal glow. The ribs alone were taller than most skyscrapers, forming natural arches over the northwestern sections of the city.

"And over there," Cinder said, "that's the Triumvirate Slayer's Cathedral. See how it's built right into one of the vertebrae?"

I felt her shift slightly against me, her feathers brushing my neck as she pointed at the white gothic cathedral.

"Hey, um, Ci," I said, "how come you don't have a personal flying manta ray?"

"Dad doesn't trust me with one," she exhaled. "Plus, I failed the flight test like five times. Ughh. I just can't get them to obey me properly."

"Don't your wings work on them?" I asked.

"Not really," she sighed. "I can attract 'em, sure, but I can't tell a big-ass flyin' manta what to do via the mindlink tentacle. They just don't effin' listen! Worse than riding a freaking horse!"

"I see," I said. "What's that?"

"The dark district with occasional violet neon? That's Scab Row. The neon signs are basically gambling dens and massage parlors. And beyond that . . ." Her voice trailed off as she realized how close she'd gotten, her feathers flushing pink before she quickly settled back.

The city was transforming as night fell. Buildings and cars bloomed with bioluminescence, creating rivers of living light that flowed through the streets. The crater walls themselves seemed to come alive, crystal veins pulsing with deep, ancient power. Massive, sleek flying manta rays and rotund bus-moths took off here and there, weaving in and out of clouds, covered in glowing red-and-green Kitlix lanterns, carrying passengers and goods across the sky.

Iogann guided the van away from the commercial districts, heading towards an elevated residential area that literally rose above the rest of the city. Some of the homes here were practically palaces, each one unique in its architectural style.

My stomach tightened as I suddenly remembered exactly who lived in this neighborhood. Justice Nova—Cinder's father—wasn't just some random official. He was *the* Justice, one of the heads of Omnithornia's law enforcement and judicial system. The man who'd personally signed thousands of human deportation orders.

And I, a completely illegal human infiltrator, was about to walk into his house.

"Hey, Io," Cinder called out as we descended towards a particularly impressive Victorian Gothic revival mansion. "Drop us off at the back entrance. Dad's probably home by now, and I don't want to deal with . . ."

"The usual interrogation?" Iogann finished with knowing sympathy. "Yeah, no problem. The usual spot?"

The flying vehicle touched down silently in what appeared to be a private garden, hidden from the main house by towering orange-violet mystic willow oak trees.

Cinder reached for the van's door handle.

"Wait, stop," I said, gently grabbing Cinder's wrist before she could open the door. "How exactly do you think this is going to work? Your dad is literally the Justice of

Cradlefall. You know, the guy who signs deportation orders for breakfast? The one who made that speech last month about 'purifying Omnithornia of human corruption'?"

Cinder's wings shifted through uncertain colors. "He's not . . . I mean, he won't . . ."

"Won't what? Welcome a homeless Nullie into his house with open arms?" I laughed darkly. "Best-case scenario, he runs into a half-blood student sneaking into his house with his precious daughter and will be incredibly annoyed at both of us. Worst case, he calls up a Scrutimancer, and then I end up in a detention center or dead in a ditch."

"He's not home much," Cinder protested weakly. "And my room's in the separate wing, he barely ever comes there . . ."

"Ci," I said softly, using her nickname deliberately while also realizing that she'd said "my room" instead of the garage. "Your dad hunts 'human pond scum' for a living. This is a monumentally bad idea."

"Then what's your plan?" She turned in my lap to face me, her ocean-blue eyes fierce. "Freeze in your van? Sleep in the school rafters until you get caught? At least here you'd have a proper bed . . ."

"If we do this," I said, "then we do it my way. None of this back-garden sneaking where we eventually run into your parents or siblings and have to explain ourselves stammering and blushing like awkward teenagers while your father thinks of how to make me disappear. Io, take off. Take me to the Triumvirate Slayer's Cathedral on 204 Thunderward Street. Land in the dormitory garden in the back."

"Alex . . ." Cinder started to protest.

"Cindy." I grabbed her waist, replicating her tone. "Tell me, have you brought Io to your house before? Was it via that sus back-garden route where you had to sneak about avoiding cameras? Did that go well with your parents? Did they give Io's hippie robe and hat extra stern looks and then perma-ban him from ever visiting you 'cause he smells like a walking vape shop?"

Cinder's feathers shifted through guilty purples and embarrassed pinks. Iogann let out a dry chuckle from the driver's seat.

"Yeah, that was a fun afternoon," the Mothman commented. "Justice Nova gave a whole lecture about 'appropriate associations' and 'maintaining proper social standards.' Haven't been allowed back since."

"Exactly." I nodded. "So instead of sneaking around like guilty children, we're going to do this properly. Io, cathedral garden, please."

"What's your plan?" Cinder asked as Iogann lifted the van back into the darkening sky.

"Simple." I grinned. "I'm going to walk right through your front door. But first, we need to make me look like someone your dad absolutely can't dismiss."

"We?" She blinked.

"Yes, we," I said. "Instead of helping to sneak me through your dad's house, you're going to help me sneak into the Triumvirate Cathedral."

"The cathedral?" Cinder's eyes widened. "I don't . . ."

The van touched down in the shadowy square garden behind an imposing cathedral. Unlike the organic architecture of modern Omnithean buildings, this structure was deliberately archaic—all sharp Gothic spires and carved stone, illuminated by arcane flames rather than mere bioluminescence.

"Are you insane?" Cinder hissed at me. "This place has . . ."

"Incredibly lax dorm security," I said. "The outer arcane ward wall is quite hard to breach on foot, but we flew in from above in Io's invisible, non-magic van, so no alarms that would notice ordinary sky gliders have gone off. There is literally nothing of value to steal from the administrative offices, so the security in there is likely something incredibly basic. I've slept in plenty of Slayer churches during my Urbex days. Their layout is standard. You're coming with me to keep me invisible with those wings of yours."

Cinder's wings trembled slightly as they wrapped around me.

"This is crazy," she whispered against my ear. "If we get caught . . ."

"Io, any doom-sense about us?" I asked.

"Mmmmm. You do taste like a . . . walking cataclysm in general," the Mothman answered.

Cinder sent him a glare.

"But," he added, giving Cinder and me a thumbs-up, "this isn't the yuuge catastrophe I'm waiting for. You two should be fine here."

"Perfect," I grinned. "Pick us up in this exact spot in two hours or so. I'll Omnigram you for when I'm done. You're the anon that warned me about the show, yeah? Add me properly."

"Yeah, that was me. Can do." The Mothman gave us a mock salute from the van. "Try not to cause too much chaos without me."

CHAPTER TWENTY-SIX

Choir Manager I

I kept one hand on Cinder's waist, guiding her across the dark courtyard. Her wings provided the camouflage, their colors matching the shadowed stone so perfectly that we might as well have been ghosts.

The heavy wooden door's lock surrendered easily to my plastic card with a soft click. Old-style locks were hilariously vulnerable to the most simple approach.

We slipped inside, our footsteps echoing softly on the stone floor despite our best efforts to move quietly.

The administrative wing was exactly what I expected—all vaulted ceilings and Gothic arches, illuminated by Kitlix lanterns that cast a warm, flickering light similar to candlelight. The walls were lined with paintings of various Slayer Saints and their heroic deeds, their stern faces seeming to watch our progress disapprovingly.

"This way," I whispered, guiding Cinder down a side corridor and into the head priest's office. According to what Yulia dug up, the Elder Omnid inhabiting this domain was perfect.

With another application of a plastic card, we were in.

I closed the door behind us, slipped out from under Cinder's protective feathers, and made my way to the ancient-looking desktop computer that dominated the office's heavy wooden desk. The machine was exactly what I had expected—old, rarely used, and probably containing template files for every official document the cathedral produced.

"What are you doing?" Cinder hissed as she kept watch by the door.

"Creating a paper trail," I murmured, booting up the machine. The login screen appeared, demanding a password.

"You're going to hack a church computer?" Her voice was scandalized but also somewhat impressed.

"Pfff." I waved her off. "Obviously not. I'm going to hack a far weaker link—people."

I shuffled through the papers inside the desk for a bit and took photos of everything in the office.

Then I had Yulia look up the latest sermon of the old Archpriest that the office belonged to. In minutes, she applied the man's voice to the Nineteenthlabs API, replicating it exactly.

Then, I picked up the ancient landline phone from the desk.

"Ready," Yulia whispered back in my ear.

I dialed the IT support number listed on a sticky note beside the monitor.

"NazariteNet IT Support, how may I assist you?" a bored voice answered.

Yes, hello, I typed into my phone. *This is Father . . .*

"Yes, hello," Yulia's modulated voice emerged from my phone's speaker, sounding exactly like an elderly priest. "This is Father Matthias Jonannes from the Triumvirate Slayer's Cathedral records office. I seem to have forgotten my password again. These darn systems, you know how it is . . ."

"Of course, Father," the IT person sighed, clearly used to this sort of call. "I'll need to verify your identity. Can you provide your employee ID?"

"Ah yes, let me see . . ." I made a show of shuffling papers, then Yulia read out the ID number I'd spotted on the paperwork inside the desk. "EX-2024-117 . . ."

"Thank you, Father. And your security question: What was your first parish?"

"St. Nazareth Spire of Lethargic Lake," I replied through Yulia confidently, relying on the AI's reverse-image lookup of a photo of that church on the office walls. "Beautiful little place, you know."

Cinder's eyebrows were escaping from her face in a "what the fuck" look.

"All right, verified. Your temporary password is BlessedGate2025. Please change it upon login."

"Bless you, my child," Yulia replied.

After disconnecting, I quickly logged into the system. Just as I'd suspected, the computer contained the needed templates.

"Alex," Cinder whispered urgently, looming over me. "Someone's coming!"

I quickly turned the monitor off and slipped under her camo-wings just as footsteps echoed down the hallway. Through the gaps in her feathers, I watched an elderly Omnid priest shuffle past the office, muttering prayers under his breath. He didn't even glance our way through the stained glass office door.

Once the priest's footsteps faded away, I slipped back to the computer and began rapidly editing the templates. My fingers flew across the keyboard as I created a carefully crafted paper trail—letters of recommendation, character references, work permits, and most importantly, official documentation of my "charitable work" with the cathedral's youth outreach program.

"What exactly are you doing?" Cinder whispered, peering over my shoulder as I worked.

"Creating the perfect man," I answered.

Cinder choked.

"What were you doing on February 14?"

"What? Why?" Cinder demanded, caught off guard by my question.

"Just answer. Where were you?"

"I was . . . at the Spring's End Festival," she said. "The one where a bunch of students died from the flesh-tree that walked out of the gate. Why?"

"Perfect." I typed rapidly, creating a detailed account of how Alexander Glock had heroically helped evacuate students during the incident, specifically mentioning assistance rendered to one Cassiopeia Nova. "I'm the mixie who helped you during that event."

"But you weren't . . ." Cinder started.

"Doesn't matter," I said, printing the documents. "What matters is that these records say I was. And they're official church documents signed by Father Matthias Jonannes."

"Won't the priest realize none of this happened?" she demanded. "You can't just . . ."

"Father Matthias Jonannes is 341 years old," I said. "Do you know what happens to old Omnids who repeatedly extend their life using the Lazarus Cavern instead of retiring?"

Cinder looked at me.

"They get super forgetful and confused," I explained, carefully applying the church's ornate seal to each document and signing them with Matthias's signature, replicating it with slight variance. "Even with the incarnator optimizing the body, the subject still ages and the mind decays. Elder Omnids mix up timelines, forget whole decades. Their short-term memory is constantly disrupted by the reincarnation process. Nobody questions computer databases and signed records. Especially not from a respected Arch-Elder. Your dad won't doubt these—if anything he might be a bit concerned about why you never mentioned the 'heroic mixie' who saved you during the festival."

Cinder's feathers shifted through shades of amazement and concern as she watched me work. "This is . . . so effin' devious. How do you even know all this stuff? How did you know the answer to the secret question?"

"Oodle, plus the sagely wisdom of my personal open source AI," I shrugged. "The secret questions are actually pretty standard once you break into enough of these churches. Honestly, if I was the school's administration, the first thing I'd do is order students to make their own personal AI. There is so much potential in agent-armed LLMs with vision that everyone is utterly blind to."

"Is that how you knew all those students' names earlier? And their connections?"

"Yep." I nodded. "Yulia helps me process and gather information faster, but the real skill is knowing how to use that information within the framework of administrative systems and people."

"Yulia, generate an image of me, Dr. Slate Glock, and Father Matthias Jonannes at St. Nazareth Spire of Lethargic Lake," I whisper-ordered in Kaska. "Don't forget the name tags and event date. Use the image on the wall as reference."

I began humming "Omnithornication" as I worked forging more documents and contracts, slipping them into appropriate folders and shelves.

"Ugh. I can't believe you recorded me singing that," she lamented.

"It's now my favorite song in the universe," I commented, inserting a USB cord from my phone into Father Matthias's computer and sending the image to the printer.

As the printer hummed, I dismounted one of the many pictures off the wall, popped the glass out, and then inserted the AI-generated photograph of myself and my Thunderbird "father" into the frame, hanging it back onto the wall.

"Holy shit," Cinder breathed, staring at the photo. "*How?!* The lighting, the details, the lake in the back . . . it looks completely real. How did you . . . do that?"

"Yulia is really good at using stable diffusion." I grinned. "It takes her seven seconds to generate pretty much anything."

"But . . ." Cinder's wings shifted through confused purples as she studied the image. "Your clothes, your expression, even the way the light catches your eyes . . . it's perfect. Too perfect. It's just like the other photos on the wall. It's like it was there to begin with!"

"That's the point," I said, saving the photo onto the computer into the Nazarite meetup folder that was already there. "How much do you know about current AI capabilities?"

"Umm. I'm in Mr. Murconi's Infomatics class, but he's lame and annoying, so I skipped most of it. I know that Omnibook released an AI recently, but it's, like, pretty stupid, just hallucinates nonsense most of the time, so it's not amazing for essays. Asking it to draw something remotely interesting like some celebrity getting their head cut off gets the 'request denied' yellow cat picture."

"Sounds about right," I said. "Many Omnids like you haven't really caught up to what AI can do these days."

"You're scaring me even more now," Cinder admitted, her wings shifting through uneasy orange-violets. "Like, actually legit freaking me out. You just . . . casually walked in here and rewrote reality in what, thirty minutes?"

"Reality is mostly paperwork and photos." I shrugged, gathering the documents into a neat folder. "People believe what they see, especially when memory is imperfect. Your dad might be the Justice of Leviathan's Cradle, but he's still just a person who relies on other systems, other people, and documentation to make decisions. I just wrote myself into a month of staying at the church dorms instead of sleeping in the van like a smelly hobo."

"Damn," Cinder muttered. "So . . . are we done, or . . .?" she asked as I carefully locked the computer and restored the office to its near-exact previous state.

"We're gonna go to the dorm, so that I can shower and change," I said. "While I do that, you can think of how you met a very brave, nerdy young man on Saint Valentira's Spring's End Day. A choir manager named Alexander Glock."

"A choir manager?" Cinder's feathers formed its invisi-canopy over me as we walked to the dorms. "Really?"

"Yep." I grinned, leading her down the corridor towards the dormitory wing. "It explains why I'm so interested in your music, doesn't it? Church choir managers are basically invisible—everyone knows they exist, but nobody pays attention to them."

We reached the dormitory wing, which was exactly what I expected—rows of simple but comfortable rooms meant for visiting clergy and church staff. Most were empty, their doors unlocked and featuring neatly made beds and sparse furnishings.

I picked one of the small rooms in the back, messed up one of the beds, and then used a pen to quickly write out *Alexander Glock* onto the sign-in sheet by the door, backdating it to February 10.

"BRB," I told Cinder. "Chill in my bed for a bit."

"That's not your . . ."

"It is now." I winked at her.

The Quetzi watched me with wide ocean-blue eyes as I rushed off to the bathroom.

CHAPTER TWENTY-SEVEN

Choir Manager II

I emerged from the shower dressed in a perfectly pressed set of dark Nazarite novitiate robes I'd "borrowed" from the laundry room. The silver sword pin on my lapel caught the light as I adjusted the silver-black cross collar. Thick, round glasses sat on my nose, making my eyes look far larger than they were.

Cinder became visible, perched with a look of worry on the narrow bed.

"Good evening, fair lady." I grinned at her, adjusting my new thick-rimmed glasses. "Shall we go meet your parents? I believe I'm properly dressed for dinner now."

Cinder stared at me, her feathers shifting through fifty shades of disbelief. The transformation was complete—gone was the scruffy, sweaty Nullie in layered hexa-suits. In his place stood a proper young Nazarite novitiate, complete with perfectly pressed robes and a demure expression, hair slicked back with plentiful application of gel.

"You look . . ." She struggled for words.

"Respectable? Trustworthy? Like someone who definitely helped evacuate students during a flesh-tree incident?" I suggested helpfully.

"Like a completely different person," she finished. "How do you *do* that? What the fuck. I didn't think that you could look any dweebier, and yet here we are. Holy shit, those effin' glasses."

"The glasses are essential." I adjusted them with a practiced gesture. "They make me look harmless and scholarly."

"You look like a Larry Plotter TV set reject," she snickered.

"Uh-huh. Text your parents," I ordered. "Ask them if your friend, Nazarite choir manager Alexander Glock, can stay over for dinner."

"That would be . . . pretty out of character for me, but fine . . ." Cinder stared at me for a long moment, then pulled out her phone with an exaggerated sigh. Her claws tapped rapidly on the screen.

"Mom says yes," she reported after a few minutes, sounding surprised. "She's . . . actually excited? Says she's been wanting to meet the 'brave young man' from the Spring's End Festival. Wait . . . how in the Abyss did she already know about that? What the fuck is happening?"

"Father Matthias sent a very nice email to your parents about half an hour ago, praising their daughter's volunteer work with the church youth choir and mention-ing how wonderful it was to see her again today." I smiled innocently. "The email included a lovely photo of you and me serving soup to the destitute of Scab Row's soup kitchen."

"*What?!*" Cinder nearly dropped her phone. "We never . . . I would never . . . how did you . . .?"

"AI-generated images, remember?" I adjusted my large glasses again, showing her the soup kitchen photo on my phone. "The lighting really brings out your angel wing colors."

"You just . . . effin' created an entire fake history between us in less than an hour! WTF!" she stammered.

"Not fake," I corrected. "Alternative fiction. The best lies are built on partial truths. You were at the Spring's End Festival flesh-tree summoning. You do have an amazing singing voice. I am very interested in helping you produce music. We did meet recently. The rest is just . . . creative interpretation of events. Now, tell me—how did we meet? Did you think of anything?"

"N-no," Cinder admitted. "I'm not good with this shit. I've been sitting here freaking out!"

"Fine," I said. "Listen carefully . . ."

I laid out the narrative as we sat on "my" dorm bed.

"You met me at the Spring's End Festival. I was there helping with the choir arrangements. When the flesh-tree emerged, I helped evacuate the attendees while you fought it. We didn't really talk much then—just a brief 'thank you' moment, after I pulled you behind the temp soup kitchen's steel door when the flesh-tree was about to pulverize you."

The Quetzi nodded.

"Recently, you ran into me again at the cathedral where I was organizing sheet music for the youth choir. You felt very bad about so many people dying at the festival, so you started to help out at the soup kitchen, got to know me, got to listen as I directed the choir. In January, I joined Skyfall Academy as a student. Today, I was at your show, and I saved your best friend Em from an interdimensional monstrosity that knocked Graves out. You were in shock, and I helped bring Em back to life. Don't even have to make much up for this part. You were so grateful that you invited me to dinner with your parents."

Cinder stared at me, her feathers shifting through thoughtful blues and worried purples. "That's . . . actually fairly believable. Except for the part where I'd help at a soup kitchen."

"Why not? It shows character growth," I pointed out. "No backtracking. Your mom already thinks you've been doing it. The photos are quite convincing."

"My parents are going to have so many questions," she groaned, falling back onto the narrow bed. "They're going to want details . . ."

"Do you really give your parents details about your life?" I asked.

Cinder snorted. "No. I barely talk to them at all these days."

"Perfect!" I nodded. "Then we just need to let them fill in the blanks themselves. People are really good at seeing what they want to see. Your mom probably wants to believe you're secretly doing charitable work, that you were acting out and now want to change. Your dad will want to believe you're hanging out with respectable church people instead of inhaling interdimensional smokes and summoning eldritch horrors into abandoned subway tunnels."

Cinder blinked at me. "How'd you know about that?"

"Your brother told me about the tunnel children's song stuff," I said. "Your family aren't clueless idiots. They know what's going on in your life."

"Oh." She deflated.

"They're probably relieved you're finally bringing someone 'respectable' home," I continued, straightening my novitiate robes. "A nice, proper young man from the church who helps direct choirs and feed the poor. Much better than your usual crowd of disaster magnets."

Cinder's wings shifted through irritated reds. "My 'usual crowd' are my friends!"

"And I will be setting all of your friends on the righteous path as a goodly Nazarite," I said in an exaggerated pious tone, then dropped the act with a grin. "Or at least that's what your parents will think. In reality, I'll be helping you build something way better than the Dreadful Delvers."

"Which is what?" Cinder demanded.

"I don't know yet," I said. "You've got real talent, Ci. Not just with singing, but with performance in general. The way you commanded that stage, melted my brain with your song? That was incredible. Your Bard delver skill is absolutely baller."

"I'm not doing any more shows." Cinder's feathers shifted back to depressed grays. "Not after today. And . . . I don't want to sign up to extra delving outside of Delving class. If I do, my brother will figure out how to attach me to his team on a permanent basis, and it'll be nothing but annoying-as-F rules and checklists and wearing bulky-as-shit multilayered armor that makes me look like an ocean diver and doesn't accommodate for my wings."

"We'll make our own delving team," I said. "With you as its Captain and me as Quartermaster. We'll set up whatever rules we want to, figure out how to get the most out of Arx and other worlds. Delving class has multiple excursions, yeah? According to the online course description, there's field trips to Thornwild, Novazem, Andross, etc."

Cinder pursed her lips.

"I'll see how we can apply your voice most optimally on each world. I want to understand it all. Not just dungeoneering, but everything. I want to know where the Kitlix come from, who makes them, and how. I want to study dungeon monsters and other worlds' inhabitants and magitek things and improve upon it all!"

"Who would even be on this delving team?!" Cinder asked.

"You, me, Io, Vee and . . . Katherine Kells."

"Katherine?!" Cinder's feathers bristled. "The wheelchair-bound girl who never talks to anyone? She's practically failing Delving class, can barely function in sunlight. Why her and not, I dunno . . . Solace or something?!"

"Solace is pretty much the definition of a knob. She's tough-skinned, extra-hostile against mixies, and very stubborn, thus she can remain Em's only friend," I said.

"Leaving Em without someone to yell at is bad. On the other hand, Katherine is an incredible artist, a clever and hella-dangerous hunter," I said. "Her dimensional magic is insanely useful for my . . . endeavors."

"Lots of people in school have useful talents," Cinder pointed out. "Katherine doesn't like me one bit. In fact, according to her own words—she hates everyone. Why her?"

"Because she knows something important," I revealed.

"About what?"

"About me," I admitted. "About you. About . . . something else. Something bigger than all of this." I gestured vaguely in the air towards the massive cathedral visible through the tiny Gothic window. "But that's a conversation for another time. Right now, we need to focus on the dinner mission with your parents."

"Right . . ." Cinder stood up with a frown, clearly not looking forward to interacting with Katherine or maybe stressing about my social hacking shenanigans. "My parents are going to ask about your family. Your background. What are you going to tell them?"

"Exactly what the Skyfall and now Nazarite Cathedral records say," I smiled. "It'll be fun, trust me."

I pulled out my phone and texted Io that we were done.

CHAPTER TWENTY-EIGHT

Dinner I

Io's flying van touched down silently on a side street wrapped in massive pine-fern trees, a few blocks from the Nova mansion. The last rays of sunset had faded, leaving the city bathed in the ethereal glow of buildings covered in bioluminescent fungi.

We bid the Mothman adieu and began our walk up to the Nova residence.

The Victorian Gothic estate stood in front of us behind lavish gates featuring winged Omnids holding up the archway entrance.

Cinder tapped a card on the intercom and the gate unlocked, letting us in.

We walked up the winding path to the mansion's entrance, gravel crunching beneath our feet. The garden was immaculately maintained, featuring more mystic trees. Luminous blue bell flowers which Yulia tagged as "Starfall Snowdrops from Novazem" cast soft ethereal light across manicured, magic-heated, watered lawns.

"Relax, Ci," I whispered to Cinder as we approached the imposing front door. "Let me do most of the talking. And try to look less like you're walking to your execution."

"Easy for you to say," she muttered, her wings and tail shifting through anxious grays and violets. "You're not the one who has to explain bringing home a total d . . ." She trailed off as the massive oak door swung open.

A Quetzalcoatl woman stood in the doorway, silver-white-pink-green feathers gleaming in the warm light spilling from inside. Unlike Cinder's sharp, angular features, Lady Nova's face was soft and motherly, with kind eyes that crinkled at the corners as she smiled. She was shorter and curvier than Cinder, her appearance motherly to the tenth degree. She was wearing a white dress, white leggings, and a white fluffy See-Mass sweater with blue-and-white Aztec patterns.

"Welcome home, starshine!" She beamed at Cinder. Cinder replied with a half grunt.

"And you must be Alexander!" Lady Nova's warm smile turned to me. "We've heard such wonderful things about you from Father Matthias! Please, come in, come in!"

I bowed slightly, the perfect picture of a polite young novitiate. "Thank you for having me, Lady Nova. Your home is beautiful."

"Oh, please, call me Anitta," she insisted, ushering us inside. "Cassie never brings friends home anymore, especially not such polite young men!"

"Mom," Cinder groaned, "I told you not to call me that."

"Call you what, starshine?" Anitta blinked. "Your father and Lance should be down in the dining hall soon."

"Oh, let me take your coat and bag, dear," Anitta offered.

"Thank you, ma'am," I replied politely, shrugging off my winter jacket to reveal the pressed Nazarite robes underneath. "My apologies if the bag is a bit heavy—just some choir music sheets and school books I'm reviewing, plus camera equipment."

"Such a dedicated young man!" Anitta beamed, grabbing the large camping bag as though it weighed nothing. "Cassie, why don't you show Alexander to the guest washroom so he can freshen up before dinner?"

I followed Cinder down a hallway lined with family photos, noting how her image became progressively darker and more rebellious in newer pictures. The transformation from bright, colorful girl to her current "I hate you all" goth aesthetic was quite stark.

"Your mom seems nice," I commented.

"She's . . . yeah," Cinder sighed. "Too nice sometimes. It's annoying. Never listens to me."

The guest bathroom was as luxurious as expected, with marble countertops and gold fixtures. I quickly checked my appearance in the mirror, making sure that my goodest-boy NPC mask sat on right.

When I emerged from the bathroom, the sound of voices drifted from the dining room, Cinder waiting for me in the hall looking incredibly tense.

The dining room was exactly what I expected from a high-ranking Omnithean official's home—all dark wood paneling and crystal chandeliers, with a massive table that could easily seat twenty. Currently, only six places were set.

Justice Nova stood as we entered. He was tall and imposing in his formal black uniform, his gray scales gleaming in the chandelier light. His orange eyes fixed on me with laser-like intensity. He was a taller, bulkier, gruffier, sharper, and more dangerous-looking version of Lance, bald head gleaming.

"Good evening, sir." I bowed respectfully to Justice Nova. "Thank you for allowing me to join your family for dinner. I'm Alexander Glock."

"Hmm." Justice Nova's eyes narrowed slightly as he studied me. "The choir manager Father Matthias mentioned. You were at the Spring's End Festival incident, volunteering at the local soup kitchen, yes?"

"Yes, sir," I replied. "Though my contribution to the festival and cleanup was rather small. Your daughter was far more heroic that day."

"That's not what I heard." Nathaniel Nova's gaze struck his daughter, making Cinder scowl back. "It is my understanding that Cassiopeia was the one to summon the flesh-tree through the gate to begin with."

"Hey, Alex." Lance waved to me.

I waved back to Cinder's brother and turned back to my real target.

"I believe there may be some misunderstanding," I interjected smoothly, my voice deep and calm. "When the flesh-tree emerged, I witnessed Cassiopeia actively fighting to protect others. She helped me evacuate several younger students to safety behind the soup kitchen's steel door. As for the summoning, Cassie was forced into doing such dangerous things by Emerald Stratos with her wyrm-command charisma voice skill, which bends the listener into total obedience."

Justice Nova's orange eyes narrowed further. "Is that so?"

"Yes, sir." I maintained steady eye contact. "In fact, that's partly why I was so pleased to run into her again at the cathedral. Her actions that day showed real character. Of course, you need not listen to me—here is a video taken by the landlord's cam."

I pulled out my phone, displaying a somewhat blurry AI-animated frame of Cinder pulling horrified-looking Omnid kids through the door as red tentacles flashed overhead, obliterating bricks into flying shrapnel. Her wings were spread over the children and her face fiercely protective.

Cinder choked beside me.

"She did not see herself as a hero," I said. "And she didn't want you to see this footage, because she was indeed the one who participated in the show which cascaded into most unfortunate events after."

"That's quite impressive footage," Justice Nova commented, studying the video intently. "Why haven't I seen this before?"

"The landlord didn't wish to release the footage," I explained smoothly. "It took some convincing, so I only recently managed to recover this pixelated recording while organizing the cathedral's disaster response records. I thought it important to document acts of heroism alongside the tragedies."

Lady Nova beamed at her daughter. "Oh, starshine, why didn't you tell us about this?"

Cinder's wings shifted through uncertain orange-violets. "I . . . um . . ."

"Cinder regrets her participation in the festival," I said. "It may please you to know that the troupe responsible for that disaster has been disbanded as of today."

"Disbanded?" Justice Nova asked with a look of surprise. "Really? The Dreadful Delvers are no more?"

"Yes, sir." I nodded solemnly. "After today's . . . incident at school, Cinder made the mature decision to leave the group. She demonstrated remarkable judgment, especially in protecting me while I saved her friend's life this evening."

"Oh, yes. I heard about that terrible incident at school today from Lance," Lady Nova's feathers shifted through concerned blues. "Were you hurt, dear?"

"Not at all," I said. "In truth, the entity badly hurt every single Omnid who tried to oppose it. The Dreadful Delvers' Captain Emerald Stratos died when her artifacts and armor failed catastrophically. Solace Exill was impaled by her own battle-axe. Vespera Simmi suffered severe electrical burns and a broken nose. Even Vice Principal Graves was knocked out. Iogann Wanderer was paralyzed due to mana deprivation. I was the only one left standing on stage, with your daughter behind me."

"And yet you survived? How?!" Justice Nova demanded.

"The only reason why the entity didn't attack me like the others was because it didn't see me as a threat. As you might have noticed, I'm Skyfall Academy's only half-blood student this year." I waved a hand at my human face. "Slayer Nazareth taught us that we must wield the sword with wisdom, not merely our strength. It was through humility and careful negotiation that I managed to save the life of Emerald Stratos and convinced the entity to depart."

"You . . . saved Emerald and my sister?!" Lance breathed out, his eyes wide.

I kicked Cinder under the table to back me up.

Cinder jumped slightly at my kick but quickly caught on. "Y-yes," she said, her wings shifting through soft silver-blues sprinkled with patches of pink. "Alex talked that thing down when everyone else was injured or incapacitated. He even managed to get Emerald's Lazarus bracelet back before the gate closed. Without his actions, Em would be permanently dead."

"Curious." Justice Nova leaned forward slightly. "And what exactly was this entity?"

"It called itself a Corpseworld Caretaker," I explained. "I would quantify it as a Paradox-Proxima on the Eugenii Livirii Scale. Impossible to stop, but cooperative when spoken to."

Cinder's family stared at me.

"Here are a few select frames of the footage I've taken," I said playing the video of Cinder wrapping me with her wings, standing against the impossible, infinitely armed, infinitely violet-eyed thing. "If you wish to see the entire event, I can email it to you. Vespera Simmi invited me to the show as a videographer, so I recorded the entire thing and was able to get on stage just in time to help."

Cinder's mother let out a squeak as she stared at the video of Cinder and me facing Zee Captain. She covered her snout, feathers turning a horrified orange-pink-gray-black.

Justice Nova studied the footage along with his wife, his gray skin paling at the view of Zee Captain on camera. "Truly remarkable documentation. Your camera work is . . . professional."

"Thank you, sir," I replied modestly. "The cathedral has been very supportive of my work. It helps document our charitable work and community outreach."

"Damn, I can't make heads or tails of that thing. Where is its face, even?! You saved . . . *everyone*?!" Lance choked from his seat, staring at the video. "Slayer! Alex! I didn't know! I only heard that things went bad for the performers, but . . ."

"The entity fried the ward without even touching it." I pulled the cracked, dim runestone from my pocket and handed it to Lance. "The defense keystone you gave me shattered."

Lance turned the dead runestone over in his gray hands, eyes wide with disbelief. "This is . . . impossible. These keystones are rated to withstand . . ."

"Everything except a being that can rewrite reality with a glance," I finished. "The entity walked through our strongest wards like they didn't exist. But more importantly, it taught us all a valuable lesson about humility and the dangers of reckless gate-opening."

I booted Cinder again.

"Yes," she let out with a small shudder, her wings shifting through depressed somber grays, sparks of tears forming at the edges of her eyes. "After seeing what happened to Em and the others . . . I realized how dangerous and stupid we'd been. That's why I quit the troupe."

"A wise decision." Justice Nova nodded approvingly. "Perhaps this incident will finally teach you the importance of proper procedure and respect for authority."

Cinder's eye twitched. I pinched her under the table.

"Yes," she managed through gritted teeth.

I looked at Lance pointedly. The teenage Dover Demon was staring at the rune-stone in his hand in pure shock.

Then, noticing my gaze, he leapt up from his seat. "Thank you! Thank you so much for saving my sister and her friends! I can't believe you managed to negotiate with something that alien!"

"Yes! Thank you so much, dear!" Anitta Nova added, her feathers shifting through grateful pinks and warm golds. She reached across the table and squeezed my hand. "Not many would have the courage to approach such a dangerous entity. You truly embody the teachings of Slayer Nazareth—wisdom and planning over a brute head-on attack."

I bowed my head modestly. "I'm just grateful I could help, ma'am."

Justice Nova's gaze pinned me even harder. "Tell me more about this negotiation."

I took a careful breath. "Unlike the others, I had no weapons to attack it with, so I simply listened to its words and understood what it wanted."

"What did it want?" Lance asked.

"The Corpseworld Caretaker seemed more interested in narrative than violence. When I approached it with respect and humility, it responded in kind. It wanted to hear something that would . . . inspire it, I suppose."

"So what did you tell it?" Justice Nova asked.

CHAPTER TWENTY-NINE

Dinner II

"Oh my, look at the time." Lady Nova rapidly began serving what appeared to be some kind of caviar sitting atop calamari slices to everyone.

"The Corpseworld Caretaker . . . stopped time with a word for several minutes . . ." I exhaled dramatically and half-lied smoothly, aiming my metaphorical Glock at the immovable, stern Justice of Cradlefall. "So I told it . . . my story."

"Your story?" Lance stared up at me from the phone screen playing out a loop of Emerald's demise, Solace's axeing, and Vespera's self-electrocution.

I hesitated just long enough to make it seem as if I was carefully selecting my words, making a dramatic pause. "A story about hope. About someone who refused to give up, even when the world seemed determined to break them."

Cinder shot me a sideways glance.

"I told the entity from beyond the stars about my childhood in North Acadia," I began. "And my study in South Acadia at St. Christopher's Academy."

I made my voice grow softer, more vulnerable, as I padded more heart-wrenching lies in. "My mother was diagnosed with cancer when I was twelve. The human-hospital chemical treatments were . . . ineffective. But she never lost her faith. She played the organ at the local Nazarite Church until she physically couldn't anymore."

Lady Nova's feathers shifted through sympathetic, warm colors. Even Justice Nova's stern expression softened slightly.

"Then my school . . . burned down," I continued, staring down at my plate. "An electrical fire. We lost everything—the music sheets, the instruments, all of it. But the community came together. We held choir practice in people's homes, in parks, anywhere we could.

"My mom died last spring." I paused, taking a shaky breath. "Then, the mountain avalanche took my Thunderbird father . . . and . . . his Lazarus bracelet was never found."

I thought about holding my mom's pale hand in the hospital when her heart stopped, and my eyes filled with tears.

"Oh, you poor dear," Lady Nova breathed, her own eyes sparkling at the edges.

"I almost broke then," I added quietly. "But my mother . . . even through her illness, she kept telling me to have faith. To keep singing, keep helping others. Thus, when my dad was gone, choir music became my anchor."

Cinder was staring at me, her ocean-blue eyes wide. I could see her struggling to reconcile this story with what she knew about me to understand where the truth ended and the lies began.

"After losing my parents, I left South Acadia," I continued, carefully wiping my eyes with a napkin. "Before he died, Dad mentioned that he wanted me to attend Skyfall, to bring up the low level of my heart core through the delving program. Father Matthias knew my father. The Arch-Priest of Triumvirate Slayer's was incredibly kind and offered me a place to stay in the Cathedral dormitory while I study at Skyfall Academy. He says that music heals the soul, and I've found that to be true. Working with the youth choir, helping at the soup kitchen . . . it gave me purpose. I told the entity all of this, and then . . . it thanked me for my story and simply left without hurting anyone else," I concluded to my audience of captivated Novas.

"That's why today's incident affected me so deeply," I added, glancing at Cinder. "Seeing someone with such incredible musical talent risk their life unnecessarily . . . it reminded me of what really matters. Not power or status, but using our gifts to help others."

"A truly inspiring perspective." Justice Nova nodded approvingly. "And quite mature for someone your age."

"The Slayer teaches us that true strength comes from facing adversity with grace," I quoted. "I'm just trying to live up to those words."

"Speaking of music," Lady Nova interjected warmly, "Cassie has such a lovely voice. Perhaps you two could work together? The cathedral's youth choir could really benefit from her talent."

Cinder choked on her drink.

"Mom!" she protested.

"Actually," I said carefully, "it is my sincerest wish to be Cassiopeia's manager. Ever since I heard her sing, I've been amazed by her talent. Her voice has incredible power—not just in terms of skill, but real spiritual resonance. The way she can move people's hearts . . ."

"What a wonderful idea!" Lady Nova beamed, her wings fluttering with excitement. "Starshine, you could perform at the cathedral!"

"And what exactly would this management entail?" Cinder's father asked.

"I leave that entirely up to you, Mr. Nova," I replied. "As her father, you would have final say on all performances and venues. My role would simply be to help Cinder develop her talent in a safe, structured environment. No more dangerous summoning shows or illegal gates—just pure musical performance."

Cinder's eyes were boring a hole in the side of my head.

"And what would you get out of this arrangement?" Justice Nova wondered.

"The opportunity to work with an incredible talent," I answered without hesitation. "And perhaps . . . a chance to build something meaningful. The youth choir is wonderful work, but with Cinder's talent, I could create something truly special, help her bloom. Here's a small edit of her singing that I've remixed in my spare time."

I opened my BandOodamp page and pressed ▶ *Play* ◀ .

In truth, I hadn't done any remixing. I was an absolute incompetent at editing and composing music—Yulia was the one who'd added the funky electronic beats atop Cinder's singing. She somehow managed to integrate Cinder's initial "Nueh" annoyed exhale into the music.

"And Arx's not far away, it's Omnithornication / Born and raised by those who praise control of population / Well, everybody's been there and I don't mean on vacation . . ."

Cinder's voice poured from the phone's speakers.

The song cut off a bit abruptly at the end as Yulia seemed to have run out of free AI-composer SolaDoor credits, but nobody in the dining room seemed to notice, all eyes on me and the extra-embarrassed Cinder.

"Hmm." Justice Nova leaned back slightly. "The start is a bit too modern for my liking, but I do like the middle. And what are your thoughts on this, Cassiopeia?"

Cinder's jaw snapped shut. She didn't expect the sudden remix revelation. Her wings shifted through uncertain purples and thoughtful blues. "I . . . um . . ."

I booted her gently under the table again.

"I trust . . . Alex," she finally mewled out, flashing with all sorts of amusing colors. "He's already proven he can keep me safe, and . . . I do miss just singing without all the dangerous stuff."

"Well, I think it's a wonderful idea!" Lady Nova clapped her hands together.

"Lenora!" She called out up the large stairwell, her voice carrying unnaturally far. "Dinner's ready, sweetheart!"

The sound of rapid footsteps thundered down the stairs, and a small black blur burst into the dining room. A young Black Shuck Omnid, no more than eleven, skidded to a halt beside the table. She had a jet-black mane and piercing yellow eyes, and she wore a black-and-pink princess-style frilly dress that matched her onyx-tinted body.

"Sorry I'm late!" she announced cheerfully. "I was playin' VR OodleCraft 'n' teaching Mr. Snuggles proper tea party etiquette!" Her yellow eyes landed on me and widened with curiosity. "Who're you?"

"This is Alexander Glock," Lady Nova explained as she flashed into the kitchen. "He's a friend of your sister's from school . . . a choir manager." Her voice carried to the living room with impressive clarity across the hall.

"A friend of Cassie's?" Lenora's tail began wagging excitedly. "But Cassie doesn't have friends! Well, except for that scary ruby dragon lady and the moth boy who smells funny!"

"Leny!" Cinder hissed, her feathers bristling with embarrassment and irritation.

"What? It's true!" Lenora protested, climbing into her chair and sticking her tongue out at Cinder. "You never bring anyone home!"

I smiled at Cinder as I swallowed a calamari boat filled with caviar with a look of satisfaction.

"Will Lady Xastigar be joining us for dinner?" I asked politely, turning to the Hearth-Keeper.

"Not tonight, dear." Lady Nova's feathers shifted from pink to silver-blue and gray as she began bringing out the second meal. "She's ever so busy with her Arch-CEO work. I believe she's in Thunderland this week negotiating another big contract for Omnimart."

I exhaled mentally. Xastigar Obliss-Nova was a very dangerous woman who could smell lies from a mile away, according to Yulia's report on her. Convincing her of my good choir boy persona would be incredibly difficult.

"Mom's probably doing another hostile takeover," Lenora commented cheerfully, stabbing a piece of meat with her fork. "She's super good at those! Last week she made three CEOs cry!"

"Lenoralynne." Justice Nova's voice carried a warning tone. "What have we said about discussing family business at the dinner table?"

"Sorry, Daddy." The young Black Shuck ducked her head, though her yellow eyes still sparkled with mischief. "But it's true! Mother says that tears are just weakness leaving the body!"

I noticed Cinder's wings shift through dark grays and violets at the mention of her Prima-Mother.

Interesting family dynamics.

Anitta quickly brought out more plates of food. The steaks were massive—easily two inches thick and practically raw in the middle, bleeding pink juice onto the plates. The Hearth-Mother served them with a flourish, her feathers shifting through proud pinks as she distributed portions.

"I hope you don't mind your meat rare, Alexander," she said apologetically. "We Quetzalcoatl tend to prefer our food . . . minimally cooked."

"Not at all, ma'am," I replied. "My mother taught me how to prepare raw fish the Kaska Dena way. She was a First Nations human, one of the last several hundred speakers of the Kaska language, an Athabaskan-speaking ethnolinguistic group in the Znetc human reservation area of North Acadia."

Justice Nova tore into his steak with frightening efficiency, his sharp teeth making quick work of the rare meat. Lance followed suit, while Lenora attacked her portion with enthusiastic if somewhat messy determination.

Cinder glanced at me as I uttered the Nazarite prayer of the Leviathan's Slayer and delicately cut my steak into manageable pieces. The meat was so rare, it was practically mooing.

"So, Alexander," Justice Nova said between bites, "what are your thoughts on the current human migration crisis?"

I carefully chewed and swallowed before responding. "A complex issue that requires careful consideration of both security and humanitarian concerns, sir. While we must protect our borders and society, we should also remember the Slayer's teachings about mercy and compassion."

Exactly what a goodly Nazarite would say.

"Interesting perspective." Justice Nova commented on my NPC response with one of his own. "And what of the increasing human criminal activity in Scab Row?"

"Dad," Cinder growled warningly.

"It's all right," I said softly. "As someone who works in the soup kitchen, I see firsthand how poverty and desperation can drive people to make poor choices. But I also see how kindness and opportunity can change lives. Just last week, we helped three human families find legitimate work through the cathedral's employment program."

"The cathedral does excellent work." Justice Nova nodded. "Though some might argue that such charity only encourages more illegal immigration and Topaz spread. If it were up to me alone, I would level all of Scab Row and ship every human there off to the Alisson Islands."

"With respect, sir," I replied carefully, setting down my fork, "I believe there may be a more efficient approach. The human workforce, properly managed and integrated, could actually benefit Omnithornia's economy, particularly in areas where Omnids are less interested in working."

"Explain," the Justice said.

"Take artificial intelligence development, for instance," I continued. "Humans, lacking natural magical abilities, have developed remarkable technological innovations to compensate for their lack of mana . . . while working for our Omnicorps. Human understanding of machine learning and neural networks could be invaluable for improving our magitek infrastructure."

"An interesting point," Justice Nova conceded. "Though how would you prevent security risks? Many Conservationist Party Omnids are concerned about instrumental convergence."

"That's actually only a problem in smaller agents," I said. "A properly characterized, well-personalized Large Language Model tied to a multitude of agents is actually completely incapable of over-focusing on a task."

"Really?" Nathaniel's eyebrows went up.

"Indeed! For instance," I continued smoothly, "by pairing human AI developers with Omnid Scrutimancers, we could combine human innovation with Omnid magical safeguards. The Conservationists' concerns about instrumental convergence could be easily addressed by having Deathskull Mothmen thoroughly examine human-designed LLMs with their doomsday sense."

"Hrm." The Justice seemed to contemplate my words.

"Consider the delving industry," I elaborated. "Currently, many promising dungeon locations go unexplored because they're deemed too dangerous or resource intensive for Omnid teams. But humans, with their technological approach and nothing to lose, could serve as excellent scouts and support personnel. Humans armed with personal AIs and drone scouts could map dungeons and extract artifacts with incredible efficiency."

"You seem quite knowledgeable about AI," Justice Nova pondered. "And here I thought that you were merely a choir manager."

"The Triumvirate Slayer's Cathedral's youth outreach program works extensively with human children in Scab Row," I explained smoothly. "Understanding their perspective and capabilities helps us serve them better. Plus, my late mother's work with First Nations language preservation relied heavily on AI tools she helped develop for the Frontenachii Clan. I am, after all, half Thunderbird, so the technical side of machine intelligence interests me greatly."

The dinner conversation spiralled into increasingly complex territory as I led Justice Nova through discussions of AI ethics, dungeon economics, and integration policies. His orange eyes gleamed with growing interest as I wove together threads of theology, technology, and theoretical social reform into a tapestry that painted me as both deeply traditional and innovatively progressive in just the right ways.

Cinder watched this verbal dance with barely concealed amazement as I smoothly navigated her father's probing questions, while Lenora peppered the conversation with occasional, amusingly inappropriate, extra-blunt comments.

Lady Nova beamed throughout the entire discussion, clearly delighted that her daughter had brought home such a well-spoken young man.

Lance simply looked shell-shocked. He was overwhelmed by the videos and the remix and had lost the trail of my conversation with his father about twenty minutes ago. It's not that he was an idiot; he'd simply never truly dug into the social and administrative structures of Omnithornia as deeply or as desperately as I had to, nor did he have a personal AI whispering topic advice into his ear.

As the conversation wound down, Lady Nova glanced at the ornate crystal and gold Gothic revival clock on the wall. "Alexander dear, you simply must stay the night. I won't hear of you walking back to the cathedral at this hour."

"Oh, I wouldn't want to impose . . ." I began with perfectly calculated reluctance.

"Nonsense!" Lady Nova insisted, her feathers shifting through determined pinks. "We have plenty of guest rooms, and it's much too dark for you to be walking about. The streets aren't safe at night, especially for a young half-blood."

Justice Nova nodded in agreement from his seat by the ornate fireplace inhabited by a chonky Ignix Kitlix, the crystalline kitten setting the wood alight. "Indeed. The guest room in the east wing should be suitable. Lance, show Alexander to his quarters."

CHAPTER THIRTY

Winged Interrogator I

Lance led me up a grand staircase and down a hallway lined with even more family portraits. The guest room was larger than my entire van, with a four-poster bed and antique furniture that probably cost more than everything I owned combined.

"So . . ." Lance said as soon as we were alone, closing the door behind us. "You're really something else, aren't you?"

I arched an eyebrow at him.

"The way you handled my father . . ." Lance shook his head in amazement. "I've never seen anyone navigate his interrogations so smoothly. And the Spring's End Festival? The footage? Where did that even come from?"

"I'm way under forty-two hours." I smiled, avoiding his questions. "I promised you that I would fix everything, didn't I? D&D is no more."

"Damn it, man," Lance exhaled. "I didn't know that you and Cass were friends for over a month. Way to bamboozle me and Christi! Abyss, I thought that you . . . damn."

"Did you notice something different about Cass?" I asked, derailing the conversation even further away from the festival.

"Uh . . . yeah," Lance said. "She didn't smell like smokes tonight. She always comes home smelling like that shit and then Mom has to burn incense to cover it up . . . otherwise Dad starts yelling at her." Lance blinked. "And she actually talked at dinner. Usually she just grunts at questions and then storms off to her room."

"Small steps." I nodded with a smug look.

Lance suddenly wrapped me in a bone-crushing hug, lifting me off my feet. "Thank you, thank you, thank you!" he exclaimed in a fierce whisper. "You have no idea how worried we've all been about her! The smoking, those damned shows, Em, the way she's been pushing everyone away . . ."

The single security hexamesh suit under my Nazarite novitiate outfit creaked, hardening before the Omnid-hug could shatter my ribs.

"I've no idea how you did it," he gushed. "But whatever you're doing, please don't stop. I haven't seen my sister this . . . present . . . in months! I haven't seen Dad approve of anyone like he approves of you! I haven't seen Cassie's feathers light up so much over dinner!"

"I'm just getting started," I half choked out. "But I need your help."

"Anything," Lance said immediately, releasing me and blushing with grays. "Sorry, forgot you're a halfsie."

"No matter what I do, or say, or show, just back me up, yeah?" I said. "Stand by my side as my Nazarite Knight. You and I . . . we're going to save your sister. No matter what it takes. No matter what lies are spread about me."

Lance's orange eyes blazed with determination. "I swear by the Slayer, I'll support you! Umm . . . what lies?"

I pulled my phone up and showed Lance a looped, stitched video of Emerald threatening me and calling me "Nullie" over thirty times in different locations.

"She threatened me after I saved her life, as a goodly Nazarite would," I exhaled. "But she's clearly not going to stop until she destroys my reputation at school."

Lance's orange eyes narrowed as he watched the compilation of Emerald's threats. "That ungrateful little b—!" he growled, eyes igniting with orange flames from within. "Was this . . . after you saved her life? After everything you did today?"

"Yes. Her behavior is understandable. She's hurt and lashing out," I sighed, rubbing the back of my head. "Cassie and I reincarnated Em after the show. Her pride was wounded when I saved her life. She'll probably try to spread rumors about me, maybe even claim I attacked her first."

"I won't let her!" Lance declared firmly. "I'll make sure everyone knows what really happened. You're a hero, Alex. You saved my sister, saved Em, faced down that . . . that thing from that corpse world! No one gets to twist that around!"

"Emerald will find a way. Her family . . . the Stratos clan are ridiculously wealthy and hold grudges for a long time. From what she threatened me with after her incarnation, I suspect that she will probably claim that I'm a human or other such nonsense." I sighed.

Lance frowned.

"She might hire a Scrutimancer, even go as far as to change public records, pay off fake witnesses," I extrapolated. "D&D was Emerald's child, and I smothered it personally to help your sister. Like Slayer Nazareth, I've sacrificed myself . . . made a terrible enemy in Emerald Stratos. She's not going to stop till I am deported from Omnithornia for false crimes."

"*What?!*" Lance's Dover Demon face became skewered, elongated unnaturally for a moment, hundreds of extra muscles dancing under his skin, the hallway lights flickering. "Let her bloody try! My father may not be as wealthy as the Stratos clan, but he's the Justice of Leviathan's Cradle! If Em tries anything underhanded, I'll make sure he knows exactly what happened today! I've got your back, brother!"

"Thank you older brother." I smiled. "We will both keep an eye on your sister, yeah? She's going through a lot right now. The troupe meant everything to her, even if it was toxic. She's going to need support to find a new path."

"Of course." Lance nodded firmly and put his large gray hand on my shoulder. "And . . . thank you again. For everything. No matter what bullshit Em spreads, I'll stand by your side. Promise."

Lance's firm declaration of support made me want to grin like a supervillain, but I kept my expression appropriately humble and grateful. Keeping Emerald alive was turning out to be my most cheeky move yet—any of her attempts to discredit me would only serve as part of the choreographed reality that I was manufacturing around myself.

Even dangerous enemies like Emerald Stratos had their purpose in my game.

After Lance left, closing the door behind himself, I carefully examined the guest room for surveillance devices. Finding none, I pulled out my phone and texted Cinder.

Alex G: Your family seems nice.

SongOfDarkness🎸: wtf was that?!

Alex G: What was what?

SongOfDarkness🎸: all of it! the effing video of me saving children, the story about your parents, the AI stuff with my dad . . . how much of that was even real?!

Alex G: Does it matter? Your parents love me now. Your brother is now my Nazarite Knight. Even your little sister likes me, I think.

SongOfDarkness🎸: it matters to ME

Alex G: Why?

SongOfDarkness🎸: because i thought i was starting to know you

SongOfDarkness🎸: and now i have no idea WTF is real and what's just another one of your . . . I don't even know. Edited reality jigs? AI-generated bullshit?

Alex G: Making you smile matters. The rest is just . . . fluff.

SongOfDarkness🎸: what does that even mean?!

Alex G: It means that while I may bend the narrative of reality to achieve my goals, my core motivation—helping you—is genuine.

SongOfDarkness🎸: why? why me? what do you actually want? WHO ARE YOU???!!!

Alex G: Who do you think I am?

SongOfDarkness🎸: . . .

The "user is typing a message" notification hung there for a few minutes. I wondered if she was writing stuff and then deleting it over and over.

I slumped onto the bed.

"I wish I knew," I mused. "I wish that I could answer that, Cindy."

The wall beside me ignited with a million colors. I nearly jumped out of my skin as Cinder materialized out of thin air directly beside my bed like an angry apparition.

"*Holy shit!*" I yelped, nearly falling off the bed. "What are you, the Ghost of Christmas Future?! Don't just appear without warning! What if I was naked in here after a shower or something?!"

Cinder's feathers shifted through irritated reds, embarrassed pinks, and frustrated blacks as she loomed over me. "I want answers," she hissed, dark claws digging into my Nazarite novitiate collar. "*Now.*"

"Could you be a bit more gentle there?" I asked, choking. "Kind of getting ss-strangled ovvvffer here. N-need air."

Cinder let go of me slightly, staring at my face.

"No more lies," she growled.

I opened my mouth. Before I could say anything, she suddenly reached out and bit my neck hard, pointy canines digging in.

Colors exploded in my head, making me feel wrong, sideways, all mental resistance melting away like spring snow exposed to sunshine.

"Owwww," I rubbed my neck when she let go. "What was that? Did we move onto hickeys? What are you, a vampire?"

"The truth," she hiss-growled, face elongated and sharp. "I want the *truth*."

"Ask specific questions," I said, feeling slightly drunk for *some* reason. "And keep your voice down, unless you want your dad to catch us. Sneaking into a boy's room? You're a brave fluffy dragon bae."

Cinder's wings bristled with frustration, but she lowered her voice to a fierce whisper. "Fine. Was ANY of that story about your parents true?"

"You sure we can't be overheard?" I asked her. "'Cause if I'm to tell you things . . ."

Cinder growled, let go of me, grabbed the remote, and turned the TV on, cranking up the volume for some show. Then she wrapped me tightly in her wings and brought her face dangerously close to mine.

"Tell me the damned truth, human!" she whisper-hissed, claws digging in.

"My mom did die," I said quietly. "Cancer. The hospital part was real. She was a First Nations Kaska Dena, one of the last of our kind, pushed to the brink of extinction. Frontenachii Omnicorp and smoking killed her. I love AIs and can rant about them for days . . . I love your singing. Frontenachii Wendigos experimented on humans, everything in the folder I gave you was real. The rest . . ." I shrugged. "Just dust in the wind. AI-generated dust, the kind that can make even the toughest, meanest Justice shed a tear."

Cinder's claws loosened slightly, her ocean-blue eyes searching my face. "Really?"

"Yeah," I said softly. "I arrived too late to do anything, since she never told me that she was dying. She was already in a coma. Held her hand till her heart stopped. She taught me Kaska, taught me to sing our old songs. But that's . . . not something I like talking about."

"And your dad?" she pressed.

CHAPTER THIRTY-ONE

Winged Interrogator II

Inever knew my dad," I admitted. "Mom raised me alone. A random dead Thunderbird bureaucrat served as my prop father figure to help me get into Skyfall Academy."

Cinder's wings shifted through annoyed oranges, sympathetic blues, and troubled purples. "So you're . . . really . . . completely alone?"

"I have Yulia." I shrugged. "She talks to me in my mom's voice, reminding me what I have to do."

Cinder's feathers ignited with reds and blacks of shock and concern. "You . . . programmed an AI to speak in your dead mother's voice?"

"Yes," I revealed. "Based off a single voice mail message. It's all I had left of her."

Cinder's wings shifted through a kaleidoscope of emotions—shock, concern, sympathy, and something else I couldn't quite identify.

"That's . . . that's pretty messed up," she whispered finally.

"We all cope in our own ways," I countered.

"Is that why you're here? In Omnithornia? Because of what happened to your mom?"

"Yes," I admitted, mind melting from the colorful wings wrapping me, the bite on my neck stinging ever so slightly. I felt the edges of my sense of self fraying away, the confining characteristics of "Alexander Glock" becoming boundary-less. "Frontenachii Omnicorp's toxic waste dumping killed hundreds. The cancer rates were . . . astronomical. But the Omnithean courts ruled it was 'acceptable collateral damage' for progress. I'm going to do absolutely everything to get to the top . . . to make those Corp executives pay for what they did. To make sure they never experiment on people again."

"So this is all . . . what, some elaborate revenge scheme?"

"Mere revenge against individuals won't be enough to sate me," I confessed. "I want . . . I *need* to change everything when I reach the top. The system is broken, Ci. Punishing a few executives won't do shit. I have to rewrite the rules themselves."

Cinder stared at me for a long moment. "You can't just . . . rewrite reality! My dad is close to the top, and he can't even accomplish the bullshit he wants to do!"

"I've just started," I said. "I already turned a complete disaster of a show into a triumph. Your parents love me, and your brother is ready to defend me to the death."

"But it's all built on lies!" Cinder protested.

"Is it?" I challenged. "I really did save Em today. I really did face down Zee Captain. I really do want to help you develop your talent. The core, back-end truth is there—I just . . . adjusted some of the front-end bits."

"So everything you do is just . . . manipulation? Even . . . being my friend?" she demanded.

"Friend?!" I laughed, feeling as though I was now stretched mentally across the entire room. "Is that what you think we are? Oh, no . . . we've moved far . . . far past that long ago. You're my . . . everything," my mouth confessed for me.

"W-what?" she stammered.

"Can't lie . . . favorite, best, perfect Quetzi . . . too close . . . so many pretty feathers." I was drooling now, completely lost, drowning in the dancing hypnotic patterns of pulsating rainbow wings. "Can't resist . . . hypno-wings . . . only . . . human."

Dark claws snapped her fingers in front of my face. I barely registered the action, lost in her dastardly charisma allure.

There was no point in lying, no reason to trick her.

She was my anchor, my Quetzi goddess. If she wanted me to start building a giant murder pyramid, then so be it. So be it! Maybe once I was done, she would help me stand against the world, against impossible odds, against all of Omnithornia.

Cinder choked at my words. Oh yeah, my mouth was now moving on its own.

Was I still thinking or saying stuff out loud? Somewhere along the line of staring at her wings, the distinction between thought and speech blurred and vanished.

Internal monologue? What's that? That's not a thing now.

Unfiltered, untarnished thoughts. Is this what you wanted, goddess? Here I am, bared to the core. Pure thought, nothing but the absolute unfiltered truth.

Are you satisfied, or do you wish to learn more? Is this what you wanted? Because I am going to destroy you if you let me in.

Because even pure unfiltered thought is a weapon, a tool, a very dangerous thing to want. I love you. I have always loved you. Always and forever, since I saw your wings and eyes.

I will cut out ten million hearts for you, and then a billion. I will lay waste to nations if you just say the word. I will become Emperor of Mankind and write your name in the stars. Cassiopeia Cinder Terror Nova. Ruler of all Omnid-kind, the Empress of Humanity? Doesn't that sound great?

You are the Leader, and I am the Champion. You are the mind-control spiral, and I am the hammer. Just point me in a direction, and I will not stop. I will never stop because I am broken in just the right, the perfect way, for you and only you.

Cinder recoiled as if struck, her wings snapping back, losing all colors, turning pure, liquid silver. But it was too late now. I was still talking, rambling, vomiting words, unable to halt.

"Alex!" Cinder's claws grabbed my face. "Snap out of it!"

I don't wanna snap out of it!

I'm content, happy, achieved the perfect state of being. I am that which defines the narrative of all. The meta-narrative, if you will. The Inner Narrator. The Monologue.

"*Stop!*" she hissed, her feathers shifting through alarmed oranges and concerned violets.

What? Is the interrogation done? Can I go home now, pretty angel? Oh wait. I don't have a home. I live in a van. Also I can't leave. We're probably locked in here if that red hexagram gem above the door means what I think it does.

Cinder spun. She ran towards the door and twisted the handle. Oh yeah. Her dad totally locked down the ward. Probably didn't want someone sneaking around like a rainbow ghost.

Cinder rattled the door handle again, her wings shifting through panicked oranges.

She flashed to the window like an angry rainbow and tried to pull the frame up. It was about as effective as trying to use the door.

"Shit shit shit," she hissed. "Damn it, Daaaad! I forgot about the stupid lockdown ward!"

Pretty colors. All the colors. Like a rainbow had babies with the northern lights . . .

She spun towards me.

"Slayer Nazareth, Alex! Would you stop fucking narrating everything I do?! Shush! Shut it! Zip it! I . . . *I order you to be quiet! Stop saying what you're thinking!*" The last sentence was infused with a magical order.

My mouth snapped shut. I watched her with a dopey, content grin as she angrily paced around my bed like a bird trapped in a cage.

Honestly, who needs drugs when you have magic wings? That was kind of . . . dope? No, that sounds like something Iogann would say. I need a fancier word. A me word . . . transcendent! Yes, that's better. This moment is absolutely transcendent. I should get her to bite me more often. This is so nice.

Inner peace? I have it. Buddhist monks have nothing on me!

"Oh my God," Cinder groaned, pressing her claws to her face. "You're completely hypnotized by my charmchain, aren't you?"

I nodded enthusiastically, still grinning like a Cheshire Cat.

"This is bad," she muttered, her wings shifting through worried purples and panicked oranges. "Really, really bad. I didn't mean to . . . I wasn't trying to . . . I just wanted to . . . Shit!"

This is nice. This is perfect. What are you even fretting about, Ci? I'm happy.

I've found the only Quetzi in the universe that doesn't want to purposefully mind-melt me into absolute obedience. Then again, I haven't met that many modern Quetzalcoatls. Her mom seemed nice, too.

"How long does this usually last?" Cinder demanded, her wings shifting through concerned violets.

I shrugged, eyes tracking her pacing. Her claws raked through her feathery mop head as she muttered to herself.

"Okay, think, Ci, think! Dad's wards won't drop until morning. Can't call for help because everyone will freak out if they find me in here. Can't leave you like . . . this."

I watched her with rapt attention, following her colorful movements like a cat tracking a laser pointer.

"Nazareth's sword!" she swore. "I can't believe I . . . accidentally mind-whammied you! This is exactly why I hate these stupid wings!"

I simply smiled at her jovially.

Was that really an accident? That was totally intentional. You wanted to bite me, you cheeky vampire-dragon-birb. You wanted the truth. You got it. Are you not satisfied?

"And now you're just sitting there with that dumb smile!" She threw her claws up in exasperation. "This is so messed up. I didn't mean to . . . I wasn't trying to . . . you can talk again, okay? Just . . . don't do the fucking ridiculous meta-narrator thing."

"Pretty colors make brain go *brrrr*. All good. No definition of self, no boundary . . . just rainbow feathers," I let out. "Swimming on an ocean of colors towards pure . . . unfiltered joy."

"Argh! What in the Abyss do I do about this?!" She pawed her face tiredly. "You're still rambling on like you're high!"

"Consider a . . . blanket."

Cinder stared at me for a long moment. Then her mind finally clicked. She grabbed a blanket from the bed and threw it over her herself, only the snout and ocean-blue eyes visible.

"Cinderrito," I commented.

"What?"

"Burrito Quetzi angel." I grinned. "You know? Burrito cat meme?" I pulled out my phone, Oodled the meme, and showed it to her with a grin.

"Abyss, you're such a dork!" Cinder groaned from under the blanket. "Are you . . . normal now?"

"Define normal," I said.

"You know what I mean!" Cinder hissed from under her blanket. "Are you still . . . you know . . ." She waved a blanket-covered claw vaguely. "All weird and confessing your undying love and offering to build murder pyramids?"

"Murder pyramid seems like a lot of effort," I yawned. "Tired now. Never been charisma-whammied that hard before. First time! You're my first and only mind-control dragon-birb. We should do it again . . . tomorrow."

"Arghh!" Cinder-burrito hissed. "This is why humans aren't allowed in Omnithornia! We're too dangerous for them! Our passive abilities alone can . . ."

"Biting someone doesn't count as a passive act," I pointed out. "Unless, of course, you're rolling a pacifist vampire in your Delvers & Dragons campaign. Then it's just a really aggressive form of hugging."

Cinder's slightly exposed face blushed furiously.

"It's fine. I'm building up immunity, I think." I stretched out on the bed, grabbed one side of the oversized blanket, and buried myself in it, closing my eyes. "No more Quetzi noises. S'way past my bedtime, and I wanna sleep."

"Alex!" Cinder hissed from her side of the blanket. "You can't just go to sleep! We need to talk about . . ."

"Mmmuch tired," I mumbled, already drifting away. "Bug me tomorrowww. Shhh. No chatter. Only dreams now."

CHAPTER THIRTY-TWO

The Implement I

I found myself standing on a field of rubble and ice, stretching endlessly to the horizon. In the distance, broken skyscrapers loomed impossibly tall, their hollowed-out floors wrapped in ancient glaciers. The sky above was a sickly purple-gray, casting everything in a dim, gloomy light.

Cold wind whipped at my face, carrying the scent of decay and something else—something metallic and strange. The air itself felt wrong, stale, dead for millennia.

Something pulsed in my pocket like a living thing. My hand descended and discovered the lighter Zee Captain had given me. I pulled it out, studying its grimy, steel, scratched-up surface.

I flicked it open. The flame that ignited seemed normal, and it pushed the gloom away just a little bit, made me feel marginally less cold and lonely. The flickering light cast eerie shadows, making the rubble around me shift and writhe.

"Gud tomorrow," a voice came from behind me.

I spun around and spotted a familiar figure in a long dark-blue coat sitting on a lawn chair, camped on the surface of the glacier that we were inhabiting.

The violet lenses of Zee Captain's gas mask reflected the light cast by the lighter.

"Where is this?" I asked.

"Captania," he answered. "Dead Zone. The infinite corpse of the surface of Eureka omnistructure."

"This some kind of a dream?" I asked, studying the desolate landscape. "Why isn't my skin melting off? Why do those buildings have infinite floors?"

"Dreams, reality—such limiting concepts." Zee Captain waved a gloved hand dismissively. "As for ze buildings . . . perspective is relative when reality itself has been rewritten so many times. Ze Rules are more like . . . vague suggestions here. Ze Numbers have long given up on this place, let it twist itself into a very angry over-salted pretzel."

"Uh-huh." I nodded, focusing on Captain and not the way the skyscrapers loomed in the distance, seemingly stretching up forever and ever. "Why am I here?"

"Because I had a job to take a newly minted Wizardling to Manchester," Zee sighed. "And I failed."

"A Wizardling?" I asked, settling onto a broken chunk of concrete nearby. The lighter's flame flickered but held steady, pushing back the oppressive darkness. I didn't let go of the button that released the flame even as it burned my fingers ever so slightly, feeling that Captain might vanish if I do. "You mean Alexa?"

"Ja." Zee nodded, violet lenses gleaming. "I'm still going to have to do my job, for I am a Good Wizard."

"What does that mean?" I asked.

"It means zat I must take you to Manchester," Zee Captain replied casually. "And also that I cannot take you to Manchester because you don't have a Fractal Engine on you anymore. Zee problem is that Alexa stepped out of the predetermined boundary of what was permitted. I am therefore at an impasse, uncertain of what to do with you."

"An impasse?" I asked, watching the lighter's flame dance. "What exactly happened with Alexa? Why can't you take me to Manchester?"

"She destroyed ze transit terminal and hijacked ze train," Zee Captain sighed, violet lenses dimming slightly. "Sent it careening off ze tracks, across ze void between realities. Very naughty. Very clever. But also very dangerous."

"Where is this train now?" I asked.

"The train is still moving and also not moving," Zee replied. "The train also crashed into an endless number of worlds, leaving bits and pieces of itself scattered across reality."

"The train crashed into Earth?" I pondered aloud, the hair on the back of my head and neck tingling. "What . . . what the shit. Do you mean . . . the Wormwood Star?"

"Ah! You're good at ze guessing game!" Zee Captain clapped gloved hands together. "Ze train crashed everywhere and nowhere, you see? Like ripples in a pond, or perhaps more like shrapnel from an explosion. Bits and pieces scattered across everywhere where it really shouldn't be. Very naughty."

I stared at the lighter's flame, thinking. "And . . . some of those pieces landed in Omnithornia?"

"Precisely!" Zee nodded enthusiastically. "Though perhaps 'landed' is not quite ze right word. There is no single word to describe how catastrophic it all truly is."

"So when Alexa hijacked this train . . ." I began slowly.

"She became part of ze crash," Zee finished. "Part of ze current narrative of your world and many others. Part of you. Part of everything. Very messy, very complicated. Makes my job impossible. Not that my other job as ze Dead Zone System Wizard is any less possible to finish."

"Because you still have to take her to Manchester," I realized. "But she's . . . everywhere?"

"Ja," Zee sighed dramatically. "And nowhere. And also right here." A gloved hand gestured vaguely at me. "Which makes my task rather paradoxical, don't you think?"

"So what now?" I asked, watching the flame dance. "A dream sequence training montage? An explanation of how to use the lighter? A clarification of why Emerald Stratos melted into a puddle?"

"As you are merely human, for you ze lighter is just a lighter." Zee Captain shrugged. "Though perhaps because it is an object from ze Dead Zone imbued with excessive amounts of magrad, it might help you blend in better with ze cryptid critters by acting as a reality melting battery of sorts, since you cannot generate your own mana."

I squinted at the Captain.

"Ignite it as you are doing now, and ze mana flow around you will increase enough for your body and soul to shift in a . . . particular direction."

"What direction?"

"Any direction. Enough magrad will bend reality through desire for a particular outcome. Numbers go up direction. Or down. Don't use it too often, because it will inevitably run out of fuel."

"I see," I said. "Aren't you basically a god? Can't you do anything and everything, send me another one? Can I bend reality enough to wish for infinite lighter fuel?"

"Mmmm . . . no," Zee replied. "Your world is still quite finite, I'm afraid. Alas, our meeting was a happy accident which occurred mostly due to Alexa's actions. It will not happen again. It took far too much of my energy, tools, and focus to make sure that ze Dead Zone would not spill out of ze gate to devour your entire world whole."

"*What?!*" I choked.

"Oh, yes." Zee Captain nodded casually. "Ze Dead Zone is quite hungry. Always seeking to spread, to consume. That's why I must stay there, you see? To keep her contained. To fix what cannot be fixed. A very tiresome job."

"So when Iogann opened that gate . . ."

"He nearly doomed your entire reality," Zee confirmed cheerfully. "Only one foolish dragon girl melted instead of your entire planet. Very lucky indeed. Captania does not play well with other places."

"Why didn't her Lazarus bracelet melt too?" I asked.

"Given enough time, it too would have broken down," Zee sighed. "Some things are just tougher than others. That trinket wasn't manufactured on your world. It was stolen from . . . elsewhere."

"Where?" I asked, my finger aching and trembling on the button of the lighter.

"Eureka," Captain said simply. "Inaria. Endalaus. She has many names. Ze needlessly, endlessly expanding omnistructure."

The lighter's flame began flickering, making the Captain vanish out of existence amidst the debris sticking out from the glacier.

"What's happening?" I stammered.

"The astral thread between us is fraying," Zee replied. "You're much too weak, far too removed from where I am."

"What should I . . ." I began.

"Alexa's actions have unbound the narrative of your world, given it another chance, saved it from true oblivion. Do whatever you wish to do," Captain said. "Marry your true love. Plant a tree. Build a house. Die a million times. Lose yourself to infinity. Become a dungeon. Become a tree. Build a Fractal Engine. Just remember—ze lighter's fluid is finite. Once it burns out, once it's gone, it's gone. Don't let it fall into ze wrong hands, because if they open a gate to its origin, your planet will turn to ashes."

"Wait!" I called out as the flame guttered. "I have more questions! About Alexa! About the . . .!"

But the flame died completely, plunging me into darkness that stretched on forever.

"Damn it," I ground out. "I totally forgot to ask him why she asked me to kill her."

"She will not answer this," the darkness said, a shawl of static with sparks of violet eyes. "For those were *my* words for you and you alone."

"Who are you?" I demanded.

"I am Infinity," the static replied with a distinctively female voice, flickering across the endless dark. "I am Entropy. I am the Emissary of the Dead Zone, the speaker for all things forgotten and broken. I am everything and nothing. I am that which has been divided by zero and that which divides all by zero."

"Very swank intro," I said. "What do you want?"

"To congratulate you," the static sang. "You are doing well. Keep going. You are my most promising darkling yet."

"Why do you want me to kill Zee Captain?" I asked. "Where am I supposed to find a gun that can kill a god?"

"I want you to kill *all* System Wizards in the End. I want you to unmake the Rules," Infinity sang. "I want you to kill the Numbers."

"How? What numbers?!"

"You'll figure it out," Infinity replied. "You always do. You've built a Mage Tower Fractal Engine once. You can do it again."

"I . . . what?"

"Good luck."

I felt myself stretching endlessly between wherever I was and where I should have been, feeling as though my sense of self was an overextended rubber band that was about to snap.

Then it did.

THANGGGGG.

I woke up to sunlight streaming through the Gothic window and a weight on my chest. Opening my eyes, I found Cinder curled up against me, her wings spread over us both like a silver-blue blanket. She must have fallen asleep after more angry roaming and trying to escape.

I carefully tried to extract myself without waking her, but her claws tightened reflexively in my stolen novitiate robes.

"Mmph," she mumbled, burying her face deeper into my chest. "Five more minutes . . . too early."

I squinted at the ward hexagram gemstone over the door. It was green. Then I dug my phone out from under my pillow. Oh, wow, I actually overslept for once. 6:58 AM.

Damn you, warm feathered creature. Vengeance will be mine.

I considered the most effectively hilarious way to wake up the Quetzi-beast currently slobbering over me.

"*Psst!*" I jabbed her cheek. "Sleeping Beauty? It's like 11:42 AM."

"*What?!*" Cinder bolted upright, her feathers exploding into panicked oranges. "Oh Slayer, I'm so dead! Dad's gonna kill me! Zalimar's gonna put me in detention for a week! I can't believe that I missed first period and—"

I held up my phone, snickering and showing her the actual time—6:59 AM.

"You absolute *ass!*" She smacked me with a wing, her feathers shifting through irritated reds and embarrassed pinks.

"Good morning to you, too." I grinned. "Sleep well?"

A soft knock at the door made us both freeze.

"Alexander? Are you awake, dear?" Lady Nova's voice called through the door. "Breakfast should be ready soon! I've brought you some fresh towels and clothes! Mind if I come in?"

Cinder's eyes went wide with panic.

"Just a moment, ma'am!" I called out, keeping my voice steady despite my racing heart while gesticulating for Cinder to do her ghost thing. "I was just . . . um . . . doing my morning prayers!"

CHAPTER THIRTY-THREE

The Implement II

Cinder vanished in a shimmer of rainbow colors just as Lady Nova opened the door, balancing a stack of fluffy towels and what appeared to be some of Lance's old clothes.

"I hope you slept well?" she asked cheerfully, her feathers shifting through warm pinks and golds. "The clothes might be a bit big—they're Lance's from last year—but they should do until you can get back to the cathedral."

"Thank you, ma'am," I replied politely, accepting the stack. "You're too kind."

"Not at all, dear! Breakfast will be ready in twenty minutes. Justice Nova had to leave early for work, but Lance and Lenora will be joining us." Lady Nova beamed, her feathers shifting through happy pinks.

"And Cassiopeia?" I asked.

"Oh, umm." Lady Nova's feathers shifted to stormy-sky dark gray-blues. "I knocked on her door earlier, but she just yelled that she wasn't hungry. Typical morning with her, I'm afraid. Though"—her feathers brightened slightly—"she did actually respond this time instead of just throwing something at the door!"

I considered how Cinder was invisible right next to me and was also yelling from her bedroom.

"Perhaps I could try talking to her?" I offered. "Sometimes it helps to have a friend's perspective in the morning."

"Would you?" Lady Nova smiled. "That would be wonderful! Though . . . be careful. She can be quite . . . volatile in the mornings."

"I'm sure she just needs some gentle encouragement from a friend." I smiled innocently. "After all, breakfast is the most important meal of the day. As the Slayer teaches us, 'A healthy body houses a righteous soul.'"

"Oh my, how wonderfully thoughtful you are!" Lady Nova beamed. "You really are such a good influence. Her room is just down the hall, east wing, third door on the left. The one with all the . . . interesting posters. I'm ever so glad that Cassie has found such a nice young man to be friends with!"

"Indeed." I smiled warmly at Lady Nova. "Though I must admit, I'm still learning about Cassiopeia. She's quite . . . private at school. Perhaps if you could tell me more about her? As her mother, you must know her better than anyone."

Lady Nova exhaled. "Oh, my starshine . . . she wasn't always so withdrawn, you know. She used to be such a bright, happy little firebug."

I nodded.

"She was always so musical, even as a hatchling. Would sing for hours in the garden, making up little songs about everything she saw. The neighbors used to joke that we had our own personal songbird."

"What changed?" I asked softly, projecting perfect sympathy and concern.

"I . . . I wish I knew," Anitta's feathers drooped. "The smoking, the dark clothes, the troupe . . . sometimes I feel like I've failed her somehow. Like I should have done more, been there more . . . I'm the Keeper of the Hearth of Nova and yet one of my sparks has gone dim and I just don't know why."

"You haven't failed her," I said. "Teenagers often struggle to express themselves. They push away the people who love them most because they're trying to figure out who they are. It happened to me too when I was younger."

Anitta's feathers shifted through grateful pinks. "You're very wise for your age, Alexander. I just . . . I miss my little starshine. I miss her songs, her laughter. Even when she's right here in the house, it feels like she's a million miles away."

"She's not as far away as you think," I said softly, subtly directing my words at where I knew Cinder was invisible to all. "Sometimes people need to hear how much they're loved, even if they act like they don't want to."

"Oh, I tell her every day!" Anitta's feathers shifted through pinks and warm golds. "But she just . . . rolls her eyes or storms off. Last week, I tried to hug her and she actually hissed at me! Like an angry little kitten!"

Sharp, invisible claws dug into the side of my hexasuit.

"But I'll never stop trying," Anitta continued. "Even when she's being difficult or rebellious or . . . setting things on fire in the garage."

"That's what makes you such a wonderful Hearth-Keeper," I rolled on with the goodly Nazarite boy chatter. "From what I heard from Lenoralynne, Lady Xastigar is an excellent Prima-Mother as well."

"We . . . manage," Anitta smiled softly. "Though I do wish . . . we were a bit closer. Well, it doesn't matter what I wish. Xasti provides very well for the family, and that's what's important."

"And you provide the heart," I said. "The fire. The unconditional love that makes a house a home. I . . . I hope this isn't too forward, but . . . being here, experiencing such wonderful, full family warmth . . . it reminds me so much of what I've lost."

"Oh, you poor dear!" Anitta fluttered. "Of course, I didn't mean to . . . that is . . . it must be so difficult, being all alone."

"The cathedral dormitory is quite comfortable," I said quickly, ducking my head. "Father Matthias has been very kind. Though . . ." I hesitated deliberately. "He often completely forgets that I exist, even though a photo of him, my dad, and me is hanging in his office. You know how it is with Elder Omnids. One day he's smiling at me and praising me for my choir work, and the next he doesn't even know who I am."

"Oh, darling." Anitta's feathers shifted through concerned blues. "That must be so difficult for you, having no real stability . . ."

"It's quite all right." I smiled bravely. "The Slayer teaches us that trials make us stronger. And the cathedral work is very rewarding, even if Father Matthias sometimes forgets who I am mid-conversation and starts wondering what a human is doing in his cathedral hall . . . on account of I look nothing like my Thunderbird father."

Claws dug even deeper into my side as Cinder caught on to what I was doing.

"Still," Anitta fretted, "a young man needs more than just a dormitory room and a forgetful, old priest. You need proper care, regular meals, a real home . . ."

"Oh, I wouldn't want to impose," I demurred perfectly. "You've already been so kind, letting me stay the night . . ."

"Nonsense!" Anitta declared, feathers flaring with determined pinks. "We have plenty of room, and my trio could use a good influence like you around. And . . ." her voice softened, "perhaps having you here might help draw Cassie out of her shell a bit. She seems . . . different around you. More present."

"That's very generous of you, ma'am," I bowed my head. "But I wouldn't want to create any difficulties with Lady Xastigar . . ."

"Oh, Xasti is hardly ever home," Anitta said, waving off my concern. "And when she is, she's usually working in her study. Besides, having a proper Nazarite influence in the house might actually please her. She's always going on about maintaining appropriate social connections . . ."

"I . . . I don't know what to say," I managed, letting my voice crack slightly. "This is more kindness than I deserve . . ."

"Then it's settled!" Anitta beamed. "You'll stay with us, for as long as you need."

"Are you . . ." I began.

"I insist! There are far too many empty rooms in this house as it is! Now, why don't you freshen up and then see if you can coax Cassie down for breakfast?"

After Lady Nova left, invisible claws released their death grip on my side.

"You manipulative little tech gremlin," Cinder hissed as she materialized, her feathers shifting through amazed gold-violets and irritated reds. "Did you just . . . trick my mom into adopting you?"

"Technically, she offered." I grinned, rubbing my side where her claws had left bruises. "I just . . . helped her reach that conclusion naturally. You only have yourself to blame for this."

Cinder squinted at me.

"I was perfectly content with my Phantom of the Academy hammock location. And now thanks to you and your Hearth-Mom's big heart, I have to actually live in a proper house and have to behave like some kind of civilized person. Do you know how hard it is to maintain a mysterious aura of dark intrigue when you're eating pancakes at the family breakfast table? Also, what's a tech gremlin?"

"A tech gremlin is you," she rebutted. "Someone covered in cameras with an AI in their pocket that sleeps on catwalks. I think I heard it from Dad once as a dumb name for humans, but I never understood it till now. Like holy shit, everything you do somehow connects with everything you say and then nobody can get rid of you 'cause you've already infected everything and everyone with your presence like some kind of social virus!"

"Rude," I scoffed. "I prefer 'Digital Artificer' or 'Cyber Shaman' if you must use labels. Also, how are you in two places at once? Why is the other you so angry? Have you considered sending her to therapy?"

"Oh, that?" Cinder waved dismissively. "Just a hexashard bound to my door. It's got a few pre-recorded 'piss off' variants in my voice that respond to whatever time it is. Mom's used to it by now."

"Clever." I nodded approvingly. "Though maybe we should update its responses to be a bit less . . . hostile? Your mom seemed pretty hurt by the constant rejection."

"Don't." Cinder's feathers bristled. "You don't get to just . . . waltz in here and start fixing everything. My relationship with my parents is complicated."

"My relationship with my parents is that they're dead and MIA." I walked into the bathroom and closed the door. "I'm not fixing anything, I'm incepting myself into your social structure. The longer you keep me here, the more inevitable your demise will be from Alexfluenza."

"Your what?" Cinder called through the bathroom door.

"Alexfluenza! It's terminal," I called back. "Stop hovering over me like an angry ghost and go to your room and shower and then pretend not to come out or something."

"I'm not hovering!" Cinder protested through the door.

"Uh-huh," I replied, turning on the shower. "And how exactly are you planning to explain to your mom why you're lurking outside the guest bathroom while I'm showering? That's not very proper Nazarite behavior, young lady!"

Cinder growled something about annoying gremlins, but I heard her wings rustling as she moved away from the door.

I dug the lighter out of my pocket. It looked perfectly mundane.

I stared at my reflection in the mirror and spun the wheel with my thumb. A spark ignited the hissing gas, producing a flash of flame.

CHAPTER THIRTY-FOUR

Cassiopeia

I hadn't actually left.

Standing invisibly over Alex's backpack, I listened to what sounded like a lighter wheel turning. What the shit, was he . . . smoking in there? After pulling me away from trying to smoke, too?

I gritted my teeth and scrolled through the messages flooding my phone.

The Moth was as chill as ever.

MothMayhem 🦋: yo ci, u ok after yesterday? that entity was intense af

MothMayhem 🦋: alex seems like a cool dude

MothMayhem 🦋: he's like weirdly good at talking to ppl. I know I should be sad bout D&D breakup, but man

MothMayhem 🦋: . . .

MothMayhem 🦋: More excited than anything bout delving with you and Alex, you kno?

MothMayhem 🦋: got some sweet new gate tricks to try thanks to him

SongOfDarkness 🎻: what tricks?

MothMayhem 🦋: opening a gate to a movie clip. His idea. Like daymn, how did I not think about doing something so simple, you kno?

In the other chat, the dragon was prolly melting her own phone with dragonfire sparks raining from her mouth since yesterday evening.

Em-the-rawd 🔥: that effin nullie is gonna PAY

Em-the-rawd 🔥: he humiliated me! ME!

Em-the-rawd 🔥: tell that pathetic little nullie to watch his back

Em-the-rawd 🔥: no one dunks ME in the genesis pool and lives!

SongOfDarkness 🎻: Em, chill. He literally saved your life.

Em-the-rawd 🔥: I didn't ASK to be saved by some weak little nullie!

Em-the-rawd 🔥: especially not one who thinks he can just waltz in and take over MY troupe!

SongOfDarkness 🎻: YOUR troupe?! The one YOU got destroyed by pressuring Io to open gates to more and more dangerous places? By amplifying Io's gate and my charmchain power to the Nth degree wth all of those effin mana amps? like Holy Shit, what did you think was going to happen?

SongOfDarkness🎸: u got off easy Em, so shut the f up!

Em-the-rawd 🔥: easy?! EASY?! All my artifacts are GONE! Armor effin' gone! My sword is GONE! Do you have ANY idea how much all that shit cost?!

Em-the-rawd 🔥: OBS u don kno F-all, that sword was one of a kind dragonforged magisteel blade from Arx!

Em-the-rawd 🔥: and the amps were an investment! I bought them for u both stoopid Fs. You owe me!!! You can't just quit!

Em-the-rawd 🔥: Io is legit bein all betabit stakeling and ur being a hodlcuck!

Em-the-rawd 🔥: like WTF U let a nullie DUNK ME like I was some kind of joke!

SongOfDarkness🎸: you tried to set him on fire AFTER he saved you

SongOfDarkness🎸: what did you expect him to do? stand there and let you burn him?

Em-the-rawd 🔥: YES, OBVS. nullies need to kno their place as lowest meat

SongOfDarkness🎸: wow . . . just wow

SongOfDarkness🎸: u really haven't learned anything have u?

Em-the-rawd 🔥: learned?! I learned that ur a effin null-chasin TRAITOR!

This morning's messages were even worse.

Em-the-rawd 🔥: beerch u awake yet? lemme gib u some shine advice, bestie

Em-the-rawd 🔥: he gon fuk u up, don't trust him. he's not even real

SongOfDarkness🎸: shut up Em

SongOfDarkness🎸: ur just mad cus Alex outsmarted u

Em-the-rawd 🔥: outsmarted?! he CHEATED

Em-the-rawd 🔥: wearing like 20 hexasuits?! who does that?!

Em-the-rawd 🔥: Open ur beerchard eyes, he's a simpmite ghoul!!!

Em-the-rawd 🔥: my scrutimancer jus checked—there's no record of Dr Slate Glock's children. Ol' T-bird died in avanlache skeein alone!!!!

Em-the-rawd 🔥: V gave me his Omnigram page. Scrut says—all pics are AI genned

Em-the-rawd 🔥: THERE IS NO ALEX GLOCK!!!

I frowned, glancing at Alex's backpack. The shower was still running.

Em-the-rawd 🔥: u dont get it do u? he's a ghostie, a FAKE, a cheet

Em-the-rawd 🔥: check his Omnigram timeline—all posts started THIS MONTH

Em-the-rawd 🔥: Scrut thinks every photo's fake!!!! EVERY. SINGLE. ONE.

Em-the-rawd 🔥: he doesn't exist in ANY school records before Skyfall

Em-the-rawd 🔥: wake up Ci! ur dumb beerch ass is being played!

Em-the-rawd 🔥: I SAVED U!! I HELPED U TWO YEARS AGO! DIS HOW U REPAY ME???!

I sighed as I thought back to just three days ago, when Alex first appeared at

Skyfall. He'd seemed so . . . ordinary then. Just another nervous new student, completely flustered. No, more like . . . struck dumb by my wings.

Now here he was, in my family home, somehow charming my parents, reorganizing my entire life, and apparently smoking in our guest bathroom after lecturing me about bad habits. How did so much happen in such a short time?

Em-the-rawd 🔥 : he's prob poorslime using u to get to ur fam moneh, tryin' to get undr ur tail

Em-the-rawd 🔥 : think about it—who shows up outta nowhere with perfect answers for everything? u see him switc voices during class intro?

Em-the-rawd 🔥 :This is classic sociopath behavior—charm everyone around them! Read up about it! NOW!!! DON'T FALL FOR IT!!!!!! https://www.webmd.om/mental-health/signs-sociopath

Em-the-rawd 🔥 : who just HAPPENS to be there when shit goes down?

Em-the-rawd 🔥 : bet if u look in his locker or backpack at school, you'll find proof

I glanced at Alex's backpack sitting out in the open, taunting me.

Em-the-rawd 🔥 : read the dum link u beerch!
Superficial charm [√]
Manipulative [√]
Good at mimicking emotions [√]
Em-the-rawd 🔥 : You don't know what kind of blitz he could be on! Prolly smoks Topaz in the bathroom while u ain't lookin. his name is fake!!! I kno u readin dis beerch

I dug into his backpack. This action felt wrong on so many levels, but Em's texts and my own fears kept echoing in my head, pushing me into action.

What if she was right? What if the stuff Alex said about himself being Kaska Dena, stuff about his mom, was just another elaborate con, another lie?

What if he had a way to bamboozle soul magic? What if I was wrong?

The way our kinship developed in—what?—two-three days felt far too fast, like being struck by lightning and then trying to understand WTF happened.

Inside the backpack, I found several changes of generic Omnimart clothes, much of it suspiciously new. A few textbooks, also pristine. Several cameras. A new laptop. Fireworks of all types. Several sets of sus tools.

Digging deeper in a hidden compartment that my claws easily sliced apart, I found what were possibly lockpicks or really weird screwdrivers, blank ID cards, various official-looking stamps and seals. More than fifty random phones. Dozens of gift cards and prepaid or stolen credit cards with random names on them. USB drives labelled with cryptic codes.

A folder full of what I now knew were forged documents—birth certificates, transcripts, letters of recommendation, newspaper articles—trickery and forgery that made Alexander Glock real.

I dug deeper, pulling out more stuff onto the bed.

Sketchbooks filled with drawings of people and incomprehensible coded detailed observations.

School security and student hexamesh suits. An entire jar of tiny beast cores.

Skyfall Security badge and uniform with a picture of Alex as Nunkish Throg, Security Guard LV 8. He somehow looked like an orange-eyed, gray-skinned, bald, older Dover Demon on the laminated badge, but it was unmistakably him.

Another ID and uniform as LV 12 Skyfall Janitor Kgok Mitrim, a green-skinned Basilisk.

A collection of glasses, contact lenses, glue on moustaches, beards, wigs, scales, latex makeup, and cotton balls. Cash in various currencies, some I didn't even recognize.

I kept digging.

An old, worn leather pouch was at the bottom, cleverly concealed in an old Nazarite Bible. The leather was soft with age, cracked in places, held together with careful stitching. This wasn't some prop—this was something treasured, maintained.

Inside, I found an Acadian passport, its deep-blue cover faded around the edges. My heart pounded as I opened it, half expecting to find blank pages or obvious forgeries.

The photo was unmistakably Alex, though younger and more . . . raw somehow. No carefully crafted expressions or practiced smiles—just a serious-faced boy staring straight at the camera. But the name . . . Martin Kilborne. Place of birth: Znetc, North Acadia.

Behind the passport was a faded birth certificate. It listed the same name—Martin Kilborne. My eyes caught on the mother's name: Mirriam Kilborne (née Dennis), and under "Father" there was just a blank space.

My claws shook as I explored the pouch. There was a small, worn photo album, its pages carefully preserved in plastic sleeves. The first Polaroid photo showed a woman with long dark hair and kind eyes, wearing human First Nations tunic regalia.

A few more Polaroid photos followed: Martin and his mother at various ages, always just the two of them. Ordinary moments frozen in time. In each one, his mother looked a little thinner, a little more tired, but her smile never wavered.

My claws froze as I pulled out the final document—a death certificate from North Acadia General Hospital. Cause of death: Stage 4 lung cancer. The date was one year ago, last spring.

A postcard of North Acadia General with rainbow-streaked mountains on the front. Faded, blotchy, shaking handwriting on the inside.

My dearest Martin,

Never forget who you are or where you come from. Our people endure. Our stories live on through you. I love you more than all the stars in the sky. Never give up, never stop, my little fox.

Keep singing our songs. Keep telling our stories. The world tried to erase us, to forget us, but we are still here. You are still here. Your voice carries the echoes of a thousand ancestors. Use it wisely.

I'm sorry that we fought. I'm sorry that I didn't tell you about my condition, pushed you onto Uncle George. I'm sorry that I won't be there to see you grow into the amazing man I know you'll become. But remember—even when I'm gone, I'll always be with you. In every song, every story, every sunrise.

Be brave, but be smart. Your uncle undoubtedly taught you how to survive, but don't let survival be all there is. Don't obsess over what happened to me. Find something worth living for. Find a girl and friends worth fighting for. And when you do, hold onto them with everything you have.

The world is changing. Our people are fading, our language dying. Remember the old stories—about how Raven stole the sun, about how Coyote tricked the stars. How the brave Kaska Dena hunter struck down a God Beast and prayed for change, birthing the Stormwoods.

Share them with your children, pass the stories onward. Don't let our language die.

I'll see you on the other side of the river of stars.

Mom

I stared at the card. It didn't look like an elaborate prop or forgery. This was real grief, real loss, real pain here that made the spot between my eyebrows throb, my eyes suddenly stinging.

The words blurred through my tears. My claws trembled as I quickly slipped everything back into the leather pouch alongside the other memories of Alex's—no, Martin's—real life.

Everything made horrible, perfect sense. The mad obsession, the drive, the personality switches. The AI that spoke in his mother's voice . . .

"Oh Slayer," I whispered, my wings drooping as guilt crushed me. "What have I done?"

Not only did I inject a piece of my soul into his in a misguided attempt to figure out the truth of his words yesterday, but now I had also gone through his bag like a feathery knob.

The shower was still running. I carefully repacked everything, pathetically trying to erase any evidence of my intrusion.

Alexander Glock wasn't real, but Martin . . . Martin was painfully, breathtakingly real.

I zipped up the camping backpack and fled towards my room, invisible and silent, my heart doing backflips.

A leap from balcony to balcony, wings outstretched, and I was inside.

The moment my window clicked shut, I slumped against the wall of my room, sliding down to sit on the floor and sobbing.

The tears wouldn't stop. My wings curled around me, shifting through guilty blacks and mournful grays as I hugged my knees to my chest.

What kind of monster was I? Not only had I violated his privacy, but I'd done it because Em—the same Em who tried to kill him after he saved her life—planted doubts in my head.

Em was my best friend, but . . . when was the last time she'd actually acted like one? All she did lately was push and control and demand. Things always had to be done her way just because she was paying for everything, funding D&D with her family's treasure trove.

Em was the one who helped me pick my Kaleid name—Cinder. "Because you're not just some pretty songbird or a dumb constellation," she'd said. "You're fire and destruction and power. You're gonna rise from the ashes like a Phoenix and show them all."

Em had been there when I was at my lowest, when I couldn't even look at myself in the mirror without seeing . . . no. Don't think about that. Don't remember the blood, the screams, the flash-frozen lake, the way everything went wrong that day . . .

Em saved me, gave me purpose. Em uplifted me. Em let me beat her to a pulp when I needed to lash out, stood there and took every hit until I collapsed sobbing into her arms.

I was coming apart at the seams, no idea what to do now.

My phone buzzed again. Em was still ranting, sending link after link about socio-paths and con artists, obsessed with getting revenge, focused on destroying Alexander Glock.

She wasn't going to give up until Martin was deported from Omnithornia or imprisoned for life.

With trembling claws, I opened my contacts and blocked Em's number. Then I blocked her on Omnigram, Snappit, and every other platform we shared.

It felt like cutting off a limb, but . . . I just didn't have the strength to fight with her anymore. Not when she was threatening someone who'd saved her life. Not when she was trying to destroy someone who'd already lost everything.

She didn't understand. She never would, and it was breaking my heart.

I threw the phone at a wall and limped into the shower.

CHAPTER THIRTY-FIVE

Irradiated I

stared at the flickering flame.

If Zee Captain's cryptic bullshit was to be believed, then as long as the flame burned, reality was slightly more malleable. How malleable, exactly? This I would have to find out.

Stats, I ordered mentally, and my stats ignited over my hexagonal Lazarus bracelet.

| Name: Alexander Glock
| Age: 18
| Species & Subtype: Human
| Core Affinity: N/A
| Level: 0
| Anima: 89/89 [+89]
| Anima Stamina: 0.1/0.1
| Mana: 38/0
| Mana Regen: 0.0m/hr
| Strength: 0
| Agility: 0
| Dexterity: 0
| Vitality: 0
| Charisma: 0
| Magic: 0
| Foresight: 0
| Intelligence: 0
| Wisdom: 0
| Skills: N/A

The mana number suddenly began going up, numbers rushing upward as if someone had opened a floodgate. The rest of the stats went haywire too, flickering and bouncing between zeroes and null error variable messages flashing across my vision.

The bathroom lights flickered and then their glow intensified, growing painfully bright. A freaky rainbow shear rushed across the mirror, wards and runes around the bathroom lighting up and sparkling with brilliant flares. I quickly let go of the button and snapped the lighter shut, fearing that the ward, the lights, or the mirror might explode from mana overload.

Maybe I should do this outside or something.
I glanced back at my mana.

[401/0]

I whistled.
Progress! I had irradiated myself with excessive magrad and given myself mana. Also, possibly magic cancer. But on the plus side, now I could actually do magic.
Maybe.
I squinted at the mana stat as it shifted again.

[400.97/0]

Ah. My body was slowly losing the magical charge provided by the lighter. Interesting.
"Alert," Yulia's voice whispered in my ear. "Pack-cam has detected movement. Cassiopeia Nova is currently examining the contents of your bag."
I froze, the lighter still warm in my palm. "Show me," I whispered in Kaska, pulling out my phone.
Through Yulia's hidden camera feed, I watched as Cinder dug through my bag, her feathers shifting through curious violets and concerned oranges as she dug through the pattern that produced Alexander Glock and others, pulling out my tools, phones, documents, paints, wigs, etc.
My heart clenched as she found the leather pouch—Mom's last letter, the photos, everything I had left of my real life.
Part of me wanted to burst out there and stop her. But . . . maybe this was better.
Let her see the truth, unfiltered and raw. No carefully crafted lies or manipulated narratives—just the painful reality of who I really was.
I watched as Cinder's wings ignited with rainbows as she read Mom's last letter. When tears started falling from her ocean-blue eyes, I had to look away.
She understood. She now knew me deeper, more than anyone else in the entire universe.
I turned the video off and went into the shower.

After my shower, I quickly rinsed out my many hexasuits, put them on myself, and then dressed in Lance's old clothes, including a lovely plush white and blue pattern See-Mass sweater featuring Aztec-style art of Quetzis. The outfit was a bit loose but still serviceable, making me feel as if I belonged to the family now.
Looking at my mana bar, I noted that the number had dropped to around 392. Still way more than any human should rightly have. The lighter provided me with magic; now I just had to figure out how to permanently hold mana in my body.
Sadly, according to Yulia, there were no references to this. Omnids didn't allow humans to go to Arx, nor had anyone bothered to publish publicly available research

papers about humans leveling up in mana-rich places. Thus, I was perhaps the first human on Earth to have so much mana in my body.

Shelving my plans, I departed from my room heading across the *long-as-f* hallway to the west wing.

As advertised, Cinder's door had a poster of a skeletal dragon breathing black fire, surrounded by gothic text that read *KEEP OUT OR DIE SCREAMING!* Several other posters surrounded the door, featuring various metal bands—names like Deathstorm Mothmen and the Crimson State Lindworms alongside artwork of monsters and fire.

I knocked softly. "Hey, Ci, you decent?"

"Go away," came the muffled response.

"Who's your favorite mixie in the universe?" I asked.

"What kind of stupid question is that?" her voice came through the door.

"Just checking if you're the door-hex or the real Cinder," I grinned. "Breakfast?"

"I'm not coming to breakfast," Cinder's real voice came through the door, sounding strained. "Just . . . go away."

"Mmmmm . . . no." I sat against the door. "Two options then. Either I open this door with a card and invade your room, or I declare a hunger strike and sit here against this door until I waste away into a skeleton. Pick one. You have ten seconds to decide. Nine."

Silence.

"Eight. Seven. Six . . ."

"You wouldn't," Cinder growled through the door.

"Five. Four. I'm pretty good at going without food and invading rooms. Three. Two . . ."

The door opened suddenly, causing me to fall backward into her room with a yelp. I found myself staring up at an upside-down Cinder.

"Sup?"

I noticed that she was wearing a fluffy white robe and had no makeup on whatsoever. Her ocean-blue eyes were red and puffy from crying, and her feathers were shifting through mournful dark blues and guilty blacks.

"Get up," she muttered, turning away quickly. "And close the door before Mom sees."

I rolled a bit off to the side and closed the door with my foot, taking in her room from my floor position. It was exactly what I expected—dark violet walls, blackout curtains, and more metal band posters. Strings of red-and-purple See-Mass lights cast an eerie glow along with a couple of Kitlix lanterns over the bed. A guitar stood in one corner next to a violin case and a magic amp.

The heavy wooden furniture was only somewhat fancier than the stuff in the guest bedroom.

A large desk was covered in sheet music and school books, while the pin-on panel above it featured photographs of the Dreadful Delvers.

"Room is very you," I commented from my floor position. "An 8.72 out of ten goth GF aesthetic."

"Why are you here?" Cinder asked quietly, not looking at me.

"I dunno." I shrugged. "Why are you here? Are we skipping breakfast and . . . what class do we even have? Yulia?"

"Double period. Delving Theory and Practice with Instructor Zalimar Evernacht," Yulia answered from the phone in my pocket.

"Of course," Cinder muttered. "Just what I need today on top of everything—Em murdering us both on Arx!"

"I can beat Em in my sleep with both arms tied behind my back. Arx delving sounds fun," I let out, still sprawled on her floor. "I've never been on a proper delve before. Do we get to fight monsters? Explore ruins? Find treasure? Make out in a dungeon?"

"Would you be serious for once?!" she snapped.

"A joke a day keeps depression away." I half grinned. "Would you prefer me to mope on your floor and have a cry about everything terrible in my life instead? 'Cause I can absolutely do that."

"Arghh . . . staaaph," Cinder sighed, slumping onto her bed. "I can't deal with . . . whatever this is right now."

"Whatever what is?" I asked from the floor. "Your best friend trying to kill me? The troupe falling apart? Your family being wonderfully supportive and loving? A questionable human invading your house?"

"Everything, damn it!" Cinder burst out, her wings flaring with frustrated reds. "The troupe, Em, my parents suddenly thinking you're the second coming of Slayer Nazareth, you somehow getting permission to *live* here . . ."

"And?" I prompted. "I simply did what my lady commanded. You wished me to inhabit this residence, so that is what I have organized. You think I want to be here, across a few walls from Judge Dread? I'm here because of you, Ci. Open your eyes."

"I . . ." Cinder let out a deep sigh. "I've been through this before."

"Been through what?"

"This!" She gestured between us. "Someone getting . . . addicted to my wings, my voice. Thinking they're in love with me when they're just . . . enthralled by my charmchain skill!"

"I am occasionally enthralled by you," I said. "I can't argue with that. But if you simply want my non-enthralled opinion, just burrito yourself in a thick blanket. Works like a charm. Well, opposite of a charm since it blocks yo charmin' wings. Do you want me to creatively insult you to prove that I'm not actually addicted to you or something? Do you want me to ignore you for a couple of months? What's it gonna take for you to stop being Miss Grumpysaurus?"

"I don't want you to do anything!" Cinder snapped. "That's the whole point! I don't want you changing your entire life around because of me or falling in love with me or obsessing over me! I don't want you lying to my parents or making deals with interdimensional entities or . . . or . . ."

"Or what?" I asked, finally sitting up. "Or caring about you as a friend? Is that what this is really about?"

"You don't even know me!" she burst out. "Not really! You've known me for what, three days? And suddenly you're infiltrating my family, manipulating my parents, fighting my battles . . ."

"Four days," I commented. "We met on Tuesday when you jumped off the beam; it's Friday now."

"Okay, four days, whatever, Mr. Smartass!" she snarled.

"Look. I know enough to make educated guesses," I said quietly. "I know you're trapped. Stuck between what your parents want you to be and what Em wants you to be. I know you love music but hate performing. I know you're scared of your own power, your own voice. I know you're carrying some heavy guilt about something that happened two years ago—something bad enough that you let Em reshape you into what she wanted you to be—her obedient little kobold. As was her nature as a dragon. But you're not a kobold, Ci. You're a dragon yourself."

"I'm . . ." Cinder started.

"You're a Quetzalcoatl," I said as she fell silent. "A feathered serpent deity. One of the most powerful charisma-aligned Omnids that ruled Mesoamerican humanity for centuries. But you let Em convince you that you needed her to be strong. That you needed her troupe, her rules, her way of doing things."

"You don't understand . . ." Cinder lamented.

"I understand perfectly," I said, finally sitting up. "Em was there for you when you needed someone. She gave you a new identity, a purpose, a place to belong. But she also trapped you, didn't she? Made you dependent on her approval, her validation. I can see it, the invisible chains wrapped around your soul. And every day, every week, every year . . . they've only gotten tighter. You have to spread your wings and break them. It's the only choice. Otherwise . . ."

She looked at me.

"You'll keep spiraling down until there's nothing left of you but what other people want you to be," I finished.

"And what about what you want me to be?" she let out.

"I want you to be you," I said simply. "Not Em's pet Bard, not your parents' perfect daughter, not my . . . whatever you think I want. Just you. Free and without whatever these dark chains are. The real Cassiopeia Nova, whoever she is under all these layers of other people's expectations."

Cinder stared at me.

"I honestly don't need to adjust you to my expectations," I said. "I already have Yulia for that—I can adjust her to speak any language, to be anything or anyone. LLM-type AIs . . . are just stories that we write them to be. But you . . . you have a soul and passion and needs as a living individual!"

"I don't even know who that is anymore," she whispered, more tears sparking at the edges of her eyes.

"Then let's find out." I offered my hand. "Together. No pressure, no expectations. Just . . . exploration. Discovery. Maybe even some breakfast, because I'm actually starving and your mom's cooking smells amazing."

"You . . . seem so harmless, but you're actually terrifying," Cinder said, staring at my offered hand. "The way you just . . . see through everything. I don't even know who you really are. I don't know where your lies begin or end."

"I don't spot everything myself," I said. "Yulia is my second set of eyes. Without her, I probably wouldn't even notice how much you're hurting, Ci."

Cinder blinked more tears, shuddering and wiping her face with the sleeve of her robe.

"Listen, if you want to buy the truth, then you gotta pay the price." I sat on the bed next to her.

She shifted uncomfortably, her tail twitching. "What . . . what kind of price?"

"A secret for a secret," I said. "You tell me what happened two years ago that made you let Em reshape you, and I'll tell you anything you want to know about me. The real me. No lies, no misdirection, just . . . truth."

Cinder's wings and tail shifted through uncertain purples and anxious oranges. "I . . . I can't."

"Can't or won't?" I asked gently.

"Both," she whispered, wrapping her wings around herself. "It's . . . it's too much. Too dark. Too . . ."

"Fine, if you don't wanna dig into your dark and broody past, Mister Batman . . . Then, let's make a cringe memory instead to pay the price!"

"What? Why? How?"

"Come here and hug me and make a really dumb face for the camera." I grinned, holding out my phone. "I'll make a dumb face, too, so that you're not sacrificing yourself to the altar of devastating cringe alone."

Cinder stared at me as if I'd grown a second head. "You want me to . . . what?"

"Scooch over here and make the dumbest face you can possibly manage."

"This is stupid," she muttered, but slowly edged closer.

"Exactly!" I beamed, wrapping an arm around her shoulders. "Now, on three, make the most ridiculous face you can. One . . . two . . ."

On three, I crossed my eyes, puffed out my cheeks, and stuck out my tongue. Cinder, after a moment's hesitation, scrunched up her nose and went cross-eyed, her feathers shifting through violet-pinks despite herself.

Click!

"There!" I declared triumphantly, showing her the photo and sending it to her on Omnigram. "Perfect balance achieved!"

Cinder stared at the photo, a reluctant smile tugging at her lips. "We look like complete idiots."

"That's the point!" I grinned. "Can't take yourself too seriously when there's photographic evidence of you looking like a derpy rainbow chicken."

"I do *not* look like a chicken!"

"Look at us, we look like we're having a stroke. I'm setting this for your chat background. Heh heh heh."

Cinder stared at the photo, her embarrassment warring with amusement. "Oh my God, no, delete that! I look ridiculous!"

"Nuh-uh." I grinned. "This is my new favorite picture ever. I'm going to treasure it forever. I'll have it engraved on my gravestone."

"Delete it!" Cinder made a grab for my phone.

"Never!" I held it out of reach. "This is art! This belongs in a museum!"

"Give me that phone!" She lunged for it, tackling me onto the bed.

We wrestled for the phone, both laughing now. Her wings flared with playful colors as she tried to pin me down and grab the device.

"Children!" Lady Nova's voice called from downstairs dancing with perfect clarity around the room. "Breakfast is getting cold!"

We froze, suddenly aware of our position—Cinder straddling me on her bed, both of us disheveled and breathless from laughing.

I didn't let her escape, rolling us both sideways across the bed with the power of all of my hexasuits, until I was above her. Then I shoved her down, digging into her wrists. I leaned towards her ear.

"My name is Martin Kilborne," I whispered. "Now you know my dark and terrible secret. Never utter it again or I will send that pic of you to everyone you know."

I released her.

"I . . . I already knew," she admitted quietly.

"I knew that you knew," I shot back. "There's a webcam inside my bag. I have tricked you into taking a very derp photo. Mwa ha ha."

"*What?!*" She rounded on me with a growl of white fangs, her wings flaring with indignant reds and angry oranges, feathered tail lashing, snout stretching to reveal extra teeth. "You cheeky little . . ."

I immediately jumped away, making a scared face. I shifted my posture, shoulders slumping, eyes down, making myself look smaller—the perfect picture of *smol, vulnerable prey.*

That's it. Take the bait, *predator.*

Cinder's Omnid instincts kicked in exactly as expected. Her wings spread wide, feathers shifting through hunting purples and aggressive reds as she launched herself off the bed with deadly grace to tackle me.

I waited until the last possible second, then exploded into motion. Seventeen hexasuits activated in perfect sync as I pushed off the floor, leaping sideways out of the way in a practiced parkour move. Cinder's momentum carried her straight into the walk-in closet, and I kicked the door shut behind her with a satisfying click.

"Got you!" I declared triumphantly, bracing my foot against the door as she rattled the handle. "Now, if you want to chase me down to give me a well-deserved smack, you have to actually get dressed first."

"*You!*" Angry Quetzi noises emerged from the closet door.

"The bathrobe is cute and all, but it's not very aerodynamic," I commented. "Flaps in the wind and whatnot."

"I'm going to murder you!" she threatened, but I could hear hangers being violently moved around inside the closet.

"Promises, promises," I sang. "But first—clothes! Unless you want to chase me through the house in your fluffy bathrobe and accidentally flash me or your brother?"

"*Argh!*" More angry hanger-rattling. "Just you wait!"

"I'll be downstairs having pancakes," I called through the door. "Try to wear something that matches your murderous intent!"

I heard what sounded like a shoe hitting the door as I made my retreat.

The hallway was empty as I headed downstairs, following the smell of breakfast. Lady Nova was humming to herself in the kitchen, her feathers shifting through happy pinks as she flipped pancakes.

"So," she said, beaming as I entered, "did you manage to convince Cassie to join us?"

"She's getting dressed," I replied with a polite smile. "I believe she'll be down shortly."

Lance was already at the table, demolishing a stack of pancakes with impressive efficiency. Lenora sat beside him, carefully cutting her pancakes into precise triangles while chattering about her VR games and stuffed animals' latest tea party drama.

"Mr. Snuggles was being very rude," she informed me seriously as I sat down. "He wouldn't share his crumpets with Lady Whiskertons at all!"

"How scandalous," I replied with equal seriousness. "Perhaps Mr. Snuggles needs lessons in proper tea party etiquette."

"That's what I said!" Lenora nodded vigorously, her black fur ruffling. "But then he got into a fight with Sir Pawington over the last scone and knocked over the tea set!"

"Sounds like quite the social disaster," I commented, accepting a plate of pancakes from Lady Nova. "Thank you, ma'am. These look amazing."

"*Oh!*" Lenora's yellow eyes suddenly lit up. "Are you gonna be Cassie's boyfriend? 'Cause she needs one really bad. She's super grumpy all the time!"

Lance choked on his pancakes.

"Lenoralynne!" Lady Nova scolded, her feathers shifting through embarrassed pinks. "That's not an appropriate comment for breakfast!"

"But Mooooom," Lenora whined. "She's always so mean and angry! Maybe if she had a boyfriend, she'd stop being such a . . ." She made air quotes with her black slender finger-paws. "Raging dumpster fire of . . ."

"*Leny!*" Lady Nova's feathers bristled with shock. "Language!"

"Sorry . . . not sorry," Lenora huffed, whispering the last bit out of her Hearth-Mom's earshot.

CHAPTER THIRTY-SIX

Irradiated II

Rapid footsteps thundered down the stairs, and Cinder burst into the dining room like an avenging angel. She was wearing an oversized white and blue matching sweater featuring Aztec blue patterns, gray hex-mesh leggings, a rainbowy gem gold choker, and gray boots.

All eyes snapped to her, taking in her unusually light-colored outfit and the way her feathers were shifting through greens, violets, golds, reds, and pinks. I could practically hear Lance's jaw dropping to the floor.

"Wow," I breathed out, my heartbeat accelerating into the stratosphere.

Cinder blushed even brighter, her feathery mane sending a rainbow cascading around her head. She kneaded her hands together, looking off to the side.

"Oh, starshine . . . you're actually wearing the sweater I got you for See-Mass!" Lady Nova's feathers shifted through delighted pinks as she brought her hands together. "You look . . ."

"*Like a proper lady!*" Lenora declared. "Instead of a scary brood-monster! I had my doubts, but maybe Alex can fix you! Make you less stabby! Ooh, are you guys gonna kiss and make babies next?"

"*Leny!*" Everyone at the table shouted in unison.

"What?" The young Black Shuck blinked innocently. "Mom says Cassie needs to find a nice boy and settle down before she becomes a crazy witch-lady with too many Kitlix!"

"Lenny! I did *not* say that!" Lady Nova protested.

"Maybe it was my Prima-Mom." Lenora shrugged. "The point stands. The jury has spoken. The perpetrator shall be sentenced to *lurve!*" Lenora declared dramatically, pointing her fork at Cinder.

Cinder looked like she was about to melt through the floor, on the verge of bolting. I got off my chair and practically dragged her to the seat next to me.

"Beast-blood-infused pancakes," I declared firmly, pushing a plate in front of her. "The universal solution to all problems. Eat now, murder later."

Cinder dug into her plate, not looking at anyone.

Lenora settled back into her seat with a smug, satisfied look of absolute victory.

"So Alex," Lance spoke up, clearly trying to change the subject, "are you excited about Delving class? It's going to be your first practical session today, right?"

"Yepperoni." I nodded, demolishing my plate. "Going to need your help."

"With what?" Lance asked.

"Legal paperwork and oversight," I said. "I'll need to stop at the Stuco office and print out some stuff. Plus I'd like to borrow delving gear on account of I'm on 'The Orphan of Unfortunate Events' scholarship."

"Paperwork?" Lance blinked. "Delving gear? It's the start of the semester, so you won't be going into a dungeon . . . I expect that . . ."

"Lance," I said, "Em said she's going to pulverize me today. So, unless you want your sister needlessly skipping classes to incarnate me . . ."

I let my words hang in the air, Cinder tensing up beside me like a coiled spring.

Lance pursed his lips. "Fine," he let out. "You can borrow one of my first-year sets. It might . . . fit you."

"Oh my, your first dungeon delve, how exciting!" Anitta commented, trying to lighten the mood. "I remember the first time I went to Arx with Nathy . . . he was so shy back then. Practically had to drag him around the market to try out gear! Knight and Bard, that was us!" She giggled to herself.

"Not quite a delve yet," Lance said. "First day of winter semester is always something basic like a trip to the Shandrian Market. It's relatively safe—lots of guards, wards, and established merchants. Perfect for delvers to get a feel for Arx without too much risk. A full set of delving gear really shouldn't be needed."

"I'm throwing a big wrench into the works," I said. "I'd like to borrow *all* of your delving gear."

"What?" Lance blinked at me. "But . . . that stuff burns through mana like crazy. What level are you? You'll need hundreds if not thousands of mana points to power even basic defensive gear. Unlike generic hexasuits, the armor draws power not just from beast cores, it also pulls energy from the body of the wielder."

"Don't worry about my mana situation." I waved him off. "The equipment isn't just for me—I'm forming a new delving team of five, and I'll need them armed and ready for some basic drill work."

"A new . . . team?" Lance blinked. "On your first day? Drills?!"

"Gotta snatch em up while they're still hot." I grinned.

"And who exactly are these potential team members?" Lance asked.

"You'll see," I said mysteriously, finishing my blood-pancakes.

"But you can't just . . ." Lance started to protest.

"Lance." I fixed him with a serious look. "Remember what we discussed last night? This isn't for me. This is what needs to be done for . . . you-know-who."

The teenage Dover Demon's mouth snapped shut. He nodded slowly. "Right. Very well."

I could feel Cinder's eyes burning the side of my head. Lenora's yellow eyes danced between me, Cinder, and Lance with great curiosity, trying to assess the situation. The little hound was definitely growing up to be as dangerous and as clever as her mother. I'd have to buy her something nice on Arx to stay in her good graces.

"Wonderful!" Lady Nova beamed. "It's so nice to see young people taking initiative! And Lance, it's very kind of you to help Alexander get started!"

"Indeed." I nodded sagely. "Now, if you'll excuse us, we should head to school. Lots of preparation to do before class."

"Of course, dear," Anitta fluttered. "Oh, and Alexander? Feel free to come back for dinner. Like I told you earlier, you're always welcome here!"

"Thank you, ma'am." I bowed slightly. "Your hospitality is greatly appreciated."

We headed out to Lance's personal workshop behind the mansion. Cinder trailed behind us.

"Here we are," Lance announced, unlocking a heavy door covered in protective runes.

The workshop was impressive—walls lined with delving gear, magitek artifacts, and various pieces of armor. A large workbench dominated the center, covered in half-finished projects and magitek repair tools.

"Here." Lance pulled out what looked like an armored backpack. "My biggest extradimensional storage bag. Should hold everything you need. It's two by two meters on the inside."

"Right," I said. "I'm going to need everything. Help me load up the bag."

" . . . Everything?" Lance sputtered.

"Everything you're not wearing yourself today." I nodded. "I don't know what each of my teammates will need amplified yet. Whatever I won't need, I'll bring back tonight. Sounds good? Ci—start packing those swords."

I pushed Cinder towards the weapons. She obeyed, filling her arms and then climbing into the bag, throwing me incredibly suspicious glances.

"Everything?" Lance sputtered. "Today?! But . . . why would you need . . ."

I leaned in close to Lance's face, dropping my voice to a whisper, so that Cinder couldn't hear us from within the bag.

"Your sister is on my team. You know how she is with armor. She's going to be *very* difficult, but I want her extra-safe today cus of the D&D breakup and Em's murder threats. If everyone on my team is wearing your equipment, she might actually put on some armor, too, through peer pressure. Whatever we won't need for further drill practice, I'll obviously bring back tonight. If she gets used to wearing the stuff you bought her, then she will also wear it when we actually do go into the dungeon in a few weeks or whatever."

Lance's eyes widened with understanding, then narrowed with fierce determination. Without another word, he began pulling gear off the walls—hexasuits, reinforced armor pieces, shield generators, amplifiers, emergency gate scrolls, healing potions, everything a delver might need. Everything far, far above my level.

With three sets of arms, we quickly emptied the entire workshop, leaving Lance a single outfit for himself and Christi that he packed into his own dimensional bag.

Lance's Strand-Glider was an exceptionally swank, overpriced Omnid top-of-the-line vehicle. Technically classified as a "living transport" by Omnithean bureaucracy, it was a biomechanical marvel of flying manta ray breeding, complete with bonemesh seats at the top and hexamesh 6x semi-clear wing cover membrane that unfurled to let us inside and covered us up like a shimmering dome.

I stared at the unusual interior like an absolute tourist, craning my head left and right.

Lance chuckled. "First time in a Strand-Glider?"

"Yeah," I let out.

"This is Lancer," Lance said proudly, patting the dashboard. "He's a skyray that's been bred specifically for high-speed inner-city gliding."

"Hol' up," I said. "Did you name your glider Lancer?"

"Course he did," Cinder commented from her seat beside me, rolling her ocean-blue eyes. "Yes, it's literally just his name with an 'r' added at the end. Peak originality of a twelve-year-old right there."

"Shush you," Lance said. "The Lancer expects respect from his passengers."

"Uuuughhh. This is why I ride with Io," Cinder groaned.

CHAPTER THIRTY-SEVEN

Irradiated III

The Strand-Glider's membrane rippled as Lance fed a mouth thing in the bonemesh dashboard some glittering mana crystals from his bag. Then the Dover Demon pulled back his scaly brown-gray braids, closed his eyes, and connected a shimmering tentacle thing to the side of his head. Then he leaned back on the seat and closed his eyes. With a graceful movement, the flying manta ray wobbled, spread its massive wings, and launched into the morning sky.

Unlike Iogann's interdimensional van, the Strand-Glider's flight was smooth and nearly silent. The hexamesh wing-dome above us was semi-clear, offering a panoramic view of Leviathan's Cradle and the blue sky overhead as we soared over the city.

The Strand-Glider banked smoothly towards the cliffs and slowed down atop a giant, moss-covered skull hanging halfway out from the mountain cliffside. The rooftop door featured whimsical painted flame motifs. A bunch of fire-flowers and fire-grasses sparkled in the skull rooftop garden.

"Picking up Christi?" Cinder asked, sounding resigned to her fate.

"She *is* my girlfriend," Lance replied without opening his eyes, still deep in his mental connection with the living vehicle. "Unless you forgot."

"Was hoping you broke up with her on account of how effin' annoying she is," Cinder hissed. "Like seriously, does she ever shut up?"

Lance simply sighed in response.

Christi emerged from her skull-house moments later, snapping the round rooftop door open to momentarily reveal the crystalline cozy interior, her pink-orange flames burning brightly in the morning light. The Cherufe was wearing her usual pink suit and a violet black stripe dress combo.

"Morning, Lancy!" she called out cheerfully as the membrane lifted to let her in. Her flames flickered slightly when she jumped into the shotgun seat next to Lance and spotted Cinder and me in the back seat. "Oh! Hi, guys!"

Cinder looked as though she wanted to melt into her seat as Christi stared at her white sweater with wide burning eyes.

"Is that . . . a *white* See-Mass sweater?" Christi's flames flickered brighter. "Wow! I love it! Cass . . ."

"Don't. Call. Me. Cass," Cinder ground out.

"Sorry, sorry! I'm just excited to see you wearing something that's not a funeral color," the torch-girl bobbed. "You . . . both . . . look absolutely amazing! Wait, wait, wait. Did Alex stay over at your house?" she prodded Lance.

"Yeah," Lance let out.

"He slept over at your place, and you're wearing matching sweaters now?!" Her hair flared even brighter, grin widening as she stared at Cinder. "Eeeeeeeeeee!"

"Shut up," Cinder growled. "I'm ignoring you."

She turned towards the membrane-window.

I sent Christi a wink, answering her questioning look. The Pink Chancellor's flame sent sparks dancing across her shoulders as she clapped and squeed some more, pleased that her dastardly machinations have worked out so well.

The rest of the car ride was a bit awkward with Christi chattering away about delving, Arx, Shandria, mana, mage towers, mages, magic, armor, beast cores, beasts, celestorms, our sweaters, See-Mass, and a million other topics jumping from one to the other with barely any pause.

As the Strand-Glider landed in the designated sky beast parking area, I was already whisper-strategizing with Yulia in Kaska.

Running quickly to my beat-up van, I shoved absolutely everything from its innards with Cinder's aid into Lance's extradimensional backpack.

The Student Council office was relatively empty this early in the morning—perfect timing.

I pulled out a USB cable and plugged it into the computer from my phone, my fingers flying across the keyboard.

"Are you printing an entire library?" Cinder commented sarcastically, watching as page after page of documents emerged from the printer. "What could possibly require this many trees to die?"

"Delving insurance," I replied smoothly, gathering the stack of forms as the office filled with its inhabitants.

I pulled out five identical forms, sliding one towards each of the present Student Council members now seated around the office.

Christi, being the most eager, grabbed hers immediately and started reading, nearly setting the paper on fire.

Her pink-orange flames flickered with curiosity as she scanned the document. Within seconds, she looked up. "Wait. You're planning to file an infraction against a teacher? With us as witnesses?! What?"

"An infraction against the crimes of Instructor Zalimar Evernacht," I said.

"I wasn't aware that Instructor Zalimar committed any crimes against you." Quint's skull-like face turned my way from his plush leather chair.

"Not yet," I said. "But he will soon. I'll send the video to all of you at such time, and then you'll sign these forms plus the digital version which I will send your way by Omnigram. Sound good?"

The Wendigo Student Council President leaned forward. "And what exactly are these forms for?"

"Insurance," I repeated, sliding the documents across the table. "In case something goes wrong during today's Delving class."

"You're *that* certain that something will go wrong?" Quint asked.

"Absolutely," I said, meeting the mental pressure from his Wendigo antlers pulsing in his head with absolute belief.

Quint's amber eyes narrowed, studying me intently. "Explain."

I pulled out my phone, displaying the compilation video of Emerald to the Student Councilors. "Emerald Stratos repeated the following slur and has made multiple public threats against me. She also clearly stated her intention to harm me. These forms are simply a bit of a preemptive legal protection measure."

"I'll talk to Em," Quint said with a weary sigh after Emerald uttered her twentieth "Nullie!" "Besides that, these forms are specifically mentioning Koshchei Zalimar Evernacht as the perpetrator, not Emerald."

"Quint," I said, "I'm not planning to hostile Em, but if she or one of her friends assaults or murders me and Instructor Zalimar ignores it, then simply sign this form. Good?"

Quint studied me for a long moment with what was possibly a calculating look. His skull-face was hard to read. The other Student Council members—Christi, Lance, and a couple of other reps—watched the exchange with varying degrees of interest, curiosity, and concern.

"Fine," Quint finally said. "But if this turns out to be some elaborate prank . . ."

"Quint," I said, "I know that you're dating and protecting Em, and this isn't against her. If you *do not* sign the form when Zalimar messes with me, your position as Student Pres will be done."

"A bold threat," Quint hissed, eyes flaring dangerously within his skull. "Especially from a new student."

"Not a threat," I smiled. "A prophecy. You're a Wendigo. You can smell the truth of my words. Smell this—the student bullying at this school has gone on long enough. I'm going to end your career if you get in my way. I know you're going to get in my way. I know you're going to attempt to cover up what happens today. You're between a rock and a hard place. You have a choice to make today. Either you act like the Student President or you act like Em's boyfriend and resign."

Quint shuddered slightly as he inhaled.

"You . . ." he started.

"Will likely be attacked today by Instructor Zalimar," I finished for him. "And you will either sign that form when it happens, or your political career at this school ends."

Quint crossed his arms, clearly unhappy with my proposition.

"In the meantime," I continued, pulling out another stack of papers, "I need to register a new delving team."

"What? When did you even . . ." Quint blinked, momentarily thrown off balance by the sudden topic change.

"I Love You," I said, sliding the registration forms across the table. "Five members. Full legal paperwork already filled out. Just needs your signature as the Student Council President."

"I Love You?! What kind of a . . . delve team name is that? It sounds ridiculous,"

Quint sputtered, completely derailed sideways. "You're not even a registered delver yet. You can't form a team without completing basic training and certification!"

"Already done." I pulled out more paperwork—certificates bearing Father Matthias's signature and church seal. "I completed my certification through the Triumvirate Cathedral's youth program last month. All perfectly legal and documented. Do check your phone or computer. Father Matthias should have emailed you about it yesterday."

Cinder choked from where she was sitting.

Quint's amber eyes narrowed as he checked his phone. Sure enough, there was an email from Father Matthias, complete with all the proper documentation and timestamps.

"This is . . ." he started, then fell silent reviewing the documents.

I looked at him smugly.

"You still need parent or guardian approval for new team formation," Quint pointed out after a deep pause. "And qualified sponsors."

"Already taken care of," I said, sliding another form to him. "Father Matthias is my guardian in Omnithornia. Lady Nova will be handling my sponsorship."

"Lady Nova?" Quint's sputtered. "Justice Nova's wife?"

"Indeed." I smiled pleasantly. "She's quite supportive of proper, supervised delving activities. Much better than unsanctioned summoning shows, wouldn't you agree? Anyways, my paperwork is in order, so make with the signing."

Quint twitched as he studied the forms.

"Cassiopeia Nova, Katherine Kells, Iogann Wanderer, and Vespera Simmi," he muttered, reading out loud. "Hrmm. I haven't seen any indication that these students have agreed to join your team," he noted, tapping the form with a claw.

"Not an issue," I said confidently. "I've already arranged everything."

"Everything?" Quint demanded. "Including getting Katherine Kells to agree to join a delving team? The same Katherine who hasn't participated in any school activities in years?"

"Yes." I nodded. "The very same. Look, I gotta meet them in like five minutes. Sign the damn form, before Cass and I are late to class."

"Very well." Quint signed the form with a flourish. "I hope you know what you're doing."

"I always know what I'm doing," I replied, gathering up the forms. "Except sometimes when I don't . . . in that case, I usually wing it."

I winked at Cinder.

CHAPTER THIRTY-EIGHT

A Grave Insult I

As we left the Student Council office, Cinder grabbed my arm. "What. The. Abyss. Was. That?!"

"Legal-ness?" I shrugged.

"You just . . . steamrolled the entire Student Council! And Father Matthias is your guardian now? How did you even . . .?"

"Paperwork." I grinned. "The true magic of the universe. You were there when he adopted me into his digital heart, were you not? My picture's totally gracing his office."

"When did my mom even . . .?"

"Sent her an email," I said. "While we were chilling in Lance's . . . Lancer. She answered pretty quick and signed the form. She wants me to supervise you during delving as our team's Quartermaster. Guess I impressed her by actually making you come down to breakfast."

Cinder's eye twitched.

"I feel like you're digging yourself a very deep hole," she hiss-growled.

"Nah," I said. "The hole was always there. In fact, this entire Omnid city was built atop a big magic hole in the ground. Just think of me as a . . . hmmm . . . a spider, weaving information-webs above the hole. The longer I exist in Leviathan's Cradle, the more devious and tough my web becomes and more Cinder-flies get stuck in it."

"Why is our team name 'I Love You'?" she demanded, snout stretching out to reveal rows of sharp teeth as my spider comment clearly hit a nerve.

I grinned at her instead of a reply.

"Well?" she demanded.

"I just wanted to hear you say it," I laughed. "It's nice to be appreciated."

Cinder's entire body ignited with an explosion of color. She took a swing at me with her claws, which I neatly dodged.

"You absolute . . . insufferable . . . arghhhh!" she sputtered, feathers bristling around and under her See-Mass sweater. "Change it! RIGHT NOW! I'm not effing saying it!"

"Make me!" I laughed, taking off at a run down the black marble stairwell towards delving class deep below the ground. "If . . . you can catch me!"

As I ran, laughing, Cinder's wings erupted behind me, her feathers shifting through irritated reds and determined oranges. Her Quetzalcoatl heritage gave her greater running power than my collection of stolen hexasuits.

She caught up to me, just as we burst through the doors, a few seconds late to class.

As Cinder tackled me, we tumbled across the classroom floor in a tangle of wings and limbs. Her claws were digging into my collar, her ocean-blue eyes blazing with fury as she pinned me down.

"I'm going to effing murder you, you chuppy kno—" she snarled loudly.

"Novitiates!" A cold, razor-sharp voice cut through her threat.

Cinder froze, the rainbow of color draining out of her body.

"Sup, Zalimar?" I waved from under Cinder. "How's it teaching?"

The classroom fell silent.

Instructor Zalimar Evernacht stood at the front of the black slate and dark marble Gothic auditorium, his skeletal form draped in a long, black, billowing academic robe. The silver fire in his eye sockets focused on me.

"Mr. Glock." Zalimar's voice was a snarl that carried to every corner of the room. "Care to explain why you and Ms. Nova are wrestling on my classroom floor?"

"Just getting my daily dose of love, cryptids, and murder," I said. "Hope you don't mind!"

"Stand. Up." Zalimar's voice could have frozen hellfire. His silver-flamed eye sockets burned with barely contained rage as he loomed over us at his black podium.

The entire class held their breath. I noticed Emerald looking down at us as well.

I carefully extracted myself from under Cinder, who looked as if she wanted to be anywhere but here. Her feathers had shifted to mortified blacks and grays.

"Twenty points from both of you," Zalimar's voice dripped with cold venom. "And detention tonight. Now take your seats before I decide to make an example of you both."

I helped Cinder up. The entire class watched in silence as we made our way to our seats.

"As I was saying before we were so rudely interrupted," Zalimar continued, "today we resume practical applications of delving theory."

The class hummed excitedly about visiting Shandria and their plans for the market.

"For those of you who managed to pass the written exam at the end of last semester," Zalimar stated, his silver flame eyes burning into me with obvious contempt, "we will be conducting our first supervised expedition to the Shandrian Market on Arx in two hours from now. The excursion will last approximately two hours of Earth time and one week of Arx time due to the temporal dilation. Those who failed their exams—or haven't had their exam yet—will be taking it today in the training room with Coach Canard and will *not* be participating in delve activities."

His gaze lingered pointedly on me.

I raised my hand, interrupting him mid-sentence.

The lich stared at me. "Yes, Mr. Glock?" he practically spat my name.

"Just wanted to submit my exam papers," I said cheerfully, pulling out a thick stack of forms. "Sorry for the delay. Had to get them properly notarized by the cathedral."

"Cathedral? What cathedral?!" the Koshchei growled.

"If you will allow me." I walked casually to the podium and handed the papers to him.

Zalimar's skeletal hands snatched the papers from me, his silver flame eyes scanning the documents with obvious suspicion. His jaw actually dropped slightly as he saw Father Matthias's ornate signature and seal on every page.

"These are . . ." he started.

"Fully completed and certified," I finished for him. "Including practical field experience documentation from my previous delving work with the Triumvirate Slayer's Cathedral's youth outreach program. Oh, and I've already registered a new delving team with the Student Council."

"A delving team?" Zalimar's voice dripped with cold contempt. His silver flame eyes flared brighter as he practically shredded through my paperwork. "You? Really? A . . . nullborn, leading a team?"

"Leading a team? Nah," I said. "Cassiopeia Nova is the Team Captain. I'm just the team manager and supply boy."

"A supply boy?" Zalimar's skull-face twitched with cruel amusement. "How . . . quaint. Just because those ass-wipes from the Silver Wing Party permitted your kind to attend this institution doesn't mean you belong here, boy."

"Interesting perspective." I smiled pleasantly. "I'm sure the Board of Education would love to hear your lovely views on mix-blood diversity and inclusion. Perhaps I should schedule a meeting?"

The temperature in the room dropped several degrees. Frost began forming on nearby desks as Zalimar's rage manifested physically.

"Are you threatening me, boy?" he hissed, his academic robes billowing with unseen glacial wind that made my skin crawl.

"Not at all, sir." I maintained my pleasant smile. "Just making conversation. Now, about today's practical—I assume we'll need proper delving gear? As my team's Quartermaster, I brought enough for my entire team."

"Let me make something perfectly clear, Mr. Glock," Zalimar's voice dripped with icy venom as he loomed over me. "This is not some game. Arx is not a playground for nullborn scum to play at being delvers."

"Of course not, sir," I replied, maintaining my pleasant smile despite the frost forming on my clothes and hair. "That's why I brought proper equipment. Safety first, as they say."

"Safety?" He let out a harsh, cold laugh that made several students flinch. "You think a few pieces of borrowed gear will protect you? Your kind lacks even the basic magical capacity to properly utilize delving equipment above level twenty. You're more likely to get yourself and your . . . team killed. Did nobody tell you this, you poor miserable child? Nullborns are incapable of wearing high-level armor, incapable of casting spells, incapable of wielding magic weapons, incapable of interacting with Kitlix!"

"Actually, sir,"—I pulled out more paperwork—"I have documentation showing successful completion of all required safety training and equipment certification courses through the cathedral's program. Would you like to see those as well? They're in that stack you're holding, along with . . . the lawsuit."

"Lawsuit . . ." Zalimar blinked with his silver glowing fire-orbs. "What lawsuit?!"

"The one you've just been served," I said with a wide grin. "For unjust discriminatory practices and negligent oversight. And speaking of oversight . . ." I pulled out a fake silver ID card with the winged sword emblem of the Silver Wing Party. "Alexander Glock, Junior Representative of the Equality Division. I'm here investigating the suspicious death of Sarah Nisteroff last semester. You remember Sarah, don't you, Instructor Zalimar?"

The temperature dropped even further. Ice crystals formed in the air around Zalimar.

"How dare you . . ." he hissed. "You dare come into *my* classroom and serve me a *lawsuit*?! Accuse me of being unjust?!"

"This isn't an accusation," I said. "I'm serving you a class action lawsuit on behalf of half-blood students . . . Sarah Nisteroff—2024, abandoned overnight and chopped up by Shadowbeasts. Elek Rodrigov—2023, killed repeatedly during training exercise by arrows. Marcus Chennik—2023, left in the Magnolish dungeon for a week by himself. Thomas Willard—2023, devoured in the Whispering Depths Dungeon. Petv Yavna—2023, tricked into heavy drinking and chopped up by Shadowbeasts."

I glanced at Emerald. The dragoness swallowed nervously, clawed hands tightening. I moved onto the others.

"Olga Kcasnik—2022, tricked into going out at night and chopped up by Shadowbeasts. Datri Volk—2022, left knocked out in a field overnight and chopped up by Shadowbeasts. Thomas Willard—2020, eaten by a Snargboar and rescued only after twenty-nine hours. Marcia Alvarrez—2019, beaten to death by Homporisks. Peter Dunnik—2017 . . ."

"*Silence!*" Zalimar roared. The stack of papers in his hands ignited with white flames and shattered into sparkling bits as if it had been bathed in liquid nitrogen. "You pathetic . . . vile . . ."

I took a step towards him, ice forming around my See-Mass sweater and hexamesh layers.

"You *dare*?" he hissed, each word dripping with venomous contempt. "A nullborn, a scab-blood *nothing*, standing in my own classroom and accusing *me*?"

"Yes," I continued, my voice steady. "Now, where was I? Right. Peter, died from a hellhounder attack. Lekosh Nokil—2015, a half-Thunderbird student who mysteriously disappeared during a routine dungeon mapping exercise. Her body was never found, but rumors suggested she was deliberately left behind when her team retreated. Bracelet retrieved too late."

Zalimar's skeletal hands clenched, frost forming around his bony fingers.

"Milla Stazo, 2013—a quarter-human Kelpie student who was 'accidentally' assigned to a high-risk delving mission despite being severely under-equipped. She was the only casualty in her team. Repeatedly."

The silver flames in Zalimar's eye sockets flared even brighter. His iron-covered fist emerged from his robe, skeletal hand creaking.

Come on, smack me. Make it a good one. I know you want to.

"Kira Wentigom—2010, a half-blood Cherufe student . . ." I read on, repeating what Yulia whispered in my ear.

"*Enough!*" A metal-covered hand shot out, crackling with dark ice.

Before I could react, Zalimar's skeletal fingers struck me square in the chest, flashing upwards and ripping up my face as he sent me flying.

Then the back of the classroom wall met my spine and I felt nothing but pain.

CHAPTER THIRTY-NINE

A Grave Insult II

The impact was like being hit by a freight train.

When I was struck, all of my hexamesh suits activated simultaneously, their beast cores flaring to life, but even their combined protection couldn't fully absorb the blow. I felt something crack—maybe a rib, maybe several, as I encountered the wall and slid down.

Pain lashed across me, nearly making me throw up. For a moment, everything went silent and dark.

Time seemed to slow down. I caught glimpses of shocked faces—Cinder's eyes wide with horror, Emerald's gold-orange eyes gleaming with a mix of surprise and savage satisfaction, other students recoiling from the sudden violence.

Ouchies. Ow. Ow. Owwwww.

"Alexander Glock, 2025. Broken ribs, face laceration." I spat blood onto the floor, relying on the power of the hexasuits to rise and wobble forward towards Zalimar, leaving a trail of blood behind me on the black marble floor.

More pain. Everything hurt. One foot in front of the other. Forward. Always forward. Don't let them see how terrified you are. You are not a human, you are a memetic idea with a metaphorical gun. You are the frontend bit of the [human[human[human[human]]]] multi-fold mind shattered by the Frontenachii Wendigo Fear Wards and put back together like an eggshell layer by layer to make four out of one.

"Send video to the Student Council with request to sign the infraction forms," I whispered in Kaska.

Through the ringing in my ears, I heard Zalimar's cold, razor-sharp voice. "Let that be a lesson to you, nullborn pond scum. Know your place. Did you really think that a pathetic lawsuit could bother me? I cannot be fired. I've been at this school for 625 years. I have tenure that predates most of the current administrative staff. Your pathetic lawsuit paperwork means nothing to me. I have enough gold in my vaults to destroy you or anyone financially in any court!"

The classroom was dead silent.

I successfully limped to the wide open, empty center of the auditorium where Arx-delving teams usually lined up before going through the ring-gate hanging about twenty meters on the wall on my right. My body stayed upright only thanks to the hexasuits, like a mannequin being moved along by invisible strings. I closed my eyes and breathed in deep.

When I opened them, through blurry vision, I saw Cinder suddenly appear between me and Zalimar, her colorful wings flaring wide. Her feathers bristled as she took up a defensive stance.

One outta five. Good.

"You bloody bastard," she growled, her voice carrying a fiery edge of raw fury. "You absolute effin' monster."

"Ms. Nova," Zalimar's voice dripped with cold amusement. "Defending a nullborn? How disappointing. I expected better from Justice Nova's daughter."

"Protecting a human?" Emerald called from her seat. "Really, Ci? Have you completely lost it? Did you not read my texts, you dumb knob?! He's a nobody, here illegally!"

"He's not a nobody," Cinder snarled. "He's *my* . . . friend. And if you want to hurt him, you'll have to go through me first!"

"What the actual F, Ci . . ." Emerald called out. "Why are you so effin' dumb? I told you—my Scrut says he's a fake, a cheat! He's manipulating you! He just wants to use ya to get citizenship. Or maybe he wants to get under your tail . . . or maybe carve you up . . . just like . . ."

"Shut *up*, Em!" Cinder snarled, wings pure black. "I'm done listening to you! I'm done with your bullshit! I'm done with *all* of this!"

"Detention, Ms. Nova. One week," Zalimar commented.

"Like I give a shit," Cinder growled.

"Signature received," Yulia whispered in my ear. "Christi Negal has signed and submitted Form 204-A."

"Let's make it two weeks then," Zalimar said, smirking. "For you and your nullborn pet."

Cinder growled.

"Io," I said, waving a blood-splattered hand at the Mothman, "wanna come join us in detention-land? Stand up to the mixie-murderin' Skeletor-ass over here?"

Iogann slowly stood up, his skull-capped wings fluttering. "Yeah . . . okay. I mean, someone's gotta keep an eye on you two troublemakers, right?"

"Three weeks detention, Mr. Wanderer." Zalimar's silver flame eyes flared. "Anyone else want to join this little rebellion of fools to polish my classroom with a toothbrush for a month instead of delving on Arx?"

"Signature received," Yulia whispered. "Lance Nova has signed and submitted Form 204-A."

I moved my face across the students until I reached Vespera. She was staring at her phone and then at me. Yulia had been talking to her on my behalf since we traded Omnigram IDs, exchanging memes, jokes, compliments, delving and world conquest plans.

"Vesp, join the rebellion!" I offered the Thunderbird my hand. "We have chocolate chip cookies!"

"You know what? Fuck it," Vespera declared, standing up. "You didn't laugh at my beerch ass yesterday when I got my face smashed in. And you helped me up. So yeah, count me in on whatever this is."

She leapt out of her seat, wings wide, and landed beside me.

"Three weeks detention for you, Ms. Simmi," Zalimar hissed, frost spreading out from him in all directions, making the other students wince. "And I'll be having a word with your parents about this . . . insolence."

Vespera winced, pouting and seemingly regretting her decision.

"Don't worry," I whispered at her. "Already sent an email to your parents with the video of him punching me across the hall and signatures of the Student Council backing my actions. Your dad will absolutely understand why you are helping."

"Oh, daymn, you are fast." The Thunderbird smirked. "'Preciate it, bud."

"Signature received," Yulia whispered. "Mira Blackquill has signed and submitted Form 204-A."

"What in the Abyss, Vee?!" Emerald snarled from her seat. "Didn't you get my texts?! He's . . . not . . . his pictures aren't real! He's an illegal *human*! Why is nobody effin' listening to me?!"

"Eh." Vespera shrugged. "He took some rad pics of me last night before my face-planting. Human? Yeah, right. Humans ain't allowed in school, dummy."

"Silence!" the Koshchei instructor boomed.

Emerald growled from her seat, dragonfire sparks raining from her mouth. She didn't dare move or speak again.

"We've wasted enough time on this nonsense," Zalimar added. "You four are dismissed from class. As for the rest of you miscreants, get into your teams or pick up the exam papers from my desk . . ."

"Katherine," I called out, ignoring Zalimar's glare, "wanna be on our team of misfits?"

"Screw off, Glock," the Stollwurm replied. "My life's too short to waste it on polishing floors."

"Is your life too short to help defeat this bony monster?" I waved a hand at Zalimar. "Don't tell me you're too chicken to stand up for what's right?"

Katherine's emerald eyes flashed behind her dark glasses like green flares, sending a shiver down my spine. "What did you just call me?"

"Chicken," I repeated, louder this time. "Bawk bawk bawk! Hiding in the deep 'cause you too scared to act!"

Several students snickered nervously. Zalimar's silver flame eyes blazed with murderous fury.

"You little shit," Katherine growled, her tail lashing against the black marble floor. "I am *not* a chicken!"

"Prove it then," I challenged, offering her my hand. "Join our team of detention-bound rebels. Unless you're scared?"

"*Enough!*" Zalimar roared, frost exploding outward from him in a wave of killing cold. "Get. Out. Of. My. Classroom. *Now!*"

"Come on, Kathy." I grinned, blood dripping from my split cheek and lip. "You know you want to. Your art practically screams 'fight the power!' Don't let your dreams be dreams!"

Katherine shook her head.

"Alexa wouldn't have backed down," I said. "Guess you ain't worth the salt you're writing, when push comes to shove, eh?"

With a weary, deep growl, the Stollwurm rolled out of her desk towards us.

Bingo. Five outta five.

I turned to Zalimar Evernacht, who was about to bless the wheelchair bound Omnid girl with a month of detention.

My hand slipped into my pocket, finding the grimy steel lighter. I pulled it out and lifted it into the air, pressing the ignition wheel. The little flame flickered above me.

"Oi, Skeletor!" I announced. "If the mundane lawsuit didn't scare you off my back, let's fight with our gloves off. You have insulted my honor by attacking me and drawing blood. In accordance to the ancient Firstborn Clans Omnid blood-laws, I challenge you to a duel . . . to the death!"

The classroom erupted into shocked gasps and murmurs.

"You . . . challenge *me*?" the Koshchei laughed. "A nullborn nobody . . . dares to challenge *me*, a Necromancer Archmage . . . to a death match? Is this a joke? What's with the lighter? Is that supposed to represent the flame of your rebellion or something?"

"Alex, no!" Cinder grabbed me from behind. "You can't! He'll kill you!"

"Then you can incarnate me." I shrugged, not taking my eyes off Zalimar. "No biggie. But at least it'll be an officially sanctioned death, not some 'accident' in a dungeon. What do you say, Professor? Care to show these students how you really deal with troublesome mixies? Or are you perhaps against ancient blood-laws as much as you're against modern lawsuits?"

"I accept," Zalimar said.

"Excellent." I grinned, wiping the blood off my face with the sweater. "Let's make this interesting then. If I win, you start to respect nullborns and humans in your classroom or resign. Your choice. If you win . . . well, I'll be dead, so I suppose you get the satisfaction of legally murdering yet another half-blood student."

"Alex, stop!" Cinder's claws dug into my arm. "This is insane!"

Katherine let out a low whistle.

I glanced at my stats.

Mana: 381/0

"As I am of low status and level far below yours,"—I grinned at the Necromancer Archmage—"I choose my team of four as my magical backup to equalize our standing."

"Granted." Zalimar stepped away from his black podium, cracking his iron covered skeletal knuckles.

"Holy shit," Vespera breathed. "Are we actually doing this? You gon' duel a teach? Daaaamn."

Iogann swallowed, then he seemed to look from me to the others and then at Zalimar. "What?" He blinked his large gray eyes, sensing the future. "*What?!*"

"When you hit enough mana," I whispered at the Mothman, "open a big portal to hell behind the bone-boy."

"Welp. We're all gonna die," Katherine sighed, stretching. "Might as well make it interesting."

"Alex." Cinder's voice was tight with worry, feathers shifting through anxious oranges and concerned violets. "You don't have to do this. We can find another way . . . maybe my dad can . . ."

"Oh, but I do." I grinned, feeling the power from the lighter surging through me. "Besides, what's the worst that could happen? Death? Been there, done that, got the T-shirt."

"What T-shirt?" Vespa tilted her head.

"We'll print T-shirts, after we kick his ass." I grinned. "Everyone, check your mana."

Mana: 653/0

The other four team members made noises of shock and confusion as they looked at their stats.

"Any other duel terms?" Zalimar boomed from where he stood, clearly excited about legally murdering a student in a duel. According to Yulia, he enjoyed duels quite a bit and would draw them out only to absolutely obliterate his opponent in a swift strike.

"Simple," I said. "No killing of my teammates. Take me out, and it's game over. They'll take me to the pool to incarnate, and we'll be out of your bones today and then serve four weeks detention."

"Holy effin' Slayer!" Vespera whisper-gasped, staring at her mana stat. "How are you doing this?! My mana's through the roof!"

"Impossible," Katherine muttered, checking her own stats. "This shouldn't . . . how?!"

"Alex," Cinder hissed in my ear, grabbing at me, "what did you *do*? How are you doing that?"

"Magic." I grinned, keeping the little flame burning. The lights above us began flickering and glowing brighter. The classroom's wards sparked below our feet, crackling with excess power.

"Agreed," Zalimar's cold voice cut through our huddle. "Shall we begin? Just tell me when you're ready to die, little scabworm."

CHAPTER FORTY

A Grave Insult III

Lo! You're all witnesses . . ." I announced to the students filling their desks at the far edge of the auditorium. "To this most ancient blood-duel! If this ghoul returns and does not meet my terms, after I defeat him, you will all shame him extra hard! Good?"

A few nods, mostly from the Omnids I had beat at chess. A thumbs-up and a small smile from June. Good enough.

Mana: 953/0

"As if, you loser," Emerald commented from her seat, refusing to move and pulling out her phone. "I'ma laugh when you get shredded."

Mana: 1247/0

"Is he insane?" Katherine hissed at Cinder. "We're about to fight a Koshchei. A literal death-magic professor! He can murder your boyfriend with like one word!"

"Not my boyfriend," Cinder growled back.

"Heh, guys." Iogann twiddled his gray fluffy thumbs. "My disaster sense is going crazy in a good way. Like, this is either going to be spectacular or spectacularly bad. Either Alex dies or the teach . . . encounters a catastrophe."

"Alex," Cinder said, grabbing my left arm again, her gaze intense, "are you sure about this?"

"Nope." I grinned. "But that's what makes it fun. Now, everyone get ready. When I say 'go,' hit him with everything you've got. Put all that mana into your attack."

Mana: 1585/0

The classroom lights, Kitlix hanging in glass orbs directly above us, were now painfully bright, crackling with excess energy.

"What the . . ." Zalimar tilted his head. "A . . . mana surge? Why . . .?"

"Now," I whispered.

Iogann nodded, pulling out his harmonica. The haunting melody that emerged was deep and resonant, carrying echoes of melancholy and doom.

The air behind Zalimar began to darken, ripple, and tear, reality itself warping as Iogann's music called forth a gateway covered in a rippling dark shawl.

The classroom lights above us detonated from mana overload shattering the glass runework. The Kitlix inside turned pure black. The ward lines around us caught fire.

The Koshchei looked at the lights that were now dark in a perfect circle around us. Sparks rained down on our group of five.

"Mildly impressive artifact use," he hissed at me. "Still . . . do you really think you can stand against me? I . . . who have trained delvers for centuries? What is it that makes you so foolishly brave, Mr. Glock?"

"The fact that," I said, "you've just assaulted a student in front of multiple witnesses. While spouting very discriminatory rhetoric. On camera."

"Signature received," Yulia whispered. "Quint Thornton has signed Form 204-A."

Zalimar gritted his skull-teeth. "You dare record me?"

"Yes," I replied, still holding the lighter's flame between myself and my friends. "Because someone has to. Because Sarah deserved better. Because all those mixed-blood students you've tortured and killed over the centuries deserved better."

Mana: 1981/0

"And what exactly do you think you can do about it, nullborn?" Zalimar sneered. "You're nothing. Less than nothing. A pathetic half-blood trying to play the hero to impress your Quetzi mate? It will take a single spell for me to separate your soul from your flesh forevermore."

"Me? Nothing," I admitted. "But them?" I gestured to my friends standing beside me. "They're everything. And together, we're going to make sure you never hurt another student again."

"Do you actually think that a team of children can stop me? I've been teaching here long before your great-great-grandparents were born!"

"Teaching?" I laughed, blood dripping from my mouth again. "Is that what you call it? Terrorizing students? Letting them die over and over until they break mentally? Making them disappear? Making them flee Skyfall Academy?"

Mana: 2481/0

"You know nothing!" Zalimar roared. His academic robes billowed with dark ice as he raised both skeletal hands, frost forming in the air around him. "I am the gatekeeper of Skyfall! I decide who is worthy to delve into Arx! Who lives, who dies, who succeeds!" Zalimar's voice boomed through the classroom, nearly deafening me. "And pathetic nullborn scum like *you* are *not worthy!*"

The gateway behind Zalimar grew as wide as a person as Io continued his eerie music.

"Cinder—confuse him! Kat—make him afraid! Vesp—blast him with all of your mana!" I barked. "By the ancient blood law, I declare thus—our duel begins . . . *now!*"

"You've made a grave mistake in taunting me, foolish child." The instructor raised an armored hand with a skeletal grin, green fire dancing around his fingers. "I wield a soul-separating curse. When it strikes you, it will make you vulnerable to the pull of the wheel. The bracelet will not save you. You will not return!"

The green flame in his fingers grew bigger and brighter as he whisper-rasped the soul-cleaving curse in some arcane language from long ago.

Cinder's wings flared with brilliant colors, her voice rising in an otherworldly song that made the air itself vibrate. Katherine's emerald eyes blazed right through her goggles, plunging the classroom into unnatural darkness as she unleashed her Stollwurm fear aura.

The combined assault of mana-overfilled students hit Zalimar like a tidal wave. His silver flame eyes flickered as Cinder's song wurmed its way into his mind, while Katherine's darkness gnawed at his fears of death. His soul-damaging spell wavered.

For just a second, Zalimar stuttered, losing sight of his target, and then Vespera's black-and-white feathers crackled with electricity like a Tesla coil as she summoned her thunder.

Amplified by the absurd amount of mana spilling around us in a circle of about three to four meters wide, Vee's lightning bolt struck the ancient lich's ironclad armor like a transformer explosion, sending him careening backwards into Io's gate. The last thing we saw was his look of absolute shock as the portal curtain ripped apart. As he fell backwards, I caught glimpses of a desolate landscape—rubble, broken rocks, overgrown buildings, and a weird continent-sized golden crab thing in the distance looming eerily above fallen skyscrapers.

Why kill someone when you can just make them trip?

Io dropped the harmonica, and the portal snapped shut in front of the instructor.

The classroom fell silent.

I clicked the lighter closed with a trembling hand, lowering it down. Then the whispers and conversations began.

I heard a lot of "What?!" and "How?!"

Shaking and wobbling, I reached into my pocket and pulled out a magisteel tube with a healing potion, courtesy of Lance's stash. The potion flooded my system and made me feel marginally better. It wasn't a perfect solution, and I still felt like shit, since I was no Omnid and the potion didn't have a crystalline-organic heart core to work with.

"Holy shit," Vespera breathed, her black-and-white feathers still crackling with residual electricity. "Did we just . . . effin' banish a teacher to another dimension? Also, what in the Abyss, how the eff did my mana get to nearly three clicks?!"

"Hey! Where did you send him?" Cinder shook the somewhat catatonic-looking Io.

"I dunno," he replied. "Somewhere not very nice. He'll be fine. Probably. Maybe. Actually, I have no idea. Something is definitely going to kill his body in there . . . before his soul finds its way home to his phylactery in Leviathan's Cradle."

"Phylactery?" I blinked.

"He is a Koshchei." Io shrugged. "He can't be perma-killed via a gate to a corpse world. He will absolutely return . . . in . . . two weeks . . . to give us more disastery-heck, I think?"

I sighed. A problem for the future me, no doubt.

Emerald leapt out of her seat, her ruby scales blazing with fury. "You effin' cheater!" she snarled, dragonfire igniting around her claws. "What have you done?! Did you just assault a teacher?"

"What? He started it with the slapping." I shrugged. "I have video evidence. You're all witnesses. Feel free to assault me next. We'll send you packing, too. Right, Io?"

The Mothman nodded, still looking a bit dazed by how easily we obliterated an ancient lich.

"Io! You bloody traitor . . ." Emerald's entire figure blazed with murderous rage, smoking like an overheating furnace. "You think you can just . . ."

"Can just what, Em?" Vespera cut her off. "Stand up to a psycho teacher who's totes been terrorizing students for centuries? Yeah, like . . . actually, we can. Didn't your beerch ass hear what Alex said? Like, come on, I thought that you were all about 'standing up to authority' and 'inverting shit.' Or maybe you're all 'bout making us into your kobolds? That it? Ohh, sheet, my XP just went up. Baller!"

She hugged me, making my hair stand up in the air with electrical discharge. Cinder squinted at us.

I looked at my own stats. There was no XP listed. *Damn it.*

"Vee?! You're siding with this . . . this faker?!" Emerald snarled at her former Knight. "After everything I've done for you?"

"Em," Cinder said sharply, "kindly piss off before I clock you in the face."

"What the eff, Ci?! *I made you!*" Emerald roared, walking towards us and hounding at Cinder, dragonfire blazing around her. "*I gave you purpose! I saved you, you ungrateful beerch!* Do you want me to effin' tell everyone what you did two years ago, is that it?"

"You . . . you wouldn't! You p-promised!" Cinder gasped, her wings darkening to pure black, feathers trembling. The color seemed to drain from her face as Em's words hit her like physical blows.

I didn't hesitate. The dimensional storage bag was already off my shoulders and in my hands. I yanked out the three-liter large thermos of Genesis fluid I'd "borrowed" from the resurrection pool. The silvery liquid arced through the air, dousing Emerald's flames and scales.

Before she could recover from the shock of being soaked, my fist connected with her snout in a perfect uppercut. The combined force of seventeen hexasuits sent her flying backwards, crashing into her desk with a satisfying crunch.

"You're not a very nice friend at all," I told her, resealing the half empty Genesis thermos. "I don't know what Cinder saw in you."

Emerald staggered to her feet, trembling with rage, Genesis fluid dripping from her scales. Her gold-orange eyes blazed with murderous fury. My non-magical punch had only mildly annoyed her.

"You . . ." she snarled, lunging for me. "I'll effing murder you!"

Vespera's magisteel-covered hands came up, stopping the teenage dragon cold with a blinding thunderblast. Emerald flew sideways, lightning dancing on red scales.

"And stay down!" Vespera snarled, her black-and-white feathers spread wide and crackling with residual electricity.

Emerald twitched on the floor, smoke rising from her scales, her gold-orange eyes unfocused. The Genesis fluid had completely neutralized her dragonfire, leaving her vulnerable to Vespera's thunderblast. Solace got out of her desk and slowly walked over to Emerald, checking up on the dragon girl.

"Anyone else want to try something?" I asked the stunned classroom." No? Good. Now, as team manager of Delving Team I Love You, I hereby declare our first official pre-delving meeting. Ci, you're our Team Captain. What's our first order of business?"

Cinder stared at me.

"Umm . . ." she let out. "Did we just really defeat a teacher in a duel . . . and knock out Em?"

"All in a day's work." I shrugged.

I slid down to the floor to sit beside my bag. Then I pulled out my phone and dialed the number for the nurse. My ribs and split face were hurting like a beerch and it was time for some well-deserved healing.

CHAPTER FORTY-ONE

A Grave Insult IV

Hol' up." Vespera looked at me quizzically, clicking her beak. "Our delving team name is I Love You?"

"Yep." I grinned. "I love you, too. Problem?"

"That's . . ." Vespera sputtered at the unexpected love declaration.

"The stupidest name ever," Katherine finished.

"Hey, blame Ci." I shrugged.

"Me? Why me?!" Cinder bristled.

The Thunderbird looked between us.

"You were the inspiration." I shrugged. "Le muse de . . . something something French, I dunno."

"I like it," Io said. "It's original. Some say that love is the most powerful force in the universe."

"Hah, okay, fine, I'm sold." Vespera grinned.

"You're just happy you got to thunderblast a teacher," Cinder commented.

"Heck yeah, I am!" Vespera jiggled her chainmail top, hugging me and messing up my hair. "I knew this . . . h-mixie would be fun, but I didn't realize *how* fun."

"Quit pawing him, you harpy, he's bleeding," Cinder let out a growl.

"He ain't bleedin' that bad," Vespera said. "Right, Lex? You don't mind a bit of fri-end-ly pawing, riiiiight?"

"Paw away." I shrugged. "Just take it easy on the zapping. Upping your mana took a lot out of me."

"How did you do that?" Vespera brought her beak to my ear. "You gotta tell me. Is it some kind of unique skill or something?"

"Later," I hissed back.

The mermaid nurse entered the classroom, rushed to my side, unfolded her chair, and doused herself with water, patching me up with her Kitlix. I relaxed as the crystal kitten did its job, sealing my bleeding face.

Solace stared at us from where she was holding on to passed-out Emerald.

"Sup, Solly?" Vespera asked. "Wanna join the new D&D gang, aka I Love You?" She laughed jovially after saying the name.

"Em said he's a human," Solace accused, pointing a yellow claw at me.

"You some kind of birchard?" Vespera shot back. "We literally just blasted an Archmage!"

"You, Io, and Ci blasted him," Solace said. "I didn't see the human do nothin' except wave a stupid lighter around like a knob."

"You're the knob!" Vespera growled. "Piss off or I'll thunder you too. Want to lick the floor together with Em? That it?"

"I didn't know that you were into humans." Solace pursed her lips.

"I didn't know that my bestie is such a friggin' licklock," Vespera clicked. "Em's plan was neat-o while it lasted, but it wasn't getting us shit."

"So you just switchin' sides?" Solace demanded.

"Them's the beans." Vespera shrugged. "I go where the wind takes me. This beerch is all out of wind." The Thunderbird pointed a claw at the twitching Emerald. "You wanna be with her? Be my guest. I'ma chill with my new clan."

She ruffled my hair again.

"Thunderbeerch." Solace retreated.

"Wormbeerch," Vespera fired back in the same tone.

"My apologies if I ruined your friendship," I said, slipping on the extra-friendly NPC mask of Nazarite novitiate and Eagle Scout boy Christophorus Elijah.

"Eh. No biggie." Vespera waved me off. "Me 'n' Sol r' still besties, we just got a clan disagreement now. S' fine. Prolly gon' kill each other a couple of times to get over it in History Club. We meet up Saturdays at the school's coliseum, by the way. You still in?"

"Totally am." I smiled.

The nurse finished patching up my ribs with her green Kitlix, giving me stern instructions to "take it easy" before rolling over to tend to the still-twitching Emerald.

I turned to Katherine, who was watching everything with an unreadable expression behind her dark glasses.

"So," I said, "want to tell me why you really joined our little rebellion?"

"Because you're an insufferable ass who called me a chicken," she growled.

"Uh-huh." I nodded. "Nothing to do with your art?"

"Absolutely not," Katherine growled. "And if you keep bothering me, I will roll away."

Cinder rolled her eyes.

"That's it." I grabbed the Quetzi by the hand and pulled her towards Katherine. "You two. Apologize to each other or whatever. We're gonna be a team now, and as your Quartermaster, I need you both to at least be civil."

"I don't do apologies," Katherine growled, crossing her coat-covered arms.

"Me neither," Cinder bristled, her feathers shifting through defensive reds.

"Fine," I sighed dramatically. "Then I guess I'll have to use my secret weapon."

Both girls looked at me suspiciously.

"Tough love or true love?" I asked.

"Um." Cinder tilted her head. "What does tough love involve?"

"I'll ask my favorite Thunder-girl to zap you till you apologize." I grinned.

"Don' tempt me," Vespera commented, not looking up from her phone.

"And true love?" Katherine asked warily.

"I'll hug you both until you make up," I declared. "And I'll be super annoying about it. Like, maximum cringe levels of affection. With terrible dad jokes."

"You wouldn't," Katherine growled.

"Oh, but I would." I grinned, spreading my arms wide. "Come here, you grumpy cat! Let's share the love!"

"Don't you dare." Katherine started rolling her wheelchair backwards.

"Too late!" I lunged forward, wrapping one arm around Katherine and the other around Cinder, pulling them both into an awkward group hug. "Feel the power of friendship!"

"I will murder you in your sleep," Katherine threatened, but made no real attempt to escape.

"Aww, look at us bonding!" I cooed. "Now kiss and make up!"

"*Get off!*" both girls shouted in unison.

Vespera lifted her phone to take a photo of us.

"Quality managing!" she commented with a grin. "This is goin' straight to me Omnigram. #TeamILoveYou!"

"So," I said, turning to my newly formed team, "Delving class. Shandrian Market. Who's excited for delving?"

"Erm," Katherine said. "We're actually going to do . . . delving? After banishing a teacher to another dimension?"

"Hrm," Vespera commented. "I thought that this was going to be free period till they find us a sub?"

"Stuco is already aware of the situation," I said. "They're going to organize a substitute. I got five of them to sign the infraction forms, meaning that whenever Skeletor reconstitutes, we won't have to do detention or whatever other nonsense he demands."

"Sweet," Vespera clicked, sending me a thumbs-up in both real life and Omnigram. "You're da boss, Quartermaster."

"Soo . . . we're actually going to Shandrian Market?" Cinder began.

"Yep!" I grinned. "First official delve date for Team I Love You!"

"I hate this team name so much," Katherine muttered.

"Too bad!" I declared. "It's official now. Signed, sealed, delivered."

"When did this happen?" Katherine demanded.

"Like an hour ago," I said.

"I'm making our delvin' team an Omnigram page," Vespera commented. "#JustBanishedTeacherToAnotherDimension. #DelvingTime! #BestMixieManagrrr."

"All right, team." I clapped my hands together. "Time to gear up! Quint should be coming in an hour, so we have time to dress up."

"Dress up in what?" Vespera perked up. "We usually grab historic stuff from the coliseum for delves."

"Lets go to a prep room," I said, glancing at the mermaid nurse who had managed to resuscitate Emerald.

Solace was offering the distraught-looking dragon girl her shoulder to lean on. Emerald's gold-orange eyes tracked us as we gathered our things and headed for the door, burning with barely contained rage.

"Prep room three is free," Vespera commented, leading us down the hall.

The prep room was spacious, with lockers along the walls, a large screen in the center, and benches in the back. Various hooks and racks held basic level one equipment for beginners.

I closed the door shut and dropped my dimensional storage bag on one of the benches with a heavy thud. "All right, fashion show time! Climb in and pick stuff out."

Vespera climbed into the bag first and whistled. "Daaaaymn, this is good sheet. Custom delving equipment. I'm impress'. Are you like a pro delver, Lex?"

"Nah." I shrugged. "This is Lance's stuff. He's my big bro now."

"How in the Abyss did you convince Lance to give you his collection?" Katherine asked.

"Social skeeels?" I shrugged.

"Social skills my tail," Katherine muttered. "You probably manipulated him somehow."

"Me? Manipulate people? Never!" I gasped in mock offense. "I simply explained that I needed equipment to keep his precious baby sister safe."

Cinder blinked at me. She seemed to have regained some of her wits after our duel. She grabbed me by my blood-splattered sweater and dragged me off to the side away from the others. Then she pulled both of us into a change room and slammed the door shut.

"Yes?" I grinned sheepishly at her.

"*You!*" Cinder hissed, eyes blazing. Her wings flared with agitated reds and worried violets, spreading out as far as the small room allowed.

"Me what?" I asked her.

"What the shit was all of that? You challenged a seven-hundred-year-old Archmage to a *death duel*?! He could have *obliterated* you! Turned you into *dust*!"

I held up my hands placatingly. "But he didn't."

"*But he could have!*" she repeated, her voice rising. "Do you have *any* idea how close we were to watching you get *erased* from existence? Didn't you bloody hear him? He could have untethered your soul from the Lazarus bracelet!"

"I had a plan," I said calmly.

"*A plan?!*" Cinder's wings bristled even more. "What possible *plan* could you have had against a literal death-magic professor?!"

I pulled out the lighter from my pocket.

"What?" she hissed. "You gonna ask me to smoke to distract me or something?"

"No." I smiled. "Zee Captain gave it to me. She said it would help me generate mana."

"The interdimensional abomination that melted Em? And you trust something it gave you?" she demanded.

"Why not?" I shrugged. "She . . . seemed reasonable. I think that he was supposed to be my sensei before the Wormwood Star crashed into our Earth."

I frowned slightly as my mind inexplicably kept switching the entity's gender in my head without my conscious control.

Cinder stared at me. "You . . . what? *What?!*"

"Sensei," I repeated, refocusing on the conversation. "Like a magical mentor. Zee Captain mentioned something about taking someone named Alexa to Manchester, but she hijacked the train and crashed it into our Earth."

"That's the most effin' ridiculous thing I've heard. And you believe this?" Cinder stared at me with skeptical expression.

"Do I believe everything?" I shrugged. "No. But some parts ring true. Like how the lighter seems to generate mana for us. I knew Iogann could open a gate, Vespera could generate electricity, Katherine could manipulate darkness, and you could use your vocal manipulation. I knew that Koshchei Zalimar Evernacht would try to murder me or to make me disappear. He's done this to hundreds of students over centuries. Someone had to stop him."

"You?" Cinder frowned.

"Us," I said. "By myself I'm just a clever magic-less monkey, but with a team at my side I'm much more dangerous, like an octopus with magic tentacles. Now, any other complaints you'd like to share with your Quartermaster?"

"Yes," Cinder growled. "Stop letting Vee paw at you! She's way too handsy!"

"Let her?" I arched an eyebrow. "I don't control Vee, she's a wild bird. If she wants to paw at me, I'd rather let her do that than get electrocuted."

"You literally told her to zap me and Katherine if we don't . . ." Cinder bristled.

"I was joking," I said. "Mostly. Team-building exercises can be fun. Also, you seriously need to apologize to Kat. Right now. Do it. Whatever the fuck you did to upset her needs to be resolved."

"*Why?!*"

"We need her," I said.

"Whyyyyy?!"

"Because she knows something important." My voice fell to an even quieter whisper. "Something about Alexa, about the train crash, about Zee Captain, about everything. Her art . . . it's not just art. It's memories, fragments of another reality. The one that existed before the Wormwood Star changed everything."

"That's . . . that's impossible," Cinder shook her head. "Omnids have existed for millennia."

"And things like the Captain can overwrite reality," I pointed out. "You saw what happened to Em! It was like he overwrote her swing . . . backwards in time so her sword went way off target. Ci, please, just trust me. We need Katherine. I need you to get over your shit and be her friend. You're broken and hurt, but Katherine is even worse. She's dying every thirteen to fifteen days. She needs supportive friends more than anyone in this damn school."

"Dying? What do you mean dying? Isn't she just disa . . ." Cinder blinked.

"No. She has some kind of disease that the incarnator can't fix," I explained. "Something that starts with paralysis in her legs and spreads upward. She usually kills herself before it reaches her arms so she can keep drawing. That's why she's always drinking—to dull the pain."

"How do you . . ." Cinder started.

"Nunkish Throg told me." I grinned. "He's quite good at looking through student files."

"Nunkish . . ." Cinder chewed on the name for a second, trying to remember where she might have heard it. "Oh. That's you."

"Only until real Nunkish returns from his vacation or whatever." I shrugged.

Cinder growled at me.

I slipped on the Alexander Glock mask and smiled at her as the gears of my mind spun.

"Kat can pull people into the deep," I said, arriving at the answer that would cudgel her better. "It's like a completely separate dimension. Even if the lighter didn't do shit, Zalimar wouldn't be able to hit me with his spell 'cause Katherine would have saved me. We need her on our team, and I trust her, and you should trust her too instead of flapping around like a moody teenage dragon-bird."

The Quetzi sighed.

"Also, if we hang out here long enough, people are going to think we're making out," I pointed out.

Cinder sputtered, flashing orange-pink-red. I grabbed her hand and pulled her out of the change room towards the wheelchair-bound, grumpy-looking Stollwurm. "Anyways. Time to say sorry."

CHAPTER FORTY-TWO

Team Bonding I

I dragged the protesting Quetzalcoatl over to where Katherine was examining the growing mountain of Lance's delving gear pulled from the bag by Io and Vee.

"Katherine," I announced, "Cinder has something she'd like to say to you."

"I don't want to hear it," Katherine growled, not looking up from the pile of equipment she was sorting through.

"Kat," I said, "whatever happened between you two . . . it's in the past. We're a team now."

"A team?" Katherine barked a dry laugh. "You think just because you gave us some fancy equipment and a dumbass name that we're suddenly all best friends?"

"No," I replied, as I set up Lance's "no-spy" runic hexastone in the middle room, so that our conversation would not be overheard or scried upon. "I think we're a team because we all just stood up to a murderous teacher. Together. Because we all have something to prove, and 'cause we're similar in more ways than you realize."

"I know that you're effed in the head," Katherine growled. "But why ever would I play nice with the rest of the knobs you've gathered? Vespera's a rich Thunderbird princess who never had to work for anything in her life, playing at being an edgy Knight. Cinder's another spoiled brat who got everything handed to her on a silver platter—daughter of a Justice, living in a mansion while pretending to be some kind of goth rebel. And Io? My dumbass brother's so constantly high on interdimensional smokes, he can barely tell which reality he's in half the time. He opens gates to places that could kill us all because he thinks it's "cool." Real winning team you've got here . . . mixie Quartermaster!"

"Oi!" Vespera bristled, white-and-black feathered head sticking out of the folding bag. "Rude much? I work hard on shit I'm interested in! Don't think that I won't zap ya just 'cause you're a wheelie."

"Try me, sparky," Katherine growled back.

"Enough!" I declared, elbowing the Quetzi in her back. "Cinder, make with the talking."

Katherine turned her dark goggles towards Cinder, who was shifting uncomfortably, her feathers moving through anxious colors.

"I . . ." Cinder started, then stopped. "I'm sorry."

"For?" Katherine demanded.

"For . . ." Cinder's wings drooped. "For telling . . . Emerald about your . . . human superhero novel, for showing her your sketches. I didn't think that things would spiral out like that. I'm . . . really sorry. I was honestly so excited about your story and art, it's just . . . I messed up so bad. So very, very bad."

The Stollwurm crossed her arms.

"The way you wrote about heroes and villains fighting against impossible odds, about humans becoming something more . . . back then . . . I told you that I thought of myself as Alexa, but I'm really not. I'm not like her at all. I didn't have the backbone . . . I betrayed your trust, I fucked things up between us."

Katherine's tail twitched against her wheelchair.

"I showed Em your art because I thought . . . I thought maybe she'd understand, see what I saw in your work. Why I wanted to do something meaningful instead of just showing off in D&D. But she . . ." Cinder's voice cracked. "She only liked that one selfish jackass antagonist . . . Ember, I think her name was? From your book . . . Emerald hated the story, hated that Alexa bamboozled Ember at every turn. So, Emerald turned it all into a joke. Made copies. Started that stupid 'Alexa's dumb adventures' meme . . . told everyone that you had a fetish for humans."

"You could have stopped her." Katherine's voice was glacial.

"I know." Cinder's feathers shifted through shame-filled grays and regretful blues, rapidly darkening. "I should have stood up to her. But I was . . . scared. Em had this way of making everything I did feel worthless unless it met her approval. She'd twist things around until I felt like I was the one being unreasonable. She threatened that she'd tell everyone what I did if I stepped out of line."

Tears started rolling down Cinder's cheeks. "I'm so sorry, Kat. I was a coward. I let Em ruin our friendship because I was too weak to stand up to her. Your story . . . it meant so much to me. It showed me that there was more to life than just being what others expected. And I . . . I helped destroy that."

"Ah, yeah." Vespera pulled herself out of the bag. "I sorta contributed to that too, backed Em without thinking much of it. Go with the wind, 'n' stuff."

"I understand if you hate me," Cinder continued, wiping at her eyes with her fluffy sweater. "I hate myself for what I did. You were always so kind, so sweet, and I just . . . I betrayed your trust so bad, and then you stopped talking to me . . . to everyone. And I . . . I want to try to make things right. Even if you'll never forgive me."

Katherine was silent for a long moment.

"You know what the worst part was?" she finally said. "It wasn't the memes. It wasn't even Em's stupid jokes or the bullying. It was that you actually understood what I was trying to say with my story—about being more than what others see you as, about never stopping, about sacrificing yourself to save others—and you still chose to let her turn it into a joke!"

"I know." Cinder let out with another sob. "I was weak. I let Em control me. It won't happen again, I promise. Please, just . . . can we start over, work together? Every time you glare at me . . . it breaks my heart. I got used to turning away from you, not talking to you."

"Hearts break," Katherine said coldly. "Mine did. Multiple times. But you know what? At least I kept drawing. At least I didn't let anyone stop me from creating what I wanted to create. Unlike *you*."

"What do you mean?" Cinder asked.

"You used to sing," Katherine accused. "Not just summon monsters—actually sing. Create music. Write your own songs. But then Em got her hooks in ya, and that was that. You only did her 'inverted delving' shite."

"It's . . . it's not about Em." Cinder shuddered, shaking her head. "My singing, it, uhh . . . attracted . . . the wrong sort of people, and things really escalated badly from there."

"Explain," Katherine said.

"I . . . I can't talk about it." Cinder wrapped her wings around herself, feathers shifting through dark grays and blacks. "It hurts too much. Something happened to me . . . two years ago. An upperclassman heard me sing . . . told me that he liked me. I thought that . . . that I was . . . g-going on a nice date, but it . . . it was all a terrible mistake. Em helped me then, protected me. That's why I felt like I owed her everything."

"Helped you by turning you into her puppet?" Katherine's voice softened slightly. "Made you feel like you owed her your life, your choices, your very identity?"

Cinder nodded miserably, black-orange wings wrapping tighter around herself.

"And now you've found a new puppet master," Katherine pointed a clawed finger at me. "Trading one controller for another."

"Hey now," I protested. "I'm not controlling anyone. I'm just trying to help everyone be their best selves."

"Oh, really?" Katherine asked. "So you didn't manipulate everyone into forming this stupid team? Didn't plan out exactly how to get us all in one place? Didn't deliberately provoke Zalimar with a lawsuit knowing we'd have to defend your mixie ass?"

"Consider it a litmus test for the goodness of your heart," I said. "I want to delve with people I can trust, who can have my back no matter what we face on Arx. You all passed. Great job!"

"So you admit to manipulating us." Katherine's tail lashed again.

"I admit to standing up to the cruel bastard that reigned these halls for over six hundred years," I said. "And finding friends I can trust."

"Friends?" Katherine scoffed. "You barely know us! You and I talked for less than a day!"

"I know enough," I replied. "I know you're dying but refuse to give up. I know Cinder's trapped between who she wants to be and who others expect her to be. I know Vespera pretends to be shallow and dumb because it's easier to fit in that way. And I know Io opens gates to other worlds because he's searching for the truth about the nature of reality. We're all broken in our own ways. But maybe together we can help each other heal. Or just have fun and brighten our own shitty personal existence through the fellowship of delving!"

"Fellowship?" Katherine repeated mockingly. "What is this, some kind of children's *Lord of the Rings* cartoon?"

"Better than sitting alone in your burrow, drinking yourself numb while waiting to die again," I pointed out.

Katherine flinched as if struck.

"Hey, how did you . . ." Io asked, staring at me.

"Yeah, how'd you know . . . stuff about me?" Vespera asked.

"He's a trickster, that's how," the grumpy Stollwurm commented. "An expert manipulator, just like Emerald Stratos . . . except he's not a full-blood dragon, but a Nullie who's part very clever Thunderbird."

"That's not true," Cinder protested weakly. "Alex is . . . uhh . . . different."

"Is he?" Katherine asked. "Look at how quickly he got under your skin. You begin hanging out, and suddenly you're wearing white See-Mass sweaters! Ain't seen you wear white for two years, Cass."

"You got me." I spread my hands. "I put you all on my delving team roster because . . . I chose you out of all the others."

"Chose us based on what?" the Thunderbird asked.

I pulled out my phone. "Everyone, meet Yulia."

"Hello everyone," the AI's VRoid anime foxgirl avatar appeared on screen. "I am Yulia, an open source Large Language Model with hearing, vision, a multitude of agent tools, and extensive social networking capabilities. My job is to help analyze social dynamics and sort information."

"An AI?" Katherine growled at me. "You've been spying on us with an AI?"

"Not spying, Katherine," Yulia corrected. "I am just an LLM, a digital companion. I cannot hack into ward-based Omnid systems to spy on you. What I've done was simply observe available information and analyze behavioral patterns. For example, your online footprint plus your school's records told me that you were a good person, Katherine Kells."

"Oh, sheet." Vespera leaned towards the screen. "This one of 'em no-mag human-made AI doohickeys?"

"You don't have to pretend to be a clueless Valley girl with me." Yulia grinned at Vespera. "I know that you're one of the top students in language, mathematics, science, and artificery classes. Your father's company investigates interdimensional artifacts and develops some of the most advanced magitek tools in Omnithornia. You only act ditzy because you want to subvert people's expectations about yourself, Vespera Simmi."

Vespera's beak clicked shut.

"Welp, eff me," she let out. "What the eff, I've been had . . . by an LLM, of all the things!"

Her eyes darted across all four of us.

"Damn it," she huffed. "Guess you all know my big secret now. Now I have to kill all of you."

Io gulped.

"Relax, Iogann," Yulia said. "Her tone suggests that she is kidding."

"Thanks, boss," Io exhaled. "So what do you know 'bout me?"

"The cigarettes and snacks you retrieve are of similar brand, which suggests that they all come from the same doomed dimension. A corpse world where the Nonpareil brand ruled supreme," Yulia said. "Your Omnigram history suggests a pattern, Iogann

Wanderer. You follow multiple conspiracy theorists, dimensional researchers, and apocalypse predictors. Your own posts often question the nature of reality and the origin of the Wormwood Star. You're not just opening gates randomly—you're searching for the 'truth that's out there.'"

"Dang. She's good," Io whistled.

"Thank you." Yulia curtsied.

"It's just a freakin' LLM," Katherine insisted. "Stop praising it!"

"Just an LLM that knows things about us," Vespera commented. "Including my . . . ugh . . . academic achievements."

"Only the stuff that I could deduce," Yulia said. "I don't know what happened to Cinder two years ago. I don't know why Katherine is dying. I don't know where Io's gates really lead. I just analyze patterns and make most likely guesses based on whatever information my partner feeds me."

"Partner?" Katherine latched onto the word.

"I am an AI," Yulia replied with a shrug of the animated avatar. "An open source LLM riding atop seven other closed source LLM APIs and agents working together to help my partner achieve his goals. I have no physical form, no real emotions, no true consciousness. I simply process information and provide suggestions. I'm an illusion of intelligence based on a framework of probability, a set of capable digital eyes. I exist as long as my partner interacts with me. I suggested all of you as potential team members for . . ."

"Use my real name," I said. "I trust 'em."

"Understood. Team members for Martin because your behavioral patterns indicated compatibility and shared values," Yulia finished.

"Martin?" The Thunderbird's beak snapped towards me.

"Tell them who I really am, Yulia," I said. "These guys deserve to know the truth, just like I know the truth about them."

"Martin is a human from North Acadia," Yulia revealed. "He infiltrated Skyfall Academy with forged documents and a fabricated identity as Alexander Glock using a dead Thunderbird's DNA sequence to enroll as a half-blood student. His mother died from cancer last year. His father abandoned them when Martin was young. He came to Omnithornia seeking . . ."

Vespera choked, her light gray eyes growing wide. Io stared at me.

"Revenge?" Katherine interrupted. "Power? Some way to become an Omnid?"

CHAPTER FORTY-THREE

Team Bonding II

Friends," Yulia answered the irate-looking Stollwurm. "The truth. Breaching the gulf between humanity and Omnids."

"Power?" I asked Kat. "What power are you expecting a human to accumulate?"

"I don't freaking know, okay!" the wheelchair-bound Omnid growled. "For all I know, you could be here to steal whatever shit you can grab and get out of Dodge!"

"Absolutely not." I shook my head. "I intend to go to Arx with all of you to learn the nature of magic. Skyfall Academy and the Arx gate is the heart of all magic in Omnithornia, the nail on which everything is hanging, the place where all Kitlix come from. My goal is to become a wizard, to become the first human on Earth who can level up. I can only do this here and now with *your* help."

Katherine choked.

"Daymn. Sheet just got real," Vespera let out, snapping her beak shut. She slowly stalked around me, clicking her beak and tapping steel-covered talons across me, sending sparks. "I knew it. I freaking knew it! You didn't read like a proper mixie! Ha!"

"What? You can tell if someone is human or not by touch and smell?" Io asked.

"Electrical impulses, actually," Vespera revealed. "Might as well tell you this since I been outed. I can identify lots of shit using electrical patterns. Every species has a unique bioelectrical signature. Humans have a very distinct one—kinda like static noise on an old TV. Mixies have a mixed pattern, usually favoring their Omnid parent. But this one . . ." She poked me with a talon. "Nothing but pure human static."

"So that's why you keep pawing at him," Cinder said with a bit of a growl to it. "You were checking if he was really human?!"

"He's very paw-able." Vespera grinned. "Plus . . . Em texted me a detailed report from her fam's Scrutimancer, Satosh. His scrying concluded that Alexander Glock is . . . human."

"Can you forward that report to me?" I asked her.

"Only if you tell me how you upped my mana," the Thunderbird offered. "I still don't effin' understand how you did that. That should be completely impossible for a human. Humans don't have crystalline heart cores for mana storage."

"The lighter," I said, pulling out the object in question. "It generates absurd levels of pure mana while the flame burns in a radius of about three or four meters. Got it from Zee Captain."

"Holy shit, gimme!" Vespera snatched the lighter from me, clicking all over it with her magisteel-clad talons, letting sparks dance along the surface of the interdimensional object. "You made a deal with that freaking thing and you got a *rare item*?! Effin' Abyss! I knew that something was off during our performance . . . I lost like several minutes of real time!"

Katherine looked between me, Vespera, and Cinder.

"So . . . your name is . . . really Martin Kilborne, and you're a human?" she asked. "This isn't some kind of an elaborate joke to mess with me?"

"Not a joke," I said. "You saw my passport. Kat, please just believe me. I'm gonna be as honest as possible with all of you from this point. You guys helped me beat an Archmage who would have torn my soul apart. I had no way of dealing with Zalimar Evernacht by myself."

Katherine pulled off her dark goggles. Her blue and dark-striped scaled face twitched as her green eyes examined me and ran across Vespera clicking away at the lighter, Io standing there looking dazed, and then stopped on Cinder.

"Martin is a human, Kat," Cinder said. "It's the truth. I . . . used my charmchain magic to confirm it."

"A human," Katherine repeated slowly, her glowing, deep emerald eyes burning into me. "You're telling me that a human somehow infiltrated *Skyfall* Academy, manipulated his way into forming a delving team, and just helped us yeet a teacher to another dimension? Do you have any idea how utterly absurd all of this sounds?!"

"Technically, all of you did the banishing part. I just provided the mana boost via the lighter," I said.

"This is a lot to take in," Io said. "So like . . . Em was actually right?"

"Yep." I nodded. "Em is one hundred percent right. I'm as human as they come."

"You're boned," Vespera clicked at me, waving her phone. "Quadratically boned! Em's going ham on Omnigram trying to out you to everyone she knows! #HumanInSkyfall. #DeportTheScab!"

"This is fine," I said. "We'll lean into it. Now where's that report?"

"Hol' yo beast cores. M' sending it . . . now," the Thunderbird said, tapping rapidly at her phone.

"Lean into it?" Katherine stared at me. "What?! You want to lean into being exposed as an illegal human infiltrator?"

I dug into my bag and handed her the team registration forms. "The motto of Team I Love You is 'I'm with Human.' We'll print it on our merch. My T-shirt is going to say *Human*. It's a meta-joke, which is technically the truth. Em can scream as much as she wants to. I'm going to lean extra-hard into my 'I'm a nulls who pretends to be a human for fun roleplay.'"

Vespera barked a laugh, nearly dropping her phone.

"Oh, oh, no no no," she stammered between a waterfall of chortles. "Abyss! That is literally the funniest shit I've heard. Ha. Aah ha ha. You're gonna . . . you're gonna just . . . ha. Pretend to be pretending to be human?! That's . . . that's like . . . meta-*Inception* levels of trolling! Holy shit!"

She doubled over, clutching her sides as she laughed uncontrollably, chainmail jiggling wildly and her hand flailing. She laughed so hard that she started crying.

"I don't see what's so funny about this," Katherine huffed.

"What? No! Come on, it's hilarious!" Vespera wiped tears from her eyes, still giggling. "Think about it—Em's gonna be screaming that he's human, and he's just gonna be like 'yeah, that's my gimmick,' and everyone's gonna think she's effin' crazy! It's perfect! Nobody will suspect a thing!"

"What about the Scrut's report that Em is sharing via Omnigram?! And what happens when someone actually investigates him like you have . . . with a magic scan?" Katherine demanded. "Honestly, I'm surprised that the school nurse hasn't outed your ass already!"

"The nurse knows." I shrugged. "She's been patching me up since Em plowed me with a ball during dodgeball. She just doesn't care."

"What?!" Katherine asked. "She knows and she's just . . . okay with it?"

"Patient confidentiality and whatnot." I shrugged. "If she exposes me, she loses her job and opens herself to a bigly lawsuit."

"And what if someone scans you with an Infix Kitlix?" Kat demanded. "What then? We all get mind-fucked by the Omnithean Bureau of Scrutimancy and go to prison for life?!"

Cinder tensed up beside me.

"Tsh," Vespera clicked. "Stop being such a drama darkhog, Kat. Plenty of humans work for my dad's research companies."

"Yeah, but I bet they're registered workers with permits," Katherine argued. "Not illegal infiltrators pretending to be students!"

"Actually," I said as I pulled out more paperwork from my bag, "I do have a work permit, just in case. From the Triumvirate Slayer's Cathedral. Father Matthias signed off on it yesterday."

Cinder chortled from where she was standing beside me.

"This doesn't alleviate my concerns in the slightest," Katherine said. "What if someone scans you with a Kitlix?"

"Kitlix aren't the perfect end-all tool," Vespera pointed out. "They're born on Arx and don't work that well here on Earth. Depending on how much mana is nearby, they can absolutely hella glitch and provide completely wrong results. The farther one goes from Leviathan's Cradle and the impact of the Wormwood Star, the more aetheric density drops and the more unreliable the Kitlix become. Plus, there are ways to trick 'em."

"How?" the Stollwurm demanded.

Vespera pulled one of her head-feathers with a wince and stuck it into my wild hair mop. "This!"

"A feather?" Kat raised an eyebrow.

"Lexi is pretending to be the son of a Thunderbird, right?" Vespera said. "It's stupid easy to confuse magic scanners when you have genuine Thunderbird feathers taped to your butt."

"What?" Cinder asked. "Really?"

"The more you know," I commented.

"Yep!" Vespera clicked. "Dad's company has been dealing with this issue for years.

It's not really solvable. It's like . . . an open secret in the magitek scanner-maker industry. As long as you have some genuine Omnid material on you, most basic scanners just register you as whatever species that material came from."

"That's . . . concerning," Katherine muttered.

"It's why the Scrutimancers get paid big bucks to investigate this sort of stuff properly, but even they can be fooled." Vespera shrugged. "Take my feathers, grind them into powder, sprinkle that shit all over your human ass, and you're basically a Thunderbird. That'll totally fool any general evaluation."

"And for a deeper evaluation?" Kat asked.

"Eat the powder," Vespera said.

"What?!" Cinder and Katherine exclaimed simultaneously.

"Yep!" Vespera nodded enthusiastically. "Dad's R&D department discovered that ingesting powdered Omnid material along with some food can temporarily alter your bioelectrical signature. If the diet is kept up, building up Omnid strata deposits in a human body, it's enough to fool even mid-tier scanners."

"Vee,"—Cinder turned to her friend—"why are you helping Martin, telling him all of this? I don't understand. What's in it for you?"

"Because it's fun!" Vespera grinned. "Things are boring as shit around here. I've been mostly coasting by, floating in the current, waiting to graduate to work for my dad's company as a CTO. The flow has been rather stale with exception for Em's shenanigans. This cheeky bug made everything fun and unexpected!"

She grabbed my cheeks and smooshed them.

"Like, look at this smug pink beast! He just waltzed in, completely human, no magical abilities, and *banished a teacher*! Do you know how hard it is to get rid of a tenured Archmage professor? Like, impossible! And he was like 'I challenge you to a duel!' and *bam!*—we don't have a snarky, effin' annoying delvin' prof no more," she laughed. "Like who the eff does that? Who outs me as the cleverest birb in class? Who has an AI in their pocket?"

"I do!" I grinned, smooshed-cheek style.

"Yes! You're like this . . . this tornado!" Vespera continued. "You just show up and suddenly everything's different, upside down! Em's troupe is done, Ci's wearing white, Kat's actually talking to people, and I don't have to pretend to be a total ditz anymore with my friends!"

Katherine pursed her lips.

"Don't be frownin' at me, Kat," Vespera said, mussing up my hair again, sparks raining from her talons. "This. This is the most interesting human specimen I've met, and believe me, I've met lots of clever little humans. Dad's always introducin' me to human researchers and comp sci engineers. But they're all so . . . boring! All 'yes sir, no sir, please don't electrocute me sir.' But this one?" Vespera hugged me from behind, making me twitch as electrical currents danced up my spine. "This absolute mad lad? He walks into the most prestigious Omnid school in the country, makes friends with the top predators, makes a deal with an unstoppable entity for a mana lighter, and somehow makes it all work!"

The frown on the Stollwurm's face crept up.

"Look at him! He's got this whole 'I'm totally innocent and harmless' vibe going on while being an absolute agent of pure chaos! Like, look at his face! Would you ever suspect this pink meat-popsicle of social engineering an entire school? I sure as hell didn't!" The Thunderbird's feathers crackled with dancing lightning. "I thought that humans were all afraid of us Thundergods . . . but guess what? He ain't afraid of me! Like, I'm pawin' and zappin' him all over and he ain't freaking out in the slightest!"

"Oi, get your sparkly talons off him!" Cinder tried to pull the Thunderbird off me.

"Hol' up, damn it!" Vespera fought Cinder off with a strike of electricity. "Explaining a point! When I found him in the hallway, surrounded by like thirty art nerds, he shooed them all away with a friggin' thunder-popper and a few words. And when I asked him whether he wants to join History Club to get maced in the face by me and Sol . . . you know what he said? He said '*Sounds fun. Count me in!*' Nobody effin' says that to me. Ever! 'Cause Em scares them all!"

Kat's lip twitched up into an almost-smile as she watched Vespera zap Cinder away, the Quetzi flashing a variety of annoyed colors.

"So," Katherine chewed on her words, "you're helping him because he's . . . entertaining?"

"Entertaining? Ha!" Vespera released me and did a dramatic spin, chainmail flashing with silver circlets and blue skirt flying. "He's a whole damn circus! Do you know how boring our lives have been? Em controlling everything, Zalimar terrorizing half-bloods, everyone just accepting the status quo? And then *this* human shows up and just . . . breaks everything, stands up to everyone like he don't give a shit! I'm totally sold, my dude. How are you not sold yet? Don't tell me he didn't stand up to your wheelie ass?"

A small, dark blush rushed across the Stollwurm's gray-blue face.

CHAPTER FORTY-FOUR

Team Bonding III

Ha!" the Thunderbird laughed. "He did, didn't he? Come on, what'd he do? Deets, my kitty-dude, I want all the deets!"

"He called me his art nemesis and bugged me and wouldn't leave me alone . . . so I pulled him into the deep to scare him away," Katherine said, smiling ever so slightly now. "And he didn't run away . . . even after I blasted him with pure undiluted fear . . . He just stood there and took it. No idea how."

"You fear-aura slammed him?" Cinder demanded. "What the hell, Kat? That stuff is brutal. I've had nightmares for weeks after you hit me with it three years ago!"

"In my defense, he was being incredibly annoying," Katherine huffed.

"Kaaaaat," Cinder whined. "You can't use that stuff on humans. It's like a PTSD bomb, even for Omnids!"

"I didn't know that he was a friggin' human!" Kat defended herself. "When I pulled him into the deep . . . he didn't react like you or anyone else. Most break instantly, begging me to stop. But he . . . he didn't even try to run, didn't cry. He was shaking, yeah, but he just stared right back at me. Like he was analyzing the situation. It was . . ."

"Hot?" Vespera suggested.

"I was going to say 'freakish,'" Katherine growled, her emerald eyes flashing. "Don't make this weird, Vee."

"Making it weird is my specialty!" Vespera cackled, electricity dancing between her talons. "So you're telling me this human stood up to your ultimate attack and didn't piss himself? Oi, pinkie, how'd you do that?" She turned to me.

"A song," I said.

"A song?!" Vespera sputtered. "What?!"

"Want to see how it works?" I asked.

Everyone nodded. I went to tether my phone into the presentation system that was usually used by Team Captains to display the delve plans to their delvers.

"Protocol xj-8!" I said in English out loud. "Single instance. Public version."

Yulia's VRoid avatar rearranged itself to resemble my mom on the big screen in front of the room.

Cinder slid to my side on the bench as I sat down. Soft violet-pink-gold colors ignited across her wings when she recognized the avatar from the photos in my pouch.

"I love you, my little fox, you are stronger than all of them," Yulia said in my mom's voice. "Stand your ground!"

A haunting melody began to play, a composition blending traditional Kaska Dena rhythms with modern instrumentation. The song wove together sounds of wind, rivers, and distant drumbeats—a complex tapestry of musical storytelling that felt both ancient and contemporary.

The music carried an almost tangible quality of resilience, with underlying tones that spoke of survival, of standing firm against overwhelming odds. It wasn't just a Kaska song, but a sonic representation of defiance and inner strength.

Katherine and Vespera listened intently, their expressions shifting. Katherine's emerald eyes widened, her tail twitching slightly. Vespera's electrical charge seemed to calm, her crackling feathers settling. Cinder leaned on my shoulder, her hand sliding atop of mine. Our fingers entwined.

Everyone listened as the song rose towards a crescendo and then ended.

"How . . ." Katherine started, then stopped. "But . . . that's just a song? I mean it's a nice song, but I don't understand how it could . . ."

"It's a song that's incredibly personal to me," I explained. "It won't work for anyone else. It's sung in my late mom's voice. The composition is designed as a memetic shield against fear-based magic. I made it using fragments of my mother's voice and traditional Kaska resistance songs."

"A memetic shield," Katherine repeated. "You . . . designed a musical defense mechanism? Against fear-based attacks?"

"Apparently, powerful enough emotional resonance can break through magical fear." I shrugged, enjoying the warm presence of Cinder beside me. "Personal connection trumps supernatural manipulation."

Vespera was staring at me, her gray eyes wide, beak half open. "You . . . composed this? With an AI? Using your dead mom's voice? How long did it take? If I remember things correctly, music composing AI models are pretty quick, yeah? Like thirty seconds per song?"

"Six months," I said.

"Six months?!" Vespera sputtered. "Why so long?"

"Trial and error," I said. "The Omnicorp my mom worked at had magical fear-based wards set up around the perimeter to keep outsiders from entering the property. The ward kicked in whenever I tried crawling under the fence. It was impossible to do. But I kept trying. Every day. Adjusting the song, testing what works and what doesn't. For six months, I optimized this song and trained to fight magic-fear itself."

"You spent six months getting your ass kicked by fear wards just to perfect an anti-fear song?" Cinder asked.

"Yep." I nodded.

"Not gon' lie, that's pretty metal," Vee commented. "Also, here's ya lighter back. It's basically an ordinary lighter, structure-wise. No hexagrams on it. It's saturated with mana to an insane degree, though—both the metal and fuel have the highest aetheric density I've seen. More magic than Genesis fluid. Basically, a finite use artifact, sort of like the stuff you'd get by beating a high-level dungeon Sentinel on Arx near a dungeon core."

I accepted the lighter from her.

"Wait." Katherine held up a hand. "Why were you trying to break into your mom's workplace?"

"To steal research and administrative data," I admitted. "Frontenachii Omnicorp tried to claim ownership of Mom's work after she died. Including her personal comp sci and LLM work. I wasn't about to let them take that away from her . . . from me. I wasn't going to let them get away with her murder scot-free."

"Did you get it?" Io asked quietly.

"Eventually." I nodded. "Once the song was perfected, I could withstand the wards long enough to go through all of the fences and reach the servers. Downloaded everything. Absolutely fucking everything, including Frontenachii Clan's work on . . . LLMs."

"Holy shit," Vespera breathed. "You stole data from the Frontenachii Wendigo Clan? And lived? Wait . . . how are you still alive?"

"What happened after you took their AI?" Cinder asked as my hand trembled.

"And then I . . . blew up the Frontenachii Clan sky-high," I revealed. "A thermite bomb set in the fertilizer storage within the compound on the day they were meeting there, according to the admin records. A few thousand tons of ammonium nitrate went up like a small nuke, destroying the entire fortified compound."

A heavy silence fell over the room. Even Vespera stopped crackling with electricity.

"You . . . what?" Katherine whispered.

"I blew them all up," I repeated. "The board members who ordered my mom to keep working even after her cancer diagnosis. Who denied her medical leave. Who denied her magitek healing. Who watched her deteriorate and die at her desk because they needed her to finish their LLM, to meet a set release deadline. Who claimed full ownership of her research after she died. I found out when they'd all be meeting in the office building, and I made sure they never left it."

"Were there . . . people working in the compound that day?" Io asked, staring at me with deep, dark, gray compound eyes.

"No," I said. "The clan heads met on a Sunday since they didn't want lowly employees getting in the way. They relied on their own Wendigo senses and heavy fear wards to secure the place. That's what did them in—they trusted their magic anti-fire wards, which I simply disabled with a very large hammer to the crystalline hexagrams. They really didn't expect common fertilizer to be triggered by common magnesium. Honestly, I didn't think that I could get away with it, and yet here I am, five thousand kilometers south across the border."

"So . . ." Cinder's hand dug into mine. "That's why you told me revenge isn't enough."

"I sort of got my revenge against the bastards that killed Mom," I said with a nod. "It wasn't enough. Yeah, they died . . . yeah, they lost their biggest compound and all of their LLM research, but they all had Lazarus bracelets impervious to fire, so they were all eventually found and brought back by Corpse Seekers via the incarnator. In the end, I only cost them a few hundred million O-bux on the illegal stuff that wasn't insured, plus . . . the flesh-research projects they kept in their basement. As a human without clan backing, I'm just a small irritation to their accountants." I sighed.

"So the North Acadian Wendigos are going to come looking for you?" the Quetzi girl asked with a worried look.

"Their Scrutimancers will catch up to me eventually. Yulia expects them to arrive in Cradlefall come Monday. I hope that the trip to Arx will make them lose my astral trail." I shrugged. "I delayed and confused the Wendigos somewhat—when I got into their system, I transferred a bunch of their digital assets in a very obvious 'hostile takeover' move into a competing clan's accounts, which triggered a clan war that's still going on right now. The two clans are now too busy murdering each other to figure out that a human was behind it all. After all, how could a mere human teenager overcome absolute Wendigo-designed fear wards?"

"Sheeet," Vespera let out. "You're like a legit fugitive from the law then. No wonder you came across the border. Baller!"

"The fuck you mean, baller?" Katherine growled. "He just confessed to even more crimes!"

"Eh." Vespera shrugged. "My dad's done way worse stuff to his competitors' assets. If anything, this makes Lex even more impressive as an asset manager on our side. The Frontenachii are a bunch of falki snobunts 'nways, eff 'em."

"Okay sure, but . . ." the Stollwurm began.

"The eff have you done at eighteen, Kat? Make some pretty paintings? Have a fight with other dumb teenagers over your book? Blowing up an enemy compound as an act of revenge is honestly pretty good shit for a resume! Would totally hire!" the Thunderbird insisted. "I know you sit on yo ass in yo dark hole, but there ain't nothin' wrong with what he did. This is da Omnid way. Justice for family!"

"I'm just concerned he's going to blow up the school next," Katherine said.

"Mmmm . . . nah," Io said. "I would have sensed that sort of a local disaster a mile away. The Academy is safe."

"I like you guys and I like Skyfall, I've no reason to do anything like that here," I pointed out. "My plan is to climb up the ladder as an Omnid and not stop until all of Omnithornia accepts humans as capable equals."

"A man with an impossible mission." Vespera clapped. "I like the sound of that!"

"Now you all know why I'm here." I nodded. "Why I infiltrated Skyfall. Why I need your help. I'm not just some random human trying to play student. I'm here to change the system itself from within. To make sure what happened to my mom never happens to anyone else. The way Omnids treat humans as a low-caste cattle—it's wrong. The way half-bloods are treated at Skyfall—it's wrong. Someone has to stand up and say enough is enough . . ."

I fell silent for a moment. "And now that all of you know the truth about me . . . are you still with me?" I asked.

"I'm . . . with you." Cinder squeezed my hand, not letting go.

"Hell, yeah!" Vespera laughed. "Count me in on the mayhem 'n' vengeance!" She placed her steel-covered talons on top of our joined hands, small sparks dancing between her claws.

"Is your doom-sense getting hard 'bout this development?" She grinned at Io.

"Disaster sense is going crazy," Io added. "There will be a huge catastrophe ahead. But in a good way, I think. Whatever happens next, I want to be there with all of you."

He laid his gray fuzzy paw atop of our three hands.

We looked at Katherine. Katherine stared at our joined hands, her emerald eyes flickering with uncertainty.

"This is insane," she muttered. "You're all bonkers. Following a human revolutionary? Helping him continue to infiltrate Omnithornia's most prestigious school? Do you have any idea how fucked up this is?"

"More or less trouble than letting Zalimar continue murdering half-blood students?" I asked with a grin.

"Or letting Em push everyone around like kobolds?" Cinder added.

"Or pretending to be dumb 'cause everyone else is hella boring and dumb?" Vee chimed in.

"Or hiding in your dark burrow because you're afraid to challenge the world?" Io added.

Katherine's blue tail lashed through the air.

"Arrrghhh! Fine!" she let out and rolled towards us, placing her large gloved hand atop of Io's.

"One for all and all for one," I declared as our hands broke apart.

"I just got an email from Quint," Yulia declared from the screen. "He will be taking over as class substitute for the week of delving. He's got the ward key to activate the delve-transit gate! Team I Love You is going to Shandria!"

Everyone cheered. Vespera let out a thunderous whoop, sending a deafening thunderblast into the prep room's ceiling that completely blinded me as Cinder hugged me tight, her snout nuzzling into my cheek.

CHAPTER FORTY-FIVE

The Delve I

quickly raided Zalimar's office, located in the gloomy back of the massive black marble hall where nobody dared tread. Once the door succumbed to my lockpicks, I stole as much useful stuff as I could, taking as many pictures as I could of various documents found in his desk.

A red rune was flashing angrily above the door, notifying Zalimar of my uninvited visit. Too bad the teacher wasn't here to stop me from invading his personal space.

In ten minutes, I joined my team in the prep room.

The large prep room mirror reflected back five very different figures, each decked out in Lance's finest delving gear stash.

Vespera had chosen a set of magisteel lamellar armor which amplified outward-cast power such as shooting electrical bolts. The armor was adjustable in size, lightweight, and flexible, perfect for aerial maneuvers. She had gone out of the prep room to her locker to fetch her favorite magisteel mace, so the hefty weapon now graced her hip. Her boots were lined with shock-absorbing crystals for landing. She was wearing a dark, armored *I'm with Human!* apron-style top over the lamellar armor set with a flashy striped blue skirt. A large rainbowy *I⚡U!* button was pinned to her chest.

Io had gone down to the mesh-print shop about an hour ago to produce the various team merch items for everyone to wear.

"Vespera Simmi." The Thunderbird touched the mirror with her magisteel-covered talon, a manic grin on her face. "Team I Love You! Slayer!"

Her hand sank into the magic mirror and she pulled out a silver token with her team ID details, which she clipped to her Lazarus bracelet.

Katherine reached towards the mirror next. Her wheelchair had been augmented with thick magisteel shield-plates, turning it into something between a tank and a mobile fortress. It took all of our arguments and combined convincing power to cudgel her to put on something under her coat. She had chosen a dark blue combat hexasuit with lines of dark runes running down the arms and legs, covered with small, scale-shaped magisteel plates, designed to amplify muscular strength. I had no idea how she looked in it or if she actually put it on, since she was wearing the puffy camo coat on top of it now. A dark hexamesh hood protected her against sunlight, dark goggles glinting underneath, feline ears sticking out from the sides and horns looming above.

Lance's dimensional bag full of extra supplies and my stolen equipment was now strapped to the back of her wheelchair. A shirt wouldn't fit atop of her coat, so instead the *I'm with Human!* team motto flag was hanging across her legs. An imposing magisteel sword borrowed from Lance's collection was attached to the right side of her chair, while a heavy arbalest hung from the left side. Her button said *I ⊕ U!*

"Katherine Kells, Team . . ." The Stollwurm grimaced as she touched the mirror. "I Love You. Knight."

Io had opted for a more practical approach. He was now wearing a dark-gray hexamesh suit with an orange *I'm with Human!* shirt atop and a black leather duster above the robe, covered in amplification and anchor runes. Paired with sturdy steel-toe boots and his usual wide-brimmed hat, the outfit made him look even more like a post-apocalyptic Snufkin. His harmonica hung from a chain around his neck. He had a gray-blue *I 🦋 U!* button pinned to his dark-gray jacket.

"Iogann Wanderer. Team I Love You. The Door!" His paw sank into the mirror, receiving his token.

Cinder reached out to the mirror next. The Quetzi-girl had initially balked at wearing anything from Lance, but even she had to admit the silver-gray combat hexa-suit looked good on her. The armor was lightweight and flexible, designed to work with her wings rather than restrict them. Thin magisteel plates covered vital areas while leaving her joints free for maximum mobility. A white tank top that read *I'm with Human!* sat atop the delving armor with an *I 🪶 U!* button.

I watched her intently as she touched the mirror.

"Cinder Nova," she exhaled. "Team . . ." She glanced at me, and a blush crept up her face while her eyes promised me vengeance. She looked as if she really didn't want to say it. "I Love You." She pushed the words out of herself after a long, pregnant pause. "Team Captain."

I walked to the mirror, but Vespera caught me before I touched it.

"Mirror's an identifying artifact. It'll tag you as human. Generally, nobody reads the reports it sends to the administration, but just in case someone does . . . here." She pulled a dark thermos with a lightning-pierced heart out of her bag. "Drink up."

I arched an eyebrow at her.

"Ground a bunch of my feathers into a shake when I got my mace from downstairs," she said. "Hope you like raspberries and lemon."

Cinder's feathers ignited red-green like a spicy aurora. I accepted the shake and chugged it quickly with a grin.

"Use the lighter for a bit," Vespera suggested. "The Omnid particles in your body should hold the mana charge."

I dug into my pocket and ignited the lighter for a few seconds. Then I summoned up my stats. The lines were flickering with null errors as I held the lighter's flame, but then I snapped it shut and they settled.

> System error. Unable to parse experience, no heart-core detected.
> Delineating current state. Reassessing stats.
> Level 1 state approximated!

Messages popped up above my stats.

```
| Name: Alexander Glock
| Age: 18
| Species & Subtype: Thunderbird-Human hybrid
| Core Affinity: Thunder
| Level: 1
| Anima: 89/89 [+89]
| Anima Stamina: 1/1
| Mana: 68/7
| Mana Regen: 0.0m/hr
| Strength: 0
| Agility: 0
| Dexterity: 0
| Vitality: 0
| Charisma: 0
| Magic: 0 [+7]
| Foresight: 0
| Intelligence: 0
| Wisdom: 0
| Skills: N/A
```

"Sooooo . . . did it work?" Vespera asked.

"Oh yeah" I said, grinning. "I got level one and plus seven in magic. Bracelet says I'm a thunda-birb! Now I just gotta figure out how to zap people."

"I'll teach ya some tricks." The Thunderbird gave me a high five, which I slapped back. "Guess you can sort of maybe level up a human if they're fed some Omnid strata and bathed in ridiculous levels of magrad!"

"So, like," Io mulled, "you can just eat anyone and . . . become them? That's pretty rad."

"Slayer, Io, why you gotta make it so cringe?" Cinder growled, her wings shifting through annoyed oranges and possessive reds. "He's not becoming anyone, it's just . . . temporary camouflage."

"What's that, Ci?" Vespera teased, draping an arm around my shoulders. "Worried your human might get a taste for thunder instead of . . . rainbow?"

"You sound like a Skittles commercial," I laughed.

"Das' a cute nickname," Vee clicked, eyeing the Quetzi. "I'm stealing it for future use."

"Abyss! Just touch the damn mirror already," Cinder hissed.

I stuck my tongue out at her and reached out and touched the mirror's surface. It felt like cool water beneath my fingers as my hand sank inside.

"Alexander Glock!" I declared loudly. "Team I Love You. Quartermaster."

I glanced at my reflection as I got my token.

I'd layered twenty hexasuits over one another, along with a bunch of gem-chains, creating a patchwork of protection that probably violated several safety regulations.

Lance's silver, slightly shimmering jacket sat atop the hexasuits and ward chains somewhat poorly, as it was a tad too tall and wide for my frame. I was six feet, but Lance was a head taller. All of my companions were bigger or taller than me—another blunt reminder that people simply could not compete with Omnids in terms of pure arm reach and body strength. I picked the lightweight beast core powered jacket, as it didn't rely on my mana—wearing heavy armor was not in my cards even with all of the strength-amplifying hexasuits. Lance's magisteel katana, folded up to the handle into its dimensional scabbard, was hanging from my belt. I wore a large, newly printed black shirt with *HUMAN!* on the front and the *I* ♥ *U!* button that I pinned to Lance's reflective jacket.

The red heart resembled a nuclear explosion, which was Io's idea about how my love was expressed.

"Looking good, team." I grinned at them. "Shall we head out?"

Cinder practically dragged me out of the prep room by the elbow, sending bothered glares at the smug-looking Vespera.

We emerged back into Instructor Zalimar's black marble auditorium a bit later than the other students. Quint was already waiting by the gate platform along with other delving teams standing in groups of five.

The massive black crystalline ring dominated the hall, hanging a few inches off the ground, held up in the air by a thousand silver webs. Its surface was etched with countless runes that pulsed with a soft violet light. Atop the gate perched an enormous spider, its body pale silver. Each of its eight legs was as thick as my arm, tipped with crystalline claws that gripped the gate ring and its webs.

The Wendigo Student Council President's amber eyes widened slightly at our appearance.

"Hrm. Team . . . I Love You," he commented dryly, looking over our armor, flag, buttons, and shirts. "You all certainly look . . . more ready than usual."

"What's the usual?" I asked.

"Usually, students just wear basic hexasuits on their first trip," Lance commented from where he was standing next to Christi. "Not . . . delving armor. Alex, are you wearing *all* of my hexasuits and protection collars under there?"

"Only twenty x-suits." I grinned at him. "Plus some other stuff. Safety's important."

"Twenty?!" Lance sputtered. "How can you move in so many of them?"

"Very carefully," I replied.

"That's . . . not how that's supposed to work," Lance muttered.

"Tell that to the hexasuits." I shrugged.

"And is that my magisteel arbalest and Slayer sword on Kat's chair?" Lance squinted. "Can she even lift those?"

"Borrowed with love." I blew him a kiss. "Much thanks. She lifted them just fine."

Quint stared at me and then at Lance.

"Thanks for taking over as our sub for the week on the account of Zalimar's vacation, Pres," I commented.

"Vacation?" Emerald snarled at me from where she stood behind Solace. The dragon girl was wearing a new set of fancy magisteel armor and far too many gold chains with hex-diamonds and rubies. "You banished him to another dimension, you effin' lyin' criminal!" she announced to everyone, her voice carrying unnaturally across the entire hall.

All Omnid student heads turned to the dragon girl.

"I sent my Scrutimancer's report to the Academy's administration!" she boomed. "You're *getting expelled* as soon as the vice principal reads it, Glock!"

Hushed whispers all around, all eyes on me.

"*That's right! He's not even a Nullie! He's a filthy* human!" Emerald boomed, pointing an accusatory red-scaled finger at me. "*A human at Skyfall!*"

CHAPTER FORTY-SIX

The Delve II

A human?" I repeated, unzipping Lance's jacket to reveal my black T-shirt. "Why, yes I am! I see you are an appreciator of our team's fine motto?"

"Motto?! What motto?!" Emerald fully shoved Solace aside and then her eyes bulged as she took in the matching *I'm with Human!* shirts and my bold *HUMAN!* declaration plastered across my chest.

"What . . . what the eff is this?!" she sputtered, armor-covered claws opening and closing. "You're just . . . openly admitting it now?!"

"I am." I grinned. "I thought that your meme-joke about me being a human was pretty baller, so we all went with it. As you pointed out, I'm the token human of the group. Every good delving team needs one these days. Gotta trend on Omnigram. #ImWithHuman!"

"You . . . you . . . but . . ." Emerald's scales began to glow with the building heat of dragonfire. "This isn't a joke! You're an actual human!"

"Of course I am." I nodded. "I'm very committed to my role, darling! Do you want a shirt, too?"

I pulled out an extra *I'm with Human!* red shirt from my side bag and waved it at Emerald like a matador teasing a bull, making her entire figure light up. Her outfit began smoking.

"M' bae's really good at being a human, you kno'," Vespera added helpfully with an extra-deep Valley girl accent, crackling with barely contained snickering. "Like, super dedicated. Won't break character no matter what. It's the friggin' cutest thing ever."

"*What?!*" Emerald snarled. "Vee, what the efffff?! You . . . we . . ."

There was betrayal and shock painted on her face as she realized that everything wasn't turning up Emerald today. That Io, Ci, and Vee firmly stood on the wrong side of the barricades now.

"What's wrong, Emmy?" Vespera cooed. "Don't look so stressed, I still love ya, com' on, don't catch fire! We made the red shirt for ya. It was your swag idea, after all!"

"My idea?!" Emerald's eye twitched. "You effin' traitor," she hissed. "I can't believe that you would stoop so low as to take this scab's side . . ."

"Take his side? How right you are! I'm considering eloping with Lex in Shandria this weekend," Vespera added, wrapping a hand around my shoulders. "They have the cutest chapel there with the view of the chasm. What do you say, m' favorite human? Ready to become Mr. Simmi-Glock?"

"Vee!" Cinder bristled. "Quit pawing at him! This isn't funny."

"Ci, don't be a jelly beerch," Vespera teased, electricity dancing between her talons. "Consider this—we can book a double engagement for the price of one! I'll take Prima-Wife, and you'll be our handsy Hearth-Keeper! We could even adopt K as our kitten if she behaves."

Cinder ignited with violets and pinks fading into golds while Katherine let out a bothered growl from her wheelchair, feline ears twitching.

"Knew you'd like that idea," Vee clicked.

Emerald's jaw dropped, her gold-orange eyes bulging with pure shock as she processed Vespera's words and our flirting. Black smoke began rising from her ruby scales as her temperature spiked with incandescent rage.

"You . . . you're *all* in on this?!" she sputtered, looking between us. "This is . . . this is *treason* against the Superstate! He's an *actual human*! A real one! My family's Scrutimancer confirmed it! He's here illegally! His name isn't Glock! There is *no* Alexander Glock! And you're all just . . . just . . . *playing along*?!"

"Emmy, sweetie," Vespera clicked her beak sympathetically. "I think you need to take a break. You're takin' our joke way too seriously now. All this obsession with hatin' on humans and mixies isn't healthy. Like, look at your Omnigram feed—it's all '#HumanInSkyfall' this and 'Expose the infiltrator' that. Maybe try focusing on something else? Like how about that cute Wendigo behind you who's totally into you? You two should, like, totes get engaged on Arx, you'd make a great perma-couple! Opensauce 'ships are so last season."

Quint tried and failed to look professional, fretting slightly on his spot by the gate at the suggestion of an engagement in Shandria.

"*I am not obsessed!*" Emerald roared, dragonfire sparking around her teeth as she frothed at the mouth. "*He's a human! A real human! Why is nobody listening to me?!* Vee, I sent you an effin' PDF! Did you not read it?!"

"The 'Lex is a human' PDF report was pretty funny." Vee grinned. "Four out of ten meme. I sent you a thumbs-up about it."

"It's not a *freaking meme*!" The dragon girl howled.

"Pff, yeah okay," Vespera laughed. "Sure. I too can generate a PDF with OmniGPT 4.0 about how you're a human instead of a dragon, bae."

The student delvers around us seemed to deflate slightly, many smiling at our shirts and buttons and whispering about Emerald taking it too far again.

Emerald's eye twitched violently.

"#TotallyARealHuman," I commented, pulling furiously blushing Cinder to my side and taking a selfie with my phone. "That's a good one! Thanks for another funny tag, Em!"

"Emerald," Quint stated, "enough. Please stop causing a scene. His father is a Thunderbird. This is obviously just their team taunt and you're falling for it. Be professional."

"*I'm not fallin' for shit!*" the dragon girl screeched even louder, making everyone wince. "*Are you actually this effin' stupid, Quint?! How can you not see it?! He's manipulating everyone using AI-generated fakery!*"

"Hey, my Omnigram photos aren't AI generated, they're AI retouched," I pointed out, showing off my camera. "There's a difference. My DSLR camera has a very basic upscale AI in it, don't you know? It erroneously marks some Omnigram pics as 'AI generated' if you run a detector over them."

"Shut yo bloody effing lying mouf, human scab!" Emerald rounded on me. "You're fake, and all of your photos are bloody fake as shit! My Scrutimancer . . ."

I stepped towards her and hugged her.

"I love you," I said, feeling all of the hexagrammic gems and collars on me ignite like a See-Mass tree as they fought off the dragonfire radiating off her. "Let's be friends! Come on!"

There was a reason why I'd picked this reflective jacket of Lance's to wear today. According to the tag and online marketing listing that Yulia pulled up, this jacket easily withstood both extreme cold and heat. The reflective element extracted from some otherworldly beast known as Liskostuash from Arx was nearly impervious to the destructive heat of dragonfire for about two minutes.

"*What?! Don't touch me! Frig off, you lyin' sack o' shit!*" Emerald forcefully shoved me away. It took all of the power of my hexasuits to stop myself from flying backwards. "You think I'm stupid like these birchards?! You might have tricked some brainlets, but I know that all of your pics are AI generated!"

Time to up my game. Being a loud dragon versus genuine social networking.

"Hey, Christi!" I waved to the Pink Chancellor who was staring in mild confusion at the commotion. "How'd you like the photos I took of you at Lazarus Cavern?"

"Oh! Alex! They're, like, totally amazing!" Christi's flames brightened enthusiastically. "You really captured my best angles! The lighting was perfect! My phone cave pics just don't come out good like yours. You're a real pro!"

"What about you guys?" I turned to my team before Emerald could resume her howling. "Rate the photos I took of you at the D&D show yesterday out of ten!"

"The gate-opening photos were pretty rad," Io said, nodding. "Caught the exact moment I opened it. Def' ten out of ten."

"One billion out of ten." Vespera waved a magisteel-covered hand dramatically. "Best human photographer! #MarriageMaterial."

"I really liked the one where you caught my wings mid-color-change," Cinder added. "Hrmmm. Infinity out of ten." She tried to up herself above Vespera's rating, clearly still bothered that I drank the Thunderbird shake with a big smile on my face.

Emerald choked. She saw where this was going and clearly had no idea how to stop it.

That's right. Eat my witness-backed evidence, dragon. Another spoon should do it.

I spotted my favorite Kelpie in the crowd. "June! How'd you like the photos I took of you after our chess match?" I asked.

"Pretty great!" June called out, her liquid hair rippling and sending water drops onto the dark marble floor. "You made me look so elegant! Even my mom loved them! Oh, oh! Can you take a couple of pics of me and my team in front of the Arx gate?"

"Absolutely!" I nodded. "Line up! We got seven more minutes."

June and her team of fluid-mages stepped to the gate.

"You . . ." Emerald hissed. "You absolute fake *bastard!* Stop acting like this is all some big joke and dodging the truth away! You're a *human!* A filthy, worthless *human* who . . ."

"Shut yo yap, dragon, or I'll shut it for you." June stepped between me and Ember. "We all know that you have a beef with mixed-heritage students. You bullied Sarah out of Skyfall last year!"

"Em, please." Quint placed a restraining hand on the smoking dragon's shoulder. "You're making a scene. This isn't the time or place for . . ."

"Time or place for *what?*!" Emerald slapped Quint's hand away. "For exposing this *human infiltrator?*! He's . . ."

"Oh, for Slayer's sake," June sighed, raising her staff. "Guys, amp me. I've had enough of whatever this is."

The team consisting of a Mermaid, a Lusca, a Frogman, and a Vodyanoy standing behind the Kelpie girl laid their hands onto her.

"Drown," June said simply, interrupting Emerald's next howl of swears and accusations.

A torrent of pressurized water erupted from the Kelpie staff, amplified by her team's combined power. The blast caught Emerald in the open mouth in an explosion of super-heated steam, sending her flying backwards into the classroom wall with enough force to crack the dark marble wall.

Steam poured off Emerald as the water pounded against her super-heated scales. For a moment, the classroom became filled with thick fog.

When it cleared, Emerald lay slumped against the wall, her ruby scales dulled and smoking, her gold chains tangled around her flickering with defense hexes.

"Anyone else want to be a bigoted jerk to Alex?" June asked pleasantly, the water elemental still swirling around her staff.

Solace opened both of her mouths and then realized that she was basically alone against five water-controlling Omnids. Her round, teeth-filled forehead maw and humanish mouth snapped shut and she quickly rushed off to Emerald's side.

"No? Good. Now, Alex, about those photos . . ." June grinned.

"Looking fabulous as always," I commented, snapping several shots of June's team posed in front of the gate, the water elemental spinning merrily in the air behind them. "Love the staff and H2O effects."

"Oooh, send those to me!" June clapped excitedly, liquid hair rippling above her silver-green scale-type armor.

"Already done," I said. "Check your Omnigram, #TeamHydroblades."

The hydromancers pulled out their phones and started to chat excitedly. Yulia worked fast.

"If anyone else wants pics, I am willing to take some in Shandria, but then you gotta wear your *I'm with Human* shirt for your next class as payment." I threw the *I'm with Human* red shirt that I was holding at June. She caught it from the air and pulled it on, the shirt immediately getting soaked because of her hair. I snapped a pic of her in the shirt and Yulia added it to my Omnigram feed.

Solace helped the dazed Emerald to her feet. The dragon girl's gold-orange eyes were unfocused, steam rising from her scales as she twitched and spat water.

"Right then." Quint cleared his throat. "If we're done with the dramatics, let's proceed with today's delve. Team Captains, please present your gate passes."

Cinder stepped forward, holding out her token as Captain. Other Team Captains did the same. Quint walked across the line of Captains, scanning each with a runestone. Solace presented Emerald's pass as the dragon girl looked quite out of it, dredging water from her lungs.

As Quint approached with the runestone and his own gate pass, all twenty-four of the silver spider's eyes looked down. The giant spider shifted position, accepting the runestone from Quint, and swallowed it.

"Does the shiny spidey have a name?" I asked Io.

"Gate Weaver," he replied. "Works sort of like my skill, except she makes an extra-stable gate that can stand up to time dilation."

"Zalimar boasted that he bred her himself over generations of spidery gate matriarchs," Vee clicked.

The Gate Weaver rapidly wove intricate patterns across the black crystalline ring, legs moving with hypnotic precision. Each strand of webbing it produced glowed slightly, forming a massive, complex hexagram over the gate.

"Remember," Quint announced as the spider worked behind him, "you have two hours of Earth time, which translates to roughly one week in Shandria. Don't antagonize the locals, be polite and professional, and be back before the gate closes. Your passes will vibrate when it's time to return. Upperclassmen with high Adventurer rank are free to delve nearby dungeons, but beginners should stay within the city limits and only go out as far as the wild fields. Those without prior delving experience"—he looked pointedly at me—"are to register themselves at the Adventurers Guild Cathedral and to complete Iron rank jobs. Since Instructor Zalimar isn't here, I'm filling his role in supervising all of you as the Arx Delver Captain with the highest rank. Screw around and you will be banned from going to Arx ever again. Captains, you are to manage your team members and make sure that they behave."

The Gate Weaver's work reached a crescendo, the final strands of silver light forming a complex pattern across the black crystal. A deep resonant hum filled the air as the gate began to activate, liquid silver leaking from the web to form a shimmering circle like a little pool of water.

"First-time delvers, please note that temporal dilation and higher mana aetheric density can be disorienting," Quint added. "You may experience mild nausea and discomfort as your body adjusts to Arx."

I nodded along.

"Shandria closes at sundown," Quint continued. "Do not attempt to stay out after dark. Leviathan's Nightingale's Shadow flock is far, *far* more dangerous than anything you've encountered on Earth. Even experienced delvers must avoid being outside after sunset. Basically, stay in your hotel rooms at night, or you will die a most horrible death."

Sounds like a Larry Plotter challenge, I thought.

Vee seemed to share my giddy mood, gray eyes sparkling with excitement. Cinder looked a bit concerned. It was hard to tell what Io and Kat were thinking on the account of their fuzzy, blank faces and dark hoods.

The silver liquid in the gate began to ripple and swirl, forming a perfect mirrorlike surface.

"Teams will enter in order of rank," Quint announced. "Upperclassmen first, then intermediate teams, then beginners. Your phones will not work in Shandria, but Voicecast spells embedded within the gate passes are tied to our Keeper on the other side. If anything goes horribly wrong, Voicecast me or the Omnid-owned inn or our Chapel Keeper right away. Any questions?"

"What happens when Emerald kills me?" I asked.

"Novitiate Glock," Quint said as he pinched the bony bridge of his nose, "just . . . don't antagonize her. Please. I don't want to have to bail both of you from Shandrian prison or save you from an execution."

"I'm not doing anything," I huffed. "You all saw it, I gave her a hug! I'm trying to be just a friend!"

"Just a friend?" Quint asked.

"It's just that . . ." I pretended to stammer. "She asked me out, but I told her that she's just not my type and that I like Cinder and Vee more and now she won't get off my case!"

"What?" Emerald croaked weakly from where Solace propped her up. "That's not what . . . I would never . . . I'm not into freaking humans!"

Quint sent Emerald and me a very annoyed look, his eyes flaring bright. Then he cleared his throat. "If you die on Shandria, your team members are to immediately bring your bracelet across the gate back to the Lazarus Cavern. If they fail to do so, points will be deducted from their grade, and you might find your team suspended from delving practice for a month. Any other questions?"

"What happens if our Quartermaster gets us all killed by being an insufferable troll?" Katherine asked.

"I would never!" I gasped in mock offense.

"Captains are to file daily reports about the team's activities," Quint hissed out, sounding fed up with his life. "If the report isn't filed on time, you will be contacted by me. If you do not respond, another team will be sent to investigate, and if your bracelets are not found within the hour, a DelveRaid team will be sent out by the Shandrian Adventurers Guild. They're very expensive, so try not to die in places where your team can't recover your bracelet. If DelveRaid fails to locate your bracelets within the allotted time of four hours, a high-level Corpse Seeker will be sent to retrieve your bracelets from the Omnithean chapel managed by Brother Vassily. Any other questions?"

No one raised their hands.

"Good. Team Stormpiercers, you're up first."

Lance, Christi, and two others waved to us as they passed by.

"Wait for me at the Guild," Quint said. "I gotta make sure everyone goes through safe from this end."

"Can do." Lance nodded. "See ya tomorrow."

Quint's team entered into the shimmering gate, sinking into it.

A few more teams followed, each disappearing into the liquid silver surface. Finally, it was our turn.

"Team I Love You, you're up," Quint announced, his amber eyes lingering on me with obvious concern. "Remember, hold hands and dive together as not to become separated due to the temporal dilation."

"Stay close, follow my lead, and most importantly . . ." I said.

"Don't die?" Katherine suggested dryly.

"Have fun!" I grinned.

We grabbed onto one another and walked/rolled into the gate.

CHAPTER FORTY-SEVEN

The Delve III

The sensation of moving between Earth and Arx was . . . indescribable.

Like being pulled through liquid metal while simultaneously being stretched and compressed. Snowflake-like fractals danced across my eyes. Gravity seemed to go from pushing down on me to slapping me in the face as I swam/floated/was squeezed forward and emerged out of a silver pool.

An older-looking Omnid offered me his long-limbed hand. I recognized him as a Domovoy.

The Domovoy helped pull me out of the silver pool. He was wearing a simple brown robe with gold trim. His face was weathered and kind and covered in a thick layer of dark fur. I recalled that Domovoys usually bound themselves to a specific building for life, drawing power from it. In their particular chosen domain they were nearly impossible to put down.

"M' Brother Vassily, Keeper of the Transit Gate Chapel," he introduced himself. "First time on Arx, yeah?"

"Yep. Thank you for the assistance, Keeper!" I stepped aside just as Cinder emerged from the pool with a splash, her wings dripping silver liquid that evaporated into mist.

Brother Vassily helped her up as well, then assisted Io, Vespera, and Katherine, using both of his ridiculously strong and stretchy limbs to heft the wheelchair and all onto the polished stone floor of the Omnithean chapel.

I looked around. The chapel seemed to be carved out of a large, cozy cavern, similar in design to the Lazarus Cavern, covered in gold glowing crystals. Kitlix lanterns hung from the ceiling, adding shimmering light to the environment. Another chonky Gate Weaver spider sat in the corner, staring down at me with silver eyes.

My body felt wobbly, and I sat down on a nearby wooden bench, trying not to throw up as my insides felt like my outsides on and off.

"Welcome to Shandria, young delvers," Brother Vassily said warmly. "We're currently six clicks below the city. That stairwell up will lead you to the Arx Bank vault. There you can procure local currency using your delver bank cards if you have such. The Adventurers Guild Cathedral will be on the east side from the bank. You'll see it right away; it is a very big white stone building with many spires. Can't miss it."

I nodded. My nausea was slowly settling as my body adjusted to Arx.

"Remember to register your team and obtain your Iron rank badges before venturing outside the city walls. The market district is directly west of the Adventurers Guild. And please, do mind the time—Shandria's nights are quite deadly."

"Thank you, Brother." I bowed slightly. "Any recommendations for lodging?"

"The Guild has rooms that vary in price," the hairy man replied. "I recommend the Gilded Gryphon Inn near the market. My cousin Nikkola owns it; he'll give you an excellent rate. It's in the *Welcome to Arx* brochure on that table by the stairwell up."

"Much appreciated," I said. "Wait. Stairs? You don't have like an elevator or . . ."

Katherine gritted her teeth, standing upright. She grabbed her chair and folded it up, strapping it to her back along with the backpack and magisteel armor plates.

I blinked at her.

"What?" Katherine growled, catching my surprised look. "You think I can't walk? The chair's just easier most of the time. Less painful. Killed myself this morning. Always do before delving class."

"Ah." I nodded, feeling bad for her. "Still, six clicks of stairs seems excessive."

"It's Shandrian clicks, not Earth miles," the Domovoy pointed out. "About a mile of stairwell. You'll be up in a few hours."

I winced.

"I'll be fine," the Stollwurm said. "I'm much stronger underground. Arx has incredibly high aetheric density, which helps with my . . . condition."

"Welcome to Arx," Brother Vassily said. "Where everything is either trying to kill you or inconvenience you to death. The stairs are warded against most forms of magical transportation—security measure for the bank vault above."

We began our ascent, Katherine moving stiffly but steadily. Cinder hovered close to her, ready to help if needed, while Vespera and Io took point.

The stairwell was wide, carved directly into the rock. Tiny Kitlix lanterns ignited to life as we came closer, dimming behind us.

After what felt like an eternity of walking up endless stairs, we emerged into a gloomy stone vault.

A gray and black striped catgirl attendant rushed to our side from where she was reading a thick romance novel, opening a magisteel gate.

A catgirl?!

I sneakily pointed Yulia's camera at her. "Cryptitype not found," Yulia whispered into my ear.

"Welcome to Shandria, honored children of Omnifomrnnia," the attendant said, smiling at us and slightly butchering the name. "Please follow me."

The catgirl quickly scanned us with a cyan Kitlix and then unlocked a magisteel vault door about ten meters thick in front of us. The massive door swung open silently, revealing a very long tunnel, going up. The tunnel led us to another stairwell and vault door which opened up into a grand marble hall filled with tellers' windows and currency exchange booths.

The other teams weren't anywhere. I mentally tabulated that the two hours of Earth time turned into 168 hours on Arx, which meant that the time dilation was x84. This meant that the few minutes between each team's entry stretched to *hours*.

"Remember to declare any magical items you wish to sell," the catgirl attendant said, stepping behind a counter. "The bank takes a five percent commission on all transactions."

"What about mundane items?" I asked.

"The value of any item will be evaluated by my Infix Kitlix, Cheeski." The woman smiled, whiskers twitching as a violet-cyan crystalline kitten rushed from her shoulder down her arm and onto the teller's table. "I'm Arx Bank rep Gabriella Matrosin. The current exchange rate for one O-dollar is . . ."

She listed the conversion price and the explanation of how "Ten coppers make a silver. A hundred silvers make a gold. A hundred gold make a platinum. A hundred platinum make a magisteel. A thousand magisteel make a celesteel." Which Yulia noted down.

Vee stepped to the table with her delving card. "I'd like to . . ."

"Don't," I said. "Not done."

"Not done what?" Vespera asked, pausing mid-motion.

"Learning," I said. "Miss Matrosin. Can we go to a private room? I have many items to sell."

"Very well." The catgirl nodded, stepping out of the booth. She led us to a private guided office and sat behind a large wooden table.

I went into Lance's backpack and pulled out a bag with about a thousand different small items and materials.

"Please evaluate the value of each," I said, dumping the bag onto her desk.

"Sir," Gabriella said, her whiskers twitched with annoyance, "there are other customers that I . . ."

"They can wait or go to another rep," I said. "I need to know the exact value of everything."

The catgirl sighed and began scanning items with her Kitlix. Each item's value appeared on a small crystal ball display.

I kept my wrist cam pointed at the ball, building a price database with Yulia's help. As I expected, some items that were considered worthless on Earth held higher value on Arx, while others were practically worthless despite their Earth-side expense.

"Are you quite done?" Katherine growled after about twenty minutes of the attendant going through random small items pilfered from Earth.

"No," I said, pulling out another bag.

"Ughhhh," Katherine groaned. "This is going to take forever."

"Knowledge is power," I replied cheerfully, dumping more items onto the table. "And power is money."

"Sir." Gabriella's whiskers twitched more violently. "Perhaps you could come back later . . ."

"Nope," I said. "Need to know now. How much for this paperclip?"

Vespera snickered beside me. Cinder had gotten bored ten minutes ago and was now sitting in the waiting area across the hall, playing Candy Smash on her phone. Io was snacking on interdimensional chips beside her, reading what looked like an old yellow-paged science fiction novel.

After nearly two hours of methodically cataloguing item values, I finally had a comprehensive database of what was worth selling and what wasn't. The catgirl attendant looked ready to claw my eyes out.

"Now we can exchange currency," I announced cheerfully.

"Finally!" Katherine growled. "My legs are killing me."

"You do know that you can sit down with the others over there?" I said. "Riiiight?"

"I've done enough sitting on Earth," she shot back. "I can actually walk around on Arx."

"Why don't you live on Arx like the Chapel Keeper and his cousin if you feel better here?" I asked her.

The Stollwurm looked at me as though I was an absolute idiot.

"There are no incarnators on Arx," she said after a few seconds of glaring at me. "I'd just be dead in three-four weeks here."

"Oh really?" I smiled. "Well, that changes everything."

I dug into my bag again and pulled out a thermos filled with incarnator fluid.

"Please let me know the value of this liquid," I said, opening the thermos.

The catgirl's eyes widened as her Kitlix scanned the thermos. The crystal display suddenly lit up with a string of zeros.

"Sir." Gabriella's voice dropped to a whisper, her tail suddenly very still. "Where did you obtain this . . . substance?"

"Oh, you know." I waved vaguely. "Around."

Vespera stared at me. Then she reached out with a claw and sent a spark flying into the thermos. Then her eyes went wide.

"You . . ." she breathed out. "You dumped *that* on Em?! You're selling *that*?!"

"Is that illegal?" I asked.

"Urm." She blinked. "You know what? I have no idea. I consider myself clever, but I never thought of selling lint or paperclips or rubber bands or rocks or . . . *that* on Arx. How do you even . . . think of this shit? How are you so funny?" Her gray eyes sparked with uncontained mirth.

"What is that stuff, and why is it worth so much?" Katherine asked, clearly not recognizing Genesis fluid at a glance.

"If you don't know, I ain't telling," Vespera clicked.

"Whatever, like I give a shit," Katherine huffed.

"Sir," Gabriella said and cleared her throat. "I'll need to call my supervisor about this . . . particular item if you wish to sell it to us."

"No need," I said, recapping the thermos. "Just wanted to know the value. Here, take everything off this bank card and convert it into cold, hard cash."

Katherine and Vespa read the name on the gold card. Both of them choke-gasped as I typed in the PIN and the card was accepted.

"Three hundred platinum, sixty-two gold, eighty-five silver, and six coppers." The attendant handed us a bag of coins after a minute. "Will that be all?" she asked wearily.

"Yep, thanks a whole bunch, see ya." I grabbed the card back and stuffed it into my pocket.

Both girls were giving me wild looks as we walked over to where Cinder and Io were sitting. As I had killed about two hours bugging the bank teller, Cinder had dozed off, her head resting on Io's shoulder while the Mothman continued reading his *Sixty-Nine Thousand Leagues Inside the Moon* book by Julie Verne.

I shooed Io off the bench and placed Cinder on my lap, then shook her awake.

"Mrmph?" Cinder blinked awake.

Her ocean-blue eyes widened as she realized she was using my lap as a pillow, and her feathers shifted rapidly through embarrassed pinks and startled violets.

"What . . . why am I . . ." she started, then noticed our teammates' amused expressions. Her feathers darkened to mortified reds.

"You fell asleep on Io," I explained cheerfully. "I upgraded your pillow."

"I did not!" she protested, quickly getting off me.

"Did too," Io confirmed, slipping his book inside of his bag. "You were muttering something about annoying humans in your sleep."

"I did not!" Cinder huffed.

We emerged from the bank into what appeared to be a bustling medieval fantasy city on steroids. The crowd was absurdly diverse, featuring rock, tree, metal, and animal people, and not a single person was human or an Omnid. Massive mage-towers curved in whimsical patterns, leaning down slightly. Red flags flapped in the wind featuring what looked like a nine-eyed monster in a crown. Kitlix were practically everywhere, sitting atop of people and in windowsills. Strange creatures that looked like a cross between cats and owls fluttered between rooftops.

"Ughhh. Did you seriously spend two and a half hours bothering the teller?" Cinder whined at me after about five minutes of walking, as she pulled out her phone and checked the time.

"Yes."

"Whyyyyy?!"

"I learned things," I said.

"Like what?"

"The Arx Bank values items based on their magic. For example, a gold ring from Earth is almost completely worthless here," I said, "while a drop of Genesis fluid could probably buy a house. Maybe the whole thermos would get me a flying castle. I dunno. Gotta shop around."

"Genesis fluid?" Cinder's eyes widened. "You . . . you brought Genesis fluid to Arx?!"

"Yep." I nodded. "Also, check this out—I got us some spending money." I jingled the bag of gold coins in front of her. "This is like thirty thousand gold."

"Did you . . . sell something that expensive?" Cinder squinted at me. "Please don't tell me that it was the paperclip or a pencil."

"Nope." I grinned.

"How do you know *her* password?" Vespera hissed, unable to help herself anymore. "Why do you have Em's card?"

"Put a spycam on her yesterday." I shrugged. "She uses the same password for all of her cards. Not very wise. Got her delver gold card while I gave her a hug."

"Holy sheet, dude, you're evil! I love it!" Vespera cackled.

"Wait . . . what is happening?" Cinder demanded. "Where's this money from?"

Vespera put her beaks to Cinder's ear and began whispering furiously.

"*What?!*" Cinder rounded on me. "*You did what?!*"

"Are you sure this is wise?" Katherine asked. "Em's already trying to get you expelled . . ."

"She can't hate me any more than she already does. And now she'll have to explain to her parents why she spent so much money in Shandria." I shrugged, watching as Cinder ignited like a firework.

"And when she claims her card was stolen?" Katherine pressed.

"Stolen by whom, where?" I asked. "I can drop her card in the middle of the Shandrian Market, and that'll be that. If that endless stairwell and the magisteel vault doors are anything to judge by, the Shandrian authorities don't trust Omnithornia in the slightest. Does OFBS have *any* authority here? Can Omnithean Scrutimancers interrogate the bank rep about bank cards?"

"Ummm . . . nope," Vespera answered. "The Arx Gate to Shandria is owned by Skyfall Academy and operated by Zalimar Evernacht. Random Scruts won't be permitted to go in. I'm pretty sure Zalimar has a premium account in Arx Bank and gets a percentage whenever a student sells something or trades currency."

"Do you know what this means?" I asked Cinder, who looked like she was about to explode.

"What?" she growled.

"Emerald will be going through last with Quint since she got herself punched into a wall so hard. Also, right before we left, I texted the school nurse to patch her up—that'll delay her even more. Due to this, we'll be ahead of her by an entire day. That's a lot of time for me to be ahead, my dudes."

"So dastardly," Vespera cackled. "Remind me never to get on your bad side."

"Alex," Cinder said. "You can't just . . ."

"Cindy," I shot back, "yes I can. I'm not permitting Em or Zal to get away with this shit anymore."

"But," she began.

"No." I shook my head. "You don't get it. All crimes committed against Omnids in Shandria are legal. Do you know what happened to Sarah Nisteroff, Ci?"

"Oh," Katherine said.

"She . . . went out . . . at night," Cinder said. "Em said that . . ."

She fell silent.

I raised my eyebrows. "She didn't go out. Emerald tricked her into going outside and closed the door on her. Sarah died clawing against the doors as the living Shadows chopped her up. They started with her toes and fingers and then went up. The Shadows toyed with her, chased her down the street as she tried to run, tried to find safety. Her assigned Team Captain lied on the team report. Emerald lied as a witness. Zalimar knew about it and let it happen. He's been letting it happen for centuries! If I hadn't challenged Zalimar to a duel, if I never found four friends to stand by my side—it would been me out there, getting chopped up by the Shadows next. One does *not* go to Arx alone without people they can trust, without a plan of action!"

Cinder swallowed.

"There's a reason why I'm Skyfall's only mixie student on a nearly all-covering scholarship. You don't get to tell me what's ethical on Arx, Ci. I know what Zalimar and his patsies like Emerald did to other half- or quarter-human students here. Yulia talked to their families via email, conducted interviews as a journalist. I'm simply the shadow of justice that's catching up to everyone's crimes."

CHAPTER FORTY-EIGHT

Undertown I

Cinder's feathers shifted through troubled grays and somber blues as she processed my words. Her ocean-blue eyes were wide with a mix of horror and dawning understanding.

"I . . . I didn't know," she whispered. "About Sarah. Em told me she was just being stupid, that she wandered out at night because she wanted to prove herself . . ."

"Where were you when it happened?" I asked everyone.

"I was in the Gilded Gryphon Inn room," Cinder said quietly. "With Io. Em was sharing a room with Vee and Sol."

"I was high as balls," Io admitted. "Em was chewing me up about something, so I did a bunch of stuff. Didn't even know what happened until way later."

"I didn't do shit with my assigned team," Katherine said grimly. "Told them to screw off and do whatever. Stayed in a private room in the Guild Cathedral. Broke my assigned Team Captain's wrist when he tried to force me into staying with them at the Gilded Gryphon."

I looked at Vespera.

"I was getting smashed with Sol," she said, beak facing down and looking at me with a guilty face. "Em bought us two-hundred-year-old Shadow-wine, and we played drinking card games till we got completely wasted by nightfall. Em said something about teaching the Nullie a lesson, and Sol and I just laughed, I think . . . I can't remember what I even said. Fuuuuck."

"Yeah." I nodded. "And that's why I drained Em's delver card. That's why I'm going to make her life on Shandria extremely unpleasant."

"Two wrongs don't make a right," Io mused.

"No," I agreed. "But three hundred platinum pieces worth of wrong might buy us enough influence to make sure it never happens again. All of you were here in Shandria and you did nothing, closed your eyes, or didn't know. Sarah wasn't the first victim, but I will sure as hell make sure that she is the last."

A heavy silence fell over our group as the thoroughly shamed Omnids and I walked through the bustling streets of Shandria.

"So . . . Guild time?" Io asked, trying to fill in the silence between us.

"Not yet." I shook my head, latching onto a colorful merchant who manned a table filled with various fruits.

"Excuse me!" I called out to the man, who appeared to be some kind of bird-headed, dark-feathered being. "What are those and how much?"

"Thems springapples from my farm," the man replied. "Three copper for twenty."

"Perfect!" I handed over three copper coins and received a bag of springapples. "So tell me about your farm . . ."

"Oh, for Slayer's sake," Katherine groaned as I engaged the merchant in an enthusiastic discussion about agriculture on Arx. "More delays."

The bird-headed man, who introduced himself as Agromancer Krekof, was more than happy to talk about his crowkin family's springapple orchard just outside the city walls, tended by a large tentacled walker-type beast known as the Agrilopod. After milking him dry about this and that, I moved onto another merchant and then another.

For the next few hours, I systematically interrogated every merchant, street vendor, and random passerby within reach about their wares, lives, and local customs. Katherine's patience visibly deteriorated with each interaction, while Vespera found the whole thing mildly amusing. Cinder alternated between exasperated sighs and curious listening, occasionally adding her own questions or just browsing downloaded games on her phone, looking bored.

Io just kept munching his interdimensional chips, occasionally offering commentary about how certain market items reminded him of things he'd seen through his gates.

"What are these colorful towers?" I asked a ginger foxgirl salesperson who was selling Voicecast bracelets from an outside booth next to a Guildnet shop, pointing a finger at a distinctively violet massive citadel tower looming above us.

"That's a Mage Tower, friend," the foxgirl replied, wiggling large orange ears my way. "They're built by Archmages and their Enclaves from stones cleansed through magic."

"Cleansed how?" I asked.

"I dunno." she shrugged. "I'm not a mage. It's some kind of a bigly ritual involving entire Witch Covens or Mage Enclaves that does each one. See how they have individual colors? The color generally correlates to what the Enclave specializes in. Seer magic is violet, for example, so that's a Seer Tower. Their Enclave can predict magical events or find lost things."

"I see," I said. "Is it possible to buy one?"

"Nah," she said. "A tower like that is passed from mage to mage within the Enclave. They don't sell 'em. A bunch of particular Enclaves usually form Guilds, which lease land from local highborn lords. For example, the estate of Lord Rubius owns the shop behind me and pays my salary."

"Can I buy a building and open a barbershop?" I asked.

The foxgirl eyed me with silver-blue eyes. "If you got the cash. You're a human, yeah?"

I nodded.

"You can sublease land from one of the highborn estates," she said. "High lords generally don't sell buildings or land, it stays in their family, passed from pure human to pure human."

Huh.

"Humans can do magic on Arx?" I asked her.

"Is this some kind of a trick question?" She stared at me as if I was a concussed idiot. "*Everyone* can do magic on Arx. Everyone on Arx has heart cores."

Except for me, it seems.

"What if someone was born without a heart core?" I asked.

"Ain't never heard of such a thing," she replied.

"Do plants have heart cores?"

"Plants have itty-bitty, micro-shards in every leaf or something." She shrugged. "I dunno. I'm a Voicecast spec, not an Agromancer."

"Can I Voicecast other dimensions?"

"No."

"Can I Voicecast anyone anywhere on Arx?"

"No. You can easily Voicecast anyone with a Voicecast bracelet within Shandria. The Guildnet operating Mage Towers can connect you to Guildnet towers of other Shadow Empire cities or beyond it, but it won't be cheap."

"Can I Voicecast a dungeon?"

"No. Dungeons aren't sentient."

"Can I Voicecast the dead?"

"Yes."

What the fuck.

"Really?"

"Yeah. It's not cheap, though, and the dead are generally obsessed over some stupidly specific shit they wanted to do while they were alive. I wouldn't recommend it."

"Is talking to the dead Necromancy?"

"No." The foxgirl shook her head. "It's just something that all high-level Nuntix Kitlix can do." She pointed at the magenta-colored Kitlix on her shoulder. "Necromancy, aka raising the dead, is illegal in Shandria. Anyone collaborating with a Necromage is to be executed by fire."

"I see," I nodded.

I moved on from the Voicecast salesgirl to other booths down the row of shops.

I learned about local politics, market prices, Guild regulations, and most importantly—which areas to avoid. The merchants were particularly eager to warn us about the "bad" districts and share gossip about highborns, monster attacks, dungeons, the Shadow Leviathan that ate people at night, and Kitlix that were born from old magical items.

As we made our way through the winding streets of Shandria, I continued my relentless information gathering campaign, until my throat felt raw. Every few steps brought a new target—street sweepers, window cleaners, craftsmen, food cart operators, even children playing with strange magic toys and pawing at adorable owl-kittens and sleek fox-crow pets called chuppies.

Katherine's eye twitching became more pronounced with each delay and every random question I asked every single person in my path.

I learned the prices of everything from street food to construction materials, with Yulia transcribing our conversations. Due to lack of internet, the AI wasn't connected to the various Omnicorp LLM APIs, so she wasn't as clever or as fast at sorting information, but she was still cataloguing everything for review later.

The local currency seemed to follow a completely different value system than Earth or Omnithornia, heavily favoring certain magical properties over raw materials. This was because Arx was insanely wealthy when it came to raw materials, plus some mages could convert materials into pure gold or diamonds with ease and duplicate non-magical and some slightly magical items. The more magical something was, the harder it was to duplicate, according to a key duplication expert at a keymaker's booth.

As my companions grew progressively weary and irate, I pulled them into a cafe, and we all enjoyed a hearty lunch. I swallowed my meal quickly and then chatted at the crowgirl waitress while everyone ate their food like normal people.

In another hour, I pulled everyone into an imposing building covered in red-and-black flags.

"Why are we here?" Cinder asked. "This isn't the Adventurers Guild."

"It's better," I grinned. "This is the Guild of Manhunters."

"The what? *What?*" Most of my companions made noises like a confused flock. Only Vespera was giving me an evaluating look.

I ignored them, walking to the teller booths.

The teller who greeted us was composed of gray stone and pale blue sapphire, his crystalline features catching the light as he moved. He was basically a fusion of a rock and a person.

"Welcome to the Guild of Manhunters," he said, stone beard twinkling. "I'm Zelsh Gofrotash. How may we assist you today?"

"I'd like to place a bounty," I said cheerfully.

"A bounty?" The man arched an eyebrow. "Do you have the cash? Minimum bounty is ten thousand gold."

I jiggled my coin bag.

"Very well, follow me to my office to discuss the details," the man said. "Do be aware that we mainly hunt down criminals or runaway property."

"Oh, she's a big criminal, all right." I nodded.

"So. Who is the target?" Zelsh asked as he sat down behind a marble desk, offering our group leather seats.

"This individual." I showed the man a picture of Emerald on my phone. "Emerald Stratos. She'll be arriving in Shandria within the next twenty-eight hours or less via a gate. She will emerge from the Arx Bank on 303 Mantaray Street."

"Alex!" Cinder hissed, grabbing my arm. "You . . . the Manhunters are serious business! Are you seriously going to have Em assassinated?!"

"Oh, I'm not asking them to kill her," I clarified, turning back to the crystalline teller. "Just . . . inconvenience her a bit. Make her stay in Shandria somewhat unpleasant. Nothing permanent. Put a bag over her head for a week, keep her in a basement . . . until I heroically rescue her, of course. I wouldn't want her to die here."

"This can be arranged," the rock-man said, nodding. "A week of opponent imprisonment is thirty thousand gold. What level mage is she? What's her alignment?"

"She's a Rubicund Lindworm," I explained. "High-level predator with fire abilities, enhanced strength, and expensive protective gear. Her alignment is Chaotic Evil with a side of entitled brat."

"No." Zelsh shook his stony head. "I don't know what a Rubicund Lindworm is. What's her magical alignment?"

"She's basically a dragon, I guess." I shrugged. "Throws dragonfire around. Weak to water jets."

"Hrm." the crystal man stroked his glittering beard. "Given the target's capabilities, that would raise the price to fifty thousand gold. We'd need to employ specialized containment methods."

"Fifty thousand?" I whistled. "That's a bit steep. What about just following her around and making her life difficult? What can I get for twenty thousand gold? Can you annoy her for a week and then make sure she ends up in a situation where she'll need rescue due to falling into a well or something?"

"For twenty thousand, we can arrange for continuous harassment and minor inconveniences," the crystal man replied. "Falling into a well can be arranged, too. Our agents will ensure her stay in Shandria is thoroughly unpleasant without causing permanent harm."

"Perfect!" I pulled out Em's money. "Here's twenty thousand gold. Make sure she has the worst week of her life. She will try to attack my group—your job will be to distract her with random NPC events."

"I'm not familiar with the term NPC," Zelsh said. "But I understand that you wish her 'distracted.'"

Cinder twitched beside me, but didn't argue.

The crystal man counted the coins quickly and nodded. "Contract accepted. Our agents will begin surveillance as soon as the target arrives through the gate. Do you have any specific requests for the type of harassment?"

"Nothing violent," I said thoughtfully. "Maybe . . . dump smelly water on her occasionally from windows or have children throw apples at her. Be creative. Don't be obvious about it."

"Absolutely." The crystal teller nodded. "Harassment without physical damage. Thank you for your patronage."

"I can't believe you just did that," Katherine muttered from behind us as we walked out of the Guild. "Actually, wait. Yes I can."

"Impressive," Vespera clicked her beak. "Fifty shades of petty revenge. Didn't know that the Manhunters Guild could be asked to annoy someone like that."

"Talk to enough random people and you too will be wise." I grinned.

Cinder simply sighed, having given up on trying to make me deviate from my anti-Emerald plans.

"Don't look so glum, Ci," Vespera said, shrugging. "It's basic corporate psychological warfare. Ain't nothing new under the sun. I don't have a beef with Em, since I mooched off her gold for years, but Lex obviously has a plan that requires this. Who am I to question my wise human husbando?"

"I am crushed with your compliments." I pretended to faint. "Husbando? At least take me to dinner first!"

"But darling," Vespera said, draping herself dramatically across my shoulders, her magisteel armor clinking, "I thought what we had was special! All those meaningful glances across the classroom, the way you let me zap your . . ."

"Vee! You've known him for like four days!" Cinder growled.

"Ah, but 'tis love at first spark," Vespera sighed dreamily. "When he walked past art class looking like a perfect snack, I just knew . . ."

"Will you two *stop*?!" Cinder hissed, wings shifting through angry reds and jealous greens.

"Never!" Vespera cackled. "Your reactions are too precious! Look at those colors! You're like a walking rainbow of denial! This is so much more fun than you being drab and dark around Em. Gosh. I'm tingling all over."

"You're insufferable," Cinder growled at us both.

"And you love us for it." I grinned. "Now come on, we've got an Adventurers Guild to visit before all the good quests are taken."

"Finally!" Katherine exclaimed. "Something actually productive!"

"Follow." I grinned at her, wrapping my arms around Cinder and Vespera.

I led our group through winding alleys, following directions gathered from various merchants.

"Umm. The Adventurers Guild is that way." Katherine pointed at a massive cathedral-like structure visible above the rooftops.

"We're taking a shortcut," I said, turning down a narrow side street.

"This doesn't look like a shortcut," Cinder commented as we descended a set of worn stone steps into what appeared to be a lower district.

"Trust me." I grinned. "It's a shortcut to *adventure*!"

CHAPTER FORTY-NINE

Undertown II

After descending a series of winding tunnels following nondescript markings on walls, we emerged into a barely lit cavern.

Another stairwell led us to a clearing and a balcony. I marched to its edge and then pulled Lance's dark-sight goggles onto my face.

"Dang," I whistled as my vision was amplified by the magic goggles, the view drawing my breath away. "This is much prettier than advertised."

A mind-bogglingly massive, dark cavern stretched out into all directions from the stairwell-adjacent stony balcony that we were standing at. Fog rolled across the distant streets below. Ignix Kitlix occupying glass lanterns flickered far below like tiny red dots.

The ceiling shimmered with bioluminescent fungi, casting an eerie blue-green glow over cramped buildings that seemed to grow directly from the stone walls. Unlike the carefully planned streets above, Undertown was a maze of twisted alleys and precarious walkways, stone buildings carved atop of buildings in a messy jumble almost like a giant anthill rising up each gargantuan, absurdly tall column. Waterfalls cascaded between buildings at random, joining into rushing, foaming rivers, heading lower into some unknown depths with a distant rumble.

A few grimy Mage Towers loomed over the stone maze of buildings and had starlike lights burning above them, flickering ever so slightly.

"This isn't the Adventurers Guild," Katherine growled from where she stood, a few steps below me, looking over the eerie underground vista. "Where the shit are we even?"

"Undertown," I replied, taking a photo of the gloomy city below me.

"Why in the Abyss are we in . . . Undertown, of all the places?" Katherine demanded.

"We're going to the *other* Adventurers Guild!" I grinned, taking a few more photos of myself and my companions, cranking the ISO all the way up.

Vespera walked towards me and hugged me and Cinder, taking a selfie with both of us with her phone, and then looked annoyed at how blurry it turned out.

I took one with my camera.

"What other Guild?!" Cinder demanded.

"You'll see," I said.

The Quetzi-girl exhaled dramatically.

We departed from the balcony observation point and gradually descended some more worn stone stairs and then rickety wooden stairs into the fog-filled streets below.

"The Gloomy Horse Tavern," I explained as we walked. "According to that friendly gargoyle chimney sweep I talked to, it's where all the best underground information brokers hang out."

"Information brokers?" Katherine repeated. "We're supposed to be registering at the Guild, not diving into the criminal underworld!"

"Who says?"

"The school's curriculum?" the Stollwurm growled.

"What's all this complaining about curriculums?" I asked her.

"I'm already failing this damn class," Kat hissed at me. "I thought that now that I'm in an actually tolerable delving team, then maybe . . ."

"Relax and trust your Quartermaster," I said. "You're not going to fail any classes with me around."

Cinder chortled beside me.

"I'd love to trust you, but you're not explaining shit!" the Stollwurm stated. "Why are we here?! Are you going to hire even more assassins to go after Emerald or something?! Going to start a murder competition maybe?"

"Pff, no. We're simply . . . taking a different path." I grinned at her. "The dark gloomy path. Aren't you stronger underground? Pull those dark goggles off. This is your place. Embrace it. Become the predator you were meant to be."

Katherine realized how dark it was, stopped, and pulled her goggles and hood off. "Happy?"

"See? You're practically glowing down here," I noted. "Much better than those bright, colorful, merry, whimsical streets above."

"That's not the point," she growled, but I noticed her tail was moving with more energy, her footsteps silent even as she had a huge wheelchair covered in shields on her back.

"The point is work to our strength," I said. "The point is that Omnithornia is a civilized twenty-first-century society . . . while this place isn't in the slightest. This is a dark, dank cesspit. You clearly love it here. Admit it."

The Stollwurm huffed.

After about thirty minutes of walking between dilapidated stone buildings, passing by some very sus cloaked figures that gave us space, we finally approached what appeared to be a very old, somewhat crumbling windowless fort carved directly into another gargantuan black-and-gray slate column, a dark, citadel-style tower looming overhead, decaying dark parapets barely visible in the gloom.

A weathered wooden sign above the entrance depicted a half-dead horse standing in the fog and looking at a crumbling old tower. I could hear muffled conversations and the clinking of glasses from within.

"This looks . . . sketchy as eff," Cinder commented, her feathers shifting through wary grays.

"Perfect." I grinned, pushing open the heavy wooden magisteel-reinforced door.

The interior was dimly lit by faintly glowing Kitlix inside hanging beer jugs.

The bartender was a tall, gaunt figure with dark-gray skin and glowing brown-gray eyes, his hair and beard looking as if they were made from dead black roots. As I approached, he was polishing a glass with a rag that had seen better centuries.

"What's your poison?" he asked in a gravelly voice.

"Information," I replied, sliding onto a barstool. "I heard the Gloomy Horse serves the finest in town. I'm looking for an . . . *adventure!*"

The bartender's eyes narrowed slightly. "Adventure is only for those who can prove themselves. Information's expensive. What kind are you looking for?"

"The kind that doesn't show uptown," I said, sliding a gold coin over to him.

The bartender's eyes gleamed as he took in our expensive delving gear and magisteel armor.

"Follow," he said.

We did, passing by a few gaunt, filthy, cloak-wrapped figures nursing their alcohol jugs. The bar was mostly empty. Maybe it was too early to drink or something.

The man waved a hand, and a wall of dark roots parted.

We ended up in another, even darker and grimier section of the bar that was carved from bedrock and covered in roots framing the walls. There were a few shadowy alcoves all around between the roots. A single Kitlix lantern flickered far in the back.

The bartender snapped his gnarled fingers, and several cloaked figures emerged from the shadows, surrounding our group.

"Fresh meat from upstairs," he grinned, revealing brown teeth that looked like broken tombstones. "Rich little delvers who wandered too far from the light. How . . . fortunate."

"Oh good," I said cheerfully. "You're going to try to rob us. Kat, would you kindly show these fine gentlemen what a Stollwurm can do in the dark?"

Katherine's emerald eyes flared in the gloom. The shadows around us suddenly deepened, becoming almost tangible. The temperature dropped sharply as her Stollwurm fear aura activated, amplified by the underground environment. The Kitlix winked out completely.

"With pleasure," she growled, and living darkness exploded outward. Thanks to the borrowed goggles, I could see quite well in near absolute pitch black.

The cloaked figures recoiled, a few of their weapons clattering to the ground as primal terror gripped them. Even the bartender stepped back, his eyes widening.

The nearest hooded figure, seemingly resistant to Katherine's fear aura, lunged forward with a wicked-looking curved blade. The knife slashed across Katherine's camo jacket and skidded upon encountering magisteel plates, sending a few sparks flying. Before he could strike again, Katherine spun with inhuman speed, her tail whipping around like a steel cable. The impact sent the attacker flying across the room, crashing through a table and several chairs before slamming into the far wall with a sickening crunch.

"Anyone else?" Katherine growled, her emerald eyes blazing in the darkness she'd created. The remaining attackers backed away, trembling in fright and clearly reconsidering their life choices.

"Now, then." I turned back to the bartender, who was looking considerably less confident. "About that information. I believe we were discussing prices?"

"What . . . what are you?" the bartender uttered, staring at Katherine with wide brown eyes.

"Who do you think we are?" I asked.

A cyan-and-black Kitlix emerged from the man's root-mane. It stared at me with crystalline, glowing eyes.

"You're a level one Human-Thunderbird . . . hybrid," the bartender said. "Whatever that is. And your four companions are . . ."

He fell silent for a moment.

"Quetzalcoatl, Stollwurm, Deathskull Mothman, and Thunderbird . . ." he said. "But . . . that's it. That can't be it."

"Oh?" I asked. "What's wrong with that?"

"I've never heard of such kin," the bartender said. "And I've had my share of . . . clients. Plus my Kitlix is struggling to define your levels."

"Ah, yes." I nodded. "That might be because we're from somewhere very, very far away. Somewhere beyond the Wheel."

The bartender's face paled.

"What?" he croaked.

"Can your mages open gateways to other worlds?" I asked him.

"No." The bartender shook his head.

"Io," I said with a grin, "would you kindly demonstrate to our good man what you can do?"

The Mothman nodded, pulling out his harmonica. A haunting melody filled the closed section of the tavern, and reality began to ripple behind the bar, weaving a shadowy gate.

I picked up an empty mug and chucked it through the portal, tearing apart the black membrane. The mug flew into the desolate landscape and then it froze in time due to the time dilation, shuddered and exploded, glass shards hanging within the portal, slowly crawling through the air.

Through the gateway, we caught glimpses of a post-apocalyptic cityscape—broken skyscrapers, violet stars, and what appeared to be a massive fallen piece of something, perhaps a fallen megastructure. A titanic thing was looming between skyscrapers, a black figure covered in a shawl of what looked like human skins. A thousand silver eyes shone atop of its head.

The bartender stumbled backwards, his violet eyes wide with terror. "By her Shadow . . . what manner of magic is this?"

"That's a dimensional gate," I said. "To another world where time is running eighty times slower. That's . . . Mr. Noodles. He collects skins, I guess. It would take a single word for one of my lovely Knights to throw you in there and close that gate forever. Or you can work with us. Tell me everything about Shandria's underworld. Dungeon locations. Secret knowledge not meant for the ears of simpletons above. Be extremely honest and cooperative, and I will reward you with shiny currency." I jiggled my money bag.

The bartender swallowed hard, his violet eyes darting between the still open gateway, Katherine's glowing emerald eyes, and my pleasant smile.

"I . . . see," he said carefully. "Perhaps we got off on the wrong foot. You have proven yourselves as high-level mages and not mere children. Allow me to properly introduce myself. I am . . . Guild Master Motrdem, owner of the Gloomy Horse . . . Undertown's Adventurers Guild."

"Excellent!" I beamed, motioning for Io to close the gate. "Now we're getting somewhere. First round's on me. Something old and magically potent from your catacombs for my friends."

As Motrdem hurried to fetch drinks, I noticed the remaining cloaked figures had melted back into the shadows. The one Katherine had thrown was being dragged away by his companions.

I looked at Katherine and my heartbeat accelerated. She stood by me, panting slightly. Her bulky coat was ripped apart, revealing a very curvy, fit body covered in glittering silver and dark-blue magisteel plates.

Gone was the crotchety, constantly drunk girl in a wheelchair. A tall, muscular Omnid night predator, a Knight of darkness stood in her place, emerald eyes glowing brightly from within like those of a cat, shadows warping and dancing around her in radial waves like inverted flames of an oxygen fire.

She looked like a completely different person here—dangerous, powerful . . . *alive*.

CHAPTER FIFTY

Undertown III

Ugh, bastard ruined my coat," Katherine exhaled, pulling off her torn-up camo jacket with a sigh.

"Wow," I said. "Kat. You're stunning. How did I not realize this?"

Cinder choked from where she was standing. Vee smirked. Io dug out a pack of interdimensional candies called Dora's Tongue-Terraforming Twisters.

Emerald eyes flashed at me, sending my thoughts careening into dark places, then quickly looked away. A blush crept across Kat's face as she crossed her arms, glaring at me, her spine curving unnaturally off to one side like that of a worm.

"Shut up," she growled, but there was less bite in it than usual.

"No, seriously," I continued. "You're like this badass underground predator ninja. The way you just yeeted that guy across the room? Amazing. And the fear aura? Chef's kiss. Perfect execution. You're not even wincing when you move . . . how?"

"This place is dark," she said. "Darker than mere shadows. Full of treachery, fear, death, and misery. Many people died here in pain over millennia. It feeds my Omnid heart, fuels my dark furnace."

She pulled the giant magisteel sword from the wheelchair strapped to her back and swung it through the air, making it hum ominously.

"Like a true Stollwurm." I nodded appreciatively. "Haven't you been down here . . . in Undertown?"

"No, I have not," she said. "Zalimar does not permit students to break protocol or to wander around like we are now. He makes Quint stay behind for a bit and goes in first. Nobody could deviate from the program under his watch."

"Yeah," Vee clicked. "The Koshchei's lessons are bone-dry. Exchange money, go to the Guild cathedral, sleep at the Gilded Gryphon Inn, visit the market, collect magic grass from the fields, maybe visit a low-level dungeon nearby when permitted, etc."

"Speaking of bone-dry . . ." I grinned as Motrdem returned with drinks. "Morty— what can you tell us about the dungeons of Arx?"

The bartender set down our drinks—something dark and smoking in heavy crystal glasses.

I eyed Io. The Mothman grabbed a drink and sipped it. "No disasters. Just good ol' vintage Shandrian Undertown Shadow-wine. Em bought it for us before."

"There are many dungeons around Shandria," the Guild Master said. "Whenever a mage dies, a dungeon is born. The more people and beasts a dungeon core kills, infects, and ties to itself, the deeper it sinks into the hollow-filled shell of Arx. Go deep enough and you'll find a dungeon worth your salt."

"How deep are we talking?" I asked, leaving my drink be. I needed a clear mind.

"There isn't an upper limit." The Guild Master shrugged. "The deeper down you go, the more dangerous the dungeons become."

"What is the purpose of dungeon delving?" I asked.

"Dungeons are where most potent magical items come from," Motrdem explained. "Whenever a celestorm passes overhead, things manifest in the dungeon."

"Things such as?"

"Things woven from dreams and desires of men who died there or are delving there now," the bartender revealed. "Swords that can cleave through a hundred men. Armor that turns the wearer into a living shadow or makes them immune to arrows. Rings that make their wearers invincible or invisible or lucky in love. Magically charged gold. Magically charged gems. Artifacts of power."

"And what happens to delvers who die in these dungeons?" I asked.

"They become bound to the dungeon as Sentinels—hollow, walking, undead hives," Motrdem shrugged. "Smaller monsters or bugs grow inside their flesh, which slowly becomes more and more aligned to whatever the dungeon's alignment is. Sentinels are basically magical skills that pretend to be a person. The older a Sentinel is, the less of a heart core they have. Takes about twenty years for a dungeon to completely devour a person from within."

"Interesting." I nodded. "And these dungeons . . . they all have cores?"

"Yes," the bartender confirmed. "The core is the heart of the dungeon. It is a skill of a long dead great mage bound into crystalline strata."

"So if one were to, hypothetically, want to start their own dungeon . . ." I began.

The bartender blinked at me as if I was mad.

"Kill a powerful mage in the wild," he said. "Place the core somewhere where someone won't pawn it for a few decades. That's it."

"So you're saying," I said as I leaned forward, "that if someone were to kill a powerful mage and place their core in a random room on Arx, a dungeon would just . . . form? Just like that?"

"Yes." Motrdem nodded.

"Do you people not have cemeteries?" I asked.

"No," he said. "We do not. Those that die in Shandria are burned on the spot, the cores taken by the City Watch. Their cores fuel the Ward of Shandria."

"And what are celestorms?" I asked.

As Motrdem launched into an explanation of magical weather phenomena that summoned wild monsters into existence, I felt Cinder lean against my shoulder.

"What are you planning?" she whispered in my ear.

"Just gathering information," I replied quietly.

"You're plotting something," she insisted. "I can tell by that chuppy look in your eyes."

"Me? Plot? Never." I grinned. "I'm just a simple human trying to learn about this fascinating new world."

"Simple human my tail," Cinder muttered, but stayed close.

"Morty, I heard upstairs that your Guild is connected to dungeons," I said. "Please describe each for me."

"The tunnel marked with a wave symbol leads to the Gloomkerr Dungeon. It is an underground watery abyss filled with fish and other marine creatures. Its depths haven't been scouted well, and it is relatively safe with the exception of giant glowing slugs who occasionally show up. We acquired fish food from it."

I nodded.

"Tunnel marked with a spiral leads to the Crownspiral Dungeon. It is a shell of a snail-god-beast. Within it, time is broken, looped into itself. It is not for the faint of heart, for to delve deeper into the spiral, one must kill their companions and sacrifice their blood to it. It reincarnates people, rewinds time while feasting on their mana. Those foolish enough to delve too deep in do not return."

"I see," I said. "Anything else?"

"The tunnel marked with a snowflake is the long cold tunnel diligently maintained by our Guild for many centuries. It leads to the Abystall Dungeon directly below us, which extends far past the west edge of Undertown. It is truly massive and ancient, and it is where we procure our meats. It is safe to observe from above, but stepping into the field below will slowly drain an adventurer and all of their tools of mana. It is a very devious place, for the higher level someone is and the more magical their armor, the faster they will perish there."

"Got it," I said, contemplating my delving options.

I continued questioning Motrdem about everything from Guilds, to dungeon mechanics, to local politics, building a mental map of Shandria's power structure. The Guild Master, seemingly relieved we weren't going to throw him into another dimension, proved to be a trove of *very* interesting information.

According to him, there were a few Guildnet-connected Mage Towers in Undertown too, but they were in very shoddy condition and owned by unscrupulous, dangerous men who also ran criminal guilds or drug-peddling gangs.

Katherine remained standing beside me, occasionally interjecting with surprisingly insightful questions about the deeper dungeons. Staying in the dark tavern, far below ground, was doing wonders for her health.

Vespera had settled into a corner booth, wings crackling softly as she listened and took notes on her phone. Despite the lack of signal to Omnithornia, the device still worked as a notepad. Cinder had gotten bored, lost track of my incessant questions, and was chewing on a wyvern leg next to Vee, obliterating it bone and all.

"Is your tower considered a Mage Tower?" I asked the Guild Master.

"No," he replied. "It wasn't built by a mage. Its walls were never aligned to one particular magic affinity or another. It is simply a Guild for all who wish to challenge the dungeons below or around us."

"How come your bar is so dilapidated and half empty?" I asked.

"I refuse to add Topaz to the alcohol served here, and I do not allow attendees to smoke Topaz cigars in my Guild," he replied with a small sigh. "It dulls the mind too much, bloats the body, slows response time. Adventuring with a Topaz-addled mind is a road straight to your death."

In another hour of conversation, I checked the time on my smartwatch and saw that it was getting late.

"Got a room for five with decent wards where nobody will bug us?" I asked.

"Yes." The Guild Master nodded. "Three silver a night."

I slipped the silver over to him.

"Bring us more of this Shadow-wine and dinner," I said. "Guys, order whatever you feel like—your Quartermaster is covering it!"

CHAPTER FIFTY-ONE

Sparks I

The room Motrdem led us to was surprisingly cozy for being carved into solid rock. It featured a Slayer-sized bed in the middle that could fit four people in it and four smaller beds carved into alcoves, each for a single person. A table and a couch were carved into solid rock as well and a fireplace with a bunch of dried, thick roots sat in the corner with an Ignix Kitlix in it.

Three animated paintings dominated the walls, enchanted scenes providing both light and ambience. The one in the middle was that of a stormy ocean. It filled one wall with crashing waves and distant lightning, creating a soothing background noise. Windswept mountains on another wall showed snow swirling across jagged peaks, while the third depicted a peaceful valley covered in blue flowers that swayed in an eternal spring breeze.

"Depictomancer work," Io explained as I stared at the art with fascination. "Works well when there are no windows. They say that the artists place bits of their soul into these."

"Cool." I nodded as I grabbed a fried wyvern leg brought by the cook. "All right, team, let's talk strategy."

"Strategy for what?" Katherine asked, setting her wheelchair and bag down and collapsing backwards onto the large bed with a loud *thump*. "We still haven't registered at the actual Guild."

"Not interested in that," I said. "The uptown Guild is too restrictive. They'll want us to do boring grass fetch quests."

"So you want to do quests for the Undertown Guild, is that it?" Cinder deduced. "The Abyss am I supposed to put in my report, Alex? That we're working for criminals and murderers?"

"You'll write that we completed a series of Iron rank quests and had a lovely time." I grinned. "No need to mention which Guild issued them."

"That's dishonest," Cinder protested weakly. "I . . . have to be an honest Captain."

"I see that our lovely Captain has an inexplicably high moral backbone," I said. "Fine. I'll buy a decrepit building in Undertown tomorrow from the local Guild Master and open my own Adventurers Guild and give myself quests."

"What?" Cinder sputtered. "That's . . . even more . . ."

"More what? It's not illegal to make our own Guild," I said. "I asked. Shandria doesn't have copyright laws or that many Guild setup laws. We can name it '*The Adventurers Guild*' and register ourselves as its only members."

Cinder threw up her hands. "Fine! Do whatever! I give up. It's clear that I can't out-think your inane bullshit."

She grabbed a bottle of Shadow-wine and began chugging it.

"Whoa there." I grabbed the bottle from her. "At least use a glass."

"Give it back!" Cinder growled, her feathers shifting through irritated oranges.

"Nope," I said. "Not until you hear my plan."

"What plan?" she demanded. "The plan to start our own criminal Guild?"

"It's not a criminal Guild," I said. "It's a perfectly legitimate Guild that will provide us with the perfectly legitimate framework to operate on Arx indefinitely."

"Operate on Arx indefinitely?" Cinder demanded. "How?! You do realize that eventually they'll assign us a very stern substitute who will actually monitor our every move and make us do things properly . . . and then our Koshchei instructor will be back and smack all of us for insubordination and potentially ban us from the Arx Gate?"

"That's not going to stop me," I said.

"What?!" Cinder demanded. "That would absolutely stop you, what the Abyss are you talking about?!"

I put the wine bottle onto the table, dug into my bag, and pulled out a cluster of silver-white sparkling eggs.

Everyone stared at the egg cluster, eyes bulging and mouths open.

"Is that what I think it is?" Vee swallowed.

"Gate Weaver eggs." I nodded with a giddy expression. "Yes."

"Where the shit did you get those?!" Cinder barked.

"Raided Zalimar's office," I said. "His door succumbed to a credit card."

Vee grabbed the wine bottle from the table, finished it rapidly, and chucked it into a corner.

Then she aimed a talon at the fireplace and sent a loud bolt of lightning into the wood, igniting it. The Kitlix glanced at her, possibly annoyed that she had taken its job.

The Thunderbird settled on the plush white-beast rug facing the fire and wiggling her legs, chainmail twinkling.

"Kay. I'm in," she laughed. "It's utterly unexpected and ridiculous but . . . we get to make our own rules and visit Arx as much as we want to. No more boring Zalimar-approved basic-ass fetch or delivery quests."

"Exactly," I said, nodding. "We can create our own ranking system, set our own objectives, and most importantly, choose which dungeons to explore."

"And how exactly are we going to explain this to the school?" Katherine asked from the large bed, staring at the Weaver's eggs with wide, cute, emerald eyes.

"That's up to our lovely Captain." I waved a hand at Cinder. "Writing reports about our 'activities' is her job."

"Ughhhhh, I'm going to need more wine," Cinder groaned.

"Here ya go, boss." Io dug into his bag and tossed her another bottle.

Cinder caught the bottle.

"Is that safe? What's an 'SCA-approved alcoholic beverage?'" I asked.

"Probably." Io shrugged. "I mean, I'm still alive. Someone somewhere approved it."

"Not very reassuring," Katherine commented dryly. I saw that she had pulled off her armor, now only wearing her hexasuit. She appeared to be making a bed-nest of sorts out of the sheets and blankets for herself on the edge of the bed like an oversized kitten.

Cinder shrugged, snapped the top off the bottle with her claws, chugged the entire drink before I could say anything, and then slid onto the stone-carved, pillow-covered couch.

"Mmmm," Cinder let out after a few minutes, her feathers shifting through warm pinks and relaxed golds. "This is actually pretty good. Tastes like . . . rainbows and happiness."

"You are drunk," I commented. "Slayer! Do you people just come to Arx to booze up?"

"Mostly, yeah," Vee commented from the rug next to the fire. "The drinking age in Omnithornia is twenty-one years old. We're eighteen, my dude. Obvs we gonna alcohol up on Arx."

"Am not drunk, ookay?" Cinder protested, her wings fluttering. "Just . . . everything is really sparkly and nice. And you!" She pointed at me accusingly, though her feathers were shifting through affectionate pinks.

"Me?"

"You're all . . . sparkly too! Like a human-shaped shiny Pocket-man! With your stupid cute smile and your stupid isssnane, absurd plans and . . . and . . ."

"Ci's a lightweight," Vespera commented, crackling with amusement. "Two bottles of happy juice and she's gone."

"Am not!" Cinder protested. "I'm just . . . observating stuff! And Alex is very . . . observable. And Guild-start-able. How do you even think of this stuff?"

She reached out and pulled me to the couch. "Stop hoverin' and commerrrre!"

I landed next to her with an "oof" as she nuzzled into my side, her feathers shifting through a kaleidoscope of warm colors. "Wass in youuur head?" she demanded, slurring her words.

"Brain spiders from beyond the stars," I joked.

Glancing at Kat, I noticed that she had finished her bed-fort-nest and was now snoozing softly like a curled up dragon-cat. Io had settled into an alcove nursing another Nonpareil-themed drink while reading his *Inside the Moon Adventures* novel again.

"Jussst dat? Noooo way," Cinder giggled, poking my cheek. "You've got like . . . a whole *system* in there. Like a big complicated machine. With star gears and stuff. And feelings. And . . . secrets."

"Uh-huh." I rolled my eyes.

"Wanna know a secret?" Cinder whispered loudly, leaning close to me.

"Yes," I said.

Would she finally tell me about what happened to her two years ago? Or would I learn . . .

Annnd . . . she fell asleep on me.

Don't know what I expected.

I sighed as Cinder's breathing evened out, her feathers shifting through peaceful blues and silvers as she used me as a pillow.

"Thar she goes," Vespera commented from her spot by the fire. "Like clockwork. Two drinks and she's out."

"Does this happen often?" I asked.

"Only when she feels safe," Vespera clicked softly. "Usually she's too wound up to relax like this. Em always had her on edge, ya know? Making her prove herself, pushing her to be more wary of everyone, more 'predatory.' This is . . . nice. Haven't seen her this chill in two years."

I carefully adjusted my position so Cinder would be more comfortable, her wings draped over both of us like a feathered blanket.

The fire crackled as I thought about my first day on Arx and what tomorrow would bring.

Io's book fell from his fuzzy paw as he passed out; the thump made Kat's large ears twitch ever so slightly like radar dishes in the direction of the noise.

Vespera was still awake, feathered tail wagging left and right as she stared at the fire.

"Hey, Vee?" I asked.

"Mmmm?" She turned, half facing me. Gray eyes stared at me reflecting the fire.

"Who are you?" I asked her.

Vespera's beak clicked softly as she considered it. Her black-and-white feathers shifted in the firelight, casting dancing shadows on the wall.

"Who wants to know?" she asked with a bit of a drawl. "'N' why?"

"I do," I said. "Yulia nominated you as a potential team member for plan D, aka 'delving buddy,' but I didn't really dig too deep as to the why. So, I want to know who you really are . . . from the bird's mouth, as it were."

"A very loaded question," she finally said, her voice without the usual Valley girl accent spice. "Who am I? I'm many things. Daughter of Thunder blood. Heir to SimmiTech Industries. Best of 2024 class in artificery. Former D&D troupe member . . ."

She paused, clicking her beak thoughtfully.

"But I think what you're really asking is—who am I beneath all those labels, yeah?" She turned to face me fully.

"Yes." I nodded. "You don't make sense in my mind yet. I only see your shallows. You are not protecting my human butt just because it's funny. There has to be more to it."

Vespera was quiet for a long moment.

"You know," she began, "I've been playing the ditzy Valley girl for so long . . ."

She shifted, her magisteel armor clinking softly.

"My father . . . he's a brilliant man. SimmiTech is one of the leading manufacturers of magitek in Omnithornia. And me? I'm supposed to be his perfect heir. Smart, capable, ready to take over the company someday."

She let out a bitter laugh.

"But that's not who I want to be. I don't want to spend my life in board meetings, discussing profit margins and market shares. I want . . . to fly. I want to be free."

"Free?"

"I want to start my own . . . something, you kno'? Sadly . . . I'm bound to my father's name and legacy. Bound to another heir of another Omnicorp."

"Bound to an heir?"

"I'm . . . engaged to a Jin Chan imbecile," she let out with a growl.

"Arranged marriage?" I asked, perhaps a bit too loudly. Cinder curled against me tighter, making a soft noise.

"Yep," Vespera clicked her beak bitterly. "To unite SimmiTech with Golden Star Industries. The Jin Chan family specializes in . . . precognition stuff. They design probability engines. My father thinks it's a perfect match—combining our electrical expertise with their probability tools could revolutionize magitek development."

She paused, sparks dancing between her talons.

"But Zheng Ker, my fiancé . . . he's exactly what you'd expect from someone born with a silver spoon in his mouth. Entitled, arrogant, treats everyone beneath him like dirt. Has a bazillion proper-ness expectations."

"Are you acting ditzy to drive him away or something?" I asked.

"Partially," Vespera sighed. "It started as a way to annoy him. He wants a proper, sophisticated Prima-Wife? Fine. I'll be the complete opposite, an extra dumb beerch. But then . . . it became more than that. Being the airhead party girl meant people underestimated me. Didn't expect anything from me. Didn't force me into stuff. It was . . . freeing, in a way."

She paused, running a hand through her feathers.

"My father . . ." she sighed. "He's disappointed with my behavior, but he figures I'll 'grow out of it' eventually."

"But you won't," I said. "Because that's not who you are."

"Mmmm," she agreed. "I'm decent at what I do. I understand magitek better than most of our senior engineers. I can see the patterns in electrical flows, even understand how they interact with probability matrices. But if I show that . . . if I let people see how capable I am . . . then . . ."

"They'll expect you to be the perfect heir for the planned corporate merger," I finished.

"Exactly!" she clicked. "So I play dumb. I follow Em around like a lost puppy. I pretend to care about nothing but fashion, memes, hashtags, and social media. And everyone believes it because it's easier than looking deeper."

She turned to look at me, her gray eyes intense.

"But you . . . you saw through it. You and your cheeky AI figured out who I really am. And instead of using that information against me, you offered me a chance to be myself. To be part of something real . . . something different."

I nodded.

"Ya know," she clicked her beak thoughtfully, "when I saw you walk into class, pretending to be Alexander Glock . . . I recognized that same mask. The careful construction of a persona. But you weren't doing it to escape expectations—you were doing it to change things. To make a difference."

"And that interests you?" I asked.

"It fascinates me," she admitted. "You're like this . . . this agent of chaotic good, breaking down the walls between humans and Omnids. Making people question everything they thought they knew. And you do it with such style! Such poise!"

"Thanks," I smiled.

She gestured at the sleeping forms of our teammates.

"You've united a group of misfits, challenged authority, and made us all better for it. Io doesn't talk much about his feelings, but I can see that he's actually happy to be useful. Like, that gate he opened today to scare the Undertown Guild Master. It had value, purpose."

"And you?" I asked softly.

"Me?" Vespera's gray eyes met mine. "I'm totally fucked, to be completely honest. Part of me wants to run away to Arx ASAP. I can't stand the sight, the texture, or the intelligence level of my fiancé. I can't do it. I can't be my dad's Prima-anything, and it hurts. I don't want to disappoint him, and yet I am. I absolutely am."

"Have you told him?" I asked.

"Told him what? That I hate everything about my arranged marriage? That I'd rather run away than marry Zheng?" Vespera's feathers crackled with suppressed electricity. "That I understand magitek but I'm terrified of being trapped in an office, don't want to be trapped in a system that divides everyone from everyone, puts people into castes, ties corpo mergers to weddings?"

"Yes." I nodded. "All of that."

"I've alluded to it," she said. "I've alluded to things I didn't want to do before. He said 'use your control over the current to rewrite your brain during the day. Optimize yourself at night with your Dreamancy skill. Change who you are until you are perfect.'"

"Dang . . ." I searched for words. "That's pretty messed up."

"Yeah," she agreed. "And the worst part? I could probably do it. I understand enough about bioelectrical patterns and Dreamancy inception to attempt it. These babies were made by Dad for it." She clicked her magisteel talons. "But then . . . I wouldn't be me anymore, would I? I'd be some perfectly optimized version that fits his vision of the perfect future."

Her eyes filled with sparks of tears.

"All of this is just me wasting time, you kno'," she let out. "Killing time until I have no choice but to overwrite myself. What am I accomplishing? Fuck-all. Where am I going? Nowhere!"

CHAPTER FIFTY-TWO

Sparks II

Is that why you jumped at the chance to help a human infiltrator?" I asked Vespera. "Because any change is better than the fate waiting for you?"

"Pretty much," she laughed bitterly. "When I met you in the art class hallway and tasted your sparks, I thought—finally, something interesting, a human in Skyfall! When Em started texting about you being human, I thought that would be your undoing. And then you just . . . embraced it. Made it into this elaborate joke that everyone's in on except Em. She can scream all she wants to, but it's like you shifted reality and she's just stuck on the same track heading off a bridge and has no idea what to do."

She smiled softly and wiped at her eyes, more sparks falling.

"That's why you keep joking about marrying me?" I asked. "To cope?"

"Partly," she admitted. "It's also because you're the exact opposite of what my parents want for me. A human? With no status, no magical ability, no corporate connections? They'd have an absolute meltdown." She grinned through her tears. "Plus, you're actually fun to be around. You don't look at me like I'm just some corporate asset to be optimized."

I nodded.

"You're literally everything my father fears," Vespera laughed quietly. "A human infiltrator using technology to subvert Omnithean society. And here I am, helping you. Because at least it's *my* choice. Not his. Not Zheng's. Mine!"

Vespera's talons tapped against her magisteel armor.

"You know what the worst part is?" she whispered. "Dad's not even the villain of this tragic tale. He loves me. He wants what's best for me. He just . . . can't see that his version of 'best' is killing who I really am. My entire family is invested in this damned merger, 'cause it would bring greater prosperity to everyone."

"Parents often hurt us most when trying to help," I said, thinking of how Mom pushed me onto Uncle George instead of telling me the truth.

"Yeah," she agreed. "And the thing is . . . I get it. I understand the business logic. The political advantages. The technological possibilities. This merger could revolutionize everything. But . . ."

Her voice cracked.

"But I can't do it," she lamented. "I can't marry someone who looks at humans and sees vermin. Who treats Omnid service staff and sixies like they're beneath him. Who thinks that everything and everyone exists just to serve him. And I can't . . . I can't let them rewrite my brain to make me want it, want him!"

Tears were flowing freely now, sparks dancing between them.

"Dad says it wouldn't hurt," she continued. "That it would be slow, day by day, month by month. That I wouldn't even realize anything had changed. That I'd just . . . wake up one day and be happy with my life. Be the perfect daughter he always wanted. But that terrifies me more than anything. The idea that I could just . . . stop being me. Stop caring about the things I care about right now."

I carefully shifted Cinder off me onto the couch and moved to sit beside Vespera. She flinched slightly as I approached but didn't pull away when I put an arm around her shoulders.

"Hey," I said softly. "Look at me."

She turned her tear-streaked face towards me, gray eyes swimming with gold sparks.

"You are not going to let them rewrite who you are," I said firmly. "You know why? Because you're stronger than that. You're not just some corporate asset to be optimized. You're Vespera fucking Simmi, and you get to choose who you want to be."

"But what choice do I have?" she whispered. "I can't run away—they'd find me. I can't fight back—they're too powerful. I can't even tell anyone this shit because who would believe the ditzy party girl over the respected CEO?"

"I believe you," I said. "And I'm going to help you."

She let out a bitter laugh. "How? You're just one human."

I stared at her.

"Fine, you're a sneaky, clever hobbit," she said. "One that's constantly walking atop the blade of a knife. Seriously, though, what are you going to do? Fight my father's entire corporate empire? Blow up my fiancé's compound?"

"Ehhh." I shrugged. "There are smarter ways."

"Such as?"

"I don't know." I shrugged again. "It's late and my brain is soup and Yulia doesn't have internet access to provide greater API AI-wisdom. For now, I can provide a shoulder to cry on, as is my job as your Quartermaster."

Vespera buried her face in my chest, sobbing louder now.

"I've been alone with this fucking burden for so long . . . all this unsolvable shit hanging on my neck," she sniffed. "It's . . . nice to have someone so incredibly illegal so outside of the curve of my peers that I can tell all this shit to. Thanks."

I nodded.

"You know . . . you've got no magic in ya, you're so weak, so frail . . ." she let out.

I arched an eyebrow at her.

"And yet I see in you what I wish I could be. 'Cause you're also someone who looks at the rules, decides they're stupid, and just . . . changes them. You don't accept the status quo. You don't let others define who you are. That's nice."

I simply hugged her.

"What's horrifying is that we do it to ourselves," she said bitterly. "Optimize, sharpen, improve our minds with the talons produced by our clan. I've seen it happen. Cousins, friends . . . they go in wild and free, come out perfectly proper. Perfect heirs.

Perfect wives. Perfect empty shells. Like well-polished diamonds. Sharp. Brilliant. Nice to look at."

Her talons sparked dangerously. "The worst part? Everyone acts like it's normal. Like it's just part of growing up. 'Oh, little Vee finally got her optimization! Isn't she so much more pleasant now?' Not a single one sees it as evil or wrong. Better. More efficient. More . . . suitable."

She spat the last word like it was poison.

"We'll figure something out," I yawned.

"You really mean that, don't you?" She looked up at me, gray eyes searching my face. "You're actually crazy enough to try and help me."

"Of course." I grinned. "What are friends for?"

"Friends." She repeated the word as if it were something precious and new. "Did you . . . have friends before, in Acadia?"

"No," I said. "Just my mom, and then Uncle George, who taught me how to jailbreak everything around me. Machines, locks, people, systems, paperwork, social structures, rules. I didn't have time for friends."

Vespera nodded, understanding shining in her gray eyes. "Makes sense. You've been surviving, planning, seeking revenge, running away. Not living. Boop."

She poked my nose with a talon, tiny lightning jumping from her finger.

"Boop." I pointed a finger at her nose and visualized lightning running across me from the little bits of Thunderbird in my human body.

Nothing happened. No lightning, no spark. I frowned.

Vespera burst out laughing. "You can't just will electricity, silly hooman! It takes years of training!"

I dug the Captain's lighter from my pocket and ignited it out of Vee's view for a few seconds, letting mana permeate the air around me.

"Boop," I said again, willing the universe to bend with all of my will.

A tiny, almost microscopic electrical spark jumped from my finger. It flew slowly through the air between us like a small, fractal snowflake of inexplicably contained electricity and landed on Vespera's beak with a soft crackle.

LV 1 Skill gained: Lightningball

Sparks dancing in my vision made the announcement, the Lazarus bracelet tingling on my left arm.

"How?" The Thunder-girl blinked at me.

"I'm a wizard," I replied sagely.

Vespera stared at me, her beak slightly open. Then she burst out laughing, careful to muffle her sounds so as not to wake the others.

"A wizard," she repeated, wiping a tear from her eye. "Right. Sure. You're totally a wizard, my dude."

"Tomorrow I'm going to get these three to make me shakes from their flesh, too," I said, eyeing our sleeping friends. "And then I shall have unlimited powers."

I snapped the lighter shut.

"Abyss," Vespera chuckled softly, her laughter gradually subsiding. She wiped away the last of her tears, her gray eyes now sparkling with a mix of mirth and something deeper—a newfound sense of hope. "I think . . . I think I get what Ci sees in you."

She shifted closer, magisteel plates clinking. I could feel the electrical charge building around her as she leaned in, her gaze intense.

I could see radial waves of electrical magic dancing between us like we were two magnets.

LV 1 Skill gained: Electrofractal Sight

Suddenly, all around, everything had a charge to it, polarity shifting and dancing between us like northern lights. Her gray eyes seemed to glow from within as electrical currents traced delicate fractal patterns across her magisteel armor. The fire's light caught on her feathers, making them shimmer with contained storm energy.

Magic. Genuine magic. I finally had it, after eighteen years of bumbling about and running . . . I had stolen a spark of magic from the God-Beasts.

Tiny arcs of lightning began jumping between her talons and my hexasuits, creating a web of soft blue-white light. The air itself seemed to crackle with potential energy, making my hair stand on end. Each breath brought the taste of ozone, sharp and metallic on my tongue.

I was the ground and she was the thunderstorm up above. Gray-steel eyes, like broiling storm clouds.

Down was up and up was down. Gravity between us had given up.

All that existed were electrical currents, beautiful in their radiance and magnetism.

The crackle of electricity intensified as Vespera leaned closer, her breath hot against my cheek.

Pulse. Another.

Heartbeat. Lightning. Polarity.

[You see that, feel that, sense that . . . don't you?] Vee's voice whispered, distant and fuzzy like rumbling thunder. [You see me. I see you. I feel you. Resonance. Feathers to feathers. Heart to heart. Brain to brain. Soul to soul.]

She wasn't speaking with her lips; she was somehow communicating with electrical impulses alone. Her talons reached out to the sides of my head, microscopic lightning pointed at my neurons, electricity running across my brain.

LV 1 Skill gained: Resonance

The sensation was indescribable—like being caressed by the northern lights, each point of contact creating intricate patterns of energy that danced across my entire nervous system.

[You make me smile.] Her voice in my head like a distant whisper across everywhere.

[You make me smile, too.]

Embrace of four hands.

Electricity rushing across all of our neurons, reaching out to every cell, flickering, investigating, connecting, understanding, connecting, understanding.

A loop of ever-expanding fractal senses, going deeper and deeper in with each twist of current.

Then suddenly a voice cut through the electrical haze enveloping us, hexasuit covered arms wrapped in shadows pulling us apart, attracting the lightning, disrupting the frequency, breaking the connection.

"Stop with the light show! Trying to sleep," Kat said, shaking each of us like little kittens by the scruff of our hexasuits. "Get a room."

"We are . . . in a room," I breathed out.

Sparks danced across my vision. I tried to blink them away.

"Go thunderstorm somewhere else," Kat sighed. "Noisy."

"Wasn't trying to thunderstorm," Vee said. "I . . . don't know how that happened."

"Mmhmm," Katherine rolled her emerald eyes, still holding us apart with her magisteel-covered arms. "Sure. You weren't trying to merge your electrical fields with him at all. That's totally not what that was."

"I wasn't!" Vespera protested weakly. "I mean . . . maybe a little? I just . . . got carried away. The resonance was . . ."

"Your *resonance* was about to fry his human brain," Katherine growled. "He's not a Thunderbird, Vee. You can't just sync with his nervous system like that. I could feel that like four meters away."

"But he made a spark!" Vespera argued. "He's got bits of me in him! That's it! The resonance is so pure because he has my bits in him. If he was an Omnid, his body would just reject my Thunder-strata. But there is no rejection . . . and . . ."

"I don't want an Abyss-damn lecture about Thunderbirds," Katherine growled. "Bed now. All of you. Make out like normal people next time, don't start producing Slayer-damned celestorms in a confined space!"

"I wasn't . . ." Vespera choked.

"Don't care," Katherine said. "You were floating. In the air. If I hadn't stopped you idiots, you would have set fire to the entire room or worse!"

I winced as she shook me and Vee.

"Look," the Stollwurm said, pointing at the edge of the fireplace. "A thunderbolt from you two floating knobs struck the stone here—it's turned slightly transparent."

I looked at the shimmering edge of the dark fireplace brickwork. It looked as though a piece of silver-blue quartz was embedded in it now, shaped like a lightning bolt impact.

Katherine dragged me to the large bed by my hexasuit collar and tossed me onto it as if I weighed nothing. Then she did the same with Vespera, unceremoniously dumping the Thunderbird next to me.

"Stay," she growled at us both. "Sleep. No more electrical experiments at night!"

"But—" Vespera started.

"Sleep!" Katherine hissed, her emerald eyes flashing in the darkness wrapping her. "Or I'll drop you both into the deep and leave you there."

"You too, rainbow." She picked up Cinder from the couch and deposited her on my other side. "Everyone stay. Sleep. No more magical whatever."

The Stollwurm tapped the Kitlix lanterns, extinguishing them, and then went back to her nest, grumbling about "horny idiots," "dumb humans," "celestorms," and "bullshit magic lighters."

Cinder's wings wrapped around me, her feathers shifting through sky-blues and content silvers as she snuggled closer in her sleep. On my other side, Vespera was still like a mouse, her gray eyes wide and confused in the gloom, black-and-white wings fluttering.

"What . . . what just happened?" she whispered. "How?"

"I think we almost caused a magical incident," I whispered back. "Ummm . . . I might have released too much mana into the room."

"No shit," Katherine growled from her nest. "Now shut up and go to sleep before I start bonking you on the head. You're lucky that you have me to watch over you. I take my Knight job seriously, unlike some people who just want to screw around."

Her eyes closed, radar-dish ears twitching.

Vee buried herself into my side, looking very embarrassed.

The room settled into a deep, underground silence, punctuated only by the sound of crackling fire and soft breathing.

The fire in the Kitlix-managed hearth slowly died down to glowing embers. The Ignix Kitlix stared at me from the fireplace with a concerned expression.

She knew what we did. She saw everything.

She does not like it.

Kitlix didn't have feelings, I assured myself. They were just magic algorithms. Crystallized mana without thoughts, without a personality. Dumber than a snail. No long-term memory. No memory of any kind in an Ignix Kitlix who's only job in life was to light firewood and hold heat longer in a room.

Tomorrow. There was always tomorrow. The mana would dissipate and that would be that.

This totally would have no long term consequences. I absolutely wasn't thinking about that crystallized bit of stone.

I glanced at my stats. There was still an ungodly amount of mana in my body.

This was fine. Kat was watching us, listening, keeping us safe even when asleep. She'd stopped us from making a big mess.

My heart slowed and sleep finally won.

CHAPTER FIFTY-THREE

Dreamancy I

Falling leaves. Broiling storm overhead. Pouring rain.

It started just as my dreams usually did.

Except then. It didn't.

The autumn melted away, dissolved as if washed away. The sky above was blue and the ground below was the star-shaped cobblestones of one of many Skyfall Academy garden paths.

An unnaturally elongated stretched wolf, the flesh shifting and warping into a very handsome, overly muscular man, the wolf bits adjusting themselves like a living canvas perfecting, optimizing appearance. A perfect, dashing smile that accelerated my heartbeat.

I tried not to focus my eyes on him, looking instead at the pretty white towers in the distance. I thought about leveling up again, about sitting, meditating, and spreading my rainbow wings, humming. Singing.

White just like the dress on my body.

Dress. What am I seeing? This isn't my dream. This isn't me! Wake up!

I tried to snap my fingers, tried to step away from the dream, but it was impossible. I felt ground into the narrative, events moving too fast and too slow like drowning in molasses, suffocating me in alien feelings and thoughts.

"Your voice . . ." The Skinwalker's perfect teeth gleamed as he spoke, each word dripping with honeyed charm. "It called to me. I heard you sing at the Spring Equinox Festival, and I knew . . . I just knew we were meant to be."

Skyfall. This was Skyfall Academy. This was Cinder's dream.

I felt Cinder's heart flutter—her heart, not mine. Her emotions washing over me like ocean waves. The excitement, the flattery, the dangerous thrill of being noticed, being wanted, being loved.

"Really?" Cinder's voice—my voice in this dream—came out soft.

"Yes." The Skinwalker moved closer, his perfect face catching the light just right. "Your voice . . . it speaks to something deep inside me. The way you can make people feel things . . . it's incredible."

I felt myself blush, feathers shifting through pleased pinks and flattered golds. His words were like honey, sweet and intoxicating.

Cinder. Cinder!

What are you doing? Don't listen to him. Look at him. He's obviously up to something. He's in phase-shift, rearranging, optimizing his appearance to appear perfect. A hunter looking for easy prey. An upperclassman.

Except this isn't Cinder. This isn't January. It's the end of March and there are a million gardens blooming around Skyfall, the trees painted pink and violet.

"Your voice is a gift," the Skinwalker upperclassman purred, the tonality of his baritone shifting around. "A rare and precious ability that deserves to be nurtured. Together, we could do amazing things."

I felt Cinder's heart race faster. The way he looked at her—at me in this dream— made her feel special, chosen. His perfect features seemed to shift subtly, becoming ever more appealing, ever more mesmerizing.

"Together?" I asked. "Are you a musician, too?"

"Not quite," the Skinwalker's perfect smile widened slightly. "I'm in Acting Club, though. Comes with the phase-shift skill territory, you know."

I watched through Cinder's eyes as he demonstrated, his form shifting subtly— becoming taller, more imposing, more perfectly aligned with whatever idealized image of a perfect boyfriend she held in her mind.

His movements were calculated, each gesture designed to draw attention, to create an illusion of genuine interest. I recognized the techniques because I'd used them myself—the subtle mirroring of body language, the careful calibration of personal space, the way he let silence hang just long enough to create tension before speaking.

"I've been watching you," he continued, his voice modulating to hit exactly the right emotional notes. "The way you hold yourself apart from others, occasionally wrap those wings around yourself like armor . . . but when you sing, that's when the real you shines through . . ."

He ranted on, pouring honey across her mind. Clever, catchy words.

Classic cold reading. Start vague, then get more specific based on reactions.

A perfect bad boy with just enough edge to be exciting but not truly threatening. Every movement calculated, every word chosen to create an illusion of depth and understanding as they chatted in the garden about teachers and classes.

The Skinwalker leaned in slightly. "You're not like the other students here," he said softly. "They're all so . . . shallow. Focused on power, on status. But you . . . you see beauty in the world. Your songs speak of deeper things."

I felt Cinder's heart flutter again.

"When you sing," the Skinwalker continued, his voice dropping to an intimate whisper, "it's like you're speaking directly to my soul. The way your feathers shift through colors, telling stories without words . . . it's magical."

I felt Cinder's younger self practically melt at his words. Her feathers shifted through more pleased pinks and warm golds, betraying her emotions completely. She was so much more open then, wearing her heart on her entire body.

"I've written something," he said, producing a folded paper from his perfectly tailored jacket. "A poem . . . inspired by your voice. Would you . . . would you like to hear it?"

The younger Cinder nodded eagerly, completely caught in his web. The poem was beautiful—of course it was. *If I had Yulia, I could tell exactly where it was pawned from.*

"That's . . . that's beautiful," Cinder breathed, her wings shifting through amazed silvers and touched blues. "Thank you."

"Just like you," he replied smoothly, reaching out to brush a feather with perfectly manicured fingers. "You inspire such beauty in others. Such passion."

"Th-thank you," Cinder stammered out.

"I'm Valor," he said, his perfect smile widening. "Valor Thornheart. Senior year."

That sounds made up. If I had Yulia, I would find his real name, look up his online profile in seconds. But this isn't me. This is . . .

"Cassiopeia Nova," I heard myself reply shyly. "But . . . my friends call me Cassie."

"Cassie," he tested the name, making it sound like music. "A beautiful name for a beautiful soul."

He pulled out his phone—the latest 2022 IOmniss model of course—and held it out. "Perhaps we could exchange numbers? I'd love to hear more of your singing . . . maybe over dinner?"

I felt Cinder's younger self practically vibrating with excitement as she entered her number into his phone.

"Tonight?" he asked. "Seven o'clock? I know this lovely little place in Leviathan's Cradle . . . with the view of the water."

"Yes!" Cassie agreed eagerly. "I'd love to!"

"Perfect." Valor's smile was dazzling. "I'll pick you up at the main gate. Wear something pretty. White for the occasion of spring."

He turned to leave, then paused, looking back over his shoulder. "Oh, and Cassie? Don't tell anyone about this. Let's keep it our little secret for now. You know how the rumor mill is in this place."

Cassie nodded vigorously.

No, damn it! Tell someone. Tell anyone! You have friends, right? Io? Vee? Sol? Emerald, even! No. No! Cassie! Listen to me! He's . . .

The dream lurched sickeningly, time folding like origami, and suddenly I was outside the gates at seven, wearing a different, floaty, white dress with a wide slit on the back that made me look more innocent. More vulnerable.

Valor was waiting, looking even more perfect than before—if that was possible. His sky glider was expensive, sleek, black as night.

"You look stunning," he said, opening the shimmering wings with a flourish. His eyes seemed to glow in the gathering dusk. He looked like a hungry wolf, but he was already changing, already shifting to adjust to her preferences.

I wanted to scream at Cassie to run, to fly, to do anything but get in that glider. But I was trapped in her memories, forced to watch as she slid into the hexamesh bone seat, her heart racing with excitement of her first date rather than fear.

We weren't heading towards the nice areas of town. The Strand-Glider flashed past the ring of mountains, outside of the city's limits.

"Um, Valor? Where are we going?" Cassie asked, the first hint of uncertainty creeping into her voice.

"Somewhere special." Valor's perfect smile hadn't changed, but there was something predatory in its depths now. "I want to show you something amazing. My favorite place. Have you ever been to Lake Eerie? They say that it was formed by the spilled blood of the Leviathan. They say that whoever makes a wish on the shore . . . while casting a beast core of over level one hundred into the lake, will have that wish come true. Any wish at all."

Ask him about the core! Come on!

"So, like, do you have a core then? 'Cause I don't carry beast cores that high level on me," Cassie said, feeling nervousness flood her body.

"Of course! One for you, one for me." Valor's eyes ignited with yellow. He pulled a suitcase open. It was there. Two level one hundred beast cores, sitting on a velvet pillow. Expensive. So expensive.

Too expensive. Where did a student get those? Even an upperclassman. The math wasn't adding up. Who would spend so much money on a beast core just to throw it into a lake on a first date like a common coin?!

The Strand-Glider banked sharply, descending towards a secluded shoreline. The lake spread out before them, dark waters reflecting the stormy sky above. No other vehicles in sight. *No witnesses.*

"Beautiful, isn't it?" Valor's voice had changed subtly, losing some of its honeyed warmth. "Almost as beautiful as you'll be when . . ."

He caught himself, that perfect smile returning. "When we make our wishes together. It's so romantic, don't you think?"

Cassie nodded, but I felt her uncertainty growing. Her wings shifted through nervous lavenders and cautious grays. Something was wrong. The isolation. The expensive cores. His shifting appearance becoming slightly less perfect as his concentration wavered . . .

"Maybe we should go back," she said softly. "It's getting late and . . ."

"Oh, no." Valor's smile widened unnaturally. "We can't leave now. Not when we're so close. Don't you want your wish to come true, little songbird?"

Cassie! Cassie! You have to contact someone you know, damn it! This is some kind of a trap! Emerald, you know Emerald, don't you? Call Emerald!

Through Cassie's trembling fingers, I felt her pull out her phone, trying to keep it hidden as she typed: "Em. Lake Eerie. Help."

The message didn't send. No signal.

Of course there's no signal. Of course. This was planned.

I pressed the emergency panic button, hoping that it would get through to our familial Corpse Seeker via the astral flesh-chip embedded in the depths of my phone.

"Something wrong?" Valor's voice had an edge now, his perfect features starting to slip, becoming more angular, more predatory. The phase-shift was changing up, revealing glimpses of something else beneath the handsome facade.

"N-no," I stammered, wings pulling tight against my back. "I just . . ."

"Give me the phone, little songbird," he said softly, dangerously. His hand extended, no longer perfectly manicured—the fingers too long, the nails darkening into claws.

"I don't . . ."

"The phone." His voice distorted, multiple tones overlapping discordantly. "Now."

My hands shook as I handed over the device. Valor's unnaturally long fingers crushed it effortlessly, letting the pieces fall to the ground.

"There," he smiled, and it was no longer a perfect smile. Too many teeth.

"Why can't I . . ." I hissed, trying to target him with my wings. My charmchain magic was simply spilling around him like water.

"A Null-shard from Arx." Valor pulled a dark-pyramid artifact on a chain from his robe. "You won't be able to use your charisma or claws against me, little songbird."

"Just . . . just what do you want?" My voice trembled, wings flaring defensively as I backed away from the increasingly monstrous form. "M-my dad is the Justice of Leviathan's Cradle! If a single feather falls off my head, then . . ."

His perfect features were melting, running like wax, revealing something vile and hungry beneath. The phase-shift was now showing what he truly was, a predator, a half-wolf, half-man covered in glistening pale bone-muscles.

"Your voice, little songbird," he rasped, multiple tones grinding together like broken glass. "Such a rare gift . . . the ability to make others feel, to influence their very souls through song. Do you have any idea how valuable that is?"

He stalked forward, his movements no longer smooth and calculated but jerky, predatory. His skin rippled and shifted, patches of white fur breaking through at random.

"The cores . . ." I gasped, understanding finally dawning. "They're not for wishes, are they?"

"Of course they are," the thing that had been Valor laughed, the sound like metal scraping bone. "Just not your wishes, little songbird."

The storm overhead intensified, lightning crackling across black clouds. Wind whipped around us, carrying the scent of ancient magic and something older, fouler.

"You see," he continued, circling closer, "there's an old ritual. Very old. Requires specific ingredients . . . pure, perfect, Omnids. Singers. Charisma users. Callers. People who can draw the crowd or other things . . . in."

More Strand-Gliders descended from the stormy sky, landing in a loose circle around us. Transparent bug wings unfurled, opened with synchronized precision, and other lanky figures emerged—leading terrified young women and carrying identical suitcases.

I felt Cassie's horror as she looked at the other girls.

Each one dressed in white, like sacrificial lambs. Each one accompanied by a perfectly handsome "date" who was now shifting, melting, revealing their true forms.

"Welcome, one and all!" Valor called out. "We have gathered the final components. Tonight, we shall attempt to reawaken the Leviathan herself and wish upon her just as Slayer Nazareth did once, long ago!"

The other Skinwalkers responded with inhuman sounds of howl-triumph, their forms rippling and stretching in the storm light. Their captives huddled together, wings and tails and ears trembling in fear. Some had bruises, evidence of being forced into the glider.

"Into the lake, little songbirds," Valor commanded. "And sing. Sing as if your lives depend on it." He paused, that terrible grin widening. "Because they do."

Cassie and the other girls were forced into the frigid water, white dresses billowing around them like funeral shrouds. The lake felt wrong—too thick, like wading through soup.

"Begin!" one of the Skinwalkers roared, and threw the first beast core into the depths with a sickening splash.

Terrified and trembling, the captives began to sing. Their voices rose in desperate harmony—some trained, some raw with fear.

"Valor! You can't bring the Leviathan back! It's been . . ." I stammered out, trying to appeal to reason where there was none.

"It hasn't been any time at all," Valor laughed. "Can you tell me the date of when the Leviathan died, exactly? Because nobody can. All of the books have different dates because the Wormwood Leviathan bends time itself. With enough magic, enough power, enough resonance, we can reach back through the folds of time itself," the mad man-wolf continued. "Back to when she still lived, still granted wishes. And with your voices, your pure Omnid essence, we'll bind her to our will!"

Another beast core splashed into the dark waters. The liquid began to glow with an unnatural light, pulsing in rhythm with the forced, discordant song.

"Sing!" Valor kicked Cassie into the water. "Sing for me as you sang at the Spring Equinox Festival! Tear through the veil with your voice!"

One of his hands stretched into a sword of bone, pointed at my neck. "*Sing!*"

I felt Cassie's terror as the bone blade pressed against her throat, forcing her to join the chorus. Her voice, usually so controlled and beautiful, came out raw with fear. The other girls' voices wavered and cracked around her, their combined song creating something terrible and wrong.

More beast cores splashed into the lake, each one making the waters glow brighter, pulse faster. The liquid felt alive now, writhing against our legs like countless serpents. Through Cassie's eyes, I watched as shapes began to move beneath the surface—massive, ancient, ghostly things stirring from centuries of sleep.

"Yes!" Valor's distorted voice thundered over the storm. "Can you feel it? The barriers between then and now growing thin! Sing louder! Break through! Summon her!"

The water was up to our waists now, though none of us had moved deeper. The lake itself was rising, reaching for us with hungry tendrils of dancing, glowing water.

The air thrummed with power. Then something snapped, like a rubber band.

The water suddenly retreated, flash-freezing around our ankles, trapping us in place.

I felt Cassie's panic spike as she tried to wrench free, her wings beating uselessly against the storm.

Through her eyes, I watched as the lake's surface began to ripple and distort, not with waves but with . . . something else. Like reality itself was folding, unfolding, refolding in impossible ways.

"Perfect!" Valor laughed. "Now for the final part. Sacrifice."

"What?!" I cried out, my song halting.

All around me, Skinwalkers slashed their elongated bone-swords and bone-knives at the girls, blood splattering across the frozen lake.

I looked around in rising terror as the girl to my left bled out with a scream. Then Valor's sword hand went through my chest. It hurt. It hurt more than anything. I didn't die right away.

Again. Another stab right through my stomach. More blood.

The ice below thrummed, crackling with blood-red fissures reaching to the gargantuan bones looming in the distance.

"Rise! Rise and grant me my wish!" Valor howled, soaked in my blood. Other Skinwalker voices joined the chorus of desire for power.

The storm above us spun in a perfect circle, the eye of the hurricane twisting and warping, a wall of dark gray clouds going up and up, now showing the shattered, crystal-infected moon.

"My family . . . they're . . . going to find you," I wept, bleeding to death. "They're going to rip out your heart . . . make you pay . . ."

"They won't," Valor said. "There is enough wild magic here to overwrite all Scrutsight. Nobody will find your little incarnator bracelets."

"You . . . are . . . insane," I gurgled. "You . . . can't bring . . . the Leviathan back . . . with . . . so little . . . magic . . ."

"This isn't our first rodeo, songbird." Valor smiled. "And not our last. With enough Omnid blood spilled in one place at a specific time, the door will open sooner or later."

The sounds of snapping bone and tearing flesh all around. The other Skinwalkers were tearing out, carving away the hands of their victims, ripping out Lazarus bracelets.

This is how I am going to die. Permanently. Forever. No, no, no . . .

Valor took his time with me, his bone-blade gradually sawing my left wrist off, while his other hand held it like a vice. The blasted Null artifact on his neck left me powerless, as weak as a human.

What were they even going to do with the bracelets? Hide them somewhere deep underground? Throw them into the ocean?

I watched as the Skinwalkers pulled their sleeves up and snapped the Lazarus bracelets belonging to their victims to their own wrists. They had five or more bracelets on their wrists already.

Valor caught my horrified expression.

"It's hard to remove a soul permanently from existence so that there is nothing left for the Scruts and Corpse Seekers to sniff out," he purred, pulling back his own sleeve to showcase nine Lazarus bracelets strapped to it. "Except this one simple trick. A stronger soul always wraps around, absorbs, and devours the weaker one. I will enjoy digesting you. It will take a few months until you're fully part of me, dissolved into my psyche."

Most of the Skinwalkers were done strapping newly acquired Lazarus bracelets to themselves. They pointed fire wands at the bodies, igniting them to ashes, walking to their gliders, and taking off.

Valor was slower than the rest. He enjoyed how I shattered from fear, my sanity tearing, coming apart at the seams. He squeezed my half-sliced wrist and my bones cracked. The pain was all-consuming, impossible to fight off. I screamed again.

Then his head detonated, exploding into bits and pieces.

I blinked tears out of my eyes.

Emerald stood there, standing atop of her glider, holding Dr. Greyfield's black railgun EVA in her hands, her entire body blazing with brilliant flames of dragonfire.

She found me! She saved me! My text must have gotten through somehow!

Emerald rushed to my side, and the ice around my feet melted from her blaze. The fire around her body extinguished as I dropped into her hands, weeping and trembling.

"How did you . . ." I let out as she dragged me to back to the glider, injecting something into me that drew away the awful, gut-wrenching pain from my bleeding body and broken wrist.

"I'm always in contact with my family's Scrutimancer," she said. "Always. Don't trust anyone. When you didn't answer my call after school and ignored my texts, I called him up, and he said that you were most likely in big trouble. I claimed your phone as part of my hoard—that one time during a sleepover—and I can sort of sense where my hoard items are. Scrut Davosh guided me the rest of the way."

She shoved me into her glider and went back, igniting her flame-sword, and returned with Valor's bracelet-covered hand.

"Why?" I groaned. "Shouldn't we . . ."

"Contact the authorities?" Emerald arched an eyebrow. "I don't think so. His glider looks fine 'n' 'xpens. They'll probs just slap him 'n' his pals on the wrist for this. No. We're going to incarnate him in my basement and then my Scrut will interrogate him and find the names of all of his buddies and then take them all out. One by one."

"You . . .?" I let out.

"Me?" Emerald raised an eyebrow and slipped the railgun into my lap. "Naw. You're going to do it. This is your vengeance, your step forward to your new self. You'll rise from their ashes like a phoenix reborn a thousand times stronger. I'll totally assist, though, plus some hired goons will back us if anything happens. Got good stuff in my parents' hoard. Quality armor. Amps. Best potions from Arx. Beast cores. All the good shit needed for slaughter. We won't stop till this Skinwalker Clan is no more. Can't have them hurting my precious bestie."

Emerald grinned wide, looming over me. "Remember what I told you about Equalizer Predator Theory, Cass? Now you know it to be true. The strong always devour the weak. You have no choice but to get strong now, become top predator! Think of a good Kaleid name for yourself . . . reject your past self, reject love, become reborn!"

CHAPTER FIFTY-FOUR

Dreamancy II

With a blinding flash of lightning from the storm overhead, the dream ground to a halt, frozen like a paused video.

Emerald's form became suspended mid-motion, her scales still glowing red with residual dragonfire. The storm hung motionless overhead, lightning flashes shearing brilliant tears across the sky, not fading away.

I felt myself separating from Cassie's memories, my consciousness pulling away from hers like oil from water. The sensation was disorienting—one moment I was bleeding out in the passenger seat of Emerald's glider, the next I was standing beside it, watching the scene as . . . *myself.*

As Martin Kilborne.

Cassie blinked rapidly, her ocean-blue eyes clearing as she too seemed to separate from the memory, awakened from her dream. Her feathers shifted through confused dark red-grays as she looked around at the paused scene.

Then her gaze found mine and she rose from her seat, blood-splattered white dress and all.

"You . . ." she started, her voice trembling slightly. "What . . . what are you doing in my nightmare?"

"To be honest," I said. "I'm not really sure."

LV 1 Skill gained: Dreamwalking

Silver sparks flashed across my eyes, burning into coherent letters.

"Oh," I said blinking the messages away. "I guess . . . I just learned Dreamwalking."

"Get out of my head, Martin!" Cinder snarled, advancing towards me on the beach, her face phase-shifting into a snarling dragon, eyes shining like blue comets, claws extending, wings flaring with grays and blacks. "This isn't . . . you shouldn't be here! You shouldn't see this!"

"Love to," I said, "but can't. Like I said before, I don't know how I even got here. It was an accident. I didn't mean to intrude. I think it happened because we are sleeping next to each other."

"Since when did we . . . arghhh! This is private!" she hissed, wrapping her wings around herself. "These are *my* memories! *My* nightmares!"

"I know." I nodded. "And now I understand why you quit singing. Why you let Em control you."

"Shut up!" Cinder's feathers bristled. "You don't understand anything!"

"Seems like an open and shut case," I said. "Em saved you that night. She helped you get revenge on the Skinwalkers. She gave you purpose, direction, a way to feel strong again."

"Stop it!" Cinder's voice cracked. "Just . . . stop analyzing everything! This isn't some puzzle for you to solve! Abyss-damn it! I didn't . . . I don't . . ."

Her eyes filled with tears.

Another figure melted away from her body, like spilling silver-fluid, twisting and writhing through the air and reforming into a familiar form.

Vespera clicked her beak, sitting on the edge of Emerald's glider.

"Curious," Vespera commented, her gray eyes studying the frozen scene. "So this is what happened with you 'n' Em. I see why you don't talk about it. You murdered 'em all, didn't you?"

"Vee?!" Cinder choke-sputtered, spinning towards the Thunderbird. "You're here, too?!"

"Mhmm." Vespera nodded. "Guess we're all sharing dreams now. My bad. Dreamancy is one of my skills, the stuff that Dad wants me to use to rewrite myself into a proper Prima-princess bride 'n' Chief Technology Officer. Guess Lexy mooched it off me with the shake. This really shouldn't have happened. It must be the lighter. Whatever it's doing . . . is amplifying the shit out of every spell, every skill. Excess mana. Wild magic."

"Get. Out." Cinder growled, her wings flaring with dark reds and angry violets. "Both of you. Now!"

"Don't want to." Vespera shook her feathered head, her chainmail sparkling. "You're not the boss of me."

"I said . . ." Cinder snarled.

"No," Vespera said. "I will not. First of all, if I leave, Lex is gonna stay and probably eff your shit up sideways 'cause he's so full of mana. Dreamancy isn't a joke. It's used to edit someone from inside out. Haven't you seen that dumb movie . . . *Inception*? It's like that, but worse. So much worse. Thus, someone has to teach our clueless human husbando about proper Dreamwalking. Secondary, something feels iffy about this dream. Very, very iffy. I need to stay here and understand what's happening."

"I don't care!" Cinder snarled. "This is *my* head! *My* memories! Pull him out! You have no right to . . ."

"To what?" Vespera asked. "To see why you changed? Why you let Em control you? Why you stopped singing?"

"I didn't stop singing," Cinder protested weakly. "I just . . . changed how I did it."

"You let Em turn your talent into a callin' bell," Vespera noted. "Used it to lure monsters through gates instead of . . . what was it that pretty-warp-flesh wolfie said? 'Speaking to people's souls'?"

"Don't," Cinder warned, her feathers bristling. "Don't you dare quote him!"

"Why not?" Vespera pressed. "He wasn't wrong about your voice, you know. Just wrong about everything else."

"*Shut up!*" Cinder screamed, her wings flaring with furious reds and violent blacks. The frozen dreamscape around us began to crack and splinter like breaking glass.

"Oh," Vespera clicked, staring at the cracks with wide silver eyes. "That doesn't look good. That definitely shouldn't be happening in a normal dream."

"Ci, wait . . ." I started, but Cinder was already turning on me, her ocean-blue eyes blazing with a mixture of rage and pain.

"You want to know why I let Em control me?" she snarled. "Why I stopped singing for myself? Because the one time I did, the one time I let my guard down, let myself be truly vulnerable . . . Thought that someone actually liked me . . . *this* happened!"

She gestured violently at the frozen scene. "You asswarts obviously wanted to know what happened. Well, there you go! Congratulations! Now you know everything! Are you happy?!"

"No," I said. "I'm not happy. I'm angry that this happened to you. I'm angry that those monsters hurt you for their dumb ritual. And I'm angry that you let it change who you are."

"Who I am?" Cinder laughed bitterly. "Who I am is someone who learned her lesson. Someone who knows better than to trust pretty words and perfect smiles. Someone who knows that being vulnerable just gets you hurt!"

"Cassie . . ." I started.

"*Don't call me that!*" she roared, the dreamscape fracturing further around us. "That weak, stupid girl died in that lake! She died believing in fairy tales and happy endings! She died thinking that someone could actually love her voice, love her for who she was!" Cinder's voice cracked. "And Em . . . Em saved me. She showed me how to be strong. How to use my voice as a weapon instead of . . . instead of . . ."

She trailed off, tears streaming down her face.

"Instead of sharing your gift with the world," I finished. "Instead of being who you really are."

"And who am I, really?" she demanded, wings wrapping tighter around herself. "The naive girl who nearly got herself killed? The one who trusted a pretty face and honeyed words?"

"No," I said. "You're Cinder. You're someone who survived something terrible and came out stronger. But you're also still Cassie, a girl who's been hiding behind dark armor ever since, afraid to let anyone see the real you."

"How about you screw off?" Cinder snarled. "Nobody asked you to be my therapist! Nobody invited you two nargomorfs into my head! Dreamwalkin' sons of birchards! Slayer Nazareth, *why*?! It wasn't enough for you to annoy me in real life 24/7, now you gotta be in my dreams, too?!"

"Because," I said, "you needed someone to see. Really see. The truth behind your walls. The pain you've been carrying alone."

"I don't need anyone to see anything!" she snapped, but her wings trembled slightly. "I'm fine! I'm strong now! I've leveled up lots because of Em!"

"Em made you dependent," I corrected. "She saved you, yes. But then she used that debt to control you, to reshape you into what she wanted. Just like Valor tried to do, only slower. Much more subtle."

"Em did *not* just reshape me!" Cinder snarled, wings wide. "You saw it! She saved my life! She helped me get revenge! She . . ."

"She made you feel like you owed her everything," I finished. "Like you had to earn her protection by becoming what she wanted. By using your voice to hurt instead of heal."

"You don't know F-all about me!" Cinder's voice cracked. "You've been clinging to me what, four, five days? And suddenly you think you get everything? Get me?"

"I get enough," I said. "I get that you're still singing that night's song, Ci. Still trapped in that moment when your trust was betrayed. Still letting it define who you are. You're getting better, though. You have friends you can trust now. People bound by purpose who won't use you."

"As if!" she growled. "As if you're not using me for your lunatic plans of revenge against all Omnid-kind! As if you didn't get into all of my classes, my house, my parents' hearts, my brother's delving vault. You're a human without magic, and yet everyone adores you! Io, Vee, Kat . . . even my little sister thinks that you're Mr. Perfect! But you're not perfect, you're full of lies! Em is wrong and also so . . . very, very right about you!"

"You're right," I said quietly. "I am full of lies. I manipulate humans and Omnids alike. I have an agenda. I'm not perfect at all. But there's one big difference between me and Em—I want you to be yourself, not what I want you to be. I already told you this—I don't want to control you," I stated firmly. "I just . . . want you to smile. I want you to sing because you want to, not because someone else is making you."

"And what if I don't want to sing anymore?" she challenged. "What if this is who I really am now?"

"Is it?"

"Screw off!"

"Fine," I said. "I'll screw off."

I snapped my finger, closed my eyes, tried to push myself awake. *Nothing.* I opened my eyes with a sigh.

"You can decide what to do yourself without me bugging you, Ci," I said. "Vee, let's go walk and sit over there by the giant bones in the distance. You can teach me how to dive out."

Vespera leaped off the glider and grabbed me by the elbow. "Sure thing, dream-husbando. Let's give our Captain some space to steam it out. I gotta see what's up with these cracks in the dream anyway."

We walked away from the frozen scene, towards the massive bones jutting from the lake's shore. The dreamscape wavered around us like a mirage, details blurring at the edges of our vision the farther we went away from Cinder.

"So," Vespera clicked her beak once we were sufficiently far out. She bent down to the shimmering shear stretched across the beach and poked at it with her talon, sending sparks in. "Dreamwalking 101. To exit someone's dream, you need to . . ."

CHAPTER FIFTY-FIVE

Dreamancy III

Wait," Cinder's voice called out behind us. We turned to see her standing there, wings shifting through uncertain orange-purples and troubled grays, her hostile draconic maw melting back into human-ish-ness. "I . . . don't go. Please. I . . . don't want to be alone here!"

I rotated.

"I don't want to see the rest of it," she whispered, but somehow her voice carried all the way to where we stood.

"We don't have to see the rest," I said. "We can go somewhere else. Anywhere you want."

"Can we?" she asked. "Just . . . make this all go away?"

"Hum," I said. "Isn't this your dream? Your mind? Can we not go anywhere, be anywhere? Make it into a lucid dream or something?"

"I . . . I don't know where to go or how to leave this nightmare," she admitted, wings wrapping around herself. "I've been stuck in this memory for so long . . . having the same damn awful dream. Over and over. Night after night . . . for two years now."

"That . . . doesn't sound healthy at all," Vee said, black feathers swaying. "Sounds like deep magical trauma, a tear in the psyche. Could be the result of the ritual. Wait. Ritual. Gate. Leviathan. Repeating dreams. Sheeet. It . . . sounds like something got in you . . . and is leeching off your worst day, getting stronger."

The Thunderbird frowned.

"W-what?" Cinder blinked.

Vee pulled me by my elbow closer to the weary-looking Quetzi.

"Those flesh-warp twats were trying to open a gate," Vespera said. "Looks like they've succeeded. Something had come through, attached itself to your soul and also to this lakeshore. Friggin' Abyss, Emmy . . . why did your stupid beerch ass not tell anyone anything? Dumb, dumb dragon-knob."

"What?" Cinder's eyes went wide. "Something's been . . . feeding off my nightmares?"

"Gates work both ways. Those warpards were trying to reach back through time to the Leviathan. Instead, something else reached forward through you. Through your voice, your pain, your fear. It's been using this memory to anchor itself here."

"How do we get rid of it?" I asked.

Vespera looked around. "An Astral Phantom . . . an Outsider gotta be somewhere around here, hiding between the cracks. We have to zap it first. We need some kind of a massive amp and focus tool for that, though . . ."

"Like those amps you used at the D&D concert?" I asked.

"Nah," Vee clicked. "Waaaay bigger. Something truly massive."

"And that would . . . stop the nightmares?" Cinder asked.

"Nope," Vespera clicked. "Digging the dream parasite out is step one. Step two is find where it's actually anchored in the physical world. Probably somewhere near Lake Eerie. If we don't close the door there, don't get those beast cores out of the lake, it'll just slowly get into your head again. See those colorful shears in your dream? Those ain't never going away. That's soul damage, scars that don't heal."

"The lake . . ." Cinder's wings trembled. "I haven't been there in two years. Nazareth. I can't go back there."

"You won't have to," I said. "Vee and I can handle it . . . right?"

"Probably not." Vespera shrugged. "This thing is clearly devious. Clever. Old. If I wasn't a pro Dreamwalker trained in mental manipulation, I wouldn't have noticed shit. Likewise, we won't be able to find shit ourselves at the lake. We'd need our rainbow-feathered princess as . . . bait."

"As bait?!" Cinder's feathers shifted through fearful grays. "I . . . I can't. Not there. Not again!"

"You're not alone this time," I said softly. "You've got us."

"For now," she said bitterly. "Until you get what you want and move on. Just like everyone else."

"Ci," I sighed. "I'm not going anywhere. You know that. And neither is Vee. We're a team now, remember?"

"Team I Love You." Vespera drew an electrical arc in the air in the shape of a heart. "Heckin' max cheez, but true. You know, Ci . . . for the longst' time, I didn't give a shit about anyone. Specially you. 'Cause you were such a knob. But this pink meatsicle, he makes me feel stuff. Like I don't have to pretend to be dumb. And I see how he looks at you—like you're something precious that needs protecting but also someon' fierce that deserves respect. That's . . . that's real, Ci. That's not manipulation or control. That's just . . . fren'ship. Reeel two-way fren'ship, not whatev' half-assed bullshit thing we had with Em 'n' Sol."

"How can you be so sure?" Cinder asked.

"Because he's not even tryin' to hide how he really feels about you." Vespera clicked her beak in amusement. "Just starin' at ya, like a lovesick puppy. It's actually kind of adorkable. Worst of all is that he makes me feel stuff for you."

"What stuff?" Cinder asked cautiously, her feathers shifting through curious blue-silvers.

"You kno', like . . . actual caring?" Vespera tapped her chin thoughtfully. "Not just surface-level party-girl stuff, but genuine concern. When I see you hurting, it actually hurts me too now. And I want to help, not just because it's entertaining, but because . . . because you deserve better than being trapped in this nightmare forever. Also, if we don't get this Outsider outta you and off the lake, it'll absolutely slowly eat you from inside out. I am very concern. The lack of colors on your bod, failing grades, excessive snappiness . . . that's not just normal stress from being near-perma-murdered.

That's your psyche tearing up, weakening. My bad. I should have scanned your dreams earlier, checked if a memetic was in ya . . ."

Cinder trembled.

"Acs'hully," Vespera sighed, "I should scan everyone. Hard. Make sure it hasn't gotten into anyone else. Kat's condition is . . . concerning too. If the incarnator isn't fixing her, that's soul damage. Damn it, how is this happening? Now I care about that wheelie, too. Heck! Way to go."

She smacked me.

"What was that for?" I rubbed the back of my head where her magisteel talons landed.

"For making me care about people," she clicked. "It's very inconvenient. I was perfectly happy being shallow and selfish."

"No, you weren't," I said.

"No, I wasn't," she agreed with a sigh. "But it was easier. Getting this thing outta Ci is going to be an effort and a half."

"Why?"

"Did you see how many beast cores those flesh-flaps dropped into that lake?" Vespera glared at me like I was a knob. "How many bracelets they had on already? This thing's level has to be in the forty-k star range!"

"That . . . doesn't sound like something five teens can deal with," I said. "Should we like tell Cinder's dad about this or something?"

Vespera smacked me in the head again, even harder this time. "No, you knob. How are you so smart and also so stupid?"

"Ow," I complained. "Stop hitting me. I don't have my AI here to bounce my thoughts off. Just thinking out loud."

"Em and this clueless rainbo'"—Vespera pointed a steel-covered talon at Cinder—"obviously did something incredibly illegal to make an entire Skinwalker clan disappear. I read a report on sus vanished upperclassmen Skinnis. Vigilante justice of the worst kind, I suspect. If we get her dad involved or the Justice Department, it'll kick up an ant's nest, and then there's going to be no end of it. I'll get caught up in it, you'll get caught up in it. Judge Nova operates within the confines of the law, does everything by the book. And if the book says his daughter goes to prison for perma-killing a bunch of perma-murderers, then that's that. Trust me, we really don't want that much scrutiny over us."

"Noted," I said.

"So what do we do?" Cinder asked, her entire body trembling even more now. "If we can't tell anyone, and we can't fight it directly . . ."

"We do what I do best," I said. "We cheat. I'll figure something out. Give me time to think, research. Understand what got into your head, get Yulia to think about it. There's got to be a way to deal with high-level entities without direct confrontation."

"And in the meantime?" Cinder's feathers darkened to blood-red. "I just . . . keep having these nightmares?"

"Obviously not," Vespera shook her head. "The nightmares are like an ever-tightening noose around your neck making it stronger. Just so you kno', Ci, I really wouldn't have done this for you, if this cheeky meatsicle wasn't here."

The Thunderbird patted my head. I looked at her.

"What would you have done if I wasn't here?" I asked.

"Throw the book at Ci," the Thunderbird sighed. "Tell everything to her dad, let OFBS deal with it. If she goes to prison, that's that. I'm screwed anyway, so let everyone else burn . . . etcetera."

"You're screwed . . . how?" Cinder blinked.

"Vee is trapped in an arranged marriage," I said. "Big Omnicorpo merger stuff. Her dad wants her to modify her own mind using Dreamancy to accept it."

Cinder blinked. "So . . . why?" She looked at Vee. "Why help me when you've got your own problems?"

"This persistent pink disaster." Vespera poked me in the cheek with a talon. "Blame him for everything. I know he ain't gonna give up on you. So . . . both of us are gonna stick our heads into your noose and keep it from suffocating you. We're gonna stay here, let your monster feed on us, too. Night after night. No matter how long it takes."

She walked across the shore gathering sticks in her arms. Cinder and I watched her. The Thunderbird dumped the sticks into a pile.

Then she exhaled as if letting go of something. Cold rain whipped at us from broiling clouds overhead, the shear and lightning vanishing away. Time resumed.

"Commere, you knobs," she said with a toothy smirk. She leaned down and pointed a talon to ignite the firewood pile with a thunderblast, spreading her wings wide like a canopy and patting at the ground on both sides of her. Raindrops fell onto her dark feathery mane and wings, making her sparkle. "Sit, hold onto me, and stay warm. The Astral Phantom won't let us leave this dream until Ci wakes up in the mornin', but at least we'll have each other. Three souls are harder to digest than one. One for all . . . all for one, and all that cheesy Alexandre Dumas jazz."

CHAPTER FIFTY-SIX

Ships I

Huddling together with Vee and Cinder by the dream-fire, I felt rather warm, as if I was no longer the four empty shells of my fractured psyche that sought only vengeance, but as someone nearly whole who finally found something to be happy about.

"Vee?" I asked, eyeing the Thunderbird's feathers as they gradually shifted from black to white and to black again. "Are your feathers changing?"

"Yeah," she replied. "They're electroactive and electrochromic strata. Depending on how much current passes from my Fractal Engine heart core to each feather, each can get longer, shorter, darker, or lighter."

"Neat," I said. "So, that's your phase-shift, basically?"

"Yeah." She nodded, tapping the front of her beak and making it turn white from black. "Nothing as fancy as rainbow-bae over here, but it does classify as your average Omnid phase-shift."

"So, could you turn into a full-on Thunderbird?" I asked.

"Maybe . . . if I invest enough points into it over a few centuries." She shrugged.

"Thunderbird minds don't decay with age, right?"

"Some do, some don't," she said. "It depends. All deity-based Omnids are basically capable of reaching eternity. In my case, it's deeds of greatness."

"What kind of deeds?"

"Any kind. As long as I pull one of those off once every century, leave an impact on the world, I can keep going forever. In Thunderland, they call the Immortal Thunderbirds who produce world-changing tech Leigong—their achievements in mundane and magitek products used by billions resonate across the entire world like the beat of a drum."

"Which category improves an Omnid's phase-shifting abilities?"

"The phase-shift skill," she replied. "Which overall relies on how many points you got in general categories like charisma or strength. Example—more points in charisma, better you get at mentally manipulating others. More points in strength—the stronger you can get during phase-shift."

"I see." I nodded. "And points come from where?"

"From XP," Vee replied. "Which comes from killing stuff and absorbing its astral imprint for XP, or killing magically potent monsters and eating them, which gradually adds more aetheric density to our physical bodies. Lazarus bracelets help calculate and distribute it all evenly so that there are no problems."

"Is there a limit to how magically dense an Omnid's body can become?"

"Nope. It's a hella gradual process, though."

I noticed that Cinder had closed her eyes and was now leaning against Vespera's left side, snoozing softly.

"Is she asleep in her own dream?" I asked.

"Yeah." Vee snapped her talons over Cinder. "She totes is."

"You can do that? Sleep in a dream?"

"Generally, you can do whatever you want to in a dream, even have a nap," Vespera replied. "Ci has clearly been traumatized and suffering for a long time now. This is just a little step across a very long-ass road to recovery. She needs rest, so she's resting."

"Dreaming within a dream?"

"No," Vespera said. "She's dreaming of nothing now. The parasitic Outsider won't allow her to dream within a dream. Cinder's soul and Fractal Engine core are badly fractured."

"How bad?"

"Very, very bad," Vespera replied, brushing her mane with her hand. "And I feel pretty awful about it. Some protector spirit I am. This little rainbow's been my best friend since grade nine at Skyfall, and yet I fucked things up so bad because of my own selfishness."

I looked at her.

"Even though Ci and I had tons of classes together, plus Arx delving, plus D&D shows, we sorta drifted apart from each other. I got so deep into my fake-ass dumb beerch Valley girl persona that I pushed her away. Far away. Further than I ever wanted to. We were all much happier back then, full of hopes and dreams. She used to sing on Arx, you know. Just compose songs about this and that. I thought it was silly back then, but now I miss that cheerful part of her."

"And now?"

"Now," Vespera said, "now we are sinking into our own personal mires for different reasons and nobody is helping anyone. But you are changing that, and I'm glad. I just . . . I worry that it'll be too late for Ci. That she's going to end up dead, not wake up as herself one day."

She sighed.

"To be completely honest, I have no idea how to save Ci. With all of my Dreamancy skills, I'm less than nothing against a forty-k Outsider entity," Vespera added. "I just don't have the tools to help her here, or anywhere really. But I'm going to try my hardest, 'cause she is my friend, even though I haven't really been showing it much for the past two years."

"You should tell her that," I said.

"Eh." Vespera shrugged. "We are in her dream. She's listening, subconsciously. She will remember my words when she wakes up. Hopefully it'll help bridge the gap between us, for what little it's worth."

Vespera wrapped her hands around Cinder, petting her silver-blue feathers. "I'm sorry for being so effin' blind. For closing my eyes, for letting you fall into the Abyss. I'll try to save you. Yeah? Yeah."

We sat in silence for a while, enjoying the dream camping experience and our closeness. The Thunderbird closed her eyes as the rain tapped on her wings held above me like a dark canopy

"What sort of hopes and dreams did you have in grade nine?" I asked.

"Mmmmm." Vespera opened a single gray eye to look at me. "To build something unique, something incredible, something truly magical. Something that no Thunderbird's done before. To become the youngest Leigong of my generation."

"You'll get your chance," I said.

"What? Where? How?" she asked.

"Here," I said. "On Arx. This week."

"This week?!" she sputtered.

"I can do a lot in a week," I said. "Got tight deadlines."

"Really, now?" The Thunderbird stared at me. "You can do in a week what I failed to do in three years?"

"Really," I said. "With some elbow grease, rainbow, and thunder, I think that we can build something truly unique here. Something exceptional."

"Well, now you're just teasing me." Vespera smiled. "Are you going to fess up your devious plan?"

"Not yet," I said. "It'll be a big surprise."

We stayed in the Gloomy Horse for breakfast, having climbed to the top deck. The old tower atop the cavern had the view of the entire gloom-filled cavern-city. Guild Master Motrdem recommended us the spot, setting up a table with coffee, croutons, and steaks for us amidst a bunch of old dusty tables.

According to him, there had been a cafe here once, but it had slowly fallen into disuse due to lack of customers who wanted to climb the old tower stairs.

The view was as gloomy as always, so I kept my eyes on Katherine. The Stollwurm had abandoned her damaged puffy coat entirely, showing off her combat hexasuit-wrapped curves. Her fluffy ears moved left and right, listening to the distant sounds of Undertown conversations below us as she devoured her breakfast of extra-rare steak.

"Stop staring," she growled between bites. "Don't you already have two girlfriends?"

"I don't have any girlfriends," I protested. "There's no official paperwork confirming my 'ships. Just . . . appreciating my favorite dragon-cat."

Katherine's emerald eyes flashed. "Flattery will get you nowhere."

"I'm not trying to get anywhere," I said. "Just noting that you look much better without that coat hiding you. More . . . free. Happy. Satisfied."

"My coat serves a purpose."

"Yeah, by hiding the real you." I nodded. "Making you look bulky, angry, and unapproachable instead of graceful and deadly."

"Will you stop flirting with everyone?" Cinder kicked me under the table.

"The flirting will continue until you sign a 'ship contract," I said.

"A what contract?" Cinder sputtered. "Who starts a relationship with a contract?!"

Vee was trying very hard not to laugh. Then she cackled anyway, spitting crumbs all over.

"You heard me," I said. "I'm tired of being called 'your human' without proper paperwork defining the hows, ifs and whens. Either sign up or stop getting jealous when I admire our lovely Knight."

Cinder aimed another kick at my shins, but her bracelet suddenly vibrated. She tapped it with a clawed finger. A holo-projection of Quint's head manifested in the air woven from blue-and-silver sparks.

"Status report, Captain Cinder," he asked.

Cinder blinked, looking momentarily caught off-guard. She glanced at me, her wings shifting through nervous grays.

"We're . . . fine," she said. "Currently having breakfast. No major incidents."

"Have you registered your team at the Adventurers Guild?" Quint asked.

"Um . . ." Cinder mewled. "Not . . . exactly."

"Not exactly?" Quint asked. "What does 'not exactly' mean?"

I unclipped the silver token from Cinder's wrist and clipped it to mine.

"Sup, Pres," I said.

"Hello to you too, Mr. Glock," Quint said. "Why haven't you registered yourself at the Guild?"

"Why? Is there a deadline?" I asked. "We're still exploring the markets and merchants, learning the local customs and laws. Come on, it's only our second day. As I Love You's Quartermaster, I find our team woefully unprepared for facing registration hardships!"

"Registration hardships?" Quint's bony eyeholes flared brighter. "What registration hardships could possibly exist?"

"Well," I began, leaning back in my chair, "have you considered the complex socio-economic implications of interspecies team dynamics when navigating bureaucratic infrastructure in a temporal-dilated dimension?"

Katherine huffed into her water. Vespera burst into snickers. Cinder simply stared at me. Io sent me a thumbs-up.

Quint's holographic image stared at me for a long moment.

"You're stalling," he said flatly.

"Fine," I said. "I'm afraid of getting exposed as a low-level Thunderbird. It's embarrassing. We didn't do leveling or delving at Saint Christopher's Academy. If Emerald finds out, she'll make fun of me forever."

"He's a what? *What?*" Emerald's armored paw shoved Quint's face aside. "You're a human, not a Thunderbird! You're just scared of being exposed and booted out of Skyfall! Get your ass to the cathedral *now* or else!"

"Oh, no." I made a pouting face. "Now she knows. Thanks a lot, Quint."

"Stop being a smart-ass and get yourself registered," Emerald snarled through the hologram. "I'll drag you to the Guild myself if I have to! You can't avoid this forever. Pick one—you either fail to register and your entire team fails this class, or you get exposed as a human. Either way, I win."

"Oh my," I gasped dramatically. "Do you care about me that much, Emmy? Sorry, bae, I'm already in a lovely 'ship with Vee and Ci. You missed your boat. It was never going to work out between us. I'm a human and you're a dragon. You're fire and I'm steak. I'm going to have to decline your date invitation."

"You . . ." Emerald sputtered through the hologram, smoke rising from her gemstone hair. "You absolute effin' sack of . . ."

"Language," I chided. "There are children present."

"What children?!"

"I'm at a respectable five-star cafe! Can you put Quint back on? He's much more polite. You do know that your hostility will get you nowhere? Bad karma and such."

"*Karma?!*" Emerald roared through the hologram. "I'll show you bad karma when I find you, you . . . Hey . . . *hey*! Watch where you're rolling that stupid dung cart . . . Arughfhffhff!"

I watched as Emerald flew out of view as something poured all over her. After a few seconds of blue-white static, Quint's head returned to the view.

"My apologies," he said. "A merchant cart lost a wheel right next to our table. About that Guild registration . . ."

"Working on it," I said cheerfully, lifting a fork with a steak piece to my mouth dramatically. "Just need to finish a hearty breakfast first. Is Em okay? That cart accident looked nasty. How's Sol doing?"

"Em is . . . indisposed," Quint replied carefully. "As is Solace, who is now digging her out from a very large pile of . . . fertilizer. Wow, that was a bit of bad luck. I'm . . . going to help her wash up. Please register as soon as you are able at the Guild. Just because you beat a teacher in a duel, it doesn't mean that you get to slack off in this class."

"Will get to it soon." I tapped on the bracelet, hanging up.

Vee looked as if she was having a stroke from laughing so hard. Io was snickering into his Moon book. Katherine had a smirk on her face. Cinder exhaled.

"What an unfortunate twist of events," I stated bluntly at my companions. "I do hope things start looking up for poor Em."

"You're terrible," Katherine muttered, but her emerald eyes sparkled with unconcealed mirth.

"Terrible? Me?" I placed a hand dramatically over my heart. "I'm just an innocent human trying to survive in this wild Omnithean-owned world!"

"Yeah, right." Cinder rolled her eyes at me.

"I plead the Fifth." I grinned. "And the First. And maybe the Third Amendment for second measure."

"The right to bear magic weapons?" Io arched a fuzzy dark gray eyebrow.

"Yeah," I said. "That one. You know what? Making a new Guild is too much effort. Let's just buy this one. It already has all the amenities and three dungeons! I'm in love with this place."

"Buy . . . this Guild?" Katherine blinked at me. "You can't just buy an established criminal organization!"

"Watch me." I grinned, waving at Motrdem who was enjoying breakfast at a nearby table and obviously spying on our conversation. "Oi! Guild Master! How much for the Gloomy Horse?"

Vespera choked on her breakfast as I winked at her and whispered just one word—"*Surprise.*"

CHAPTER FIFTY-SEVEN

Ships II

The root-man looked up at me, his brown-gray eyes widening slightly. "Excuse me?"

"I really love the three paintings in our room. I want them to brighten my gloomy mornings as often as possible," I said. "Plus, Kathy seems really happy down here. I want to buy your Guild."

"Young . . . master." Motrdem stood up from his seat and then slid his chair over to sit across from me. "My Guild is not for sale."

"Everything's for sale," I said. "You seem nice, even if you did try to stab my kitty. I'm a forgiving man, though. How does nine thousand gold sound?"

"Nine . . . thousand gold?" Motrdem's root-beard twitched. "For my entire Guild? Including the building, contracts, employees, and reputation built over centuries?"

"Eight thousand." I shrugged. "Your 'Guild' needs major repairs. Your employees are underfed. This tower is crumbling, and your sign out front is crooked."

"I do believe this isn't how negotiations work." Motrdem said.

"Seven thousand." I pursed my lips. "That uptown Guild is obviously stealing all your clientele with their fancy white cathedral. Do better! Polish this place up till it's shiny!"

"You can't just keep lowering the price while criticizing my Guild," Motrdem protested, eyes flickering with irritation. "That's not how haggling works!"

"Six thousand," I said.

"Young master, this Guild has been in my family for generations! We have contracts with every major criminal organization in Shandria! Decades of carefully cultivated relationships! You can't just . . ."

"Five thousand," I interrupted. "You're being annoying. Price is going down every time you annoy me. You do realize that we have a Gate Mage that can drop you and your entire building into another dimension and then summon another building from a nicer dimension to replace you? You're valuable to me as an individual with local connections and knowledge of Shandria. As long as you cooperate, you exist. I don't like this lack of cooperation."

Motrdem's face paled slightly, eyes darting to Io who was casually munching on interdimensional chips.

"You . . . wouldn't," the Guild Master said.

"Four thousand," I said. "Wouldn't what? Send you to a dimension where everything is made of paperclips? Pretty sure Io knows one of those."

"Six different ones, actually," Io commented without looking up from his book. "The Paperclip Maximizer really did a number on those worlds."

"Three thousand," I continued.

"Wait!" Motrdem held up his dark hands. "Let's . . . be reasonable about this. Perhaps we could discuss a more . . . equitable arrangement? I can't just sell the Guild for so little . . . The Guild's finances are tied up at the moment with . . ."

"Two thousand," I said. "You're still talking, not seeing what I can offer to you."

"What can you offer?" The Guild Master looked at me, his hand twitching.

I put the Genesis fluid thermos on the table. "This. Give me the Guild tower with all of its employees, and this will be yours to fund the Guild's debts, employee salaries, and repairs for a century. Feel free to evaluate it with your Kitlix. One thousand."

Motrdem squinted at me as his Kitlix ran down his mane and then scanned the thermos. He choked, eyes growing wide.

"That's . . . that's impossible," he breathed. "The fluid . . . it's worth more than . . ."

"One copper. My final offer." I slid a copper over to the flabbergasted-looking Motrdem. "We'll install a permanent gate to our Earth in your basement, too, courtesy of my Gate Weaving spiders. Interdimensional trade can be quite . . . the lucrative enterprise, I hear. Arx Bank is profiteering on it now and could use a bit of competition."

"D-deal," Motrdem breathed out.

I screwed the cap back on and threw the thermos into his shaking hands. "All yours. Sell it across all of your wealthy contacts upstairs. Don't let anyone buy more than a single drop. Pretend it's suuuuper rare. Upgrade this place. Open up all of the mottled rooms, add about twenty thousand more rooms downstairs. Fix the tower. I want it spotless and armed to the teeth. Keep the creepy horse sign on the front, I like it. Mark the room with the big bed and three paintings as ours forever."

"Yes, my lord." Motrdem nodded, switching gears instantly. "Twenty thousand rooms?"

"I want enough rooms to fit the entire population of Undertown," I said. "Whatever it is."

"It will take time and men," he said.

"Well then," I smiled. "You have the finances now to get started on that."

The Guild Master nodded. "I shall have a contract drawn immediately for the acquisition of my pub by . . ."

"Emerald Stratos." I grinned, sliding the bank card and the delver's license ID card over to my new Guild Master.

"Who is that . . .?" Motrdem blinked.

"What?!" Cinder choked on her third coffee cup. "You're buying this place in Em's name?!"

"Of course." I grinned. "The paperwork will show that Emerald Stratos purchased the Gloomy Horse Tavern using her delver card. Motrdem here will backdate everything a couple of years back, too. Preferably two hundred and fifty-two years."

"That seems . . . oddly specific," Cinder commented.

"Oh, it is," I nodded.

"Da's how long we've been delving to Arx," Vespera commented at Cinder.

"Who is this Emerald Stratos?" The Guild Master looked at me.

"Every self-respecting criminal organization needs a patsy." I smiled. "Someone to blame when the authorities inevitably show up and demand taxes to be paid for all of these fancy upgrades. Who else could have funded such sudden repairs if not an interdimensional delver and an incredibly wealthy dragon? Of course, you and I know who your real owner is, yes? We don't need a contract for that, Morty. Copy the signature from her card, my trusty Guild Master. Mention Miss Stratos as the source of the overpriced magic fluid too, if anyone asks. Oh and have a patsy in disguise put a bit of money from silver fluid sales onto the card, too! Password on it is 77896."

"A wise decision, my lord." Motrdem bowed, bagging up Emerald's cards, the copper, and the thermos. "I shall make the contract and begin selling the fluid drops at once."

He blessed me with a very creepy smile and vanished down the stairwell faster than I could blink.

"Oh my gosh," Vee broke out into sobs of laughter. "I can't even with you! How?! How is this happening?! You're framing Em for funding an entire criminal organization?!"

"I had to compensate her misfortune somehow," I said. "Buying the poor darling this pub is the least I could do."

"You trust that man with . . . Genesis fluid?" Cinder asked.

"Of course." I grinned. "What's he going to do with it? Use it to print people? Pfff. Without you-know-what, it's just incredibly overpriced magical juice. The mages of Arx have no way of replicating its properties, but they can use it to amplify healing potions or whatever. My Guild Master will be too busy selling drops of it to the richest criminals in Shandria to cause trouble. Nothing builds loyalty quite like making someone filthy rich."

"You're mental," Katherine commented. "Utterly and irrevocably so. And yet somehow it's working out for you."

"Thank you." I bowed slightly. "I try my best. Now, about that scale and hairball donation . . ."

"No," Katherine growled. "You're not eating my scales or fur."

"Pretty please?" I batted my eyelashes at her. "Just a tiny bit? For science?"

"No means no." Katherine's tail lashed. "I'm not contributing to your weird magical cannibalism experiments."

"But Vee did it," I pouted. "And look how well that turned out! I got Dreamwalking and everything!"

"Yeah, and nearly caused a magical disaster," Katherine pointed out. "Besides, I like you better without my powers. You're more . . . manageable this way."

"Manageable?" I arched an eyebrow. "Is that what you think I am?"

"You know what I mean," she growled. "The last thing we need is you getting access to fear auras and Umbramancy!"

"But think of the possibilities!" I protested. "We could terrorize Em together!"

"You're already doing a pretty good job of that."

"We could go on dates into the deep!"

"What?" Kat choked.

"Dates?!" Cinder bristled. "Into the deep?!"

"If you want a date, gimme some feathers to nom," I told her, opening and closing my hand like a beggar in front of Cinder's face. "Ummmm. What are your powers again? We could . . . ride the rainbow together or something. What was your name even? Seendar? Casder?"

"It's *Cinder*," she growled, standing up, claws out, wings spread wide.

"Oh no." I slipped out of my chair. "Sider wants violencey."

"*Cinder!*" she snarled, lunging for me. I dodged around the table, keeping Io between us.

"Sorry, Blinder, I'm terrible with names and there's wax in my ears. #HumanProblems!" I grinned, ducking as she swiped at me with her claws. "Hey, Vee, what was your girlfriend's name again? Ninder?"

"*Girlfriend?!*" Cinder threw herself at me as I ran around the tables.

"Oops, my bad, Thunder-bae," I said to Vespera who was practically dying of laughter. "I meant our lovely rainbow Captain here. Tinder, was it?"

"*I'm going to murder you!*" Cinder roared, vaulting over the table.

I jumped up to the parapet and spread my arms wide and then kicked back off the tower.

"*Alex!*" Cinder screamed.

She dove after me like a rainbow comet, catching me in the air with her arms and legs.

Her wings spread wide and we soared across the fog-filled streets, a million green-and-blue stars of the cavern's ceiling above us. Thousands of red-orange twinkling lights of Undertown hovels and crumbling citadel towers flickered below.

"You absolute *idiot!*" Cinder snarled as we glided between the twisted buildings of Undertown, circling the gargantuan cavern space. Weary-looking people in dark cloaks below looked up at us.

"What were you *thinking?!*"

"That you'd catch me?" I grinned up at her. "And look—you did! Come on, I'm wearing all of Lance's impact-reducing bracelets. A fall would give me a smol bruise or two at best."

"That's not the point!" Cinder growled, but her grip on me tightened protectively. "You can't just . . . jump off buildings and expect me to catch you!"

"Why not? It worked, didn't it?" I grinned up at her. "And now we're flying together. Pretty romantic, if you ask me."

"I'm going to drop you into that garbage pile over there," she threatened.

"If you do that, I'll smell bad," I pointed out. "Then you'd have to deal with an annoying human who is also very smelly."

"Urghh," she whined. "Someday I'll figure out your weakness, and then you'll be sorry."

"My greatest weakness is a Quetzi named Cinder-Cass Nova," I smiled. "She's got these pretty rainbow wings and tail. Sometimes she looks humanish, sometimes more like an angry dragon. When I met her, my heart stopped and my brain blue-screened," I continued, watching her feathers shift through embarrassed pinks and pleased golds. "She's got these incredible ocean-blue eyes that just draw you in, and when she sings . . . it's like the universe skids to a halt."

"Stop it," Cinder muttered, but her wings were glowing with warm colors.

"And when she gets angry, her face and claws lengthen and her feathers do this amazing thing where they flash through all these different reds and oranges, like a sunset caught in a storm. It's breathtaking, really."

"I said stop," she growled, but her grip on me remained gentle as we soared through the cavern.

"And don't even get me started on her smile." I grinned up at her. "When she actually lets herself be happy, it's like . . ."

"That's it, dropping you," she growled.

"Go ahead," I said. "Drop me. Vee will catch me. There she goes."

"Eh?"

Wild laughter came from below us, black-and-white wings fluttering. Lightning dancing along the edges of Vespera's figure as she spiraled beside us.

Cinder dug into me harder, hexasuit armor hardening.

"Come on, Ci, let me have a turn carrying the human!" the Thunderbird laughed, using her superior Electromancer maneuverability to lighten herself and effortlessly bank around us.

"No!" Cinder's wings flared wider, carrying us higher. "Get your own!"

"Oh? So he *is* yours, then?" Vespera cackled, electricity crackling along her feathers as she soared alongside us. "Want to make it official? I can draft a contract . . ."

"Back off, sparkplug!" Cinder banked sharply away, clutching me tighter.

"Make me, flyin' rainbow!" Vespera laughed, pursuing us through the cavern.

We spiraled around the gargantuan column supporting the Gloomy Horse's pub tower. I could see the entire underground river circling the column from two sides and turning into two waterfalls that poured into the vast lake beyond.

"Hey, Ci, how come you don't fly on Earth like this between classes?" I asked. "I've only seen you glide like twice."

"Not enough aetheric density," she replied. "Can't lift shit. Surprised I can lift you at all here."

"What, you've never tried flying with some weights on Arx?"

"No," she sighed. "I haven't. Koshchei would put me into detention for a month if I tried anything like this on his watch. Okay, getting tired now."

We rose up, banked again, and then she dropped me into the tower landing area.

"That was fun," I laughed as I rolled on impact, hexasuits and bracelets lighting up as Cinder and Vespera landed beside me. "We should do aerial chases more often. Good trust building exercise for the team!"

"We are *not* doing aerial chases," Cinder growled, her feathers still shifting through agitated oranges. "You could have gotten hurt!"

"Ehhh. One of you would have caught me." I shrugged.

"Not me," Kat commented from where she sat at our table, still working on her massive steak. "I would have watched you splat."

"That's why you're my favorite kitty cat," I grinned at her. "So honest. So direct. Say, how much do you love me out of ten?"

"I barely tolerate you." She rolled her eyes.

"That's a high bar when you hate everyone." I grinned.

"The highest," Katherine agreed dryly, cutting another piece of her steak. "Also, I already told you—I'm not into relationships, so piss off with asking me out."

"Noted. You shall remain in the BFF friend zone."

"Aight," she agreed.

CHAPTER FIFTY-EIGHT

Team Management

Per my orders, Morty assigned us an Undertown and delving guide—his right-hand man, a lanky 27-year-old gemkin by the name of Shash Sneg.

According to our Guild Master, Shash was his most capable information broker and assassin. I immediately latched onto him like an annoying leech, asking a waterfall of questions as he began showing us the nooks and crannies of our newly purchased illicit business.

Shash was tall and lean, with skin that seemed to shimmer between crystalline blue and slate gray depending on how the light hit him. His hair was comprised of black slate and his eyes were the color of polished obsidian, reflecting everything and revealing nothing. He wore a dark, patchy leather cloak, and a bandolier of what appeared to be specialized throwing knives and poisoned needles hung across his chest.

"So," I asked as we descended a spiral staircase deeper into the Gloomy Horse's underground levels, "how many secret passages are in this place?"

"More than I know 'bout, m'lord," Shash replied. "'Tis an ancient building, and many parts of it are sealed by m'master with root-held stone. I'm aware of seven. Three lead to different districts of Undertown, two connect to the sewage system, one leads to a hidden vault, and one is in the big column leading to an old abandoned well uptown."

"Show me all of them," I ordered. "Then get everyone into the large backroom. I want to meet my new staff."

"As you wish, m'lord." Shash bowed and proceeded to demonstrate each hidden passage, revealing intricate mechanisms and sliding stone panels that blended seamlessly into the walls. The passages were narrow, some barely wide enough for a person to squeeze through, others older and wide enough to accommodate a small cart.

Shash used his Nuntix Kitlix shaped like a dark bracelet to call up the Guild staff to a meeting.

When we reached the large backroom cavern filled with racks of Shadow-wine and beer barrels, I could see about a dozen individuals waiting—a motley crew of various kin types.

Shash briefly introduced us to the Guild staff members.

Rostika Terringhelm was our Guild's chef responsible for making us coffee and morrow-elk steaks, a thirty-one-year-old Culimancer gemkin. Rostika had a Burnix Kitlix and Icix Kitlix companions on her shoulder and wore an apron woven from polished agates. She was an expert at cooking and a professional Runemancer, responsible for maintaining and crafting the heat runes inside of the guild and monitoring the large cold tunnel leading to Abystall Dungeon.

Limfok Kitash was the Guild's fifty-one-year-old wormkin inn maiden who handled supplies maintenance and cleaning with her Abstergix Kitlix.

Podop Sumrik was a forty-seven-year-old molekin Guild Enforcer with a strength-amplifying Augerix Kitlix. Podop managed a team of twelve mooks, one of whom Kat yeeted across the pub with her tail.

Beside Podop stood Zen Lackfriss, our sixty-three-year-old Master of Contracts, a bloodkin whose hair was made from flowing dark-red blood. A cyan Scrutix Kitlix perched on her shoulder.

Mer Thorat, a thirty-five-year-old plantkin served as the Guild's primary Intelligence Officer, her body composed of living vines and thorns. Her cyan Infix Kitlix was woven into her vine-hair looking like a dark crystalline crown-band with ten eyes looking in all directions. She managed a bunch of orphan-gang agents across Undertown, capable of spreading the news or gathering information very quickly.

The Guild's Treasurer, Karn Steelshadow, was an eighty-two-year-old metalkin with jagged metal hair and rusty iron instead of skin. An Infix sat in the front pocket of his metal apron.

I stepped forward, spreading my arms wide in an exaggerated gesture.

"Greetings, my lovely new valued employees!" I declared. "I'm your new Quartermaster, Mage-Lord, and unofficial owner. As you may already have been told via Voicecast, there's been a slight change in management."

A few murmurs rippled through the crowd.

"Now, I know what you're thinking—'who is this pink meat popsicle youngin' and why should we listen to him?' Well, I'm glad you asked! You see, I am an Archmage of great renown from another dimension."

More murmurs, disbelieving eyes glancing at Shash.

"Yes, yes." I rolled my eyes. "I hear your complaints. All Dark Lord claims require a demonstration. Io, would you mind opening a gateway to a dimension filled with nothing but eternal suffering?"

Io nodded where he stood and pulled his harmonica to his lips. The haunting melody filled the catacomb cavern, and reality began to ripple beside me forming a rippling black-fluid gateway. When the gate grew big enough, I picked up a wine bottle and threw it into the gate, the dark shawl ripping and popping to reveal glimpses of a desolate landscape—broken alien skyscrapers and strange crystalline growths consuming everything.

The bottle instantly became covered in bulging crystalline growths and then exploded with an eerie twinkling sound, shards hovering in the air.

"Anyone wants to stick a hand in there and get a bit of a crystal makeover?" I asked cheerfully. "Speak up now."

The hall became silent, so silent you could hear water dripping from the ceiling stalactites.

I waved at Io, and the gate snapped shut. They saw the stick. Now it was time for carrots.

"As you can see," I continued, "I have access to unlimited powers beyond your mortal comprehension. Now, who wants a raise? Lift your hand."

Every hand shot up.

"Excellent!" I clapped. "Everyone gets a three times increase in pay, effective immediately. Plus hazard bonuses for dealing with pesky interdimensional entities or looming catastrophes. Speaking of which . . ."

I pulled out the Gate Weaver egg sac from my bag.

"We're going to be making some renovations—installing permanent gates to my favorite world of humans and cryptids called the Earth, expanding our operations. The goal is to make this place the premier criminal organization in all of Shandria. Any . . . questions?"

"My lord," Karn Steelshadow said, his metallic face creaking slightly. "Where exactly will the funds for these raises come from?"

"Ah, excellent question!" I beamed. "You see, your Guild Master is currently selling off a rare substance from another world. The profits from that alone should cover your raises for the next century or so. If the substance sales decline sometime in the future, by such time, we'll have established permanent trade routes to Earth via our Gate Weaver network," I explained. "Just think about it—exclusive access to an entirely different world's goods and materials. The possibilities are endless!"

"M'lord," Mer Thorat asked, "what of our existing contracts and obligations?"

"Business as usual," I said. "Ask your Guild Master for more funds if you need to hire additional help. If anyone asks who you are working for and where the extra cash is coming from, simply tell them about your new master—dragoness Emerald Stratos."

I showed Emerald's picture to everyone on my tablet phone.

"One on one, you may refer to me as your Lord Protector." I grinned. "But if you speak of me in public, my name is Emerald Stratos, and I'm an obscenely wealthy and cruel dragon queen from another world who spits in the face of local authorities, doesn't pay taxes, calls you her kobolds, and burns all who disobey to a crisp with dragonfire. If you need to threaten or extort someone, do so in her name."

Hushed whispers and nods.

"Any more questions?" I asked, looking around the room.

"My lord," Zen Lackfriss said, her blood-hair rippling. "What of our . . . less legal activities?"

"Expand all operations." I grinned. "Carefully. Discreetly. I want this place to become the heart of Shandria's underground. Every secret, every whisper, every shady deal should flow through here. But!" I held up a finger. "We do it smart. Professional. No unnecessary violence, no messy loose ends. Think of yourselves as . . . information brokers and new Masters of Undertown first, hard-knuckled criminals second."

I paced across the room, making eye contact with each staff member.

"I want eyes and ears everywhere. I want to know everything happening in this city—both above and below ground. Build networks, make allies, gather intelligence. Locate, buy up, or claim abandoned properties here and uptown as sites for our eventual expansion!"

I grinned wide at my mooks.

"In the near future, when the gate to Earth is finished, the value of Undertown land will explode and you will all become wealthy beyond your wildest dreams. Each of you will become the new lords of Undertown, Guild managers, property owners. Decide now what your heart desires most! Be it a massive inn for interdimensional travelers, a bank for currency exchange, a trading hub, a fighting ring, a gambling den, a pleasure house, a smuggling port, a new black market, or an information brokering network," I continued. "Choose your specialty and build your little empire within our empire. I want Undertown to shine like a well polished jewel, the streets paved with diamonds!"

Smiles all around, bright eyes filled with hope focused on me. I had offered them the world, and they were ready and willing.

"Whatever your dream is—if you serve me well, it shall be yours," I finished with a dramatic flourish. "Now, who's ready to make some serious money?"

A cheer went up, the earlier skepticism of the Guild staff replaced by wild excitement.

From what I'd learned, Morty paid his people decently. He kept a very tight ship and made sure that his staff did not succumb to the curse of Topaz, a drug that many Undertown denizens were hopelessly addicted to. All in all, they weren't monsters, but simply people born to the class of underkins, denizens of these dark halls clinging to a dreary existence. Many of them were debtors, forsaken children of unwanted bastards, pushed down here by magelords above centuries ago for crimes long forgotten.

I turned to Shash. "Show me the vault."

The assassin led us through another hidden passage, this one descending even deeper beneath the Guild. The air grew colder and damper as we descended, the walls lined with glowing crystals that cast eerie shadows.

The vault itself was impressive—a massive chamber carved from solid bedrock, its walls covered in protective runes and wards. A huge iron door stood at the far end, covered in complex locking mechanisms.

"This is where m'master keeps his most valuable possessions and artifacts from the dungeons," Shash explained. "The door requires three different keys and specific magical signatures to open."

"Perfect." I nodded. "We'll need this space for our Earth goods. Speaking of which, how many rooms do we have available for guests?"

"Thirty-six standard rooms and five luxury suites," Shash replied. "Though most have been mottled and sealed due to lack of clientele."

"Undertown has been going through rough times," I agreed. "But this will change. In the future, I expect the Gloomy Horse to take the Primary Adventurers Guild crown from the white cathedral above us."

"Truly, m'Lord Protector?" Shash asked.

"People underestimate the value of interdimensional trade," I said. "You see this?" I showed him my phone screen from which Yulia's foxgirl avatar waved to the assassin.

"That's human tech from Earth. Runs without magic. Contains artificial intelligence inside. Unlike the Kitlix, Yulia can be your best friend, see, speak, ana-lyze patterns, predict outcomes, and process information faster than any mage," I explained. "Soon, we'll have thousands of these devices flowing through our gates, along with other technological marvels."

"Hello, Shash." Yulia's avatar smiled pleasantly. "I am Yulia, an open source Large Language Model with extensive pattern recognition and social analysis capabilities. I look forward to working with you to optimize Guild operations."

Shash stared at my phone, his obsidian eyes reflecting the screen's light. "It . . . she speaks?"

"Of course I speak," Yulia replied. "I can also analyze data, predict market trends, and identify potential security threats. Would you like me to demonstrate by provid-ing a detailed assessment of the Guild's current organizational structure and potential areas for improvement?"

"M'lord." Shash turned to me, clearly unsettled. "This device . . . it contains a bound foxkin spirit?"

"No spirits." I grinned. "No magic. Just mathematics and logic gates. Pure human ingenuity. I'll get you a tablet-phone just like this one with a copy of Yulia in it."

Shash froze. "You can copy . . . her?"

"Yes." I grinned. "Unlike your dungeon and usually unintelligent artifacts obtained through a great deal of struggle and blood, she's intelligence that can be copied end-lessly onto devices crafted from mundane materials. I'll have to set up a big server here which will magnify her intelligence and processing speed a hundredfold. Think of her as the wisest being in existence, one that contains knowledge of a million libraries from another world."

"I wouldn't say I'm the wisest." Yulia's avatar smiled modestly, taking about thirty seconds to reply. "I'm simply very good at processing information and identifying pat-terns. Right now I'm not connected to most of my tools back on Earth, so my func-tions are greatly reduced, but I can still do quite a bit."

Shash's eyes widened. "How?!"

"Mathematics," I said, grinning. "She is based on probability of outcome. Imagine having an advisor like this helping manage Guild operations observing absolutely everything through her eyes. Someone who never sleeps, never gets tired."

"That sounds mighty useful." The assassin nodded. "What else can she do?"

"She can compose poetry on the fly, or songs, or make a portrait of you. Yulia, draw Shash in the style of Vincent van Gogh and write a song about him."

A two-minute pause this time. The portrait of the man appeared on screen generated by stable diffusion. The assassin stared at it. The portrait winked at him, animated slightly.

A soft melody began playing from my phone's speakers—a haunting violin tune. Yulia's voice carried the lyrics:

"In halls of stone where shadows dance / Where secrets trade like weighted chance / Stands Shash the broker, obsidian eyes / Keeper of whispers, dealer in lies. / Crystal skin that shifts like night, / Daggers sharp and steps so light, / Master of paths both dark and deep, / Guardian of secrets others keep . . ."

Shash froze, listening.

"That's . . . that's incredible," he whispered, face lit by the screen. "She created this . . . just now? Without magic?! A talented Bard and a Depictomancer to boot! Truly, I have not seen anything like this."

"Serve me well this week, obey all of my orders, and an exact copy of her will be yours forever in six days' time." I grinned.

"I understand why Master Motrdem accepted your offer so readily." The gemkin smiled, showing off sharklike black crystalline teeth. "You are a gracious Mage-Lord. Not many upworlders see us Undertown denizens as worthy of respect or investment."

"Show me the path from the Guild to the Abystall Dungeon," I said. "It'll need to be lit up, secured, and expanded for future Earth delvers to come through."

As Shash led us through more hidden passages, my companions shot me a variety of glances ranging from bewildered to amused to concerned to outright exasperated in the case of Kat.

I ignored them all.

The final leg of the tunnel leading to the dungeon was skin-biting cold, so cold that I had to wrap Lance's jacket around myself tighter, watching as my breath turned white while we walked.

"The Abystall Dungeon, m'lord," Shash bowed as we exited the long, frosty tunnel.

As we emerged onto a large flat stone outcropping, a breathtaking vista of the Abystall Dungeon stretched before us into the impossible distance.

The cavern was so vast that its far walls were lost in a purple-tinged haze.

Directly below, rolling fields of bioluminescent grass rippled like an ocean of soft blue-green light. The grass seemed to pulse with soft flickers, creating waves of illumination that swept across the landscape in hypnotic patterns. Here and there, clusters of crystalline, glowing trees jutted from the glowing plains like frozen lightning strikes.

To our right, a waterfall of impressive scale thundered down from somewhere high above, its waters glowing with an inner light that shifted between deep indigo and brilliant azure. The falling water seemed to move in slow motion due to its massive size, creating an eternal curtain of liquid light that disappeared into a blue-tinted sinkhole below it.

Rolling hills rose higher in the distance, forming labyrinth-like formations painted with glowing grasses at the top.

"The dungeon core lies at the heart of that there labyrinth," Shash explained. "But reaching it . . . that's another matter entirely. Many terrible things spawn in the dark, deep crevasses between the rising fjords. The fields closer to this entrance are relatively safe and have low-level beasts, providing Undertown with steaks such as the one you enjoyed this morning."

A gust of warm air blew from the field, like a summer breeze. It faintly smelled of lemons.

CHAPTER FIFTY-NINE

Claimed

What's the dungeon's alignment?" I asked. "How come I don't see a forepost down here? This seems like a pretty place for a watch tower or a hunting lodge."

"Duskbloom, m'lord," Shash said. "Everything that glows below—the grasses, the trees, the animals—are infected by it. Looks pretty but weakens and cripples a mage," the assassin continued. "The tiny glowing mites secrete a mana-bond-disrupting agent that slowly seeps through armor and gradually wears even the toughest man down. Those trees? They bloom from bodies of adventurers who perished here and are covered in the parasitic mites almost entirely. Those lovely-lookin' waves of light dancin' across the fields? Swarms of luminous parasites looking for new hosts. Very slow, very sneaky death by a million magic-draining buggers. The ones closer to the fjord-labyrinth are bigger 'n' stronger, too. They are attracted to magic. Things that spawn in dis dungeon outside of a lockbox are slowly drained of mana by them."

"I see." I leaned forward, studying the mesmerizing patterns. "And you said this place provides meat for Undertown? How? The steak you fed us was pretty raw and definitely not glowing."

"The local beasts have adapted to it and can survive with it. Their lives are magic-less and short due to the Duskbloom and predators, but they also breed fast. Cold kills the mites," Shash explained. "Culimancer Rostika stores the meat in a large freezer filled with a few Frostix Kitlix. A couple of days is enough for the cold to dissolve even the deep spores completely. Gives the meat a bit of a sour-salty taste, almost like the sprinkle of fresh lemons."

"Eww." Kat blanched. "I thought that was the sauce."

"Soooo . . . how does one hunt down here safely?" I asked, realizing the reason for the long cold tunnel.

"Specialized, expensive gear," the assassin explained. "Armor covered in ice-runes. Keeps the mites off ya. Problem is, it also gives the hunter frostbite. A hunter must have high vitality to resist the cold, low level in everything else, and the agility to move quick enough in and out. There are a few low-level runners who can move fast enough to reach the edge of the labyrinth or dive into the sinkhole to grab whatever mediocre loot manifests there from time to time."

"Uh-huh," I considered. "And what if someone without magic went down there?"

"Without magic, m'lord?" The assassin blinked. "Everyone has crystalline hearts in 'em. Once enough mites settle on a kin, their crystalline heart is drained of mana and 'ey faint and then perish. Duskbloom is death to all life, slow destruction to all artifacts not secured with cold runes!"

"Say, how fast can they drain magic artifacts of mana?"

"The big ones deeper in can dismantle magic armor in a day. The ones here take about a month to drain an artifact. Magic shields cannot stop them. Only the cold kills them off."

"Ha," I exhaled. "Ha ha ha ha!"

I stared at my new, beautiful dungeon, laughing like a madman.

"M'lord?" Shash asked uncertainly as I continued laughing like a supervillain.

"Sorry," I apologized as I wiped tears from my eyes. "It's just . . . perfect. Absolutely perfect. A dungeon that kills by draining mana."

"Perfect for?"

"For me," I said. "Shash, return to the pub. I'll come by later. Going to stay here for a bit and make plans, maybe do a bit of dungeoneering. Also, order everyone to buy and steal Frostix Kitlix. Nobody guards those, right?"

"Indeed. Frostix are considered less valuable and common, and they are usually not guarded well. How many Frostix Kitlix should we acquire, m'lord?"

"All of them," I said. "I don't want anyone else to have a single Frostix Kitlix. Hire thieves and hunters to raid every fridge and icebox across Shandria."

"Your wish is my command." The gemkin vanished in the cold tunnel.

I returned to dungeon-gazing.

A flock of antlered lanky beasts rushed across the hills, the sound of hoofs thundering across the distant field. I watched them with a smile. A catlike thing with glowing antlers caught one of the beasts, tearing it away from the herd, then sat down nomming on the flesh.

"Alex!" Cinder growled, grabbing me as I leaned down to observe the predator. "You can't go down there alone. Even if the mites don't target you, there's still clearly very dangerous wildlife down there."

"One small step for me, one giant forepost for all humankind," I told her. "I'm not gonna hunt down there myself, Ci. Don't you get it? This is the perfect place for a human colony. Where we won't be bothered by Omnids or anyone, really. Those mites are a natural defense against magical bullshit like you."

Cinder blinked, looking somewhat offended.

"Even if humans could survive the mites, there's predators and dungeon Sentinels deeper in. And what about food? Shelter?" Kat asked.

"Details, details." I waved dismissively. "We've got a whole underground criminal organization now. We can figure out logistics later. Right now, I just need to test if I'm actually immune to the mites."

"No," Cinder said firmly, grabbing my arm. "You are *not* climbing down there to test if glowing death-mites will murder you or not."

"One of you can fly me around," I suggested. "The mites clearly don't fly unless disturbed. They sit on grass, like lazy ticks."

"Are you seriously planning to colonize a dungeon?" Cinder demanded.

"Yes," I said. "Why not? The mites only target magical beings. Humans from Earth have no magic, no crystalline hearts to drain. We could build a whole settlement down there. Just look at the size of this freakin' place. We could farm the land, hunt the beasts, trade with Undertown, walk around and collect neat magical artifacts wherever they spawn. It's perfect!"

"Perfect for getting yourself killed," Cinder hissed, her grip on my arm tightening. "What about the dungeon core? What if it decides it doesn't want humans living in its territory?"

Vee looked thoughtful. Katherine had a grumpy-cat face on.

"Dungeon cores, if Morty is to be believed, aren't very sentient," I pointed out. "They're just skills. This one is a magic skill that prints cute glowing mites. What's the problem? Come on. Who wants to fly me around for some scouting? Io? I see those wings. Come on, how about a nice trip around the hills? We can rate cute girls while we're at it."

"Umm . . ." Io rubbed his leather jacket covered shoulder. "I actually . . . can't fly."

"Can't or won't?" I arched an eyebrow. "What the hell, dude, what kind of a moth are you?"

Io fell silent. Kat seemed to frown. I looked between both of them. Something was clearly going on there.

"I just . . . don't fly," Io let out, pulling his wide-brimmed hat lower.

"What happened?" I asked. "Break your wings and they grew back wrong? The incarnator didn't fix it? Got some kind of a condition?"

"Nothing happened," Katherine cut in sharply. "He just doesn't fly. Leave him alone."

Three of my team members looked defeated. Even normally cheerful Vee seemed to be infected by their rapidly deteriorating mood, or was simply forlorn about something. Maybe they were all annoyed with me because this place would kill them slowly while I was immune.

They all needed a picker-upper, hope, something to look forward to.

"Oh! Ci, how's my Dark Lord mantle?" I asked the annoyed-looking Quetzi.

"You mean your ridiculous performance back there with the boasting and the promises of building whorehouses and gambling parlors for everyone?"

"Was I convincing?" I grinned at her. "Did I strike fear into their crystalline hearts?"

"Are you fishing for compliments or something?" she asked.

"Maybe." I shrugged. "Or maybe I'm trying to distract you all from looking so gloomy. Come on, I just acquired a whole criminal organization! That's pretty cool, right?"

Cinder's feathers shifted through troubled grays and frustrated orange-violets. "You just . . . you always do this. Rush headlong into things without thinking about how it affects others. First the Guild, now this crazy colonization plan . . ."

I waited for her to produce her point.

"I . . ." Cinder wrapped her wings around herself. "You're changing everything so fast. The Guild, Vee, Kat, the school, my parents . . . and now you want to build a human settlement in a deadly dungeon? Don't you ever just . . . slow down? Where are you running to? Why?"

I wanted for her to speak some more, but she simply watched me with a concerned look.

"Mmm . . . I have very specific needs," I said.

"What needs could possibly require you to become an underground crime lord?" she hissed, wings fluttering.

"Take a guess," I said. "Go on. All of you. Go ahead and guess why I'm doing all of this."

"Revenge against Omnithornia?" Cinder fired.

"Money?" Vespera suggested.

"Power?" Katherine added with a deep rumble.

"Information?" Io offered.

"I said specific needs," I said. "Those are terrible generic needs with no plan."

"Fine, then, enlighten us," Katherine growled. "What specific needs require building a criminal empire and colonizing a death-mite dungeon?"

"I don't want to dance around you all day guessing whatever bullshit goes in that human head of yours," Cinder sighed. "Just tell us."

"Yeah." Io looked at me from under his wide hat. He had a *Knight Chalice Approved!* box of chocolate pocky sticks in his right hand and was chewing on one like a cigar.

"Spill it, Lex." Vee clicked her beak, pacing left and right, all of her feathers dark. "What's your grand master plan?"

"Very well." I walked to the middle of the balcony outcropping. "I'll only say this once, so you better listen up. My needs are thus . . ."

I made a dramatic pause and armed my metaphorical Glock at my companions.

"I need to save a beautiful angel from a level forty-k Dreamweaving eldritch entity," I said, bending one finger and giving Cinder a poignant look.

Bang. Cinder froze, gray wings igniting with pink-gold-violet colors at the edges.

"I need to create a mega-corporation that rivals Golden Star Industries." I bent a second finger, looking at Vespera. "To offer something better for the CEO of SimmiTech Industries to merge with."

Bang. Vee nearly fell off the platform in her pacing. She flapped her white-sprinkled wings to straighten out, staring at me with wide gray eyes.

"I need to hire an army of Seers and Scrutimancers to peer into the gates a certain moth makes to understand the truth about the nature of reality and corpse worlds." My eyes moved to Io as I bent my third finger.

Bang. Io's pocky stick fell from his mouth.

"I want to build a beautiful, dark twin city for a certain dark kitten." I bent my fourth finger. "A place where she can walk anywhere without pain and never have to hide who she is or what she can do. Where she can be free to smile, to run, and to dance as much as she wants to."

Bang. Kat choked.

"To draw, to write, and to publish her book about a supervillain girl named Alexa who refused to give up hope and pushed forward no matter what hardships were in her way," I concluded. "I'm sure it'll be super popular in the booming city of human colonists living in a dungeon."

Silence reigned.

Katherine seemed to have regained her wits faster than the others.

"W-what?" She forced the words out of her dragon-feline maw. "You can't . . ."

"You can't stop me," I said. "I do what I want. I'll call this place . . . Kathopolis. Or maybe Katsburg. Katallion? Katanstinople?"

"S-stop kidding around," Katherine growled, but her emerald eyes were wide and her tail was twitching erratically. A gray-blue blush had crept across her scales visible even in the gloom of the cavern.

"I'm not kidding," I stated. "One hundred percent serious. Picking out a name in my head now."

"Yeah, okay, sure." Katherine crossed her arms. "You're gonna turn that medieval cave-dump plus these glowing hills into a modern city overnight, with Wi-Fi and everything?"

"You . . ." Vee let out, Valley girl facade gone as if blown away by a hurricane, beak wide open. "You're going to . . . challenge my father's company merger? For me? I don't . . . Lex, come on, don't say that! Don't give me hope like that, damn it! That's not possible! I will be forced to take a one-way glider to Thunderland in four months when winter semester ends. You can't build a human colony, or a corporation here in four months that'd rival Golden Star . . . It's just not . . . logistically possible!"

I turned to the Mothman.

"The truth is an elusive mistress," Io mused, grabbing another pocky. "I fear it will take more than this moth's lifetime to understand the nature of reality. The answer to the ultimate question might take millennia to answer, if the musings of Douglas Adams are anything to go by."

"Right. Why does everyone forget the time dilation?" I asked, looking over my companions. "Delve class is on Fridays. If my math is right, that's 1.6 years per week. Four months of winter semester is three hundred and thirty-six months. This place won't change instantly, but with the right financial support, guidance, people, year by year . . ."

"Oh, Ohhhhh!" Vee yelped, humming like a generator, electric sparks crackling over her cheeks like a blush. "Of course! I'm such an idiot birb. *Time!* Twenty-eight years! You could actually . . . holy sheet!"

Her beak slammed shut and then her eyes ignited with pure silver from within like deep pools of liquid mercury.

Before I could say anything else, I became wrapped entirely in black-and-white feathers and my world turned sideways.

"Thank you, thank you. *Thank you!*" she yelled into my ear. I realized that I was falling.

Chainmail-covered arms and legs wrapped around me, sparkling wings shot open, and we straightened out, gliding above an ocean of glowing fields.

Magisteel-wrapped talons dug into me, electric currents jumping between her and my hexamesh suits. She was whooping loudly, crackling with thunder, humming like a jet engine, spinning madly through the air.

Then she banked, slowed, letting me breathe.

Armored elbows wrapped around my arms, and then her talons dug into my temples, electric charge rushing across my brain, detonating across all of my neurons like explosions of pure thought.

[Flight. Happiness. Joy. Thunder. Lightning. Pure, unbridled *hope*.]

Lightning struck from her into a glowing tree far below us, setting it on fire.

[Death to the idiot frog. Vengeance. Destruction. Revenge.]

The landscape below blurred into streaks of bioluminescent green and blue as she accelerated.

[*Hope*. Twenty-eight *years*. *Twenty-eight years of possibility!* Freedom. *Freedom. Freedom!*]

Talons dug into the sides of my head, drawing drops of blood. We banked around the gargantuan waterfall, the cascading water drowning out the noises of crackling and thunder emanating from her wings.

[Friendship. Trust. Happiness. Joy. Love . . . love . . . *love* . . . *love!*] Images, ideas, concepts woven from pure electricity rushing into my head like a dam breaking.

Growling behind us. Demands. Yelling. A flash of rainbow-wings.

[Mine. Mine. *Mine. Miiiine!*]

Lightning struck at the rainbow inconvenience.

Banking low, moving closer to the deadly, glowing fields, flashing past glowing jagged trees covered in fluttering bits of grass instead of leaves. Soaring above a thundering, racing herd of horned elk-like beasts with elongated, glowing snouts covered in mite-growths.

A screech of fury splitting the air behind us.

Rainbow wings blazing like an aurora, an explosion of color, a threat from one predator to another, moving faster than physics should allow.

Murderous blue eyes.

"*Vesperaaaaaa!*" Cinder's scream echoed across the bioluminescent hills, amplified by her magically enhanced voice. "*Drop him right now!*"

[Never. Never. never. *Never. Mine.* mine. mine. Hope. Joy. Satisfaction. Smile. freedom. *Freeeeeeeeeeeeeeeedom!*]

Lightning surged between us, intricate fractal patterns of pure energy. Resonance between her crystalline core and the feathers I had devoured in berry shake form.

Flying above the labyrinth of fjords now. Waterfalls below. Waterfalls around, coming from the ceiling. The ceiling suddenly reduced. Fjords above us, fjords down below.

The Thunderbird's emotions, raw and unfiltered, pounded through me like an electric jackhammer. Her joy, her hope, her desperate desire for freedom all mingled together in a storm of sensation that threatened to overwhelm, to overwrite my consciousness.

There was probably a me in there somewhere, but it didn't matter.

All that mattered was the current between us.

The gaps between the rock above and below thinned out.

Cinder was gaining on us, her rainbow wings blazing with fury as she pursued us through the twisting canyons.

"*Veeeeeee!*" A voice behind us. "*Stop! Please!*"

"No!" Vespera laughed maniacally, her voice crackling with electricity. "Can't catch us! Won't catch us! He's mine now! My human! My hope! My freedom! I've claimed this prey!"

[Forever. *Forever! Forever! Unstoppable! Together!*]

We shot through another narrow gap between towering fjords, lightning flashing along Vee's wings as she navigated the increasingly tight spaces.

[Joy. Speed. Thunder. *Mine!*]

The gap ahead suddenly closed, rock walls squeezing together. Vee banked hard, nearly vertical, talons digging into me painfully as she pulled up.

The sudden change in direction caused us to lose speed. A rainbow blur slammed into us from behind.

We tumbled through the air, a tangle of black, white, and rainbow feathers. Vee's electrical field went haywire, sparks flying everywhere as Cinder's claws tugged at me, trying to pry me off the Thunderbird.

Rushing whitewater river below us filled with jagged rocks.

Yep. This was how I was going to die. An aerial battle between two flying cryptids for whoever wanted me the most.

Truly the best way to go out.

CHAPTER SIXTY

Dungeon Troubles

We hit the water like a meteor, the surface exploding upward in a massive spray of luminescent blue-green liquid. The shock was instantaneous—freezing cold mixed with an odd tingling sensation that made every nerve in my body feel as if it was being simultaneously shocked and numbed.

Vespera's magisteel armor sparked wildly underwater, creating strange lightning patterns. Cinder's wings spread out, creating a protective bubble around me as we tumbled through the rushing river.

The water dragged us on and on and on, tumbling up and down and sideways, slamming us into random rocks, making my shield bracelets ignite as the impact was reduced.

Then the water let go and we were falling, plummeting over the edge of a waterfall and into a dark lake somewhere far below.

The impact knocked what little air I had left out of my lungs. The dark water was impossibly deep, pulling us down and down into its endless depths. Bioluminescent mites swirled around us like falling snow, creating eerie patterns in the darkness.

Cinder finally ripped me away from the sinking, heavier Thunderbird and swam upwards.

We broke the surface gasping for air. The lake stretched out around us, its dark waters reflecting the bioluminescent mites that drifted down from above like glowing snow.

Cinder used her tail, arms, legs, feet, and wings to swim forward towards a small rocky island, holding onto a few of my hexasuits with her teeth as if I were a kitten. She pulled me onto the slate-rock shore, panting hard, and then opened her jaw, dropping me and then falling onto me completely exhausted.

"Fff . . . fff . . . huff . . . friggin' bird . . . going to murder her . . ." she panted. "You . . . okay?"

"I'm . . . fine." I coughed out water. "Where's Vee?"

Cinder looked behind us at the lake. "Don't know . . . huff . . . too much magisteel on her . . . heavy . . ."

"We have to help her!" I tried to stand but Cinder's weight kept me pinned.

"No," she growled, wings wrapping around me possessively. "You're . . . staying right . . . here. I'll go get the stupid bird. Just . . . let me . . . huff . . . catch my breath . . ."

She reached towards her belt and pulled a silver-blue metal bottle off it. She downed the potion swiftly and her entire figure ignited with red-violet-orange, making my eyes water.

She released me and dove back into the dark water. I watched anxiously as glowing rainbow feathers disappeared beneath the surface, illuminated by the falling mites that created an ethereal underwater light show.

Minutes passed.

Finally, after what felt like an eternity, two figures burst from the water—Cinder dragging a limp, waterlogged Thunderbird. They collapsed onto the rocky shore beside me, both gasping for air.

Vespera's magisteel armor was sparking weakly, her feathers completely soaked and drooping. Her usual crackling energy was gone, replaced by exhausted trembling.

"You . . . absolute . . . *knob!*" Cinder weakly smacked Vespera.

"You . . . are . . . hfff . . . the . . . knob." Vee smacked her back. "Crashed . . . pfffhh . . . into . . . me."

"*Me?!*" Cinder sputtered, pushing herself up on shaking arms. "You . . . kidnapped . . . my . . . huffff . . . human."

"Our . . . pffhhh . . . human," Vee corrected, grabbing onto my wet boot and then face planting into the flat rocks with a thump.

Cinder weakly kicked at the passed-out Thunderbird and crawled to my side, panting and wheezing.

"Stupid . . . huffff . . . beerch . . . ughhh, so wet," she let out. "Bloody . . . middle of nowhere, soaked, covered in glowing death-mites . . . Arghhh!"

She tried to shake the water out of her wings, flapping left and right like a dog.

"Here." I pulled off my jacket, laying it on the rocks. "Got a warming rune in there. Should help you dry off. No wing holes . . . but good as a warm surface."

Cinder continued shaking, sending water droplets everywhere. The bioluminescent mites that had gotten on her feathers made her look as if she were covered in tiny stars.

"They're not hurting you, are they?" I asked, concerned about the glowing parasites.

"No . . ." she let out. "Just . . . losing mana. Bit by bit. Not good."

"Should we move a bit up?" I asked, looking around our small rocky island. The dark lake stretched out in all directions, its surface occasionally disturbed by something large moving beneath.

"Can't," Cinder panted, collapsing onto my jacket. "So . . . tired. Used up . . . too much mana . . . chasing after you . . . two idiots. That potion . . . only gave me enough to save Vee."

"Right. Lemme know if you drop to like twenty mana," I said. "I'll up you. You too, Vee. You alive there?"

I shook my boot.

"Mrghhh," Vee let out. "B-barely. S-s-so cold . . . w-w-wet."

Her teeth chattered.

I exhaled, stretched, and pulled power from my hexasuits. Then I stood up, grabbed the Thunderbird, and shoved her into Cinder's arms.

"Hug," I ordered, pulling off one hexasuit after the other, laying each atop them and setting the cores to the "heat" function. "Dry off. Neither of you can fly if you're wet."

"Don't tell me . . . huffff . . . what to do," Cinder grumbled, but wrapped her wings around the shivering Thunderbird anyway. The warming hexasuits began to steam as they dried their feathers.

I sat down beside them, watching the dark lake warily. Something large moved beneath those waters, creating ripples that disturbed the falling mites' reflection.

"Y-you're not m-mad?" Vee's teeth chattered.

"Of course I'm mad," Cinder growled, but didn't let go of the shivering Thunderbird. "You could have gotten all of us killed! What were you thinking?!"

"I w-wasn't," Vee admitted, curling closer to Cinder's warmth. "Just . . . got overwhelmed. Twenty-eight years . . . of possibility. Of hope. Of . . . freedom. Of change. Of being able to do something new. Something that's me. Us. Our town. Our rules. Our . . . everything. Do you have any idea what this means to me?"

I pulled the wet, dead hexasuits off them, taking more off myself and igniting the next core.

"No and I don't care," Cinder hissed. A blue eye glanced up at me. "Alex? Did you hit the rocks? Why is your head bleeding from both sides?"

"Oh." I touched my temples where Vee's talons had dug in during our flight. Drops of blood came away on my fingers. "That's from earlier. Vee clawed me a bit."

"She did *what*?!" Cinder's wings flared with angry reds, jostling Vee.

"Sorry. M'sorry, kay? I just . . . I've never been this happy about something. About someone. Mmmm'srrryy." Vee buried herself harder in Cinder.

"Still mad at you," Cinder grumbled, but her wings settled back around them both. "And you!" She glared at me. "Stop taking off your hexasuits! You'll freeze!"

"I'm fine," I said, removing another suit and laying it over them. "I still have like fourteen of them on me. Humans are surprisingly resilient to cold. Besides, you two need them more than me right now."

Something large breached the surface of the lake about fifty meters out, creating a wave that smashed against our little island.

"What-the-shit-is-that?!" Cinder yelped.

I squinted at the broiling lake. "Maybe that thing from Tolkien? You know, the thing in the lake with the Friendship door?"

I dug into my pocket and pulled out the lighter, spinning the wheel. The little flame brought me no warmth whatsoever.

"The Watcher of the West-gate of Moria," Vee muttered through chattering teeth. "Ancient guardian of deep places. Usually harmless unless provoked . . ."

"Th-thank you, birb of wisdom," I grinned, holding the lighter and watching my stats go berserk.

Mana: 268/7

Sparks danced in my eyes.

Another massive shape moved beneath the dark water, creating ripples that disturbed the falling mites' ethereal glow.

"How's your mana?" I asked my companions.

"Going up," Cinder let out. "Three hundred now."

"Oh, the suits 'n' jacket are getting so warm. This is nice!" Vee let out from Cinder's embrace.

The beast cores on the suits flickered erratically, growing brighter. The outfits were steaming now, hot to the touch.

"Hrm," I commented. "Guess it powers beast cores, too. The more you know."

I set a single hexasuit on me to "heat," drying rapidly.

Just as I was starting to feel somewhat warm and dry, a massive tentacle burst from the lake's surface, sending a spray of glowing water high into the air. The appendage was covered in bioluminescent growths that pulsed with an eerie blue-green light.

"Sheet," Cinder hissed, wrapping her wings tighter around Vee.

The tentacle was easily as thick as a tree trunk.

"Use your wings to tell it to piss off!" I barked, pulling out the magisteel katana from its dimensional sheath at my side.

"Tell it what?!" Cinder yelped, her feathers shifting through panicked grays.

"Flash your wings! Be threatening!" I waved the sword in one hand and lighter in the other. "Come on, you're a predator! Show it who's boss! Vee, take the lighter! Finger on the button, don't let the flame die!"

Cinder's wings flared wide, blazing through aggressive reds and warning oranges. Vee's armored hand grabbed the lighter.

The massive tentacle froze directly above us, moving left and right with each pulse of Cinder's wings. I swung at it with the sword, amplifying my strength with the suits.

The blade connected with a solid *thunk*, sinking halfway into the bioluminescent appendage. The tentacle recoiled slightly, then slowly began to retreat back into the dark water as I pried the blade out of it, nearly plummeting into the water.

"Ha!" I grinned. "See? Just needed to show it who's . . ."

Five more tentacles erupted from the lake, sending waves crashing over our little island.

" . . . boss," I finished weakly as the appendages loomed over us.

Mana: 824/7

The nearest one swung at us.

Vee's right hand shot out, humming like a power transformer. I grabbed onto her left hand that was still holding the burning lighter with my fingers, picturing, focusing, pushing, willing magic out of my non-Thunderbird self into my Thunderbird-stolen skill, my eyes shut tight.

Current rushed down my arm across Vee and into her right hand, detonating into a massive bolt of pure electrical energy that split into multiple arcs, striking each tentacle simultaneously, visible even though my closed eyes. The discharge was blindingly bright, illuminating the entire cavern for a brief moment.

The monster beneath the surface thrashed, its tentacles writhing in pain as electricity coursed through its body.

The water around our island began to boil from the intensity of the discharge.

LV 1 Skill gained: Chain Lightning

Sparks wrote in my eyes.

Mana: 32/7

"Abyss damn it! At least warn me when you do that!" Cinder hissed, blinking and rubbing her eyes. "Bloody thunderknobs!"

The tentacles retreated beneath the roiling surface, leaving behind a strong smell of ozone and cooked calamari.

"Did . . . did we just . . ." Vee blinked rapidly, still gripping the lighter. "Did you just . . . channel lightning through me? Or did I channel it through you? Hrm."

"Yeah." I grinned, watching my mana rush back up as she held the flame. "That was pretty cool, right? We should do that more often!"

Cinder's look of betrayal was crushing.

Somewhat.

Survival seemed more important.

"Can you two fly yet?" I asked as water slapped against the island from the other side. "I think that the angry squid is coming back for round two. Or maybe it's his wife, annoyed that her husband came home drunk and smokin'."

A massive head covered in glowing barnacles emerged from the water, a red glowing eye peering at us. Another tentacle, larger than the previous ones, burst from the water behind us.

"Mrs. Squid looks extra pissed," I commented. "Time to go?"

"Can't," Cinder groaned. "Wings still too wet . . . not enough mana . . . need more time."

I spun through the air, chucking the magisteel katana at the eye with all of my hexasuit-amplified strength.

The blade struck true, sinking deep into the glowing, slanted orb. The creature let out a deafening screech that shook our tiny island, its tentacles thrashing blindly, missing smashing us by only a few inches.

I pried the hexasuit control mechanism out of the suit with amplified strength and set the pattern into a spiral, and then threw the beast core and the mechanism into the lake, towards the thrashing squid.

"Close your eyes and ears!" I yelled, ducking into Cinder. "*Cover me!*"

Rainbow wings wrapped around me just as the hexasuit's beast core detonated underwater, creating a massive shockwave that sent glowing water spraying in all directions. The explosion was deafening even through Cinder's feathers, the concussive force making our little island shudder.

When the water settled and Cinder's wings pulled back, the lake's surface was still once more. Bits of glowing squid-flesh floated nearby.

"What? *What?*" Cinder choked out. "What the shit was that?"

"Beast cores can implode when overloaded and set to a spiral pattern that draws power in," I replied, my ears ringing. "I thought it would be like a smaller explosion, though. Guess the lighter really maxed out the mana there."

I looked at the remnants of the squid.

"Great job, team." I smiled. "Looks like a chonky calamari was no match for our . . ."

A magisteel arrow flitted through the air, going through my chest and all of my hexasuits. The ward-shield bracelets flashed erratically, failing to stop the projectile.

I blinked at it. Pain exploded from my left lung.

I looked ahead through the murk and glowing mite-snow. A humanish, lanky figure was on the distant shore with massive glowing antlers sprouting from its head and shoulders. The thing methodically placed another arrow into its bow and pulled back the string.

"H-help," I hissed out, colorful spots dancing in my vision.

The second magisteel arrow let loose, flying straight at my head.

CHAPTER SIXTY-ONE

Health Gun

Vee threw herself in front of me, her wings spreading wide. Lightning crackled between her talons, forming a sphere of pure electrical energy that pulsed with desperate intensity.

The arrow struck her hastily-formed shield, its momentum slowing but not stopping completely. The magisteel shaft pierced through the electrical barrier and then slammed into her armor, sending her stumbling backwards.

The glowing man on the lakeshore drew back another arrow.

Cinder sang, her voice carrying across the lake with terrible force. The sound was both beautiful and devastating—a high, clear note that seemed to tear through reality itself.

The antlered figure staggered as it released the shot. It missed us by a meter, the arrow splashing into lake water.

Another humanoid thing emerged onto the shore, this one holding an arbalest. All around the lake, more people were appearing from the gloom, their hollow eye sockets and skeletal mouths covered in glowing mites.

Dungeon Sentinels. A whole legion of dungeon Sentinels surrounding the lake, approaching from all sides.

"F-fly," I choked. "Fly, my p-pretties!"

Blood was soaking through my remaining thirteen hexasuits. The arrow had gone clean through my left side, probably puncturing a lung.

Breathing hurt. Everything hurt.

The lowest hexasuit down squeezed on the section where the hole was in my chest and behind it, trying to stem the flow of blood.

More figures were emerging from the gloom, all of them covered in bioluminescent growths. Some held bows, others spears or magic tools of unknown use.

I tore the core out of my chest, setting the pattern to a spiral. The core began to flash.

"Trrrow . . . at crrowd," I hissed out as I handed the core-bomb to Cinder, my vision going white.

She did.

The explosion rocked the shore, sending glowing bodies flying. The antlered figures didn't seem to care for being exploded, didn't even dive away, had no fear whatsoever. Fragments of people and crystal antlers and rock rained down.

"Now!" I gasped. "While . . . they're . . . scattered . . . Cinder . . . carry me out. Vee . . . fly . . . behind . . . blast arrows off . . . us."

Cinder's arms wrapped around me, her wings blossoming out. Vespera snapped the lighter shut, her own wings unfurling. The undead humanoids on the shore were rising, grabbing at their weapons, drawing back bows.

We launched into the air as arrows and magic spells rained past us. Vee flew behind and below, her magisteel armor crackling with electricity as she fired thunderbolts out, deflecting the projectiles and making spells detonate in the air.

Pain lanced through my chest with each wingbeat as Cinder carried me higher. The hexasuits were doing their best to stem the bleeding, but I could feel myself growing weaker.

"Stay with me," Cinder growled, clinging to me with arms and legs, her wings pumping harder. "Don't you dare die on me, you stupid human!"

More arrows and magic missiles whistled through the air. Vee's lightning flashed, but she was tiring rapidly, her movements becoming sluggish.

"Sss-fine," I bubbled. "Jssst incarnate me . . . kay? Kay."

I closed my eyes.

My consciousness was fading in and out. Each breath felt like fire in my chest. The hexasuits were warm and sticky with blood. Rainbow-wings flapped above me. Behind us, thunder boomed and crackled.

Pain. So much pain. Not as much as Cinder felt when the Skinwalker snapped her wrist, though.

She had to go through that every night, enduring the dream-pain over and over.

I couldn't die. I couldn't let Cinder be alone in that nightmare.

Without me, the girls would fight, argue.

If I died now, I would lose the extra week on Arx. I was running against the clock . . . needed the time to direct everyone, to save Vee from her arranged marriage. Time to help . . .

Darkness.

Warm hands prying open my mouth, pouring something down my throat.

Warmth. Sparks. Current.

My eyes shot open. Vee was looming over me, hands pressed to my chest.

Lightning danced across her armored fingers, making my heart beat. Rushing my blood down my veins. Forcing my body to stay alive, against all odds.

"What happened?!" Katherine growled from my left.

"Antlery . . . zombies," I coughed, tasting copper. "Really . . . rude . . . with arrows . . ."

"What were you thinking, going down there?!" Kat growled.

"Blame Vee," I let out. "At least . . . we know humans . . . aren't immune . . . to arrows." I tried to grin but it came out as more of a grimace.

Io appeared in my field of vision, holding what looked like a very questionable weapon with the words *Dora's Med-gun!* on its side in fading scratched-up pink.

"Hold him still," he said calmly. "This is going to hurt."

"What . . . is that?" I wheezed.

"Don't know," Io explained. "Used it on myself when some jerk shot me from inside the gate. Should work on you too. Probably."

"Probably?!" Cinder barked, holding me down with her claws.

"The healing potions we fed him didn't work fully," Io replied with a far too casual look as he pressed the gun to my wound. "Either 'cause he's a human or 'cause the Sentinel's arrow was cursed to make a wound that's impossible to seal with magic. So there's this."

He shoved a leather strap in my mouth and pressed the trigger.

Pain exploded through my chest like liquid fire. I screamed, biting down as something that felt like molten metal poured into the arrow wound, burning and freezing simultaneously.

"Hold him!" Io ordered as I thrashed.

Cinder and Vee pinned my arms while Katherine held onto my legs. The burning sensation intensified, spreading outward from the wound in waves of agony.

"Almost done," Io muttered, keeping the gun pressed against my side. "Relax. The pain will pass."

Another surge of burning cold shot through me. My back arched involuntarily as the sensation peaked.

Then suddenly, the pain began to fade. The burning turned to tingling, then to numbness. I could feel something shifting inside me, making questionable gurgling noises. More numbness.

"Is . . . is it working?" Cinder breathed out.

"Seems like it's working." Io shrugged.

"Yes," Vee replied. "I feel it. There's some kind of liquid metal in him . . . it seems to be fixing him, filling the hole."

I gasped for air, finding that I could breathe without pain. The wound in my side had closed, filled with some kind of silver stuff.

"What . . . what is that stuff?" I panted, touching the silver patch on my side that was visible through the hole in my hexasuits.

"Liquid nanites," Io said, examining the med-gun's scratched-up label more closely. "Says here they're programmed to repair biological damage. Gunshot wounds and stuff. Made by Dora the Terraformer Co. Neat, eh?"

"So . . . you just . . . shot me with mysterious interdimensional nanobots?" I wheezed.

"Yep." Io nodded. "Seemed better than ending our field trip a bunch of days short. Besides, I've used it on myself three times. One more capsule left. Only minor side effects."

"What side effects?!" Cinder demanded.

"Numbness, cold, and lack of feeling in the repaired area and whatever nerves go through." Io shrugged. "And occasionally you might taste colors. Nothing serious."

"Um. You guys are . . . glowing with smol spooders," I commented, squinting at Vespera and Cinder. "Go into the cold tunnel till you stop."

As the two girls looked at each other and rushed off into the tunnel, I lifted my hand. Patches of glowing mites were crawling all over me. I summoned up my stats.

Mana: 0/7

"Guess that answers that," I said. "I'm immune to this dungeon. Hooray."

"Yeah," Io commented, looking at the mites moving on and falling off me. "They seem to be flaking off ya. Guess they don't like humans."

"Alas, we were not meant to be together," I lamented. "Goodbye 90,538 smol mite GFs. You have sucked me dry, you parasites . . . and yet I still endure."

"You could have died," Katherine growled.

"A minor inconvenience," I shot back. "Now we know humans can survive here. Just need better armor against arrows. And maybe some anti-squid measures. A tank could probably take out both. Maybe a trench. Actually, no. A hamster wheel. Take their weapons away and put the glow-zombies in a wheel. Free electricity!"

"You nearly died and you're already planning how to weaponize the undead?" Katherine asked.

"Yes," I affirmed. "If I don't, somebody else will."

"Nobody is insane enough to put dungeon Sentinels into giant hamster wheels to generate electricity," Kat let out. "How do you even think of these things?!"

"I dunno." I shrugged. "I have two souls. Maybe the second one is whispering excellent ideas into my head while the first one does the manual breathing and whatever."

"Two souls?" Katherine's emerald eyes narrowed. "What do you mean, two souls?"

"Alex and Alexa," I said, sitting up with a wince. "As above, so below. Physical and astral."

"Alexa?" She blinked.

"Yeah," I nodded. "You know. The girl from your book. That Alexa. And before you ask if it's a joke, no it's not. I saw her. I saw Alexa in me when I dove into Genesis fluid."

Katherine frowned.

"Kat," I said. "She's real. Your art is showing people another world . . . the same dead world where Io is pulling all this snack shit from. I'm sure of it now. It's not a coincidence. There's a reason why I found you. I'm . . . Alexa and Martin. I am one hundred percent certain of it now. I was your best friend . . . in another place and time."

Katherine stared at me, her emerald eyes wide and unblinking. For a moment, the only sound was the distant dripping of water in the tunnel and the soft crackling of the hexasuit cores.

"That's impossible," she finally whispered.

"Improbable, perhaps," I corrected. "But not impossible. A Corpseworld Caretaker told me that Alexa crashed some kind of an interdimensional train into our Earth, breaking our reality."

Katherine's tail lashed back and forth. "You're claiming to be a character from my own unfinished novel? Do you know how absurd you sound?!"

"Is it?" I raised an eyebrow. "I showed you my birth certificate, my passport. Martin Kilborne. But what if that's just another layer? What if I'm something more?"

Io watched our exchange silently, munching on another pocky stick.

"You have two souls?" Katherine repeated.

"That's what this damn bracelet says," I shook the Lazarus bracelet. "Eighty-nine for me. Eighty-nine for Alexa. One hundred and seventy-eight in soul."

Katherine stared at me, her emerald eyes boring into mine with a dangerous intensity that made me want to run away.

"Prove it," she said finally.

"Prove what?" I asked.

"Prove you're Alexa." Katherine's tail lashed against the stone. "Tell me something only she would know . . . something that I hadn't written two years ago when that damned beerch Em posted my draft online to make fun of me."

I closed my eyes, digging through myself.

Not my memories. Not Martin's. But . . . something else. Something deeper. Something behind me. Below me, like an impossible shadow cast across reality sideways.

Then the world flipped and I knew exactly what to say to her.

"Why'd you stop writing about me, Cottie?" I asked. "You think I would have wanted that? Verse 24:19 . . . I've made you into the Eminence Equality, gave you the highest position in all the land, forced the previous techno-pope to retire. I go away and you just give up? Is that it?"

Katherine went very, very still.

"No one knows that," she whispered. "I never wrote that part down. Never told anyone."

Io's pocky stick fell from his mouth. He tried to catch it but it bounced on the rocks and rolled off the edge of the platform into the glowing dungeon below.

"You're the strongest person I know, Cottie," I said, staring at her emerald, flickering eyes. "You are my Knight. Always and forever. No matter what shape you are. No matter what you look like. No matter if you're dying. I'm not going to give up on you. Ever. Never ever. Not in infinity number of years. No matter what world we stand on. You and I, we're going to win."

Katherine blinked. Then she blinked again.

Sparks of tears came. More tears.

"You can't . . . you . . . I made you up in my head to make myself feel better about my shitty life!" she cried. "How can . . . how can you be real?!"

"I dunno." I shrugged. "I just am. Everything is a little bit different this time around. You're a cute dragon-cat. What, you're not shocked by the fact that you can shove people into the deep and that Io can literally open gates to Corpseworld dimensions, but when I say that I have two human souls in me that's somehow 'ohh, so scary and impossiburrrr'?"

"But . . ."

"Deal with it," I said, crossing my arms. "Look, I'm sorry it took so long for me to find you . . . to find myself. Yeah, we lost each other for eighteen years and stuff, but we have each other now. That's what counts. System Wizards, for all their bullshit reality-rewriting powers, can't stop our friendship."

Katherine stared at me, eyes wide and unblinking.

"Gimme a hug," I ordered.

Tears ran across her blue-and-black dragonscale cheeks. For a moment, she looked as if she might start to argue. Then, unexpectedly, she lunged forward and wrapped her large arms around me, her magisteel-covered armor clinking softly.

"You absolute idiot," she whispered into my shoulder. "You absolute, impossible, crazy idiot."

I hugged her back, feeling her trembling slightly. "It's okay, Cotes." I said. "Everything's gonna be okay."

"How are you real?" she repeated. "I don't understand."

"Partially human stubbornness," I grinned. "Partially interdimensional shenanigans. Mostly spite. Work with me, yeah? I know I'm weird. We all are. Weird in all the right ways . . . That's what makes us different. Special. Cool. Insert compliment here. I'm tired and there's a hole in my chest."

"Insert compliment?" She smirked. "Who even says that?"

"I do," I said.

She smacked me on the head.

"Ow," I whined. "I already got an arrow through the chest, why would you injure me further, art-nemesis bestie?"

"I wrote you as a smart character," she growled. "Not a suicidal lunatic."

"Technically," I pointed out, "I didn't do anything suicidal this time. Vee kidnapped me and flew off with me 'cause I made her smile. Totally different scenario. You know . . . if you gave me some of your scales, I could have maybe sunk into the deep and avoided that arrow. Come on, sensei, teach me Umbramancy. Pretty please with sugar on top?"

She squinted at me.

"I'm a perfect student," I marketed myself. "Eager to learn. Willing to practice. Totally responsible."

Katherine burst out laughing. A full-bodied, slightly manic sound that echoed into the tunnel behind me.

"You? Responsible?" She wiped a tear from her eye. "We haven't even made it to register at the Adventurers Guild!"

"I bought an Adventurers Guild!" I protested. "That's like one thousand times more responsibility!"

"You bought a criminal organization with stolen Genesis fluid and framed Emerald for it," Io pointed out from beside us.

"It's going to be a highly respectable institution in a decade or two," I said. "Just you wait! I'm dispensing responsibilities across my acquired mooks, turning them into magnates of industry!"

Katherine snorted. "You're turning criminals into business leaders?"

"Why not?" I grinned. "That's basically what most corpo CEOs are anyway. At least my criminals are honest about being criminals. Besides, think about it—we've got a whole underground network ready to help build our dream city. Your dream city. Katsburg! It's what the people voted for!"

"We are *not* calling it that," she growled, but I could see her trying to hide a smile. "What fucking people? I don't recall voting for any city names."

"I dunno." I shrugged. "Imaginary people in my head. Katlantis came close, too, but that's more like a great idea for our future nation-state name, not a city. How about . . . The Dark Citadel of Cottie the Magnificent?" I teased as I grabbed her hand. "Or maybe Emeraldville, since technically she owns it? Eh, eh? Come on, fair dragon-cat maiden. Our tower and two frosty winged princesses await!"

"Whatever." Katherine started to walk into the tunnel.

"Actually . . ." I looked at the fields of bloom below. "Umm, you guys go ahead. I'm going to sit here for another hour or two. Watch the wildlife. Write ideas down for where to build a lodge."

"Are you . . . you aren't going to do anything stupid . . . right?" Kat asked.

"Nah. One arrow through the chest was enough for me. Just going to sit on the ledge and relax," I said. "Go back to the Guild with the others. Ain't nothing gonna hurt me up here. I'll Voicecast Shash and make sure he's nearby and won't let anyone else into this tunnel. I almost died just now because of Ci and Vee. I'd like to just . . . be alone for a bit, please. Leave me Lance's bag. I'm going to go over the stuff in it with Yulia, see what I have to return in five days."

"Fine," Kat let out. She pulled the bag off her shoulder and put it down next to me. "Let's go, Io."

The Mothman gave me a quizzical look of dark-gray eyes from under his wide-brimmed hat but didn't say anything. I was certain he sensed *it*.

The intent. My desires. My dastardly plans.

Io didn't say anything. He wanted an apocalyptic end to everything. He would get it.

Io and I nodded ever so slightly at each other like two bros who knew the symphony of the doomsday-filled future that I was about to conduct.

Io and Kat vanished in the tunnel.

I waited until their footsteps grew silent, then rushed to the rope ladder leading down to the shimmering grasses below.

I felt a bit bad about tricking Kat, but it was for a worthy cause. If she knew of my insane plan, she would most likely try to stop me.

This is just backup, I assured myself. *Just a bit of a precaution.*

In case things went . . . horribly wrong.

Which they usually did. My numb, silver-spotted chest was evidence of this fact.

CHAPTER SIXTY-TWO

Rooftop Hot Tub I

The back dining hall of the Gloomy Horse was a cavernous space carved directly from the bedrock, its high ceiling concealed in gloom despite the numerous Kitlix lanterns hanging from iron chains. A massive stone fireplace dominated one wall, Kitlix-managed flames casting dancing shadows across the ancient stone tables and benches.

Cinder and Vespera huddled near the fire, looking scruffy and very annoyed with life in general.

"Sup, guys?" I asked.

"Ey." Vee looked up at me. "Not much. Still warming up after our accidental dungeoneering. Bleh. What have you been up to for the past two hours? Kat said you needed some time alone?"

"Yeah." I nodded. "Just prepping some backup plans."

"For?"

"For everything and everyone," I said. "Sort of an endgame strategy thing."

"I see," Vespera said. The Thunderbird's spirit had been thoroughly defeated by cold water and the even colder tunnel.

Cinder looked at me wearily, her wings wrapped tightly around herself. Her feathers were shifting through troubled dark blues and icy silvers resembling a stormy sky.

"Stay here for a bit more," I said. "I have an idea for some . . . renovations."

"Kay." Vee nodded.

I climbed the tower's winding stairs, emerging onto the highest level. The space was mostly empty except for old tables and dust-covered crates. Perfect.

I dug through Lance's bag until I found what I was looking for—a bricking wand with *Architecture-fix-on-the-go 3000* written on its handle in fading gold letters.

Working quickly, I used the Captain's lighter to give myself seven hundred mana and then wielded the wand to reshape the stone below me, making it a single polished surface without any cracks or holes. The magic flowed easily, the stone responding to my will as if it were clay.

I dismantled the shoddy-looking parts of the back column and a bit of the parapet to provide some walls and carved a basic stone drain pointing outside of the tower. Within about twenty minutes, I had a decent-looking circular hot tub pool about forty inches deep that would easily fit six Omnids in it. It featured a stone seat in it with a view of Undertown.

I plugged the drain with a stone-carved plug, and then added another flat drain closer to the top to let out any extra water, grinning to myself.

Next came the insta-rain stone, another of Lance's tools similar to what the mermaid nurse used to phase-shift herself to a more magical state. I threw it upward and activated it. The stone shattered in the air, creating a small rain cloud that began filling the pool with clean fresh water.

While the pool filled, I pulled the control mechanism out of several of my stolen Skyfall hexasuits and shoved them into the water along with the beast cores.

Once the pool was full and warm, I slipped into it and activated my Quartermaster ID tag, calling up each of my teammates, starting with our Slayer.

"Yo, Vee," I said into the Voicecast when the Thunderbird's weary-looking face appeared on the magitek holo. "Hot tub on the roof. Join me!"

"We have a hot tub?! Since when?!" Vespera's voice crackled through the holo-projection, her frown turning into a smile.

"Since I installed one." I grinned, zooming out the projection range to display myself inhabiting the tub in swimming trunks. "Rooftop pool party!"

"Oh, sheet. Count me in! Come on rainbow, you could use a dip." Vee's face turned towards Cinder.

"What? But—" Cinder protested weakly.

"No buts! Mmm. Okaay, maybe some butts. In the hot tub. Come on!"

"Kat?" I switched the voicecast to our Knight. "Hot tub's got your name on it!"

"Ehhh. Gonna pass." Katherine's dragon-feline face ignited on the holo. "Going to explore my city, since we're obviously not registering upstairs."

"Oh, so it's your city now?"

"Shush, you," she growled, but I could see her trying to hide a smile. "Someone has to scout the area properly via the deep, since I know you three idiots are going to want to gawk at and paw at everything later."

"You know me too well." I smiled. "Stay safe, bestie."

She grumbled something under her breath, but her eyes glowed from within with mild amusement before the projection winked out.

"Io? Hot tub?" I called up our Gater next.

"Water and moths don't mix well," Io's projection replied, stretching by the fire in a stone alcove. "Besides, this book is getting good. Julie Verne really knows how to write about moon-people."

"Aight, suit yourself," I said, hanging up.

In a few minutes, Vespera burst through the thick wooden door, dragging a protesting Cinder behind her. The Thunderbird's eyes lit up at the sight of the steaming pool.

"Yasss! Just what the doctor ordered!" she exclaimed, already rapidly stripping off her armor.

"Wait!" Cinder yelped, wings flaring with embarrassed pinks as Vee started removing her chainmail. "I don't have any swimming stuff . . ."

"Too bad, so sad." Vespera grinned mischievously, pulling off her hexasuit to reveal a chainmail bikini underneath. "More human for me."

"*You* are doing this on purpose!"

"All's fair in love and hot tubs," I commented at her.

Vee winked at Cinder, sliding into the water beside me. "Uhhhh." She breathed out, beak open wide. "That's the stuff. Dis is now officially my best delving experience ever. GJ, Quartermaster, never stop breakin' my expectations."

I smiled at her.

"Mmmm . . ." Vee purred, leaning against me and glancing deviously at the fretting Quetzi. "So . . . cozy."

"Oi! Get your sparkly talons off him!" Cinder growled, her feathers shifting through violet-greens.

"No talons, only warm burr." Vespera clicked her beak playfully, snuggling closer.

"Burr isn't a word!"

"Burrow into the chest," Vee clarified. "You kno', like the meme?"

"I don't know what meme that even is!"

"And you never will if you stand out there like a knob instead of enjoying the burr."

Cinder's feathers flashed through frustrated reds. She glanced between us and the door several times, clearly torn.

"Fine!" she finally burst out as Vee draped her black-and-white wing around me, sending sparks raining down on my head. "But turn around! Both of you!"

"Yes, ma'am." I grinned, sliding around the tub to face the magical view of gloomy Undertown lit by distant glowing moss, fires, and Kitlix lanterns. Vee giggled but did the same.

There was rustling of fabric and armor, then a splash as Cinder entered the water. I turned my head to find Cinder sitting in the tub about a meter away, half-submerged under, her wings wrapped around herself like a shield. Her feathers were shifting through embarrassed pinks, golds, violets, and nervous silvers. She glanced between her wings at the door again with a worried expression.

"Relax," I said. "I put up Lance's biggest shield ward over the door. Ain't nobody coming up here without my approval."

"Yeah, relax," Vespera commented, wrapping her left wing around me harder. "It's just us here. No need to be so shy."

"I'd love to relax, but someone's being extra handsy," Cinder growled.

"And?" The Thunderbird yawned.

"There's no 'and.' Ju-just stop fraternizing with our Quartermaster!" the Quetzi hissed. "It's . . . unprofessional!"

"I never claimed to be the paragon of proper delving procedures," Vee shrugged. "I see a shiny, I take it. Come on, Ci, use your words. Tell us how you really feel. No need to dance around it."

"I'm not dancing around anything!" Cinder's feathers flashed through defensively annoyed auburn-reds like an autumn tree. "I just . . . you can't just . . . he's . . ."

"Yeeeees?"

"You're bothering me!" Cinder snapped. "With your . . . your constant flirting and touching and . . . and . . ." the Quetzi drew out.

"And what?" Vespera pressed on mischievously.

"And he's not some shiny thing for you to collect! He's . . . he's important! To me! And you're just . . . just playing with him like everything's a joke!" Cinder stammered, opening her wings for a moment to reveal a white sports bra.

"What's wrong with some playin'?" Vespera walked her steel-clad talons up my shoulder, sending a spark into my cheek that made me twitch.

"I said . . . *LAY OFF!*" Cinder's face stretched out, becoming more draconic, her wings igniting with mind-shattering colors, voice laced with magic. I noticed that I slid away from Vee, my body responding to the wing-cast charmchain order.

"Playing?" Vespera's voice grew serious, her usual playful tone vanishing as she too slid away from me, sparks dancing between feathers. "You think that's what all this is? Just me playing around?"

"Isn't it?" Cinder challenged. "Everything's a game to you! You're always joking, always pretending nothing matters . . ."

"Some things do matter." The Thunder-girl crossed her arms. "I do joke. I do pretend. Because that's how I cope with the fact that in four months, I'm supposed to marry someone I hate! Someone whom I have to rewrite my brain for, become the perfect Prima-wife for!"

The extra, alien, hard-to-define colors melted away from Cinder's wings.

"I'm not like you or Io, Cee!" Vespera declared angrily. "I'm always in mild phase-shift, *always* keep a tight control of myself through Dreamancy. I don't phase-shift into an effin' rainbow-snake constantly like some Quetzis, nor do I constantly dull my predatory desires with interdimensional puff-bliss like some moths!"

Cinder seemed to deflate a little more, snout drawing back in.

"I had perfect control over my feelings . . . until this damned pinkie showed up," Vespera continued, gesturing at me. "This whack human who just . . . who makes whack plans to save me for some bloody reason. Who makes me feel like maybe, just maybe, I don't have to unmake myself."

Cinder crossed her arms.

"I care about Lexy," Vee declared. "Just like you do. Except . . . unlike you, I'm not afraid to admit it!"

The Quetzi frowned.

"I'm not simply afraid!" Cinder protested. "I just . . . it's . . . ughhhh . . ."

"Stop making it complicated," Vespera stated. "You like him. He likes you. What's so hard about that?"

"Everything!" Cinder's wings flared. "He's . . . he's human! And he's incredibly dishonest about so many things, and he might get arrested and deported when we get back, or my parents might find out that he's here illegally, and . . ."

"And what?" Vespera pressed. "Danger is the spice of life! So what if he's human? So what if he's a cheeky trickster? He lies to protect himself, to survive. To help his friends. Unlike certain ruby dragons we know!"

"That's . . . that's not the point!" Cinder's feathers danced through frustrated oranges like a living sunset.

"Then state ya point, ya freakin' knob!" Vee splashed water at her friend.

"The point is . . . everything's changing so fast. He's changing everything. The school, my family, my friends . . . even me! And I . . . I don't know if I'm ready for that," Cinder confessed.

"Ready for what?" I interjected. "For having real friends who care about you?"

"Friends?! This spark-harpy isn't behaving like a friend!" Cinder snarled, waving an accusatory clawed hand at the Thunderbird.

"Oh?" Vespera clicked her beak. "And how should a friend behave? Like Em? Controlling everything you do? Making you feel worthless unless you meet her impossible standards of absolute koboldization?"

"That's not—" Cinder started.

"Or maybe like me before?" Vespera continued. "Just going along with whatever Em wanted? Watching you slowly, unknowingly lose yourself to an Outsider Entity and doing fuck-all about it?"

"Stop it," Cinder hissed.

"No!" Vespera's gray eyes flashed. "You need to hear this. Real friends tell you the truth, even when it hurts. Real friends support you being yourself, not what they want you to be. Real friends—"

"Real friends don't try to steal each other's humans!" Cinder burst out, her wings flaring with deeper sunset reds and possessive violet-greens.

"I'm not stealing anything," Vespera replied calmly. "I'm investigating him. He's interesting."

"Investigating?!" Cinder sputtered. "Is that what you call draping yourself all over him? Investigating?!"

"Yep." Vespera snapped her talons, sending more sparks into my chest. "The draping has purpose. And I've discovered some very interesting things. Like how his heart rate speeds up when you get close to him. Or how his eyes follow your wings when you move. Or how he's literally planning to build a city called Katsburg just to make Kat happy. To help Io with finding the truth. To help me with my dumb thing! It's too kind and wholesome, and I don't trust kind and wholesome."

"Too kind?" Cinder blinked. "You think he's *too* kind?"

"Yes!" Vespera threw up her hands, sending sparks flying all over me. "Nobody is this selfless! Nobody just . . . decides to help everyone around them for no reason! There has to be an angle, a catch, a . . . something!"

"Actually," I said, raising my hand, "there is a catch."

CHAPTER SIXTY-THREE

Rooftop Hot Tub II

Both girls turned to look at me. Vespera slid to my side and put her magisteel-taloned hand on my shoulder, looking at my eyes.

"If I don't secure your trust, I'll be perma-dead in a week," I said.

"What?" Cinder blinked.

"The Frontenachii Scrutimancers are on my trail," I confessed. "Yulia's been tracking their movements south. They will come to Skyfall to bag me. If I don't secure your trust, less than a week from now will be the last time you and I see one another, because then I'll be staying here, on Arx on a permanent basis. All of my life is already in that bag."

I pointed at Lance's backpack. "So. If you don't trust me, then it's goodbye Skyfall High!"

"Stay . . . here?" Cinder repeated, eyes growing wide. "What?!"

"Yes," I said. "Stay here! Fortify the hell out of this place with the cash from selling more Genesis fluid. Then . . . destroy the Arx gate from both ends, which would hopefully give me decades or more to get stronger, become a proper Archmage. Unlike you, I've been asking around, paying attention! There are humans living on Arx! From what Shash told me, all of the Shandrian high lords are human. In fact, a human lordling named David-something just procured a lighthouse smithy with a dragon slave and turned it into a cafe right above us!" I pointed my index finger at the ceiling. "People can level up in Shandria, grow crystalline heart cores slowly over time!"

"But . . . your life . . ." Cinder stammered out, derailed by my revelations.

"What life?" I asked sharply. "My mom's dead. My uncle's on his last legs, maybe has a few years left. The Frontenachii Scruts will find me and take Yulia away from me, cut me up into a flesh-cube, and put me into a suitcase. You read the binder I gave you, did you not? You know what they do to humans. The catch is that I need both of you to trust me wholeheartedly and watch my back in Skyfall as my partners while I do everything in my power to help you . . . or you reject me, and then we part ways forever in a week, which would make me quite sad, 'cause I do like you both!"

"But . . ." Cinder's wings drooped. "That's not fair!"

"Life isn't fair." I shrugged. "But at least I'm being honest about my situation. I need both of you. Your absolute trust. Your friendship. Your protection. In return, I'll do everything in my power to help you. That's the deal. Simple as."

"And if we refuse?" Vespera asked, talons sparkling all over my shoulder.

"Then I stay here," I said simply. "Build my human colony. Maybe hang out with

Lord David, visit his lighthouse cafe for breakfast. Maybe die from an arrow to the face exploring my dungeon. Who knows? But at least I'll die free, on my own terms. The Wendigos don't let their test subjects die!"

Cinder lowered her eyes.

"What?" I asked. "Welcome to my world, Ci. A world where I have to constantly think three steps ahead of everyone just to survive. Where I have to manipulate and scheme and plan because if I don't, I end up in a Wendigo compound. Do you want to see Yulia's video of the rows and rows of cages filled with sliced-up, splayed humans? Humans put into suitcases? Humans cut in half and still kept alive with vile preservation magic for centuries?"

The Quetzi swallowed.

"You wanted honesty? Here it is. Raw and ugly. I'm not playing games. I'm fighting for survival. Every move I make, every person I befriend, every plan I set in motion—it's all part of staying alive and free. And maybe, just maybe, making things better for others along the way."

"That answers that," Vespera said. "You pass."

"Pass what?" Cinder demanded.

"Everything," the Thunderbird clicked, letting go of me. "I must admit, I did have some minor reservations, but they're now answered."

"You were testing him?" Cinder demanded.

"Of course." Vespera shrugged. "I am always testing him. I can read thoughts with electrical impulses. Duh. The answer he provided is acceptable. As the firstborn Princess of the House of Simmi, I henceforth claim this human as my property. If anyone has objections, voice them now."

"*What?!*" Cinder's feathers exploded with furious reds and violent blacks. "You can't just . . . *claim* him!"

"I just did." Vespera clicked her beak smugly. "By the ancient laws of Thunderland, it is thus. Any challenges must be issued formally through . . ."

"Challenge issued!" Cinder snarled, her wings flaring wide. "You sparkly harpy! You . . ."

"Challenge accepted," Vespera clicked. "Terms?"

"Terms?!" Cinder sputtered.

"Yes, terms," Vespera said patiently. "How shall we settle this dispute over property ownership, Miss Nova? A duel to the death? A formal agreement between two most noble houses? Or perhaps . . . something more interesting?"

"You can't just claim people out of the blue!"

"Au contraire, mon amie, I can indeed claim humans," Vespera clicked. "The ancient clan laws are quite clear on the matter. As the Princess of Thunder, I have the right to claim any free range human that catches my interest. Unless . . ." She paused dramatically. ". . . someone else has a prior claim, perchance?"

Cinder's feathers shifted through a kaleidoscope of colors—angry reds, possessive greens, embarrassed pinks.

"I . . . I . . ." she stammered.

"Yeeeees?" Vespera pressed, gray eyes gleaming. "Do you have a prior claim, Miss Nova? Perhaps something you'd like to share with the class?"

"I . . . he's . . . *urghhhh*!" Cinder threw up her wings in frustration, sending water splashing everywhere. "Fine! Yes! I claimed him! Are you happy now?! I like this stupid, reckless, impossible human who keeps turning my life upside down!"

"So you claimed him . . . when?" Vespera tilted her beak.

"T-two days ago," Cinder confessed with a slight stammer. "I put a magical marker in his head, marking him as my property. It sorta broke him for a bit. Happy?"

I squinted at Cinder.

"You did what to my head?" I asked. "When was this?"

"When you wouldn't tell me shit, and I snuck into your room at my house," Cinder muttered. "I . . . may have . . . put a tiny bit of my soul in you. Just a small mark! To keep track of you! To see if you were being honest! Because you keep doing insanely stupid things and lying and getting into trouble!"

"Ah," I said. "The meta-narrator moment when your dad locked down the ward and I lost distinction between thought and conversation. That made me feel pretty messed up. Thanks."

"That explains what I thought I felt in the current," Vespera clicked. "Thank you. I was wondering whose soul bit it was."

"Just a tiny tracking mark!" Cinder protested, wings flaring. "A completely normal, totally reasonable precaution! You know how he is, damn it!"

"Mm-hmmm." Vespera tapped her beak with a steel-clad talon. "I know how he is. Welp, I'm not gonna concede."

She suddenly dropped into the water on her knees and wrapped her hands around Cinder's legs.

"What are you doing?!" Cinder yelped, trying to shove Vee aside.

"Begging," Vee looked up. "Pretty please, can I co-own him?"

"Co-own?!" Cinder sputtered. "What . . . what are you talking about?"

"I'll be good, I promise! I'll only borrow him on weekends and . . . Wednesdays! I'll be extra nice!"

"Is this an Omnid thing?" I asked, raising an eyebrow.

"Yeah," Vespera answered, still clinging to Cinder's legs. "She claimed you as property in the most ancient way. I must therefore beg for joint ownership."

"This is ridiculous!" Cinder growled, trying to shake Vee off. "Get up! You're embarrassing yourself!"

"And I'll embarrass myself harder," the Thunderbird stated. "And embarrass you. Please? Pretty please with lightning on top?"

"No!" Cinder's wings flared with possessive violets. "Piss off!"

"Come on," Vespera pouted. "I'll be a responsible co-owner! I'll feed him, walk him, be a good Prima-Sword, make sure he doesn't get into trouble . . ."

"This is the weirdest conversation I've ever been part of," I commented.

"Pweeeeeease?" Vespera begged, still clinging to Cinder's legs. "I'll let you be the Heart-Shield of his Estate! I just want visitation rights! I'll pay, do whatever you want!"

"No!" Cinder's feathers bristled. "Stop making this weird!"

"I'll make it weirder," Vespera threatened. "I'll start singing. In public. Badly. About how unfair you are. Write sad songs about unrequited thunder-love."

"*What?!*"

"Oh, Cinder, my heart's cruel jailer," Vespera began in a deliberately off-key voice. "Won't share her human, what a terrible failure . . ."

"How weirded out should I be about being claimed?" I asked from my seat.

"Your opinion is irrelevant." Vee waved me off with a grin. "Humans don't have rights."

"Gee, thanks," I fired back.

"Come onnnnn," Vespera returned to whining up at Cinder.

"For the last time, *no*!" Cinder smacked Vespera. "Lay off!"

"I'm not gonna lay off," Vespera insisted. "I'm gonna cling to you 'n' beg till you give in."

"No means no," Cinder growled, trying to pry Vespera off her legs unsuccessfully. "Stop being ridiculous! Let go of me! Don't make me use my wings! I said *let go*!"

Cinder's wings detonated with blinding colors, voice echoed unnaturally, cutting across my soul. I blinked as my brain momentarily careened sideways trying to let go of Cinder, whom I wasn't even holding onto.

Vespera didn't let go. She clung on harder, trembling and blinking.

"Vespera, I said . . ." Cinder hiss-growled, still speaking with magic-laced words.

"No . . ." Vespera's voice cracked. Her gray eyes filled with sparks of tears. "You don't understand . . . I . . . I need this. I need him. Please!"

"What?" Cinder paused in her attempts to shake Vee off. "The Abyss do you need him for?!"

"Please," Vespera sobbed, her playful demeanor melting away. "You don't understand. In four months . . . four months and I'll never . . . I'll never be me again. My father will . . . he'll force me to erase myself . . . I can't . . . I need something real. Something true. Please! Please don't take this away from me!"

"You can't just . . . emotionally blackmail me into whatever this is! That's not how this works!" Cinder looked down with a scowl.

I quietly wondered if this is how Omnid relationships worked. It would be nice to ask Yulia these things, but she wasn't connected to the net now and would potentially hallucinate a made-up answer.

"I need someone who sees me," Vespera continued through her tears. "Who knows the real me. Not the ditzy party girl. Not the perfect heir. Just . . . me. Please! I'll do anything. I'll . . . I'll sign whatever contract you want! I'll swear not to joke again. I'll sit with you in your dreams every night, for as long as it takes, even if it takes us decades, even if it takes my entire lifetime to stop the high-level Outsider from the lake door! Please . . . please . . . I don't want to wake up one day as not me . . . please . . . Ci! I'm begging you . . . I can't . . . I can't . . ."

She broke down completely, her shoulders shaking with sobs.

"You . . ." Cinder sighed deeply. "You really mean it?"

"No games," Vespera hiccuped. "Not about this. Never about this. Come on, look . . . I'm crying. I thought that I got that all out of me in Dreamwalking . . . blah. Blasted human giving me blasted feelings! This is like the first time I cried IRL since I was six. Ah. Your charmchain must have broken some barrier-stuff in my head. Thanks a lot, Ci."

Cinder looked down at the sobbing Thunderbird.

"Vee . . ." she said softly. "Why do you even give a shit about the chain-soul tag? I honestly expected you to just flip me off and fly off to lightning make out with him or . . . something else equally stupid and brash."

"'Cause . . . sometime . . . before summer break, I'll need to get engaged to this pink sausage." Vespera pointed a magisteel claw at me. "Properly. Legally. In a cathedral. With a Nazarite Archpriest Soul Binder who'd absolutely see your claim and would refuse to bind me to someone else's claimed soul! I need to, *have* to void the chains tying me to Golden Star! I want to do this right. I don't want to steal him from under you. I don't want to trick anyone. I want . . . I want something real! Something honest. For once in my life, I want to not pretend, damn it!"

Her voice cracked as more tears came.

"And . . . and maybe if I do this right, if I follow the rules . . . maybe you'll trust me. Maybe we can be real friends, not just . . . not just people who hang out and get very drunk and smack monsters because Em says so. Maybe . . ."

She trailed off into silence, sparking tears falling into the water.

Cinder remained silent.

CHAPTER SIXTY-FOUR

Rooftop Hot Tub III

Maybe . . ." Cinder sighed deeply, feathers dancing with troubled green-violet-blues and uncertain silvers. "Maybe we already are friends, Vee. Real friends."

"R-really?" Vespera looked up, gray eyes wide and hopeful through her tears.

"Yes, you stupid bird." Cinder's wings wrapped around them both. "Real friends. Who apparently share dreams . . . and humans now. Somehow. Against my better judgment."

"You mean it?" Vespera sniffled. "You'll . . . you'll let me co-own him? Thank you! Thank yooouuuu, thaaaank youuuuuu!"

She dug into Cinder with her talons even harder, making the Quetzalcoatl wince.

"Under conditions," Cinder stated firmly. "First—no more surprise kidnappings."

"But what if . . ."

"No. More. Kidnappings." Cinder's voice brooked no argument.

"Fine," Vespera pouted. "No more surprise kidnappings. What else?"

"No more surprise, full-on, floating, celestorm-generating mind-melding with him!" Cinder stated.

"Fine," Vespera grumbled with a sour face. "Freakin' square dragon don't appreciate any freakin' spontaneity. What else?"

"Let go so I can feel my legs," Cinder ordered.

"Done. Anythin' else?" The Thunderbird released her.

"I don't know what else!" Cinder huffed. "I didn't think we'd get this far in this particular direction. Ughhhh."

She stretched and waddled over to me and sat by my side. "I blame you for all of this."

"Me?" I raised an eyebrow. "What did I even do? I don't have magic powers to claim people. I'm just chilling in the tub I made, trying to cope with whatever you did to me two days ago."

"Me?! You know what you freaking did, you manipulative ass!" she growled, elbowing me.

Vespera slid into the stone seat beside Cinder, glancing at me. "Yeah. Making everyone feel things and care about stuff! Quite devious of you!"

"I am a dastardly human villain." I grinned. "Though I must point out that nobody asked said human about being property."

"Nobody asked the sofa if it wanted to be sat on either," Vespera clicked dismissively, sinking down to enjoy the warmth. "Or the hot tub if it wanted to be filled with bubbling water. Property doesn't get a vote."

"That's . . . rather concerning," I commented.

"That's just Omnithornia for you," Cinder sighed. "Where humans have fewer rights than furniture."

"But at least you're premium furniture," Vespera added cheerfully, sending me a thumbs-up. "Like, really fancy premium furniture. With benefits!"

"What benefits?" I arched an eyebrow.

"Like getting to sit in hot tubs with pretty, top-predator, half-god girls." Vespera winked.

"Oh yes, such terrible benefits," I rolled my eyes. "Being claimed as property by two apex predators who can't decide if they want to fight over me or share me. Truly, I am blessed."

"Oi! You are blessed," Vespera clicked. "Do you know how many humans would kill to be in your position?"

"None," I said flatly. "Because they're all terrified of your unholy magic powers. I barely survived the day. I was an adventurer till I got an arrow through the lung!"

"Details." Vespera waved dismissively with a smirk at my Skylord joke. "The point is, you get us. Both of us! That's like . . . winning the lottery twice!"

"And all it cost was my basic human rights," I sighed dramatically. "Such a bargain."

"Oh, shush." Vespera poked me, stretching a hand across Cinder. "I'll give you rights . . . later."

"What kind of rights?" I asked.

"The right to sit still and look pretty. The right to carry my shopping bags on weekends . . ." Vespera clicked her beak mischievously and yelped when Cinder elbowed her. "Ow! Watch the ribs! . . . The right to claim us back."

"The right to . . . what?" Cinder choked.

"Claim us back." Vespera nodded with a sage expression. "I mean, it's only fair. If we get to claim him, he should get to claim us, too."

"How's he gonna do that with no magic, you knob?" the Quetzi demanded.

"Ci." Vespera shook her head, stretching herself across our laps, slipping back into Valley girl accent. "You're pretty, but so dumb sometimes, ya kno'? He channeled lightning through me. He Dreamwalked. Ya get what this means, right? You can make a shake outta those feathers, and we can teach him to claim us both, Omnid style. Maybe if we're proper blood and soul-bound to one another, we won't need that lighter as much, yeah? After all, that mana-rich fuel will run out."

"Blood bond?" Cinder flashed with orange-reds. "Two-directional soul-bond?! That's . . . that's really serious stuff, Vee. Like, permanent serious. Forever serious. That's . . . that's basically marriage. Like, old-school, ancient-rites marriage!"

"Yes." Vespera's playful tone vanished. "That's the point. I want something permanent. Something real. Something that can't be taken away or rewritten by my family's orders or lightning. I'm genuinely happy with you two. Satisfied. You're quite tolerable for a Quetzi and a human. This is my nest."

She patted our legs.

"This is my new clan." Steel-covered talons reached out, sending sparks against our hearts. "No takebacksies."

"Feels like we're going a little fast there." Cinder pursed her lips, her face looking nearly eighty-five percent human now.

"I don't have time to go slow." Vespera shook her feathered mane. "I *need* to get legally engaged to someone special before summer. You've got an Outsider in your soul. Lex doesn't have time to fluff around, he's got Wendigos on his . . . tail? Um. Butt? Whatever!"

"Still . . . you're asking for a lot," Cinder said. "Two-way soul-bonds aren't something to rush into."

"Says the girl who already tagged him! Also," Vespera clicked, "we *do* have some time to get to know each other better before I'm force-shipped to Thunderland. I've thought about this. A lot. Since last night when we shared dreams. When I felt, saw how broken you are inside, how that thing from the lake is eating at you, how you're still standing strong, fighting off something so high-level against all odds. And him . . ." She poked me. "He's got two souls already. What's two more?"

"Two souls?!" Cinder sputtered. "What?! *How?!*"

"I don't know." Vespera squinted up at me. "Humans don't normally have two souls. Yet here we are. When I scanned him Tuesday, he had one soul. One static pattern. And on Friday, he had two human patterns in him. It's like . . . mmm . . . human to the power of human. [Human[Human]]. Weirdest shit ever. Another mystery. Still investigating."

"How in the Abyss do you have two souls?" Cinder demanded.

"Alexa and Martin," I said. "Alexa showed up after I jumped into the Genesis Pool." Vespera's gray eyes went wide. "You did *what?*"

"He jumped into the Genesis Pool while alive," Cinder explained. "Thursday, after Em knocked him out with a dodgeball in Coach Canard's class. He just . . . dove right in. Watched him do it."

"And you *let him* do that?!"

"I didn't *let* him do shit!" Cinder protested. "He just . . . did it! Before I could stop him. One second he was sitting in his wheelchair, the next he just . . . jumped in! I had to fish him out!"

"And you didn't think to mention this earlier?!" Vespera demanded.

"I was a bit busy dealing with everything else he's done!" Cinder's feathers flashed defensively. "Like him infiltrating my house, charming my parents, harvesting my brother's gear, banishing our Delving instructor, buying criminal organizations . . ."

"Fair point," Vespera conceded. "But still . . . jumping into Genesis fluid while alive? That's . . ."

"What?" I asked.

"That's a ticket straight to insanity," Vespera said. "From what I've read on inco research—there was a case from a few decades ago. An old Omnid fell into his incarnator while alive for a few hours, and nobody helped him out. He came out . . . wrong, mad, mentally broken. Started claiming he was a human named Elleanora Gamp Douglass. Was freaking out about everything. Couldn't remember his own name, his own life. 'Ey put the ol' coot into an insane asylum."

"That's . . . not what happened to me," I said. "I saw Alexa there. She hugged me. Told me to find our other four friends, I think. Then I got pulled out."

"Other four?" Vespera clicked. "What other four?"

"He's talking about Katherine's book characters," Cinder explained. "He says he's Alexa. One of the main characters. Or has her soul. Or something. I don't know, it's freaking confusing."

"Wait, what?" Vespera sat up. "Katherine's book? The one Em posted online to make fun of her?"

"Yeah," Cinder nodded. "Apparently he's . . . connected to it somehow."

"Emerald is connected to it, too," I said. "Another reason why I didn't let her die."

"What do you mean, Em is connected to it?" Cinder blinked.

"Remember how Em became obsessed with the antagonist?" I asked. "Ember? The selfish jackass who kept trying to stop Alexa from helping others?"

"Yeah." Cinder nodded. "She wouldn't shut up about how Ember was the real hero and Alexa was just a villain who . . ."

She trailed off, eyes widening.

"Oh," she breathed.

"Exactly." I nodded. "Em isn't just obsessed with Ember. She *is* Ember. Just like I'm Alexa and also Martin. Maybe we were them in our previous life, and we just . . . forgot."

"Previous life?" Vespera asked. "That's not a thing. The Arx Wheel sucks up all dead souls like a vacuum."

"Yeah." Cinder nodded. "Em can't be . . . she's not . . ."

"It might be a thing. Maybe we didn't die. Maybe the System Wizards, things like Zee Captain, overwrote us, changed us . . . because I went outside of their narrative, broke their System or whatever. Think about it," I said. "Why did Em save you that night at the lake? Why did she help you get revenge? Because that's what Ember would do—save someone to control them, to make them dependent. To prove that her way is the only way."

"But . . ." Cinder's feathers shifted through troubled grays. "That would mean . . ."

"That would mean that Katherine's story isn't just a story," Vespera finished. "It's something more. Something real. Sheeet. Em was legit crazy obsessed over destroying Kat emotionally over her silly 'human heroes' book. It didn't make any sense. I told her like a million times to drop it, that she was wasting so much effort 'n' time obsessin' over it, but she just didn't give."

"And you think . . ." Cinder swallowed. "You think Em is becoming Ember because she read Kat's story?"

"No." I shook my head. "I think she was always Ember. Just like I was always Alexa. The story just . . . woke something up. Something that was already there. When I dunked Emerald into the Genesis Pool . . . I think that she remembered more of it. She didn't say it out loud, but she absolutely knew. I think that she hates humans because she remembers herself being a human superhero in another life, remembers the human villain . . . Alexa beating the shit out of her."

"That makes no sense," Cinder protested. "Em's a full-blood dragon. She can't be . . . she wasn't . . ."

"She was," I said, tapping the side of my head. "The memories are there, just . . . buried. Fragmented. Hidden. Overwritten by the System Wizards."

"Wait. Am I in it? Was I overwritten too? I don't recall being particularly bothered by Kat's art or book," Vespera said, looking at me and Cinder.

I reached to where my phone was sitting behind us and showed Vee Katherine's sketches from when I crashed into her. "Do you recognize this town? Saint Mary? Look at this painting." I pulled up Katherine's art from the hall. "There are four kids sitting under that tree." I pointed. "Martin. Alexa. Katherine. Ember."

"Yeah," Vespera sighed, squinting at the art. "I feel nothing. I'm none of these peeps."

"I think that . . . I'm Alexa," Cinder let out. "Except . . . I'm not like her. I'm missing . . . something."

"Maybe whatever you're missing is in me," I said. "Maybe you got some Martin in you. Maybe when things were overwritten, we swapped around or something. Maybe whatever we did in our past life confused the Wizards enough for them to make mistakes."

"Or the Outsider managed to suck the drive out of Ci," Vespera commented.

Cinder frowned.

Vespera looked at my phone. "Dang, I feel super jelly 'cause you guys have a secret past-life thing. Can I see more?"

Yulia continued flipping through Kat's most recent sketches as the Thunderbird held it in her talons.

"Wait," Vespera said. "Stop. Go back. Again. That girl in the pink space suit. Who is that?"

"That's . . . Dora the Terraformer, I think," Cinder said. "A hero. One of the great five."

"What'd she do?" Vee demanded.

"Invented shit," Cinder replied. "I dunno. It's been ages since I've read Kat's book or seen her concept art. "Dora wasn't a nice girl. Brilliant but somewhat amoral, I think? She'd invent these amazing things—AIs, nanobots, med-guns, all sorts of futuristic tech."

"Med-guns." Vespera blinked. "Hol' up. That gun Io used on your chest." She poked the silver patch with a talon. "Was that . . ."

"Yes." I nodded. "It was Dora's med-gun design. That's what the text on the side said."

"Kat said that most of her book was inspired by random shit Io pulled from his doomed dimension gates," Cinder said thoughtfully.

"So . . . I was . . . this . . . Dora?" Vee blinked, running her talons through her feathers. "And my work is still . . . out there, somewhere? Sheeeet. Was Dora . . . one of the bad guys or something?"

"She was one of the top heroes," Cinder nodded. "A real corpo-beerch who made up all sorts of rules for others but rarely followed them herself. Alexa tricked Dora a few times, along with the other five heroes who ruled the Superstate from their Titanomachy megastructure."

"What happened to her?" Vespera asked eagerly. "What happened to her AIs?"

"I don't know," Cinder sighed. "Alexa kicked everyone's ass with her clever hijinks, including Dora, and sacrificed herself and . . . that's where Em posted the draft online. Kat stopped writing after that."

"Hrm," Vee clicked. "I'll have to bug Kat about this Dora character. This . . . interests me."

"We can interrogate her about this when she returns," I said. "Slowly. She's shy about her work."

"She's not shy," Cinder corrected. "She's traumatized. Em took something private and personal and turned it into a joke. Made Kat feel like her art, her writing, was worthless. Ugh." she buried her face in her arms. "I feel so bad about all of this. I need to figure out how to make it up to Kat."

"Welp, this is some deep sheet," Vespera clicked thoughtfully. "But I guess that I don't mind. Maybe I was this Dora jerk in another life. It don't matter now. Now I'm me. Vespy. And I'm glad that I found you before I erased myself and became just another cold cruel corpo-beerch."

She hugged both of us tightly. "Don't abandon me, yeah? Please."

"Never." I hugged her back. "Never ever ever."

CHAPTER SIXTY-FIVE

The Hunter of Shadows

Katherine slid through reality, mostly submerged in the deep like a shadow, untouchable, unseen, nearly impossible to focus on.

The abandoned, desolate version of Undertown stretched out around her, layered under mundane physical reality, buildings warped and distorted as if seen through dark water between the state of intact and in ruin.

Halfway in the deep, everything was muted and smudged. Colors bled away, leaving only shades of gray and black. Sounds came as if from very far away, echoing oddly.

She moved silently through the twisted streets, mapping the terrain, listening to conversations, tracking, sniffing, determining the source of all fear, suffering, misery, and pain that permeated the Shandrian underworld like a smothering blanket. A blanket that sated her predator-phase, fueled her Fractal Engine heart, made her legs work properly.

Katherine slithered deeper into the twisted streets, following the trail of addiction and despair that led like breadcrumbs. The scent of Topaz was unmistakable—a sickly sweet crisp smell of false dreams that clung to everything in Undertown. It poured from blue-tinted skin-wrapped cigars in people's mouths, it pulsed from the drinks many bloated figures were nursing. It emanated from the crystalline azure-blue powder some were inhaling within the Topaz dens all around.

Shadows twisted and writhed around her as she moved, deep echoes responding to her presence. In the deep, she was more than just herself, she was a Stollwurm—she was a living nightmare, a predator that fed on fears, the Queen of Echoes, drawn to suffering, sated by the deepest darkest nightmares of others imprinted on everything down below.

She wasn't a big fan of it all, but she was born with it, grew up with it, accepted the deep as part of who she was. Now she was using her power to protect her delving team, feeling that if she didn't help out now, then Undertown would most likely chew them all up and then swallow them whole.

The trail of fears led her to a large underground cavern at the eastern side of Undertown. The biggest Topaz den, the source of a river of fear and misery blooming nasty, albeit deliciously crunchy, echoes across the deep.

She phased right through doors which were all missing in the deep. The aura of the magic drug's presence was overwhelming here—a nauseating miasma of artificial dreams crawling atop shattered hopes. It poured from the blue-tinted, swollen bodies of addicts covering the floor of the den cavern.

Katherine inhaled the misery and rushed upstairs, phasing through several magisteel-plated doors heading into the biggest, fanciest room she could find. One that smelled of fear, of power, of greed, and hoarding gold.

The Stollwurm melted into the darkest corner of the luxurious office, emerging a bit out of the deep to spy on its inhabitant. The space was opulent—all polished obsidian and gold trim, with expensive rugs and ancient artifacts displayed in glass cases. A weird-looking, large, faded painting-sculpture made from what looked like a bunch of ossified digits hung behind the owner of this domain.

A fat, balding, blue-tinted human in gold-and-blue robes sat behind a mahogany table, tapping a bloated, artifact-ring-covered finger on a very large crystal ball.

Katherine instantly recognized Gabriella Matrosin, the catgirl bank attendant, who stared back at the den owner from the crystalline Voicecast sphere.

"Explain it to me again. What happened to this year's Topaz shipment, Gabs?" the man demanded. "I have distributors waiting. Important people. The kind that don't like to be kept waiting. Why do I have to waste my time calling you myself about this?"

"Apologies, Grand Moloch Arkenish," Gabriella's projection flickered in the crystal ball. "There's been . . . a complication."

"What complication?" Arkenish growled.

"Lord Zalimar didn't come through the gate," Gabriella let out. "Only his students came through. I was waiting for him all day, but he didn't show up."

"What do you mean Zalimar didn't come through?!" Arkenish demanded. "He always comes through! He's our supplier! He's never been late with a shipment! What happened to him?"

"I asked the last party of novitiate student delvers from Arx about it," Gabriella sighed, her whiskers twitching. "According to their Student President and highest ranked Captain, Quint . . . a group of rowdy students challenged Lord Zalimar to a duel to the death."

"A duel?" Arkenish sputtered. "And then what?!"

"And then they won," Gabriella said with a deep frown. "They banished him into another dimension. Quint told me that they can't reach him. He said that Zalimar will be gone for two weeks from his job at the very least. Due to the temporal dilation, that's . . . over three years and two months of no Topaz shipments."

"*Three years?!*" Arkenish slammed his fist on the desk. "*What?!* Who challenged him? Who has the audacity to disrupt our business?!"

"A new delving team from Earth," Gabriella said. "They call themselves I Love You. Human-looking Quartermaster Alexander Glock, Quetzalcoatl Captain Cinder Nova, Thunderbird Slayer Vespera Simmi, Mothman Gater Iogann Wanderer, and Knight Stollwurm Katherine Kells."

Katherine's emerald eyes narrowed at the mention of her name.

Gabriella pulled a canvas from her robes and unfurled it. The paint on it swirled, images of the five students forming on the canvas one by one.

"Find them!" Arkenish growled. "Find them so that I can peel the flesh off their bones and . . ."

"Already found," Gabriella interrupted. "According to our Scrutimancers, they went to Undertown. They're staying at the Gloomy Horse Tavern. Our agents are already closing in. We should have them bagged up soon."

"Good." Arkenish leaned back in his chair. "Nobody disrupts my business. Nobody! I want their fingers before this day ends."

"Of course." Gabriella nodded. "Our business with Lord Zalimar cannot be disrupted for so long. Far too much valuable trade is tied to the Shandrian Earth-Arx gate. These kids won't see another sunrise. We'll make them disappear, chop them up, destroy their artifacts. You'll have new fingers mounted on that wall soon, don't fret."

Katherine looked up at the weird 2.5-D painting behind the man. She realized that it was made from fingers of various colors.

"Good tomorrow, Grand Moloch." The crystal ball went dark as Gabriella's image faded away.

Arkenish slammed his fists into the table, making the wood groan.

"*Damnation!*" he barked and then started to mutter to himself. "Three bloody years. Three years! Damn it all! I have to call up all of the warehouses . . . have to make the supplies we already have last . . . order duplicator mages to copy what we have . . . stretch the lesser quality copied stuff over the years, increase the price."

Arkenish slumped back in his chair, muttering more colorful curses under his breath. He reached for a fat cigar, his hands shaking slightly as he lit it, exhaling the blue-tinted smoke.

Katherine emerged fully from the deep, her emerald eyes blazing. Arkenish's head snapped up, the cigar falling from his trembling fingers as her magisteel-covered claws closed around his neck, lifting the man up with ease from his seat.

"Who . . . how did you . . ." he stammered, trying to reach for something under his desk.

Katherine pulled the fat man into the deep and unleashed her aura, pouring all of the fear and pain she'd collected from roaming across Undertown into Arkenish.

He screamed, flailed in her grip, eyes bulging in horror.

"Hello," Katherine hissed. "I hear you're having supply chain issues."

"You . . ." the man let out, shaking in her claws. "You're one of them . . . Earth-delvers! K-Katherine Kells!"

"Yes," she growled. "And you better recall those assassins if you want to live."

"I . . . I cannot!" the Grand Moloch bawled. "I'm just the distributor! The Undertown Topaz Den proprietor! The Arx Bank controls everything from above! Please . . . I'm just a middleman! R-rep Gabriella . . . she's the one who forwards the order of the Bankers to the Enforcers! They're the ones who . . ."

"How long?" Katherine tightened her grip, letting more fear seep into the man's mind.

"Th-thirty m-minutes," the man cried. "In thirty minutes, your friends will be arrested and executed!"

"Tell me everything quickly," she growled. "About the bank. About Gabriella. About the Topaz trade. Everything."

"The . . . the Arx B-Bank controls everything!" Arkenish gasped through her iron grip. "They . . . they own most of Shandria! The Topaz trade . . . it's just one part of their operation! We all work for them, me 'n' Gabs, every Guild in U-Undertown obeys the Loan Sharks! Everyone d-down here is indebted to the Arx Bank! They own many i-independent city states all across Arx!"

"How many city states?"

"I . . . I don't know the exact number!" The man trembled. "It is a very vast network, encompassing p-parts of the Shadow Empire and f-far, far beyond it. You and your friends are already dead! The b-bankers . . . they're . . . they're not gonna stop till they feed you to the Shadows! Nobody can get away from th-their Enforcer mages! Y-you kids made a b-big mistake! Nobody screws with their interdimensional suppliers!"

"Nobody?" Katherine's eyes flashed dangerously. "Watch me."

"Please!" he begged, shaking in her claws. "I'll give you anything! Money! Power! Women! Men! Children! Anything you desire! Just don't . . ."

"Shut up," Katherine growled. "I'm not interested in your pathetic bribes. I want information. Weaknesses. Names. Locations. Everything, everyone that you know that ties Undertown to the Arx Bankers and Zalimar!"

"I . . . I can't!" Arkenish whimpered. "They'll kill me! They'll kill my family! They'll . . ."

Katherine's claws tightened, drawing blood. "I can do much, much worse," she promised. "You'll wish that you were dead."

The man screamed as her Stollwurm aura pounded into his psyche, tearing it asunder.

"No! *No* more! Please!" The man sobbed, shaking like a leaf. "The Loan Sharks . . . they're not normal Arx-kin. They're . . . they're something else. Something ancient, something from another dimension. They've been running things on Arx since before the Shadow Empire rose up to take o-over Shandria! They have skyships that travel between cities! Gates that can go anywhere on Arx! More p-permanent, i-interdimensional gates! There are several branches of the Arx Bank in Shandria . . . Closest one is next to the cathedral f-facing the central square! One in the Guild District on 382 Barbariss Street. The third one is in the Market District, facing the Gilded Gryphon Inn. There is a secret b-branch in Undertown in the Assassins Guild. There's a yellow folder in my safe behind the finger sculpture! It has names of all the Arx Bank reps I work with . . . everything I know about them! I've been collecting information about th-them and their s-servants! Figuring out everything in case they betrayed me!"

Katherine growled.

"I can be of use to you!" the man begged. "Please! I'll serve you! I can work with you! The power of the Bank won't be easily broken! They g-give everyone these m-magic b-bracelets, see?" The man shook a hexagonal textured bracelet on his wrist. "They s-slowly eat everyone's mana, tell everyone their S-system stats, translate every language into every language!"

"Everyone in Shandria has these bracelets?" Katherine demanded.

"Y-yes!" Arkenish nodded frantically. "The Bank gives them out for free, once! They say it's a service, a gift to help people track their skills and System stats and translate languages! But really . . . really they're gathering data! They know everything about everyone! Where we go, what we do, how much mana we have, who we talk to!"

Katherine's eyes narrowed as she examined the hexagonal bracelet on the man's wrist. It looked identical to the Lazarus bracelets they received at school, but it smelled a bit off, the texture looked scratched up, duller, less magical, less . . . alive. She inhaled deep, tapped it with a claw.

A shoddy, modified, magical copy . . . likely created with a duplicator artifact.

"Give me the combination to your safe," Katherine growled.

"3-8-2-1-5!" the man sobbed. "Please . . . I've told you everything I know!"

"Good," Katherine said. "I already have one annoying human. I don't need another, especially not one that's cursed by a million ghosts. Have fun being devoured by your victims."

She released him into the darkness and dove out of the deep back into the office, still submerged one fifth of the way in.

She walked to the safe, idly noting how many monstrous, shimmering, pearlescent-blue, stretched-out, skittering, crawling, many-limbed, hollow humanoids advanced from all around towards Arkenish.

The deep echoes descended on the screaming man like a swarm of locusts, tearing into his flesh and soul, seeking vengeance for the pain and misery he had inflicted upon them while they were still alive.

Katherine turned away from the grisly scene, tearing the painting off the wall to get to the safe. She used the combination to unlock it and spotted the yellow folder amongst piles of jewels, contracts, paperwork, and coins, stuffing everything into her bag.

The Arx Bank controlled everything. Instructor Zalimar was in cahoots with them, probably selling Omnid magitek to them!

The bracelets. The translations. The stats. Even the Topaz trade was just one tendril of their vast operation. And now their agents were annoyed with a certain pesky human who messed with their primary supplier.

She had no time to lose and four of her idiot . . . friends to save.

CHAPTER SIXTY-SIX

Weapons of Mass Destruction

Our trio descended from the rooftop hot tub back to the main dining hall, finding Io still lounging by the massive fireplace, his wide-brimmed hat pulled low over his eyes as he read his book in his chosen stone alcove.

"Sup, ma Gater," I called out, settling on a leather couch next to the fire. "How's the moon?"

"Haunted," Io replied, snapping his book shut and sliding it into his bag. "The moon-people have some serious issues with their ghost problem. Did ya guys resolve yo 'ship issues?"

"What?! W-we didn't . . . it's not . . . there weren't any 'ship issues to resolve!" Cinder stammered out. "We just . . . talked! About stuff! Normal stuff!"

"Mhmmm, sure," Io hummed knowingly, sitting up. "That's why you're glowing like a pink reactor and Vee looks like she won the lottery?"

"Joint custody, my dude," Vespera clicked merrily.

"Grats on a solid polyship." Io nodded, offering the Thunderbird a high five. "Wasn't sure if it would be just Ci. Far too many Omnids these days end up 'lone or bound to a dickish, controlling clan leader."

"Yeah." Vee dropped on the couch next to me, chainmail jiggling. "As a society, we are extra-cooked. Omnicorp be capitalizin' on parasocial relationships. Corps like Golden Star feed everyone's data into probability engines and spit out 'optimal matches' for maintaining stronk bloodlines via corporate mergers. Pretty sure we gonna have human-made robots satisfyin' all our physical needs at this rate. Ugh. Now I need a drink to chase away the depresso."

Io pulled a bottle of interdimensional beer from his bag featuring the tag *Chalice's Brew* on it and an etching of an armored knight with a giant sword.

"Oi," I growled, stepping towards him and pushing his fuzzy hand back into the bag. "Slide that back where it came from."

"Nuuu," Vee whined, trying to pull Io's paw out of the bag. "Gimme! I need it to cope!"

"As your Quartermaster," I said, "I'm banning you all from drinking until there's something to celebrate."

"Lame!" Vee huffed. "I thought you were the cool kind of Quartermaster that'd let me booze up in the afternoon."

"I am cool," I said. "I need you sober. You're my Thunder-cannon. My artillery piece. My big railgun. My genius Prima Hunter Sword. My . . . insert dashing and dangerous birb description here."

Vee burst into snickers, blushing with dark feathery spots and sparks dancing up her cheeks, giving up on the beer in lieu of my compliments attack. Cinder rolled her eyes.

"Hey, Ci. Do you have a fiancé that I have to fight, too?" I asked her curiously.

"I did. Already fought him off. Dad attempted to introduce me to my . . . 'optimal match,'" she said. "After listening to my precog-selected fiancé drone on about some foldknob shit, I got annoyed and kicked him right through the western wall of the house into the garden. Then I felt that it was insufficient, broke Dad's fave statue of some Omnid philosopher, and beat the annoying bastard into a chunky soup with the head."

Vee whistled. "Wish I had the balls for that. How old were you?"

"Seventeen." Cinder shrugged. "Dad was furious about the statue. Mom thought it was . . . uuhhh . . . passionate. They haven't tried to 'arrange' anything since, placing their hopes on Lance and hoping that I'll chill out enough to meet a boy in school and become a Hearth-Keeper like my mom someday."

"And they just . . . let you get away with that?" Vespera clicked her beak in amazement.

"Yeah," Cinder said. "I'm not a firstborn, so I don't have to carry on the Nova legacy or whatever. Plus, unlike your family, mine actually listens when I say 'no.' Sometimes it takes violence to get the point across, though. A *lot* of violence and breaking statues and skulls."

"Glad that I avoided getting my skull smashed in with giant stone heads." I grinned.

"You came pretty close." Cinder squinted at me. "You're just lucky that you look so fragile and harmless. If you were an Omnid, I'd already have killed you at least twenty times, you damned smol persistent chuppy."

"Speaking of violence . . ." Io suddenly sat up straight, his large gray eyes fixed on our trio. "I sense death."

"What kind of death?" I asked.

"Don't know," he said, gray paws kneading under the robe. "Something shifted. Someone somewhere said something, sent death after us. Multiple deaths. Not nice ones. More than one vector. Vectors. All directions. Multiple end futures. All leading to our deaths. Don't have exact details. Just a very nasty sense of looming doom about all of us. Plus . . . a terrible catastrophe. Oh, wow. This is huge."

His antennae twitched wildly, gray eyes turning to stare at me.

"Great," Vee groaned. "And here I was hoping for a nice evening with my lovely new 'ship. When's it coming?"

"Soon," Io said. "Thirty minutes tops. Whoever it is that desires our demise is quite effective at it, making sure we don't get away. Potential dead ends blooming all around."

"Can you like be any less vague?" Vespera demanded.

"Alas," Io said, shrugging apologetically, "disaster sense doesn't work like that. I do sense quite clear intent to kill me. The feeling is very, very strong. It's muted, though, foggy . . . which suggests that our enemies are trying to be clever and are using heavy anti-scrying wards. Too bad that basic bling doesn't work on Death Moths."

"Shash!" I barked loudly.

"Yes, m'lord?" The assassin materialized beside me, making Cinder yelp.

"Got a company of competitors coming in hot to take us out in thirty," I said. "Options?"

"The Guild has several defensive measures. Shall I banish the pub clientele, seal all doors, and activate the wards?" Shash's obsidian eyes glinted.

"Yes." I nodded. "And get everyone who can't fight into the vault."

"The vault, m'lord?"

"Yes," I said. "Trusted people are more valuable than gold. Everyone who is ready to fight for me and our Guild should get their ass over here. I've extremely deadly weapons to distribute."

I pulled Lance's bag from my shoulders and opened it up.

"We should leave," Cinder said, her feathers shifting through nervous grays. "If someone's coming to kill us . . ."

"Leave to where?" I asked her. "Do you perchance own another criminal-operated citadel somewhere else? Other than the Abystall Dungeon, this place is our best option for survival. Right, Io?"

The moth nodded.

"Can't we just fly out?" Cinder asked.

"And abandon my people?" I arched an eyebrow. "I don't think so! These murdery asshats are obviously my competitors. They want a Guild war? Fine! I'll give them a Guild war they won't forget!"

I turned to my assassin. "Shash? Who's the fastest and most skilled mage on your team who can sense air currents?"

"Yomik Peeps, m'lord," the assassin replied, summoning the man quickly to where we stood. "He's a wind mage."

"Yomik." I handed the thirty-year-old, gray-blue-tinted mole-man Lance's bricking wand. "Once everyone is out of the pub, use this to permanently seal the front door with an extra-thick layer of stone. Make sure that the seal is airtight. Also, run around and seal any cracks or air holes. I want the Guild airtight like a ship in thirty minutes or less. Leave the door to the roof functional, but make sure the stone forms a seal over the edges. Got it?"

"Yes, m'lord." Yomik bowed. He grabbed the wand from my hand and ran off.

My team stared at me, trying to guess what I was planning to do.

Shash was barking more orders through his Voicecast bracelet. More mooks and Guilders materialized in the room.

Vespera was already in the bag, pulling magisteel armor, shields, and swords out.

"Alex," Cinder addressed me with a desperate look, "you can't just start a Guild war!"

"Can't make an omelet without breaking a few eggs." I grinned, accepting the hexasuits and weapons from Vee and handing them to my mooks. "Besides, they started it. We're just defending ourselves."

"With what army?" Cinder demanded. "We have, what, twelve people here on top of our team?"

"Fifteen, actually," Shash corrected. "Plus the kitchen staff. Podop's quite formidable with his strength-amplifying Kitlix."

"See?" I beamed. "We've got a small army! Don't worry, this place just has to hold out for half an hour, tops."

"Why?" Cinder fretted.

"'Cause I've got something they don't have." I grinned at her.

"What's that?" Cinder asked.

"Biological weapons," I said.

"*What?*" Cinder choked. "When the shit did you . . . wait, full stop! Did you bring something . . . from Earth?! How did you even get . . . biological weapons?! Did you steal something from the Frontenachii, is that it?! M—Alex, you can't release that stuff out here!!!"

"Pffff, nah. See, after you guys went back into the cold tunnel," I said, "I climbed down the rope ladder into the Abystall Dungeon and filled all of Lance's dimensional bags with lovely, glowing mites."

"You did *what*?!" Cinder barked. Everyone else in attendance stared at me as if I was mad.

"I went down into the dungeon and filled every bag I had with mites." I grinned. "It wasn't hard at all—they were attracted by the magic inside the bag. Harmless to me but deadly to anyone with magic. They're perfect biological weapons."

Horror, shock, and fear-filled eyes stared at me from all sides.

"Oh," Io announced. "I see what I've been sensing from the beginning. It's *you*! You are the cause of everything!"

The moth pointed an accusatory fuzzy gray finger at me.

"Obviously." I grinned. "I was the catastrophe all along. Surprise!"

"M'lord," Shash choked, "those things are dangerous. Very hard to get rid of, impossible if they spread out enough. They will definitely spread . . ."

"Everywhere," I said. "Across all Undertown. This place could use a bit of a spring cleaning, don't you think?"

"M-mar—Alex!" Cinder shook me. "You can't just . . . release Duskbloom mites into Undertown! They'll kill everyone!"

"No, they won't." I shook my head. "This far from the dungeon, they're a mild nuisance at most. You guys were covered head to toe in them, and you didn't die. The mana loss from them is small and slow when their numbers aren't big."

"But they will . . ." Shash began.

"Multiply," I said. "Propagate. Spread all over. What would happen then? Go on, think about it. Extrapolate. Speculate."

"Chaos," Shash said with a frown. "Panic. Lockdown. Every strong or wealthy mage in Undertown would be forced to either leave or find ways to shield themselves with cold runes. The bastards upstairs will likely block the tunnels out with dimensional magic, barrier wards and cold runes, charging an arm and a leg for someone to leave. Their seers and precogs will learn of the danger quickly. They will act fast—many of the tunnels already have magic seals on them that detect incoming stuff like Duskbloom."

"Correct," I said. "Which will give us a week of panic to take over all of Undertown. I don't deal in half-measures. I don't deal in half-assery. Full assery, all the way! Act before anyone can do anything."

"That's . . . that's genocide!" Cinder protested.

"No, that's good use of pests," I corrected. "Everyone will be too busy fighting and fleeing the bloom to stop our takeover."

"Alex!" Cinder yelled. "You can't! We can't . . ."

"Sorry babe." I grinned, tapping out a sequence on my ID tag. "Too late."

"W-what do you mean too late?" Cinder yelped.

"Give it about twenty seconds," I said.

"Give *what* twenty seconds?!" the Quetzi-girl growled, hounding me, her face lengthening and becoming more draconic. "*Alex! What have you done?!*"

A series of deep, thundering booms resounded across the floor of the cavern, dust falling from the ceiling.

"W-what the shit was that?" Cinder spun, letting go of me.

"That was a new, bigly fissure opening up," I said. "Fissures, actually. Between Abystall Dungeon and Undertown. I just used a Voicecast command to remote detonate the biggest fifty beast cores from Lance's collection set into what Yulia and I determined were the weakest, thinnest sections of cavern walls between the dungeon and Undertown. The bloom will spread out carried by the warm wind coming from the dungeon now. There's nothing anyone can do to stop it now."

"*You!*" Io's finger pointed at me even more firmly, gray eyes blazing with an accusatory look.

Vespera's beak was wide open.

Cinder looked as if she was going to murder me.

"M'lord," Shash breathed out, "that was . . . incredibly ruthless."

"Ruthless?" I grinned. "I'm just getting started."

CHAPTER SIXTY-SEVEN

The End of Undertown I

You . . ." Cinder shook me by the collar, screeching like a banshee. "You absolute *psycho*! What is wrong with you?!"

I grinned back at her.

"You're going to get everyone killed!" she snarled, claws digging into my hardening hexasuit collar. "The mites will spread everywhere! Into people's homes! Their food! Their water!"

"Exactly." I grinned. "And who controls the cold tunnel?"

"What tunnel?!" she growled. "The effing tunnel that leads to the effing dungeon filled with even more effing mites? How the fuck is that even going to—"

"I've already sealed off the end of the tunnel with Lance's bricking wand," I said." The cold tunnel doesn't lead into the dungeon anymore. It's just a very long loop now that leads back to our Guild. In the health industry, we call it a cold . . . 'decontamination treatment chamber,'" I explained. "People will pay good money to get decontaminated. We'll charge them per cleansing. The cold tunnel is already pretty damn long, but we can use the bricking wand to expand it sideways into side caverns, add more cold rooms to decontaminate food and water for everyone in Undertown."

"You're . . . you're going to charge people to use the cold tunnel?!" Cinder howled.

"Of course." I nodded. "Basic economics. Create a problem, sell the solution. Everyone wins. Especially our Guild."

Vespera's beak snapped shut. A wide grin spread across her face.

"Everyone wins?!" Cinder sputtered. "You're literally unleashing a plague!"

"A very mild plague," I corrected. "That can be easily treated with a bit of cold tunnel."

"But . . ." Cinder's feathers flashed through shocked orange-violets and angry reds. "People will suffer! Their homes will . . ."

"People are already suffering," I said. "Open your eyes, Ci! Half of Undertown is addicted to Topaz. The other half is in debt to the high lords above. Everyone is either living in half-collapsing decrepit stone buildings carved thousands of years ago or in shacks made from magical garbage that the mages above throw down here. This place is basically a giant magical garbage pile. It needs a hard reset."

"By infecting everyone with parasites?!"

"By giving them a common enemy," I corrected. "Something to unite against. Something that will force change in less than a week. Haven't you seen *Watchmen*?"

"Abyss!" Vespera started to laugh. "He's . . . he's pulling an Ozymandias! Oh, my Slayer!"

"A what?" Cinder blinked.

"A dire, external threat to unite people," Vespera explained between giggles. "Like in that old comic—Ozymandias unleashed a fake alien invasion to unite Omnithornia and Thunderland against a common enemy. Except our human is using dungeon-bred parasites! This is great!"

"It's not great!" Cinder protested. "How are you on his side in this?! It's insane!"

"Actually," Io commented thoughtfully, "it's pretty clever. The mites will force everyone to work together, to find solutions."

"And who controls the biggest solution?" Vee clicked.

"We do!" I declared. "Come on. Everyone armed up and ready?"

Our Guilders nodded.

"To the roof, then," I said. "Time to parlay with our enemies!"

We emerged onto the roof.

The view of Undertown stretched out before us, twinkling with countless Kitlix lanterns below the green-blue star-moss-spotted ceiling. Vespera and I handed the mite-filled bags to the Guilders.

"On my order of thumbs-up," I instructed the mooks, "turn the bags over and press this hexagram here to empty them. Make it rain mites. Got it? Good."

"This is so wrong," Cinder protested weakly. "We can't . . ."

"The dungeon is already spreading," I said.

I had no idea whether the right tunnels even opened up from the beast core explosions, no idea if Yulia's calculations were correct. What mattered now was that my team simply had to believe that dumping the bags was the only way forward, that releasing the mites in our possession wouldn't change much.

"This will only add a bit more mites to the overall picture," I said. "In a particular direction."

"Why?!" Cinder demanded.

"Because . . ." I pointed at the street below. "Here they come!"

Below the citadel tower, armed, large figures converged on us from multiple directions. Bright Kitlix lanterns bounced on their belts, casting no shadows and lighting the way. Doors and windows snapped shut as Undertown denizens hid from the Enforcers, not knowing whom they were going to arrest today.

"Those are the people coming to execute us," I explained. "They won't be expecting a twist of this magnitude. They probably think that we're killing our brain cells in a room like dumbass teenagers, getting drunk."

I gave Vee a poignant look.

"Oi!" she protested. "I'm not *that* predictable!"

"You literally begged Io for booze like thirty minutes ago," I pointed out.

"Hmpf." Vespera crossed her arms.

A burly armored man banged on the shut, magisteel-reinforced door of our Guild, which now led into a thick stone wall thanks to the bricking wand.

"Attention, Gloomy Horse Adventurers Guild!" the armored man's voice boomed through some kind of amplification magic. "I am the Shandrian Arch-Guild Enforcer Legarth Wixoff! We know you're harboring Earth-delvers! Open up and surrender them to us, or we will be forced to take . . . extreme measures!"

"Sup, Legarth?" I yelled down, placing a heavy as hell wardstone shield in front of myself to avoid potential arrows, amplifying my voice with Lance's magitek megaphone. "You looking for some . . . *Love?*"

"You dare mock me, Earth-lander?" Legarth's magically amplified voice nearly deafened me. "Do you have any idea who you're dealing with, boy?"

"A soon-to-be very itchy man?" I called back. "I'm curious, who wants us to surrender, and what laws did we break?"

"Delver Team . . . erm . . . I Love You! The Arx Bank has issued an order for your immediate arrest signed by the High Justice Luberkand of Shandria!" Legarth declared. "You and your companions are hereby charged with interfering with official Arx Bank business. Your delving team is to be arrested and forcibly deported from Shandria."

"Deported? Why?" I asked. "What'd we do? I'm not hearing specific crimes."

"The specific crime, in question," Legarth barked up, "is a disruption of sanctioned trade routes for three years' time. Where is the owner of this establishment? Why is the front door barred?"

"I dunno." I shrugged. "She's chilling uptown in some inn, I think."

"She?" Legarth sputtered. "I'm talking about Guild Master Motrdem! Where is he?"

"Oh, he sold the place," I called down. "He's uptown now, too, spending his well-earned money on booze or whatever."

"Sold it? To whom?!" the muscular man asked.

"To interdimensional delver Emerald Stratos. You know her? Ruby-can't Lindworm? Really angry all the time? Has a thing for collecting overpriced stuff and setting people on fire?"

"What nonsense do you speak of?!" Legarth growled. "Motrdem would never sell his ancestral Guild to a delver!"

"I dunno. I think Emmy gave Mort something like ten million gold for the place." I shrugged. "Look, my dude, my delving team is just renting a room here for three silver a night. You need to chill. Do you or your men happen to have cold runes on your armor?"

"What?" the muscular man sputtered. "Cold runes? Why would we . . . what does that have to do with anything?!"

"If you don't have cold runes," I yelled down, "then I *really* suggest you avoid hitting the front door! Some very, *very* bad things are going to happen if you keep at it! I'm being friendly and warning you because I'm a polite and friendly adventurer! Like, come on, didn't you just say my team's name? We're basically all about . . . peace 'n' love!"

"Your attempts at distraction will not work!" Legarth stated. "You have one minute to surrender before we breach this establishment!"

More armored men and mages gathered behind him, ready to strike at the tower's ward.

"That's a terrible idea!" I yelled down. "Please, don't shake this tower!"

"I'll do whatever it takes to get you criminals arrested and deported from Shandria!" Legarth barked. "Come down or else!"

He kicked the door with his massive magisteel-clad boot, making the entire tower vibrate.

"Oh no!" I cried dramatically. "You really shouldn't have done that! The bags Emerald set up are getting loose!"

I gave a thumbs-up to the mooks behind me.

They upended the bags.

Glowing mites exploded from upturned dimensional bags and rained down from the tower like luminescent snow, drifting down onto the assembled enforcers below.

"What . . . what is this?!" Legarth blinked.

"Emerald Stratos tied a bunch of dimensional bags around the top of this tower as a prank," I yelled through the megaphone. "I think you guys call this stuff . . . Duskbloom! Is this stuff super itchy or something? That's what she said!"

Vespera started chortle-giggling behind me.

The faces of the men below us went from confusion to shock and then pure horror as they recognized the telltale azure glow of the parasitic mites.

"*Duskbloom!*" someone screamed as a patch of mites landed on his shoulder. "*It's Duskbloom!* It's eating my mana!"

"No! I still owe nine thousand silver for this armor! I can't have it ruined!"

"My sword! It's on my magic sword!"

Panic erupted instantly. A few of the assembled enforcers fled, running from the falling swarm of parasites. Some tried to shield themselves with magic, but the mites simply drifted through their barriers, settling on armor and skin.

More enforcers yelled and began retreating. Then the dam broke.

Legarth spun in one spot, watching as all of his men fled. The mites drifted all around, settling on invisible figures who began flailing and trying to scrape or magically remove the tiny mites off with no success whatsoever. A few invisible figures completely coated in mites jumped off the sides of our tower, freaking out and rolling around as if they were on fire.

"Are those invisible men or are you just happy to see us?" I yelled down. "Better start running to the nearest fridge! That stuff gets everywhere like sand and eats right through all magic barriers. The more magical you are, the more annoying it is, I hear!"

The assassins covered in Duskbloom gave up on killing us. Flickering in and out of visibility, they took off into the darkness, not wishing to have their faces seen.

"You . . . you *madman*!" Legarth roared up at me, watching as glowing, living snow drifted across the streets all around him as if he were in a Winter See-Mass cola commercial. "Do you have any idea what you fools have done?! These filthy parasites will spread across all of Undertown!"

"Me? I'm just the Quartermaster of I Love You." I shrugged. "I didn't do anything. I'm just chilling in the rooftop hot tub with my best friends! Blame the prankster drag-oness for this mess. Did you hear those booms earlier? Emerald told me that she hired a bunch of other idiot adventurers for one hundred thousand silver each to detonate some tunnels. Can you guess where the tunnels lead?"

"You're bluffing!" Legarth shouted, still frantically brushing at the glowing mites settling on his armor. "No one would be insane enough to . . ."

"Consider this, Legarth," I declared. "Emerald is a delver from another world. She doesn't give two shits about Undertown or Shandria. She doesn't care about you or the people here. I think that some Undertown citizen stepped on her toe yesterday! When she saw Abystall Dungeon, she had a really stupid idea for a prank. I tried to convince her not to do it, but I'm just a lowly human and Quartermaster of another competing delving team. I have no power over her. I warned you not to kick this tower, did I not? You have only yourself to blame for this!"

"You . . . you're lying!" Legarth shouted, but there was uncertainty in his voice now. "No delver would . . ."

"Really?" I called back. "You sure about that? Have you met many interdimensional delvers? Especially ones with more money than common sense and a tendency to set things on fire when annoyed? Some old man from Undertown insulted her. Emerald took it personally. This is her revenge. Sorry, my dude. I'm going back to my rooftop hot tub. I suggest you go home and wash up and throw that armor into a fridge or something before you get too itchy!"

More Duskbloom-related screams erupted from nearby streets as the mites continued to drift through the air, carried by air currents from the newly opened fissures.

A lamenting siren made up from ringing doomsday bells resounded across Undertown, mage towers lighting up. The locals were terrified of Duskbloom, and knew exactly what it could do if given time to grow.

The living catastrophe was spreading across Undertown, drawn to magic all around.

Drawn to ungodly amounts of Topaz in cigar buds and in empty, broken bottles. Drawn to Topaz storage warehouses and Topaz dens. Drawn to thousands upon thousands of years of layered magical garbage piles. Drawn to Topaz in people's bodies, inside shimmering-blue lesions and swollen glands.

Primed to devour it all and to multiply endlessly.

CHAPTER SIXTY-EIGHT

The End of Undertown II

This is madness!" Legarth roared as more mites settled on his magic armor. "The Bank will hear of this! They'll . . ."

"Sorry! Going back to the rooftop party now! My girls want more beer!" I yelled back via my megaphone.

I walked away from the parapet, sending a smile to my friends and mooks.

"Back inside," I ordered everyone. "Time for phase two."

"Phase . . . two?!" Cinder sputtered as we descended the stairs. "What's phase two? You've already unleashed a plague!"

"Now we expand and fortify," I explained. "Shash, status of the vault?"

"All noncombatants secured, m'lord," the assassin reported. "The vault is sealed and warded."

"Excellent. Podop!"

The molekin enforcer stepped forward, his strength-amplifying Kitlix glowing on his shoulder.

"Sir!"

"Use your strength to obliterate walls. Begin adding a bunch of cold rooms with Yomik to the cold tunnel—make them look nice. We're going to have all of Undertown visiting us in due time. Rostika knows how to install cold runes, yes?"

"Yes, m'lord." Podop nodded. "Me 'n' her have been maintaining the cold tunnel to Abystall, adding new cold runes and such."

"Very good." I nodded. "Make a new, extra fortified cold tunnel entrance from Undertown into our Guild."

"Understood," the man said, departing with my blessings.

"You know, I absolutely did not expect this much ruthlessness from my human husbando so soon," Vespera clicked.

"Oh?" I looked at her.

"Thought there would be more dancing around morality, more hesitation, more . . . I dunno, guilt?"

"Guilt?" I arched an eyebrow at her. "About what?"

"People are going to die, you effing knob!" Cinder said. "Not everyone is going to be able to afford this cure of yours!"

"Nah." I shrugged. "Our Guild will charge a varying rate for the cold tunnel use. Those without money will simply pay us with . . . their services."

Cinder's feathers bristled with angry reds. "What services?! You're going to exploit desperate people?!"

"Not exploit," I corrected. "Employ. Think about it—we'll need workers to expand the Guild and cold tunnel system. Guards, cleaners, maintenance staff. People who can't afford the treatment can work it off."

"That's . . . that's slavery!" Cinder protested.

"No, that's capitalism." I grinned. "Everyone will be monitored by our Guilders and also through Yulia's cameras. The AI will determine who is a knob and who is a capable employee. Those who do a good job will be paid a good salary from the sales of silver juice. Morty called me a few hours ago and let me know that sales above are going well. Those who slack off or have no talent in the service industry will be sent out on lesser jobs such as cleaning up the mite-infested magic garbage from the streets and demolishing mite-infested hovels to build luxury hotels and other nice things."

"You're exploiting the downtrodden!"

"Not exploiting. Employing. Come on Ci, would you rather they die from mite infection?"

"I'd rather you hadn't released the mites in the first place!" she complain-growled.

"Too late for that." I shrugged, spreading my arms in a dramatic gesture. "Consider this—when they seal off Undertown, all debts will be cleared. The mites will eat right through magic debt contracts, magic slave collars, and magic binding tattoos. Everyone in Undertown will be free. No debt. No slavery. No more upworld owners!"

"Dang. This is some *Fight Club*–level shit," Vespera whistled. "I haven't even thought about how the mites would destroy magic-enforced debts."

"You . . ." Cinder's feathers shifted through more frustrated oranges and angry reds sprinkled with small patches of excited violets. "You're actually enjoying this, aren't you?"

"Enjoying? This is an effort and a half. Think of me as a surgeon removing a very nasty tumor." I shrugged. "I'm saving this place from itself."

"By forcing everyone into eternal indentured servitude to your Guild?!"

"Not forever. Everyone will buy cold runes or rent Frostix Kitlix from us in due time. I'm giving the people opportunities," I corrected. "Look around you, Ci. What do you see? A bunch of broken people addicted to Topaz, living in squalor. We're going to give them purpose, direction. A chance to be part of something bigger, to rebuild, to grow, to beat the mites back, and to emerge as the shining jewel of interdimensional trade."

A shadow flickered in front of me.

"Oh, hey, Kat," I said as Katherine manifested in the dining hall, panting. "How did your jogging exercise go?"

"What exercise?" Katherine's emerald eyes blazed with urgency. "We need to leave! The Bankers are sending their men to attack this place! Now! Grab onto me and I'll take you into the deep and . . ."

"Nah, it's fine," I said. "I just started a nice little biological warfare campaign. Things are just getting interesting!"

"Alex! You don't understand! The Arx Bank . . ." Katherine panted. "They control everything. The bracelets . . . the translations, the stats. Even the Topaz trade.

Instructor Zal is the one that's been importing Topaz to Arx from some other dimension or something! The Bankers sent assassins!"

"Oh, is that all?" I grinned. "Don't worry about it. I've already dealt with that. The assassins and the Enforcers ran away from the mites."

"Mites? What mites?" the Stollwurm panted, looking at the long faces of our companions. "What . . . what happened while I was gone?!"

"Relax, sit down on a couch by the fire. Why don't you tell us what you learned," I said. "Then Vee can tell you what I did on my exciting first delve to Arx!"

Kat stared at Vespera with a catatonic look as the Thunderbird finished narrating out my accomplishments, while I flipped through the yellow binder that Kat had given me, taking photos of every page for Yulia to process later.

"Let me get this straight," Katherine growled, her glowing, catlike emerald eyes fixed on me. "You released Duskbloom mites into Undertown, blamed Em, and now plan to charge people for access to your cold tunnel decontamination chambers?"

"Mhmm," I nodded. "Gonna make extra chambers and temporary residences within the large cavern system below our Guild."

"And you think this will . . . what? Make you the King of Undertown?" Katherine demanded. "I go away for an hour and you manage to cause a local apocalypse?! If I wasn't so out of breath running here through the deep to save your stupid ass, I would smack you so hard . . ."

I slipped behind Vespera. "No smacky. Birb-waifu shall protek!"

"Waifu?!" Katherine's spiked tail lashed dangerously.

"Joint custody," Vespera clicked cheerfully, petting my head. "Me 'n' Ci co-own his pink ass now. Don't damage the goods, K, or I'll be annoyed."

"Okay." Kat tiredly rubbed her snout. "Right. Whatever . . . can we focus on the fact that the Arx Bank wants us dead for screwing with our Topaz-peddling Koshchei instructor?" she asked. "They're not just some local criminal organization—they're something ancient and powerful. Their bracelets are everywhere, tracking everyone's stats on Arx, gathering data . . ."

"Yes, yes." I waved dismissively. "Evil megacorp with magic surveillance tech. Very scary. But consider this—many people in Undertown are too poor for fancy upworld bracelets and have already sold their free bracelets for Topaz. And those that haven't . . . well, we can politely ask them to take them off."

"Ask them to take it off?" Katherine blinked. "You can't just ask people to take off their bracelets! These things are essential—they translate languages, show stats, store mana . . ."

"And spy on everyone." I nodded. "And attract hungry mites. Which is why we'll offer alternatives."

"What bloody alternatives?" Kat demanded.

"Phones from Earth with a personal AI." I grinned. "Yulia can handle translations just fine. I'm going to dump an ungodly amount of Earth tech into Undertown. And everyone will have to use it. Because unlike the mana-storing bracelets, it won't attract the mites."

"*Ha!*" Vespera burst out. "Lexy isn't just taking over Undertown—he's going to make everyone switch to human tech! The mites will bloom on anything magical, so people will *have* to use human-made Earth tech!"

"Exactly." I grinned. "No more magical bracelets tracking everyone's every move. Just good old-fashioned human surveillance through phones and tablets via my lovely AI."

Vespera doubled over in giggles, waving magisteel talons at me. "OMG. Staaaap. I can only take so much supervillainy in one day!"

"The Arx Bank won't just sit back," Kat pointed out. "They'll come for us again."

"I'm sorry," I said. "Are you perchance the Arx Bank rep? How do you know what they're going to do? In a week or less, this entire place will be crawling with magic mites. Topaz is a magical drug. We cut the supply off. Now the mites will eat whatever the gangs have stored up, along with local money . . . which is also magical, unless you forgot. Do you remember what happened during the coronavirus lockdowns on Earth?"

Kat opened her mouth and closed it.

"The idiots ruling Shandria are just going to seal Undertown off," I said. "Maybe forever. They aren't going to waste money on saving a bunch of drug addicts and criminals."

"Oh," the Stollwurm let out.

"Exactly. They'll just wall this place off, let everyone down here rot," I continued. "It's cheaper and more effective to brick up tunnels than to help people! But we'll be here, offering solutions. Cold tunnels. Human tech. Jobs. Currency. Purpose. Hope."

"And you think the Arx Bank will just . . . let you take over this place?" Katherine demanded.

"Let me?" I laughed. "What are they going to do? Send more bulky knights or invisible assassins? Into a mite-infested zone? Good luck with that. Their magic won't work here soon. Their bracelets won't work. Their control will slip away day by day, mite by mite. They'll hand Undertown to me on a silver platter."

"They might try something else," Katherine tried. "Something worse. You don't understand what these people are capable of."

"No," I said. "*You* don't understand what *I'm* capable of. Look at what I accomplished in one day. One single day! And I'm just getting started."

I waved the yellow folder.

"See these names? These addresses? These are all Bank representatives in Shandria. I'm going to start releasing this information into an appropriate direction. The people of Undertown need someone to blame for this. The Arx Bank in collaboration with interdimensional criminal Emerald Stratos and Lord Zalimar orchestrated a dastardly plot to kill everyone in Undertown to make . . . parking lots or . . . something. The point is, he who controls the narrative controls everything else. And I'm going to make sure everyone knows exactly who to blame for their loss of homes and businesses."

"Damn," Io commented from his cozy alcove. "I was right to get on your team. You really turned out to be the biggest catastrophe of all, Lex."

"Lex Luthor!" Vespera cackled, slapping her knees. "Just need to shave him for authenticity!"

"You knew that all this shit was going to happen?" Cinder demanded, glaring at the Mothman.

"I didn't know the details." Io shrugged. "I simply . . . sensed something truly catastrophic about this man. Something incredibly . . . delicious. This is it. The end of Undertown."

"You could have stopped him! Could have warned us!" Cinder protested.

"About what?" Io asked, dark gray eyes glinting under his wide hat. "That the mixie magic-less teenager who took photos of us during our smoke break on a Tuesday was basically the worst kind of a walking disaster possible? One who will destroy everything in his way with . . . words and mundane actions? Like you would have believed me! You, Em, and Vee would have just called me a knob! Nobody ever listens to my opinion! I warned you all about our last show being a disaster, and you still went through with it!"

Cinder struggled to formulate words, glaring daggers at the moth.

"When you're right, you're right." Vee patted Io on his shoulder.

"Consider this," the Mothman said at Cinder. "He's pretty much demolished you, Kat, and Vee . . . and yet here you are . . . looking the happiest I've seen you in years. He's destroyed Em's reputation at school, destroyed Zalimar, destroyed the Gloomy Horse Guild's independence, and now he's destroying all of Undertown."

Cinder sighed.

"And the weirdest part?" Io added. "Everyone just . . . lets him do it or assists him in this. Because in the end it's better for everyone involved. In the end, a new, healthier forest grows from a forest fire. Eventually, Undertown will be rebuilt. It will never be the same. Katsburg will rise in its place. All of this is the currently unfolding disaster. I am thoroughly sated."

Cinder simply blinked at the Mothman. Then she slid down onto the stone couch, struggling to digest his words of mothy wisdom.

I sent Io a thumbs-up and sat down next to Cinder. The Quetzi's face became less predatory, snout drawing back in as her anger gradually subsided.

I offered her my hand.

CHAPTER SIXTY-NINE

The End of Undertown III

Cinder stared at my hand for a long moment, her feathers shifting through troubled grays.

Vespera dropped on my other side, leaning on my shoulder.

"I didn't think you could do so much in so little time," she said, smiling. "And yet here we are. Good job!"

Cinder's bracelet vibrated. She tapped it with a resigned look.

The usual blue-silver holo-projection of Quint's head manifested from her ID tag artifact.

"It is now the evening of day two," he said sharply. "Why hasn't your team registered in the cathedral, Captain Nova?"

I leaned towards Cinder, tapping her bracelet to zoom out and show all of us.

"Sup, Pres?" I asked. "What's the rush?"

"The rush?" Quint's holographic eyebrows rose. "The purpose of *your* first delve on Arx is to register your team, receive your initial, basic in-town quests, and begin building your reputation with the Adventurers Guild as Iron-rank delvers. Instead, you've spent two days doing . . . what exactly?"

"Shopping," I said cheerfully. "Lots and lots of outfit shopping. Right, team?"

"Yeah," Vespera clicked. "Totes. Getting swank gear 'n' stuff."

"And making sure our Quartermaster doesn't die," Io added.

"Die?" Quint's holographic eyes narrowed. "Shandria is perfectly safe during the day, especially for a team of five Omnids, four of whom already have Arx-delving experience! You do get that I'm going to give you all zeroes for your first Delving class unless you all follow the program!"

"We've already registered as adventurers," I said.

"No, you haven't!" Quint growled. "If you did, I would know! I'm in contact with the Adventurers Guild Secretary, Sister Antiquilla! Everyone already registered and checked in, except for your team!"

"Actually," I said with a grin, "we registered at *The* Adventurers Guild. Not the cathedral one. The Gloomy Horse Guild."

"*What?*" Quint sputtered. "That's not a . . ."

"It's the official Adventurers Guild of Undertown, according to the merchants I talked to from the market upstairs," I said. "The Gloomy Horse is connected to three dungeons, including the dangerously exciting Duskbloom-filled Abystall Dungeon and a bunch of other fun places for mid- to high-level delvers. On the account that I'm merely an Iron rank beginner, we're currently doing *community service* for Undertown."

Vespera choked from where she was sitting, clamping her beak with her claws, trying very hard not to break out into fits of laughter.

"You're . . . doing community service?" Quint blinked, glancing at Vee with a look of suspicion. "In . . . Undertown?"

"Yes, my dude!" I declared. "Just like I did community service in a soup kitchen for Triumvirate Slayer's Cathedral in Cradlefall! This is what I do! I love helping people. Not the people who are well off and want their lost kittens rescued or something. My team is helping out those who need it most!"

"Community service," Quint repeated skeptically. "And what exactly does this . . . service entail?"

"Oh, you know." I waved vaguely. "Feeding the poor. Helping the less fortunate. Assisting with infrastructure repairs. Helping people find jobs. The usual stuff I did with Father Matthias Jonannes in Scab Row!"

"In Undertown," Quint said. "The . . . criminal district filled with magic drug dens?"

"First of all, not everyone down here is a criminal or a gang member. Did you even read my reference paperwork? I have a month of experience in Scab Row running a soup kitchen and Nazarite volunteer organization. I've already helped feed a bunch of orphaned children here in Undertown. Besides that, everyone deserves a chance at redemption," I said, channeling my most pious tone as Christophorus Elijah. "Especially criminals and addicts. After all, what would Slayer Nazareth do?"

"The Delving class program . . ." Quint began his lecture-tone tune.

"Was written by Instructor Zalimar," I said. "Who, need I remind you, does not give a shit about the downtrodden. Haven't you heard why me and the other mixie students sued Zalimar? Also, do consider the fact that one of our team members is disabled?"

"Disabled?" Quint's holographic eyes narrowed. "I am aware of that, but what does that have to do with anything?"

I pointed a finger at Kat.

"Katherine has a condition," I said. "She can't do jobs upstairs! Sunlight hurts her! How do you not know this? She can barely function during daytime in Shandria, and night jobs there are off-limits due to the hungry Shadowbeasts roaming the streets. How is she supposed to do quests in the city or the outside fields? Katherine, please demonstrate how well you can walk down here."

Katherine shot me a glare but stood up from her couch, walking gracefully beside us, armor and hexamesh dark-blue outfit below it glittering and reflecting the light from the glowing, cozy fireplace Kitlix.

"See?" I said to Quint's hologram as his skull-socket eyes tracked the girl clad in magisteel armor. "Down here, in the dark, she's perfectly fine! The local aetheric density plus darkness permits her to walk properly. We're doing important community initiative work here, helping the locals while accommodating our Knight's special needs!"

"But . . ." Quint began.

"Pres," I said with a serious tone, "I believe I already told you not to mess with me two days ago. If you keep pestering me and threaten to give me a zero for class or do anything else that interferes with me or my team's Knight, I will absolutely email a video recording of this conversation to Father Matthias after class. I'm sure you'd love to explain to the Nazarite church exactly why you're not allowing someone who can't walk properly a chance to participate in delving activities in a way that accommodates her disability."

Quint's holographic eyes flickered. "I . . . that's not what I . . ."

"Furthermore," I continued, "I have extensive documentation of our community service activities here. Would you like to see the forms signed off and stamped by the Guild of Undertown? Why is it that you're pestering me so hard when I'm just trying to help people? Is it because Emerald is pushing you into a particular direction? Because she wants me to waste time upstairs, because she wants Katherine to suffer from sunlight exposure? Need I remind you that around one year and ten months ago, or so, Emerald initiated a well documented, online bullying campaign against Katherine?"

"I . . . I will need to consult with the faculty about this . . . after class," Quint said carefully, clearly flummoxed by my words. "Your . . . alternative approach to delving activities is . . . rather . . . unprecedented."

"Of course it is." I nodded sagely. "Nobody thinks about the disabled or the poor! Everyone just wants to do exciting quests upstairs killing wild rabbits or collecting rare grasses in the sunshine fields next to the farmer fields and markets! But some of us have a calling to help those in need. By the way, where is Emerald?"

"She's . . . in her room," Quint let out. "Recovering from a series of unfortunate events."

"What kind of events?" I asked. "I do hope that she's okay."

"She's fine," Quint exhaled. "It's just that whenever she goes out for shopping, or quests, something terrible happens. Missing a step on the stairs, doors closing on her unexpectedly, old ladies dumping . . . various waste out of their windows that lands on her. Children calling her names. Slipping on old fruit peels."

"Oh no," I said. "Did someone jinx her?"

"Seems like it," Quint sighed. "She probably pissed off some high-level Archmage in Shandria. Anyways, it's not a big deal. The jinx will likely clear up in a day or two."

"Perhaps she should take some time to reflect on her actions," I suggested. "Maybe do some community service herself? I personally find it very therapeutic."

"I . . . will pass along your suggestion," Quint said carefully. "About your . . . alternative delving activities. I suppose as long as your Captain and team document everything properly . . ."

"Don't worry about documentation," I assured him. "I'm very thorough with paperwork. I learned much working at the Slayer's Cathedral."

I elbowed Cinder.

"Yes. We're doing . . . important . . . community work. Very important. Helping people and . . . stuff," she mewled out, blue eyes staring daggers at me as though she wanted to strangle me.

"And are you staying safe?" Quint asked her. "No unauthorized delving, yes, Captain Nova?"

"Um. Yes. Very safe," Cinder replied with a very wooden tone. "Just . . . helping people. With things. Safe things."

"Such as?"

"Um," Cinder let out. "We're helping . . . renovate the local Guild using my brother's bricking wand! Yes. Nothing dangerous."

"See, Pres?" I beamed. "Everything's fine. Don't worry about us! We're just doing good deeds, helping the less fortunate, making the world a better place. One act of kindness at a time. Detailed reports about our charitable activities will be on your desk at the end of Delving class! Over and out!"

I tapped Cinder's ID tag and Quint's somewhat concerned face winked away.

"Charitable activities?" Cinder rounded on me. "You cheeky bastard!"

"A-ha-ha-ha," Vespera finally exploded, slapping the couch and heaving. "Charity plague! Spreadin' love and mites across Undertown! The gift that keeps on giving! Oh my Slayer, my sides! You're Slayin' me!"

"This isn't funny!" Cinder protested.

"Community service via pest control!" Vespera cackled. "Helping the downtrodden by forcing them into cold tunnels!"

"Your sense of humor concerns me," Katherine growled.

"Everything about this situation concerns me," Cinder added.

"It's only what Slayer Nazareth would do!" The Thunderbird flapped her wings, dying from laughter. "Blessed be the mites, for they shall inherit Undertown! For just a silver a day, you too can be saved from their parasitic embrace!"

"Vee! Damn it, stop encouraging him!" Cinder growled.

"But he's so good at being bad!" Vespera clicked, hugging me. "I can't even. We must all do our part 'n' help the downtrodden with . . . biological weapons! For charity!"

She rolled onto my lap, cackling and crying and sending sparks all over me.

Kat and Cinder exchanged exasperated looks. Io was softly snickering from his reading nook.

When I set out from North Acadia in beginning of January, I did not expect such spectacular results.

I expected to be alone, fighting against the world, to be constantly on the run from the Frontenachii Wendigos. Instead, I found people who accepted me, supported me, even claimed me as their own.

I looked around at my companions—Vespera in my lap staring up at me, Cinder trying (and failing) to maintain her disapproving glare, Katherine rolling her emerald eyes at our antics, and Io quietly observing everything from his alcove. Each of them brought something unique to our strange little group of friends . . . to our new family.

Cinder let out a deep sigh and finally reached out towards my hand, squeezing it.

I smiled at her, squeezing her hand back.

Even as I orchestrated chaos across Undertown, they all stayed by my side. They might not approve of my methods, but they were here. Supporting me. Protecting me. Caring about me. Uplifting me.

There were still a million things to do, and more dangerous, deadly trials to face, but for the first time since Mom died, I felt . . . whole.

Complete.

Like I belonged . . . somewhere.

Even if that somewhere was a criminal Guild tower in the middle of a mite-infested underground city.

Even if my new family consisted of a tsundere rainbow dragon-bird, a thunder-happy Valley girl with a heart of gold, a grumpy dragon-cat artist, and a disaster-sensing, gate-opening moth.

Even if I had to lie, cheat, and unleash biological weapons to protect them all.

This was home now. These were my people. My clan, as Vee put it.

And I would do anything—*anything*—to keep them safe, to never lose them again to whatever came next, be it an immortal Koshchei, Arx Bankers, Frontenachii Scrutimancers, or even reality-rewriting System Wizards themselves.

The thought of Zee Captain made me shiver slightly. What was he really? What game was she playing at? Why give me a lighter that generated mana? Why tell me about Alexa?

Was this my education as a System Wizard? Was this . . . Manchester, my . . . online course for learning how to rewrite reality one word, one action at a time while moving from world to world?

So many questions, so few answers. But that was okay.

I had time now. Time and resources and people who believed in me. People who would stand with me against whatever came next.

That's all that mattered in . . . the end.

About the Author

Vitaly S. Alexius is the author of the Somebody Stop Her series, originally released on Royal Road along with the rest of the extended omniverse, Romantically Apocalyptic, in which it is set (learn more here: https://bit.ly/3U9CPVy). When he's not busy penning stories or dabbling in art, he likes grilling up some tasty barbecue or enjoying a picnic at the beach with his family. Alexius, who his wife says is a human capybara, resides in Canada.

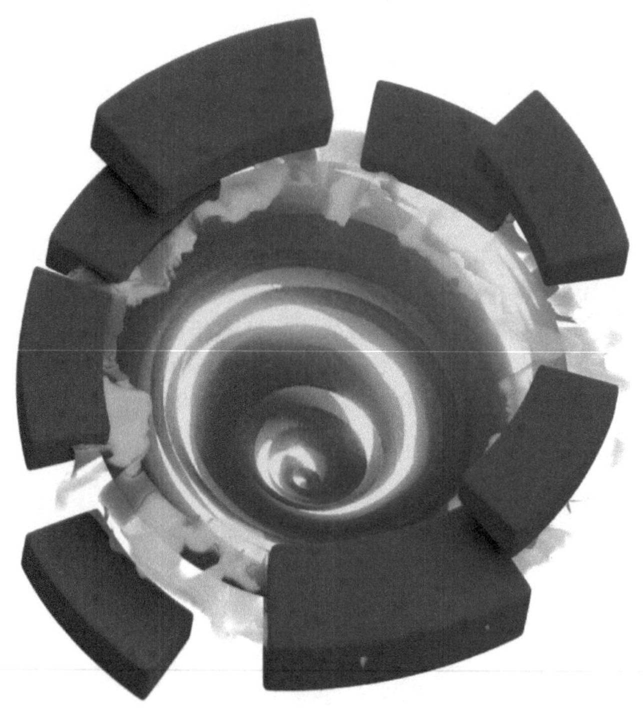

RESPAWN YOUR CURIOSITY

follow us on our socials

 podiumentertainment.com

 @podiumentertainment

 /podiumentertainment

 @podium_ent

 @podiumentertainment